NEMESIS

ALEX LAMB

First published in Great Britain in 2016 by Gollancz
an imprint of the Orion Publishing Group Ltd
Carmelite House, 50 Victoria Embankment
London EC4Y 0DZ

An Hachette UK Company

1 3 5 7 9 10 8 6 4 2

A CIP catalogue record for this book is
available from the British Library.

ISBN 978 1 473 20612 0

Typeset at The Spartan Press Ltd,
Lymington, Hants

Printed in Great Britain by Clays Ltd,
St Ives plc

MIX
Paper from
responsible sources
FSC® C104740

www.alexlamb.com
www.orionbooks.co.uk
www.gollancz.co.uk

For Louis the Inappropriate,
who made it all happen.

0: PROLOGUE

0.1: TOM

The end of civilisation looked like two angry red points. Captain Tom Okano-Lark scowled at them as they sat there in the centre of his retinal display, unwelcome and persistent. From the warning tags clustered around them, he knew what they represented – a pair of small gunships racing towards him at about a tenth of the speed of light. Both vessels bristled with cheap tactical weapons showing fire-ready signatures.

It wasn't the response to his friendly hail he'd hoped for, but after forty-six hours surveying the Tiwanaku System, Tom had all but given up on civilized dialog. Since their arrival and the initial unpleasant surprise, his expectations for the outcome of the mission had darkened steadily, along with his mood.

The settlement on the planet in front of him shouldn't have existed. The fact that it did was going to make a lot of people very upset for one simple reason: it represented the end of thirty years of interstellar peace.

Wendy Kim, the IPS *Reynard*'s first officer, broke the silence.

'Four minutes to engagement radius, sir. Do you want to deploy gravity shields?'

Wendy ran the *Reynard*'s blunt-sensor ops. Nobody had a more detailed or more disconcerting view of the approaching ships than she did. She lay prone on the crash couch opposite Tom's on the other side of the *Reynard*'s tiny central cabin while the other four crew members lay in the bunks stacked below them. None of them dared speak a word.

'Not yet,' said Tom. 'We have to play this *exactly* by the book otherwise they'll string us up the moment we get home.'

He hated risking his crew but the face-off had to be done right, which meant waiting and pretending the approach wasn't threatening until after a legally unambiguous dialogue had taken place. The moment news of what they'd found got back to Mars, the finger-pointing would start. Shooting would follow.

Until Tiwanaku, unregistered squatter settlements – otherwise known as *Flag Drops* – had always sprung up near well-established colonies, so they could leech off the existing infrastructure and avoid the legal hassles that came with registering a new planet. IPSO law was remarkably forgiving when it came to protecting the inhabitants of an established world, no matter how they had got there. Frontier-jumping, on the other hand, was *verboten*. The fact that one of Earth's sects had now established a colony on an independent world without telling anyone implied they were finally ready to forgo the law altogether.

Tom hated how unfair that felt. He'd spent his career in the service of the Fleet, struggling to uphold the delicate balance of power between Earth and the Old Colonies. He'd spent far more of that time protecting Earthers than he had Colonials. Now Earth had gone and ruined it all. And for what? Money, as usual.

Had it been a simple scouting run, Tom would have turned back immediately and headed straight for New Panama, home to the Fleet's Far Frontier HQ. But the *Reynard* was escorting families. A modified nestship ark, the IPS *Horton*, trailed behind them crammed with a thousand coma-stored colonists. And it had just dropped warp about 20 AU out, which meant his time for lying low had ended. Fecund nestships, even human-modified ones, did not arrive quietly. They left a gravity signature like a brick thrown at a pond.

'Sorry to put you all through this,' Tom told the others. 'Stay glued to your displays and wait for my word.' He knew his crew considered him a stubborn perfectionist. This time, though, they'd just have to humour him. The stakes were simply too high.

As the gunships raced towards them, he tried to get himself into a calm and diplomatic frame of mind. After all, who could blame the Flags for wanting to move here? Tiwanaku Four was a superb planet sitting square in the habitable zone, swathed in salmon-coloured dunes, with a decent level of atmospheric nitrogen and fat, healthy ice caps: a classic Mars Plus. It loomed in his display like a ripe peach. Not to mention the masses of Fecund artefacts drifting in the outer system, the signs of surface ruins on the planet itself, or the traces of non-terrestrial organic activity in the atmosphere.

Fecund ruins meant money. For decades now, mining the remains of that long dead race for technological marvels had driven humanity's economy. Treated properly, Tiwanaku could become a thriving research centre and home for millions of Earth's struggling poor. But onto this gem of a world the Flags had dumped a clump of rickety habitat modules and a couple of thousand people, along with a cheap off-the-shelf industrial base that looked barely usable. Three orbital habitats hovered in geostationary orbit housing at least as many more settlers.

Given how much Earthers hated orbitals, that really said something. Whatever sect ran this place had clearly been shuttling people out here faster than they could put homes on the surface. And all this in the nine months since the last survey pass, when the planet had been registered as 'colony pending'. The Horton's passengers were going to be seriously peeved. Presuming they didn't all die first, of course.

'Their orbital suntap stations are targeting,' said Wendy. He could hear the strain in her voice. 'Even at this distance they might be able to nail us.'

Just the fact that they had suntap weapons here was insane. As far as Tom knew, nobody had been stupid enough to actually fire up a suntap weapon since the Interstellar War. Maintaining half a dozen suntap platforms and two orbital drone-stations for such a tiny colony was like protecting a family-size hab-tent with a squad of titan mechs. The settlers had obviously expected trouble. They'd practically courted it.

Thank Gal they hadn't noticed the Reynard's arrival until now, otherwise Tom knew he'd already have a disaster on his hands. Most of the time, he cursed the fact that scouts were little bigger than soft-combat ships. This time, it had probably saved his life.

'Sir,' said Faisal Koi from the bunk beneath him. Faisal ran the fine sensors – the Reynard's most delicate and specialised scanning equipment. 'We've got audio from the incoming.'

'Let's hear it,' said Tom. Close enough to talk meant close enough to kill. He couldn't stall any longer.

'IPSO vessel, this is the captain of the war-shuttle *Sacred Truth*,' said the voice over the comm. 'You are in violation of our territory.'

The speaker sounded about fifteen. He had a heavy Earth accent, though Tom couldn't have guessed from which part. It didn't make much difference these days.

'You are instructed to leave this system immediately,' said the Flag. 'Failure to comply will be interpreted as threatening action.' It sounded like he was reading from a prompt screen.

Tom replied on the same channel. 'Whose territory is that, may I ask?'

'That not your business,' snapped the Flag.

'This is the IPS *Reynard*,' said Tom carefully. 'We are representatives of the Interstellar Pact Security Organisation here in a peaceful escort capacity for the colony ark IPS *Horton*. We intend no violence. We are, however, legally obliged to give you notice that your settlement is unregistered and therefore illegal. We also note that: A, you are occupying an unexplored alien ruin site in contravention of Social Safety Ordinances; B, you are inhabiting a foreign biome without a licence; and C, you are using suntap technology at an unlisted star. All this will have to be reported. We strongly recommend that you power down your weapons and declare your funding body immediately. If you comply, you will not be held responsible for this settlement's existence.'

He didn't expect a reasonable answer but had to try. Flags seldom understood the game they were caught up in. They were suckers a long way from home who believed they'd won a future among the stars. Meanwhile, the real bad guys made a fortune off them. A peaceful outcome would help everybody. Even so, Tom's finger hovered over the button for the gravity shields.

The reply came fast. The optical lag on comms had dropped to a matter of seconds.

'This an independent human settlement!' the Flag shouted. 'We don't recognise your IPSO and don't want your colony ark. If you don't charge engines in two minute, we open fire.'

Tom glanced at Wendy. Two days of stress had drawn lines on her usually serene oval face. Her dark eyebrows sat knitted together into a single, intense line.

He muted the channel. 'Can you believe this?' he said.

4

'I think they'll do it, sir. These Flags are set up for a fight – they've been waiting for this.'

'Send a warning to the *Horton*,' said Tom. 'Tell Sundeep to keep his engines warm and plot a course back to sanity.'

He flicked the channel back open. '*Sacred Truth*, please be reasonable. Consider the consequences of this course of action. We're not here to make trouble. If you force us to leave at gunpoint, we'll have to return with a frigate and evacuate all of you.'

Not to mention that the breakdown of IPSO authority would likely kick off a bloody scramble for control of the remaining Fecund stars and the alien riches they sheltered. They weren't supposed to acknowledge that fact in negotiations, even if everyone knew it.

'Your words mean nothing, Fleetie!' yelled the voice over the comm. It trembled with rage. The video remained blank. 'We know you here to kill us but we defend our home to the last man. Go now and spare yourself a fight. No more talk. I mean it!'

Tom couldn't remember hearing a man sound so scared. Yet they were the ones pointing all the guns. He'd been told that Flags received a lot of political conditioning but someone had wound this guy up to breaking point.

'*Sacred Truth*, we acknowledge your request. As a sign of peaceful intentions, we will remove to a safe distance.'

'You will leave!' the Flag screamed.

'Okay, *Sacred Truth*, we're heading out. Please do not open fire. I am legally required to give you the opportunity to make a statement of claim before disciplinary action becomes unavoidable. If you want to keep any rights over the world you've settled...'

He let the sentence hang as he fired up the engines.

'Jawid, buffers to full strength. And quickly, please – we're leaving.'

'On it,' said his roboteer. 'Casimir-buffers sizzling in five.'

'Brace for thrust, everyone.'

Throughout the four-kilometre-wide sphere of the *Reynard*'s mesohull, robots raced to their action stations. Around the tiny central refuge of the ship's habitat core, a dozen huge rad-shielding machines hummed into life, swaddling the cabin with a protective foam of pseudo-vacuum bubbles.

Their timing made all the difference. Two seconds after the *Reynard*'s shields saturated, a radiation wave slammed into the buffers just beyond the cabin walls. Red warning icons splattered across Tom's display like blood spots as warning clangs filled the air.

Tom blinked in confusion. 'Jawid, what was that?'

'Buffers at forty per cent, sir! Compensating.'

'We've lost fine sensor function,' said Faisal. 'Looks like g-rays. They fried the primary bank. Compensating with secondaries.'

Tom flicked the comms-link back on and set it to broadcast. 'Unregistered colony, I said *do not open fire*! We are prepping to depart.'

Silence filled the channel.

'I don't think it was them, sir,' said Wendy nervously. 'I'm picking up damage signs from their ships, too – that blast fried them worse than it did us.'

Tom selected one of the cameras that still worked and zoomed in for a closer look. Sure enough, both gunships had started drifting. One showed a rebooting engine. The other showed no activity at all.

His brow furrowed. 'Then who nuked us?'

'Scanning now,' said Wendy. 'Pinpointing the origin of the blast.' She paused, holding her breath.

Tom glanced across and saw her frowning into her data.

'Sir, I think you should take a look at this.' She posted a view to his display.

On the other side of the system, about ten AU from Tiwanaku's star, a cloud of *something* twinkled. Whatever it was, at that range it must have fired its blast more than an hour earlier, and with prescient accuracy. Either that or the wave had been broadcast to scour the entire system.

'Those bursts look a lot like tiny warp flashes,' said Wendy. 'And I'm seeing visible growth in the cloud radius.'

In other words, it was headed their way. They could have company any minute.

Tom checked the *Horton*'s position. Compensating for light-lag, it was still more than half an hour from the blast-wave.

'Jawid, prep a message drone,' he said quickly. 'Overcook its engines and send it to the *Horton*. If we can give Sundeep even a minute's warning on that radiation, it'll be worth it.'

'On it.'

'Wendy, Faisal – I want to know what that cloud is.'

'Whoever they are, they're sending video on tight-beam,' said Faisal. 'We're getting it and so is the colony.'

'Patch it through.'

In the video window that opened before him, Tom saw a grainy picture of a young man lying on a concrete floor. As he squirmed backwards away from the camera with panic in his eyes, he raised a desperate hand as if to ward off a blow, then nothing. The video reset and started again. Played over the top of it was a track of warbling, poor-quality audio – the sort you might hear from a broken vending machine.

'Trespass detected,' the audio cheerfully informed them. 'Punishment cycle initiated. Damage imminent.'

The message looped over and over in the same flat, chirpy tones.

Tom's skin prickled. Their situation suddenly felt sinister. First a colony that wasn't supposed to exist, and now this? It almost smacked of some kind of prank. But pranks didn't usually start with a near-fatal radiation blast.

'Hold on, everybody. I'm putting some distance between us and whatever *that* is.'

Tom pointed his ship back towards the *Horton* and fired the engines. The thud of warp kicked them into their crash couches. The slow, steady rhythm of gravity bursts picked up tempo, but not nearly fast enough. While the illegal colony shrank, the twinkling cloud kept growing. Whatever it was, it had to be closing on the star incredibly fast.

Tom stared at the cloud anxiously. 'Any guesses, people? What are we looking at?'

'It looks like a munitions burst,' said Wendy. 'SAP analysis suggests a classic drone swarm, but it's way too big for that. I'm seeing warp flashes from more than ten thousand sources and no ship signature behind them. Just empty space.'

'So this is a local phenomenon?' said Tom.

'Unclear,' said Wendy. 'We saw no signs of anything like this from our early system scan. There'd have to be some kind of base for these things to hide in, and we didn't find one. No moon, no engine signature, no comms, nothing. They just sort of ... appeared.'

'Could they have launched from the Fecund ruins?'

Wendy shook her head. 'Very unlikely. That cloud came in way above the ecliptic. There's nothing up there – we looked.'

'I'm matching the flashes to known drone profiles,' said Faisal.

'They're weird. They don't look like anything in the book – the radiation spikes are too short and bright. Whatever they are, we didn't build them. Sir, do you think this is what made the Flags so paranoid?'

'No idea,' said Tom. 'Wendy, are those things following us? Are we clear?'

'Hard to say. They appear to be focused on the planet. I'm taking a closer look … They're closing on T-Four now, sir. Orbital insertion in five, four, three …' Wendy gripped the edge of her bunk. 'Whoa!' she shouted.

'Share it with us, Ms Kim,' said Tom sharply. 'Don't make us guess.'

She posted a view to Tom's display. It was a drone cloud all right. A huge one. The space around the planet had been filled with some kind of warp-enabled munitions and both colony gunships were already balls of slowly blossoming flame. Beams lanced out from the suntap stations, frantically trying to lock on to the blur of targets. Drones exploded everywhere but there were far too many to fight. Tom watched one station after another detonate, bathing the planet below in scorching light.

'There are over two thousand people down there,' he said. 'Jawid, I want a full record of this event on a secure message drone. Immediate release. Destination: New Panama System, Frontier Fleet HQ.'

'On it.'

'Keep a channel open to the drone – I want them to see and hear everything. Faisal, do these profiles match any speculated Fecund drive signatures?'

'Sir?' said Faisal. He sounded confused.

'I want to know who the Flags pissed off. Is it possible that someone was living here already? Someone the original survey flights missed?'

'Sir, the Fecund went extinct ten million years ago.'

'I know that,' Tom snapped. 'Check anyway. And look back over those scans you did on our approach – is it possible that the out-system ruins actually belonged to someone else?'

'N-no, sir. The match was very tight. And no, Fecund warp wasn't that different from ours, sir. If anything, it was messier. Though if they'd somehow survived for ten million years, who knows what they'd have by now?'

Tom knew he was clutching at straws. 'Maybe another human colony that was here before us, then? One with its own weapons tech?'

Even as he said it, he knew that answer wasn't right, either. For a start, colonies with weapons this advanced wouldn't have any trouble with Flags. But still, the threat had to be human, didn't it? Otherwise how had they sent a message in English, no matter how cryptic?

'Give me a matching tight-beam,' said Tom. 'I'm going to talk to them.'

'Sir!' said Wendy. 'I have to point out that we don't even know if there's a pilot guiding that swarm. It could be autonomous. If it is, you may trigger target awareness.'

'They might not spot us without help, Lieutenant, but they're sure as shit going to notice the *Horton*. That ark lights up like a Christmas tree every time it warps. Which means we either assess the threat now or get ready to defend the *Horton* against whatever those things are.'

He thumbed the comm. 'Unidentified drone swarm, this is Captain Tom Okano-Lark of the Interstellar Pact Ship *Reynard*. We are unaware of the political situation in this system but know that there are civilians on that planet. Please end your assault. If there has been an injustice here, rest assured that the full weight of IPSO law will be applied. We will assist in making whatever amends are necessary. I repeat: please end your assault.'

He waited for the message to creep at light-speed towards the swarm, his heart in his mouth. Next to him, Wendy shifted uneasily on her bunk. Meanwhile, the message kept repeating.

'Trespass detected. Punishment cycle initiated. Damage imminent.'

'Sir!' said Wendy. 'Some of the drones have changed course. They're headed this way. I recommend immediate retreat.' Her tone said what she didn't need to: *told you so*.

Tom spat curses. 'Hold on, everybody – we're repositioning to defend the *Horton*. Wendy, let Sundeep know we're coming. Engaging combat mode.'

The *Reynard* was a small ship, but a tough one. It had been designed for two things: environmental scanning and punching well above its weight when necessary. Changes rippled through the vessel from the tiny cabin kernel right out to the exohull surface kilometres above them.

Tom's arms went numb as his simulated replacements came online and his skeletal reinforcements kicked in with a jolt. He felt a sudden flush on his cheeks as the micromesh around his augmented heart started pumping. Elsewhere in the cabin, his crew sank back into their couches as similar machinery buried in their bodies woke up and flexed.

Tom boosted the engines, throwing as much power at the drive as he could without giving someone a concussion. It was like piloting a road-driller.

'Deploy countermeasures,' he ordered. 'Disrupters at maximum spread.'

'Already on it,' said Jawid.

'We have company,' Wendy said grimly. 'Sending you the bearing.'

The Casimir-buffers snapped like the jaws of dragons.

'Shields at twenty per cent, sir,' said Jawid.

'Engaging evasives.' Tom picked a program at random and fired it. Better to live with broken limbs than not at all.

The cabin filled with the clamour of alarms.

'Faisal, I want g-ray scatter. Lots of it. Don't spare the juice.'

'On it.'

Tom grimaced as he watched the horrid blur of action outside his ship. The drones jumped around like crickets and were nearly impossible to hit.

'Drones headed for the *Horton*, sir,' said Wendy. 'No sign they've been able to manoeuvre and they're not responding to hails. The radiation wave might have hit them.'

'Shit,' said Tom. 'Diving to intercept.'

His virtual hands flashed over the keyboard, modifying their tumbling flight onto a course that would head off the threat. He struggled to breathe as gravity pulses hurled him from side to side. Outside, the drones from nowhere flashed ever closer. The growl of the drive became a deafening roar as the ship's autopilot SAP struggled to compensate.

'Deploy everything,' said Tom, his artificial breath labouring. 'Jawid, recondition gravity-shield buoys for self-destruct. Release them all. We're going to buy the *Horton* as much time as we can.'

Tom watched the buoys tear away from his hull in dizzying arcs.

'Fuck you,' he told the drone swarm. 'Leave my colonists alone.'

Space lit up with a cascade of eye-searing nuclear blasts.

The closest drones popped and died like soap bubbles but hundreds more raced up to replace them, apparently undeterred. They winked and flashed like a cloud of fairy dust closing around the *Reynard*.

It was the last thing Captain Tom Okono-Lark ever saw.

1: BEGINNINGS

1.1: MARK

In a grubby rec room smelling of cabbage and bad coffee, at the top of a New York supertower, Mark Ruiz sprawled in a beanbag chair. A beaker of lukewarm stimmo hung in his limp right hand. His glazed eyes stared emptily into the middle distance. An idle passer-by might have mistaken him for a drug addict or a student taking an unscheduled nap; it had happened before. Mark, however, was a roboteer. He was working late and hating it.

He barely perceived the rec room. The body his mind currently inhabited hung in the air eighty kilometres away in the form of a struggling Wheeler Systems aerolifter about thirty seconds from being dashed to pieces against the ground. He wrestled with the New Jersey weather, edging the lifter back towards the tower while the air around him screamed and threw itself at the vehicle like an army of crazed angels. The jagged peak of the Princeton Environmental Sampling Station jutted dangerously below, visible as a streak of smeared yellow light in the storm studded with flashing warning beacons. The ground beneath lay black as pitch. A greasy charcoal-grey sky glowered overhead.

The lifter was, at the end of the day, a blimp. And the weather outside was, whatever they liked to call them these days, still a hurricane. No matter that the blimp in question had nuclear engines with more thrust capacity than the average orbital shuttle, or that its dynamically flexing frame was studded from end to end with near-indestructible air-sculpting microfins. Dealing with two-hundred-kilometre-per-hour winds in a glorified balloon required attention.

Unfortunately, the people trapped in the sampling station weren't going to rescue themselves – either from the storm or the approaching rebels. It would all have been a lot easier, and a lot less frustrating, if Mark hadn't been doing it to a deadline.

The NoreCorr regional government, under the auspices of the FiveClan Cooperative, had finally given in and sold the rights to the now-defunct Philadelphia District. With the city's remaining housing modules air-shuttled to New York at last, control had been scheduled to turn over at midnight. The buyer: the Barrio Eighteen Corporation – the only eco-speculator crazy enough to bother.

FiveClan, predictably, wanted to get as much high-end equipment out of the area as possible before the site changed hands. In true NoreCorr style, they'd ignored the meteorological reports and sent a team of engineers into the tower to remove the quantum processing cores: by far the most valuable items inside.

Equally predictably, Barrio Eighteen wanted them to fail but couldn't be publicly seen to object. So when rebels from the Shamokin Justice Movement had arrived unannounced to try to prevent the removal of staff and equipment on cultural grounds, nobody had been particularly surprised. The Shamokin had a very elastic sense of cultural priorities and a history of taking on dodgy contracts. Less than an hour after the engineers entered the tower, the Shamokin shut down all ground transportation, forcing evacuation by air.

FiveClan had sent Mark in to resolve the problem and now the Shamokin were taking potshots at him from the ground to try to prevent him from docking. He could see them in the infrared, stomping over the remains of the abandoned kudzu plantations in exosuits, angling against the weather, bolt rifles cradled in their ceramic arms.

Mark hated exosuits. Nothing smacked of the abuse of human labour like an exosuit. Why put a person in a dangerous situation when they could just teleoperate a robot? Only people who cared more about money than human lives.

In his mind, Barrio Eighteen and Shamokin Justice were as ridiculous as each other. What was the point of a land-grab on Earth in this day and age? Particularly in NoreCorr. This was the third supercyclone this month and by far the worst. Most of Earth's sects had enough sense to focus their energy on planets that weren't dying.

A sudden shift in the storm threw the lifter sideways just as Mark closed on the tower for the fourth time. He twitched in his beanbag chair and diverted a little more of his focus to the SAP running the struggling engines. The SAP doing aerosurface sculpting complained wildly at the sudden neglect. Fortunately, Mark was an Omega, genetically engineered to handle as many Self-Aware Programs as it took to run a full starship. Splitting his mental focus to guide multiple pieces of equipment came naturally to him, so long as he didn't push it too far.

Ricky B called him from the tower. 'It's no use, Mark. I think those Shamokin bastards have cracked door security. Don't worry about us. Just get out of here.'

'I'm not leaving you.'

'Don't be a fool, Mark. It's not worth it.'

'I'm going to get you out,' Mark insisted.

'Why?' Ricky snapped. 'What's the fucking point? It's just a couple of weeks in a Shamokin shelter and a ransom demand. We both know FiveClan's good for it.'

Mark snarled to himself. For a team of trapped engineers about to be kidnapped at gunpoint by armed rebels, Ricky and his people sounded surprisingly blasé. But then, that was Earth for you these days. Life was cheap, loyalty expensive.

'Can you get the dockbot back online?' said Mark. 'If I had some help from your end on the tethering arm, we could nail this.'

'I've told you,' said Ricky tersely. 'The dockbot refuses to work under these conditions and there's nobody down here who can persuade it to accept an override. If you can't make the join to a static arm, you might as well call it a night.'

'Fine,' said Mark. 'Just send me an address, then. I'll talk to it myself.'

'Why? You can't run the fucking arm and the lifter at the same time, so what's the point?'

Mark gritted his teeth. It had been enough of a pain in the ass to come out here tonight. No way was he going home empty-handed.

'If you don't think I can do it then you won't mind sending me the address.'

Ricky muttered curses at him. 'Don't be stupid. Nobody can do shit like that.'

Ricky was right, of course. Nobody with normal modifications could. But Mark seldom had to worry about the limits of his handling skills.

Thanks to Will Kuno-Monet, his genetic editor and erstwhile mentor, all he had to worry about was being discovered.

'The address, please,' said Mark, 'or I'm putting this in the report.'

'Whatever!' said Ricky. 'It's your funeral, buddy.'

The tribunal-mandated nanny-SAP running in the back of Mark's head sent him a warning jab. [*Exposing the extent of your abilities jeopardises Fleet security,*] it reminded him. [*Remember that your interface is the exclusive, classified property of the IPSO organisation.*]

How could he ever forget?

'Fuck you, and fuck Will Monet,' he told it. The SAP had heard it before.

The secure link appeared in Mark's sensorium. With significant effort, he calved off a share of his attention and pointed it at the dockbot. Immediately, his mind flooded with a wave of terror. For a moment, it looked like he'd get leak-back to the other SAPs under his command, but Mark brought the dockbot's mood under control just in time. Giving the lifter a panic attack would undoubtedly send it crashing into the tower or the ground or both: not an ideal outcome.

He reached out mentally to understand the dockbot's problem. Three of its sensor plates had been left exposed after the last storm and it could no longer feel its second elbow. Consequently, the weather was freaking it out. It was convinced it was going to break. The tiny software minds installed in equipment like the dockbot seldom had enough sentience to think rationally in situations like these. They responded reflexively, like all simple machines. It took a human handler to instil enough logic to overcome their basic programming.

Mark pressed cool reason into the dockbot's tiny mind, reassuring it that everything would be okay. He ignored the plaintive warnings from the aerosurface SAP and coaxed the tethering arm out of the lock position. At the same time, he nudged the lifter closer to the ground, while stray bolts fired from below bounced off its armoured hull. He brought the tethering arm up to kiss and bind.

'We have a link,' he told Ricky with satisfaction. 'Get everyone into that transit pod. We probably have a minute, tops.'

'You're fucking crazy, you know that?' said Ricky. 'Fucking moddie roboteer. You're not normal. Fine. We'll all get in the transit pod in a *hurricane* and crawl up a docking arm into your blimp while they shoot at us from the ground. Sounds great. No problem at all.'

14

Mark smiled to himself and let his mind surf, spreadeagled between the various SAPs he was managing. It was a little like juggling on a unicycle, he decided. Hard, but not impossible.

A minute slid by while Mark watched the rebels mass near the base of the tower fifty storeys below. The last group brought an antique siege-walker with a mounted rail gun. Not good.

'Are you coming or what?' said Mark.

'Yes, we're fucking coming. We're getting the cores in.'

'*What?* Why are you still bothering with the cores?'

'Because management will skin us if we show up without them, *retard*. Or didn't you figure that out? They're worth more than we are.'

Mark rolled his eyes. Classic NoreCorr reasoning.

'Okay,' said Ricky. 'Loading the pod now. You'd better be ready.' His voice oozed reluctance.

The transit pod full of engineers began its climb up the tethering arm, motors squealing. The rebels chose that moment, of course, to fire their rail gun. A depleted-uranium shell tore up through Mark's lifter envelope at three kilometres per second. The aerolifter lurched as ten per cent of its lifting capacity vanished. Every SAP in the vehicle screamed at him simultaneously.

Mark had less than a second to react. Fortunately, his machine-assisted reflexes could handle that. He shot out a command to the tethering arm to blow its rear emergency bolts and the arm snapped with the transit pod still climbing up it.

A cry of terror issued from the engineers inside the pod as they swung free. The arm dangled from the lifter, spurting sparks and hydraulic fluid into the rushing air. For four uncomfortable seconds, the pod ground its way up the arm before the airlock mandibles could seize it. Mark released the top bolts and dropped the arm. Several hundred tons of steel plunged towards the rebels below and he felt a moment's satisfaction watching them scramble. The arm landed squarely on the siege-walker.

'Are you *out of your fucking mind?*' Ricky yelled. 'Some of us are physically fucking *here*, you sonofabitch. Did you forget that?'

Mark pulled the lifter up, gaining altitude and turning back towards New York.

'The airlock to the cabin is now open,' Mark told his passengers. 'Please find a seat and make yourselves comfortable. ETA at New York

Terminus is approximately twenty minutes, weather permitting. Thank you for flying FiveClan.'

He switched off the comms, silencing Ricky's shouting, and stretched out on the chair. He'd spilled his stimmo, he noticed with a wince. Still, rescued engineers: check. Rescued data cores: check. Seriously annoyed Shamokin rebels: check. All told, it wasn't a bad end to a night's work. He might even make it downstairs before the bars closed.

1.2: ANN

At the Plaza Café in Stichin City on the planet Yonaguni, Ann Ludik sat with a cappuccino and a touchboard, hard at work like the dozen or so white-collar types around her. Her two heavies, Carl and Mimi, lounged under the fruit trees a few seats away, dressed as students and chatting over some interactive magazine. In their flickering vid-smocks and gel-boots, they looked for all the world like a pair of nice, ordinary kids. Overhead, somewhere in the deep mauve sky beyond the habitat bubble, the IPS *Griffin* lurked, ready for action. From where she sat, Ann had an excellent view across the pink marble plaza to the entrance of the presidential offices – a nine-storey block of open-fronted levels carved into the canyon wall.

Unlike the government workers around her, the data light flickering in Ann's contact lenses did not show spreadsheets or code-maps. Instead, it displayed a video feed of the aerial drones her crew were tracking from orbit – drones she suspected were laden with chemical explosives. The UAVs in question had already flown just over two hundred kilometres from Stichin City and were racing towards the Flag settlement of Pyotor's Dream. There could no longer be any doubt about their intended destination.

The touchboard in front of Ann contained the passive end of a state-of-the-art quantcomm device that gave her an untraceable, instantaneous data link to her crew. Ann spoke in a subvocal mutter which the implant in her throat dutifully turned into complete speech that only her crew could hear.

'Ara, drop the stealth-shield, please,' she said. 'Carol, bring the spectroscopy SAP to full awareness, and River, a low-intensity X-ray on target three, if you wouldn't mind.'

A lance of invisible energy spat out from the *Griffin*'s hull, skewering one of the drones. It ballooned into a sphere of yellow flame, littering the surrounding desert with debris.

Ann surveyed the blast site with grim satisfaction. 'Do we have a signature?'

'Yes, ma'am,' said Carol. 'Trace presence of naznite confirmed.'

'Disappointing but expected,' said Ann. 'Carol, can you land those other drones at this point?'

'On it. I've still got their drone security cracked – they haven't even tried to cycle it yet. I'll take control and land those puppies now.'

'Excellent. And please download a copy of their flight plan. Make sure it tallies with the information our crawlers provided.'

'Of course, ma'am. Correlating... We have a match. Confidence is one hundred per cent.'

Ann sighed to herself. After more than a week of waiting, the entire grubby episode was finally at an end. She hadn't enjoyed the mission. Her cover as an SAP sanity inspector had bored her. She disliked the bland Frontier-fare that Yonaguni offered for food and entertainment and found the smug attitudes of the colonists downright objectionable. The fact that the kind of plot she'd witnessed here could unfold at a colony a mere three light-years from New Panama struck her as a worrying sign of the times. Three light-years was practically next door. How long before the unrest reached the regional capital itself?

During the course of her career, Ann had watched tensions at the Frontier steadily worsen and IPSO's job grow ever more difficult. After the end of Earth's crusade and the fall of the Kingdom of Man, IPSO had been little more than a symbolic presence – an armed statement of unity to encourage cooperation during the difficult adjustment that followed Interstellar War. Over the years that followed, it had become the most thinly stretched and poorly funded policing body in human history.

In part, that was down to the sheer amount of space they were supposed to look after these days. On top of the fifteen original human colonies, they now had thirteen new ones to protect in that region of the galaxy formerly dominated by the extinct Fecund – the so-called *Far Frontier*. But the real problem wasn't the distances, it was the people. These days, every time an IPSO monitoring mission turned its back, another fight broke out.

Krotokin and his people simply hadn't expected the beleaguered Fleet to notice and so had barely bothered to hide what they were doing. They didn't expect the Fleet to care, either. Sadly, they weren't far wrong. Krotokin had been spotted simply because of his startling incompetence. Ann dearly wished they could have delegated the entire sting to a package of legal SAPs, but you didn't arrest a planetary president without showing up in person.

'River,' said Ann, 'please forward a copy of our findings to the local Fleet office and send another to Messaging Central for release on the next scheduled mail-flight.'

'Done, ma'am.'

'Lovely. Now put in a call to President Krotokin, please, override code *Balmer*. We're on our way.'

Ann got up from her seat and strode around the sauntering pedestrians, heading straight for the presidential office. Abruptly, her two heavies dropped their student act, jumped up and followed her. They moved with animal menace, their clean white smiles now tucked out of sight. Warning lights in Ann's view-field told her that their killtech had come online.

Through the buds in her ears, she heard the incongruous music of the wait signal on the presidential line – some kind of Bhangra-Mahler hybrid.

'He's not answering,' said River.

'Of course not,' said Ann. 'Are you tracking him?'

'He's still in the boardroom. Wait. Scratch that. They're moving. In the corridor, going east.' He threw a window into the corner of her view-field.

At the entrance to the offices, a couple of guardbots advanced towards her. They stopped the moment her override hit them and moved quietly aside.

'Is transit locked down?' said Ann.

'Yes, ma'am,' said River.

'Good, because we're at the stairs.'

Ann marched straight up from the lobby level to Admin One, a huge expanse of near-empty workspace dotted with loungers and sports equipment for the bureaucrats to use. A few of them looked up in confusion as her team passed.

'He's down a level. Make that two,' said River. 'He's headed for the events area.' Ann's map updated.

'Perfect,' she said. 'I'll meet him there.'

She bounded up another two floors in the mild gravity to the expansive ballroom where Krotokin held his parties. She scanned it rapidly.

'Not seeing him.'

'In the back,' said River. 'Building specs say it's a kitchen.'

Ann jogged across the carpeted acres with Carl and Mimi right behind her. How typical of Krotokin's administration to install a physical kitchen. Here they were at the Far Frontier and he still wanted to show off by having his event food prepared by *people*? Still, she supposed, it created jobs for new arrivals. No doubt that was how Krotokin justified the budget for it.

Ann rounded the partition at the edge of the ballroom to find Krotokin striding towards her with four of his cronies behind him. He stopped abruptly. Carl and Mimi took up position, hands flexing in readiness.

'Ah, Mr President,' said Ann. 'So glad I found you. Taking a tour of the facilities, I see.'

Krotokin regarded her coolly with his jowly, bulldog frown. He adjusted his formal hoodie, tugging at the platinum-tipped cords.

'Who am I speaking to, please? And do you have an appointment?'

'I am Captain Andromeda Ng-Ludik of the IPS *Griffin*, and I'm here to notify you that the drones fired by your administration at the unregistered settlement of Pyotor's Dream have been seized. You and your cabinet are hereby formally charged with intent to commit an act of war.'

Krotokin regarded her with displeasure and managed to look bored.

'Those drones weren't *fired*, Captain Ludik, they were sent. We received a request for battery materials. We were delivering them. You have made a mistake, I fear, and an embarrassing one.'

Ann smiled. 'Spectroscopic analysis of a detonated sample drone indicates otherwise. The material you were delivering contained trace quantities of the hyperoxidizing agent naznite, rendering it extremely combustible. That's an unlikely ingredient for a battery mix, wouldn't you say?'

'Ridiculous. And if it's true, I have no idea—'

'Spare me the bluster, Mr President,' said Ann. 'Your planet has been under continuous observation for the last nine days. We followed the delivery of naznite into your system and know both where it was sourced and who it was delivered to. We know the name of the shell company your administration used to hide the purchase and have a complete record of their transactions over the last business quarter. If you didn't want to be noticed, you shouldn't have tried to save money by sourcing the chemical from a lab on New Panama rather than manufacturing it yourself. You are at liberty to debate these details, of course, but please keep your protestations for the tribunal. My crew and I are bored of watching your world. We would like to move on to filing your arrest and concluding this unfortunate chapter.'

Krotokin's face wrinkled up. 'Arrest? What do you mean, *arrest*?'

'What does it sound like?' said Ann. 'If you connect me to your legal SAP, I will present the charge via download for you to consider at your leisure. Once the local constables have taken you into custody, of course.'

'Since when did this become a matter for arrest?' Krotokin sounded genuinely surprised.

'Since you started breaking IPSO law,' said Ann patiently.

Just listening to the man made her angry. The fact that he'd shown little more creativity in his actions than the average janitorial SAP did little to blunt her frustrations.

Krotokin glared at her with a wounded expression. 'Are you aware that in the last year, three more Flag Drops have settled on this world?' he said, his voice rising. 'Or that eight of my people have died in terrorist raids? Or that we have lost millions in research revenues due to the mindless looting of scientific sites? The people you're protecting here have even tried to hold our water supply for ransom, for crissake. Yet because of *IPSO law*, we're still expected to provide them with protein, heavy metals and whatever else they decline to bring for themselves. Every damned year our planet has thousands more immigrants to feed. Immigrants who arrive with complete disregard for legal process and who expect us to support them while they operate without any respect for our laws.'

Ann couldn't have felt less moved. 'You may want to be careful about incriminating yourself further, Mr President. These remarks could be taken as a confession.'

'My point is this,' said Krotokin. 'If one of my people, for their own misguided reasons, chose to tamper with a delivery to these parasites, I could hardly blame them. One might ask why nothing happens when the habitats of legitimate colonists are under attack. But the moment their frustration drives them to make a single mistake, the Fleet shows up to punish them!'

Ann summoned a sense of calm and tried not to shout her reply. 'Perhaps it's because the crimes you're describing are minor and should be handled by your local IPSO representative. Whereas the deliberate bombing of a population site occupied by more than four thousand people is an act of outright war.'

'If it is such a thing,' Krotokin growled, 'then clearly you're on the wrong side of it, Captain Ludik. I will have my people investigate this matter and identify the actual culprit. In the meantime, I recommend you take this up with Commissioner Bak, who I believe needs to be consulted before charges can be filed.'

In other words, the local IPSO representative in question – the person who should have been on top of the conspiracy from the start.

Krotokin waved urgently to his aides. Abruptly, a call icon appeared in Ann's view-field.

'Incoming call,' said River Chu. 'It's Commissioner Bak.'

'Now *there's* a coincidence,' Ann drawled. She turned to her heavies. 'Make sure they don't leave.' She swivelled and stepped back towards the ballroom for a little privacy.

'Put him through,' she said.

Commissioner Bak's chiselled features appeared on the video feed wearing an expression of thinly concealed anxiety. Ann could see a swimming pool behind him, backed by one of Yonaguni's more ostentatious faux-Parisian villas.

'Captain Ludik!'

'Commissioner Bak, I assume you received my report.'

'I did!' said Bak. 'Welcome to Yonaguni! I do wish you'd called when you first arrived.' He pushed a strand of damp blond hair aside and tried for a winning smile.

'As do I, Commissioner,' she lied. 'However, the mission profile required stealth – given the rank of the suspects involved, I could not contact you without risk of interception. I do hope you understand.'

'Of course!' said Bak. 'And please, call me Darrel.' Ann could see him struggling to figure out exactly how badly compromised his position had just become. 'Though I strongly advise you to be circumspect in your choice of next steps,' he added earnestly. 'The political situation here on Yonaguni is very delicate. We've had a great deal of difficulty keeping the Flags and Colonials from each other's throats, as you can see. But what may be less clear is that a conviction for the president would likely only cause a more radicalised faction to take power, which would lead to further violence and yet more convictions. Do you get my drift?'

Unfortunately, Ann did. While she questioned his motivation, he was probably right.

'And I think we both understand that there are also certain *moral* issues at play in this case,' Bak continued. 'It would send the wrong signal for the Fleet to be seen siding with Flags, surely? It would certainly make things harder for *our organisation* to function.'

Ann tried not to grimace at his clumsy subtext. He was clearly referring not to the Fleet, but to the Frontier Protection Party. When legal colonists became infuriated with the Flags' constant nibbling on their turf, they joined the FPP. The movement had started out reasonably enough but subsequently degenerated into rabble-rouser politics and anti-Flag bullying.

'I can see the difficulty of your position given your assigned mission goals,' said Bak. 'But maybe we can find a way to help you meet your targets while ... softening the impact on local politics?'

Ann tried to contain her disapproval. She knew Bak was an FPP supporter from the pro-Colonial events she'd attended that had been arranged by the Rumfoord League. Having seen her at those same meetings, Bak no doubt assumed he could take her politics for granted. But then, like most people, Bak had no idea that the Rumfoord League existed, or that there was anything going on at those events other than the usual Flag-bashing rhetoric. All Bak knew was that she appeared to be deeper into Colonial politics than he was.

Nothing made Ann more uncomfortable than reactionaries assuming she shared their views. Being mixed up with idiots like the FPP made her feel dirty. She'd suspected Bak of being in on the entire Krotokin affair from the start, which was why she'd kept him out of the loop. His attitude now did little to alleviate her suspicions.

'Commissioner Bak, my position here is clear,' she said. 'I have no choice but to uphold the rule of law.'

A second icon appeared in her view. This one had River Chu's marker on it and a private security code. Her words dried up. An icon like that could only mean one thing – fresh data from the League. Besides her, River was the only other person aboard with access. He must have received a reply ping from Messaging Central when he submitted their report. Something had been waiting for them on the stack while they were in stealth mode. It could have been there for days, she realised with alarm. They'd never expected Krotokin to take more than a week to make his move.

'One moment, please,' she told the commissioner. She paused the comms feed and opened the attached message. It contained a single phrase: *Constant Flies.*

Her insides crunched tight. It had finally happened, then – the moment the League had been planning for. The dreadful years of creeping around behind the backs of the Fleet were finally over and all the awful secrets they'd kept from the rest of IPSO would finally come out. But who knew how long the message had languished? She didn't have a second to waste. They'd have to return to New Panama immediately.

Frustrating though it was, her current mission would have to be resolved without her. Her crew would be confused, of course, and probably upset, so she'd need to concoct some explanation for why they weren't sticking around to nail the crooks to the wall. It could have been worse, though. At least they got to catch the president.

She turned the feed back on.

'Commissioner ... Darrel. I have considered my options and one alternative has just come to light.'

'Please,' said Bak. 'Go on?'

'Effective immediately, I am handing over resolution of the case to you.'

Bak blinked at her, suddenly wary at being handed his ideal solution with so little effort.

'I'm not sure I follow.'

'I have an executive order permitting me to delegate responsibility for concluding this affair. If it would smooth local politics, I could delegate to you.'

'It undoubtedly would,' said Bak, 'but are you sure you're comfortable with handing it off?'

'No, Darrel,' she said. 'Not comfortable at all. But then I don't imagine you will be, either. A final report must be filed at local Fleet HQ within twenty days showing a satisfactory resolution. If I leave you in charge, an interim report will have to go with me, containing my recommendations for legal next steps. You will need to reconcile any decisions you make with those findings and register them with the War Crimes Court. Do you accept responsibility for the case?'

Bak peered at her, trying to comprehend her sudden U-turn. The risk of professional entrapment clearly scared him. Ann could tell she was going to have to make it easy for him.

'It would benefit *our organisation* if you were to resolve this locally and let me get on my way,' she said.

Bak's eyes lit up. 'Of course! I see what you mean – clearly this matter must be taken seriously.'

'I need to be able to trust you on this,' she said, knowing full well she could not. '*Our organisation* cannot afford for the rule of law to be seen to weaken. Do you understand?'

'You can rely on me,' said Bak earnestly. 'I won't let you down.' With the twin prospects of career disaster and jail apparently indefinitely postponed, his smile broadened. 'Those responsible will be dealt with most severely.'

'River,' said Ann, 'please send the report codes for the case to Commissioner Bak.'

'Done.'

'Darrel, how fast can you get here?'

Darrel blinked. 'Er, how fast do you need?'

'Can you be here in five minutes?'

Darrel glanced back at something or someone in the pool, looking uncomfortable.

'I can,' he croaked.

'Good. Please do.' She swapped channels again. 'Carol, please assemble some of the building's guardbots. Swap out their SAPs for Fleet enforcement standard and bring them up here.'

'On it,' said her roboteer uncertainly. She clearly did not understand what had just happened, but Ann's crew was nothing if not loyal.

She walked back to where her heavies stood grinning at the president.

'Something came up,' she said. 'We're leaving.'

Mimi looked disappointed. 'What about them?'

Three standard-issue guardbots clad in wasp-striped tact-fur clumped around the corner, their camera-lights winking.

Mimi's face fell. 'You're kidding.'

Krotokin's shoulders sagged in relief.

Ann regarded the president coldly. 'Don't think you're off the hook,' she said.

She gestured for her heavies to follow, then turned and walked away. It chafed to be leaving the scene of an arrest like this, but what else could she do? Events had overtaken them, which meant that petty Frontier conflicts like this one would soon be fodder for the history books. There was some relief to be had in that, along with a healthy serving of fear.

'Ara,' she told her pilot, 'please prepare for immediate departure. Destination is New Panama HQ. We'll be coming up via shuttle within the hour.'

1.3: WILL

Will Kuno-Monet stood alone at the window filling one wall of the IPSO senatorial lounge and struggled for calm. Beyond the glass, the city of Bradbury stretched under a dusty lavender sky. Ranks of fin-shaped supertowers marched to the low horizon, each proudly displaying some architectural quirk intended to make it look somehow more important than the others. At least half of them were still unfinished – webbed over with support fibre and crawling with construction spiders.

Dense traffic flowed between the buildings through a sprawl of glassy tunnels that made the vehicles look like blood cells racing through a network of capillaries. To Will's mind, the whole city resembled a farm of giant, interconnected lungs – which wasn't far from the truth. Bradbury produced so much atmospheric leakage these days that you could see real clouds over the city.

A lot had changed since his first visit after the war. Back then, Bradbury was a scatter of neo-deco palaces left over from the Martian Renaissance, pockmarked with bullet holes and mingled with ugly Truist block-architecture. All the original buildings were gone now – vanished under the tide of change along with his optimism.

Will breathed deep and tried to sweep the worry and the anger to the corners of his mind. Ira was counting on him. This next senate session needed to go right or their funding woes would only increase. He just wished the nightmares hadn't picked this particular week to return.

Will had suffered from war-dreams for most of his life and had developed strategies to handle them. This time, though, they were worse than ever. Instead of seeing Amy screaming in the Truists' torture chair, which had actually happened, he saw Rachel. Her last word before they fried her brain was always *Mark*. He felt sick just thinking about it.

When he'd told Nelson about it, his friend had calmly suggested that Will had unresolved guilt issues relating to the loss of his wife's ship and his *almost-son*'s subsequent attempt to rescue her. No shit. He didn't need a trained psychologist to tell him that. He'd not been able to sleep properly ever since the tribunal that had crippled Mark's career. What Will craved was some way to get the screaming in the back of his head to stop. He rubbed his tired eyes.

Behind him, the door to the session chamber slid open. Will turned to see Parisa Voss, the senator for Antarctica and his staunchest political ally, step out and stride across the slowly evolving gold-patterned carpet to meet him. Like most home-system politicians, Pari always looked both immaculate and overdressed. She'd changed outfit since their last session together and now wore a magenta foil skirt-suit and a gold Martian Renaissance tiara. Her contact lenses had been tinted a shocking turquoise to match her shoes. Will could make out the subtle play of data light across her pupils. She'd looked about thirty years old for the entire thirty years Will had known her.

'Are you ready?' she said.

He nodded.

She peered at him. 'You okay, Will?'

'Just more dreams, that's all.'

She winced and laid a hand on his arm. 'I'm sorry. Did you talk to Nelson about it?'

'Yes, but I think he's a bit preoccupied with the refurb of the *Ariel Two* at the moment. He's got his starship-captain hat on this week and doesn't have much time to play therapist. Don't worry, I can manage.'

'Let me know on the private channel if you need a time out,' she said gently. 'I'll cover for you. The committee's in fine form today. They're even more annoying than usual.'

Will tried for a smile. 'Great.'

'Speaking of which, we have to change your ten o'clock. Representative Bose has ducked out on us. I think Ochoa is pressuring him.'

Will groaned. In the virtual space of his home node, he brought up the bewildering multicoloured mess of his calendar. A wide lane of appointment slots peppered with thousands of memory keys led off into the distance.

'I'm thinking we slide that session with the Transcendist bishops in there,' said Pari. 'They'll take what they can get.'

'Done.'

As Will's time-management SAP dutifully moved the slots about, he couldn't help glancing off into the far, unbooked future. Somehow, that wonderful empty land always receded as he moved towards it. Apparently, you couldn't be the first person in human history to make contact with an alien civilisation, end an interstellar war and claim control over a planet-busting starship the size of a small country without people noticing. And since they'd noticed, his involvement in government had proved unavoidable.

The promises Will had made to Gustav Ulanu after the fall of Truism didn't help, either. When Gustav ascended to the ecclesiastical throne as Prophet, he'd begged Will to ensure that Earth remained a fair partner in IPSO affairs. Since Gustav's assassination at the hands of his own people, Will had felt more duty-bound than ever to maintain that balance. Consequently, he had little time these days to function as a starship captain or even a roboteer. He was, as Gustav had once put it, 'an icon of incontestable power'. His duty was to the entire human race. And apparently that meant meetings – lots and lots of meetings.

'Okay,' he told Pari. 'Let's do this.'

She led him back towards the chamber where IPSO's Defence Funding Committee was in session. As he walked, Will prepared.

Over the years, he'd developed a Self-Aware Program for political discourse – a persona to hide behind. It worked well but came with costs. The SAP guided his body but didn't filter emotions, and Will had found that his anger in meetings tended to accumulate. Nevertheless, he reached for the icon labelled *Statesman* and pressed it against his mind like a mask, turning himself into a Teflon-coated lobbyist yet again.

At the same time he stretched his mind wide, syncing it with the building's pervasivenet. Fingers of his awareness slid out to cover the senate's secure communications traffic. The political backchannels, supposedly invisible to all but the chosen few, fell open to him. Will knew he wasn't supposed to use his powers to spy on his adversaries, but he'd realised years ago that they were already spying on him. All he was doing was balancing the game. When he'd told Pari, she'd expressed astonishment that it had taken him so long to pick up the habit.

Will plastered a diplomatic smile on his face, took a deep breath and stepped into the high-ceilinged session chamber. A mahogany podium faced a ring of tall chairs clad in real vat-leather where the funding committee's members sat waiting – a rainbow-dressed bunch with expensive physiques and flawless hair. The Earther habit of dressing in patriotic sect colours, or House colors, as they now liked to call them, had been making a comeback. Behind them, anti-snooping baffles in Fleet-blue twisted on the walls.

'Everyone, I think most of you have met Captain Ambassador Kuno-Monet,' said Pari Voss. 'And those who haven't will of course recognise him and understand what a privilege this is for all of us.'

Will waved the flattery away with a self-deprecating hand.

'Captain Monet has come to speak to us on behalf of Fleet Admiral Baron. I'd like to thank him on behalf of the senate for finding room in his schedule to make that possible.'

Lukewarm applause rippled around the room. In reality most of the senate thought of him as a political halfwit and an annoying obstruction to their plans, just as he regarded them as oily, money-grabbing crooks. But they were all too seasoned to let their opinions show, so the game ticked along as ever. Will surveyed the unwelcoming faces around him and smiled.

'Ladies and gentlemen of the committee, thank you for your time. I'd like to say a few words today about the organisation we represent. IPSO was established with a single goal – to protect a balance of power that would permit Earth and the colonies to prosper together in peace. For thirty years, we have succeeded in that ambition.'

[*Hah!*]

That response came on the private channel for Earth's Free Movement faction – the political face of the Flag-Drop industry. Will ignored it. He'd learned long ago that hearing your opponent's sarcasm was far more useful than pretending it wasn't there – presuming you could hold your anger in check, of course. He spoke on.

'Since our founding, humanity has pushed out beyond the gateway-lobe at New Panama and now inhabits over a dozen star systems that formerly belonged to the Fecund species, as well as our own.'

[*As opposed to fifty systems.*]

'On each of our new worlds, settlers from Earth and the Old Colonies live side by side, creating new economies together. That is an extraordinary achievement.' He paused for effect.

{*Extraordinarily short-sighted.*}

This latest witticism came from the other side of the house – Isambard Visser, senator for Drexler and champion of furious Colonials everywhere. The anti-Flag bullies in the FPP loved him. Will hesitated for a moment, regaining his poise.

'We have expanded cautiously,' he went on, 'because early experiences proved that unchecked growth results in destabilising conflicts. We have seen time and time again that people will squabble over the scientific advances waiting to be discovered in the new territory, often at the cost of their own lives. And our caution has borne fruit. IPSO has developed a formula for growth, and while it does not please everyone all the time, it has worked.'

{*Monet apparently can't please any of the people, any of the time.*}

Will heard stifled chuckles erupting around him. Anger pulsed in his veins. He suppressed it.

'At the end of the war, people told us that a shared police force couldn't function without a shared government to back it up. The continued existence of IPSO has proved them wrong. People told us that Earth and the Colonies couldn't trade. They were wrong, too. The success of the IPSO peace-coin has disproved that. And we were told that genetics and robotics would destabilise the economy, producing a crisis that would plunge us back into war. Had they been right, I would not be standing here before you today.'

[*We wish you weren't.*]

'However, we now stand at a crossroads. Under consideration for a vote at the next senate plenum is Bill Eight-Eight-Two. If this bill passes, the funding support for starship construction will be reduced by a third. This proposal comes at a time when conflicts on the Far Frontier are occurring at an ever-increasing rate. This bill is only before us because certain members of IPSO's governing body have begun to lose faith in the balance we espouse. There are some who believe that the Colonial governments should be allowed to police their worlds without IPSO oversight. This would please representatives of the Old Colonies but probably mean the deaths of tens of thousands of Earth's unregistered settlers across the Far Frontier.'

{*Monet makes it clear he stands against the rule of law.*}

'There are others who believe that the planetary registration process should be disbanded, permitting human expansion to accelerate. This would allow individual Houses of Earth's estate to effectively claim worlds for themselves in isolation, creating a scientific gold rush likely to end in a bloodbath.'

[*Or human diversity, perhaps – a nightmare prospect.*]

'Both of these visions require IPSO to adopt a passive role in human affairs. I can see why slashing the Fleet budget might look appealing at first glance – extracting fees from governments who do not welcome our support is never easy. However, giving in to either of these agendas bolsters one party at the expense of the other. In reality, the alternative to balance is chaos. Thus, in my capacity as special adviser to the senate and representative of Fleet Admiral Baron, I move for Bill Eight-Eight-Two to be struck from the agenda. Ladies and gentlemen, if we don't act as guardians of the human peace, no one will. We all stand to lose if the bill is passed. For the sake of humanity, please stand with me. Thank you for listening. May I count on your support?'

Silence followed. The senators shifted in their seats. Finally, a large, cadaverous man in a floor-length tangerine coat raised a hand – Gaius Ochoa, the senator for Titan and the leader of Earth's Free Movement faction.

'Captain Monet, thank you for speaking,' he said. 'You have lost none of your oratorical flair.'

Chuckles filled the backchannel. Will smiled sweetly.

'Please be assured that we understand your concerns. We share them, in fact. However, we just *can't* be seen to prioritise ship-building at this time. It's as simple as that. Money is tight all around, Captain. IPSO has half a dozen major projects badly in need of support.' He held up a bony hand and marked them off. 'You've got the Earth Exodus shuttle project; the housing programmes throughout the home system; the lottery programme for colony relocations ... The lottery programme alone has been begging for extra money for nestship berths for the last five years.'

Will nodded with sage understanding. 'Absolutely. I'm aware of the difficulties.'

'Are you?' said a pale-skinned woman in a green – Constance Fon, the senator for Africa. 'Did you read the most recent *Emergency Earth* status report?'

Will shook his head politely and pretended he couldn't guess what he was about to hear.

'It will, they say, take about forty more years to get Earth's fifteen billion offworld,' she said. 'That's assuming no population increase, which looks unlikely given the current boom in life-extension technologies. At the same time, weather stability has deteriorated by another fourteen per cent. Earth's climate is projected to slide into the Galatea Zone within the decade.'

Will understood that term from personal experience. The Galatea Zone was the period between habitability and sterility in which a planetary ecosystem exhibited violent, chaotic behaviour. The Galatean colonists had encountered it during their misguided attempts at terra-forming. Earth, they'd since discovered, was now approaching the same state from the other direction as its ailing biosphere finally gave out.

'Under conditions like these,' said Fon, 'the approaching disaster on Earth must inevitably be a priority.'

Pari raised a manicured finger. 'Of course,' she said. 'But Earth's weather has been a known issue for years. It's not necessarily an IPSO problem, though. It's a local one.'

'I beg to differ,' said Fon. 'IPSO must weigh the social benefits and step in where it can effect the greatest good. Disaster relief is written clearly into our charter. And how many people are involved in your Frontier conflicts, Captain Monet? Thousands? Perhaps tens of thousands? The Far Frontier colonies are all but empty. By comparison, the problems on Earth involve the lives of billions. Earth may be a local crisis, but it dwarfs the skirmishes you're worried about, and for that we need ferries, not battleships.'

'A fair point, madam,' said Will. 'However, if the brakes come off at the Frontier, there's no telling where it will end. Do I need to remind you that it only takes a single starship to threaten a world, regardless of how many people are on it?'

'Captain Monet,' said Gaius Ochoa with a sly smile, 'the only person

31

in history who's jeopardised a planet with a starship is *you*. You're not threatening *us*, I hope?'

The backchannel erupted with laughter again. This time Will struggled not to respond. Putting the *Ariel Two* in orbit around Earth to end the war had been one of the hardest and most frightening things he'd ever done. He'd hated every fraught, desperate minute of the ordeal. It was amazing how nobody ever thanked him for it.

'No,' Will snapped. 'But I would point out that there is nothing to stop us from simply moving Earth's population down into subcities or up into orbitals. Not every single citizen needs to be laboriously relocated to another gravity well at IPSO's expense.'

The Statesman SAP sent him a worried squeak. He got a warning look from Pari, too. He'd been too blunt. He saw some of the senators' expressions tighten. Two of them folded their arms.

'Unfortunately, subcities don't work,' said Fon. 'The tectonic consequences of the Galatea Effect make that painfully obvious. And orbitals are no better. We learned from the debacle at Drexler nine years ago that we can't force people to live a certain way. They won't accept it. Accidents happen. People die.'

Will gave up pandering and swiped the SAP aside. 'The Drexler disaster was sabotage,' he said. 'It happened because we weren't there to stop it. Just like we won't be if you let this damned bill pass.'

Will knew he'd lost his cool. He should have let the SAP do the work, but spending his days as a puppet to his own software did not sit well with him. They'd always known it was a long shot asking the committee to drop the bill. Both sides wanted the Fleet starved so they could access the money hiding in the Far Frontier.

'You're right,' he said. 'Why should the Fleet's policing efforts be spread so thin in the face of the bigger problem? I mean, if the Fleet *really* wanted to make a difference, then by your logic most of them ought to be right here, focusing their efforts on the contractors who run all those Exodus projects and rooting out all the white-collar crime. After all, there have been some mighty unusual prices charged for some of those relocation programmes.'

The senators bristled. Statesman let out a silent wail.

'Might I suggest that we all step back for a moment and *take stock*?' said Pari brightly. This was her safety phrase for Will, to let him know when he'd gone too far.

Gaius Ochoa pointed a bony finger at Will's chest. 'You're on thin ice with that remark, Monet,' he said. 'Pricing pressure on contractors would only cause them to look for savings elsewhere, and that would mean a reduction of safety protocols. We don't have control over how those businesses are run.'

'The prices wouldn't have to change,' said Will, 'just the oversight. Do you have a problem with that?'

By now, Gaius Ochoa's face had taken on an unhealthy hue. 'Captain Monet,' he growled, 'oversight of Exodus projects is not the job of this committee. Did you accidentally come to the wrong meeting?'

Will knew he'd scorched the negotiation but it wasn't as if he'd ever had much of a chance. Talking with these people always felt pointless. He could have killed all of them with his bare hands, of course, but what good would that do? So he gripped the podium in front of him instead, the strength of his augmented fingers drilling holes in the organically sourced hardwood.

'You're right again,' he said. 'We shouldn't be funding the Fleet to investigate corruption. And you certainly shouldn't have to put any pressure on the people robbing us blind. I tell you what – why don't I do it instead? That'd be more fun than meetings, anyway. I'll get Admiral Baron to okay it for me to start doing random spot checks on private cargoes,' he said, idly making a pattern of dents in the podium's surface. The wood cracked under his hands. 'Let's see who I can catch. No need to use Fleet ships, just *Ariel Two*. We already know that dozens of sect outfits are breaking the law, and some Colonial companies, too. Now, who should I go after first?'

He glanced around the room at the senators, sizing each of them up. They regarded him with expressions of stunned alarm. All except Pari Voss, whose face bore a look of weary despair.

'Any recommendations?' Will prompted. 'I'd love to get my hands on some of the people who're screwing us over, wouldn't you?'

For once, the senators had no reply. They'd never seen such an overt threat in a political meeting. Who else but Will Kuno-Monet would be allowed to get away with it?

The human race only had one super-person. When the galaxy-spanning Transcended race offered Will support and decided to spare humankind rather than torching them – as they had the unfortunate Fecund – their help came in the form of gifts. Along with granting

Will control over the most powerful ship in human space, they'd also changed his body. He could move faster than the eye could see and crush steel with his hands. Pepper him full of bullets, as people had tried to do on numerous occasions, and his body healed in minutes. At the end of the day, political manoeuvring with Will only worked because he always played nice. Always. These days, though, his patience was wearing awfully thin.

Pari Voss opened her mouth to say something placating, only to be interrupted by a ping from the room's SAP.

'Excuse me, Captain Monet, but we have a message marked *Urgent Alpha*, executive eyes only.'

Will blinked away his anger. That rating encompassed both him and the senate but almost nobody else. It couldn't be good.

'Put it on the screen, please,' he said.

The committee room's monitor wall swapped to video display.

'This is a recording taken at Survey Star Nine-One-Nine, provisionally named Tiwanaku,' said the SAP. 'It was recorded by the escort scout IPS *Reynard* and forwarded via emergency messenger drone. The events captured occurred approximately four weeks ago, local frame time.'

The video started and Will saw what Captain Tom Okano-Lark had seen. After the *Reynard* initiated battle mode, the perspective jumped to grainy footage from the drone's onboard telescope, pointed back towards the ship. The picture flickered with every pulse of warp. They caught a brief final glimpse of the *Reynard* accelerating to avoid the unidentified swarm closing on it, and then nothing.

A cold silence fell across the hall. One senator nervously cleared his throat. The hair on Will's neck stood up straight.

'Have we heard from the *Reynard* since the drone's release?' he said.

'No,' the room replied.

If the *Reynard* had survived, it would undoubtedly have followed up with an *All Clear*.

'How was this message forwarded?' Pari asked in a hushed voice.

'Via Far Frontier Headquarters in the New Panama System and priority fuelling stars. Security Level Freddie has been applied since initial receipt.'

'Then we're the first in the home system to know.'

'Along with Admiral Baron, yes,' said the room.

Will looked back at the senators' faces, their expressions now blank with surprise. This had been an unusual morning for them. In Pari's eyes, he saw something like compassion.

'This rather changes things, doesn't it?' she said.

Will nodded. Suddenly, the tables had turned. If they moved to a war footing, he wouldn't have to worry much about senate approval any more since the democratic functions of IPSO were suspended during a Fleet emergency. Funding battles would be the least of their problems.

Will didn't find himself enjoying that knowledge. Instead it made him feel obscurely guilty, as if he was no longer playing by the rules he'd set himself.

'I'll get this sorted out,' he told the staring faces around him. 'Don't worry. I'll make sure it's resolved.'

'We'll help however we can,' said Pari.

'Thank you,' said Will. 'Now if you'll excuse me, I should probably go and speak to the admiral.' He nodded his respects and headed for the door.

If the attack had actually been perpetrated by aliens, who knew what else they'd be capable of? The Transcended who helped Will end the war had been able to remotely blow up stars on a whim. Nevertheless, Will felt excitement bubbling up. Here, at last, was a problem worthy of his abilities. Maybe he'd get a chance to actually do some good for once.

2: GATHERING

2.1: WILL

Will paced the transit pod as it whisked him across Bradbury to the Admiralty building at three times the legal speed limit. The SAP begged him to take a seat with every wild turn it took through the transport web. Will ignored it.

The pod segued onto a vertical track and raced up the side of the building, shunting others aside with override warnings, and deposited him at the entrance to Ira's suite. The doors leapt open just in time to miss Will's striding feet.

Ira's office filled a four-hundred-square-metre slice of sparsely decorated tower-habitat with cyber-thyme flooring and off-white organic walls. At the far end, a huge window-wall looked onto the glassy, peach-tinted ruins of the Mars Pioneers Historical Park. Ira stood near it, instructing most of his entourage and furniture to leave.

'. . . Monet is here, I said. Everybody out except you two chairs. That's right, you two.'

He ushered them through the archway into the planning chamber beyond. As soon as the doors had shut, he turned to greet Will with an urgent grimace.

'You heard, then?'

They'd both changed since they first flew together during the war, but Will always felt that Ira had managed the last thirty years better than him. Sure, Will hadn't aged a day and had beaten everything from cancer to chemical attacks, but Ira had found ways to be happy. When his role in history forced him into politics, Ira adapted. Now, instead of managing a ship, he managed a civilisation – or at least that part of it which pertained to interplanetary security. Ira hadn't balked when IPSO's Social Engineering Division insisted on increasing his height, or straightening his nose, or electing him Fleet Admiral six times in a row. Will wasn't sure how he'd stuck with it. When Will asked, the only answer Ira ever gave was: *If I don't do it, it'll be some other poor shmuck whose decisions I like less.*

They'd let him keep his trademark bald head, at least – for brand-persistence reasons, apparently.

'The room is secure,' said Ira. 'We can talk.'

Will had already checked for himself. He habitually managed his own security and had never been happy handing off control to the Fleet, not even with a friend like Ira in charge.

'I have a question,' said Will. 'Am I still ambassador to aliens?'

That title hadn't meant anything useful for twenty years, just hung around his neck like an albatross – a convenient label for his enemies to mock him with.

Ira nodded. 'Of course. And handling this is definitely your job. With the scale of threat this event implies, we need the big guns out there, and that means you and the *Ariel Two*. But realistically speaking, we both know this isn't likely to be an extraterrestrial problem.'

After humanity's interaction with the preeminent Transcended race, a flurry of research had been conducted regarding the probabilities of various kinds of contact scenarios. Hugo Bessler-Vartian, the irascible physicist who'd accompanied them on that fateful mission which led to first contact, had taken the fortune he made from his work on Fecund technologies and poured it into research on aliens. Specifically, on what he perceived as the alien threat to humanity.

The conclusions had been stark: the probability of encountering a species as old and powerful as the Transcended far outweighed that of finding one of a similar age to humankind. The apparent rarity of intelligent species in the universe made sure of that. With so few civilisations to be discovered, the likelihood of finding one the same age as your own was almost zero. Consequently, the probability of finding aliens who would attack the human race in any recognisable way was also vanishingly small. Humanity was far more likely to be wiped out as a pest before they'd even noticed.

'You think it was some kind of power grab by a sect, then,' said Will, 'dressed up to look weird.'

Ira glanced at him sidelong. 'Don't you?'

'Sure – it's the logical conclusion,' Will admitted. 'But why bother?' Part of him wanted the attack to be exactly what it appeared to be simply because it would give him something practical to do. 'Think of the expense,' he said. 'The drones, the radiation blast, the modified engines. Not to mention hiding all the construction beforehand. It'd cost billions to pull off. And for what?'

'That's what we'd like to know,' said Ira. 'Since that message showed up ten minutes ago, our research cluster has been hard at work trying to find out.'

He waved a hand at the nearest wall, which screened-on to display a freeze-frame of the terrified youth from the video the *Reynard* had intercepted.

'We just received this,' said Ira. 'We don't know who he is yet, but that jacket he's wearing is a giveaway. Our SAPs traced the buttons on his lapel – those insignia belong to the Knights of Kolob, which is the underground Truist Revival branch of the Smithite sect, a group known to have invested heavily in Flag-Dropping.'

These days, every sect on Earth had a Revivalist branch of some kind. Even with his augmented memory, Will struggled to keep track of them all. Before the war, there had only been Truism – the belief in the supremacy of man over all of nature – with Earth's church at the top. While foreign to Will's sensibilities, he could at least wrap his head around it.

Then, at the end of the war, Gustav Ulanu had realigned the faith under Transcendism: the idea that there were benign mentor species in the universe hoping to guide humanity towards God's truth. For a while, it had looked like the new doctrine was going to convince everyone to cooperate. But after years of silence from the Transcended, religious politics had slid inexorably away from them. After Ulanu's assassination, that process had accelerated dangerously.

'But the Knights are small fry,' said Ira. 'They only have a tiny share of the Flag movement, which makes me wonder: if this attack was some kind of inter-sect warning, why bother? The Smithites can hardly be the target – they're not worth the investment.'

Ira brought up a freeze-frame of the two ramshackle gunships. 'Then there's the shuttles the *Reynard* encountered. We can't say for certain but we think they belong to Truth Reborn, the Revivalist arm of Theravad Plus – a bigger player, for sure, but still hardly worth this kind of attention.'

'You think all this is a message for the Fleet, then?' said Will.

'Maybe,' said Ira. 'The fact that both Flags *and* legit colonists were attacked suggests that whoever did this wants everyone to be afraid. Our strategy software thinks the subtext here is a group making a play to set themselves up as a separate government. They're using the alien motif to make everyone back off till they can get it together.'

'But who?' said Will. 'The Old Colonies wouldn't bother, and there can't be more than a handful of sects on Earth with the money to pull that off.'

'That's what I want you to find out,' said Ira. 'To minimise the panic, the public will be told it's a hoax and that we're sending an investigation team. At the same time, we're telling the senate that an exodiplomatic mission is unavoidable, just in case this is exactly what it looks like – a first-contact situation.'

Will frowned. 'Why the double message?'

'Because it gives the Fleet the most leeway to operate. And it rules out any political argument for keeping you off the mission – after all, you're still humanity's expert when it comes to dealing with aliens. The negotiation around this is going to be fast and nasty, I'm afraid. We need ships out there as soon as possible, but Earth's senators will be pushing for control. They'll try to delay things to force us to accept more of their people on the team. They're already furious that this event makes their sects look like a bunch of planet-grabbing, warmongering assholes.'

Will snorted. 'Imagine that.'

'The good news is that Parisa Voss is on the Committee for E. T. Affairs, as is Bob Galt-Singh from Galatea. You'll have to babysit some VIP diplomats and all that shit, but with luck they'll cover the chit-chat, leaving you free to work.'

'I can handle that,' said Will. 'When do we start?'

Ira reached out and took Will's arm. His expression softened. 'Soon, Will,' he said. 'Very soon. But first, my old friend, can we sit down for a moment?'

Ira's sudden change of pace took Will by surprise but he knew better than to second-guess it. While he and Ira had remained close since the war, they'd spent little time relaxing together. If Ira had something to say, there had to be a reason, so he let Ira guide him to one of the chairs near the window.

The view from Ira's room was far humbler than that from the senate's executive suite. Probably no more than thirty storeys off the ground, the window looked out on a park that had been crowded around by modern architecture, leaving it in shadow for half the day.

'Will, I have something to ask of you,' said Ira, sitting across from him. 'Something about this mission.' He leaned forward.

'Go on?'

'I need you to bring me back a miracle.'

Will frowned. 'Not sure I follow you,' he said.

'We're in trouble,' said Ira. 'The Tiwanaku Event makes it obvious that the sects aren't bothering with legal channels to build settlements any more. Once that gets out, IPSO loses the last of its credibility. War is just around the corner and this might be the start of it.'

'I know things are bad right now—' Will started.

Ira cut him off. 'Unfortunately, you don't know the half of it. The sects are gearing up – we've tracked the arms shipments. They've been waiting for this for years. And if we have another war, it won't be like the last one. Suntaps and nestships *ended* that war. Next time around, that'll be what we start with. Presuming, that is, the Transcended let us get that far. It'll be the end of everything, Will, believe me. We tried to build the future, you, me and Gustav,' he said. 'We let them put us in starring roles and we still fucked it up.'

Will folded his arms. 'What else could we have done?'

Ira shrugged. 'I don't know. When I look back, so much makes me cringe. Like the whole senate business, for a start. Do you know why we settled on the Old American model for the IPSO council? So we could bake inequality into the system.'

Will wrinkled his nose. 'Come on,' he said. 'Nobody wanted to make things unfair.'

'No, but we did want to give a bunch of tiny colonies the same voice as a planet of billions. We *created* the Flag problem, Will, by giving ground on both sides, even when it didn't make any sense. We forced the registration of new worlds with one hand while demanding fair treatment for all inhabitants with the other. We effectively manufactured an incentive for people to show up unannounced. The sects are going around us now precisely because that's the only option we gave them.'

Will disliked the idea, particularly given how his last meeting had gone. 'Sure, but still, I don't think we could have predicted all this.'

'Maybe not. Hindsight's twenty-twenty and all that. But here's my point: you need to bring something back, even if it's only new technology. Whatever those faux-aliens used to nuke the comms, for instance. Had the *Reynard* encountered nothing more than an unlicensed colony, that would have been it – war. As it is, this weird attack will keep that door shut until everyone figures out what's going on, but it won't hold them for long. We need something to buy us some breathing room to figure out how to fix this mess. A diversion. An opportunity. Anything to pull us back from the brink. Otherwise the sects are going to trash the peace and that will be the end of us all. If I could go and do this myself, you know I would.'

A cloud of deep sadness passed over Ira's brow. For a moment, Will had a glimpse of the inner man, and what he'd given up to turn himself into a politician.

Ira drew a heavy breath and looked out at the historical park below, where the broken towers of Mars's early habitats stood.

'Do you know why I picked this office?' he said.

Will shook his head.

'Because of that,' said Ira, pointing at the ruins. 'Those buildings changed history. They built them for volunteers in a reality-based entertainment. Did you know that? They printed them out of the local dust. They glassified it. Terrible radiation shielding, of course, but the company that funded them didn't care; the volunteers from Earth were on one-way tickets. But when Earth saw those people living in pink fairy castles with all that room and all that light, it changed how everyone thought about Mars. They looked around at the shit they were living in and said: *I want that.* It saved the economy, Will, when it looked like everything was going south.'

Of course, everything had still gone south, Will thought. About a century later, after the Martian banks had sucked all the other planets dry. He chose not to point that out and stared dutifully down at the remains. Then he dropped his bombshell.

'I want Mark on my team,' he said.

Ira looked at him hard. 'Have you talked that over with Nelson?'

'Nelson's my *subcaptain*, Ira. Are you really suggesting I need to talk something like this over with him first?'

'Mark's a dangerous liability.'

'Ira, you chose to trust me. You asked for a miracle. I can do that, but those are my terms.'

Ira's face took on a weary cast. 'Will, he hates you, remember?'

'How could I forget?'

'And he's not your son.'

'I *know* that,' Will snapped.

'And the senate are going to hate it,' said Ira.

'I don't give a shit,' said Will. 'He's the best and I trust him. If you want a fucking miracle, he's where you start.'

Ira sighed. 'Is this really the time to call in favours? There'll be other moments for Mark. Better ones.'

'Is that true?' said Will. 'Because if so, where are they? It's over a year since the court case that screwed him over and I'm not seeing things get any better. And given your cheery prognosis, I'm not holding my breath. If there's one thing I've learned since I watched the Truists pump bullets into Gustav's face, it's that around here, you have to push. Nobody is going to hand me what I want on a platter. And given what we're talking about right now, I don't see a reason to fuck about with a substandard crew. He's the best and you know it.'

Ira rubbed his eyes. 'Will, we all know he can fly, but he doesn't follow orders. He stole a *starship*, remember?'

'A fact that nobody outside IPSO's inner circle is even aware of,' said Will. 'And you know why he did it. She might have been my wife, but she was also your engineer, remember? You worked with Rachel for how many years? And none of us lifted a finger to try to help her.'

'For the very obvious reason that there was nothing we could do.'

'And yet she's still out there, Ira. Frozen in space and probably waiting in cryo. How are you sleeping these days, may I ask? Everything hunky-dory?'

Ira stared tiredly into the middle distance. 'Not that great, if you must know,' he said softly. 'Will, I'm not sure you understand what you're asking for.'

'Don't play with me, Ira,' said Will. 'How could I not?'

Ira shot him a bleak look. 'If there's one thing you have in common with that kid, it's your mutual inability to notice the shit happening around you when you're upset. We've been covering for you, Will. Me,

Pari, everyone. Since we lost Rachel you've been a liability. And that's one of the hardest things I've ever had to admit.'

Will felt his cheeks flushing. He considered shutting his blush response down but there was little point in trying to hide from Ira. They had too much shared history.

'First there was that tribunal,' Ira went on. 'Then there was the self-cloning fiasco. Then all those "off-the books" trips out to the edge of the Depleted Zone in humanity's most obvious starship. How do you think it makes the Fleet look when we indulge you at every turn? We've tried everything to pull you out of your tailspin, Will, up to and including hiring the Fleet's most highly qualified life-coach as your sub. If this mission doesn't get your mojo back, I won't be able to protect you any more. Politically speaking, you'll be on your own.'

'If this mission doesn't succeed, it sounds like there may not be a civilisation left to come back to,' Will retorted.

'Which is why I'm saying yes.' When Ira glanced up to meet Will's eyes, he saw a kind of finality in them – a hardness he hadn't glimpsed for years. 'You get your wish. I'll add him to the plan. Maybe some good will even come of it. Plus the senate hates it when I surprise them. It throws all their predictive modelling off.'

Ira managed a wry smile, then looked wistful. He rose and stuck out his hand. Will recognised the signal to leave and blinked in surprise. He'd been dismissed. He stood, shook his friend's hand and hugged him.

'Good luck,' said Ira. 'You're going to need it.'

'Thanks,' said Will and headed reluctantly for the door.

'By the way,' said Ira suddenly. 'How did the meeting go?'

Will paused and exhaled. 'Terrible. I couldn't keep to the script. That podium's going to need mending. I think I scared everyone.'

Ira smiled. 'Good. I was rather hoping you would. There wasn't much else that could shift them. Your unreliability is at least... reliable.'

Will blinked at the realisation that Ira had played him.

'It may not sound like it, but I have confidence in you,' said Ira. 'I know you can bring me that miracle. It's what you're best at. But one last thing, Will – try to enjoy it, huh? You get to go and chase aliens.'

Will saw that sadness again. Suddenly Ira looked small in his enormous office.

'I'm jealous of you,' said the Fleet admiral. 'Make the most of it.'

Will nodded. 'I'll try,' he said.

2.2: MARK

Mark sat at the back of the event room at the Atlantic Environmental Research office, waiting for the meeting to end. Jim Dutta, his boss, had run long with his weekly round-up.

The AER office occupied a slice of New York Supertower Three, high up the east face of the building. The office was, in Mark's opinion, a dump. The first-generation biofabric walls and floor had come down with tower flu eight years before, leaving them yellowed and blotchy. Nobody had bothered to vax them because the building was overdue for decommissioning anyway, and they lent the air a slightly sour, vegetal smell.

At least the view was decent. That last big storm had cleared the air and there was no sign of smog or haze, not that NoreCorr got much of either any more. From the meeting room you could see out across the choppy grey waters of the Brooklyn Crumbles all the way to Sunnyside Island and the Long-Eye Towers beyond. Streaks of high, white cloud hung in a blue-green sky. Unfortunately, the room's inhabitants were rather more depressing.

Jim stood at the front, going through recent stats, looking uptight in his over-formal FiveClan corporate hoodie, smiling as always. Along the top of the presentation wall ran his jokey slogan for the day: *Hey, look on the bright side, at least nobody has to go to New Jersey any more! :)* Underneath lay his three main bullets: weather is worse, politics is worse, budget is worse. In the bottom-right corner a timer ticked down, showing how many hours remained before the next supercyclone hit, along with the afternoon's oxygen levels and expected temperature spread. Long after Earth's industries had all been shuttered, the biome was still collapsing. And with each slow, inexorable phase of the ecotastrophe, the weather grew wilder.

'So yes,' said Jim, 'we *are* going to shut down the sampling tower at Newark. With the others gone there's no point keeping it. Our major operations are all being moved to Pittsburgh.'

There were grumbles around the room.

'I know, I know,' said Jim. 'But realistically, this is not a big issue for us. The silver lining with this new storm pattern is that model confidence is way up, so local sampling is less of a priority, which means an easier time for you guys. And more opportunities for great travel!'

A hand went up.

'Yes, Tina,' said Jim.

'Does this mean more lay-offs?'

Jim spread his palms. 'No decisions have been made about staff redeployments. It's likely that some of you will be invited to relocate to other NoreCorr sites.'

'Any offworld?' said Tina.

Jim winced. 'Probably not.'

Muttering from the engineers kicked off again.

'What is this shit, Jim?' said Tina. 'They're closing all the sampling towers. If my wife and I don't keep up our booking payments, we'll lose our flight out. Then it might be what, two more years till the next open berth we can afford comes on the market. What am I supposed to do – sign up as a Revivalist and beg for a posting as a Flag? I'm not spending another two years on this shit-hole planet watching cities get smashed flat, Jim.'

'Nobody here is going to miss their booking payments,' Jim insisted. 'Everyone will get their ticket offworld. FiveClan has you covered, remember? Everyone here is Made Gold or higher, am I right?'

Mark didn't speak up. He hadn't invested in any of the Made Premium programmes. But they hardly mattered to him.

'In any case,' said Jim, 'could we get back to the agenda, please? And let's save the questions for the end, okay? On a final positive note, the Princeton operation was a complete success. Management are delighted that we extracted the cores with everyone intact – everyone's going to receive a quarterly bonus, so kudos to Ricky and his team for all their hard work!'

Everyone clapped. Those nearest to Ricky slapped him on the back.

'And very special thanks to Mark,' Jim added, 'for pulling them out in the nick of time with some incredible flying!'

The applause slacked off. Some of the clapping grew slow enough to be heavy-handed even for irony. Mark got a couple of sidelong glances.

He folded his arms. Everyone in the room knew that without him there'd be no bonus, no cores, and everyone on Ricky's team would be screwed on their booking payments. Fuck them all. This was not what he thought it would be like when he came back to Earth. He wondered for the thousandth time if he'd just picked the wrong city.

Before he moved he'd heard that, what with all the major urban relocations, sect affiliation didn't mean much any more. Everywhere was a melting pot these days. Supposedly. He'd realised that was bullshit in week one. Outwardly, Earth's sects might operate as a bloc, but within Earth society affiliation counted for everything. Everything that wasn't already determined by class, at least.

'Okay!' said Jim, trying to hold on to the enthusiasm that had already fled the room. 'That's it for now, I guess. Next meeting one week from now. Everyone enjoy your weekend!'

The engineers started filing out, muttering in small groups.

'Mark, could you stay back a minute?' Jim added. 'I'd like to chat about something.'

Mark watched the others leave with a mixture of resentment and dread. His *little chats* with Jim had been getting steadily more awkward over the passing months. Jim had sunken, sad-looking eyes in a pale brown face that was always smiling, and you could read his emotion by how much stress that smile was hiding. Today, it hid the most Mark had ever seen.

Jim waited until the last engineer was gone before speaking.

'Hey, Mark. Look, sorry for the vibe there.'

Mark shrugged. 'I did my job. I got them out. If they don't appreciate it, that's their problem.'

'Yeah. That's the thing. Look, Mark, I've no idea what to do about this. I know that whole transit pod thing was an accident—'

'What else was I supposed to fucking do?' said Mark. 'Leave them to the Shamokin? Just fly away?'

'*Management's* very happy with your choice,' said Jim, 'but the guys think... Well, the guys blame management for sending them there in the first place when they should have just let the whole issue slide. And if management ended up having to pay extra to get them out, well, then maybe it would have served them right.'

'Except that's not how it works, is it?' said Mark. 'Management would have found a way to pass the fucking buck, because that's what they did last time.'

'You know that and I know that,' said Jim earnestly, 'but the guys think they're likely out of a job anyway. They don't feel there's much left to lose.'

'Can I help what they think?' Mark snapped.

Jim laughed nervously. 'Well... maybe yes. You see, the guys feel... well, they feel like you're showing them up, Mark. Like they can't compete and you make them look slack.'

Mark seethed. 'What?'

'It's hard for them,' said Jim. 'You're so... different – you do the work of, like, ten guys at once, and you don't even *try* to fit in.'

'Don't I?' said Mark. 'I've attended every single fucking work social since I showed up here.' But he knew that wasn't what Jim meant.

'Yeah, but they don't care about socials,' said Jim. 'I mean, you still haven't declared an affiliation. And it's been what, over a year?'

Here it comes, Mark thought.

'Did you consider that last offer I sent you...?' said Jim, his voice trailing off as he hit the end of the sentence.

Jim kept sending Mark invitations to join his faith group. His congregation was Standard FiveClan Transcendist church-lite – about as watery as religion got. As a Fleet roboteer, Mark would be highly regarded. There'd be special roles for him in their prayer meetings, no doubt.

Mark quietly suspected that was one reason he'd got the job, but it was the last thing he wanted. And he had no desire to join some gang of Truist Revival bullies, either. He didn't see why he had to join somebody's church to be considered an Earther. He was aware of the historical context, but surely the planet was better than that? However, he knew not to say such things to Jim's face and hurt the man's feelings even more.

'Look, Mark, I know you're not super-fond of religion,' said Jim anxiously, 'but church doesn't have to be about belief. It can just be about community. Making friends. Letting the guys feel like you're on their side so everyone can relax a little. There are hundreds of congregations in the tower, Mark. Not joining any of them just makes you look weird. Like a Colonial. Like you don't care. And besides, you've been here for over a year and you don't have a girlfriend. I know you're straight from your stats, so don't you want to get laid? What girl will go for you if you're not signed up?'

'One who's not religious?' Mark offered bluntly.

In truth, Mark had actually gone on a few dates since he'd arrived, but only with other roboteers. He wasn't great with norms. He'd never quite worked out how you were supposed to trust them when you couldn't share thoughts. Plus they always talked too much.

Finding women with handler interfaces in the depleted remains of New York was rough. Earthers hadn't exactly lined up for genetic modification after the war. Losing to a tiny colony of gene-tweaked atheist intellectuals didn't leave them particularly receptive to the idea in the immediate aftermath and the prejudice still hadn't eroded. However, locating potential dates turned out to be the least of his problems. All three of the women Mark had met felt he was hiding something from them. Which, of course, he was.

The words *I'm a secret government experiment* had hovered on his lips a hundred times, but he'd never said them because his job would have vanished along with what was left of his freedom. In the end, loneliness had proved easier. He was used to loneliness. His childhood had featured plenty.

Jim sighed. 'Look, Mark, your skills are unbelievable. I never thought I'd get a roboteer on this team, let alone one from the Fleet. When I heard you were available and wanted to come here, it was like my dream come true. Really. But frankly, it's screwing everything up. You told me when you first arrived that you were supposed to be lying low, yet you show off every chance you get. Half of the guys have already figured out you're something special and the others are only in the dark because they don't know enough about roboteers to tell the difference. You scare the shit out of all of them and it's damaging morale.'

Jim stared at his shoes – stuffy regulation trainers with FiveClan logos on them.

'I want your skills, Mark, but not at the cost of my team.'

Mark breathed deep. He couldn't believe he was at risk of losing another job after all the compromises he'd made.

'I came here because I believed in this project,' he said. 'I wanted to understand Earth, and to help save it. That's what I've tried to do all along.'

'Earth's not just a ball of rock,' said Jim sadly. 'Maybe the colonies are like that, but Earth is about people. Lots and lots of tired, anxious people who dream of getting off this planet before it kills them. You – you could go anywhere. You just came here to make a point. They feel that, and it makes them afraid. They wonder if there will be anything out there for them if they ever get off. Or if everyone out there is as different from them as you are.'

Jim squinted out at the view. 'So, after we drop Newark, maybe this would be the right time for you to move on. Either that or you find some way to fit in. Join a church. Come to a meeting – you never know, you might like it. Everyone wants to meet you. My wife still hasn't met you.'

Jim looked up at him with puppy-dog eyes, begging Mark not to hate him. Mark tried to figure out what to say as he oscillated between anger and despair.

'You don't have to decide anything now,' said Jim. 'Just think about it, okay?'

Mark wanted to utter some witty comeback. Instead, he just glared out at the dying sky. In the quiet that followed, the room pinged them.

'Incoming message, Alpha Zero priority,' said the room's hoarse, hissing voice. Its speakers were as sick as its walls. 'Recipient-only content for Mark Ruiz. Immediate receipt required.'

'Take the call,' said Jim, sounding relieved by the excuse to leave. 'You can't say no to an Alpha Zero. Use my office.' He briefly met Mark's gaze. 'I'm sorry,' he said, and patted Mark timidly on the shoulder before letting himself out of the room.

A kind of hot, helpless fury boiled up inside Mark. There was only one person in his life who called him up using IPSO top-security overrides: Will Monet.

His mind jumbled over a dozen different cruel things he could say as he stormed into Jim's tiny office and manually slammed the door behind him, scaring the room's SAP into a string of bleating apologies. A badly balanced stack of crystal cores slid off the closest shelf and clattered onto the floor as the wall wobbled.

Mark reached mentally into the room's controls and punched the privacy icon. Then he dropped out of his body and into his home node. He grabbed the link and dived up into the virtual meeting space that had been prepped for the call.

'What?' he demanded, before noticing that the person across the virtual table wasn't Will after all. It was Nelson Aquino.

Nelson was seated in a velvet armchair in a well-appointed study somewhere – an orbital, probably, given the curving view of immaculate forest beyond the window. Dressed in a pinstripe Nehru suit and old-fashioned data shades, the look was classic Nelson: understated and under control. The expression on his regal, hawk-like face was grave.

'Good morning, Mark,' he said. 'Did I call at a bad time?'

Mark folded his arms. He looked down at his virtual self to see that he was still wearing his crumpled FiveClan one-piece. It wasn't a great look, but who cared? He wasn't here to impress anyone.

'Let me guess,' he growled. 'Message from Will fucking Monet.'

Nelson nodded. 'Got it in one.'

Nelson had been popping up ever more frequently in Mark's dealings with Will over the last few years. He'd been promoted to Will's subcaptain – his closest aide and the man responsible for looking after the *Ariel Two* while Will was doing everything but flying. He was the kindly therapist type everyone was supposed to like. Mark disliked him anyway.

'For a man I'm not supposed to know, he calls a lot. You know that? Does he want to try saying sorry again? Because quite frankly he can stick it.'

Mark had suffered badly the first time he became estranged from Will. For the first eight years of his life, Will had been closer than Mark's parents, as only a teacher with an interface could be. Then, without warning, the classified roboteer programme Will had created for the Fleet was disbanded. For Mark and the other kids, Will practically disappeared. Mark and his family had been sent offworld with barely a word of explanation.

Years later, their relationship had changed again when Will became a secret mentor – a magnetic figure tantalisingly unavailable most of the time. For a while, Mark had felt that his interface was something special again rather than a burden. Then, after the tribunal and the unpleasant truths it revealed, Mark had given up trying with Will. The Fleet had made it clear they considered Mark's mind their property, and him an embarrassment to boot.

Will's excuse for trashing Mark's life had always been the same: security. He'd done it all to keep Mark and the others safe, apparently. It was funny how those security problems appeared to make everyone suffer except Will.

'This time it's something rather more pertinent than an apology, I'm afraid,' said Nelson. 'We both thought it would be better if I spoke to you.'

'So what are you now,' said Mark, 'his handler or his errand boy?'

Nelson ignored the jibe. 'I see that you're angry,' he said. 'Clearly the timing of this call is imperfect for you. Unfortunately, what I have to say will not wait.' Nelson interlaced his long pianist's fingers. 'Four weeks ago, local-frame-time, two IPSO ships and a variety of Earther sect vessels were destroyed in what appeared to be an extraterrestrial conflict. We lack enough data to know whether non-humans were genuinely responsible, but in the unlikely case that they were, this is the single most important event since humanity encountered the Transcended. It might mean anything from interspecies war to outright annihilation for the human race.'

He said it all with a breezy coolness that suggested he wasn't fussed either way.

Mark peered at him. 'You're shitting me.'

'Sadly not. I have a memory file for you, if you'd like to see for yourself.'

Nelson waved a hand and an icon appeared in front of Mark, floating in the air. Mark snapped it up and swallowed it. Full situational awareness of the Tiwanaku Event blossomed in his mind. He blinked in awe, his anger dissolved.

'Okay, heavy times,' he said. 'Why call me? I'm not Fleet any more, remember?'

'Your status is actually listed as *voluntary indefinite sabbatical*. But in any case, your erstwhile guardian Will Monet is assembling the mission being sent to investigate. He has asked me to let you know that there is a position available to you as captain of the attached diplomatic vessel if you want it. A service to IPSO such as this would give Will ample political material to force the Admiralty Court to grant you sole ownership of your interface. It is, in short, a ticket to your independence. You would become the only non-Fleet-aligned Omega roboteer in human space, free to pick whatever job you choose, in whatever star system you like – presuming you could find a ship able to match your talents, of course. You wouldn't have to interact with Will Monet ever again, if that's what you desire.'

A part of Mark quivered at the promise that offer held. But he had

51

too much emotional scar-tissue around failed Fleet promises to accept it at face value. He looked at Nelson askance.

'So come back and do one last job, is that it?'

'Will has asked me to point out that you and he would be on different ships throughout the mission,' said Nelson. 'Because this ... alien event is most likely some kind of scam, once you arrive at Tiwanaku there will probably be little for you to do but look after your high-profile passengers. You would be at liberty to fly home while we resolved the situation militarily. Needless to say, if whoever is responsible tries to stop the diplomatic team from leaving, your specialist skills would prove extremely useful.'

Mark laughed. 'So one minute I'm the Fleet's dirty little secret and the next I'm playing cruise-captain to a bunch of celebrity stiffnecks? Doesn't that strike you as ridiculous?'

For the first time, a glimmer of frustration showed through Nelson's calm veneer.

'Unsurprisingly, it's not proving an easy sell with the senate, but that's the only role available. Will has made it clear he wants to give you a full captaincy, and as the other two ships are military, they must be captained by currently active Fleet personnel.'

Mark realised Nelson was hating this. He guffawed and shook his head.

'This is bullshit. It's just another attempt to suck me back in, and even more cack-handed than the rest.'

'Hard though it may be for you to imagine,' said Nelson with a little acid in his tone, 'Will has only ever wanted the best for you. He feels responsible for the trajectory of your life and career and is now burning significant political capital in an attempt to give you what you want. Namely, your freedom. Will has most definitely made mistakes, particularly regarding his relationship with you, but can you not find some room in your heart to see what he's trying to do here?'

Mark didn't reply. He stared out at the sloping bank of pine trees beyond Nelson's shoulder. It was ages since he'd been on an orbital. There were no forests left to visit on Earth. He'd spent the last year and a half telling himself he didn't care, and that his cause made his presence on the Old World worth it. He'd insisted that doing his part for Earth was a far better thing than breezing about with a bunch of Colonials who didn't understand their own heritage.

In truth, though, his options really had been heavily constrained by the Fleet's claim on his interface. They were terrified of letting someone with his skills out of their grasp. But without it, he was nothing. Beyond roboteering, what did he have? Were they to take away the artificial section of his mind that had shaped him since birth, he knew he'd go crazy in under a week. He'd feel less confined if they snapped his spine.

The fact that the Fleet owned the circuitry in his skull had given his anger something to feed off for a long time. Normal roboteers couldn't be bound by that kind of contract. It wasn't legal. But Mark had never been normal. They'd tried to take his interface from him once already by claiming he was unfit for duty. Mark had to admit that Will had blocked that attempt, but nothing could stop the Fleet from trying again at any time.

Nelson tapped an impatient finger on the arm of his chair. 'I knew it was a mistake to call,' he said. 'I anticipated your response, and frankly, I don't blame you for it. The position would involve ingratiating yourself with a group of *stiffnecks*, as you put it, after all. As captain, you'd be the lowest-ranked person on the ship, barring your subcaptain, of course – little more than a pilot, really. Hardly the sort of position you'd relish. Still, it was my responsibility to let you know the offer had been made. I shall tell Will that you declined and no more will be said about the matter.'

'I'll take it,' said Mark.

Nelson raised an eyebrow. 'Pardon?'

'I said I'll take the job.'

'You're sure?'

'I said yes, I'll take the fucking job.'

Nelson looked peeved. 'Splendid,' he said, unconvincingly. 'Will is sure to be pleased.'

'No doubt,' said Mark. 'Are we done?'

Nelson nodded. 'I will follow up with travel arrangements via a secure channel.'

'Fine,' said Mark, then dropped out of the meeting and back into the blotchy yellow cupboard that was Jim's office.

Accepting this olive branch scared him. He knew full well that Will would use it to try to drag him back into the Fleet and his old life. The prospect of returning to that existence of tedious charter flights, combat drills and existential despair made him shiver. But pissing Nelson off helped Mark feel more comfortable with the deal. And there was a secondary bonus: he could tell Jim to stick his church meeting where the sun didn't shine.

2.3: YUNUS

Yunus Chesterford reclined on the enormous gel-filled couch beside the other panellists and waited for the recording icon to appear in his contacts. Bradley Yao, the host of the interactive, lolled beside him in azure pantaloons and a bronze shirt open to the waist.

As the icon appeared, Bradley leaned in towards the closest camera-drone, his Angeleno-perfect features locked in a suave smile.

'Hi. I'm Bradley Yao, and this is *Greater Matters*, the feed that brings you the deepest discussions on today's thorniest topics.'

They sat together in an opulent passive-broadcast lounge near the top of Bandung Tower Five, complete with hookah, diamond jars of spiced tea and this year's most fashionable type of intelligent rug. The windows commanded striking views over the ruins of the old city, where another supercyclone was approaching. That one lamentable feature of their setting, though, would of course be edited out of the final broadcast to give the impression that it had been shot somewhere fashionably offworld.

'This show is the latest in our series on the role of alien influences in human development,' Bradley told the drone. 'And, as usual, once we've met our guests and got the ball rolling, everyone will be welcome to ping in and participate in the discussion. We have Avatoids by Physi-presence waiting live for you here in the studio. With me today I have Yunus Chesterford, founder of the Chesterford Exocultural Initiative and author of *Human Destiny: Our Role in the Universe*.'

Yunus nodded towards the drone hovering closest.

'For those of you who don't already know,' Bradley continued, 'Professor Chesterford is the man who cracked the Fecund navigational code and single-handedly founded the field of Exocultural Studies. He's a proud Reconsiderist and has accolades from Saleh, Baxter and Lowell Universities. Professor Chesterford, welcome.'

'Hi, Bradley,' said Yunus with a warm smile. 'It's great to be here.'

'On his left is Venetia Sharp, one of humanity's leading specialists on Fecund psychology and social behaviour. A native of Esalen Colony, she is senior exo-psych consultant to IPSO's Exploratory Division. She also holds an endowed chair at Bryant University on New Panama.'

As usual, Venetia had come to the interview dressed in a T-shirt and slacks that looked about three days out of the printer. The bob of black hair that framed her face hung loose and uncovered. He could only imagine what Citra would say. Still, the editing SAP would be live-tweaking the image to give Venetia the modest skirts and head-sleeve their Earth audience preferred. Her sharp features were not unattractive, to Yunus's mind. However, she had a kind of cynicism and intensity he found unbecoming in a middle-aged woman. That kind of fiery attitude was for little girls who hadn't found husbands and settled down yet.

'Venetia, thank you for coming,' said Bradley.

Venetia nodded. 'Hi.'

'And beside her is Professor Harare Tam, a senior partner at the Vartian Institute, the most highly regarded exodefence think tank in human space.'

Yunus smiled to himself. The Vartian Institute was the *only* such think tank. Nobody else bothered. Tam looked as stuffy and professorial as ever in his purple Institute hoodie, which he always wore fully zipped. The patches on his sleeves were peeling. They always wheeled Tam out when they needed a good crackpot, and Tam never disappointed. His wild eyebrows alone were enough to boost the feed's hit-rate.

'Thank you very much for inviting me, Bradley,' said Tam. 'I am glad to be here. Really very grateful.'

Yunus thought of Tam rather fondly, ridiculous figure though he was. He and the other top names in social exoscience didn't really get along that well, but they'd all known each other for years and developed an inevitable camaraderie. Often, he and his fellow pundits found themselves competing for the same patches of limelight and the same scant government grants. Except Tam, of course, whose insular organisation never appeared to want for cash.

Yunus knew that most outsiders regarded his field as something of a joke. The healthy doses of speculation required, along with the backing from politically biased sources, tended to make it look less than rigorous. He didn't care. It had worked very nicely for him.

This show was a perfect example. Yunus's allies in government arranged things like this to keep him in the public eye. It was high-class propaganda, really, but for the best possible reasons. Two pro-balance pundits with differing philosophies had been brought in to fight it out, leaving him to be the voice of moderation. The Colonials didn't get a voice, let alone bigots like the FPP. Yunus knew he'd come off in a good light; the event had been set up that way.

'Today's topic,' said Bradley, waving expansively, 'is this: in our modern age, do we still believe in benign alien mentorship? Doctor Sharp, how about we start with you?'

'Sure, Brad. First, I feel I should clarify that when we're talking about alien mentors, I presume we mean the Transcended. As far as I'm aware, humanity hasn't encountered any *other* galaxy-dominating civilisations. So the question you're asking really is: do we still trust *them* given that we haven't heard anything from them since Monet's first encounter?

'The answer is yes, absolutely. And now more than ever. The reason is simply that, despite all the speculation to the contrary, nothing bad has happened to the human race since we started using the suntap technology the Transcended gave us. We're still here running our own affairs. I'd say that leaves little room for paranoid speculation. On top of that, we have to add all the advances that access to Fecund space has given us – advances that would never have been possible without their intervention. There are the nestship technologies, all the new methods for building orbital habitats, and the unexpected bioscience benefits of having Fecund bacteria to play with, life-extension being the most obvious among them.

'Then you have to factor in the suntap's effect on energy prices. The ability to quantum-channel energy straight out of a star's corona is an incredible boon for humanity. Everyone focuses on the threat of using suntaps to power weapons but that's not their only application. Suntap power stations have made antimatter cheaper and more plentiful than at any other time in human history. If that's not benign mentorship, I don't know what is.'

By this time, Tam was practically vibrating in his chair.

'Professor Tam,' said Bradley. 'It looks like you've got something to add. You disagree?'

Tam sat up straight and fiddled with the zipper on his hoodie. 'Well, yes, with all greatest possible respect to Ms Sharp, she is wrong. I know that the line she's taking has been the popular norm for some years now, but it remains a dangerous and reckless one.'

Bradley struck a thoughtful pose. 'How do you square that, Professor? It's hard to argue with the Transcended silence, or the benefits we've gained from the Far Frontier.'

'Neither point is strictly relevant,' said Tam. 'For a society such as the Transcended, thirty years is the blink of an eye. In that time, we've done exactly what they wanted, which is spill out into a region of the galaxy over which we already know they exercise tight control. In the meantime, we've learned nothing about their intentions. They're as opaque to us as they were when they first announced their presence via the lure star. The simple fact that they haven't once told us how we're supposed to improve as a species or "constructively self-edit", as they so colourfully put it, should serve as a warning.'

'But if we don't know what they want,' said Bradley, 'should we automatically assume that their goals are malign?'

Tam nodded like a badly calibrated housebot. 'We still only know two things about the Transcended. First, that they hand out weapons to younger species. Weapons of unspeakable power. And second, that they use the stellar signature imprinted by those weapons to eradicate any species they don't like. The only race at peer-level development to humanity that we know of is the Fecund, and our best estimates suggest that the Transcended wiped them out in a coordinated remote assault that took a little under a week. A week! This despite the fact that the Fecund had come to occupy at least twenty different star systems spread over dozens of light-years. The moment a star-faring species begins using the suntap, they essentially hand a kill-switch for their own civilisation to a race of entities about which they know *nothing* except for the nebulous agenda they choose to promote. Does that sound benign to you? A Faustian bargain is what it sounds like to me – and one we have already foolishly entered into.'

Yunus saw his opportunity to wade in. He waved a hand.

Bradley took note and shifted his attention. 'Professor Chesterford – you see it differently?'

'If I may, Brad. I have the utmost respect for both of my colleagues' positions, but I think there's room for a middle ground here. Doctor Sharp's position is the one we've grown used to hearing. But as Professor Tam points out, it may be a little naive. I think we'd be crazy to dismiss Professor Tam's concerns out of hand simply because they sound paranoid to our culturally conditioned ears. The real problem is that we don't have a frame of reference for this topic. As Doctor Sharp mentioned, we only know of one "galaxy-dominating civilisation", and quite frankly, we know so little about the Transcended that the actual extent of their abilities remains a mystery. It's my opinion that we should withhold judgement until we know more. Simple as that.'

'You appear to be suggesting that there's more to know,' said Bradley, one eyebrow arched. 'Isn't that the problem, though? That they're not talking to us?'

'Who's to say they're the only voice out there?' said Yunus. 'Perspective might come from anywhere. We only have the Transcended's word that they're the ultimate authority in this galaxy, yet we've never even laid eyes on them. We only need one data point to disprove their claim. And if that happens, we'll have to start rethinking human significance in the galaxy. If it turns out that the Transcended are lying to us, as Professor Tam implies, we might have to consider whether some of our own home-grown notions of moral authority might hold a little more weight than those we've imported from a supposedly superior race.'

His line wasn't the Transcendist Church orthodoxy, but that was deliberate. The people Yunus worked with were trying to reseed some of Truism's better ideas in the public domain, particularly among the upper end of the Following class – the show's core audience.

'I'm sorry,' said Venetia with a sneer, 'but is this a discussion about aliens or church policy? Because, last I checked, we don't *have* that other data point you're referring to. We have ruins left by one peer-level species – the Fecund – which are ten million years old, and that's it. Are you honestly proposing another such species exists out there for us to find? A living one?'

Yunus shrugged. 'I'm proposing that we can't know the answer to that question yet.'

She smiled darkly. 'And if there is one, it automatically validates the idea of human supremacy, I take it.'

Yunus frowned. Venetia was leading them off-topic. Her remarks would lower her popularity ratings, which he didn't mind, but ideally she shouldn't be poking around so close to the show's political agenda. Yunus framed a pithy reply but the recording light in his view-field snapped off. A call icon replaced it.

Bradley's face fell. 'I'm sorry, everyone,' he said, glancing about. 'Looks like we had to suspend recording. Not sure why.'

'That's my fault, I'm afraid,' said Yunus. 'It came in high priority. I'm sorry. I told them not to ping me here. I'll be back in a moment.'

He hurried out of the recording lounge, his cheeks burning. The camera-drones darted aside to let him pass. He stopped in the waiting room to take the call.

'Who is this?' he said. 'It really isn't a good time.'

A call window opened in his contact-display. In it hovered the blandly handsome face of Ezekiel Wei, his top contact in the IPSO House Proportional.

'Zeke!' he said, astonished. 'I'm sorry, I was recording a show. What can I do for you?'

'Something's come up,' said Zeke tersely. 'Do you have a secure line? You need to see this.'

Yunus glanced around and strode for the nearest privacy chamber. He waited for the anti-surveillance light to come on.

'I'm clear,' he said, looking into the nearest camera. 'Show me.'

'Word of it only just hit the House,' said Zeke.

A separate video-window opened in Yunus's display. In it, Tom Lark's recording began to play.

Yunus's skin tingled as he watched – partly in anger and partly in awe. The recording made it obvious that one of Earth's Houses had engaged in some very public frontier jumping. Under normal circumstances that would have been cause for celebration. Earth would finally have enough political momentum to force IPSO to change the laws around planetary registration or risk war. However, the violent ending ruined everything.

Instead of a clean political lever, they had chaos. IPSO would undoubtedly assume Earth's sects were responsible for the attack, despite the fact that it muddied Earth's own cause. They'd point the finger because they could.

Yunus felt sure he had enough traction with Earth's leadership to know the attack wasn't Earth's doing, and he doubted the Colonies would pull a stunt like this. It wasn't their style. Which meant this was *it* – the big moment his career had been leading up to. He could forget grubbing around in Fecund garbage heaps. This event would change the human race for ever.

'There'll have to be a diplomatic mission,' said Yunus breathlessly.

'Without a doubt,' said Zeke.

'I want to be on it,' said Yunus. 'Whatever it takes, I want a place on that ship. I'm calling in my favours, Zeke. All of them. Earth's going to need a representative.'

Zeke smiled. 'We were hoping you'd say that. Your name was top of our list, along with Citra's, of course. I'll talk details with you later but for the time being, keep this quiet, okay? We can't afford for it to go public on our watch.'

'Of course,' said Yunus. 'I understand.'

As soon as the call dropped, Yunus reached for his wife's icon and pinged her with the priority ramped to the max. Her face appeared, backed by shelves full of lab equipment.

'Yuni?' she said, looking confused.

'Citra, dear,' he said. 'Get to a privacy box, quickly. You're never going to believe this.'

2.4: ANN

Ann watched impatiently through her display as the *Griffin* slid towards port. She'd made the run from Yonaguni in record time but still feared it wasn't fast enough. Ahead of them loomed the ungainly octopus that was the local Fleet HQ, straddled between the vast, dark masses of starships and buzzing with shuttles. Hundreds of kilometres below, orbital habitats formed a glittering band of pearls around their parent world: New Panama, jewel of the Far Frontier.

Despite being so close to her adopted home, Ann's stomach refused to settle. It churned in anticipation of her meeting. The cloak-and-dagger nonsense her Rumfoord League work required sat poorly with her. Policing the Frontier had been difficult enough before she'd been required to start lying to her own people.

She'd have given anything for a day off on the surface. New Panama was, to her mind, the most optimistic of worlds – close to what she'd hoped the future would be like as a child. Bryant City was all broad, domed spaces and habitat canyons. None of the horrid supertowers that blighted other worlds. On rest days, she liked to visit the McKlusky Museum and attend the public talks. Everyone there appeared to be making deals or showing up with some new discovery. The mood of excitement the place contained just from being the gateway between the old and new frontiers hung in the air like fragrant smoke.

Before Baron and Monet's fateful voyage, humanity had been restricted to an onion-skin layer of stars all the same distance from the galactic core – a region defined by the limitations of warp drive. But with the discovery of the nearby Penfield Lobe, everything had changed. Now they had access to a second layer of stars crammed with the ruins of the Fecund civilisation. New Panama lay at that solitary junction, a hub for trade, science and exploration.

Bryant City had half a dozen different research institutions just for studying the lobe and a dozen more dedicated to the alien remains that littered the outer system. The place had come a long way since Monet's discovery of it. And business decrypting the Fecund technology found in the new territories never stopped booming. Ann loved the world for the hope it offered when the rest of the Far Frontier seemed so squalid.

Slowly, Fleet HQ slid up to obscure the view. Ann found herself looking out at a silver-grey horizon of metal and ceramic struts that stretched for dozens of kilometres. Here and there, sensor towers rose like gothic spires into the star-spattered sky.

The *Griffin* slid to a gentle halt and a soft bonging sound filled the cabin as the locks engaged. Ann fought down another wave of excited unease as she unclipped from her bunk and drifted into the cabin's central well.

'I'm proud of all of you,' she told her crew. 'We did a great job.'

They'd already guessed she had some kind of important meeting to attend. She could see the curiosity written in their eyes.

'I'll be gone for a while,' she said. 'Hours, maybe, so please shut down without me. And in case you finish before I get back, enjoy your break. You all deserve it.'

She tried for a winning smile and fought down a stab of jealousy towards her own team.

River shot her a concerned look as she made for the airlock. 'Hope it goes well,' he said.

'Me, too,' said Ann as she sealed herself in.

The *Griffin*'s docking pod slid up through the ship's mesohull and mated with the standard-issue transit pod waiting at the end of the tethering arm. As the doors swung open, Ann glided across from one bland, biocarpeted interior to the other.

'Welcome back, Captain Ludik,' said the transit in a friendly, feminine voice as it accelerated away from the ship. The main screen showed her a map of her location on the station and various useful facilities she might want to visit.

'Where would you like to go?' it asked eagerly. 'I can deliver you to your office in four-point-eight minutes or the officers' lounge in five.'

'There's a project I need to check on first,' said Ann. 'The details are here.'

She pressed the chip in the back of her hand against the reader in the transit's wall.

An ungainly pause ensued. The pod momentarily slowed and then accelerated again as its usual identity went to sleep and another one woke up.

'Secure reboot complete,' said the SAP in a new voice – one with a deeper, more directive tone. 'Lie back, please, Captain. Transit will be swift.'

Ann clipped herself into the furry lining of the pod using pull-out straps from the wall and held on tight as the transit routed her out of the human pod channels and into the ones designed for freight. Freight-pods didn't operate under the same acceleration limits, which meant the ride could be rough.

'Do I have a meeting point?' she asked as she was jounced and jerked through a complex web of girders between boxes of machine parts and canisters of coolant. The shadows of tubes and walkways flashed past on the monitors.

'Yes. Your end point is confirmed. Your contact is waiting for you. Surveillance cover for this meeting has also been arranged. Details will be deposited in your chip on your return trip.'

When Ann or one of the other members of the Rumfoord League needed to take time out, they were simply listed as *not available*, which usually meant working on one of IPSO's secure projects. And there were enough such projects in the Fleet that the conspiracy was easy to hide, particularly with the high-level support the League commanded. But that didn't stop Ann hating every minute of the subterfuge.

The pod lurched to a halt, tilted ninety degrees and slid her under the carapace of a large crab-shaped maintenance robot. The screens' view swapped to the crab's primary cameras. Ann felt a surge of acceleration as the robot sped away from the Fleet station and out into empty space.

Though she felt badly in need of conversation, she knew better than to try to talk with the pod. The stealth SAP now in charge of it had deliberately filtered access to information and was designed to flag a warning if she asked too many unexpected questions.

'Can I get a status update?' she said instead.

'One has been prepared for you,' said the SAP. 'Passive-vid will play it on screen two.'

The screen flared into life as the SAP began its presentation. The League's stylised Taj Mahal logo showed briefly, followed by dense tables of statistics.

'Our Nemesis machine deployment at Tiwanaku achieved objectives but with unanticipated losses,' it said.

Ann groaned. The Nems made her nervous, but she wasn't alone in that.

'Human error caused a delay in initiating the swarm surge. Consequently, warp exodus was delayed by approximately one standard day. Rather than encountering a system in post-swarm fugue, the *Reynard* and *Horton* arrived prior to engagement. Both ships were lost. Fortunately, swift action on the part of the *Reynard*'s captain meant that knowledge of the event still passed to Fleet control.'

Ann shook her head at the awful waste. That was some terrible timing. The *Horton* had been full of families. She reminded herself that a lot more innocent people would die before the project was over. Their loss would make this tragedy a footnote by comparison.

'Nemesis machine activity ran entirely as predicted by the mean standard model with the exception of a single behaviour – the incorporation of a broadcast message into the attack pattern.'

The presentation played the message loop. Ann watched the terrified boy backing away from whatever piece of alien machinery had come to get him and nausea rose as she imagined what must have happened next. She put a hand over her mouth.

The fact that the message appeared to represent a certain level of autonomous intelligence – not to mention malice – disturbed her, but she knew that wasn't a fully rational response. There'd always been evidence that the Nems were smart. They appeared to be almost on a par with human SAP technology. What they weren't, though, was flexible, creative or self-aware. The League would never have dared use them if they had been.

The last war had brought hard lessons about the misuse of alien technology. The League overcompensated by modelling and testing everything to the *nth* degree. Some of the conspirators called it overkill. Ann called it wise.

The Nems always incorporated a small amount of foreign material into their matrix after each attack, and this showed up as subsequent modifications to their behaviour. To Ann's mind this meant you could never be too careful. Thankfully, the Nems' overall sophistication never wavered.

'The message has been subject to significant subsequent analysis,' said the SAP, as if picking up on her alarm. 'Concerns were raised that it constituted an entirely new behaviour. However, closer examination of the records of previous Nemesis machine operations reveals that a broadcast message has always been associated with attacks. Prior analysis had erroneously assumed this message was some kind of targeting signal. In fact, what occurred during this attack was a translation from the Nemesis machine language to an approximation of our own, using material culled from the protocols of co-opted machines.'

That came as something of a relief, though it did little to quell Ann's overall sense of unease.

'The one remaining concern regarding the attack was that the presence of the two extra ships increased the size of the target, and therefore the mutation risk incurred through ingestion. The League notes, however, that recent scans of the Tiwanaku System suggest that the machines are operating entirely within tolerances. The presence of extra biological samples does not appear to have distorted machine behaviour patterns. This may be because the samples in question were destroyed during acquisition.'

In other words, everyone died before the machines could get to them. Ann hoped so, for their sake. Not for the first time, she shuddered at what she'd become involved with. Had she not considered it absolutely necessary, she never would have joined the Rumfoord League. But the discovery of the Snakepit System and its attendant technologies had left the conspirators in an impossible position.

It had started with the realisation that Earth's sects had been keeping discoveries in Fecund space secret from IPSO, a move clearly aimed at strengthening their hand if war broke out. After that, it was only a matter of time before certain Fleet captains had started doing a little off-the-books exploring for themselves to even the odds. They'd only been looking for an extra Fecund secret or two, but the world they found changed everything. After that, keeping their discoveries secret became a necessity. Had they made it public, the debate over control of Snakepit would have sparked a conflict all by itself. The planet was, as Sam had put it once, 'the dirty great toyshop the Transcended always meant us to find'.

Snakepit's own Nemesis machines had proven by far the most effective way of keeping the frontier safe and open. Whatever Ann thought about the Nems, they were clean, discreet and incredibly reliable. While nobody really understood how they worked, they followed simple cues with reassuring consistency. And they had staved off outright war for over two years without the true cost appearing on anyone's balance sheet.

The Rumfoord League's existence hinged on that fact. The sects' secret colonies simply disappeared without them knowing why. Had the Nems not been doing the heavy lifting, such an ambitious operation would have become obvious long ago. Now, though, the sects' increased aggression had made the ugly endgame inevitable. For all the horror it entailed, Ann looked forward to the resolution and transparency it would bring.

The rest of the report made grim, dry reading. Ann was supremely grateful when, after twenty minutes of silent, anonymous flight, her pod slid back out of the robot and into the exohull of an orbital habitat. She enjoyed a brief, thrilling ride down from the orbital's hub, looking out at the curving ring of immaculate suburb below. The pod finally deposited her at a small domestic station in the centre of a well-maintained municipal park.

Ann stepped out and took a deep breath of artificially fresh air. It was balmy and scented with pine. There was birdsong, she noticed, though it was almost certainly piped. Attractive-looking apartment buildings peeked over the treetops. The glass-and-ceramic sky above her had been tinted a carefully calculated blue.

What struck her most, though, was the quiet. But for the birdsong, the place was absolutely and surreally empty. This had to be one of the many structures left over when the orbital building market collapsed – what people these days were calling *ghost-cans*.

'Nice, isn't it?' said Sam Nagano-Shah as he stepped out mischievously from between the trees.

Sam was a powerfully built man with an apparent age of about fifty, dressed in a blue Fleet uniform. Laughter lines crinkled the edges of his brown eyes and his curly fair hair faded to grey at the temples. Ann had always found him attractive but unsettling. His kindly face didn't quite match up with the occasionally harsh things that came out of his mouth.

She nodded. 'Very.'

'It's amazing to me that people don't want to use it,' said Sam. He gestured at the trees. 'You'd think the Earthers would be lining up.'

'Indeed,' said Ann.

Everyone knew why the Earthers hated orbitals. Even if you set aside the engineered political anger the sects spread about them, the core reasons to fear orbitals were primal. A refugee camp was still a camp, even if it was a pretty one. And a camp where people could accidentally shut off your air was never likely to feel homey, particularly after that nasty string of 'accidents' involving the habitats around Drexler. It would be years before the places were fully populated and New Panama had a dozen of them, which made them perfect spots for discreet meetings.

'We picked the nicest one, of course,' said Sam with a grin and a wink. 'The one they gussied up to show visitors.'

'Of course,' said Ann with a tepid smile. 'Why pick an ugly one if you don't have to?'

Which was, of course, exactly what the League should have done, she thought. Picking an obvious habitat felt like a self-indulgent security risk. But besides being the head of Fleet police operations at New Panama, Sam was also the local League chief and a master at political subterfuge, so she kept her opinions to herself. In all probability, the factors guiding his choice had nothing to do with appearances.

'You're sure the location is secure, then?' she asked, squinting into the open distance. An immense arc of unoccupied suburb curved away from her into a haze overhead.

'Absolutely,' said Sam. 'We keep the Ulanu cultists and other weirdos out of this habitat. You won't find any drug addicts up here. Or pure-food enthusiasts, for that matter.' He gestured at the path. 'Shall we walk?'

'Certainly.'

'How's the family?' said Sam.

His feet crunched on the gravel as they wound between the trees. A robotic gardener clad in shimmering green tact-fur pruned a branch ahead of them and clambered politely out of the way as they approached.

'Fine,' she said. 'All fine.'

In truth, she didn't have much contact with them. She found them dull and slightly upsetting. She didn't like the way they chivvied her to 'be less cold', and to 'open up'. Her mother was a particular culprit. What was Ann supposed to do – sit there and tell them all about the burned bodies they'd had to suction out of the last Flag ark they'd found? Or perhaps they'd have liked her to explain why the habitat-building plans they sounded so excited about were dangerously ill-conceived? Her parents didn't appear to have ever got over the fact that they'd had her modded for intelligence and critical decision-making and got exactly what they'd paid for.

'Mostly boring, really,' she added. 'You know how it is with Gala-teans – they don't call it the Switzerland of space for nothing.'

This was a running joke between them. Sam was also from Galatea. Most of the Rumfoord League's top people were. The planet was still wrestling with an ongoing environmental catastrophe that had started long before the war, brought on by a failed attempt at terraforming. Barely a week went by without some kind of emergency.

Out of desperation, they'd long ago tinkered with genetic engineering in an attempt to create minds smart enough to fix their problems. It had left them with more than their fair share of eccentrics. Consequently, their society had a high tolerance for quirks. Ann found Sam's love of chat somewhat taxing, but that was just Sam. Sam had been bred for leadership, not logic. It took all sorts.

'Overcaptain Shah,' she said, 'please forgive me for being blunt but could we cut to the details? My assumption is that we're here to discuss the fallout from the Tiwanaku assault – is that correct? You must have heard back from Earth by now.'

Sam smirked, apparently amused by her reaction. 'Sure,' he said. 'Of course. The answer is yes, there will be a mission, as we expected, and we want you on it.'

Ann breathed deep. 'How many ships?'

'Monet expected two,' said Sam. 'Our people pushed for three, for the obvious reasons. Monet seemed flexible in that regard.'

'So you need a first officer?' said Ann optimistically. 'Someone to help you keep the game from getting out of hand?'

'No, Ann. I need a captain.' He pivoted to face her.

Ann's eyes went wide. 'A captain? For which ship?'

'The *Chiyome*.'

'But I thought you were going to take it?'

Ann felt flattered but confused. The *Chiyome* was the ship the Fleet wasn't supposed to have. It used hybrid Human/Fecund technology, with both a quantum stealth-shield and third-generation tau-chargers. It was, to all extents and purposes, invisible.

Sam shrugged and let some frustration show in his expression.

'That I was, but Monet has made things a little complicated for us – he's insisted on bringing in Mark Ruiz as a pilot for the *Gulliver*.'

Ann's brow creased in confusion. 'Ruiz. Isn't he the man you told me about – Monet's protégé? The one who stole a starship and nearly killed everyone aboard?'

Sam nodded and set off down the path again.

'I thought he was out of the picture,' said Ann. 'Didn't that get resolved?'

'It did,' said Sam. 'Monet unresolved it.'

'I can't imagine the senate will agree,' said Ann. 'Given what you said, Ruiz must not have held a command for over a year.'

'The senate already bought it,' said Sam. 'Admiral Baron threw his full weight behind the request and threatened to invoke emergency powers. We didn't anticipate that.'

'And did Ruiz consent?'

'We haven't heard back yet, but given the time-lag involved, we have to assume he will and prepare for that eventuality. League agents on Earth will no doubt be trying to figure out how to passively remove him from the proceedings without arousing suspicion. It goes without saying that they'll have to be incredibly careful. Monet's role is central to our plans and by now everyone will be watching Ruiz, from the senate, to the sects, to Monet himself.'

Ann exhaled as her mind raced through the implications. The League plan was, in broad strokes, simple. Having used the Nems to fake an alien attack, they'd lure Will Monet to Tiwanaku. Once there, they'd goad the *Ariel Two* into igniting a Nem swarm-response, having laid a convenient warp trail all the way to Earth. They'd then divert Will to Snakepit to make sure he couldn't prevent the invasion that would inevitably follow. The Nems' assault would be shut down almost as soon as it started, just after the Earther interests in the home system took a hit. The sects' power would crumble while the Fleet would come off looking like heroes. With minimal loss of life, the political stalemate would be broken, with Colonial interests favoured. Even better, Will's culpability would leave him conveniently malleable in the new order to follow. A return to IPSO's current compromises would be out of the question.

The devil, though, was in the details. Getting Monet and his ship to Tiwanaku and soliciting a violent response from the Nems were both trivial tasks. Shutting down the Nems at Earth wasn't likely to be a problem, either, given the League's extensive knowledge of the machines' weaknesses. Getting the *Ariel Two* to Snakepit, however, required finesse. The plan hinged on the careful manipulation of Will Monet – a process that had been underway for years. Unless Will took himself out of the picture at the critical juncture, the most powerful starship in human space would remain dangerously – and unpredictably – in play.

In that context, Ruiz's involvement was something of a wild card. Ruiz had been their leverage – their means of ensuring Monet's compliance. Their plans for abducting the young roboteer would have to be scrapped.

'That makes control over the *Gulliver* somewhat uncertain,' she said. 'I mean, if he has helm control, how are you going to get the ship to Snakepit?'

'A good question. Which is exactly why I've added myself to the diplomatic team,' said Sam. 'I'm going to take on the role of strategy specialist and manage him directly.'

Ann paused, unsure of what to say.

'Do that and you're putting your life on the line,' she said eventually.

The *Gulliver* would be in the thick of it when the Nems reacted to their visit. Their response would be swift and terrible, and the *Gulliver* was unarmed.

Sam nodded. 'Because that's my responsibility. Which means that I need you to play the outfield in the *Chiyome*.' He grimaced. 'Let me come clean with you. I'm asking you because I need someone totally rational on that ship. Someone who will stay on top of things. I know your politics aren't aligned with most of the League but you understand better than anyone why we're doing this. You were the one who built those models. You know how many more people will die if we don't act. We're talking about billions here. We're talking about the end of civilisation itself.'

Ann nodded. Her predictive work on frontier conflicts had attracted the League's attention to her in the first place.

'It may get *unpleasant* in there,' said Sam. His face darkened into a scowl. 'We've never used the Nems on a target as large as Tiwanaku. It's more than twice the size of the settlement the sects tried to dump at Nazca, and you know what that was like.'

Ann wished she could forget. After laying the warp trail to Nazca to lead the Nem swarm to its prey, she and the other conspirators hid at the edge of the system and listened in on the emergency broadcasts from the doomed Flags. Worse still, she'd been part of the surface clean-up team after the Nems had finally fallen torpid.

She'd stood in the sterilised dust where the illegal settlement had once sat and stared at the weirdly organised heaps of dismembered human bodies and machine parts. Immobile Nem surface-workers loomed all around her, clumsy and insectile, vapour still venting from their backs. The eyes of the not-quite-dead machines tracked her as she passed, the fine orange hairs that covered them quivering in the planet's feeble breeze. Her skin crawled just thinking about them.

It had taken weeks for the Nem activity at Nazca to peter out, and probably weeks for their last victims to die. During that time, the Nems had busied themselves with cryptic, purposeless tasks, like dying ants bereft of a queen. The League had held its breath waiting for them to stop so they could safely descend to the planet and clean up the remains.

It appeared that the larger the target they used the Nems to clear, the longer it took for them to shut down afterwards. The League's scientists had speculated that above some threshold, the machines would take on a different behaviour – probably the creation of a new colony. That in itself wouldn't be such a bad outcome. However, it'd leave the League with plenty of explaining to do when the next IPSO scout flight arrived.

'This puts the whole operation way outside our comfort zone from the get-go,' said Sam. 'We're playing with fire but absolutely cannot afford to get burned. Do you understand me?'

Ann found his change of mood intimidating. She nodded. She never knew with Sam whether to treat him like a superior officer or some kind of friend.

'Isn't that what everyone does these days, though?' she said defensively. 'Since the war, the whole economy's been built on borrowing alien tech. And there have been fewer surprises with the Nems than with the Fecund ruins.'

'People don't use Fecund ruins to carry out mass executions.'

Ann flinched inwardly and changed the subject to lighten the tone. 'What about Ash? Wasn't he going to captain the *Gulliver*?'

'Ash becomes Mark's second. And the moment the shit hits the fan, I'll issue an executive order and slide him into the hot seat. You don't need to worry about the *Gulliver* – I'll cover that angle and rendezvous with you at Snakepit. You keep your eyes on Monet.'

'And who's my second?'

'Jaco Brinsen-Nine,' said Sam. 'Do you mind?'

Ann shrugged. 'Of course not. Jaco is a dedicated contributor to the League and an accomplished officer. I can see why you picked him.'

Jaco was part of Sam's own staff. She couldn't have asked for a more attentive second, even if he was an FPP zealot.

'So that's a yes, then?' said Sam. 'You'll take the position?'

'Of course,' said Ann. 'I could hardly say no.'

Sam's expression darkened again. 'I wanted to give you the option. If someone offered me this job, I'd be shitting my pants. We've set a juggernaut in motion here and we have to stay the course. A lot of people are going to die. The next fifty years of political history are about to be shaped by what we do. Maybe the entire course of human development.'

'Desperate times—' she started.

'Desperate times doesn't even begin to cover it,' he said, his gaze fierce. 'If we had a government that was awake enough to solve this problem without us, it would have happened by now. But we don't, which means we have no choice but to go around them. We won't make any friends doing this. The best possible outcome will be that nobody ever realises what we've done for them.'

He stared at her, waiting for something. She had no idea what to say.

'I won't let you or the League down,' she told him.

'Just understand that your primary responsibility now is to make sure that Monet gets out of there alive and heads straight for Snakepit. It is *imperative* that he take the bait. The predictive models we have for him are only about sixty per cent reliable, as evidenced by this Ruiz business, despite him being the most modelled man alive. Whatever happens, we need him to be a part of what follows. He's too dangerous anywhere else. Whoever controls the *Ariel Two* has the edge in human space. And that needs to be us.'

'Understood,' said Ann.

The idea of manipulating her childhood hero wasn't a comfortable one, but they all had to play the hands they were dealt. She understood how important it was that Will remain in the dark, even while she hated the necessity of it.

'What will happen to the *Griffin*?'

'River Chu will take over,' said Sam. 'The *Griffin* will conveniently be sent on a tour of the home system. That way, River will be able to participate in the clean-up process.'

'Of course,' said Ann.

She'd have preferred for her crew to be a long way from Earth when disaster struck but knew that Sam couldn't spare the staff. The reach of the Rumfoord League might be long but its members were few. They relied on their network of uninformed FPP sympathisers for almost everything. And at least half of the League's effort was taken up just keeping that network functioning.

'One more thing,' said Sam, his voice softening again. 'I need a favour.'

'Whatever you need,' said Ann.

'It's not part of our core mission plan, but there's a way we might be able to safely, gently resolve this Ruiz business before the mission even starts. I think we have to try.'

She glanced at him nervously. 'What do you have in mind?'

'I'm planning a small scandal to disqualify Ruiz from taking command – something that Monet would find disappointing but plausible. I think it should be easy enough to arrange. I'm asking you because you've got more undercover police experience than just about anyone else in the League and you'll be there on Triton at the right time. All you'd need to do is make contact with a certain member of the Triton underworld and set up a suitably embarrassing episode – anonymously, of course. I'll handle the rest. Think you can manage that?'

'Easily,' said Ann.

'Once you've made the connection in person, everything should run by itself. I'll forward you the details via the League channel. Does that work?'

'Sure,' said Ann.

'And, needless to say, do keep this quiet,' Sam added. 'Best not to even share it within the League. If anything goes wrong, we want our people to have plausible deniability, as usual.'

'Of course,' said Ann.

She tried to hide her dismay at the prospect of carrying yet more secrets. But in a matter of weeks it'd all be over. She could hardly complain at this point.

'Terrific,' said Sam, breaking into a smile. 'Time is of the essence, I'm afraid, so you'll be leaving directly. You have a passenger berth on the *Dolittle* – it's leaving for the home system in two hours.'

Ann was astonished afresh. 'That doesn't leave me much time to pack.'

'River is doing it for you right now,' said Sam.

'That's a relief,' she lied. Apparently she wasn't going home even for a day.

Sam stopped as the gravel path looped back to face the transit station and stuck out his hand for her to shake.

'Look, I know this is a tough call, but you're the best I've got. The next time we meet will be on Triton, and I won't be able to be half this chummy. So this is me saying good luck now. I know you'll do great.' He offered her a rough half-smile.

'I appreciate it, sir,' she said, feeling pride and terror in equal measures as she shook his hand. 'And thank you.'

'Welcome to the most dangerous mission in history,' said Sam. 'See you in a couple of weeks.'

She managed a watery smile and a salute as she stepped towards the pod.

3: ARRIVAL

3.1: WILL

Two days before he was due to depart, Will met Pari Voss at the Bogota spaceport. They transferred to her private lifter and made for Mexico City with all haste. Pari's lounge had a window-wall where passengers could take in the view. They drank Nibiru sours and caught up while jagged, grey mountains slid past beneath, reaching up out of a pale and furious sea.

'How's it going?' she asked.

'Great,' said Will guardedly. He knew Pari wouldn't have asked him to come down if there hadn't been a pressing need. 'Scrambling to pull everything together in time but enjoying it.'

He'd spent most of the intervening three weeks feeling impatient to leave while IPSO's bureaucracy had dragged its heels at every turn. Fortunately, getting Mark involved had lifted his mood immeasurably. His dreams about the war had stopped, which came as an incredible relief.

'How about you? What's the deal?'

Pari had been handling the political fallout from Ira's announcement of the mission and her request to see him here was undoubtedly related. However, she hadn't forwarded him details about their upcoming meeting which usually meant that, legally speaking, it wasn't happening.

'Not so great. Somebody leaked the fact that you have a link to Mark to the E.T. Affairs group in the House Proportional.'

Will rose out of his chair. 'They did *what*?'

Only a handful of people in the senate knew about Mark's past and all of them had been sworn to secrecy. Will had worked for years to keep the young roboteers from his failed Omega Programme out of the public eye. It had been an endless source of stress and misery for him and after the tribunal it had only grown harder.

'Now E.T. Affairs think you're packing the mission with your cronies and trying to pass them off as allies of Earth. Or that's what they're saying, at least. They're threatening to cry foul and block the mission.'

'Who did this?' said Will, his fingers curled into claws.

Pari threw up her hands. 'We're still figuring that out. For all we know the information has been sitting out there for a while and the House has just been waiting for the right time to apply it. In any case, the good news is that we have a solid commitment that word hasn't gone any further.'

'From whom?' Will growled.

'From my guy in the House Proportional,' said Pari. 'His name is Ezekiel Wei. Zeke knew my husband. Our kids used to play together. He's okay. Really.'

Pari didn't like talking about the loss of her family. A Revivalist splinter group had killed them all while she was away on senate business. It had been a sad, bloody affair, so Will didn't push it further. He sank back into his chair and glowered at the dead ocean.

'Don't worry,' said Pari. 'He's got our backs. And that's who we're going to meet. We're going to Mexico to show willingness to compromise.'

Will frowned at her. '*Are* we willing?'

'Of course not,' said Pari. 'Unless you've changed your mind.'

Will peered furiously into his glass. 'I thought they couldn't block the mission in any case.'

'No, but they could tie us up in paperwork for weeks. And by that time, every sect and colony will have sent their own missions.'

'That's not going to happen,' said Will. 'I don't care what they fucking want. I'm done with this shit. I'm leaving in two days whether they like it or not.'

'And you can do that,' said Pari. 'Just realise that if you do, Mark won't be coming with you. Nobody can stop you leaving on the *Ariel Two*, but the *Gulliver* is a diplomatic ship under IPSO control.' She looked at the expression on his face and sighed. 'Will, don't go in confrontational, I beg you. You'll hurt our cause. This should be a very quiet meeting. Trust him and leave him room and we can probably resolve this.'

Will downed the rest of his drink. Alcohol hadn't touched his metabolism in thirty years – a fact he lamented from time to time. Still, the drink's bite helped stiffen his resolve.

'Fine,' he said. 'Do we know what they want?'

'That's the other piece of bad news,' said Pari. 'They want you to hand off diplomatic leadership of the mission to Yunus Chesterford.' She glanced down at his hands gripping the arms of the chair. 'Will, please don't break the furniture. Titanium loungers are so difficult to replace.'

'Yunus Chesterford is a dick,' said Will. 'No way. That guy has tried to fuck me over more times than I can count. He's gone on record as a Transcended-denier, for crying out loud.'

'I know, Will,' said Pari. 'I know. He's Earth's pet exoscience pundit. If he could roll the clock back and bring Sanchez out of the grave, he'd probably do it.'

'That's because he has no fucking idea what the High Church was like. They used to string up intellectuals like him and flay their skin off with nanowire.'

'Let's just see what Zeke has to say, huh?' said Pari. 'We'll be there in a few minutes. We can get angry later.'

The conversation petered out after that, leaving Will alone with his thoughts. His last run-in with the Chesterfords on the biosphere world of Davenport loomed in his memory.

Humanity had discovered several biospheres during its expansion, each as useless as the last. Earth's organisms appeared to either destroy alien life or wither before it. One biochemistry always found a way to dominate and co-opt the other. So rather than wrestle with the ecological nightmares biospheres caused, colonists tended to seek out lifeless Mars Plus worlds instead. They lived contentedly under plastic domes and left life-bearing planets for scientists and thrill-seekers with no fear of cancer.

Davenport was an extreme case. Its life was among the most virulently disruptive that humanity had ever found. The entire planet had been cordoned off to prevent the risk of its flora and fauna being weaponised by terrorist groups.

Which was why Will had chosen that site for his experiment in personal duplication. Away from prying eyes where nobody could get hurt, Will had taken over a small lake between two moss-spattered hills and consumed enough of the local biota to build a backup copy of himself. Or a near copy, at least. The experiment, like most of his endeavours since the war, had been a flop. Something in the structure of his smart-cells prevented him from making a complete duplicate. The clone had been a sort of shadow Will, halfway between himself and a walking SAP. Useful, perhaps, but not the reserve copy for the human race he'd hoped for. After three days of life, it committed suicide, but not before sharing the full extent of its personal anguish about Rachel with him.

To Will's dismay, it turned out that Citra Chesterford, Yunus's wife, was leading one of the Davenport research teams at the time. Despite signing the Fleet nondisclosure agreement and promising silence to his face, she passed knowledge of the failed experiment to Yunus the moment he'd left the system. Yunus had promptly turned it into a political weapon. Will was still living out the consequences.

With some difficulty, he forced himself back to the present and tried to concentrate on the view that Pari's senatorial lifter afforded. Like many of the world's metropolitan areas, Mexico City had acquired its share of supertowers. They jutted out from between earlier, less battleship-like forms of architecture, most of which had been allowed to dissolve in the worsening weather. As they nosed towards their destination, a tethering arm reached out of the building to meet them, bearing an old-fashioned transit pod with real windows.

Zeke met them there. He turned out to be a dapper individual with small features and tidily oiled hair tinted a conservative blue to match his jacket.

'Parisa, Will, wonderful to see you. Thank you so much for coming. Only chit-chat until we reach the safe room, please. Security in ArcoCinco is not what it used to be.'

Will stared at the man and tried to restrain himself from saying something unpleasant.

The pod took them down into the body of the tower, granting some impressive views over the grey infinity of Mexico City's rubble-maze on the way.

'I see you have vegetation down there,' said Pari, pointing to some feeble patches of green. 'That's impressive.'

Zeke shrugged. 'Small-scale projects. It's all for show. Surface plants cost more to manage than they give back. All the real farming is underground nowadays, like everywhere else.'

The pod swapped track and descended into the tower's vast hollow interior. The top floors had been well maintained, Will noted, at odds with his expectations. They looked, if anything, better off than some of the habitats he'd seen on Mars. About forty levels below, though, things got ugly. Down in the building's central well, Will could make out the scars of flenser damage on the ceramic walls, and long, dark streaks of something unpleasant on the plastic windows.

The pod dropped them at a penthouse meeting room with a real lawn and apple trees. They sat down around an antique Formica meeting table to talk.

'We're ready to pull the plug and start over,' said Zeke cheerfully.

Pari sighed. 'Do that and we'll all lose valuable time, the sects and the Fleet both. Plus any mission the sects send by themselves will lack credibility.'

'Granted. But my committee can't green-light something when they've been taken out of the loop altogether.'

'That hasn't happened,' said Pari.

Zeke shot her an incredulous glance. 'Really? Then how come you're recruiting already?'

'Some parts of the mission are negotiable and others aren't,' she said. 'It makes sense for us to make progress on those elements that aren't.'

'So the nepotistic inclusion of Will's protégé is non-negotiable?'

Will pressed his hand against the table, being careful not to break it.

'First up,' said Will, 'ship's captain is a Fleet position and we'll pick staff for Fleet roles as we see fit. Secondly, the selection is not nepotistic. I picked Mark because he's the best starship pilot the Fleet has ever produced. Bar none. Or did your source forget to mention that while they were laying out the juicy titbits? We'll be risking our lives out there and we need to make choices which reflect that reality. And frankly, I'd have thought your people would relish the appointment. I picked the only Omega-rated roboteer who's from Earth. Doesn't that mean anything to you? Your alternative was Ash Corrigan-Five, from Drexler – the FPP's favourite planet. You're telling me you'd prefer that?'

'No, of course not,' said Zeke. 'And honestly, the gesture did mean something, right up until it turned out that Ruiz was one of your people, not one of ours. The sects thought they'd won something at first, then they started to feel cheated. Now they need some kind of concession so they know you're not trying to screw them over.'

'What's wrong with the House just doing its job?' said Will. 'The military positions on this mission were never open for debate. You're supposed to be helping us source scientists.'

Zeke threw his hands open. 'And that's what I'm trying to do. But help me out here! I'm sympathetic to your needs, but you have to realise that the House Proportional is *not* like the senate. Most of the representatives know about the Tiwanaku Event now and they *hate* it. They're all from Earth, of course, and to them this whole thing looks like an attempt to demonise Flags.

'For the sects, an independent colony like the one the *Reynard* found out there isn't a sin, it's an inevitability. Sure, such things aren't legal yet, but they expect that to change and they're quietly furious that it hasn't already. This event, though, makes it look like Earthers run around fomenting interspecies war. The sects need to feel like they're a part of this process otherwise they'll go it alone. I can think of at least three groups with Revivalist wings that could reach Tiwanaku easily. They have armies of Truist zealots just begging to recreate old glories. Any one of them could send a mission out while we sit here in bureaucratic hell.'

'What about the fact that one of these groups of yours is probably the outfit that caused this situation in the first place?' said Will.

'Of course,' said Zeke. 'But what about the others? They're not going to break ranks until they know who to blame. And they already hate the fact that you're still ambassador. I've heard people calling you the *Alien Satan* again, which I haven't heard for years. And the fact that you're putting your own people in key positions only makes that worse. As far these people are concerned, Will, the Transcendist experiment failed years ago, back when the Transcended stopped talking. IPSO became a prison then, not a promise. They want Earth's primacy back. For them, this just looks like another delay to their destiny.'

'We're already making compromises,' said Pari. 'We're sourcing the diplomatic ship from the Vartian Institute rather than using one of our own, and we've reduced our contribution to the diplomatic team to a single strategic advisor.'

'That doesn't help much,' said Zeke. 'The Vartian Institute will insist on putting one of their own paranoid agents aboard, which only leaves three places to fill.'

'Make them count, then,' said Pari. 'Who have you picked?'

'Venetia Sharp is a definite,' said Zeke.

Pari wrinkled her button nose. 'The woman who wrote all that vitriol about the FPP?'

'The same. But you can't debate the fact that she's an excellent scientist.'

Will said nothing. He'd read plenty of Venetia's work and found it rock-solid.

'As for the other two slots,' said Zeke, 'that's where the Chesterfords come in. If you put Mark Ruiz in the captain's seat, we want Yunus Chesterford to head up the diplomatic effort. He gets to be the public face of this mission, with executive command over that ship.'

Will fumed silently.

'Come on,' said Zeke. 'You get what you want and Earth gets what it wants. It doesn't cost you anything. We both know the mission will go from diplomatic to military the moment you find out who pulled the stunt at Tiwanaku. When that happens, control of everything reverts back to you anyway. So what's wrong with handing Earth the *appearance* of a victory?'

Zeke's eyebrows rose optimistically as he waited for a response. Will just glared.

'It's not that simple,' said Pari. 'Yunus would have to explicitly hand off override control in the event of an emergency and he won't be in a hurry to do that. If he thinks there's an angle in it for Earth, he'll just sit on his thumbs.'

'What can I say?' said Zeke. 'I've managed things so far, but the alternative is that information about Mark's background leaks a little further. It's out of my hands at this point. Unless I can bring a compromise for the sects, they'll act on that knowledge regardless of what line I ask them to take. As it is, we just need this one small concession to gain their silence.'

'You realise that's blackmail,' said Pari.

'I realise it's business,' said Zeke. 'This mission is very high-stakes. What did you expect?'

'Yunus Chesterford is a grandstanding idiot,' said Will. 'He'll be worse than dead weight if anything serious happens.'

'He's a widely respected thought-leader on alien interactions,' said Zeke. 'And his wife is an award-winning exobiologist.'

Pari shook her head. 'You're on thin ice. All we have to do is swap the roles to put Ruiz in the subcaptain slot and your leverage evaporates. You won't have a chance of pushing a leadership position for Chesterford then, and you'll end up with a captain you like even less.'

'Except that's not going to happen, is it?' said Zeke.

'Don't be so sure,' said Pari. 'We're not ruling anything out.'

'Fine,' Will told Zeke. 'You've got a deal.'

He could see where the negotiation was leading and he didn't like it. If Earth wanted Chesterford to lead the mission, there were ways he could work around that. And after all, he'd be aboard a different ship. Plus the thought of inflicting Mark Ruiz on the Chesterfords gave him a certain perverse satisfaction.

Pari turned to face him, her eyes wide. 'Will! I'm not sure you meant that. Why don't we all just *take stock* and think this over for a moment?'

'Nope,' he said. 'The man gets what he wants. I'm bored of fucking about.'

'Works for me,' said Zeke. His grin threatened to split his face apart.

Will leaned forward and fixed Zeke with a cold look. 'And now here's a threat for a threat,' he said. 'You get what you want today, and the information about Mark goes away *for ever*. If it leaks any further, I will personally seek out you and every member of your committee and remove all of you from the human race, by hand. Do you understand me?'

Zeke's smile evaporated.

'Will,' said Pari.

'Do you get me?' said Will.

Zeke nodded. 'Very clearly.'

'Good,' said Will. He stood up from the table. 'Thank you for having us over. It was a long way for a short chat, but I'm glad we've ironed that out.'

He nodded his respects and headed for the transit pod with Pari trailing after him. On the way back up to the lifter, her mouth was a thin, bloodless line. As soon as they headed south, she spoke up.

'I had that under control,' she said curtly.

'Sorry,' he said. 'I know I lost it. I don't care.' His patience had burned out.

'Now what are we supposed to do?' said Pari. 'You'll be leaving Mark on a ship run by your public enemy. Yunus will screw you over the moment he gets a chance.'

'Mark will manage. And if Yunus finds out about him, then the good Professor and I will have words.'

'But what if something goes wrong?' said Pari. 'Yunus will have all of the overrides. So long as he's on that ship, it'll belong to him.'

'I said, *Mark will manage*. Look, I'm sorry, Pari. I know you're doing your best for me, but this is my limit. Mark gets that captaincy and the next person who tries to block it has to go through me.' He hoped the tiredness in his voice would make her realise how serious he was.

Pari rubbed her temples. 'You can be an asshole sometimes, you know that? In case you didn't notice, making sure the sects don't screw this mission up is in my best interests, too. We're supposed to be on the same team, remember – the one that wants the human race *not* to burn itself to a cinder?'

They didn't talk for the rest of the flight. Will thought about apologising a dozen times but lacked the energy. He just wanted to get the hell off Earth as fast as he could.

3.2: ANN

Ann's clipper got her to the home system just forty hours before she was due to head back out. That barely gave her enough time to follow through on Sam's request. So, as soon as she'd arrived at Triton's Delany Station and checked in with Local HQ, she got to work. From her bland little room in the officers' dorm, she used the League toolkit Sam had provided to set up a web of silent proxies in Delany's public network. With untraceable routing in place, she sent a message to the contractor Sam had picked out using a security weave borrowed from NoreCorr's FiveClan sect. Ten minutes later, an equally anonymous reply arrived with a rendezvous attached.

10 p.m. Ocean Magic Shuttle. Alone. Reuse this message as ident match.

Ann leaned back in her chair, surveying the reply with a mix of anticipation and dismay. The job was on. She had no excuse not to act.

The details of the 'favour' Sam wanted had come as a disappointing surprise. It wasn't that the task itself would be difficult, per se – simply that Sam had set her up with the kind of persona she found uncomfortable. According to her briefing, she was supposed to be a Leading-class Earther heiress and the daughter of the contractor's previous point of contact. Whether that was Sam or one of his other underlings, she had no idea. In any case, she needed a look that was dressed-up and dumbed-down – not her forte.

She left her room and stopped off at the undercover police desk two floors below, where her League chip convinced the wardrobe octobot to part with a shoulder-carry and a few simple props. With her equipment assembled, she strode out through the drab, bustling corridors of the Fleet Headquarters and boarded the next available private transit heading hab-south.

The pod took her down through the stack of rings towards the end of the station where the space elevator connected. She got off at R3 – the privacy area. As she marched along the empty carpeted corridors, Ann used her contacts and subvocal mic to rent a high-end space nearby. A destination icon appeared in her heads-up map.

The suite turned out to be a pleasant one with furnishings in soft, neutral beige and a modern tactronic desk. She dumped her bag on the floor and used the chip in her arm to put a freeze on the local security. Then, with the suite running on passive, she configured one wall as a digital mirror and stripped.

Ann had no body-image issues. She looked like what she was: tough. Hard planes defined her face and she made no effort to soften them. She kept her hair pragmatically short. Most men, she knew, found her more off-putting than attractive. However, Ann liked being that way. To her mind, her body was exceedingly functional. When she asked it to do something, it responded efficiently. What more could she want?

She synced the touchboard on the wall to her subdermal augs and initiated the undercover program she'd picked out. She started with the easy part and dropped the pigment in her skin by several shades, toning it fashionably retro-cauc, the way the Leading-class women liked it these days. As soon as she had it right, she fired off a program of physical adjustments. This always hurt like hell but never failed to confuse surveillance SAPs. The contractor Sam had chosen would never be able to trace the job back to her, or to the Rumfoord League. Even if he snooped for skin DNA, he'd draw a blank. Ann's augs had tools for that, too.

She breathed through the pain as her nose reshaped itself and her lips plumped. Her chest ached like fury as her body's fluids rebalanced. She'd contemplated pain-suppressors, but they always left her groggy and she had work to do. Over agonising minutes, the machines inside her remade her as a woman for whom personal appearance was a priority.

Outside the Fleet, nobody had augs like these. The public tended to be extremely wary of implanted tech for the simple reason that it could be hacked, usually with unpleasant consequences. The soft assaults on roboteers after the war had made that pretty clear. Consequently, the closest most people came to sticking machines in their bodies these days was a pair of smart-contacts and an ident in their hand. For many years, the Fleet had been even warier and gone as far as refusing to use contacts on military flights, opting instead for easily replaceable visors. But eventually the security became solid enough to make the risks worth taking.

Ann tested her voice as her vocal cords reconfigured, getting squeakier by the second.

'Wreck a nice beach,' she said. 'Bah bah bah.'

To her own ears she sounded ludicrous, but apparently neo-girlish was all the rage. She pulled a dress and an organic wig from her bag. Some swiftly programmed instructions to her chromatophores removed the need for cosmetics. As she donned the heels that went with the disguise, she gave thanks for the muscular support her augs provided. She hated heels. They were for idiots. Who voluntarily wore torture devices on their feet?

Five minutes later, Ann looked very convincingly like a Leading-class Earther princess from Triton's private orbital estates in town for a little partying. She fluffed her hair and tried a few facial stretches, getting used to the peculiar tightness of her new features.

With the transformation complete, Ann altered the privacy suite's records to show it as still in use and stepped out, locking it behind her. She took another private transit to the shuttle waiting lounge, via some route-laundering detours, then sat in a cafe to kill time until her flight out.

Like many of Triton's watering holes, the cafe had been decorated with high-class glitz for Earth's rich, most of whom had never set foot on the planet where their money came from. Instead of ordinary chairs and tables they had mismatched Surplus Age antiques made of non-biodegradable plastic, all artfully battered. Static physical prints made of tree-pulp paper hung on the walls. Table service came in the form of human staff dressed in coquettishly robot-themed attire. The lighting was low, gold-toned and constantly shifting.

While Ann found the ostentatious styling objectionable, she could hardly avoid it without dropping character. Since the war, the home system's outer planets had become the playground of the Leading class. These days people even talked about them as 'greater Earth' without a hint of irony. Her role required her to breathe that privilege like air without even noticing.

She had over an hour to burn, but that suited her just fine. She was probably under observation already and the extra chance to snoop would just put her contractor's mind at rest. She ordered a glass of bubl-brite, then brought up a fashion magazine on the table in front of her and pretended to read.

The drink tasted as revolting as Ann had known it would. Children and halfwits with sugar addictions drank bubl-brite. She ignored the craving for a decent cup of green tea to wash the syrup down with and tried her best to look like a bored debutante.

The minutes passed slowly. By the time her boarding announcement appeared, she'd fended off a couple of attempts to hit on her and shooed away a robot selling garish transgenic flowers. Relieved, she made her way to the docking pod and held on tight to the handles as the gees fell away. A quarter of an hour of dull embarkation protocols later, she found herself reclining in a pink-furred shuttle interior listening to crosbystep remixes, on her way to Ocean Magic – one of Neptune's less popular public-access pleasure palaces. The cabin was almost deserted.

Twenty minutes after the craft untethered, a boy floated over and hovered next to her. At the same time, an icon appeared in her display. This was her guy. Animated tattoos writhed on his cheeks and his unnaturally huge brown eyes were like something out of a children's interactive. Wavy blond hair hovered around his face. He looked more like a soft rich kid on his way to pick up girls at a float-party than a professional criminal. But then, that was the point.

'Mind if I sit here?' he said smoothly.

'Please do,' she replied in a carefully modulated NoreCorr accent. As he sat, she swapped the local privacy settings to full.

'I got your message,' he said. 'You need a job done?'

'Yes. The details were all in the packet. Did you receive it?'

'Sure. You want my people to find this guy and rough him up a little. That's easy to arrange. Mind if I ask why, though?' He looked her up and down, his eyes stalling on her augmented chest. 'I mean, girls like you don't often resort to buying a fixer, you know? What did he do that made you want to take such extreme action?'

This was where the acting came in. Ann arranged her features in a furious pout. She blushed.

'Do you really need to know? I thought your kind of people didn't care.'

'We have to ask, miss. Got to be careful in this business, so we always check out a job before we take it.'

'Why? Aren't my FiveClan credentials good enough for you? Daddy said they should be enough for anything. He said you know him.'

'And I do. Your daddy's been an excellent client. But still, I'd like to understand.'

'It's private,' she said weakly.

The man waited.

Ann squeezed her hands into fists, being careful of her overdecorated nails.

'He *left* me, if you must know. That Fleetie bastard left me. He thinks I'm just some little Earther ditz he can use as he pleases and then vanish on the next shuttle out. But that's not how it works. Nobody treats my family that way. It's like he doesn't have the first idea who he's dealing with.'

The man nodded. 'I get it. He's a Colonial, I take it?'

She snorted. 'Of course. He calls himself Earther, but he doesn't understand anything. He didn't grow up here. He's got no sense of class. He isn't even *affiliated*. I should have known what that meant right from the start. He thinks he's some kind of handsome flyboy and that girls will fall all over him, just like that. With no consequences.'

'So you'd like his legs broken.'

Ann feigned a shudder. 'Nothing so drastic. Just teach him a lesson, that's all. Some bruises will do.'

'Do you want to leave a message for him?' said the fixer.

She shook her head and adopted a wistful expression. 'No. I don't want him back. Not now. It's too late. He mustn't even know it was me. My family shouldn't be involved.' She glanced out through the false window to her left. 'If he comes back to me afterwards, I won't even have him. It's that much over.'

The fixer scrutinised her for a moment, trying to conceal a smile. 'Okay, miss. You've got it. The fee will be sent to the Made account in your message packet. After that, we'll never have contact again. Do you understand?'

Ann nodded quickly. 'Daddy already said that.'

'Your daddy is a smart man. Let him know we took good care of you, okay?'

She nodded.

'When you see him, I want you to give him this.' The fixer pressed a memory bead into her hand.

Ann tried not to look too shocked. This wasn't part of the script.

'What's that?' she said.

'It's for your dad. He's a hard man to reach. He'll know what it is. Tell him from me that we've been trying to get hold of him for months. He needs to install this or he's going to get both of us in trouble and that would be bad for everyone. Do you understand?'

Ann nodded mutely.

'Good girl.'

As the shuttle slowed on its approach to the next orbital, the man unclipped.

'Bye now,' he said. 'Hope you find a decent boyfriend. You can't trust Colonials, you know. They're all the same.' He winked a huge eye at her as he pushed off towards the airlock.

Ann turned the awful crosbystep back on and tried not to look concerned. She slipped the memory bead into her party-pack and watched out of the corner of her eye until the fixer had disappeared through the airlock.

She exhaled deeply as the hatch cycled shut. Her job was done, thank Gal. Sam could rest easy. However, Ann knew she wouldn't be able to call it a night until she'd taken a careful look at that bead. If it contained tracerware, she'd have to find some in-character way of disposing of it before dropping her cover.

She waited until the next stop before disembarking and boarding a return flight. Getting back took twice as long, with more waiting in lounges and more tedious advances from idle young men. Ann endured it all, counting down the minutes until she reached Delany.

Once there, she used a public study-booth to scan the bead. It came up blank – there was no active code in it at all, or at least none the public booth could detect. It contained a single passive file encrypted using a standard FiveClan protocol. Ann sucked air over her teeth. She was either facing a serious professional-level threat or none at all. She saw no choice but to take a risk and head for home.

It was another hour and several route-laundering episodes later before she made it back to her privacy suite. By then, her whole body craved release from the disguise. She wanted nothing more than to rip off the dress, relax the awful machines in her nose and settle in for a nice long kickboxing workout at the Fleet gym.

She ignored her body's protests and instead sat down at the tactronic desk. Using the same code package that had sealed off the privacy suite from the public network, Ann rigged up a sandbox-harness for the file. It wouldn't protect her from the worst species of malware, but she'd be safe from all the mundane varieties of soft assault. With her heart in her mouth, she transferred the file to the desk's processor web and used the Made account Sam had given her to open it.

Inside lay a string of perfectly ordinary-looking software patches. From the file names and interface keys, they appeared to be for pharmaceutical industry code. Closer examination using the harness's analytical tools revealed tidy packets of audit-screened liarware bolted into otherwise entirely vanilla statistical packages. It was the kind of code that corrupt middle managers in sect businesses used to lie on their quarterly reports – hardly super-spy material.

Ann squinted at them in confusion. What in Gal's name would Sam want with code like this? The League's own stealthware could achieve exactly the same results effortlessly without needing attention as old-fashioned as a hand-written upgrade. Sam, or one of his agents, must have acquired the software the patches belonged to, because otherwise the fixer would never have chased him with them. The poor guy had obviously been concerned that his earlier version might fall foul of a security scrape and wanted to keep them both out of prison.

Was Sam involved in black-market drug production? It seemed insanely unlikely. The best explanation she could think of was that Sam's previous agent on Triton had been running some kind of business on the side without the League's knowledge. However, given the do-or-die loyalty the Rumford League demanded, that answer felt ridiculous, too.

Ann leaned back in the chair and stared at the code diagrams hovering over the desk. She realised then, with some discomfort, how little she actually understood about Sam's operation. The League hinged on his work, and all their lives with it. She dearly hoped that somewhere on the other side of all that subterfuge and secrecy, he knew what he was doing.

3.3: MARK

After clearing out his New York appartment, Mark took the interplanetary shuttle to Triton. He registered with the Fleet admin SAP at Delany Station and checked into the dorm remotely. It was still afternoon, local time, so he found himself with a few hours to kill before he effectively became part of the Fleet again. He was in no hurry to put a uniform back on, so instead he went to the squeeze-bar at Cantaloupe National Park.

All the business on Triton, and most of the leisure, happened at Delany, where a comfortable one-gee of spin could be counted on. That was also where you found all the ghastly overpriced restaurants and the shrieking crowds spilling out onto the walkway from the thousand-peace-coin-a-ticket nightclubs. Consequently Mark preferred the surface, despite the feeble gravity. Sadly, there weren't many places to visit at the bottom end of the space elevator, but of all of them, Cantaloupe was undoubtedly his favourite.

The weird maze of ridges and bumps that made up Triton's cantaloupe terrain lay just beyond the window-wall, lit by the frail light of the distant sun. The deep shadows and oddly organic twists and knobbles of pinkish ice make the place look like a world-sized exercise in surrealist art. The light was amplified, of course, otherwise the place would have looked like midnight in a tar-pit. But then, even the best bits of Triton were, in Mark's opinion, slightly fake.

He sat there for hours drinking whisky out of a bulb, staring at the ghostly landscape and trying to figure out where his job on Earth had gone wrong. His blood-engines could fix the booze later.

Leaving New York had been hard. He'd gone there to make a point, to connect with his roots and to try his hand at something that was really his own. After a lifetime of being groomed to fit the needs of the Fleet, Earth had felt incredibly honest and refreshing. New York actually needed him, and he was happy to share his talents with them. With time, though, the place started to feel as much like straitjacket as the one he'd left behind.

The core problem was his lack of freedom. Without the rights to his own interface, he was only half a man. Every decision he made or job he took had to be run past a committee of bureaucrats – people he'd never met who nevertheless felt they deserved a piece of him. When ordinary people were treated like that they called it slavery.

A polite cough from behind interrupted his brooding. He turned around to find a guy in a gold jacket smiling unctuously at him.

'Hi!' said the man. 'My employer would like to use the table you're seated at. Would you mind moving? We'll pay, of course.' He pulled a gaudy transaction stub from his pocket.

Mark glanced around at the rest of the bar. It was mostly empty, which was precisely why he'd chosen it. There were dozens of empty tables.

'Can't he sit somewhere else?'

'My employer thinks you have the best view in the house,' said the man jovially. 'Well chosen, my friend! How much would you need? Fifty? A hundred?'

'I don't want to move, thanks,' said Mark.

'My employer would be disappointed by that. He's a very powerful man. And he's asking you to name your price, that's all.'

Mark glowered at him. 'I don't have a fucking price.'

'You're FiveClan, right?' said the man, knowingly. 'Don't make a choice you'll regret later.'

Mark looked down at the branded one-piece he was wearing. Was this guy assuming things about him because he was dressed like a working Earther? Was he assuming that Mark could be ordered about just because he hadn't been born into the Leading class?

'This conversation is finished,' said Mark.

The man looked disappointed and more than a little confused. 'That's one expensive seat you've got there, my friend. Enjoy your evening.'

'I'm not your fucking friend,' Mark muttered at the man's departing back.

Mark hated Triton. It had only two kinds of people: Fleeties and the Leading crowd – billionaires in from their private worlds with their entourages. It made the place as hypocritical as it was polished. Clean-cut types with blue uniforms and high-handed morals rubbed shoulders with drugged harem girls artificially re-aged to a subjective twelve. Mark wasn't sure which group he liked least. Earth's Leading were the ones sucking it dry, in his opinion. They gave the planet a bad name. When most people from the Colonies looked at Earth, they saw only idle Flags and the rich scumbuckets who funded them. They didn't look any deeper. On the other hand, at least the Leading weren't hypocrites.

Someone tapped him on the shoulder. Mark turned again and found himself looking at a young Adonis. He was seven feet tall, perfectly muscled and dressed in gold velc pantaloons. His eyes were the icy blue of glacial meltwater. Or, more likely, a numbered option from the premium range of a New Angeles surgical catalogue. On his arm hung a girl with a flatly unrealistic physique and slow, doe-like eyes. She had a bland, empty smile parked on her exquisite lips.

'You're in my seat,' said the young god, an impatient frown creasing his chiselled features. 'I always sit here.'

Mark looked around at the almost empty cafe. 'I didn't hear the cafe SAP complaining,' he said.

The god looked bored. 'This isn't a formal request. It's a polite one.'

'Sorry, but it doesn't sound that polite,' said Mark, his anger mounting. 'Why don't you try a different spot tonight? You might like it.'

'Do you know who I am?' said the rich kid.

Mark couldn't believe someone had pulled that line on him for real.

'No fucking idea,' he said. He launched a background search to find out and kept talking. 'But whoever the hell you are, you should be fucking ashamed of yourself. Asking for special privileges in an IPSO park?

91

Do you imagine you've got extra rights based on whichever trophy wife happened to squirt you out into the world? It's people like you—'

The youth shrugged and wheeled his girlfriend away before Mark could finish. Mark seethed and considered calling the man back as he drifted off elegantly in the low gravity. He mentally glanced at the results of the search request. He'd apparently just insulted the first son of some high-profile sect baron. Whatever. He'd be in Fleet hands as soon as he finished his drink.

However, in the wake of the altercation, Mark found himself unable to relax. His already sour mood worsened. People weren't allowed to get away with that kind of shit in the New York towers, so why should they be able to here?

He downed the rest of the bulb and shoved it into the table-slot along with his other empties. He got up to leave, unclipping himself from the chair. However, navigating to the pod bank at the back of the room proved challenging. He'd grown unused to low-gravity conditions over the last year or so and the whisky wasn't helping. He bumped the ceiling a few times on his way over.

Once there, Mark asked the transit SAP to take him to his room, picked a pod and leaned himself against the wall inside as the vehicle raced up towards Delany Station. The increased gravity felt good, but his head – not so much. His interface connection remained muted and slippery. He'd clearly drunk more than he'd meant to. That had been happening a lot since he moved to Earth.

He pinged the pod's SAP for an arrival check. It wouldn't do for him to show up at a Fleet dorm with his blood chemistry all messed up. He'd need a little time to self-scrub before arriving. But the transit SAP didn't respond. Mark frowned in confusion. Was he sending bad packets? Was he too fuzzy to frame his requests properly? He started a metabolic cleaning program to straighten his head out and pinged the pod again. This time he asked for a basic protocol check and looked over the message for flaws before sending it.

Still nothing came back – not even a repair apology. Mark suddenly got the sense that something was wrong. Someone had co-opted his ride. Who'd bother to do that, though? It was the sort of prank he and his friends used to play on each other back in the Omega dorm.

His self-scrub had barely started when the pod pivoted and dropped him down a gravity well to somewhere in Delany – one of the lower rings, at a rough guess. The doors slid open to reveal two large men with thick necks and folded arms.

'What's going on?' said Mark.

'You were rude to someone important today,' said the one on the left. 'That's not how we do things on Triton. We're here to teach you some manners.'

Mark gazed at them in disbelief. What century did they think they were living in?

'You've got to be kidding, right?'

What kind of cretin sent in *human* enforcement? He dumped a third of his submind bandwidth on cybernetic liver assist, a third on breaking the security wall they'd locked around the pod, and the rest on combat readiness.

[*Warning,*] said his nanny-SAP. [*Exposing the extent of your abilities jeopardises Fleet security . . .*]

'Whatever,' Mark muttered.

From the beige, soundproofed walls behind the men, he could tell he had to be on a level with privacy suites. Triton had plenty. A lot of the business the billionaires did wasn't exactly Fleet-kosher.

'Step out of the pod, please,' said the man on the left. 'We don't want to make a mess of a public facility and it's not going anywhere until you do.'

Mark stayed put, waiting for his moment. His unarmed-combat program, bleating a little from being woken after years with no updates, nevertheless fed him a barrage of tactical data. Right Thug stood slightly asymmetrically, suggesting weakness in his left arm. Left Thug showed trace signs of a former neck injury, indicating a potential weak spot. And so on.

The man on the left reached into the pod to grab Mark by his shirt. Mark sidestepped, swivelled and pushed, using the man's momentum to send his face crashing into the back of the pod.

'Are we really going to do this?' he asked. 'Didn't you guys look me up first? Didn't you spot that I'm a Fleet roboteer?'

Mark had more gravity-support modifications in his body than most people even knew existed. He realised with a groan that his identity had probably been shielded since arrival for mission-security reasons. Most likely, the thugs had no idea who they were dealing with. Unfortunately, the security hold on the pod was *really* tight.

'I don't want to have to hurt you,' said Mark, though it looked like he'd already failed on that count. The man picking himself out of the pod wall had a broken nose. He'd have to chalk that up to the booze. He was still too fuzzy to fight properly.

While the first man grasped his face and groaned, the second lunged for him. Mark twisted and dragged Thug Two into the pod, tripping him as he entered. The thug went sprawling to the floor.

Mark stepped around both of them into the privacy suite behind. The men came after him, breaking out stim-sticks from their jackets.

Mark regarded the weapons with disbelief. 'Come on, guys. What is this, junior hoodlum night?'

The first thug, the one with the bloody nose, now looked unprofessionally angry as he dropped into a fighter's crouch. Mark's combat SAP pointed out the veins on his neck showing that he'd just got a bump of reinforced heart function. Probably some heavy stimulants, too. It recommended a twenty per cent improvement in response times to compensate. Mark obliged, despite the strain on his already struggling metabolism.

The thug came at him, stim-stick slashing for his chest. Mark chose his microsecond, dived in following the arm-sweep and drove his fingers into the man's exposed shoulder pressure point. He followed up with an elbow to the man's jaw, sending it cracking upwards. The thug toppled back.

Thug Two saw his opportunity and sprang. Mark adapted his spin, sidestepped and used it to propel the man forward again, this time at the suite doors. They dutifully opened for him and he landed on his chin in the corridor beyond.

'This has been nice, guys,' said Mark. 'A special moment, really. But I have to be going.'

He jumped over Thug Two, avoiding the man's swipe for his ankle, and walked quickly down the hall, checking behind him as he went.

Now that he'd left the suite, the habitat guarantee of zero surveillance did not apply. However, Mark found he still couldn't get a handle on the network. Was it possible that the entire corridor was on some kind of lockdown, or even the entire ring, maybe? The thought made him nervous. He looked back to check on his pursuers. As he did so, he bumped into a young woman emerging from the door next to him.

She yelped in surprise. She had short purple hair and a look in her eye halfway between panic and outraged affront.

'Why don't you watch where you're going?' she said, rubbing her elbow.

'My apologies,' said Mark. 'My fault entirely. I was distracted.'

He glanced back again and this time saw the two thugs rapidly approaching, stim-sticks in hand. Both men now looked scared and angry. He could see them assessing the risk involved with a witness. Mark knew he needed to shut this down quickly or someone innocent was going to get hurt.

'Excuse me a minute,' he told the woman.

'Go away, please, miss,' said Thug One. 'You don't want to be involved in this.'

Mark strode up to meet them. The first jabbed wildly with his stim-stick. Mark swapped his weight to his back foot, stepping out of range and swinging his front leg up to kick. The stick sailed out of the man's hand. He grunted in pain. Mark followed up with a second kick to the man's chest as his leg descended, sending him toppling back towards Thug Two. As Thug Two darted sideways to avoid the collision, Mark took the opportunity and turned in while his assailant was unbalanced. He drove a fist into the man's sternum, knocking the wind out of him, and followed up with a jab to the pressure point on his neck. Thug Two crumpled. Mark turned back and kicked Thug One in the head before he could stand.

He paused to breathe and looked up to see the woman staring at him, appalled. This looked terrible, he realised. He was supposed to participate in a high-stakes mission tomorrow and here he was beating up two local heavies in a public corridor. He checked the network again – still no surveillance, thank God. A chance remained of him cleaning this up.

'Would you be okay with not talking to anyone about this?' he said to the woman, trying for a winning smile.

She looked disgusted by the offer. 'This is a privacy deck,' she said levelly. 'I don't have to notice the men you assaulted, the booze on your breath or the pain you inflicted on my elbow. We don't have to notice that either of us was here *at all*.'

Mark couldn't help but notice a catch in her phrasing.

'I could pay you,' he suggested.

She wrinkled her nose at him. 'No, thank you. I want *nothing* to do with this. Frankly, I assume this is how most Earther business gets done so it's all part of the local colour as far as I'm concerned. Let's just pretend we never saw each other here.'

Mark bit back a riposte. There was no point in picking on her prejudice.

'That sounds ideal,' he said. 'Many thanks.' He hoisted one of the thugs over his shoulders. 'I'll be back for the other one shortly.'

'No matter,' said the woman. 'I won't be staying to watch.'

Mark declined to make a remark. Instead he retraced his steps with the hoodlum dangling across his back and deposited him in the privacy suite. By the time he returned for the other, the woman had left.

Mark felt slightly relieved. Her company had been uncomfortable. His mood dived again, though, when he turned the second man over. His eyes lay open and staring. Foam filled his mouth and his fingers and face kept convulsing. He must have fallen on his stim-stick. Mark groaned. He checked the man's pulse and found an erratic mess.

It was a disaster. If this got out, he'd be without a job in New York and no Fleet gig, either. Mark hefted the twitching man and dumped him down next to the first. Then he shut the door to the privacy suite and spoke to the door SAP.

'I know you're awake because you're still running,' he told the little program, 'so give me your command chain.'

The SAP began the process of polite refusal. Mark reached out via his interface to the SAP's public API and wedged self-opening commands right up its primary comms channel. The SAP squawked as Mark prised open a path to its central command listing. He grabbed a link to the command chain and used it to iterate up until he hit the governing intelligence for the entire level. While smarter and more slippery than its tiny minion, it soon succumbed to the same blunt intrusion. With access rights in his virtual hand, Mark reluctantly called Will.

A very surprised Will Monet appeared in the home node of Mark's sensorium. He looked exactly as he always had – tall and awkward, with weirdly intense eyes and a shock of badly behaved hair that he'd artificially greyed at the temples in a vague attempt to look distinguished. The light-lag was nil, meaning Will was already on the station. He glanced around.

What Will always used to say when he visited Mark's home node was, 'Why don't you clean up around here?' To which Mark would always reply, 'It's not a mess, it's a hashing function.'

The grey, granite cave Mark used still looked the same. The splatter of floating icons was, if anything, bigger and messier. This time, though, Will made no comment about that.

'What's up?' he said simply.

Mark didn't feel like talking. And because they were both roboteers, he didn't have to. He just sent Will a memory dump instead. Will's brows rose in surprise.

'Still drinking, I see,' he said.

'I didn't fucking call you for judgement,' Mark snapped. 'I called you to see if you were prepared to help.' He immediately felt like a child again. Amazing how Will could do that to him with a single sentence. What was the issue, anyway? Mark could drink enough to kill a horse and be sober again within an hour. The involuntary augs he'd received as a child had made sure of that.

'Of course,' said Will. 'I'll send robots to handle the two men.'

Will scowled suddenly. For a moment, his virtual form split into an army of shadowy figures and recongealed. Weird shit like that happened a lot with Will.

'Odd,' he said. 'The security here is badly compromised. But you'd guessed that already. I'll look into it.'

He held out a hand and an icon appeared. It shimmered and juddered in a way that icons weren't supposed to. Whatever it was, it was lousy with the dubious alien software that Will ran on.

'Here are some security enhancements for you, to make sure this doesn't happen again.'

Mark waved the offer away. 'Thanks, but I don't need them. I'm going straight to my room anyway.'

'Mark,' said Will, 'do you think it was a coincidence that this shitty little sect scion happened to descend on you like that? You're being watched. This was someone's best attempt to take you out of the mission without tipping their hand. I'll lay you any money that the social profile you saw for that guy is about an inch deep. And that crappy hooch you were drinking – they were doubles, I notice, on special. Ever stop to wonder why the price was so low? Did it never occur to you that someone might have actually *wanted* you to get drunk? Someone doesn't want you to fly, Mark, and chances are they're coming with you on that ship.'

Mark realised with a sinking feeling that Will might be right. The man moved in a world where paranoia took on a life of its own. He'd forgotten what it was like.

'If you want to keep the job, please accept this,' said Will. 'The Fleet will be all over you tomorrow, insisting on upgrades, and they'll want to see recent memory logs. This will save you time and make sure that this episode never sees the light of day.'

'Fine,' said Mark.

He snatched up the icon and tossed it back like a piece of cake. He could feel the program crawling through his memory stacks like a spider, delicately inserting itself. He shuddered, but could tell Will was relieved.

'I'll see you tomorrow,' said Will. 'Please don't leave the suite until the robots show.'

'Of course not,' said Mark sharply.

Will winked out.

Mark returned to his physical body and slumped against the wall. He felt like a teenager again and hated it as much as he hated the fact that Will's assessment was undoubtedly right. The straitjacket angst of being locked in a former version of himself was one thing. The growing sense that this entire decision had been a huge, horrible mistake was quite another.

3.4: WILL

As Will slid back into his body, a sense of quiet victory hummed in his veins. His luck finally appeared to be turning. The mission had come together despite the political and logistical obstacles that everyone had been so keen to throw in front of it. And now he had Mark on board, too.

He opened his eyes in his private lounge at the other end of Delany Station. Pari and Nelson were still sitting there, watching him intently. Nelson stared with earnest concern while Pari regarded him with barely concealed anticipation. The mission plans from the meeting they'd been having before Mark's call had all been cleared away. As he took in the looks on their faces, Will's sense of achievement began to fade.

'You're back,' said Pari. 'What happened? Where did you go?'

'Two thugs came after Mark,' said Will. 'It was a set-up. Someone wanted him to look violent and unreliable just before the mission. It didn't pan out that way. I've got two unconscious bullies to clean up but other than that, we're in the clear.'

He dumped a summary of the experience into the room's blackboard space for them to pore over.

Nelson shook his head as the data scrolled up in his contacts.

'This is bad news,' he said. 'We're incredibly lucky this didn't go public. If he hadn't called you when he did—'

'I know,' said Will. 'It would have made for a very effective smear. As it is, we're golden.'

Pari lurched to her feet and started pacing. 'Golden, my ass. This isn't a near miss,' she said. 'It's the tip of the iceberg.'

Nelson crooked an eyebrow. 'Meaning what, exactly?'

'If the sects are resorting to mission sabotage at this late stage, we're already in trouble. Specifically, Mark is in trouble – he's clearly the target. I know you didn't mean to put him at risk, Will, but that's what you're doing. Do you honestly believe that Yunus wasn't aware of this? And by this time tomorrow, that bastard will have full control over the *Gulliver*, and Mark along with it. That could be a death sentence. And a screwed-up mission to boot.'

'Are we completely wedded to the idea of Mark as captain at this point?' said Nelson. 'Couldn't we just make him sub and slide him out of the hot seat before something worse happens?'

'Don't even go there,' said Pari. 'Will and I have had this conversation. Will isn't keen on compromise.'

'You're dead right I'm not keen,' said Will, his anger bubbling back up. 'And we can drop that line of reasoning right now.'

Pari shot him a hurt look. 'Excuse me, Will,' she said, 'but did you just issue me with an *order*? I'd rather you didn't treat me like an adversary or a minion, please. I find it hurtful.'

'Sorry,' said Will. 'I didn't mean it that way.' Still, his mood refused to settle.

'We're not here because we're your groupies, Will,' she said. 'Please remember that. We're peers, and we're all trying to solve the same problem. Do I need to remind you who's been looking after your agenda for the last *two years*?'

Will shook his head. 'You don't.'

'Had it not been for me, there'd be no research ships mapping the Depleted Zone,' she said. 'There'd be no Omega Oversight Programme keeping all your little roboteers safe. Do you think it's easy to make money from the IPSO budget disappear to cover all that? You haven't so much as *looked* at that stuff in years. Do you think I take on that work just for fun?'

Will knew she was right, even if it didn't sit well with him. After Rachel's ship had been lost in the Zone, he'd stopped managing his own side-projects. He'd just given up and delegated almost everything to his friends to give himself room to grieve. Somehow he'd never got around to picking up the reins of leadership afterwards. There'd always been too much to do.

'And what about Nelson?' she said, gesturing. 'Who do you think has been looking after your bloody ship while you attended all those charity dinners? Who do you call up every time you have another damned war nightmare?'

'Please,' said Nelson. 'I'm not sure that's strictly relevant. I suspect Will is just trying to clear out some of his familial guilt issues and this mission will run more smoothly if he does. I think Mark's involvement is a terrific idea, even if it does complicate matters.'

Will rubbed his temples. 'Look, I appreciate everything you've both done, more than I can say. I'd have come apart by now if I didn't have you two. But the flip side of that is that I've been running on rails for far too long and letting you both cover for me. Now I'm fixing that. I need to.'

Pari snorted. 'You chose a fine time to do your fixing.'

'I chose the one opportunity I had,' Will snapped. 'I've had no chance to do anything better, stuck in bullshit meetings every goddamn day. The reason why I put Mark in the captain's seat is because he's a better fucking pilot than any of the alternatives. What would be the point of sitting him in there as a sub? Decoration?'

Pari's eyes narrowed. 'Is that what you think those meetings are, Will? Bullshit? Have you any idea what would happen to your credibility and your precious political balance if I hadn't been packing your calendar with friendly faces for all those months? You'd be a joke already if it wasn't for me. Or more of a joke, at any rate.' She threw up her hands. 'I'm done for tonight,' she said and strode for the door. 'I hope you know what you're doing, Will, because out there I won't be around to wipe your ass for you.'

The door leapt open at her approach and crept shut afterwards as if anxious at her departure.

'Well,' said Nelson, slapping his knees, '*that* was interesting.' He stood and offered Will a warm, amused smile. 'Something tells me we're not going to get a great deal more useful planning done this evening. I propose that we all reconvene in the morning before the mission briefing when everyone has cooled down a little. How does that sound?'

Will stood. 'Fine.'

He felt more embarrassed than he wanted to let Nelson see. Giving Mark a ship had been his last great attempt to clear his moral decks, but it felt as if he was simply sliding closer to failure yet again. With every step he seemed to alienate someone he needed.

'I hope you don't think I'm being a fool,' he said.

'You're taking risks,' said Nelson, 'but you're also taking control and being proactive. It's an appropriate reaction under the circumstances. Not the one everyone would take, I admit, but appropriate, so don't worry about it.' He nodded to Will from the doorway. 'Goodnight, Boss. See you on the morrow.'

Will waved as the door slid shut. As soon as they left, he fell back into the couch, covering his face with his hands. Guilt and embarrassment slurped around inside him – a storm in own his personal teacup. Yet as he sat there, he found a smile inexorably drawing itself across his face.

Mark had looked as uncomfortable as ever. Trouble still followed him like a shadow and Will knew he should have guessed something like this might happen. Mark's software had been way out of date despite the nanny SAP he carried. He'd never have been so easily targeted otherwise. He probably hadn't touched his interface code since moving to Earth. Will felt a little guilt for having not predicted that, either.

It shocked him, too, how naive Mark still appeared to be. Will saw now, with hindsight, the foolishness of trying to shield his protégé from the risks his life entailed. He probably shouldn't even have tried. Nevertheless, he felt a certain perverse satisfaction in resolving this new problem quickly and quietly. He hadn't told the others about the software patch he'd rigged. He doubted they'd have approved.

Nelson would have said that by intervening, Will had exposed himself. That he was acting out his need for personal contact and jeopardising the very relationship he wished to foster. Will lacked the energy to talk it through. He called up a submind and sent it off to tweak the Fleet agenda for the following day – removing certain checks and tests from Mark's list so that nobody would find out what had happened.

With that done, he looked back over the web of security bypasses woven around the habitat ring that housed the privacy suites. It was a remarkably thorough job for some sect baron to have cooked up on short notice. So thorough, in fact, that it made no sense.

Will paged through visualisations of the data till he found one that worked for him. The messaging protocol for the suites took on the form of a landscape of networked nodes, and the security alterations became spiderlike structures straddling it. Presented that way, the truth stood out: there hadn't been one set of security alterations but two. One set had been designed to unlock and broadcast content when triggered. Had that happened, Mark's actions would have wound up fully documented and in the hands of the receiving party – almost certainly the same people who'd arranged his fight.

A different set of alterations had been imposed over the top, seemingly without knowledge of the edits already in play. While far less intrusive than the first, they'd successfully prevented the first set from releasing their message payload.

That the House representatives who wanted Mark ejected from the mission had cooked up a scandal came as no surprise. That there were conflicting security objectives layered over the same site worried him deeply. Deeper forces might be at work than he'd surmised.

Security had been a big concern for Will ever since the war. Repeatedly being shot, burned and poisoned in assassination attempts had taught him to pay much closer attention to the intentions of others than he'd ever dreamed would be necessary. That in turn had led him to keep Mark's genetic heritage secret from everyone, including Mark.

All the children from the Omega Programme he and Rachel had launched so disastrously contained the same set of genetic mods he'd received himself. Only one of them, though, contained genetic material from *her*. He could see her in Mark every time he looked. Mark had the same compact, muscular build, the same dark, brooding complexion. They'd tried to prevent all those children from becoming political targets, but Mark first and foremost.

Pari had a point. If Will really wanted Mark safe, he couldn't be too careful. Maybe he'd be able to find someone on the mission to help cover that base. But in the meantime, he shouldn't leave things to chance.

He opened up a channel to the new software in Mark's interface and tightened the security a little more, adding a self-aware routine to watch for trouble. Mark didn't even need to know it was there. Yunus wouldn't be able to touch him now. Will sprawled, satisfied with himself and feeling childish for it. However it panned out, tomorrow was going to be an interesting day.

4: DEPARTURE

4.1: ANN

It was two in the morning when Ann received an unexpected second message from the fixer. She sat up in bed and fumbled around for a touchboard to make sure her security filters were still in place, then tapped the icon with trepidation.

My men are half-dead. Meet me in the back room at Poseidon's in one hour to renegotiate. Otherwise I will go public about Fleet operatives hiring criminals for cash.

Ann stared at the message and didn't breathe. She thought back through the steps she'd taken and the software fail-safes she'd put in place to cover her tracks. At no time had there been any evidence that the FiveClan fixer had seen through her cover. His checks on her phoney sect status had all been perfectly managed. There'd been no evidence of a trace from the memory bead, either. So where did the accusation of Fleet involvement come from?

She desperately wished she could contact Sam, but that'd be the last thing he'd want. In the League, once something screwed up, agents dealt with their problems independently unless they absolutely needed backup. That way, the screw-ups didn't spread.

Ann thought over her options. The one that leapt out as the most responsible was also the one she liked least. She had to find out just how compromised the League had become and take action accordingly. She composed a status report for Sam and put it in a time-locked address in the Fleet's database. If she got back before the lock opened, the message would disappear and Sam would never have to know what had happened. If she didn't, everything he needed to take the next steps would be delivered to him via one of the League's secure pipes.

Ann started her preparation by testing the waters. She composed a short reply to the fixer and sent it.

WTF? Is that really you? You said no more contact!

She rebuilt the security shield she'd need to cover her actions in the field while she waited to see if he'd ping again. His next reply came swiftly. It contained just two words.

One hour.

Below that, he'd included a snippet of an error statement from a broken piece of SAP code. Fleet headers were all over it, along with all manner of time and address stamps that made it clear whose security software had been running on the privacy ring around the time when Ruiz was supposed to be intercepted by the FiveClan heavies.

Ann couldn't have asked for a more incriminating log file. She hadn't been told – and hadn't asked – how word of Mark's behaviour was supposed to get back to the Fleet after the fight. As it was, she could now make a pretty good guess. Sam had chosen that particular fixer because he'd already sold the guy a compromised security-blackout kit. In other words, the tools for a possible covert op on Triton had been carefully deployed by Sam months ago. She updated her status report, finished her security shield and headed down to the undercover desk as fast as she could.

Fifty minutes later, Ann was back in disguise and pushing her way through the drunken throng at the entrance to Poseidon's Bar on the lo-gee level of Ring Nine. Between all the shouting and the endless slamming beat of the kiddicore they were playing, she could barely hear herself think. The syrupy blue illumination kept surging on and off.

As she squeezed towards the bar, someone elbowed her in the ribs. A minute later, another clod accidentally tipped half their drink down the back of her barely adequate dress. Ann buffered up her claustrophobia and pressed it into a sense of purpose. This was all just part of the day's work. A badly botched, frightening day, for sure, but just a day.

She forced her way to the bar and pinged the room's SAP for some human attention. When a cocktail-bot tried to take her drink order, she waved it angrily away. Eventually, a woman in a skintight blue bodysuit decorated with mermaid scales came grudgingly through a door and slouched towards her. She didn't bother trying to talk over the din, just subvoked a message straight to Ann over the public channel. The text appeared in her view.

'Can I help you?'

She didn't need to sound bored. Ann could see it in her eyes. Bars on Triton required a live human attendant in case of emergency. That didn't mean they liked being disturbed.

Ann replied in kind. 'Someone's waiting for me in the back room.'

The woman rolled her eyes. 'We don't have a back room.'

'Yes, you do,' said Ann. Using a silent command, she pulled up the message the fixer had asked her to use as ident on their first meeting and briefly pasted it back into her public persona.

'Oh – *that* back room,' said the woman, her eyes suddenly alight with attention. 'Follow me.'

She led Ann around the side of the bar and down a corridor where the music was a little less deafening. Other than a few couples making out, the place was empty. The woman took her to a blank plastic wall panel at the far end decorated with animations of cavorting sea-sprites. It slid aside at their approach. As soon as Ann was through, it slid back into place.

On the other side lay a room with black, deactivated walls and a large interactive table of the sort gamblers preferred. The fixer sat behind it dressed in a charcoal grey mocksuit, arms folded. A pair of men in black gym-wear with grotesquely augmented muscles flanked him on either side. The fixer's huge brown eyes radiated contempt. He didn't look so young any more.

'My boys are almost dead,' he said. 'They showed up in the hospital about twenty minutes ago with some convenient memory problems. One of them also had motor-neurone damage. He'll be on myelin support for about a year. We didn't sign up for that, so I want money to cover their medical bills.'

While he talked, Ann's shield scanned the room for the inevitable surveillance and quietly shut it down.

'How much?' said Ann.

'Two million peace,' said the fixer.

'I don't have that kind of cash,' she said. 'And neither does my dad.'

The fixer slammed the table with both hands. 'Don't fuck with me!' he yelled. 'Your fucking *daddy* is a Fleet operative, you little bitch, and so are you. And if you don't fucking pay me what I'm due, I'm going to spill that SAP-dump on every public channel I can find.'

'I don't understand,' said Ann, feigning fear. 'What's all this got to do with an SAP-dump?'

'Listen to me,' said the fixer. He waved a finger at her. 'You think I don't know when I've been stitched up? Your fucking *daddy* is the man who gave me that blackout code in the first place. I traded with him in good faith. I thought he was *Clan*. Do you think I'd ever have passed him a trial-rigger if I'd known I was messing with the Fleet?'

Ann no longer had to feign confusion. Unscrupulous pharma corps used trial-riggers to fake the results of drug tests. At least she now knew what the software patches were for, but knowing raised more questions than it answered.

'That blackout code was supposed to keep the whole privacy level locked while my boys were in there,' said the fixer. He sounded hurt. 'And it worked fine for months before you showed up. Then tonight, it almost shut down halfway through the job. Surprise surprise. When I tried to unhook it afterwards, it started spewing that shit I sent you all over my view. *Fleet* script, I note.'

'I don't get it,' said Ann. 'A *trial-rigger*?'

'Don't,' said the fixer, fighting down apoplexy. 'Don't play dumb with me. We're way past that. If I'm on the hook to the Fleet I've got nothing to lose, do you understand? I might as well go public. I'm here because I'm a *businessman*, and I had this dim, dim hope that maybe we'd be able to sort this all out like grown-ups. I don't care who you're trying to bust. So long as it's not me, you can do what the fuck you like, but I still need to cover my fucking costs. I don't expect to be used like a fucking *noob*.'

Ann spread her hands as if in confusion. At the same time, she subvoked the safeties off the stun-wands embedded in her forearms. Darts flashed out, burying themselves in the bodies of the two huge bodyguards. The fixer had half a second to look surprised and dive sideways. Ann's third dart sliced through the air behind him.

'Wait!' he yelled, but Ann was already in motion, vaulting around the side of the table in the low-gees, her heels lost somewhere in the air behind her. Her fourth dart caught him in the neck as he scrabbled for cover. He slumped face down on the floor.

Ann took a moment to catch her breath. She rubbed her arms and grimaced as she inspected the tiny wounds the weapons had left. She'd need a little surgical attention when she returned to the dorm, but that problem was for later. First, she had to figure out how to get out of the mess she'd landed in.

As soon as he woke up, the fixer was likely to follow through on his promise and go public with his data. Furthermore, he almost certainly had the package on a timer, so killing him would only guarantee the release of everything he knew. If he was a smart man, he'd have timed the package to need a check-in after their meeting, which meant she might have just minutes to figure this out. She needed leverage and couldn't secure it with the tools she had on her. Time to ask for help.

The prospect of calling Sam still didn't appeal. He'd take a dim view. Furthermore, he'd be likely to use a rather absolutist approach to clean-up. The fixer would probably suffer until he divulged the key to the package and then vanish for ever. Given the kind of stakes the League played for, she doubted that dispatching a few crooks would stack up as relevant for Sam. Her new first officer – Jaco Brinsen – would almost certainly favour the same approach.

If she could find one, Ann wanted a less fatal way to resolve the problem. The fixer's business operation couldn't be that big, otherwise he wouldn't have bothered meeting his clients in person. Furthermore, he'd been liberal enough with his information to look almost honest. Executing him didn't feel right.

She brought up the *Chiyome*'s crew listing in her view – just six names including her own. Everyone on that ship's roster was a League operative. They had to be, given what the *Chiyome* was there to do. Of the officers arrayed before her, one leapt out: Kuril Najoma, the ship's engineer. She'd worked with Kuril before. He was a good man – a professional and definitely not a killer.

Ann routed a call through her security shield to Kuril at his dorm room with a League security seal attached. An icon in her view pulsed as she waited for the link to open. Twenty long seconds later, he answered. Ann exhaled with relief as Kuril's broad, earnest face filled a window in her display, his forehead wrinkled in confusion. She could tell he'd been asleep from the scrambled thatch of brown hair on his head.

'Captain?' he said. 'Can I help you?'

Ann subvoked a message and sent it as raw text. The sight or even the sound of her right now would only confuse him.

Need a favour. Go to the pharm counter downstairs and get me a dose of field-issue stun-gone, two doses of Redact, one vial standard-issue medical micromachines, and an on-site programmer. Then come to this address immediately. Tell no one, and keep your traffic tag visible only to me.

His eyes went wide. She watched him quickly check the security seal on the message, worry drawing creases in his features.

'All right,' he said. 'I'm on my way. I can be there in ten.'

Make it five.

She brought up a local map for him and watched his traffic tag light up in red as it changed status. While she waited for Kuril to arrive, Ann carefully reached out into the bar's security system via her contacts, acquiring the command code for the door and prepping some database requests for the task to come. As soon as Kuril's tag showed him at the building, Ann sent him a follow up message.

Go straight through the bar. Take the passage at the back on the left-hand side. Walk as far as the end wall.

As Kuril reached the hidden door, Ann slid it open to admit him. He stepped inside.

Kuril was a huge bear of a man with a gentle, introverted temperament. How he'd ended up involved in the desperate business of the League, Ann had never asked. He took in the sight of the unconscious criminals and then stared at her like a stranger, his eyes flicking back and forth between her face and her cleavage.

'Captain?' he said incredulously.

'Good to see you,' she said. 'Did you bring the things I asked for?'

Kuril nodded absently, still not quite sure what he'd walked in on.

'It's me,' she said. 'Don't ask me to change my face or voice right now, it hurts like hell. If you need proof, try this: three years ago I beat you at Go in a guayusa shop on Harmony that had live locusts in the window display.'

Kuril's mouth fell open and then shut again. 'You look ... different,' he said, blushing slightly. 'What do you need me to do?'

'Give those two meatbots the Redact doses. The scrawny one gets the micromachines. We target the pain pathways in his central nervous system.'

He regarded her anxiously. 'We're torturing someone?'

'Not if we can help it,' said Ann.

109

Kuril moved quickly from body to body, administering the drugs while Ann picked up the programmer box, tethering it to the processor in her contacts and setting up the configuration she wanted. As soon as she was ready, she had Kuril help her prop the fixer up in his chair.

'Now get behind him,' she said. 'It's best if he never sees your face.'

She sat the programmer-box unobtrusively on the floor under the fixer's chair. From there, it had enough network range to reach the tiny devices they'd injected without being obvious. Then she applied a quarter dose of the stun-gone to the fixer's neck.

His eyes fluttered as he drifted back into consciousness. As his eyes took her in, his mouth curled into a sneer.

'You're a fool,' he slurred. 'Data's on a timer. Who doesn't these days?'

'I guessed that,' she said. 'So I put you on a timer, too.'

She opened up the link to the programmer in her display and sent him a short jolt of pure pain. The fixer bucked in his chair with surprising force for a man still doped to the eyes. He didn't scream. He was too busy trying to suck air into his struggling lungs.

'I put something inside you,' she said. 'I'm not saying what, but you know how it feels now. Your agonising death is keyed to your own data release. The moment you go public, my crawlers will notice and post a signal to your spine. If we lose, you lose.'

He stared at her with a mix of panic and outright loathing.

'In case it wasn't already obvious, you're in over your head,' she said. 'But you strike me as a decent enough guy, so instead of killing you, I'm going to save you. When you leave here, you're heading straight to the shuttle port. When you get there, you'll find a ticket waiting for you on the next nestship out to Nazca under the name of Sundar Kim, courtesy of ISPO undercover ops. You're going to start a new life on that colony. A good one. You get one network call out, and that's to shut down the timer on that data packet. Don't bother trying to call anyone else. We'll be listening. Do as you're told and you'll be safely in coma within the hour, otherwise you'll be dead. And believe me, you'll be a hell of a lot safer out there than you are here.'

'You wouldn't do that,' he wheezed. 'You're Fleet.'

Ann smiled like a shark. 'That's where you're wrong. You need another jolt to convince you?'

'No!'

'Good. And now you get to walk out of the room a free man. Congratulations, you win.'

She applied the rest of the dose to his neck and stood back to give him room. She gestured at the exit.

'I'm Made Platinum,' he said. 'You'll be hearing about this.'

'No, you're not,' she replied. 'You're Sundar Kim, an unaffiliated project manager with a modest bank account and good prospects. Enjoy it. It's more fun out there than this dump, I can assure you.'

The fixer shot her a look of pure spite, staggered to his feet and walked silently to the door. As soon as he was gone, Kuril exhaled noisily.

'Sooner or later that man's going to figure out he's not on a timer,' he said. 'Without a stabilising framework, those micromachines will drain out of his body within hours.'

'He'll be far away before that happens,' said Ann. 'And by tomorrow morning, so will we. We're looking at the end of civilisation, Kuril. We can afford to play a little fast and loose.'

On paranoid instinct, she quickly checked the fixer's movements in her security shield, but he was headed out of the bar as ordered, having made a single call to a nondescript secure address. The tail she'd put on him was operating perfectly. It'd warn her if anything weird happened.

Kuril sagged against the wall. 'Why me, if you don't mind me asking? Why not Jaco?'

'Jaco would have insisted we mind-clamp the guy for his data key and then dump his body out of an airlock. He doesn't like loose ends. I was prepared to bet you felt differently.'

'You bet right,' he said.

'But I'm going to need you to keep quiet about all this,' she said. 'The League won't like it. It's not their style. Can I count on you? You know how they feel about mistakes – they burn them out before they spread, no matter who makes them.'

'Of course.'

She clapped him on the shoulder. 'Then thank you,' she said. 'And sorry for involving you. The way I see it, everything we're doing is an attempt to minimise the loss of life in the big picture. Which means that every life counts – even a scumbag like our Mr Kim.'

'Don't worry. I'd have done the same thing. Or tried to, at any rate.'

'Now get out of here,' said Ann with a companionable smile. 'My

111

security will cover your exit from the building. I'll follow in ten minutes. That should give us a solid hour before these two guys wake up with a bad case of memory-blur.'

Thankfully, the problem had resolved itself with plenty of time left over to remove her status report from the network. Presuming there wasn't further fallout from the event, she and the League were in the clear. Still, Ann knew she'd be counting the hours till she left port the next morning, checking the tail she'd set every time her anxiety bubbled up.

She wasn't kidding herself about why all this had happened. She'd agreed to follow through on the favour for Sam without having the first clue as to how his operation at Triton worked or who was involved. She should have made him explain more. Not understanding had nearly ruined everything.

With Ruiz involved, the game was changing too fast for her to rely on simply following orders. In the IPSO Fleet, officers were expected to ask questions and act independently to achieve their commander's intent. The same applied in the League. Ann knew she needed to step up to that plate. If she didn't understand the role she'd been asked to play, they might not get through the next few months alive.

4.2: MARK

After several hours of tedious Fleet upgrades, medical checks and legal paperwork, Mark floated out of a transit pod into the lounge of the most spacious and well-appointed shuttle he'd ever seen. The entire interior had been lined with reactive biopolymers. Curving padded walls with a mother-of-pearl sheen swept down to meet at a discussion area with bio-nouveau couches, luminous clamber-web and projector bubbles. It was like visiting the inside of a designer pumpkin. A cluster of people dressed in shipwear floated down near the central meeting area, chatting like old friends – his fellow explorers, apparently. He felt a stab of awkwardness just looking at them.

Nelson drifted up to meet him, dressed in Fleet blue today rather than his usual slick duds, but no less immaculate for it.

'Hi, Mark. Good to see you,' he said, extending a warm hand. 'I'm glad this all worked out so well.'

Mark accepted the gesture and tried for a smile. If Nelson had any idea what happened the night before, he showed no sign.

'I trust you slept well?' said Nelson.

Mark had not. The Fleet dorm had been as blandly acceptable as always. But between the blood-scrubbing, the adrenalin come-down from the fight and too much thinking about Will's words, Mark had struggled to relax.

'Well enough.'

'Great,' said Nelson. 'Let me introduce you to some of your ship-mates.' He pushed off the wall, back towards the conversation below. 'Ladies and gents,' he said, 'may I introduce Mark Ruiz, our captain aboard the *Gulliver*?'

On entering the secure shuttle, Mark had deliberately chosen not to take the memory download of mission personnel the security SAP had offered him. He always found that meeting people with total foreknowledge made him behave too much like a classic roboteer – overfamiliar, mechanical and creepy. There wasn't much he could do about who was coming, he reasoned, so he might as well meet them first-hand and treat them like equals. That strategy had worked well for him in New York.

The first person to turn around was Ash Corrigan-Five – formerly his Omega dorm buddy and childhood friend, and subsequently someone he never wanted to see again. Ash was all blond hair and apple-pie looks, as ever. He greeted Mark with easy good humour.

'Mark! Great to see you!' He grabbed Mark's hand and pumped it.

Mark tried not to show just how unwelcome the surprise was. In the back of his head, he scrabbled to turn on introduction-assist. Ash, apparently, would be his subcaptain. It'd be their first opportunity to work together since Ash had given evidence against him at the trial.

'So you're back,' said Ash. 'Just like old times, eh?'

'I guess so,' said Mark.

Great, he thought. *Let's pretend you never sold me out, you pushy Drexlerite fuckhead*. He kicked himself for not coming in as prepared as possible. That was the Fleet way of doing things and he'd just end up paying for it if he didn't get with the programme, particularly as his role was so central.

The *Gulliver* was a ro-ship – geared for roboteer pilot and command. Ro-ships were the fulfilment of Will Monet's childhood dream that one day roboteers would captain and control their own vessels. That had probably sounded like a grand and fitting dream for a generation of pre-war roboteers trapped in terraforming work. What that vision had created for the Fleet, though, was a giant headache.

Roboteers were subject to digital infection risk, attention overload and numerous other personal limitations, not to mention attacks of good old-fashioned autistic behaviour. To compensate, ro-ships had their own pattern of command. Each captain was required to fly with a sub on board, at least one non-roboteer passenger-witness and an extensive battery of backup software. Where possible, two subs were preferred.

While ro-ships were capable of fast and delicate flying that ordinary pilots couldn't match, they generally weren't allowed to take on high-pressure missions. Most roboteer captains ended up as glorified ferrymen, running modified nestships packed with supplies and colonists to the Frontier. Mark should have guessed that someone he knew would be in the number-two seat on his ship. A mission this significant called for someone Omega-rated, and there weren't that many of them to choose from.

The discomfort of the moment, though, paled in comparison to the one that followed.

'And may I introduce the physicist with our scientific team?' said Nelson, pointing back over Mark's shoulder. 'Doctor Zoe Tamar.'

Mark turned around to see the girl with the purple hair gliding down from the pod bay.

'Doctor Tamar is also the mission's representative from the Vartian Institute,' said Nelson. 'She's more familiar with the workings of the *Gulliver* than anyone else, so you'll be working with her closely.'

Dr Tamar's expression suggested she was at least as disappointed as he was.

'Oh, but we've met,' she said, before clapping a hand over her mouth in mock-regret.

Mark's heart skipped a beat. Nelson regarded her in confusion.

'We had a lovely conversation in a hallway,' said Zoe. 'Something about contemporary privacy issues, if I remember correctly?' She glared at him with a cryptic kind of anger, as if his being in the same room as her constituted an affront.

'Oh, yes,' said Mark stiffly. 'I'd *forgotten*. How nice to see you again.'

114

'Super,' said Zoe. 'We get to fly together? How unexpected.'

Now that he had an opportunity to look at Dr Tamar properly, it was also easy to tell what kind of company she was likely to be. She had big dark eyes, full lips and curves under her one-piece. She also clearly considered him dirt. Her bio said it all. She was a year younger than him but had published a dozen seminal research papers already. Her resume said *I'm out of your league and you know it.* Mark liked his crewmates a little less obviously acid in temperament. It was shaping up to be a fun trip.

'And may I introduce the *Gulliver*'s exopsychology specialist, Venetia Sharp?' said Nelson, gesturing to the woman behind Zoe Tamar.

Mark found himself being scrutinised by a thin woman in her subjective forties with a severe black bob and a sly smile.

'Nice to meet you, Captain Ruiz,' she said. 'Your reputation precedes you. I admire your work.'

She appeared to find this statement quietly amusing. To Mark's ear, it sounded like a veiled slight.

Great, he thought. *A comedian.*

Venetia stuck out a hand and Mark shook it distractedly. Between Ash and Zoe Tamar, his attention was already scattered; his focus didn't split nearly so neatly when human relationships were involved.

'Excuse me,' said a loud voice with a strong Leading-class accent.

Mark and the others looked up to see a man floating into the centre of the crowd with his arms raised. He was tall, with a scrawny build and weak chin but an impressive mane of professor hair.

[*Yunus Chesterford,*] his introduction SAP informed him, [*mission leader.*]

Mark frowned and shot a silent request back to the program.

[*I thought Will Monet was in charge?*]

[*Will Monet is the senior Fleet officer,*] said the SAP. [*Yunus Chesterford is the head IPSO representative.*] The top diplomat, in other words.

'The shuttle tells me we're all here,' said Yunus, 'so we'll be leaving shortly. May I recommend that you all take a seat and we'll begin the briefing?'

Mark grabbed the nearest strand of clamber-web and made his way down to the meeting space. He spotted Will as he moved to clip

115

himself into a seat. Will sent him a short electronic *hi*. Mark declined to respond.

'First, welcome,' said Yunus. 'I see some new faces here and plenty of familiar ones. It's not often that people in our line of work get to put their talents to the test, and these are hardly ideal circumstances. Regardless, I'm delighted to see you all. With luck this mission will achieve something wonderful for the human race, and at the very least it should help resolve a dangerous situation.'

He glanced down at his hands with a wry expression.

'And to all of you who, like me, have been required to take on some Fleet augmentations for this mission, apologies on behalf of IPSO. Apparently they're necessary for flight safety under possible combat conditions. They assure me that, upon conclusion of this mission, anyone who wants the augs removed can have them taken out. Now, before we begin the meeting proper, I'd like to share a message from our senate sponsor – the head of the Senate Committee for E. T. Affairs, Parisa Voss.'

Yunus gestured at the central projector bubble, which sprang into life. Auntie Pari's face appeared against a majestic background of stars. It'd been years since Mark had seen her. She looked exactly the same. Just as plastic. Just as prissy. Her nose was, if anything, even more eerily button-perfect than he remembered. Will liked her, of course. But she'd never had a particularly good effect on Will, in Mark's opinion, particularly after Rachel's loss. Through her, Will had been dragged further and further into the very politics he hated.

'The mission you are about to undertake is the most important in recent history,' said Auntie Pari. 'You are travelling to meet a very real threat, some of you unarmed. That threat is unquantified in its scope. Whether we face extinction or the beginning of a golden age may depend on the actions you take. There has been precious little time to prepare for this mission, which means that all of you will need to cooperate and improvise at the highest levels of Fleet performance. I know you're capable because we've chosen our best. For what you are about to do, on behalf of IPSO and all the Human Worlds, I salute you.'

Polite applause sounded around the room. Mark played along.

'Fine words for a fine mission,' said Yunus, waving a professorial finger. 'I'll be brief as we have a lot to cover today. In outline, this

116

mission will comprise three ships: one diplomatic, one enforcing and one silent backup. The diplomatic ship is the *Gulliver*.'

The projector bubble gave them a slowly rotating 3D view of the ship. Like all human-built ships, it looked like a dull metal ball covered with the broken-umbrella spines of warp inducers.

'It will be unarmed, of course, except for two highly trained Spatials who will remain in coma, except to provide support if we engage in any face-to-face diplomatic activity. In accordance with Vartian Institute recommendations, this ship will not carry messenger drones in case alien tampering leads to soft contagion.'

Mark tried not to groan. That was classic Vartian Institute reasoning for you – paranoid to the last. Rather than keep something useful aboard, they threw it out to prevent the one-in-a-billion scenario that someone might try to use them to spread viruses.

Hugo Vartian had been obsessed with alien software infections. At the end of his life, he'd lived in a recreation of a twentieth-century home, apparently, without a single data hub in it. He even had a human cleaner, if the rumours were true, and cooked his own food on gas burners like someone out of a period drama.

'At the recommendation of the senate, the ship has been configured for maximum security,' said Yunus. 'It will run under a segmented security regime. This means it will comprise three independent modules, each with its own software domain – one for science, one for diplomacy and one for pilot control. This should prevent any software incursion that *does* arise in any section from spreading to the others. Each module will have its own primary officer. The science section will be run by Professor Citra Chesterford, the diplomacy section by Overcaptain Sam Nagano-Shah, and the Fleet section, of course, by the ship's captain, Mark Ruiz. I will be the only person with emergency overrides for all three.'

Mark tried not to look chagrined. Who had ever heard of a captain not having full control over his own ship? He couldn't help but wonder if this gem was a direct result of Will getting him the job.

'This also means that instead of a single set of cut-outs for your surgical augs, there will be three,' said Yunus. 'If a software incursion occurs in one part of the ship, hitting the aug cut-out will drop body support everywhere. It's our hope that this will enable the team to avoid being even partially exposed.' He pulled a droll expression. 'Reassuring, isn't it?'

The regal-looking woman in a conservative head-sleeve sitting next to Yunus let out a peal of tinkling laugher. His wife, the biologist, the SAP informed him.

'Having said all that, the *Gulliver*'s objective will be to engage in *peaceful* dialogue with whatever force is responsible for the Tiwanaku Event. If that objective proves impossible, the *Gulliver* will withdraw. While unarmed, the ship does possess some of the most sophisticated warp engines ever devised.'

Yunus brought up some engine specs. The *Gulliver* really was eye-wateringly fast. It could manage two kilolights, which was ridiculous. Mark didn't doubt the ship guzzled antimatter. He hoped they had plenty of fuelling stops set up.

'The enforcer ship is, of course, the *Ariel Two*,' said Yunus. The familiar flower-bud shape of humanity's only weaponised nestship appeared in the bubble. 'As usual, it will be under the command of Will Kuno-Monet and subbed by Nelson Aquino and his crew. The *Ariel Two*'s objective is to observe the diplomatic exchange while providing the promise of force if negotiations are not held in good faith.' Yunus raised a cautionary finger. 'It will be paramount for the *Ariel Two* to maintain a safe distance from the proceedings unless called upon to act. If physical threat becomes apparent and the *Gulliver* is forced to withdraw, then – and *only* then – will the *Ariel Two* take over as primary point of contact.'

Mark glanced across at Will to see how he was taking this but Will had his Statesman face on and was impossible to read.

'The backup ship is the *Chiyome*,' said Yunus, 'under the command of Andromeda Ng-Ludik and subbed by Jaco Brinsen-Nine.'

He pointed to an athletic-looking woman with a buzz cut and *don't fuck with me* eyes who looked like she'd be equally at home in a lab-coat or at the safe end of a sniper's rifle. He'd heard of Andromeda but never met her in person. She had the reputation of being scary effective and about as warm as a nice day on Triton.

When Yunus brought up a picture of the *Chiyome*, Mark sat up and blinked. It looked like a human rebuild of a Fecund ship on a much smaller scale, with a heavy emphasis on the quantum shield. Mark had never seen a ship like it, and he'd seen plenty. Someone in Fleet Research had been busy.

'The *Chiyome*'s objective will simply be to observe,' said Yunus. 'It uses a new kind of cloaking technology that extrapolates from the Fecund quantum shield principle and will be effectively invisible throughout the mission.'

'Wait, *what*?' said Zoe. 'You've got a working *gravity cloak*? When was that problem solved?' The purple-haired scientist managed to look excited and appalled at the same time.

Yunus shrugged. 'I don't have any data for you, I'm afraid. And in any case, after this briefing, the *Chiyome* will operate as a separate entity. It will be deployed only in the unlikely case that the *Ariel Two* encounters difficulties. If that happens, the *Chiyome* is well prepared to resolve conflict. It is equipped with both a modified suntap energy-capture system and a boser canon. As you can see, we're taking no chances with this mission.'

Mark's mouth fell open. So the Fleet was building stealth ships with bosers now? The boser was another Transcended giveaway technology like the suntap. It accelerated coherent iron to near-light-speed and fired it like a laser. It was also banned by just about every law that IPSO had. Even the ones on the *Ariel Two* had special locks on them that only a few people could open. With a ship like the one he was looking at, you'd be able to slide up to the planet of your choice undetected and butcher the population with the flick of a switch. It was a blatant invitation to war.

Mark glanced around at the other faces in the room to see if anyone else was worried by this. To her credit, Venetia Sharp looked disgusted and was scowling from under her black bob. Zoe Tamar looked stunned. Will was as carefully blank as ever.

'For obvious reasons, our fuelling stops will all be at secret locations.' Yunus showed them a star map. 'We've picked out two stars in the local shell, here and here. They have the survey names Gore-Daano and Tontoundin.'

Their flight plan went out of its way to avoid the primary traffic routes on the Penfield Lobe that lay between the old and new frontiers. Mark scowled. He'd assumed they'd be going via New Panama. Anything else seemed crazy and nothing in the high-level briefing he'd received had suggested otherwise. This last piece of Fleet secrecy was going to cost them.

The lobe was the Transcended's artificial bridge between the navigable sheet of stars referred to as the human galactic shell and its neighbour closer to the core: Fecund space. You couldn't get from one shell to the other without going through it, which meant that all the cheap, efficient crossings were crammed with traffic. Any other route came with delays and serious fuelling overheads.

'I'm sorry,' he blurted. 'What's obvious? Why won't we be stopping at New Pan? Don't they have data and resources we need? Like the latest scans of the target system, for instance? And other neat stuff that will help us not die?'

'The *Chiyome* can't be seen at—'

Mark cut Yunus off. 'Okay, fine for the death-ship, but you just said it'll be operating independently. Why should it affect anyone else? We'll be going in blind, otherwise.'

A warning ping from Will appeared in Mark's sensorium. [*Remember, you have to fly with this guy.*]

Mark ignored it. His opinion of the Fleet had dropped plenty in the last five minutes. If they were going to distort the entire mission so they could bring this war-crime-on-rails along with them, Mark wanted to know why.

Yunus looked peeved at being interrupted again, which was fine in Mark's book.

'The mission is being conducted quietly so as to not create panic,' said Yunus. 'Which is why we're here today.'

'New Pan has ships routed via quiet stops in the out-system all the time,' said Mark. 'There are police missions every week. Plus didn't you just say that ship was invisible?'

'The senate decided—'

Mark raised his eyebrows. 'Obviously. But *why*?'

Yunus pulled a face that suggested he was working hard to stay civil.

'Maybe I can help out here?' said Sam Shah.

Mark recognised Sam, of course. Overcaptain Shah was regional head of Far Frontier police operations and one of the heaviest hitters in IPSO. He was the man most people credited with keeping the Frontier safe and open. In person, Sam had a kind of cheerful gravity like a well-mannered neutron star. When he entered the room, all eyes bent towards him. The fact that he was even on this mission was astonishing to Mark, let alone that he'd agreed to come as a passenger.

'Essentially, this is a matter of Fleet secrecy, I'm afraid,' said Sam sadly. 'There are strategic reasons for our routing. You've all signed the Fleet non-disclosure so I see no point in not telling you. The alliance of sects that spearheads the Flag movement has found and repaired an intact network of Fecund fuelling stops.'

Mark's eyes went wide. '*Intact?*'

Muttering filled the room as Sam's explanation continued.

'They're at brown dwarf stars that didn't nova during the Fecund extinction event, which means they're in nearly perfect condition even after ten million years dormant. Many of these sites have biological remains and devices that are still under analysis.'

Mark shook his head in disbelief. This was *huge*.

'In some ways,' said Sam, 'the sects have been more innovative about tracking down Fecund artefacts than the Fleet has. Needless to say, this represents a technological goldmine for Earth's Truist Revival movement. And it explains how they've been able to get so many people to sites at the Far Frontier without Fleet detection. To the best of our knowledge, they don't know we're on to them – we still hold the technological edge. But the Tiwanaku Event calls that supremacy into question. As you can probably guess, we developed the *Chiyome* to even the odds in case of a sneak attack. Obviously revealing it to you all on this mission constitutes a calculated risk. But frankly, if we can't pull this mission off safely, it wouldn't stay secret much longer anyway.'

Mark realised then that human civilisation was teetering a lot closer to the point of meltdown than he'd ever imagined. The fact that the sects hadn't announced so huge a find and just made a profit off it spoke volumes. Behind the clotted crap of IPSO politics, forces were aligning. The Flag settlements might depend on loopholes in the law right now but there was no reason they had to stay that way. It cast the presence of a ship like the *Chiyome* in a whole new light.

'Naturally, we don't want to give the game away any more than we have to,' said Sam. 'So our route to Tiwanaku remains quiet, in case someone decides we should have an accident before we get there. And indeed, several of the scenarios our modelling SAPs have raised show exactly that outcome. In those cases, the Tiwanaku Event functions as a kind of lure to get the *Ariel Two* out of the picture, leaving the Far

Frontier open for a bolder military move. If the sects have the resources to cook up a scheme as ornate as the Tiwanaku Event, we have to assume they also have the ability to attack colony worlds on multiple fronts. In light of this, the data we need for insertion will be provided by stealthed sentinels posted at the edge of the Tiwanaku System rather than from New Panama itself. So don't worry, Mark – you'll get the data you need. Nobody is going to send you in there blind.'

Mark nodded absently. He could now see the dual standard the mission represented. Yunus was there for the fluff. The likes of Will and Sam were there to make sure that whatever group was behind Tiwanaku got nailed to the wall before they started a war. Will had brought him in because, for all their history, Will knew exactly where Mark's allegiances lay. And he wasn't wrong.

Silence hung over the meeting room as everyone digested the political reality they'd just been presented with.

'Glad we've got that covered,' said Yunus brightly. 'In a nutshell, our job is to visit, understand and report back to New Panama. If our ships are split up for any reason, we are to rendezvous here.' Another star map appeared. 'This system has the survey name Nerroskovi. It's just two light-years from Tiwanaku, which should make the process straightforward. Of course, if the location is needed, it's likely that your ships will have engaged in evasive manoeuvres, so we've modelled expected rendezvous windows and included them in your flight plans.'

Mark watched Yunus scan the room, surveying the distracted gazes of the participants and trying to recapture some semblance of control over the proceedings.

'As you're all aware, despite the military speculation behind this mission, it will be carried out under the working assumption that *aliens* are responsible, not humans. And it's important we make that possibility our focus and our number-one priority. And this presents us with a paradox,' he added enthusiastically. 'If the aliens are as malign as they appear, why have the Transcended not intervened in their development as they threatened to do with ours? Yet if they are not malign, why did they attack? I have my own theories, of course, but it would be wrong to bias you this early.'

Mark looked at the man and wondered where he was managing to get his zeal from. Hadn't Sam Shah just made it horribly clear what they were really there to do?

'And while this scenario will sound unlikely to most of you,' Yunus went on, 'there are some good reasons to believe that these aliens are, in fact, real. I have decided on a name for them, by the way – Photurians – on account of the synchronised warp flashes of their drone swarms and its similarity with that of fireflies.'

That's nice, thought Mark. A good old-fashioned command decision to spare anyone else from having to think creatively. Not that it mattered.

'For instance,' said Yunus, 'have a look at these follow-up scans taken since the tragic loss of that first contact. As soon as word of the event reached New Panama, drones were sent out to monitor the area from a safe distance. This is what they found.'

The bubble showed a dense weave of shifting drone traffic around the captured colony world. It looked aimless and hypnotic, like a school of sea creatures of some kind. The bubble zoomed in to show orbital stations being carefully disassembled and bundled up in knots of webbing by weird, definitely non-terrestrial-looking robots. Just watching them made Mark's skin prickle. Whoever had laid on this show had done one hell of a job.

'As you can see,' said Yunus, 'there is persistent, unusual activity at the site showing complex patterns of behaviour. Not what you'd expect to see if this were some kind of scam, but exactly what you might expect from intelligent life forms.'

Venetia Sharp chimed in, waving a narrow hand to catch his attention. 'With respect, Professor, while fascinating, these patterns don't necessarily indicate the intelligence I'm sure you'd love to see there. They look to me like the sort of activities hive insects might engage in, or drones designed to mimic them.'

Yunus's lips pulled into a tight little smile. 'And yet they communicated with us in English. Hardly the behaviour of insects.'

'Hardly the behaviour of an alien species, either,' she replied. 'If anything makes the case for a hoax, it's that message. If we examine the semantic content alone—'

Citra Chesterford shook her head and interrupted. 'Our initial modelling survey looked for matches with both machines and hive species. That swarm pattern you're seeing doesn't match any known species or SAP variety.'

'So what?' said Venetia. 'Designing a new drone-swarm dynamic would take what – a day? Less for a talented roboteer.' She shot a quick, pale-eyed glance at Mark.

'To *that* level of detail?' said Citra. 'I doubt it.'

Mark kept his mouth shut. Without a closer look, he wasn't sure.

'There's also the matter of the warp-drive signatures, is there not?' said Yunus. He gestured at Zoe Tamar. 'They don't resemble anything produced by either human or Fecund vessels, correct?'

'They do not,' said Zoe.

Yunus shot Venetia a smug glance. 'Innovations in warp technology are an unlikely achievement for mere insects, wouldn't you say? Or even for humans staging a hoax.'

'But there's something very wrong with those drives,' Zoe added. 'They shouldn't even work. The mere fact that they operate at all points to Transcended involvement.'

Yunus's smile dropped away. 'I don't think there's enough evidence to jump to that conclusion.'

'Why not?' said Zoe. 'It's just Occam's razor. We know of one operational alien species in IPSO space, so why propose another?'

'I consider it highly unlikely that a species at that level of development would bother engaging in petty warfare of this sort,' said Yunus.

Venetia emitted a short, impatient laugh. 'Yunus, dear, this is not one of your staged chat shows. We're not engaging in idle speculation now. This is exocultural research in the raw, with a significant human price-tag attached. Leaping to convenient conclusions in this context is actually *dangerous*. So while I can't agree with Zoe's interpretation, I at least respect the fact that she might have a point.'

'The only person here *not* displaying the proper respect,' said Citra Chesterford, 'is *you*, Doctor Sharp. Do I need to remind you that my husband is leading this mission?'

'No, Citra,' said Venetia, wryly. 'Do I need to remind *you* that this is an IPSO project, not an Earther one? Outside the home system, we generally *earn* respect rather than assuming it will be automatically bestowed by class.'

Citra looked daggers at the smiling psychologist. Yunus's gaze shuttled rapidly back and forth between the two women with growing anxiety.

'There will, of course, be follow-up science talks for the diplomacy team on the *Gulliver*,' he said quickly, 'which is perhaps the best forum

124

for such robust debate. I have no doubt that we'll be able to derive a range of plausible scenarios before reaching Tiwanaku.' Yunus pointed at the ceiling with evident relief. 'In any case, the shuttle informs me that we have docked with the tethering arm for the *Gulliver*. I recommend that our teams proceed to their respective ships where we can continue our discussions.'

He gestured to the pod bay where the doors slid open, then led the way towards them.

Mark hesitated and looked around at all the high-profile people suddenly in his charge. Sam Shah had made the dangers alarmingly clear. The science was a sideshow. Treating Tiwanaku as anything other than a war zone would be crazy. And he'd be piloting the only ship with no guns. Keeping hold of his interface rights would be the least of his problems.

4.3: ANN

Ann waited in the shuttle with the others as they made their way towards the *Ariel Two*. Her difficult night had left her fuzzy. Two cups of stimmo hadn't helped so she'd resorted to Fleet-issue fatigue-displacers. She'd pay for it later, of course, but it beat falling asleep in the briefing in front of Sam. Instead, her mind had whirred throughout the presentation, repeating every anxious, uncomfortable moment of her last meeting with the fixer.

Will Monet sat across from her, his expression serene but his body radiating a kind of knotted tension that she associated with combat troops before a drop. His eyes held something hungry and tragic in their gaze as he watched his ship approach on the central bubble. Far from the kindly superman she remembered from their first meeting years ago on the *Ariel Two*, this Will looked haunted and old.

His demeanour worried her. His actions would be her responsibility from the moment he stepped out of the meeting room. Everything that followed would depend upon how Will reacted to the scene the League had created. All at once, the security leak that had been dominating her thoughts for the last eight hours felt utterly trivial. Her main problem hung right in front of her. *This* was the part of Sam's plan that she needed to understand. As she stared at Will, suddenly all the psych reports and model profiles felt woefully inadequate.

'I'm proud to be working with you, Captain Monet,' she blurted. 'You should know that my team and I will have your back throughout this mission.'

Will turned his hollow, searchlight eyes in her direction. 'I'm delighted,' he said, not sounding for a moment like he meant it. He paused, his head tilting, as if something had just occurred to him. 'Would you mind if I had a word with you in private?' he said.

Ann looked around at the other assembled crew. 'What, *now*?'

Will nodded. 'This shuttle has a privacy chamber, doesn't it? They usually do.'

Ann knew that it did, in the opposite direction from the pod bay.

'You and I are captaining the two armed vessels on this mission,' said Will. 'It makes sense for us to confer before we start.'

Ann quickly considered her options. Disappearing for a private chat at the last moment would look downright odd to the rest of the mission team. But when had Will Monet been anything other than odd? It was too good a chance to pass up. Even thirty seconds of private conversation might give her crucial insights into how he'd react under pressure.

'Okay,' she said with a half-smile. 'Great idea. It should have been in the mission plan already – we need to understand each other.'

'My thoughts exactly,' said Will and pushed off towards the chamber.

Ann followed, acutely conscious of all the eyes on her back.

The chamber was a compact cylindrical space lined with the same opalescent padding as the main cabin. Will shut the door behind them.

'What can I do for you, Captain Ambassador?' said Ann.

For the first time in years, she stood face to face with the most powerful human being who'd ever lived. He smiled awkwardly at her, looking more like a lost little boy than a political titan. She felt an unexpected surge of guilt at her desire to understand him. After all, what else could she do now but lie to him?

'What do you think of this mission, Captain?' said Will.

'How do you mean, sir?'

'Do you believe in our mission goals? Do you think there are aliens out there? Or do you think this whole thing is a cynical set-up to try to force someone's political agenda?'

Ann recalled that Will could see in the infrared and read emotions via

126

skin temperature. She wished she'd thought to activate her subdermal augs before stepping into the shuttle. If she blushed in front of him now, it'd be blindingly obvious.

'The latter, sir. I think the likelihood that aliens are behind this is extremely slim.'

'Me, too,' he said, nodding. 'I have a favour to ask.' He met her eyes suddenly and didn't blink. 'I know you're here to provide extra military support and that your presence is the senate's best idea for ensuring everyone's safety. But I'm going to ask you to focus on the *Gulliver* out there – to keep them safe, and to ignore me and the *Ariel Two*. Nelson and I can take care of ourselves. Our ship is old and it's seen battle before. The *Gulliver*, on the other hand, is defenceless. It's going to need you. Badly. Can I rely on you to do that?'

Ann struggled internally while his gaze drilled into her. 'Of course,' she said. 'Though the mission plan inevitably limits what I can do.'

Will waved her comment away. 'The mission plan will mean nothing from the moment we hit that system. What I'm asking for is personal and outside the plan. It would mean you being ready to act the moment that ship is in trouble, not just because you think it's time to invoke a backup. Can I count on you? If I can't, just say. I won't hold it against you.'

Ann held her breath. *No!* she suddenly wanted to yell. *You can't count on anyone. Nothing will ever be the same again.*

'I'm sorry, Captain,' said Will, peering at her. 'Am I making you uncomfortable?'

Ann exhaled and started to feel stupid. Will had taken her aside to lean on her, of course, and now she was leaking information without even opening her mouth. She cursed the sloppy reasoning that had brought her here. She needed to regain some control of the dialogue before he noticed exactly how embarrassed and regretful he was making her feel.

His request was really about Mark. That was his vulnerability. Maybe she could use it.

'Of course I can help,' she said. 'If you explain why.' She watched him with as flat an expression as she could muster.

'I'm sorry?' said Will.

'I mean, if you want me to go outside the mission profile, you must have a reason, and I'm guessing it's a personal one. If you can tell me what that is, I'll consider your request.'

She blinked at him and waited.

Will regarded her with surprise. Apparently he'd expected her to simply accede to his demand. Of course he had. He must have encountered little else from Fleet officers for decades.

'There's someone on that ship whose life you want to protect,' Ann ventured. 'That's clear. My guess is either Mark Ruiz or Ash Corrigan. Perhaps both. They were both participants in your Omega Academy, were they not?'

When hidden anger lit in Will's eyes, she knew she'd gone too far. She wanted him off-balance, not cornered.

'My guess is Corrigan,' she said breezily. 'He's the public face of what's left of your programme. You can't afford to lose him.'

Will relaxed. 'You guessed right. He's a good kid. And it's not just what he represents. He doesn't deserve the risks.'

'I tell you what,' said Ann. 'How about a trade? You may not remember this, but I was a very junior officer aboard the *Ariel Two* years ago when you took that last trip back to visit the Transcended.'

Will's eyebrows went up. She saw vagueness enter his eyes as he rifled his digital memories for the record and felt momentarily hurt. He didn't remember. Why would he?

'So you were,' he said, surprised.

'I saw what that mission did to you,' said Ann. Her throat tightened. It wasn't a happy memory. 'I remember your disappointment. Your confusion. We all felt it. That was the mission when I decided to devote my career to helping maintain the kind of balance you espouse. All my work at the Far Frontier came out of that choice. But you shut yourself off on that return flight. You didn't talk to anyone. It was awful for everyone on board, and it made explaining the details of our failure to the senate review board incredibly difficult. It took me months to escape debriefing and get a new post. So I'm asking you not to shut me out this time. Instead, I'd like you to talk with me so that if the worst happens, the rest of us will be properly equipped to handle it. I want to know how you're thinking when the time comes for us to act. If you agree, I'll contact you on tight-beam to make that possible.'

Sam wouldn't like the idea, but Sam didn't have to know.

Will appraised her anew. 'I thought your ship was supposed to run

128

silent from the moment we leave port. Aren't we required to avoid contact?'

Ann shrugged. 'If we're going to abandon the mission plan, we might as well do it properly. What do you say?'

Will stared at her in confusion for a minute and then slowly broke into a grin. The idea that they'd made some pact to break the mission guidelines appeared to amuse him greatly.

'Done,' he said, with a laugh. 'You have a deal.'

Ann almost laughed with him. Amazingly, her ridiculous gambit had worked. The shuttle chose that moment to interrupt.

'Docking with the *Ariel Two* achieved.'

'I wasn't sure about the senate's push for a third ship, you know,' said Will as he made for the door. 'It looked like mindless overkill to me. But you're making me glad you're here.'

As he pushed back into the main cabin, she allowed herself to breathe. She'd established her bond and managed to get through the meeting without risking the League, and all in the two and a half minutes it had taken for them to reach the next ship. Were it not for the knot of confused guilt writhing around inside her, she'd have felt proud.

As it was, she felt painfully conflicted instead. Will Monet, for all his flaws, was not a bad man. He was just desperately lonely, as only someone with no peers could be. What they were going to do to him, however, was terrible. Her promise to protect the *Gulliver* was hollow. She'd be watching and monitoring Will's ship every second of the mission until they could coax him as far as Snakepit, where the shooting would start. Ann would never have been able to bluster through without total confidence that Sam and Ash would cover that base on her behalf.

Jaco Brinsen watched her approach, a look of hungry curiosity on his square, clean-cut features. However, he kept his mouth shut as the *Ariel Two* team slid across to their docking pod and bid them farewell.

Conversation in the shuttle remained almost comically muted after that. The League conspirators who'd been picked to man the *Chiyome* avoided each other's gazes until they reached the sanctuary of their own docking pod. Now, at last, they could speak without fear of leaking information to the rest of the Fleet.

'What did you say in there?' said Jaco with a knowing smile. 'Will went in looking like death and came out with a huge grin on his face. Nothing naughty, I hope.'

'I established a connection, that's all,' said Ann, knowing she sounded cryptic. 'I attempted to maximise the amount of tactical information we have about our target so as to increase the likelihood of mission success.'

'Hah!' said Jaco, obviously disappointed that she didn't volunteer more. 'It was impressive, in any case. They told me you have ice-water in your veins but I didn't believe it until now. You've got him figured out, I'd say. Wrapped around your finger, even.'

She pulled a sour face and looked away. 'Let's not go that far,' she said.

She knew what Jaco was trying for. He wanted to build a sense of camaraderie and mutual support right out of the gate so they'd be better able to work together. However, a joint celebration about duping Will Monet wasn't what she needed.

The pod locked home against the hatch to the *Chiyome*'s habitat core and Ann led the way through. For a ship capable of delivering so much silent death, it didn't look like much on the inside. Standard-issue self-cleaning panels in soft white clad the walls. A triple-stack of crash couches lined either side of the main cabin – the same layout the Fleet had used aboard small ships ever since the war. But for the serial numbers on the walls, she could have been inside the *Griffin*. As her crew moved wordlessly to their bunks, Ann felt a stab of profound loneliness, as if some of Will's isolation had rubbed off on her.

On the *Griffin*, her crew had felt like family even though she'd been forced to keep secrets from them. On the *Chiyome*, there'd be nothing to stop her from talking about everything she knew, yet she felt more distant from her colleagues than she had in years.

Kuril paused as he manoeuvred past her bunk to reach his slot.

'Just wanted to say, ma'am, proud to be serving with you. I know you'll do good.'

Ann smiled. 'Thank you,' she said. 'I'll do my best to live up to that.'

Perhaps not totally alone, then. One friend was a start.

Will smiled as he descended towards the *Ariel*'s primary habitat core. Ann had been right, of course. His behaviour on the return leg of the failed lure star mission had been self-indulgent in the extreme. Maybe he'd have the chance to atone for another lesser sin while doing his job.

Nelson hovered beside him, his gaze probing.

'If you don't mind me asking, Will,' he said, 'what did Ann say to you?'

Will shrugged. 'Not much.'

Nelson pulled a face like a man dining on lemons. 'It's just that you look rather distracted, considering.'

In truth, Will was. His agreement with Ann didn't amount to much. It was the fact that it existed at all that pleased him. That and the no-nonsense style with which she'd challenged his request. It had been years since someone had treated him that way – direct, honest, but rooted in compassionate instinct. The sudden discovery that he could still be treated as something other than a god or an embarrassment held remarkable appeal.

Acceding to her request had been a spur-of-the-moment decision. It didn't cost him anything, and the choice felt very unlike one the person he'd been for the last two years would make. This mission was bringing out sides of him he'd believed were long dead.

'She's blunt,' he said. 'I like that.'

Nelson's eyes went wide. He looked long and hard at Will's expression.

'Will,' he said heavily. 'Please don't kid yourself. That woman is hard as nails – she's more machine than person. Don't you dare go gushy on me at a time like this. And particularly over a shark like Andromeda Ludik. Don't go confusing her with Rachel just because they're both tough. Will, I know her and you don't. Expect nothing of her except orders well executed and you won't be disappointed.'

'I'm not confusing her with anyone,' Will snapped. 'That's the last we'll see of her, anyway. After this she's on her own.' He clapped his hands and rubbed the palms together. 'Onwards and outwards, then, I guess,' he said, pushing the conversation forwards with false brightness.

He tucked his smile inside. Ann's persona might be that of the efficient machine, but Will sensed that he'd perceived something rather different in her. Her request hadn't been all pragmatism. Will's instincts told him there was more to it than that. He would have to see how it panned out, of course, but if she did decide to check in with him, Will had already decided he was going to enjoy it.

4.5: ASH

Ash tried not to look at Mark as the *Gulliver* team descended into the core of their ship in the tiny docking pod. It had been hard to keep his emotions in check. Just seeing Mark made him angry, and having to listen every time he interrupted someone made it worse.

So many memories he'd forgotten came flooding back. Mark the smart-ass. Mark the favourite. There were eighteen of them in the aborted roboteer crèche, all closer than siblings at one point, in the way only roboteers could be. But over time, it became clear that in the eyes of their all-important mentor – Will Monet – only one of them mattered. The rest might as well have been invisible.

Then came the relocations and the secrets. When they next met, years later, siblings had become rivals as good at screening their thoughts from each other as they'd once been at sharing them. Just thinking about it made Ash seethe. He had been proud of himself for putting it all behind him and becoming a real asset to the League. Now Mark had reappeared and pulled the rug from under him all over again.

Ash didn't feel jealous, exactly, though there was some of that. What made him itch was how much harder Mark's presence made his job, when it had been scary enough to start with. His role in the League plan had originally been simple: fly in, wait for the cue and fly out to Snakepit, then watch Will get his well-deserved comeuppance. Now he had his boss aboard watching over his shoulder and they both had to be ready to act in an instant. Rather than fret, he tried to concentrate on what their resident Vartian Institute lunatic was saying as she babbled at them about the ship.

'...in fact, the *Gulliver* was designed fifteen years ago,' she was saying, 'in a collaboration between the Fleet and the Institute. The scenarios they envisaged for its use mostly involved dialogue with the Transcended, which is why the project got shelved. Construction of this ship was only completed two years ago. We designed it to protect against intrusive hacking and any other kind of alien incursion we could dream up. So, short of being shot at, we should be pretty safe.'

Ash bit his lip. As if that would do them any fucking good.

'As Yunus mentioned, there are three modules: fleet, science and diplomacy. Control over one cannot be used to usurp control of another.'

'Doesn't this create control problems?' said Mark. 'It sounds counter-productive, frankly.'

Ash watched Zoe Tamar shoot him a cold glance. Classic Mark. The guy hadn't changed. He could barely open his mouth without pissing somebody off. And this was who they put in charge of a diplomatic ship? Ash tried not to laugh. At least no one was likely to complain when he took over.

'Remember, our stated goal is to make contact with antagonistic aliens,' said Sam. 'Anything intended to make that process safer should be welcomed.'

'The ship does have a shared central data core,' said Zoe, 'but it only records information and can't act as a comms channel. It uses a transparent non-blocking intercept protocol that we believe should be impervious to abuse. And while the ship has no weapons, we do have two shuttles equipped for first contact, plus some of the most extensive analytical tools you'll find anywhere. Not to mention some fairly slick living quarters.'

The pod docked against the ship's habitat core and opened its doors. One by one, they spilled out into the interior. Ash had seen it before but remained impressed by just how plush a ride the *Gulliver* was.

Every inch of inhabitable space on a starship came at phenomenal cost as it had to be buffered against the ferocious radiation that filled the rest of the hull. This meant that most modern ships usually featured just four or five compact chambers, usually serving double duty. Fittings were invariably utilitarian and the decor served exclusively to keep the crew from going nuts under such confined conditions.

The *Gulliver*, in contrast, had been designed to carry diplomats and executives in style. It featured private cabins, a bio-lab, a study centre and a circular meeting space. In reality, the habitat core wasn't that much bigger than on a regular ship, but no expense had been spared in hiring designers to make the ship feel special.

Inspiration had come from the hallowed halls of Mars's Lowell University. The padded walls resembled redwood panelling and screens like picture windows filled much of the available space, showing three-dimensional views out onto the rust-tinted perfection of Martian Zen gardens. The guide-strips and touch controls resembled polished brass while being warm and soft to the touch. The air smelled mountain fresh, tinged with a hint of Burroughs pine. Even the acoustics had been tailored to give the auditory sense of a much larger space. So long as you stood still and didn't touch anything, the place wasn't a claustrophobic nightmare.

Mark whistled as he looked around. 'Wow. This makes a change from cargo-lifters, I can tell you.'

Citra Chesterford shot him a nervous look down the length of her elegant nose.

'Cargo-lifters? Your bio said nothing about cargo-lifters. I thought you were a starship captain.'

'I've been on sabbatical,' said Mark.

'To fly *lifters*?'

'Mark's credentials are not in question,' said Sam. 'I can assure you he's the best pilot in the Fleet.'

'*And* he has a personal endorsement from Will Monet,' Ash couldn't help adding.

Sam peered at him pointedly. He was making it sound like Mark's selection had been an inside job. Which, of course, it had been. It was exactly the kind of nepotistic pandering Ash had witnessed since they were little. It was funny how he'd never been the recipient of that attention.

'The habit core has three levels,' said Zoe. 'The top is an astrogation and immersion lab. Most of the action is here on the central ring. This corridor links all the work and cabin spaces, and your retinal implants will tell you which segment you're in. And down here, at the bottom of the core-sphere, we have something special.'

She led them to the access tube that ran down to the meeting area below. It had been styled after one of the university's grand discussion chambers. Beyond the circle of velvet-lined crash couches, the wall-screens made it look as if polished floors stretched away to gothic windows where the cliffs of the Valles Marineris beckoned. Faint scents of leather and paper books hung in the air.

'We have a fucking *lounge*?' Mark exclaimed.

'People who think for a living function better in a pleasant setting,' said Zoe.

'Everyone on a starship thinks for a living,' Mark retorted. 'They just usually get by with fewer cushions.'

'I think the Vartian Institute did a terrific job,' said Ash. 'I've had some experience flying the *Gulliver* and it's a great ship. All the features make sense once you get used to them. I'll make my memories available to you, Mark, so you're not starting from scratch.'

Venetia Sharp's owlish gaze flicked from Mark's face to his own. She peered at him like a lab specimen.

'Interesting,' she said. 'Our most experienced pilot isn't our primary captain.'

Ash squirmed a little under that gaze. Psych-types made him uncomfortable.

'Oh, Mark's very good,' he said. 'Prior to his unexpected sabbatical, he was winning all kinds of awards for mock combat.'

He noticed Sam's mouth tighten and knew he had to back off.

'I hope your skills extend beyond combat,' said Citra. 'This mission will require a rather different kind of flying.'

'That's why you should be pleased to have a lifter pilot in charge,' said Mark with a dry smile. 'My experience is very diverse.'

Yunus clapped his hands together. 'Well, clearly this will be an excellent base of operations. We should prepare to leave, I think. Triton Control will be awaiting our signal.'

'Absolutely right,' said Mark. 'Please make yourselves comfortable, everybody, while Ash and I retire to the bridge.'

What passed for a bridge on the *Gulliver* was a minuscule cabin on the main level with two crash couches arranged like bunk-beds and just enough room to walk or float beside them. Ash and Mark took their places, coupled fat-contacts to their necks and met virtually in the ship's metaphor space. It resembled a circular obsidian platform situated in the Zen garden that lay beyond the simulated windows. Afternoon light slanted across the rocks and a cool breeze tickled Ash's virtual skin. Like most other features of the ship, no expense had been spared on detailing the helm-arena.

Ash sighed to himself. He'd tagged all the metaphor spaces in the *Gulliver*'s subsystems with his own designs weeks ago. Now Mark would want to use his own, obsessively Earth-biome-orientated imagery. Flying with Mark, he recalled, was like piloting a shrubbery.

Mark's avatar appeared. 'Enjoying yourself?' he said with a scowl.

'Not sure I know what you mean,' said Ash.

'I'm not stupid,' said Mark. 'You're trying to make my life harder. It didn't take you long.'

Ash laughed it off. 'I'm sorry,' he said. 'You're right. My bad. Old habits die hard. You make it easy, though. I'm trying to think if there's anyone on this ship you haven't annoyed already.'

He conjured a flock of control visualisations out of the red sand like birds and busied himself checking their slowly rotating glyphs.

Mark exhaled slowly. 'Let's start this again,' he said. 'You were slated to be captain of this ship. Then I showed up. Now you're not. That must piss you off.'

Ash shrugged. 'It's no biggie. We're both professionals.'

'For what it's worth,' said Mark, 'I'm sorry. I'm not here to rain on your parade. This whole thing wasn't my idea, and we both know whose it was. I'm just here to do a job. After that I'll get out of your life and you'll never have to see me again. In the meantime, I'll take any advice you have to offer because you're better with people than I am and you understand this crowd in a way I never will. While we're out there, I'll do my best to make you look good, so that you get something decent out of this trip, career-wise. Because I'd really, really like this mission to go well so that we can both put it behind us. How does that sound? Can we have a truce?'

Ash felt his smile crumbling and tried his damnedest to prop it up. That was the problem with Mark. He might be a self-indulgent little prick, but he was still capable of acts of deep humility. Ash wished he wasn't. He'd be a lot easier to hate that way. Ash took the guilt that threatened to well up inside him and screwed it down tight.

He'd sold Mark out during the tribunal and Mark hadn't even mentioned that. Sam had asked him to do it to prove his loyalty to the League but it had come at a huge price. It had put him at odds with most of the other Omegas. It didn't help that Ash had never really believed he deserved the Omega ranking in the first place and felt like he'd been faking it his whole life. He'd always suspected they gave him the grade because he was good with people, and the Fleet was desperate for a friendly face for its roboteering efforts. That fear had messed with his confidence ever since. Or at least until Sam made him a true insider and brought him into the League. These days he worried more about who *did* accept him rather than who didn't.

'Sure,' he said, uncomfortably. 'We can have a truce.'

'Great,' said Mark. 'Thank you. I mean it.'

Ash turned back to his station and summoned up a stack of flight-path sheets like a tower of luminous tea trays. He tried not to think about what the League had in store for Mark. After the nasty surprise would come the imprisonment, followed by despair or death. Mark would never forgive him then. Ash knew he might as well enjoy the companionship while it lasted.

5: UNDERWAY

5.1: MARK

Mark spent his first shift out from Triton checking over the *Gulliver* and familiarising himself with its features. While the pretentious academic decor wasn't to his taste, the ship was, as Ash had suggested, a beautiful piece of engineering. It made him realise how much he'd missed flying in space. Besides the extraordinary engines, the *Gulliver* had impressive redundancies built into the robots that teemed in its outer hull layers. They had enough robotic support on board to rebuild the ship from the inside out.

There were frustrations, of course. The diplomacy and science sections had been walled off from him due to those ridiculous security concerns. He hated having two great dark patches in the cabin where his eyes and ears couldn't roam. But, for the most of part, the *Gulliver* was a pleasure.

Best of all, Mark loved the ship's *feel*. His unusual interface design dispensed with many of the metaphor layers roboteers customarily relied on to manage a ship's systems. Instead, it made heavy use of the trick Will had learned from the Transcended: employing sketched copies of a roboteer's own mind in place of SAPs to manage each function. Input from each copy filtered hierarchically into the pilot's consciousness as seamlessly as feedback from his own body. This gave him an intuitive, immediate grasp of the vessel around him.

The fit was never perfect, of course. Balancing subminds often felt like choosing between different ways to see an optical illusion. The worse the system's design, the more jarring the distinction between each perception. But the *Gulliver* had been designed with Mark's type

138

of interface in mind, so the merging of ship facets was almost perfect. Getting used to it felt as easy as sliding his hand into a velvet glove.

And what a glove! The *Gulliver* didn't drive between stars, it *soared*. It didn't turn with boat-like ponderousness the way most ships did. It banked effortlessly, gravity bursts slewing around Mark like a cloak made of thunder. Hooked up to the *Gulliver* he felt like some kind of huge vacuum-dwelling avian, slipping through warped space as if it were no more complicated a medium than air. By the time his shift finished, Mark was in love.

When he checked out, though, reality wasted no time intruding. He found a message waiting for him in his home node from Sam Shah. What Mark craved was a good night's sleep. He certainly didn't feel like attending a meeting. But his confidence was up and it was surely better to start behaving like the master of his own ship sooner rather than later.

He reluctantly made his way around the *Gulliver*'s faux-spacious companionway, past the holographic gardens with their sand fountains and cool, rusty light, to the privacy chamber where Sam waited. He'd set the ship's drive to provide a steady one-gee of pull. The *Gulliver*'s engines purred so smoothly that the gravity almost felt Earth-like.

Sam welcomed him in, flicking aside screens full of numbers and maps. The walls returned to their garden-view default, making the tiny chamber slightly less claustrophobic.

'Hi, Mark, thanks for coming. Want to sit?'

A chair slid out of the wall, momentarily breaking the illusion.

Mark sat. 'What's up?'

'I want us to get off on the right foot,' said Sam. 'I may be here in an advisory capacity, but I'm still the senior Fleet officer on this ship and you deserve to know where I stand. First, you weren't my preferred choice for captain, but you probably figured that out already.'

Mark wasn't surprised but didn't enjoy hearing it anyway. He brushed his resentment aside.

'Second,' said Sam, 'you're a brilliant pilot and a great officer for this job. And, if we're honest, were it not for a few past mistakes you'd have been my top choice for this position from the get-go.'

'Okay,' said Mark, relaxing a little. 'Thank you, sir, I guess.'

'I understand that you probably want to make a point with this trip,' said Sam. 'Were I in your shoes, I'd want to redeem myself and put the past behind me.'

'That's the plan,' said Mark.

'Great. Because I have an offer. Let me mentor you on this trip and I will give you my complete support in the business that follows. I'll throw myself behind the case for the complete restoration of your interface privileges.'

Mark wasn't sure what to say. He hadn't needed oversight running a starship since he was sixteen. Had they given him a captaincy or not?

'Mentor me, sir?'

'In a manner of speaking, yes.'

Mark tried not to feel insulted. 'I really appreciate the offer, sir, but I would hope that such a deal isn't necessary. It's my intention to follow the mission profile to the letter.'

'I don't doubt that,' said Sam, 'but I think we both know this mission isn't going to be that easy. For a start, these people you're carrying are all VIPs and they all know each other. They're used to being treated like little gods. Any one of them could probably put the stoppers on your career with a single call after this trip is through.'

Mark said nothing. Sam undoubtedly fell into that same category himself.

'Maybe you think that just sticking to the mission profile will be enough,' Sam went on, 'but again we both know conditions might arise where the profile is exceeded. We're heading into a very uncertain situation.'

'Even so, I'd like to think that you'll be pleased with my performance,' said Mark. 'Extra input shouldn't be necessary for someone at my career level. And the best way for me to make a point to the Fleet is surely to do my job properly without oversight.'

Mark knew how Fleet courts worked. Any evidence on his report that he'd abdicated responsibility for his actions to another officer during the mission would give them an excuse to hold back his interface rights. No matter how well intentioned Sam might be, Mark couldn't be seen to let someone else guide his command choices for a minute, not even a more highly ranked officer. Plus being seen to take sides among such heavy – and politically charged – company might prove more dangerous than staying neutral.

Sam spread his hands and chuckled. 'Fair enough. Excellent attitude.

Let me try to be a little more... candid. As a member of the Fleet strategic board, I am sometimes privy to information I can't share. And it's... possible that this information may have a bearing on our mission.'

'I get it,' said Mark. 'And of course I'll welcome your input at all times.'

'I wish that were enough. But we may find ourselves in a situation where the reasoning behind my recommendations might be opaque, or even counter-intuitive.'

Mark tried not to squirm on his chair. 'And if you signal that, I will give your input the corresponding weight. I'd love to do more, sir, but I can't agree to automatically accept your proposals without due process. That would be less than the Fleet expects of me.'

Sam's expression slid a little, betraying some frustration. 'I *do* see the bind you're in, but I'm trying to give you a way to offset the responsibility if something actually goes wrong. You're basing your reasoning on the assumption that there even *needs* to be a court session at the end of this. If you get my drift.'

In Mark's experience, there was always a court session.

'What I'm offering you here is a free ticket to a clean slate,' said Sam. 'I just want to help.'

Mark wondered what anyone reviewing the surveillance tape from the mission would make of all this. Sam appeared to be extremely confident that circumventing Fleet process wouldn't be an issue, even in the event of disaster. Unless, of course, Sam was setting him up. Will's words suddenly came back to Mark with a jolt. *Someone doesn't want you to fly, Mark, and chances are they're coming with you on that ship.*

'But that's the thing, sir,' he said. 'I don't want a free ticket. I want to earn it.' He got to his feet. 'I'm sorry I can't do more, sir,' he said. 'Thank you for taking the time to talk with me, and please know that I take your input extremely seriously.'

He let himself out, not sure whether to feel insulted or worried by how the conversation had gone. Hopefully the entire subject would be moot in a few weeks when Sam had a chance to see him in action. Either way, Mark no longer felt ready for sleep. He needed a distraction. A book, perhaps, or a few minutes of light interactive. He made his way to the ladder that led down to the lounge but paused at the top when he spotted Zoe Tamar seated below, reading a tablet in a shaft of artificial sunlight.

He sighed to himself. The prospect of sitting with an attractive, talented woman who considered him something between a brawling mobster and ship's dogsbody didn't strike him as particularly restful. However, short of disappearing back into the ship's metaphor space, there was nowhere else to go. Like all starships, the *Gulliver* was crowded.

He decided to retreat anyway just as she looked up and noticed him. Mark smeared a smile onto his face and grudgingly descended. He picked the chair closest to the wireless node and slumped into it with his arms folded. He peered out at the simulated canyon and hoped she'd keep reading.

'What's up?' said Zoe. 'Someone piss in your crash couch?'

Despite her tone, she sounded curious, not critical. Mark had no idea how to avoid talking to her without coming across as even ruder than usual.

'Are you sure you really want to know?' he said. 'I don't want to dump on you. We haven't exactly hit it off so far, and that's almost certainly down to me.'

'We need to be able to work together,' said Zoe, 'so you might as well talk. Otherwise I'll just sit here wondering why you're in a shitty mood.'

She paused uncomfortably and ran a hand through her hair. Mark belatedly noticed it was the same purple as the Vartian Institute logo.

'I was short with you last night,' she said. 'Your presence spooked me, I admit that. I may have blamed you a bit, which wasn't strictly rational. So now I've done the easy part of opening up and you've got nothing to lose by talking. Who knows, my opinion of you might go up.'

Mark regarded her nervously. He recognised an olive branch when he saw one and couldn't really turn it down, though chatting lacked appeal. He reluctantly decided to return the gift of transparency.

'I just had a meeting with Sam,' he said. 'Didn't go so great.'

'Why not?' she said. 'What happened? Is he upset with you or something?'

'No, nothing like that.'

Zoe waited expectantly.

Mark writhed inside and wondered how much to say. He hated situations like this. With another roboteer, he'd just hand them a memory file and let them figure it out. With norms, you had to tortuously work out what you were and weren't supposed to disclose. Whatever. If she wanted honesty, he might as well do it properly.

'He seemed to want some kind of concession from me. I'm not even sure what it was. We didn't get that far. He offered to *mentor* me. Which, first off, I can't allow, and, secondly, is kind of insulting. It's just one more reminder to me that I don't really like Fleet work. I can't wait for the mission to be over so I can get the hell out of this project and leave all this political shit behind. It's the little things like this that make me wish I'd never said *yes*.'

'That's ironic,' said Zoe, folding her arms. 'I had to fight so hard just to be included. The Vartian Institute was forced to offer up millions in tech patents to get me my slot.'

Mark winced. He'd managed to scorch the mood already. Amazing.

'Sorry,' he said. 'That came out badly. Look, ignore me. My life is weird. I don't need or expect sympathy.' He sat there and smouldered, wishing he'd never opened his mouth.

Zoe looked at him oddly. 'Can I offer you a little advice?' she said.

'Sure,' said Mark. 'Go for it.'

'For the next few weeks, our lives are in your hands,' she said. 'And as you point out, you're a little weird, and you're clearly not happy. Most of us don't know the first thing about you except the *very* short bio the Fleet gave us, and that you have some kind of link with Will Monet. So don't be surprised if people on this ship are a little concerned about that, and maybe look around for ways to exercise some control over their destiny. Like offering to mentor you or cheer you up or find out who the hell you are, or whatever. That's just human nature.

'If you don't want to be on the receiving end of that, why not try reframing how you look at the mission? I don't know what your reasons were for taking this job, but I can tell you why I'm here, and why I'm excited about it.' She leaned forward in her chair. 'I think this is the start of a new phase of history. We've been given all the clues: the radiation flash, that message, their warp signature. I believe the Transcended are involved in all this and that their agenda will be revealed. We'll know what they're angling for, at last. For better or worse we'll know where the human race is headed. And this ship will be right there when we figure all that out. That's worth getting a bit ramped about, surely?'

Mark saw the glee in her eyes. It certainly felt nice having someone want to share their enthusiasm with him, but even so, he couldn't help himself. Suspending disbelief didn't come that easily.

'So you don't think it's all some kind of a bullshit scam, then?' he said. 'That's what Will and Sam seem to think.'

Zoe sat back and offered him a slightly wounded smile. Mark immediately regretted his words.

'No,' she said. 'I don't. I'm pretty sure they're wrong.'

'Really?' said Mark. He felt a desperate urge to explain his unpleasant remark and sound consistent at the same time. 'I mean, I take your point about the warp drives – it's a good one, and you're the expert. But if I was going to try for something like that, I'd trick out every drone with tau-chargers to hide their signature and then just dump out a tailored g-ray flash every time they warped. They could make it look however they liked. And at the kind of distance the *Reynard* was sitting at, I can't see them having the sensor resolution to tell the difference.'

Zoe's smile stiffened. Something a little like worry showed in her eyes. Mark guessed she hadn't explored that option – probably because it was the kind of kludgy approach a starship engineer would think of, rather than the clean, clever solution that would occur to a scientist.

'Not possible,' she said. 'The peaks in their emission spectrum don't correspond—'

'Simple,' said Mark before she could finish. 'If they timed it right, they could use the gravity distortion of each warp pulse to impart a little redshift to the bursts. Your spectroscopic peaks would all slide. Then they follow each burst with another a nanosecond later using a different configuration. Voila – fake spectrum. Who could tell the difference? Unless you had sensors sampling at an insanely high rate, of course.'

Zoe crossed her legs and looked anxious. The idea that she might have been out-thought by a jumped-up flyboy didn't appear to sit well with her.

'Maybe,' she said quickly. 'But that sounds like a very expensive solution. How practical is it, really?'

Mark shrugged. 'No idea. But if the alternative is a plot by dead aliens who haven't bothered to talk to us in the last thirty years...?'

'There's no evidence they're dead,' said Zoe.

'Sleeping, then,' Mark offered. 'Stoned, lazy, whatever.'

He watched her shoulders tense and realised he wasn't making friends. He rubbed his eyes.

'I'm sorry,' he said. 'I didn't mean to rain on your parade. We shouldn't rule anything out at this point, in any case. And my problems aren't your problems.'

'You got that right,' she said.

'I'm going to hang out in my cabin,' said Mark. 'Thanks for the advice. I mean it.'

He climbed out of the lounge, more convinced than ever of his goal: prove himself, quit and get as far away from the Fleet and all its hangers-on as he could. The ship had plenty of virtual space to offer, all of it free of passengers. It suddenly looked surprisingly appealing. A few weeks tucked away might not be so bad after all.

5.2: YUNUS

Two days into the flight, Yunus sent his captain a meeting request. Ten minutes before Ruiz was due to arrive, Yunus made his way to the study space he'd chosen as an office and looked over his first-contact plans while he waited. He hadn't used such a cramped workroom in years, but that was space travel for you. At least the decor was tasteful. Most starship interiors looked like hospital cupboards.

Right on time, the door notified him. 'Captain Mark Ruiz is here.'

Their pilot was punctual. That, at least, boded well.

'Show him in,' he said.

Ruiz stepped inside, a guarded expression on his face. Yunus took that moment to assess the man properly. Ruiz was both a roboteer and an Earther – an unusual blend. His build was pure Earth, if perhaps a little wider and stockier than most, and he had the dark, mixed-race looks you found in almost every city these days. But the way he carried himself was something else. He had the loose, expansive gestures of a Colonial, and angry, hunched shoulders that were all his own.

Yunus wondered what had made Mark Ruiz quite so bitter and reclusive. Since they'd come aboard he'd practically been invisible. Yunus needed to know how the man thought, and whether he could be trusted. With a skilled ally at the helm, his goals at Tiwanaku would be a lot easier to achieve.

'You wanted to see me,' said Ruiz.

'Yes. Thank you for coming. Please sit.'

Yunus gestured for a chair. The room obliged.

Ruiz glanced around at the walls as he settled.

'Can I ask what this is about?'

'I want to get to know you,' said Yunus. 'I'm leading this mission and you're my captain. It's as simple as that. We've had a couple of days to settle in. Now feels like a good time.'

Ruiz folded his arms. 'What do you want to know?'

'Who you are. How you think. What your priorities are. Your bio says you're an Earther, for instance, but you appear to have spent less than two years living on Earth. That's unusual.'

'It's what I could manage,' said Ruiz. 'I consider myself an Earther, if that's your point. My parents are from there.'

'Not a Galatean?' Yunus indulged in a playful smile. 'You were at school on that world for a while.'

Ruiz's expression didn't waver. 'I grew up on Mars, New Panama, Galatea, Europa, and even spent some time on Saint Andrews. I don't consider myself from any of those places.'

'I see,' said Yunus. 'And what do you think about this mission you've found yourself on? Do you believe in it?'

Ruiz regarded him warily. 'I believe it's a job. And I believe I'm the best person for it. Look, you have my bio – what more do you need to know? Is there something specific I can help you with?'

Yunus restrained a sigh. He tried to stay gracious.

'Of course,' he said. 'You respect directness, I can see that. Frankly, I want to understand your politics because I believe they may impact this mission.'

'I try not to have any.'

'You chose to spend two years flying in the North Atlantic Disaster Zone. That's not what I'd expect from someone who doesn't care about politics.'

Ruiz exhaled and appeared to relax a little. 'I care about Earth, if that's what you mean.'

Yunus smiled. So the young man did have some humanity after all.

'That's what I hoped you'd say. How about Freedom Camps? How do you feel about them?'

Ruiz looked confused. 'Freedom what?'

'I prefer not to use the expression "Flag Drops",' said Yunus. 'I consider it a pejorative that our society appears to have accepted into common parlance. I prefer Freedom Camps, or Free Camps, if you like.'

'I think they're sad,' said Ruiz. 'I think there are a lot of poor people on Earth who'll do anything to escape, including claiming to be Revivalist zealots for one bunch or another. They get shipped off to the Frontier and treated like dirt.'

How sad – another citizen who'd absorbed the Colonialist propaganda without even noticing.

'You don't think they're being given a chance to build a new life?'

'From what I've heard,' said Ruiz, 'the conditions are usually shit.'

Yunus winced a little at the language; Colonials had such filthy mouths. And Ruiz *was* a Colonial, whether he believed it or not. For starters, he didn't appear to have a grasp of the basic concept of respect for his betters.

'May I paint a different picture for you?' he said.

Ruiz shrugged. 'Go for it.'

'Consider how much it costs to take people to the Far Frontier. The Free Camps are privately funded. They're usually poor because almost all the available money has been spent just getting people there.'

'Okay,' said Ruiz. He fell silent.

Yunus pulled an amused expression. 'Have I convinced you already?'

'If you want to convince me, you'll have to tell me why there are so many of them. Why not just build fewer and give people a decent quality of life?'

'Because,' said Yunus patiently, 'unless Earth builds them, billions of people will be locked out of the economy. The Far Frontier gold rush is happening *now*. Whoever is out there making those discoveries is going to own tomorrow's businesses. What do you think will happen to all those people on Earth if they don't get a share in that? That's also why they bend the rules. Earth leans on IPSO as much as it can because the alternative is leaving billions on Earth penniless, eking out a life in dismal prefab warrens while the Galatea Effect smashes everything on the surface.'

Ruiz looked out of the corner of his eyes as if scanning for an escape route.

'I don't know, it still sounds exploitative to me. I don't see the Leading classes out there getting their hands dirty.'

Yunus struggled to maintain his composure. Mark was obviously a classic *Eno*, an *Earther in Name Only*. Shame. Yunus had hoped to find something of a kindred spirit. He'd found it hard enough to endure the way the mission had been set up and was appalled by the things he'd learned about the Fleet's recent behaviour – the existence of the *Chiyome* first and foremost. The assumption of Earth's guilt appeared to have been written into the mission plan from the outset. And, given that, he still wasn't sure why the Fleet had chosen to show their hand and reveal the awful ship's existence. There was something off about the whole business.

Yunus had told himself since first joining the mission that it was worth all the schmoozing with ignorant Colonials, given what Earth stood to gain. However, being trapped in a closet under several kilometres of radioactive starship surrounded by bigots made that difficult. He had to remind himself of his duty every time they shoved their prejudice in his face. None of them had even taken the time to understand Earth's society before they dismissed it. None of them showed him an ounce of the respect he was due.

'Actually, there are members of the Leading class in every Free Camp,' he said. 'Who do you suppose runs things?'

For a moment, Ruiz's guarded expression slipped. His eyebrows twitched upwards. Yunus felt a surge of satisfaction.

'You didn't know that?' he said brightly.

Mark shook his head.

'I thought not. Despite the propaganda, not all of the Leading class are greedy billionaires,' said Yunus. 'Most of us are just people who happen to be born into clerical families and who accept the social responsibility that comes with that privilege. Many of us volunteer to work in the camps. A classful society is a two-way street, you know. *Noblesse oblige* is an oath we take seriously.'

Ruiz exhaled noisily. 'I'm glad to hear it. But did you really ask me here to talk about the Frontier? Given our mission profile, it's not exactly relevant.'

Yunus sighed and decided to get to the point. Chit-chatting with a foul-mouthed misanthrope had started to wear on him.

'Actually, it's very relevant. You and I both know that this mission comes at a critical time. The future of the Frontier is being decided right now, which makes the timing of the Tiwanaku Event either suspicious or miraculous.'

'Agreed,' said Ruiz. 'Can we just say suspicious?'

Yunus grimaced. 'Ah, but here's the thing, Mark. The Fleet is completely convinced that one of Earth's Houses is responsible for the attack, but I don't buy it. You may be aware that I'm well connected in Earth politics. I *know* senior representatives from all the major sect groups, even if only slightly, and I will tell you this: the Far Frontier is so important right now that I cannot think of a single House that would break ranks in order to fake something as unlikely as first contact. It would ruin their credibility with their allies at a time when alliances mean everything. Their power in the senate *requires* that they act as a unified bloc.'

Ruiz looked genuinely unsettled. 'So you think a colony's responsible?'

'No,' said Yunus with a smile. 'Not even Drexler would try this. Consider the implications. Such a masquerade would not stand for long, and if news got back to the home system, the Colonial cause in the senate would collapse. Only Galatea would have the money for this, and Galatea is obsessed only with itself. As the Prophet Sanchez said – once you remove the impossible, whatever remains, however improbable, must be true. In this case, logic requires us to entertain the belief that the aliens are real. Whether the timing is driven by the Transcended or inspired by God, I do not know. What matters is the *possibility*.'

'Okay. Fine,' said Ruiz. 'Let's say they're real, then. Regardless, what do you actually want from me?'

'I want room to pursue my diplomatic agenda,' said Yunus, leaning forward. 'Let's not fool ourselves – we both know why Sam Shah is on this mission. If there *are* aliens at Tiwanaku, Sam will try to take control of the situation immediately. He'll use it to try to create an advantage for the Colonial faction he represents. He has links to the Frontier Protection Party, you know.'

Ruiz shook his head. The spark of interest in his eyes appeared to be fading.

'No. I didn't know that.'

'All I want is for you to give me the benefit of the doubt for long enough to secure an advantage for the billions of people stuck on Earth. The same people you spent those years trying to save.'

Mark's mouth became a thin line. Yunus's cheeks flushed with contained annoyance. Somehow, asking for a simple favour appeared to have tipped Ruiz into a kind of emotional lockdown. Didn't the young man see how much of a difference he could make? Control of the helm at Tiwanaku meant control over the comms channels. It meant being able to position the ship to prevent the *Ariel Two* from firing. It would govern who made contact first and how fast. Yunus's ownership of the override codes would be worth nothing without a supportive hand at the controls.

'Can you do that for me?' Yunus pressed.

Mark fixed him with a steady look. 'With all the greatest respect, Professor, I'm committing to exactly nothing that's outside the mission plan. I don't mind telling you that Sam has already spoken to me.'

Yunus's stomach lurched.

'And I turned him down, too,' said Ruiz. 'I can't afford to take sides on this ship. I couldn't even if I wanted to. I'm here to do a job and that's it. I hope you'll be pleased with the outcome, but straight dealing is all I can offer you.' He stood and headed for the door. 'Do you have any other questions?'

Yunus gazed at the nasty little Eno with dislike. 'No. You may go. Thank you for your time.'

In the quiet that followed, he pondered what he'd learned. Sam had already angled for Mark's allegiance, which suggested that Sam had already guessed the Photurians were real, regardless of the act he maintained to the contrary. It also meant that his agenda had to be different from the Fleet's, otherwise a private discussion with Ruiz wouldn't have been necessary. It was imperative that he understand what Sam was up to.

He sat with eyes narrowed, his fingers idly tapping on his knee while he tried to think of a strategy for winkling that secret out. He suddenly wished he knew more about Sam besides his ponderous reputation.

'Where is Sam Shah?' he asked the room.

'Sam Shah is in this sector,' it replied. 'He is speaking to your wife in her lab, two doors down.'

Yunus leapt to his feet. It was too good an opportunity to miss. He strode the short distance around the central corridor and waved Citra's door aside.

She was sitting on her lab bench, laughing. She stopped and blinked as she noticed him in the doorway around the side of Sam's shoulder.

'Yuni! There you are, dear,' she said. 'Did you know that Overcaptain Shah has an interest in the Davenport biosphere?'

Sam turned and nodded to Yunus in greeting, his broad, handsome face crinkled with smiles.

'Professor,' said Sam, 'your wife and I were discussing Frontier biosecurity. She's extraordinarily well informed.'

'I'm surprised you ever imagined otherwise,' said Yunus as he struggled for poise. 'If she wasn't an expert, she wouldn't be here, would she? Overcaptain Shah, may I have a quick word with you in private?'

Sam glanced at Citra and then back in his direction.

'Of course,' he said simply.

Yunus gestured for Sam to join him in his study. They made the very short walk in silence. As soon as Yunus sealed the door behind them, Sam looked at him expectantly.

'How can I help you, Professor?'

'I just learned that you had a private chat with Mark Ruiz. Do you mind if I ask why?' Sam's omissions would be as informative as his remarks.

Sam's eyes widened in surprise. The man had the good grace to look embarrassed, at least.

'I did. He told you, I suppose. I was trying to feel him out.' Sam fixed Yunus with a level gaze. 'I'll be blunt. You and I have different political interests. You'd like our investigation at Tiwanaku to result in benefits for Earth without advantages for the Colonies. I'm biased in the other direction. I think we're both man enough to acknowledge that. And I think we also both understand that this mission *is* a political one. But while you and I may see Tiwanaku as a human problem, I suspect Will Monet has a different take. I was very effectively outmanoeuvred when it came to selecting a captain for this ship. Ash Corrigan was my choice. I thought the fact that he's got so much experience on diplomatic ships would be a strong sell for Earth's senators. His record is spotless and he's been their captain of choice for official flights to the Far Frontier for the last two years.'

Yunus contained his surprise. He hadn't known that.

'Clearly, though,' said Sam, 'any pilot from Drexler, no matter his record, could hardly compete with an Earther for the job. So Monet got his way before anyone had the chance to notice the connection, or to look deep enough into Ruiz's background to see how odd an appointment that was.'

'I see,' said Yunus. He wasn't sure what he'd expected from Sam, but it wasn't this disarming directness.

'I'm not used to being tactically outplayed, Professor,' said Sam. 'I don't mind telling you that. What concerns me, though, is when it's members of my own side doing it. When you and I find out which group is responsible for Tiwanaku, we won't have much time to negotiate a deal. We'll both want to take point in that conversation and tight control of this ship will make all the difference. I can live with that problem. Here's the thing, though. You want an advantage for Earth. I want the same for the Colonies. So what does Monet want? Why did he put his man in that chair? We may be at odds, Professor, but I think it's safe to say that neither of us wants war, which is why I'd like to know what's really going on aboard this ship. And if that means a little sleuthing on my own time, I don't mind doing it.'

Yunus gazed blankly as it dawned on him that it wasn't Sam who'd figured out about the Photurians, but Will Monet – a far more serious adversary. Yunus saw then that he'd made the mistake of conflating Will's erratic behaviour with a lack of subtlety. He'd grown used to thinking of Monet as a washed-up relic, but it was logical that an event like this would bring him back to the fore.

It all made sense now. Of course Monet was more likely to have noticed an extraterrestrial hand in affairs than the plodding policeman before him. Monet had put Ruiz in the captain's chair precisely because he wanted control at Tiwanaku. And that was also why Ruiz was so hard to reach. His opacity wasn't an accident. Yunus wondered how he'd been so blind.

'I won't promise to share what I learn with you,' said Sam. 'You're too much of a professional to expect that from me. But I hope we can agree to respect each other as adversaries and make sure this mission doesn't get blood on its hands. Can I rely on you for that?'

'Yes,' said Yunus distantly, his mind spinning. 'Of course. Thank you, Overcaptain Shah, your honesty has been extremely refreshing. I think we understand each other better now.'

Sam nodded curtly as he retreated to the door.

'Agreed,' he said. 'May the best man win, Professor. And I meant what I said – your wife is very impressive. You're lucky to have an ally like her aboard.'

'Thank you,' said Yunus as Sam let himself out.

He sat alone for a few minutes after that, calculating his next move. He needed a better handle on Monet's game, and he needed it quick.

5.3: WILL

The *Ariel Two* arrived at the Gore-Daano fuelling station right on schedule. Will found himself surveying a desolate little system – just rocks and dust looked over by a sullen, underfed star. An automated Fleet outpost had been left there to handle the ships. Were SAPs able to feel loneliness, Will didn't doubt this one would. He'd hoped for more distraction.

The view from the ship's interior cameras didn't help, either. The last refurbishment had updated the *Ariel Two*'s cabins significantly, under Nelson's careful supervision. The comparatively large spherical space of the central habitat core had been split into pleasant cabins lined with pale, luminescent clamber-web and softly carpeted walls that changed colour to taste. Their new crash couches had a sleek, fluid design. Will couldn't have cared less.

He'd spent too many of his off-hours during the two weeks of voyage so far with Nelson and his three-person team: Mitra, Peter and Devi. Competition for a posting to the *Ariel Two* was fierce, with positions almost always going to Fleet personnel who doubled as research scientists. Only those who wanted to spend years inspecting the bowels of a working nestship applied.

Consequently, the in-flight conversation had tended to involve animated speculation about details of the *Ariel Two*'s design over glasses of low-alcohol wine in the ship's central dining space. Will had sat through the debates with Nelson's tight-knit clique and tried to make the best of it, but there were only so many discussions of hydraulic transport eddies he could take.

As the days without meetings had crawled by, Will had found himself increasingly drawn to a bad habit: living in the past. Nelson had repeatedly counselled against it, but with the team now hard at work refilling the *Ariel Two*'s antimatter reservoirs, he had time on his hands.

With a twitch of thought, the *Ariel Two* fell away. Will found himself back in the apartment on Mars he'd shared with Rachel. He flushed with the heat of replayed emotion.

'I just don't think it's a good idea, that's all,' he said.

Rachel got up from the sofa and strode to the window. He took in the sight of her compact, muscular back and ached, even through the veil of recall.

'It's got to be better than sitting here letting this shit play out, hasn't it?' she said.

She turned to stare at him, her dark eyes fierce. Rachel had always been at her most beautiful when in motion – when animated by something, as she was now. The man he'd been that day had barely noticed. He was too caught up the moment.

'You're drowning here and you don't even see it,' she said. 'You're getting sucked deeper and deeper into Earth's poison. I feel like I've lost you already, Will. So why shouldn't I try fixing it?'

'Charting the most dangerous part of deep space is fixing our relationship?' he said. 'Forgive me for not understanding how that works.'

[*Tell her you love her,*] Will yelled at his prior self. [*Tell her you're afraid you'll lose her. Be honest!*] The prior Will didn't hear. He never did.

'Do I really need to spell it out for you?' she said. 'You've made fixing *you* about fixing civilisation. Did you ever stop to think about how nuts that is? And we both know you can't fix civilisation while everyone's fighting over the Far Frontier. So if I can't fix you without fixing that first then I might as well try. I'm going to go find something else for the human race to get excited about because that's all I have left.'

The old Will pulled a grimace of confused distaste.

'All you've got *left*? What the hell's that supposed to mean?'

She turned away again. 'I barely see you,' she said. 'I'm not having any fun here, and neither are you. I hate Mars. *You* hate Mars.'

[*Don't say it,*] Will shouted into the past. [*Don't say it!*]

The memory froze. It took Will a few seconds to pull himself free of the moment and notice the incoming call icon from the *Gulliver* in his sensorium. He shook off the old pain, closed down the memory and opened the channel.

When the window opened, he found Yunus Chesterford seated before him in one of the *Gulliver's* executive workrooms. He wore a bespoke one-piece in Reconsiderist brown with his mission-lead stripes proudly displayed.

'What's up?' said Will. Embarrassment vied with impatience at the edges of his mind.

'Nothing so far, thankfully,' said Yunus. 'I'm just calling you to check in. Anything to report?'

'No,' said Will tersely. 'It's been an uneventful week. I can send you a summary, if you like.'

'Please do,' said Yunus. 'I'm glad it went smoothly. There is one topic I want to broach with you. It's not mission critical, but it may become so.' Yunus began to look uncomfortable.

This, Will thought, would be the real reason for the call. 'I'm all ears,' he said.

'I've received multiple reports about our captain,' said Yunus. 'He doesn't appear to be integrating well with the rest of the team.'

'I see.'

'Citra and I started from a sympathetic position,' said Yunus. 'Mark is both an Earther and a roboteer, a combination that cannot have been an easy one to live with.'

'That's true,' said Will.

'So after I started receiving complaints—'

'You received formal complaints?' Frustration started to build in the back of Will's head like storm clouds on a muggy day.

Yunus shook his head. 'Not formal ones, exactly. No one has been so blunt. Just comments.'

'Okay. You received comments. And then?'

'Well, we reached out to Mark to try to amend matters. To extend the hand of friendship, as it were. Citra invited him to join a prayer group that I wanted to start. As a fellow Earther it felt like the least I could do. And the response she received . . .'

'Yes?' said Will.

'Frankly, it was rude.'

'He declined, I take it.'

'He did more than that,' said Yunus. 'He suggested it was an inappropriate activity for the crew of a diplomatic starship.'

'A position I agree with,' said Will sharply.

Yunus's cheeks coloured.

'But we're discussing Mark Ruiz,' said Will. 'You have additional concerns. Please go on.'

'I don't even know where to start,' said Yunus. 'When not running the ship out of that little cupboard of his, he's sitting in the lounge in the same chair, not talking to anyone. I've held scientific talks every day and he hasn't attended a single one. I don't know how he can expect to be ready when we reach Tiwanaku.'

'Did you record the talks?'

'Of course.'

'And they were held in the diplomatic zone, I take it?' Will ventured.

'I don't see how that matters.'

'My question is, how do you know that Mark wasn't replaying the talks when he was sitting in the lounge? Your captain is a roboteer, remember?'

'There is more to the talks than their informational content,' said Yunus. 'There is also the social component, in which he is making no attempt to participate.'

'A valid concern,' said Will. 'I'm sorry he isn't behaving as you expected. Can I ask you, though – is there a single thing actually wrong with the way the ship is being run? Something that might require my disciplinary involvement? Your gravity, for instance? Your schedule? Food? Air? SAP support?'

'No,' said Yunus. 'But that's not the point. My point is simply that the captain would do a better job if he had a closer bond with a member of the diplomatic team and some tighter supervision.'

'You're volunteering, I take it?'

'Absolutely, I'm volunteering. And frankly, I consider it necessary. If you were to encourage him to approach me—'

Will's patience began to evaporate. 'Why me? Sam is the senior Fleet officer on the *Gulliver*.'

'Mark was *your* pick for this mission, was he not?' Yunus stared at Will openly, watching for a response.

'Where did you hear that?'

'It is common knowledge on the *Gulliver*,' said Yunus. 'I believe Subcaptain Corrigan was the first to mention it.'

'Was he indeed?'

'Did you imagine that such a significant piece of manoeuvring would go unnoticed, Captain? No one is surprised that you attempted to put your man at the helm of this ship. Politics is politics. I'm simply asking that you assist in guiding him. At least if you don't want it to become entirely obvious that his posting was contrived.'

'Firstly, his posting was based on my assessment of his talent,' said Will. 'And secondly, I can assure you that my intervention would be entirely counterproductive.'

Yunus smiled. 'I find that hard to believe.'

'However you may imagine my relationship with Mark Ruiz works, I can assure you that it is not founded on mutual respect.'

Yunus looked confused. 'Nevertheless, you must have some influence over him, and it is *imperative* that this mission be correctly managed. In any case, I would like you to ask him to work with me.'

'No,' said Will.

Yunus scowled. 'I'm sorry?'

'I'm not doing it. It's not my job, and Mark is not, as you so colourfully imagine, privately taking cues from me. We are captains of independent ships. If you want to win him over, do it yourself. Use your *charm*.'

'Fine,' said Yunus sharply. 'Let us pursue a different tack. Perhaps if you can explain to me why you wanted Mark on board in the first place, I will know better how to find common ground with him.'

'I chose him because he's a good pilot,' Will snapped.

'Certainly his flight stats are impressive. But that's not *really* why he's here, is it?'

Will glared at Yunus and contemplated saying something harsh, but managed to keep his mouth shut.

'It's because of the Photurians, isn't it?' said Yunus triumphantly. 'Admit it. You know there are real aliens present who have nothing to do with the Transcended and you're scared that your entire narrative will fall apart.'

Now it was Will's turn to feel confused. But the eager *I-have-you-now* expression on Yunus's face rapidly turned his astonishment into

157

mirth. Up until that moment, he'd harboured a small fear that Pari might be right. Maybe Yunus was lining up some kind of threat to Mark's life. In that second, though, he'd seen Yunus for what he was – a fool. He stifled a burst of laughter.

'I'm sorry, Professor Chesterford,' he said, 'but I think we've pursued this line of discussion as far as I'm interested in going.'

'Are you *refusing* to say more?' said Yunus.

'Yes. That's exactly what I'm doing.'

Yunus glowered. 'We appear to be having a little misunderstanding of authority here,' he said. 'Do I need to remind you that I head this mission? I appreciate that you may have some bitterness over the fact that responsibility for the Tiwanaku fleet was handed to me, but I would hope that you are professional enough to overcome that and grant me the respect I'm due.

'I wish to be compassionate about your position, Captain Monet. For a man such as yourself, it can't have been easy to experience as much *failure* as you have. But the fact is that you did, and authority now resides in fresh hands. If possible, I would like us to have a clear and civilised understanding of our relationship, without animosity. Is that clear?'

Yunus stared at him, his eyes bulging slightly, his nostrils wide.

It occurred to Will how easy it would be to reach through the *Gulliver*'s security, co-opt the nearest robot and crush Yunus's scrawny neck. As usual, exercising his power would do little good and a lot of damage. Yunus's opinion would be moot within a matter of days, in any case.

Will let out a long breath. 'I hear what you're saying,' he said.

'Good,' said Yunus. 'You have convinced me, at least, that your assistance would be counterproductive. I will attempt to further matters on my own.'

'That sounds like a great idea,' said Will. 'I wish you luck. Do you have any other concerns?'

'None, thank you.'

'Terrific,' said Will. 'In that case, I wish you all the best with your refuelling.'

He dropped the connection, jumped to the home node of his sensorium and paced back and forth in the Galatean trench apartment he still used as his primary metaphor. He wouldn't have to suffer fools much longer, thank Gal. He'd break the Tiwanaku plot wide open, find his miracle and bring an end to this whole lamentable period of history. Anyone who stood in his way was likely to get their head split open. Maybe he'd even put some old ghosts to rest at the same time.

A new request icon appeared in the simulated air before him. It was Nelson. Will threw open a channel and Nelson's image appeared.

'What?' said Will.

'As soon as your ship-link closed, I thought it best to seek you out,' said Nelson. 'I heard it all via the public store and thought it likely you'd be upset.'

'That obvious, huh?'

'Indeed,' said Nelson, inclining his head. 'Your relationship with Yunus Chesterford is not so much predictable as baldly deterministic, I'm afraid.'

Will resumed his pacing. 'Why do I do it?' he asked. 'Why am I so fucking *nice*? Why do I let these people talk to me that way? Why do I let politics and bullshit affect what I do? Look what a fucking mess of IPSO it's made, and yet I still do it.'

'You know why,' said Nelson calmly. 'Both in the large and in the small. In the large, you are trying to honour the promises you made at the end of the war – not to control humanity, but to guide it. That path is always the harder one, but it is by far the most laudable. And in the small, you made sacrifices for Mark. You knew he and Yunus would not see eye to eye. You expected it and knew it would annoy you. And here you are.'

'But still, it sucks,' said Will. 'Yunus called me a failure. Would he rather I start asserting myself? Because I could do that. If that's what mankind really wants, maybe I should start giving it to them. Smashing some shit up and seeing how they like it.'

Nelson sighed. 'Will,' he said, 'we've gone over this. Let's take a look at these so-called failures that make you so anxious. You couldn't speak to the Transcended after the war because they refused to talk. Not your fault. You couldn't have children because of the mess they made of your DNA. Not your fault. You lost Rachel because her ship deliberately probed a wall of curvon-depleted space which turns out to be thousands of light-years wide. Once again, not your fault. And you failed to transform the politics of the entire human race through the force of your personality. Hardly surprising. You set out to change everything, Will, and it turns out that fixing humanity is not as easy as blowing a hole in the side of a planet. And now you're trying to claw back the one thing that stops you from feeling totally alone – your relationship with Mark – and it turns out that's not so easy, either.

'Here's the thing, Will. You can't force the universe to give you what you want. You must have figured that out by now. Does it help you to alienate Yunus just because he's ridiculous? I suggest not. In all likelihood, it makes Mark's job harder. You push yourself and others too hard, my friend. A superman you may be, but just because you were given extraordinary gifts does not mean that suddenly solving everyone else's problems is your exclusive responsibility.'

Will stared at the walls. Part of him wanted to shout back. *They didn't stuff you full of nanomachines*, he thought. *They didn't make it your job to save your species from extinction. Do you think I'll ever get away from that?* He didn't speak, though, because listening to Nelson made it clear to Will just how irrational he was being.

'You're right. Thank you, Nelson,' he said quickly, feeling none the better for the advice. 'I'm not sure what I'd do without you here.'

'Blow up more planets, I expect,' said Nelson. 'In any case, it's my pleasure. I'll put together a gently worded message for Mark and pass it on to him.'

Will nodded. 'Thank you. Again. I appreciate it.'

'Why don't you drop out to the rec room?' said Nelson. 'Devi has put some plots together about the Tiwanaku data, along with a few rather playful speculations. I think they'll be fun. Want to join us?'

'Not right now,' said Will.

Nelson shrugged. 'As you wish. I suggest you find some way to relax, though. You need it.' He winked out.

Will sat down on his home node's grassy floor, hugged his knees and wondered how he'd come to feel so alone. Nelson's words had failed to touch him. He considered restarting the memory but found he lacked the desire. He'd only feel dirty wallowing in past sins.

It took him a moment to realise there was another message request icon in his queue. This one had come in very quietly without any alert markers on it, via a directed tight-beam. He hadn't seen any sign of the *Chiyome*'s arrival but it could only be Ann. With a flutter of surprise, Will routed the connection through a private buffer that would bypass the ship's public data store and flicked the channel open. He'd half-expected her to abandon the pact as soon as they were en route.

Ann's hard gaze appeared in the video feed. 'Captain Monet,' she said. 'I'm checking in as per our agreement. How are you doing?'

'Fine,' he said, rubbing his head. 'Okay. All on course.'

Her eyes narrowed. 'You don't look fine. You look unhappy. Do you want to explain?'

Will hesitated.

'This is what we agreed,' she said. 'You give me an effective read on your mental state, I watch out for your interests in the target system. Do you still intend to honour that agreement?'

So Will explained. Short of actually admitting a specific connection to Mark, he recounted everything he'd discussed with Yunus, with growing relief. Ann listened impassively, nodding from time to time. At the end, he found himself babbling through his anger, trying to explain to her the constant strain of having been handed so many weapons that he could never in good conscience use. The sort of things he'd wanted to say to Rachel. That he should have said, but never did. When he realised he was running off at the mouth, he stopped.

'That's it,' he said, waving a virtual hand. 'It's no big deal, really. Just everyday frustration. Nothing more.'

'You know what I think?' she said. 'I think you should cut yourself some slack. You'll be busy enough when we get to the target so focus on that instead. Ignore Yunus. He's irrelevant.'

Will blinked at her. There it was – the Gordian knot of his emotions, cut. This was what Rachel used to do for him. Before that stupid fight. Before she'd left.

He deflated, his anger draining away.

'Yes,' he said quietly. 'Thank you.'

'My pleasure,' said Ann. 'Thanks for the update. For what it's worth, your *everyday frustrations* constitute the kind of pressure that would crack a normal person wide open. You're doing remarkably well, considering. Feel proud of that. Ludik out.'

It took him a moment to realise she'd shut the channel already. She, and the *Chiyome*, had vanished again. Will stared through his sensors at the featureless night around him and laughed. He couldn't see her anywhere. It shouldn't have been comforting, but it was. For no good reason at all, he felt poise rushing back into him like water.

Mark sat in his favourite chair in the lounge and replayed memories from the ship's science talks while he waited for the others. In his mind's eye, he watched Venetia expound on her theories while the image of a beaked quadrupedal monstrosity with chameleon eyes and eerily human hands revolved slowly on one of the screens.

'...but besides the Transcended, the only race we know of that reached star-faring status was the Fecund,' she was saying. 'So what does studying these creatures tell us about what might be waiting for us at Tiwanaku? Well, for starters, their social organisation was very different from ours. Fecund society revolved around the extensive use of disposable children. A single pair of clan-parents would produce tens of thousands of spawn over the course of their lives, most of which became non-reproducing workers, often surgically modified to fit specific tasks. While not strictly eusocial, there is a lot that is insect-like about Fecund society, including the way that knowledge was socially shared and integrated. Most significantly for us, it's clear that the Fecund valued life very differently from the way humans do, in fact...'

Mark checked the time. He needed to take over from Ash at the helm in less than an hour. His passengers were late, but he wasn't surprised. He'd received a warning from Nelson days ago. Apparently he'd been doing everything badly, including sitting in the lounge the wrong way. Well, fuck that. Where else was he supposed to sit while he went over the mission science? Or perhaps he was supposed to randomly use chairs further from the wireless node just to mix it up for the benefit of others.

Nelson had pointed out that he'd missed all the talks. Not missed, Mark wanted to say: avoided. Still, Yunus and his little gang appeared to imagine it mattered. It was ridiculous. How could he possibly avoid learning about them all? He hadn't been able to escape them for a month now and their quirks had become grindingly apparent.

Yunus and Citra had the objectionable habit of praying up the lounge, as if it was their solemn duty to advertise on behalf of the Reconsiderist Lite-Church. Zoe, in contrast, spent most of her time frowning into her contacts and tapping furiously at her touchboard, whether people were praying next to her or not. That was, of course, when Ash wasn't chatting her up.

When Sam wasn't blocking access to the ship's exercise space, he was usually to be found sitting cross-legged in the lounge, ostentatiously reading from an ancient physical copy of Sun Tzu's *The Art of War*. Ash hid in his room when he wasn't trying to schmooze people and Venetia just watched everyone when they thought she wasn't looking. For some of the supposedly most brilliant minds in human space, they looked like a fairly lame bunch to Mark. Nevertheless, he'd reluctantly convened a meeting. It was a good time for it. Tomorrow they were scheduled to rendezvous with the watchers at the edge of the Tiwanaku System.

As the first of them began to descend the ladder to the lounge, Mark shut down the memory. He suspected they'd all been muttering with each other in the corridor so they could present some kind of a united front.

'Good morning,' he said, aiming for brisk professionalism. He received reserved expressions from his assembled shipmates. 'Thank you all for coming. As you're undoubtedly aware, tomorrow is a big day and I want to make sure I've understood your needs correctly for the mission phase that follows. My intention is to check in with each of you in turn to make sure I have everything straight. Does that work for you?'

'It's a little late,' said Yunus, 'but the gesture is appropriate. We're amenable to discussion, of course.'

'Terrific,' said Mark. He turned to Sam. 'Overcaptain Shah, do you mind if I start with you?'

Sam spread his hands.

'As I understand it,' Mark said, 'your primary concern for our insertion into Tiwanaku is that if these *Photurians* are actually a sect ruse, it's unclear what the motivation behind them is. A charade like that couldn't possibly last, which implies a short-term objective rather than a longer one. So you're concerned that the entire purpose of the event was to draw Fleet attention, exactly as it has done. Hence, we need to treat each event that draws us deeper into the system with extreme suspicion. Scanners should be on full sweep the entire time, and we should have an array of tactical predictors going, treating the insertion as a military engagement to ensure that it doesn't actually become one. Is that a fair summary?'

163

'That's about the size of it, yes,' said Sam, looking unimpressed.

'Lovely,' said Mark. He turned to Zoe. 'Doctor Tamar, your main concern is that the Photurian warp-burst signature looks physically impossible. It doesn't conform to any known decay pattern, and without tapping the galaxy's curvon flow, there's no way it could possibly generate the spatial distortion burst necessary to create a warp envelope. You and I have already discussed possible ways that signature might be faked, but you'd ideally like us to get close enough to their machinery for a thorough scan. We should be sampling at the highest possible rate while observing Photurian warp so as to distinguish between true warp pulses and artefacts. If possible, you'd like a physical sample of one of their drives. Correct?'

Zoe nodded.

'I'll see what we can do,' said Mark. He turned to Citra next. 'Your talk concentrated on what we might be able to learn from a valid Photurian biosample. You point out that a simple test of their base-pair lexicon will tell us immediately and unambiguously whether we're dealing with a new form of life or an impostor. That leaves us, of course, with the question of how to collect such a sample without exposing the *Gulliver* to danger.'

'My talk covered a lot more than that, Captain Ruiz.'

'I'm well aware of that. What I'm trying to do here is summarise your needs. Is there anything else you'd like me to try for while we're in there?'

Citra shook her head.

'And how about the other Professor Chesterford? Yunus, for you, adherence to the diplomatic protocol you've invented is paramount. We should assume that humanity has transgressed into Photurian territory and that the Photurians are our peers. We should behave as visitors to sacred ground and make no assumptions as to what is safe to look at, sample or visit.'

'We're still debating this,' said Venetia. 'I don't think that approach holds water.'

Yunus scowled at her. 'It's the most cautious strategy.'

Venetia rolled her eyes. 'You saw the video dump that was waiting for us at Gore-Daano,' she said. 'The alien machines started by packing up the colony and porting it to space. Then they gave up and started milling about. I'm more convinced than ever that your Photurians are like broken robots or confused eusocial insects.'

'Are you proposing we walk into a potential first contact assuming we're meeting with broken robots?' said Yunus.

'I'm not proposing anything at this point other than keeping an open mind,' said Venetia. 'For starters, the way Mark has framed it, it's pretty obvious that we can't be totally respectful and collect the data we want at the same time. I think that's sort of his point.'

Mark smiled. 'Thank you for listening, Doctor Sharp,' said Mark. 'However, I propose you leave the solution of that conundrum to me. And while we're on the subject, I confess you're the one person whose needs I don't fully understand yet. I enjoyed your talk on the Fecund, and the whole idea of sentience frameworks, but you didn't articulate a specific mission agenda.'

'You're right,' she said. 'I did not. But I might still think of something.'

'I'll make sure to keep a comms channel open, in that case,' said Mark. 'Just let me know if you do.' He surveyed the room. 'Did I miss anything? Would anyone like to add any thoughts?'

Zoe raised a hand. 'Sure. I'd have preferred it if you'd actually come to my talk rather than just nerding it afterwards. We still hardly know you.'

'My apologies,' said Mark. 'I meant to spare you my company, not hurt your feelings. I see now that that was a mistake. I'm truly sorry. Anything else?'

A leaden silence fell. It sat there until Yunus broke it.

'Captain Ruiz,' he said, 'this isn't easy, but I think we need to be realistic. You've had weeks now, and at no time have you shown the necessary level of engagement that would convince us you're a suitable commanding officer for this ship. We're flying into a very uncertain situation and need to feel absolutely confident that we have the best man at the helm. You haven't given us reason to believe that, which is why we're asking you to step down.'

The silence fell again.

Mark's brow creased in astonishment. 'I'm sorry. You're asking *what*?'

Sam spread his hands. 'Look, Mark,' he said, 'it's great that you've got us all here, but from tomorrow onwards we have to be functioning

165

like a team, not one vid-star and a room full of groupies. Ash could have taken those shifts during the talks. You know that. And now Ash is better informed about the upcoming risks than you are. I don't know about everyone else here,' he said, looking around, 'but I'd feel more comfortable with him in the hot seat tomorrow. He at least feels like part of the team.'

'You have to be joking,' said Mark. 'You want to take me out of command? But I haven't done anything.'

'And that's precisely the point,' said Yunus.

Mark glanced around at their closed faces and began to realise just how screwed he was. His one chance for career redemption had disappeared already and he hadn't even noticed. So much for hiding away to avoid pissing anyone off. He'd managed to achieve that without even opening his mouth.

'You need a unanimous passenger vote to unseat a ro-captain.' The words sounded pathetic and defensive to his ears even as he said them.

'Which is why we all agreed to come. As the only other non-voting crew member, Ash has already been informed.'

'Look,' said Mark, raising a placating hand, 'I'm an Omega roboteer, for crying out loud. You all know that, but maybe you don't know what it *means*. It's a curse as well as a blessing. I've got digital access to information that makes a lot of human interaction irrelevant. That's why roboteers tend to be bad with people. Ash may be an exception, I admit, but I'm not. When I talk to ordinary people, I either have to deliberately screen information from myself or pretend I don't have it. I didn't come to those talks because I didn't want to patronise or infuriate anyone.'

'The fact remains,' said Yunus, 'that we have a roboteer aboard who *does* have social skills.'

'Wait,' said Mark. 'Let me finish. I know I've got that limitation, so I haven't been hiding from you all that time, I've been compensating. I didn't just watch your presentations once – I watched all of them eight times. I spent my rest hours doing follow-up analysis on every topic you raised. I had analysis SAPs combing your prior work and integrating subminds for my use during the upcoming insertion. There isn't a paper any of you have published that I don't currently have SAP-memorised. I didn't come along to ask you questions because I already knew the answers.'

166

He couldn't tell whether they believed him or not. Either way, it was clear they didn't want it to be true. He felt his hackles rising.

'Here's a question,' he said. 'This one's for all of you. Did *any* of you watch one of those presentations again after the fact?' He glanced around again, trying to meet their evasive eyes. 'Anyone?'

He knew the answer, of course. And they knew he knew. He could tell he wasn't making friends, though. Only Venetia wasn't frowning. She appeared to be hiding a smirk.

'And it's precisely that kind of adversarial attitude that will ruin this mission unless we do something about it,' said Yunus. 'I'm sorry, Captain Ruiz. Your technical skills may be impressive, but this mission calls for a deft, socially aware hand.' He looked to the others. 'I call for Captain Ruiz be removed from his position on the basis of unsuitability for the post.'

He raised an imperious finger. Mark's heart sank as he watched other hands go up – first Citra Chesterford's, then Sam's.

'I'm sorry, Mark,' said Sam. 'It's for the best. I'll still support you when we get back to HQ.'

Two hands stayed down: Venetia and Zoe.

Sam turned to the physicist. She stared at her feet.

'Zoe, this is a serious matter,' he said softly. 'You need to have total confidence in Mark not to register a vote right now.'

'I just think it's a bit mean,' said Zoe. 'We're going to kick him out of command and trash his record because he failed to come to some slideshows?'

'That's not the point,' said Sam. 'Think about those things you told me earlier. About that corridor on Triton.'

Mark's cheeks flushed.

'I'm asking you point-blank if you can have total confidence in this man tomorrow,' said Sam.

Zoe's hand crept upwards. Her eyes did not. Sam turned next to Venetia.

'Doctor Sharp, I don't think I have to explain the weight of this moment to you. May I ask you why your hand is still down?'

'Me?' said Venetia cheerfully. 'Well, it's because I *do* have total confidence in the captain, Sam. I was undecided when I came in here, but he's addressed every one of my concerns quite adequately.' She tucked a strand of straight black hair behind one ear and looked pleased with herself.

'I'm sorry?' said Yunus. His face had turned an unhealthy beetroot colour.

'Captain Ruiz,' said Venetia, 'could you tell me the title of Professor Chesterford's third linguistics paper?'

'Sure,' said Mark. 'That would be "A Comparison of Semantic Network Structures Derived from Fecund Hierarchical Glyph Language Nine".' He stared at her with a fluttering realisation that someone might actually be on his side.

'That's correct, is it not, Professor?'

'Parroting technical information doesn't prove anything,' Yunus said sharply. 'A research SAP could do it just as well.'

'You're right,' said Venetia. 'So can you tell me in your own words, Captain, what were the main criticisms of that paper, and your opinions on them?'

Mark tried to resist grinning. Against all expectations, he'd suddenly started enjoying himself.

'Of course. You were the most vocal critic, Doctor, as I recall. You had issues with the specific mapping technique Professor Chesterford used to derive those networks. You claimed it lacked foundation and didn't take account of the Nazca out-system data-core findings. My guess is you chose to ask me about this particular paper because of the way that whole controversy was resolved. The entire issue became moot a couple of years later, I believe, when Yingling Bo's work on SAP-simulated Fecund worker-groups was published. Your concern is probably that without the same level of deep simulation, making assumptions about any language patterns we encounter at Tiwanaku is likely to be dangerously biased due to our own semantic priors, just as it was then.'

'A fair answer,' said Venetia, 'and a thoughtful one.' She turned to give Yunus a wicked smile. 'You see, you should have listened to his explanation a little more closely. Ash isn't the best-trained pilot on this ship any more. Mark is.'

'This is beside the point,' Yunus snapped. 'We're not contesting his capacity for recall but his ability to participate as a member of the team.'

'And I'd be able to get behind that concern, Yunus, dear,' Venetia replied, 'if it wasn't so transparently politically motivated. You think you're in some kind of contest with Will Monet, a position made obvious by the fact that you've brought his name up at coffee every day since you talked to him. And you see Mark as his weapon. But if you actually wanted to involve Mark with the team there are a dozen different ways you could have done it, none of which you tried. So rather than messing with the ship's command structure, I propose we let Captain Ruiz absorb this lesson and get back to work. I'd be surprised if he isn't *extremely* attentive when we enter that system tomorrow.'

Yunus erupted to his feet. He looked daggers at Venetia for a long second and then clomped to the ladder. Citra took an extra moment to give Mark a withering, disdainful look before following him. Sam sighed and rubbed his eyes.

'I hope you know what you're doing, Doctor Sharp,' he said. 'That's not how I would have run things, but it's your call. Good luck, Mark, I'm confident you'll do your best.'

He heaved himself up the rungs, shaking his head.

Zoe stood, too, but lingered, squinting into space, on the brink of saying something.

'I don't blame you,' Mark said quickly. 'Not for a moment. They put you in a tough spot. I'd have probably done the same thing.'

She looked at him and a quick, fragile smile blossomed on her face. Something in Mark's chest squeezed tight as he tried to return it but it was too late. She was gone already, swarming up the ladder after the others.

Mark turned his gaze to Venetia and found her watching him closely with a dry smile curving one corner of her mouth. He'd given her less attention than she deserved. He'd been too caught up in his opinion of everyone else.

'Thank you,' he said. 'I don't know what to say. Why did you...' He couldn't finish the question.

'I thought you deserved another chance,' she said, shrugging. '*And* I knew your mother.'

Mark's face fell. 'You knew Bella Ruiz?'

It sounded unlikely. Why would a high-powered scientist like Venetia know a part-time molecular engineer with a second-rate degree from Earth?

'No,' said Venetia. 'I'm talking about your *other* mother.'

169

Mark instantly saw the truth behind the joke. She meant Rachel Bock, of course. Rachel had spent her whole career in exoscience. She and Venetia must have been crossing paths for years. He should have guessed it from day one.

'She wouldn't have had much patience for this lot,' said Venetia, her eyes sliding to the top of the ladder. Then she fixed him with a hard look, her smile dropping away. 'Listen, Mark, I'm as surprised as you are that we're on this ship together. I had no idea until I showed up for the shuttle briefing. So don't get me wrong, I didn't do this out of some sense of allegiance. I did it because I thought you deserved better. But you need to up your game. People like Sam and Yunus thrive on attention. Give them as much as you can. Kowtow. Laugh at their jokes. And don't take a single thing they have to say seriously. Stick to that formula and I'll make sure you come out of this trip in one piece. Got it?'

Mark nodded mutely.

'Good,' she said. 'Nice job with the science research, by the way. That paper of Yunus's was a stinker. You were very diplomatic.'

She winked at him as she headed out. Mark just stared. He actually had an ally. Who'd have guessed?

6: APPROACH

6.1: ANN

When the *Gulliver* and *Ariel Two* warped in to meet with the observation ship outside the Tiwanaku System, the *Chiyome* flew alongside, silent and attentive.

It had been a tense, dull flight. Sam's hand-picked crew were polite, professional company. Ann had tried to build a bond with them, but as the days creaked into weeks, the sense of distance between her and most of the others had deepened.

The only bright spot in the trip had been the occasional opportunities to work with Kuril. The rest of the crew watched their unexpected friendship develop without comment. Now, at least, they'd all have something to do instead of stewing and feeling out each other's loyalties. This close to Tiwanaku, the *Ariel Two* needed to be monitored constantly. Ann felt glad of the change, even through her fear.

The observation ship sent from New Panama, the IPS *Samyaza*, had chosen a spot just beyond the heliopause, far enough out to make detection by the Nems statistically impossible but still close enough for surveillance. Ann tuned in when the comms channel from the *Gulliver* opened.

'Good morning, *Samyaza*,' said Yunus Chesterford. Ann could see the diplomatic team clustered in the *Gulliver*'s faux-opulent lounge and immediately felt jealous of their space.

'We're ready for insertion,' said Yunus. 'Do you have anything for us?'

The feed from the *Samyaza* showed the round, earnest face of the chief observer, Meleta Keth, with beige crash-padding behind.

'Plenty,' said Meleta. 'First, and most significantly, we've witnessed two exit events on the same bearing.'

'Fascinating!' said Yunus. 'Information about the origin of our visitors, perhaps?'

Of course, Meleta had seen no such thing. And even if there had been an exit, Meleta's team wouldn't have been able to trace it. The Nems' warp system made that almost impossible.

Meleta sent across the coordinates. Ann immediately recognised the local vector for Snakepit. No change to Phase Two, then – something else to be thankful for. She watched Yunus's eyes light up.

'That's outside IPSO space!' he said.

'Indeed it is,' said Meleta. 'Which surprised us, I can tell you. It's highly suggestive. There's a star on that bearing on the local shell, too. G-type.'

'This is momentous!' said Yunus. 'That could be their homeworld.'

'We're trying not to assume too much,' said Meleta, 'but I grant you it's exciting. Secondly, though, you should know that there's been a change in the aliens' activity.' She passed across a video feed, then added, 'The system now contains more than four million drones and a low-density cloud of quasi-industrial by-products about six light-minutes wide. Orbital factories have been churning stuff out at a crazy rate.'

The image showed a dense belt of material around Tiwanaku Four, far too heterogeneous to analyse at that distance. Still, it gave Ann pause. They were looking at a *very* active reflection phase. That particular Nem behaviour clearly hadn't scaled linearly with target size. She'd have to keep a close eye on it during the hours that followed.

'There's also activity down on the planet's surface,' said Meleta, 'but it's hard to classify. We're not close enough for a proper look.'

'This is all interesting stuff,' said Sam, 'but we have to remember that it could just be a smokescreen. Nothing in this data so far rules that out.'

He was, Ann thought, a gifted actor. Had she not known, she'd have assumed Sam was completely on the level.

'And lastly and most weirdly,' said Meleta, 'there's some sporadic weapons fire in-system. We're not seeing a pattern to it, mind you. It looks random.'

'Some kind of interior conflict, perhaps,' said Yunus. 'Maybe our friends have factions, or are part of a militaristic society.'

'Or it's weapons testing,' said Sam. 'In any case, if people are shooting, that's an extra reason for us to stay on our guard.'

'Agreed,' said Yunus.

'I'm sending you the full observation package,' said Meleta, 'and forwarding a copy to the *Ariel Two*. Good luck in there.'

'Thank you, *Samyaza*,' said Yunus. 'Keep an eye on us. We're going to make history.' He was grinning as he flicked off the comm.

The *Gulliver* adjusted course and headed cautiously in-system. The *Ariel Two* prowled along behind, as subtle as a tyrannosaur.

Now they had to wait. The *Samyaza* had better sensors than the *Chiyome* and would release a coded ping on a League band when they were confident it was safe.

'Looks like Chesterford's thoroughly taken the bait,' said Jaco as they lurked there. 'It's hard not to enjoy that. He imagines he's going to win a trading pact for Earth or something.' He chuckled. 'Yet more money for the grasping thieves he represents. It doesn't even occur to him that he's ushering in the end of his own vile kleptocracy. That's fitting, somehow, don't you think? It's times like this when the significance of what we're doing really hits home. It's the other shoe finally dropping for those bastards at long last.'

Nothing underlined Ann's discomfort more than this – her relationship with Jaco Brinsen. Ann steered clear of political discussions, while Jaco courted them. For the entire flight, he'd claimed whatever soapbox shipboard conversation supplied and used it to orate about the righteousness of their work. It appeared to be his way of rationalising the dark deeds ahead.

Ann didn't want moral reassurance. Their job made her sick. Their choices might be driven by unavoidable mathematical facts, but that didn't make what they had to do any more laudable.

'That's enough, Mr Brinsen,' she said. 'Let's not get too proud of ourselves. Nobody planning to kill millions should be too smug. It's unseemly, wouldn't you agree?'

Jaco fell quiet for a minute before replying. 'You're right, obviously, Captain. We should avoid unseemly behaviour at all costs and stick to the mission plan, right? Just do our jobs and try not to let it affect us too much.'

This was a veiled criticism. Of the crew, only Jaco knew she'd been checking in with Will Monet at their fuelling stars, in contravention of both their Fleet orders and the League plan. As her first officer, he had access to all the same comms records that she did.

Ann let it slide. 'Exactly, Mr Brinsen. Adherence to the commander's intent, to the best of our abilities.'

'Ma'am,' said Zoti, her sensor-jockey, 'I'm reading an encrypted local ping from the *Samyaza*.'

'Good,' said Ann. 'Open a channel on tight-beam, please.'

'Already on it, ma'am.'

Meleta's face reappeared in a new window in her display.

'*Chiyome* here,' said Ann. 'I don't like the look of that reflection activity. Anything else we need to be watching for?'

'No, ma'am,' said Meleta. 'I don't believe so. The machines are behaving normally but at the high end of the envelope. We've run a few extra scenarios to be sure – I'm sending you the results now. What we're seeing here is still very similar to what happened after the operation at Nazca. It's scary to look at, but it's within anticipated parameters. It does mean we need to keep our eye on the final ingested target size, of course,' Meleta added. 'Every extra human sample they get hold of takes us closer to the edge of that envelope. Human costs should be kept to an absolute minimum.'

In other words, try not to get people killed. That would be tricky, of course. The whole point of bringing Will here was to solicit a violent response from him. In the seconds and minutes that followed, some very swift action would be required to make sure that situation didn't spiral out of control.

'My goal in any case,' said Ann. 'Do you have the package?'

'Sending it now,' said Meleta. 'Drone should be with you in five.'

Ann watched as the tiny stealth-drone containing the all-important biomaterial made its way between the ships. When it finally came to enforcing Will Monet's compliance, this little package would do more than an entire fleet of starships. She feared the stuff and wished she didn't have to carry it on her ship.

'Zoti, a reading on the package, please, as soon as you're able.'

'I have it, ma'am. The material has about six days of stability left, which should be enough.'

'A word from Snakepit on that,' said Meleta. 'The bioscience team wanted to stress the need for extreme caution. So far as they know, that stuff won't interact with ordinary human tissue, but they can't make any promises. The denaturing process is still in the experimental stage. They say that the genetic code in those cells is so dense there may be petabytes hiding in there that they haven't noticed yet.'

'In that case we'll only use it if we have to,' said Ann. 'And on that note, I should be off before my charges get themselves in trouble. If this place is anything like Nazca, that won't take very long.'

Meleta managed an awkward smile. 'Rather you than me,' she said. 'We'll be thinking of you. Please be careful.'

'Thank you, Meleta,' said Ann. 'See you at the Pit in a few days, I hope.'

Ann charged her engines and hurried off after the other ships. She couldn't afford to fall too far behind. The Nems might kick off a defensive surge from the moment they saw company. From this point onwards, every second counted.

6.2: MARK

As Mark headed into the Tiwanaku System, Ash came onto the bridge and took up his position. The mission plan required that they have the subcaptain on standby, which made perfect sense to Mark. Whether headed towards first contact or into the jaws of a sect trap, a second pair of eyes was likely to help.

Ash's avatar appeared in the helm-arena. Mark had swapped out the Zen garden for a direct view of the system ahead, overlaid with colour-coded threat data from Sam's tactical SAPs. Ash's avatar stood at the centre of that mess of ruddy icons and looked grim.

Mark turned away from his scans to face his ex-friend. 'You okay?'

'Fine,' said Ash. 'Just a little apprehensive, that's all.'

'Understandable. Want to take over the long-range-threat scanning?'

Ash cracked a smile. 'You bet.'

'Between you and me,' said Mark, 'all the weird shit the observers reported sounds like a smokescreen. This still feels like a set-up. I'm just waiting for the shooting to start.'

'Sounds reasonable,' said Ash, turning to face his displays. 'I'm not looking forward to this regardless.' He said nothing for a few seconds, then added, 'I heard about what happened with the others, by the way. Sorry about that.'

'Not a problem,' said Mark. 'I'm not blaming you. Like you said before, we're all professionals here.'

'Yes,' said Ash quietly. 'I guess we are.'

Mark opened the gated link to the lounge, pulling up a video window. 'Checking diplomacy team feed,' he said. The data connection to the lounge had to be routed through the many layers of the Vartian Institute's secure cut-out bus. It took a surprising amount of work. 'Do you have my view on the bubble? You should see the helm-arena on screen one and an in-system schematic on two.'

The lounge displays had been set up to provide a window onto the *Gulliver*'s virtual space along with whatever data the team called for. Mark disliked giving them eyes into his world, but at least this set-up gave him eyes into theirs.

'We do,' said Sam. 'We're good to go.'

Mark might have been imagining it, but he thought he heard a kind of clipped frustration in Sam's tone. Yesterday's tension hadn't resolved. Still, this was the moment they'd all been waiting for and Mark intended to ace it.

'Great,' he said. 'Fine sensors going live in five.'

Almost as soon as Mark activated the fine-sensor mesh, he discovered the broadcasts. Signal-dense low-power transmissions saturated the entire in-system region. They were all the same, and they all sounded like garbage.

Mark forwarded an audio stream to the lounge. A scrambled mess of music, static, data and garbled voices filled the air. Yunus looked delighted, Zoe appalled.

'What the hell is that?' she said, holding her hands over her ears. 'How many channels are you playing at once?'

'Just the one. But they're all like that. As far as my subminds can tell, it's a mix of DNA sequences, pop songs, machine code, Bible readings, enzyme pathways and all kinds of other crap.'

'But why?' she said, wrinkling her nose. 'What's it for?'

'Is there anything recognisably alien in there?' said Venetia. 'All I'm hearing so far is mashed human content.'

'Not unless you count the mashing algorithm,' said Mark.

'Could this be an attempt to communicate with us already?' said Yunus.

'Unlikely,' said Mark. 'There's no evidence we've been spotted. We're still too far away – light-lag alone pretty much rules out dialogue.'

'So this is internal traffic,' said Citra. 'But why would they be sending each other DNA snippets?' She started working feverishly at her touchboard, picking the message apart.

'As yet unclear,' said Mark. 'I'm tracking a few outlier objects from the swarm that are close enough for us to look at. They appear to be artificial. Zooming in on one now.'

Mark maxed out the *Gulliver*'s telescope resolution and took his first look at one of the alien artefacts. The scowling face of the Prophet Sanchez filled the screen.

'Jesus!' said Ash. His avatar jumped about three metres across the virtual bridge. 'I didn't see *that* coming.'

Of all the things Mark had imagined they might find, the sour countenance of the man who had kicked off humanity's first interstellar war was not one of them. The head appeared to be sculpted out of dirty ice and was approximately half a kilometre on each side. It tumbled in the lonely darkness, snarling at the stars.

'What should we make of this?' he asked the science team. 'Are the aliens Truists?'

'It certainly suggests this is sect activity,' said Sam. 'I just didn't expect to see evidence so soon.'

'I disagree,' said Venetia. 'Look at the styling on that head. See those hair curls? The iconography here is consistent with the Truth Reborn group, the one we suspected of founding the initial colony. Which makes me wonder – why would an invading group decorate the star system with their victims' religious material? Or are you suggesting that Truth Reborn faked the invasion to protect their own colony?'

'Okay,' said Sam, 'so maybe that thing's out there because the invaders trashed a temple and tossed it into an elliptical orbit. I grant you we'll have to look at more artefacts before we reach any conclusions.'

Mark had read about Truth Reborn. It was one of the weirder groups Earth had turned out, but was well funded by its parent sect and hugely successful. Each Flag colony they founded had its own Sanchez clone grown from reconstituted genetic material from the great man himself.

Unsurprisingly, the clones lacked independent neural function and only spoke to make religious proclamations on behalf of the sect.

The creepy thing about them was that they weren't life-sized. The sect manufactured them like little Buddha dolls which sat on shrines. Each one was about the size of a three-year-old, but ancient-looking and fierce. Mark could easily imagine such a thing scaring the pants off a congregation of the Following. What a giant replica of one was doing way out here was anybody's guess.

'Scanning for another target,' he told them.

He zoomed in on a new artefact. A rounded triangular structure the size of a tower-block loomed out of the night. It had a shiny, wet-looking mottled surface and flickered occasionally with spastic electricity.

'What the hell is *that*?' said Zoe. 'Is that a statue of *faecal matter*?'

'No,' said Citra. 'I can answer that one. It's a liver.'

'Actually,' said Mark, 'I think it's a drone reshaped into a human liver.' He passed them a spectroscopic analysis, disbelieving what it told him even as he did so. 'Note that this thing has remnants of warp inducers, and appears to still have antimatter containment running.'

Zoe shook her head. 'I don't get it. Why disguise a drone as a liver? That's the craziest thing I've ever heard of.'

He shared her confusion. Whatever was going on here, it didn't feel right.

'Targeting again,' he said. 'Scanning for consistent themes and patterns this time.'

The *Gulliver*'s cameras swept the system. One by one, a bewildering array of objects appeared, most of them made out of repurposed munitions twisted and squeezed to resemble everything from body parts to domestic robots.

Mark found what at first appeared to be a survival bubble filled with human corpses. On closer examination, the bodies proved to be four times life-size and fashioned out of frozen hydraulic solution from a Fecund nestship. Their perfectly duplicated faces bore expressions of terror and agony. A model of a domestic cleaner robot he found turned out to be made from compressed human meat, partially carbonised. Grotesque hybrid figures, half-human, half-machine, hung lost between the worlds, like disused mannequins from the staging of a nightmare.

It was as if, Mark thought, someone had taken a medieval artist's depiction of hell and rendered it in space on an unimaginable scale.

'It feels like we're being mocked,' Mark told Ash over their private channel. 'Someone's fucking with us. I don't like it.'

Ash didn't reply.

Mark turned his attention back to the swarm. 'There's still no evidence we've been spotted,' he told the team. 'There's a lot of drone traffic in here, and none of it has changed course since we arrived. All that clutter around the colony world? That's drones. I'm seeing some warp flicker, yet we're not even getting sensor bounce off the hull. It's as if they're not interested in us.'

As they closed on the swarm and the planet it enveloped, a team of Mark's sensor SAPs came back with some digitally resolved images of activity from the surface. Mark posted them on to the team in the lounge.

They showed odd nodes of activity surrounded by what looked like grounded drones. They appeared to be industrial centres of some sort, except they weren't obviously making anything. The contents of the human colony buildings had been dragged out onto the sand and arranged in aimless spirals or long, meandering lines.

'I need a deep sweep on that atmosphere,' said Citra. 'Look for unusual biomarkers.'

Mark refocused the sensors and posted their data feed to her view.

'I'm not seeing any,' he said. 'Just your ordinary Mars-Plus— No, wait. What the hell is *that*? Is that biological or industrial?'

He sent Citra the molecular profile of some high-atmosphere residue hovering above the equator. The *Gulliver*'s analytical SAPs couldn't make head or tail of it.

'They're long chain molecules of some sort,' he said. 'That's about as much as I can tell you.'

'They're not matching anything in my database,' said Citra, her eyes feverish with interest. 'Which is an excellent start. But this could just be noise. We need to get closer. Much closer.'

'Wait,' said Zoe. 'First can you show us more data on the drone cloud, please? What I'm seeing here is confusing. These things can't possibly be functional.'

Mark called up a suite of engineering SAPs and blackboarded them together to examine the dense cloud of flickering vehicles. Many of them had been so deformed that they could no longer warp effectively.

'But that data must be wrong!' said Zoe. 'These don't match the scans made by the *Reynard*. And that unusual warp signature is gone!'

Just then, a group of three drones set upon one of their observation targets, scorching it with g-ray pulses. With the lone drone disabled, the others sliced it into pieces with scything blasts from scavenging lasers and scooped up the remains. In seconds it was gone.

'What the fuck was that?' said Mark. 'Are these things *feeding* off each other?'

He surveyed the drone swarm with renewed alarm and ran a second round of analyses, looking for predation patterns. Before they intercepted the swarm, it'd be useful to know just how violent it was likely to get.

The SAP came back with a confused mishmash of readings. The drone traffic was neither exclusively random, predatory nor organised, but a confused mix of all three. He saw reports of drones modifying themselves or each other, and occasionally, for no apparent reason, self-destructing.

'I guess now we know what the weapons fire is about,' muttered Ash.

'Okay,' Mark said to the science team. 'I admit I'm changing my opinion. This place isn't human. I can't think of a single group in human space weird enough to invent all this.'

'It doesn't look alien either, though,' said Venetia. 'Everything we're seeing here has a human origin. It looks like a psychotic, almost parodic rehashing of the Earther colony that was here when the Photurians arrived.'

'So long as you discount the atmospheric data,' said Citra. 'Which we shouldn't.'

'The rehashing may be important,' said Yunus. 'Maybe they're reaching out to us. They anticipated our arrival and this is their way of saying hello.'

Mark could hear the excitement in Yunus's voice. Whatever was actually going on in the system, he was loving it. For Yunus, encountering the unknown was apparently enough.

'As your ship's exopsychologist,' said Venetia sternly, 'I have to absolutely disagree. That's anthropocentric confirmation bias. You're seeing what you want to see. Where are the open comms channels? Where are the attempts at symbolic language? Let me ask you this: what kind of person takes something apart and then puts the pieces back together in random combinations?'

'You mean scientists?' said Zoe.

'That's right,' said Venetia. 'If anything, we're being analysed here, not spoken to. Think about it: we've got models and samples at different levels of representation and attempts to mix them. We've got randomised reassembly, both in message and physicalised format. One way to look at this mess is as a kind of actualised dream or filtering process. I can't help but wonder if we're seeing a single intelligence here that's using the entire star system as a cognition blackboard.'

'But what for?' said Zoe. 'If we're looking at something that can form a system-wide intelligence, why in all the worlds would it bother to attack us? And why would it even be struggling to understand us at all? It didn't take the Transcended an hour. They did it all in a single software incursion.'

'I have no idea,' said Venetia.

Zoe shook her head as if appalled by the lack of order to it all. 'Why this system? Why now?' she said.

'Of course they're trying to understand us,' said Yunus. 'That's a given. We invaded their territory. They've never seen anything like us before. They're figuring us out.'

'Bullshit!' said Venetia.

Yunus sighed at her. 'You said yourself you had no idea why they attacked. That's an answer for you.'

'There's a difference between *an* answer and the *right* answer,' said Venetia.

'And we lack the information to assess in any case!' said Yunus, throwing up his hands. 'The only thing that matters is that we choose the safe interpretation – the one that's least likely to create a disaster for the human race. We proceed with the utmost respect because anything else is madness. It's time to invoke the diplomatic protocol and hail them.'

'That's the *safe* option?' said Venetia. 'In case you hadn't noticed, this entire system is full of several million cannibalistic warp-munitions.'

'Won't you please shut up and let my husband do his job?' said Citra. 'I mean, what else is supposed to happen here? Is your plan for the diplomacy ship *not* to engage in diplomacy?'

'Shouldn't we carry out a little more research before making ourselves known?' said Mark.

'What do you imagine the watchers at the edge of the system have been doing for the last month, Ruiz?' Yunus snapped. 'We have their data already. Are a few more minutes of prevaricating honestly going to make a difference?'

'Mark,' said Sam, 'why don't you ready a comms channel for Professor Chesterford? And keep the engines warm. *Really* warm.'

As the *Gulliver* slid into the shifting haze of the drone swarm, Mark grimaced to himself and prepped the comms-buffer. Yunus inserted a simple audio message, mimicking the style the Photurians had used in their initial assault.

'We are humanity. We come in peace. We wish to talk.'

With grim reluctance, Mark forwarded it to the transmitter array and pumped it towards Tiwanaku Four. The Photurian response was almost immediate. It came back on the same channel, audio only, delivered by the voice of a human child. The accent was Earther, Tigerbelt – New Bangkok, perhaps.

'We will talk,' it said serenely. 'Bring all your people to the surface of the planet.'

Yunus laughed in delight.

Sam blinked in surprise. 'I'm not reassured,' he said.

6.3: WILL

Will watched the camera feeds as they bore down on the drone swarm surrounding the occupied colony. Whatever was going on here, it wasn't a scam, or at least not the kind he'd expected. The sects simply didn't have the resources or imagination to create something this wasteful and random. On the other hand, every alien site and memory he'd seen when he encountered the Transcended had one thing in common – purpose – and this place didn't appear to have that, either.

From the carefully targeted puzzles to the borrowed experiences in unfamiliar bodies, everything the Transcended had shown him was designed to broaden his perspective. In contrast, the senseless display of symbols and artefacts here just left him feeling lost.

'Who'd do this?' he asked himself. 'What's it all for?'

Nelson watched from beside him on the *Ariel Two*'s bridge.

'I'm starting to rule out human origin,' he said, scanning the swarm for the fifth time. 'Could this be another kind of a Transcended test?'

'I can't think of a justification,' said Will. 'This place isn't a puzzle. It's just nuts.'

He listened in as the *Gulliver* sent out their message to the swarm and brought his weapons systems as close to full readiness as he could without them being visible to a direct scan. The simple, straightforward reply it received surprised him just as much as the surreal junk that had preceded it.

We will talk. Bring all your people to the surface of the planet.

He waited for the *Gulliver*'s team to compose a reply and regretted afresh that he'd let Yunus Chesterford take the diplomatic lead. The mission plan called for Will to play a passive role until he had justification to act otherwise, which meant sitting and listening. He wasn't sure he could stand it.

'You want to meet us in person?' came Yunus's voice from the *Gulliver*.

'Yes,' said the swarm.

Will zeroed in on the origin of the response. It appeared to be coming from a loose mass of orbital machinery built around one of the Flags' suntap stations.

'Why isn't he using a fucking video channel?' Will muttered to Nelson. 'Politeness, or something else? I want to know where that voice is coming from.'

'We need reassurances,' said Yunus. 'Can you tell us why you attacked this colony?'

'You attacked the body,' said the swarm. 'We are punishment.'

Another pause while the diplomatic team deliberated.

'We did not attack you,' Yunus assured the swarm.

'Clearly you did, as we are here.'

'When and how did that happen?'

'We do not know how to make this answer yet,' said the swarm. 'Bring your people to us.'

'Wow, *that* sounds inviting,' Will muttered.

He set his sensors to make another deep scan of the alien machines, scrambling for clues as to what was going on. At least the other drones weren't moving to surround them. They appeared indifferent to the ships sliding through their midst.

'We are uncertain,' said Yunus. 'What are your intentions regarding the human race?'

'We have no intentions.'

'Then what do you plan to do next?'

'Learn to defend the body. Repair the body.'

'Where is the body?' Yunus asked.

'We do not know how to make this answer yet. Bring your people to us.'

Will struggled to contain himself. 'Ask about the voice!' he shouted into the air of the *Ariel Two*'s bridge. 'Why does it sound like a child? Get them to show you their face! Why aren't you collecting as much data as you can?'

'If we brought you a map of the stars on this shell, would you be able to show us where the body is?' said Yunus.

'Yes.'

'We can send you one now.'

'Bring it to us with the people,' said the swarm. 'We will need more information for the map-making.'

There was a pause from the science team. 'How did you learn to speak English?'

'We learned from you the last time your type attacked us.'

Yunus and his team deliberated again before trying to answer.

'We have *no record* of attacking you before,' he said at last.

'Clearly you did,' said the swarm, 'as we speak English.'

'Do you intend to attack us again?'

'We attack in retaliation to an assault on the body.'

'What constitutes an assault?'

'We do not know how to make this answer yet. Bring your people to us.'

'It's a machine!' Will yelled. 'You're talking to a machine.'

He couldn't stand being cut out of the conversation any more. He could feel the situation getting dangerous. He wasn't sure how yet. He just knew.

He sent a tight-beam request to the *Gulliver*, captain's eyes only, requesting a real-time feed to the diplomacy team and prayed that Mark would be reasonable about it. To his credit, Mark didn't hesitate.

The link appeared in Will's sensorium with a two-word note attached: *They're crazy*. A view of the *Gulliver*'s lounge appeared. Will groaned with relief as he patched himself in.

'...but this isn't getting us anywhere,' Sam was saying. He looked more anxious than Will had never seen him. 'We barely know any more than we did before we hailed them.'

'Will Monet here,' said Will. 'I have to agree with Sam. This encounter doesn't match any of those we planned for. We need to exercise extreme caution. We need time to analyse and think. I recommend that we pull back to the edge of the system and investigate with probes.'

'Ditto,' said Venetia. 'This swarm just sounds more and more like a SAP to me and less like a full sentient, which means there's nothing to lose by sending an automated investigation. I want to know whose software we're talking to and why it's here. If a SAP wants us on the planet, it's not going to be to learn about our culture.'

'No,' said Yunus. 'We're not giving up. We came here to speak with these people, and that's what we're going to do.'

Venetia looked exasperated. 'Yunus, didn't you even hear us? They're not *people*.'

'I heard your *theory*, yes. I just don't agree with it. Of course Monet thinks we're talking to machines. That's what he's bred for. And a retreat to the system's edge would conveniently revert control over the mission to him. In doing so, we lose all hope for establishing a diplomatic dialogue. I'm not going to simply hand off control for this mission on the basis of a hunch.'

Here they were, Will thought, in exactly the position that Pari had warned him about.

'Then let me prove it to you!' he said. 'Open a video channel to the swarm. Let's take a look at them.'

'We decided not to do that,' said Yunus. 'We didn't want to risk cultural snap judgements about appearances.'

'*You* didn't want to risk it,' said Venetia. 'And I told you culture is irrelevant at this point.'

Yunus didn't appear to care.

'For crying out loud,' said Citra, 'please at least acknowledge that my husband knows what he's doing. You're all so confident that we're talking to a machine, but why should that surprise you? Isn't that exactly what would happen at Earth if aliens visited us? The fact that they have a translator program running is hardly surprising.'

'First, that's not a translator,' said Will. 'I know what a translator sounds like. And second, they're using the voice of a human child. That's a pretty unusual choice. Don't you want to know why?'

Yunus arched an eyebrow. 'Why so curious, Captain Monet? So you can judge them? What if they have a toddler wearing a neural shunt? And what if they had no idea what a child was before they attacked those ships? Does that make them evil?'

'What are you fucking talking about?' said Will. 'This isn't about good or evil, or any of that shit. It's about *risk assessment*.'

'Do I need to remind you that you're not part of the diplomatic team, Captain Monet?' said Yunus. 'Your participation in this conversation breaches our mission plan.'

'But Will has a point,' said Sam. 'Trying to talk to this thing isn't working. We need to do better than this. Yunus, if you can't find a way to make your diplomacy programme work, I'll have to request that the Fleet take over so we can go with Will's approach.'

'You don't need to worry about that,' said Yunus. 'I've decided to attempt first contact. Mark, can you wake our Spatials from coma, please, and make sure they're briefed?'

'Sam,' said Will pointedly. 'That isn't a solution.'

Sam nodded. 'Yunus,' he said. 'Professor Chesterford. Are you sure you want to do this? Whatever is out there sounds very keen to meet in person. Ominously keen. And there's nothing to stop us sending a drone to meet them instead. Plus, I have to remind you that if we *are* facing aliens, they may have live human hostages. I can't recommend that we expose any more of this team to danger than we absolutely have to, as that may only make that situation worse.'

'Your perspective is welcomed, Overcaptain Shah, but this isn't one of your police operations. We're not talking about a hostage negotiation here. We are dealing with the unknown, and it has asked to meet *us*. Not a drone or a robot. A limited demonstration of trust is called for and that's what we came here to do. Based on what happens when we extend that trust, we may have a solid reason to treat the Photurians as adversaries, but we *cannot* proceed on that basis. This may be the first live peer intelligence humanity has ever encountered and we can't risk ruining that opportunity. I accept that the probability of a fully sentient system is lower than we'd both like, but we're talking about aliens here. We shouldn't expect to understand them at first glance. And if we don't meet them with trust, we may incur a disaster for the whole human race.'

In the invisible privacy of his home node, Will clutched his hair. Yunus was clearly too much in love with the promise of a place in the history books to see the danger staring him in the face.

'That being said,' Sam insisted, 'the risks here are huge. The team must be minimised.'

Yunus shrugged. 'First contact requires only one.'

Citra looked pained. 'You don't need to do that, Yuni. I'll go with you. I'm not afraid. I can't get decent biosamples up here, in any case.'

Yunus shook his head. 'Sam has a point, my love,' he said. 'And I couldn't forgive myself if they hurt you. The diplomacy team should have minimum exposure and this is my responsibility. I'll take the soldiers and leave it at that.'

'Don't,' she said. 'You deserve this moment, Yuni, but don't go alone. Please.'

He took her hand. 'Don't worry, my love. I'm not a fool. The soldiers will be with me and the contact shuttle has safeguards. I'll use the telepresence kit, okay? You're with me on this, though, right?'

Citra nodded, though Will couldn't help noticing the cords of stress lining her neck.

'We came here to do this,' she said in a strangled voice. 'This is your dream.'

'And my job,' said Yunus. 'Someone has to find us answers. And that person should be me. I'll send you the data you need.'

Yunus reached for the control for the communication channel.

'We will come to the planet,' he told the swarm. 'Can you meet me wherever I land?'

'Yes,' came the reply. 'Come quickly. We want to meet all your people.'

Yunus closed the channel and smiled. 'Mark, please ask the Spatials to prepare for shuttle departure. I'm going in.'

'I don't recommend it,' said Mark bluntly.

Yunus scowled into the closest camera. 'Did I ask your opinion, Captain Ruiz?'

'Just do it, Mark,' said Sam. 'You can't stop him. Please.'

'Whatever,' said Mark. The shuttle ready-warnings came on.

Will contemplated reaching in and trying to secure remote control of the *Gulliver*. He was pretty sure he could do it, but the Vartian Institute defences might make the process take hours. By then, Yunus would be long gone. He turned to Nelson.

'What do I do here?' he said. 'Is this where I start asserting myself?'

Nelson shook his head. 'I think Sam's up to something. He's trying to give you a graceful way out of this. The moment Yunus puts himself at risk, you'll have control and he'll thank you for it. If Yunus wants to expose himself, that's his problem. We just have to stay professional and let this game play itself out, crazy though it is. And after all, he might even be right.'

Will nodded grimly. 'So be it,' he said. 'Fire up the suntaps and get ready for action. Instinct tells me we're out of our depth.'

Nelson nodded. 'Already on it.'

6.4: ANN

Ann watched the dialogue unfolding between the *Gulliver* and the Nem swarm with mounting alarm. A long reflection phase, she could accept. The fact that the clean-up phase had, if anything, gone into reverse, she could also just about handle. They'd seen elements of those behaviours before. But this *conversation* was freaking her out.

Nems didn't do conversation. They pinpointed threats and responded to them – ruthlessly. The *Gulliver*'s interaction window at Tiwanaku was supposed to have been measured in minutes, not the hours it had taken for the ship to reach the colony itself. The machines were being *way* too nice.

Why hadn't they fired? And why in Gal's name did they even want to talk at all? She couldn't imagine how much stress Sam must be under at that moment. Without a violent response from Will, all they had on their hands was a nest of dangerously over-informed Nems and a massive security problem. The way this was going, they'd be lucky to fire a single shot.

Kuril spoke up. 'Ma'am, are we off mission plan already? What do we do? Do you want me to warm the boser? Are we going to have to make the shot ourselves?'

'Not necessary,' said Jaco, calmly. 'This is just a manifestation of reflection-phase crosstalk. Those Nems aren't distinguishing between our ships and the pseudo-human activity they've created for themselves. For them, this is all play.'

'But the reply format—' began Kuril.

'Is within model tolerances, Mr Najoma. During reflection, the Nems always mimic the incoming format from a peer bounce, and that's exactly what they've done here. The fact that the format was ours rather than theirs doesn't matter.'

'Unfortunately, Kuril has a point,' said Ann. 'Jaco, I agree with your analysis that this is down to the long reflection. But it's our job to be paranoid and this swarm is already at the edge of our modelling envelope. We might be able to explain this response but we still didn't expect it. So move us in a little closer, please. I want to be able to get a clear shot at the Nems, or at *Ariel Two*, whichever becomes necessary.'

Jaco paused, his frustration palpable. 'On it, ma'am,' he said eventually. 'Though I must point out that the closer we get, the more likely we are to be spotted.'

'Point taken, Mr Brinsen. However, we still have Nem-cloaking. If it comes down to it, we'll have to rely on that.'

Her job was to make sure that the plan went off without a hitch. Personal risk didn't factor into it. Much more of this chatting and everything was likely to unravel.

7: CONTACT

7.1: YUNUS

The salmon-coloured mountains of Tiwanaku Four loomed large in Yunus's view-field as they descended. On that dusty, frozen world, mankind's greatest adventure lay waiting to start. He was sure of it. He had butterflies in his stomach, though of course that could have been down to the violent lurching of the shuttle.

Side windows in his display showed him views of the seats in front of him where his two Spatials were hard at work, piloting the shuttle and surveying the local airspace. The names of his escorts were marked at the bottom of the displays: Nico Ratan and Lisa Markus. Neither of them looked particularly fazed by being woken up at the eleventh hour for a shuttle drop to an alien world. They behaved as if this was the sort of thing they did every week.

On the other hand, he reflected, both soldiers had been sourced from the Fleet's Covert Ops Division. Who knew what they did every week? It didn't bear thinking about.

'I'll be using the telepresence rig,' he reminded them to break the silence. 'The secure set-up. As soon as we hit the ground, one of you will be on shuttle defence, the other will be manning the cut-out and will double as a human pilot if we need one. Does that work?'

Both Spatials nodded.

'Textbook operating practice, Boss,' said Nico. 'We're on it.'

'I want to thank you for your bravery,' said Yunus. 'What we're about to do is momentous. It's a first in human history. Nothing like this has ever been done before.'

He wanted to touch them somehow. To make them understand the significance of what they were walking into. However, they accepted his remarks with nods and blank faces.

'Yes, sir,' said Nico. 'That's why we volunteered. Not every day you get a job like this.'

'We'll have you in and out in no time,' said Lisa. 'Safe as houses.'

Fast and safe was hardly the point, Yunus thought. But both soldiers had probably been extensively briefed on protecting the diplomats and weren't thinking far beyond that. They both looked to be the classic military type. No sense of awe. No interest in the unknown. Bodies lousy with killtech, no doubt. Nobody should be carrying that amount of artificial augmentation. It was against nature.

He blamed the Galatean influence. Between augs and genetic modifications they were reducing the human race to specialised pieces of machinery. It would have been better for everyone if that particular genie had never escaped the bottle. The Truists had tried, of course. They'd fought the war to keep mankind human, and they had lost. The old-style Truist Spatials would have at least been humbled by the gravity of their task.

Colonials were so self-righteous in their assumptions, changing everything they came across and throwing out their moral compass along the way. His colleagues on this mission were perfect examples of that smugness. They all imagined they were so smart, yet their vision was so narrow. Everyone on the *Gulliver* had been applauding themselves for their caution. Yet they didn't appear to realise that *all* human reasoning came from assumptions.

For all they knew, they'd be incurring a risk for mankind by *not* trying to communicate. What mattered in life was the assumptions you chose to work from and your willingness to adapt, not how far you got from the set of faulty axioms you'd started out with. Yunus had lived his whole life by that logic. And he'd been waiting all his life for a moment like this one. He'd known that one day, it would happen.

Meanwhile, the others on the *Gulliver* just sounded keen for the Photurians to not be real, despite all the evidence to the contrary. It was the only way they could keep their blinkered understanding of the world alive, he suspected. Should they be surprised that the Photurians used a machine to communicate? Of course not. Should they be surprised that they couldn't understand what they were looking at? He didn't think so. Monet and the others regarded him as some kind of fool. He was aware of the risks. He was simply ready to face them, that was all.

The Spatials brought him down at the carefully selected point he'd chosen near the planet's equator. It was close enough to Photurian activity sites to make communication easy, but far enough away that they wouldn't be able to impede his exit if something went wrong. Outside lay a bland expanse of pinkish desert under a dirty orange sky. It looked like half the worlds he'd visited.

'Okay,' said Nico. 'Ground checks complete.'

Yunus unclipped from his couch and clambered down the narrow access tube on his left that led to the telepresence tank. The tank was one of the more impressive pieces of kit the Vartian Institute had installed. It enabled him to link with a biodroid perfectly shaped in his likeness, specifically designed for missions such as this. While his real body remained secure inside the shuttle, all his physical sensations would come from the remote bot.

The bottom of the tube opened into the access ring for the body-sleeve below. It looked like a wet, green rubberised sock large enough for a person to slide into – quite revolting, really. Yunus removed his ship-suit and stashed it in the small locker in the wall. Then he sat on the edge of the ring, dipped his feet into the unpleasant aperture and slithered after them. He pushed himself down, testing his body against the simulant gel surrounding it as darkness swallowed him. It was, surprisingly, like floating in a bath of warm nothing. The tank linked to his retinal implants, showing him green status lights all across the board. He was ready.

The comms between the biodroid and Yunus were highly secure. Once inside the telepresence tank, he had only a one-way link to the shuttle – they could hear him, but he couldn't hear them. That way, the mission could still collect data about his experiences while preventing the kind of feedback hacking that had notoriously co-opted the original *Ariel*. It also meant he'd be on his own. Yunus wasn't that fussed. He'd just have to spend less time listening to the witterings of his colleagues. His droid also came equipped with sensors for all manner of dangerous technology. They could detect the presence of everything from enzymes to nanobots to radiation. Yunus suspected he wouldn't need any of them.

His view showed the shuttle bay opening and the contact rover heading out across the sand. It travelled five hundred metres, stopped and deployed the inflatable neutral-zone habitat-bubble it carried. The invitation beacon atop the habitat started winking its message to the Photurians nearby.

Yunus felt a brief stab of regret. The Photurians had asked to meet *him*, not some artificial substitute. On the other hand, the biodroid would, in effect, be a part of him – if the Institute scientists were to be believed. To an observer, it would look like him, smell like him and even scan like him. And the light-lag on the line-of-sight comms was effectively zero. Besides, if he took any more risks than this, Citra might never forgive him.

The countdown in his view clicked from five to one. Then the droid came online and Yunus's concerns instantly vanished. He felt as if he was actually standing alone inside a small transparent dome on the surface of a barren world. He patted his chest, looking down at the crisp ambassadorial uniform his double wore, and then out across the rosy dunes. He suddenly felt profoundly exposed. He could hear the squeak of the dome shifting in the planet's feeble breeze, and the hiss of the air recyclers. The canned atmosphere felt dry and chilled his skin. Were it not for the status icons winking at the corners of his vision, he'd have had no way to tell that he wasn't really there.

Yunus looked around at the empty, sterile pocket of habitability and felt like a figurine in an antique snow globe. Typical, he reflected. The Vartian Institute had thought of everything except proper furniture. And without a feed from the shuttle, he had no idea when the Photurians would send their envoy. He sat down on the rubberised floor of the bubble to wait.

He shifted on the uncomfortable plating and wondered what the crew aboard the *Gulliver* would be saying. Not much of value, he suspected. A few snide remarks. More pointless panicking. In any case, Citra would fill him in as soon as he got back.

In the meantime, God had given him his chance. Just five minutes with the aliens might be enough to establish himself as the trusted point of contact. If he could manage that, power would follow. With an interspecies relationship to manage, the Earth would regain its rightful primacy and all this foolish talk of war would be over at last. If anything was worth the wait and the risk, it was surely that.

As it was, the Photurians didn't take long to arrive. Just fifteen minutes later, a very ordinary-looking rover appeared on the horizon and headed straight towards him. Yunus felt a twinge of disappointment. He'd hoped that the contact vehicle would be somewhat more exotic. But given the extent to which the Photurians were reusing human material, it was hardly surprising.

As the rover neared, his heart began to race in anticipation. Yunus got to his feet as the rover drove up and docked with the bubble. The airlock opened. Yunus held his breath, peering into the shadows beyond.

Out of the rover limped a teenage boy. He had no hands. His arms ended in damp orange sacs. A Sanchez clone head had been rather clumsily glued into his neck, along with a complicated system of rubber tubing. Pouches of organic machinery stuck out of his skin at irregular intervals. He wore a torn ship-suit that looked and smelled like he hadn't changed it in weeks. He was clearly terrified. The boy scratched his stomach mournfully with one elbow. The ripped flaps of his ship-suit parted briefly to reveal a piece of a coffee machine that appeared to have been inserted there.

Yunus shivered in disgust. This wasn't what he'd hoped for. Still, maybe he could salvage things. He should trust his own protocol and not put too much stock in appearances.

'Who are you?' he said carefully.

Everyone back on the *Gulliver* would be watching through his eyes. He had to play this out with dignity, whatever the consequences.

'Ryan,' said the boy sheepishly. He looked away.

'We are Punishment,' said the horrible clone head under his chin. 'You only have one person? Where are the rest of your persons?'

Yunus chose not to reply to that one. 'What happened here?' he asked.

'They changed me,' said Ryan. He started to cry.

'The pest site was claimed and integrated,' said the Sanchez head primly. 'Pattern dictates that we remain at pest site to destroy stragglers. However, integration is behind schedule as we do not understand the human components. They have no clearly defined function. Their system protocols are strange wrong with many level. They are challenging!'

Yunus tried to keep the revulsion off his face and struggled to understand what he was looking at. If this was a straight physical subversion, it was terrible job. Human surgeons had developed more impressive

194

puppet-hacks decades ago. What had been done to Ryan resembled a cliché of alien control as executed by halfwits. Even the most botched alien fake made by a sect group would look more plausible than this.

'Please kill me,' Ryan blubbed. 'I hurt so much. I don't want to be like this any more.'

The Sanchez head talked over him. 'You will help us understand,' it said enthusiastically.

'We will do what we can to facilitate peaceful coexistence,' said Yunus. 'We will provide you with knowledge and tools for trade. However, we will need our human components back.'

'The components are integrated,' said the head. 'We do not need for trades. You will supply further instance of person to enable us derive more harmonious interface.'

'What happens if we don't want to do that?' said Yunus.

He hoped the Spatials were watching this closely. He was counting on their instincts as to when to pull the plug.

'Integration is preferable to destruction,' said the head. 'Through integration, pest species may serve the body and become useful. Integration is good! Enjoyment of integration will be inserted. Enjoyment will be applied to all persons.'

Yunus started to see contagion alerts in his display.

'We'll have to consider your offer,' he said hurriedly.

'You delay,' said the Sanchez head. 'Do not delay. There is not need of delay.'

Ryan screamed. Abruptly, the bulbs on the ends of his arms burst, filling the air with a fine orange mist. He collapsed sideways.

At the same time, Yunus's control over the android started to deteriorate. Contagion warnings piled in his view and he watched in horror as his hands started to dissolve.

Nico pulled the plug. Yunus gasped with relief to be back in the shuttle. He started desperately clambering out of the pod as the sleeve retracted, his lungs labouring for air.

'Let's get the hell out of here!' he yelled.

'Already on it, Boss,' said Lisa. 'We'll have you out of here in no time. Safe as houses.' The shuttle's engines started to whine even while Yunus was clawing his way up to the hatch. He had never heard so lovely a sound.

7.2: MARK

As Mark watched the feed from Yunus's android, his unease about the man's departure melted into outright horror. The Ryan-thing had been both pathetic and hideous. He no longer had any doubt that Will was right. Their adversaries were machines, and not very smart ones.

Citra Chesterford pinged him from the lounge.

'Captain Ruiz, is there anything we can do to get closer to that shuttle?'

'Not yet,' he told her. 'They need to hit the stratopause before I can compute a decent intercept vector. There's too much drone traffic in low orbit. I can't risk it until I know where they're going to be.'

'Please let me know as soon as you can,' she said. 'I don't want to leave him out there a second longer than we have to.'

'I'm on it, Professor,' said Mark. 'Don't worry.'

He powered up a trajectory computation SAP and set it racing over the vector options while he watched the shuttle creep up through the atmosphere.

'If a drone so much as twitches near them, they've had it,' said Will over the comms. 'I have low orbit on lockdown.'

Then, as they watched, the inconceivable happened. One of the huge, misshapen drones parked in low orbit abruptly suicided. It blew its antimatter containment out sideways, punching a mass of white-hot shrapnel towards Tiwanaku Four. That close to the surface, the effect on the planet's atmosphere was instant and catastrophic. Huge shock waves of ionised gas ballooned outwards and surged around the globe.

'What the fuck?' Will yelled.

Mark froze in horror. Downing a shuttle that way was like using a rail gun to crack an egg.

'Jesus,' said Ash. 'This is where it gets real.'

Even with seconds to react as the air-tsunami tore around the planet, there was nothing Mark or anyone else could do about it. The wave hit, picking up the shuttle and spinning it like a leaf in a hurricane.

Yunus had barely clipped into his couch when the wave hit. It saved his life. The shuttle jolted as if smacked by a gigantic hand. Impact foam erupted around his body to prevent his neck from snapping. A roar like the end of the world filled the air, backed by a chorus of shrieking sirens. Yunus found himself spinning end-over-end. He squeezed his eyes shut and prepared to die.

To his astonishment, the roar slowly transformed into a wail. The tumbling stopped, replaced by a furious juddering. The sirens fell silent. When he opened his eyes, the view outside the shuttle on the screens showed a swirling nightmare of gritty darkness punctuated by explosions of lightning. The shuttle bucked wildly.

Yunus could only stare. What in God's name had happened? Had someone dropped a nuke on them?

'Brace yourselves, please,' said Lisa calmly. 'We have limited control. Landing is going to be rough.'

To Yunus's astonishment, she was managing it. For all that he might not like their style, Yunus had to hand it to the Spatial Corps. Their troops weren't fazed by anything.

'This is Lisa Markus to *Gulliver*,' she said over the comms. 'Contact Shuttle One has experienced aileron damage. Currently attempting a thruster landing. Will commence repairs immediately upon grounding.'

Yunus's terror came back, redoubled. A thruster landing in conditions like these? How was that even possible?

Lisa showed him. The shuttle jerked in mid-air. The storm became a bone-jarring shake and the shuttle dropped, leaving the pit of his stomach far above. Then it bounced horribly and fell again. Step by step, it lurched its way closer to the ground.

Impact with the desert made the hull ring like a bell and the ship immediately began to vibrate furiously. Yunus realised that they must have been travelling far faster than he'd imagined. The shuttle slewed sideways, metal shrieking, and slid for what felt to Yunus like an impossibly long time.

Suddenly everything stopped. Yunus became belatedly aware that the sirens had all started up again. He hadn't noticed during the landing.

Lisa cut them off, leaving only the sound of the ticking hull and the screaming sand outside.

'Contact Shuttle One to *Gulliver*,' Lisa said over the comms. 'Are you still reading us?'

Yunus held his breath while he waited.

A faint reply made it through the lightning-swamped hellscape that Tiwanaku's atmosphere had become.

'This is *Gulliver*. We see and hear you, Contact Shuttle One,' said the voice of Mark Ruiz. 'Do not commence repairs. We are prepping Shuttle Two for your rescue.'

'Fucking Fleeties,' Lisa muttered under her breath. 'That is not recommended, *Gulliver*,' she said. 'Conditions down here are *extreme*, and we have repairbots.'

'Understood but overridden,' said Mark. 'Sending you data now.'

There was a pause from Lisa before she said anything more.

'Oh, holy fuck,' she whispered at last.

'What?' said Yunus. 'What's going on?'

She forwarded the information to his view.

It showed a surface scan from orbit. On one side was the atmospheric schematic of the antimatter event that had boiled the atmosphere. On the other was a close-up of their position. Bright points denoting several dozen vehicles had poured out of the nearest Photurian habitat nodes. All were converging on their site, despite the raging oblivion of the storm.

'They're coming for us,' said Nico in a hushed voice. 'The bastards are coming.'

7.4: WILL

Will cursed himself over and over. He never should have let things go this far.

'That's it,' he said. 'Fuck this first-contact bullshit.'

He redeployed his subminds, tracking every single object as far out as geostationary orbit. Should one of them so much as move, they'd get a boser in the face. He reached for the comms channel Yunus had used to speak to the swarm. Sam was already on it.

'Move away from that shuttle!' Sam was telling the swarm. 'That shuttle is ours. Aggression will not be tolerated. Retaliation will be total. Be aware that you are declaring war on an interstellar species!'

The Photurians didn't appear to give a damn. Their vehicles kept closing in on the grounded shuttle.

'Mark,' said Will. 'Don't launch that second bird.'

'We don't have time for repairs,' said Mark.

'You don't have time for a rescue, either. Photurian intercept is in six minutes. Even on full burn, your shuttle will need nine. You have to give me a clear shot.'

He swapped back to the comms. Sam was still there, repeating himself over and over, applying different weird filters and urgency warnings to his message as if it would make some kind of a difference.

Will drowned him out. 'Get any closer to that shuttle and I'll destroy you,' he told the swarm.

The Photurians maintained their approach.

'Hold on tight, everybody,' Will told Nelson and his crew. 'Things are about to get interesting.'

He fired eight g-rays at the surface on minimum strength, aiming for the Photurians closest to Yunus's crash site.

Kilometres of desert turned to molten glass in a ring around the shuttle. Twenty-seven Photurian rovers vaporised. Weird, bright holes momentarily formed in the storm clouds as eight columns of atmosphere turned instantly to plasma. At the same time, Will aimed his primary boser at the largest orbital factory hub he could see and fired a microsecond shot. The factory hub popped like the devil's own soap bubble, splashing the planet's atmosphere with another wave of hideous thermal violence.

'Do you get it *now*?' he asked the swarm. 'Leave our shuttle alone.'

The response was swift and, at first, curiously beautiful. In a ripple that raced out through in-system space, the aimless, drifting flight paths of the countless drones began to change. They shifted and realigned as if waking in unison from a shared dream. Then, in waves thousands strong, they dived towards the *Ariel Two*.

Will regarded them with alarm that melted rapidly to shivering anticipation. Aliens had taken from him his chance to have a family, his credibility and finally his wife. If he was honest with himself, he'd been waiting years to punch one in the face. Now, apparently, he was about to get his chance.

He opened up a channel to the *Gulliver*.

'Mark,' he said. 'It's all down to you now. This is why I brought you. You know what you have to do. Get those scientists out of here and keep them safe. Leave Yunus and these assholes to me.'

8: DISASTER

8.1: MARK

Mark sat mutely watching the madness play out while Sam raged at Will for taking over the comms.

'Damn you, Monet!' he yelled. 'What have you done?'

Citra was dumbfounded. Then Will's message came through for everyone to hear.

Mark's chest tightened. A wash of guilty anxiety he hadn't felt for years washed over him. His youth had been filled with Will's speeches about protecting people. The story about Amy Ritter's death had been drilled into him about a hundred times.

Do not expose your friends to danger, Will had always said. *It is your duty to use your talents to help humankind. You have been given a gift and IPSO is counting on you to use it wisely.*

Mark had heard it all. He'd never expected it to matter.

'Everybody strap down,' he told the team in the lounge. 'We're getting out of here and there may be some fancy flying.'

The Casimir-buffers fizzed into life. He greased the rails for warp and kept them humming. But instead of clipping in, Citra lurched up out of her couch.

'No!' she said. 'We have to go back for Yunus!'

'Not possible, I'm afraid,' said Mark. 'He's in Will's hands now.'

He brought up the positions of all the closest swarm drones, turned the ship and dived carefully for the largest gap between them. Citra bounced off the crash padding.

'Strap in, please,' he told her. 'I don't want you to get hurt.'

He put half of his submind attention on vector analysis and dumped as much neuro-accelerant into his bloodstream as he could without triggering epilepsy. The world rammed into high gear. He bounced and spun the ship simultaneously, nudging several cubic kilometres of elastoceramic alloy framework for the simple purpose of kicking Citra Chesterford back into her couch. He managed it almost perfectly. She cried out in pain and grabbed her arm as it hit the edge of her seat. She'd live. He piled on the gees to keep her there.

'Venetia, you're closest. Fasten her in, please. Now.'

Venetia leaned over fast as Citra cradled her elbow.

'Mark, the shit has hit the fan,' said Sam, his voice labouring against the sudden acceleration. 'Yunus is gone, which leaves me in charge. I'm passing the captaincy to Ash. He has more flight hours on the *Gulliver* than you and right now we need that experience.'

'Negative,' said Mark coolly. He didn't even bother getting angry. He had too much to think about. 'I have my orders, and with respect, Ash can't fly worth shit under combat conditions. Right now we need to leave and I'm already on it.'

Mark brought up the vector cloud, merged with it and swooped around as sixty drones headed towards them on different converging paths. Fortunately, their attention appeared to be on the *Ariel Two* rather than him, which made life easier. He watched the *Ariel Two*'s quantum shield shiver into life, coating the ship in silvery armour. He envied it.

The *Ariel Two*'s defences came online just in time. The drones burst harmlessly against it, flooding the planet below with blasts of poisonous light. The *Gulliver*'s Casimir-buffers smacked and crackled as the radiation waves hit.

Another two hundred and eleven drones lay dead ahead. Mark saw them charging for warp.

'Shit,' he muttered.

As soon as conventional acceleration wasn't enough, the *Gulliver* was going to have real problems. The drones wouldn't be able to go superlight this deep in-system but they'd still wreak havoc with his trajectory models. Mark bumped his vector-support allocation to seventy per cent and braced himself for the flying to get chewy.

'Mark!' Sam shouted. 'This mission is now under military jurisdiction. Ash has been trained for alien-incursion events. You have not. Relinquish the helm.'

'Back off!' Mark yelled. 'That is *not* standard procedure and I'm trying to concentrate!'

Suddenly, Mark's grip on the ship wobbled. Security override flags popped up all over his display with Sam's signature on them. They started vanishing as soon as they'd arrived but the ship's systems didn't recover as fast. Half the hull management SAPs went into forced reboot.

'What the *fuck*?' he shouted.

The ship's engines cut out, waiting for the management circuits to re-engage. But the drones kept coming. Warp-light crackled around their hulls. Mark glared into the lounge camera. Sam looked astonished.

'Ash,' said Sam. 'Do you have the helm?'

Mark rounded on Ash's avatar. He was standing there looking dumbly at his hands, panic in his eyes.

'N-no,' said Ash. 'I do not.'

'Are you fucking *insane*?' yelled Mark. 'I don't know what kind of shit you tried to pull there but that was some unbelievably bad timing.'

'Mark,' Ash breathed. He gathered himself together and practically squeaked. 'Give me control!' He started fumbling with the hull albedo subsystems, tinkering with them like a lunatic. Mark ditched Ash's avatar, flicking it out of the helm-arena.

Ninety-seven drones hit warp, all dangerously close, and the *Gulliver* juddered backwards like a body peppered by bullets. Mark saw damage warnings from warp inducers and sensor arrays all over the hull erupting in the helm-space around him. A dozen different system management SAPs started keening at him simultaneously.

'*Holyfuckingshit!*' Mark yelled.

As they sat there helpless, the *Ariel Two*'s mighty g-ray banks opened up. Ninety-seven Photurian drones died simultaneously, sending another tidal wave of radiation smashing into the *Gulliver*'s side. Rad-management SAPs screamed at him as Casimir-buffer support dropped to twenty-one per cent. The *Gulliver* wasn't built for this kind of abuse.

Mark backed some of his submind attention off vector analysis and threw it on emergency repair. Several hundred robots raced down tracks in the mesohull, prepping replacement inducer components even while they moved.

'Sam, were you trying to get us *killed*?' Mark shouted. 'Do not touch those system controls again or God help me, I will break your neck if we don't die first.'

'You are in breach of your command chain!' Sam shouted back. 'I will have your interface rights revoked.'

By this time, Citra had recovered her wits.

'We have to go back for Yunus,' she announced. 'Take us back. We have to get down there. As his wife, I'm *ordering* you.'

Mark ignored them both.

Citra unclipped from her couch again. With the engines down, her seat-lock had released.

'Just give me the shuttle, then,' she said. 'I'll do it myself!' She headed for the hatch.

Mark's engine control started coming back online and not a moment too soon. A new wave of seven hundred and nine drones had swerved towards the *Ariel Two*, with the *Gulliver* right in their path.

'Will someone *please* restrain that woman,' said Mark. 'We have nine seconds. After that, the turns we need to take are likely to kill her.'

Venetia and Zoe responded as one, surging out of their couches. Zoe tackled Citra while Venetia flew to the wall where the emergency medkit sat. She yanked out a sedative, kicked off against the wall and flew back to where the two women tumbled in the air.

Citra was punching Zoe repeatedly on the back.

'Let. Me. Go!'

Venetia slammed the sed-gun into Citra's side. She grunted and flopped free. At the same moment, the engines sprang back into life. Mark brought the injector rails up to full power.

'Hurry, please!' he said. 'We're out of time.'

Venetia and Zoe dumped Citra's unconscious body into the crash couch and clipped her in with frantic hands before diving back to their own seats. Mark applied the emergency straps. Zoe glared across at Sam, who hadn't moved a muscle.

'Thanks for all the help,' she snarled.

Mark fired the warp guns, kicking everyone back into their seats. The thud of warp rose rapidly to a growl as Mark veered out of the path of the oncoming wave. Eight gravities of acceleration squeezed the air from their lungs.

As he skirted the edge of the wave, his warp envelope scraped those of the closest drones. They veered wildly off course, crashing into their neighbours in a cascade of searing blasts. Mark watched the explosions in his wake with mounting frustration. Whoever programmed these Photurian pilot SAPs had done a really shitty job.

'I know everyone's upset,' said Mark, swapping to his virtual voice as his chest squeezed tight. 'I wish there was something I could do for Yunus, but right now, everyone needs to *back off and let me do my job*! I will meet as many of your needs as I can.'

'What are you talking about, Mark?' Sam subvoked through gritted teeth. 'We have just one need, and that's for you to *get off the fucking helm*!'

Sam still didn't think he could fly. Maybe the guy needed some gentle re-education.

'Zoe,' Mark said sweetly. 'You wanted data on Photurian warp drones, did you not? Well, there's now plenty of shrapnel we could collect. There may even be biosamples.'

She stared at the camera with terror in her eyes. 'What do you mean?'

'Wait!' said Sam. 'Insubordination is one thing. Don't go adding to it with crazy. Take samples and you turn this ship into a target!'

Mark snorted. As if they weren't one already. He threw his ship into a loop, dived around and between the waves of oncoming munitions and raced back the way he'd come, heading for the spinning debris field the cascade had created. At the same time, he dropped some very accelerated submind attention on the collection scoops.

With millisecond timing, Mark swapped the orientation of his warp envelope, smacking the ship's gravity field flat in less than a second. The *Gulliver*'s hull squealed like a bag of pigs as rampant gravitational eddies raced through it. There were reasons why Fleet had banned this particular manoeuvre.

He slalomed back through the radioactive ruins in the drones' wake on conventional velocity, siphoning up bits of smashed munitions while thruster-braking as hard as the drives would allow. He had to prevent the shrapnel from hitting so fast that it punched holes through the hull. Warning sirens competed with thunderous crashes in the mesohull as the remnants piled up in the backs of the scoop buffers.

'There we go,' said Mark as the *Gulliver* hurtled out of the other side of the debris field. 'Nice and easy. Plenty of research material for everyone.' He'd like to have seen Ash try that one. Ideally from a safe distance.

Unfortunately, the trick had dropped his conventional velocity and dumped him in the patch of curvon-depleted dead space behind the drone wave. The timing wasn't optimal as another wave of drones had powered up to drive straight through them. This time, the drones numbered in the thousands. His target identification SAP started whimpering.

Mark muttered to himself. He should have spotted them gearing up. He'd spread his attention too thin. Sam let out an incoherent yell as he caught sight of the oncoming wave.

Mark threw power to the thrusters, pushing them way beyond tolerances and *guessed* which direction would have the cleanest space.

Fortunately, he guessed right. The warp engines kicked back in, giving him just a fraction of a second's clearance as the next wave of drones surged past to detonate themselves against the *Ariel Two*'s titanic defences.

Nineteen seconds later, he had reached the edge of the cloud. By then, though, the drones were following him. Four hundred and fifteen drones flicked out of the cloud behind him, like a pseudopod from an angry, oversized amoeba.

'Really?' said Mark. 'You want a race?'

The *Gulliver* was in its element now. With clear space ahead, the drones didn't stand a chance. Their distorted engines were no match for his. Mark piled power onto his remaining warp inducers, bringing the engine growl up to a frantic whine. Artificial gees squeezed them into their couches as the *Gulliver* shot away from the drone cloud, leaving it dwindling in the distance.

Mark sucked air as he eased off the drives and blinked at the ceiling of his bunk. He guiltily checked his passengers' life signs. All still green, thankfully, though everyone was probably going to need some bones set. Next time, he'd remember to deploy the gel-sleeves on the crash couches *before* the fancy flying. Nevertheless, they were all still alive. Just.

He kicked off a program of extremely gentle warp-scatter manoeuvres, set the autopilot SAP on course for Nerroskovi and exhaled with relief.

8.2: WILL

Eleven hundred warp-enabled munitions thundered towards the *Ariel Two* in a desperate bid to rip a hole in Will's hull.

'Piss off,' said Will.

The *Ariel Two*'s g-ray banks opened fire, eviscerating the swarm and smothering the massive hull with blooms of light.

In the lull that followed, Will fired a squadron of dropbots at the ravaged planet below, programmed to seek out and defend Yunus before the Photurians could get to him. Whether anyone down there was doing anything except cowering from the world-spanning radioactive grit-storm was anyone's guess.

'Where the fuck is the *Chiyome*?' said Will. 'If this doesn't qualify as an emergency, I'd like to see something that does.' He eyed the next wave of incoming drones. The entire cloud was centring on him and there were millions of them. 'That's the problem with an invisible ship. You can't tell if it's even fucking there.'

'Give Ann some credit,' said Nelson. 'You asked her to look after the *Gulliver*. Maybe she's doing that. She's probably en route to Nerroskovi right now.'

Will realised with a start that Nelson was absolutely right. Given what he'd seen of the woman so far, that was exactly what he should expect. It upset him that she hadn't tight-beamed him to at least let him know what she was doing – probably more than it should have.

'We live in hope,' Will muttered.

He watched through the dropbots' eyes as they plunged into the ruined atmosphere, their descent envelopes ablating dangerously fast. Will didn't care. If even a handful made it down there in time, it'd be enough. He pulled up his scans of the planet's surface, paging through infrared wavelengths to find one that would give him a clear look at Yunus's position. He set a SAP working through every possible combination of imaging filters.

The situation on the surface leapt into focus. Where Yunus's shuttle had been, a pile of frenetic Photurian activity now buzzed. They appeared to be trying to build some kind of shield around the shuttle and themselves for protection against the raging storm.

Will roared his displeasure. Who knew what had been done to their diplomat by now? Everything was going to hell in a handcart. He'd come here for a miracle and instead he'd built himself a clusterfuck. And it was all because he'd let halfwits like Yunus have a say in the mission instead of trusting his intuition and shutting them down the moment they'd started acting stupid. Because of that, he was now left with the unpleasant choice of leaving the away team to the mercy of alien machines or glassing them from space. There didn't seem to be much in it. With disgust, he released his links to the dropbots and turned his full attention to the swarm.

'Right!' he yelled. 'Who wants some?'

A shimmering sheet of drones light-seconds wide was curving in towards him, wrapping slowly around the nestship like a shawl of death.

'Merry Christmas!' Will yelled and threw the *Ariel Two* towards them, his g-ray banks scything space like a thousand flaming swords.

Drones died and died and died. Will's blood surged in his veins. These pathetic robots didn't stand a chance against him. Even the Earthers thirty years ago had put up a better fight. At least half of the machines were too malformed to fight. Nevertheless, his heart sang at the destruction. If felt good to smash something up after decades of tiptoeing around, trying to forgive everyone else's terrible behaviour. So seldom did he get a chance to exercise the strength the Transcended had burdened him with.

But his sense of satisfaction waned rapidly, leaving a hollow ache behind. No matter how many drones Will obliterated, there were always more, just as easy to predict as the last wave and just as expendable. It would take him days to clear out the entire system – pointless days that would remove any chance of Tiwanaku Four ever hosting life again.

'We're achieving nothing,' said Nelson as he winced from another blast-wave hitting the shields. 'And for all we know, those drones are carrying human hostages.'

Will paused his onslaught and flicked his view to a camera in the habitat core. Nelson looked drained, his crew terrified. Peter and Mitra lay there with eyes pressed shut, their view-fields off. Even Devi looked distressed. She'd never seen Will in full fury before. None of them had.

He realised his friend was right. Whatever or whoever had been the guiding intelligence behind the invasion, it wasn't here now. Most of the drones weren't even in fighting shape. The clever warp technology they'd exhibited in their initial attack on the *Reynard* was nowhere in evidence. Instead, these drones appeared to be low-grade approximations of the craft that had launched the initial assault.

He was fighting ghosts. He wasn't achieving anything except scaring his own people. For all its baroque decoration, the system was effectively empty and the away team no closer to being retrieved. By now it looked obvious that the Photurian machines had got them. Will hoped for Yunus's sake that the storm had killed him first.

'If we want this situation fixed, we'll have to try something else,' said Nelson. 'We're still in the dark as to the cause of all this.'

Will nodded as he looked out at the damage he'd done. The space around the *Ariel Two* had become a rosy haze of plasma and shrapnel so bright it obscured the planet below. Tiwanaku Four would have a ring system for centuries. A tide of embarrassment swept through him.

'You're right. We're going to that system the watchers identified,' he said. 'I want to know who's behind this shit. I'm going to find them. And I'm going to fix all this.'

Nelson shot him a reproving look. 'You realise that's outside of the mission parameters. The only place you're supposed to go after this is the rendezvous star or home.'

'Fuck the parameters,' said Will. 'I should never have let those bean-counter fuckwits set them in the first place. I haven't got my miracle yet, and I'm not going home without one.'

Will brought his ship about and headed in the direction of the uncharted star. Whoever was out there was going to get a piece of his mind.

8.3: ANN

The moment Will warped out, Ann groaned in relief. He'd fallen for it, thank Gal. The whole process had taken way longer than it should have, and had been far uglier. Watching the feed from Yunus's shuttle had made her want to puke.

In the wake of this mission, she knew she'd never be able to think about herself the same way again. The weight of guilt incurred, regardless of the intended goal, was just too high. The ends, as it turned out, did not justify the means. Ann watched the *Ariel Two* flicker out of the system with lead in her heart.

She stared down at her sweating hands and rubbed them together.

Look at me, she thought. *I'm the Lady Macbeth of deep space.*

What would Sam think of her in this state? She hadn't even remembered to check the *Gulliver*'s exit vector. Not that it mattered, next to everything else they'd seen. She didn't doubt that Sam had a better handle on things than she did right now.

'Ma'am,' said Kuril. 'Do you want an immediate tail?'

She blinked, grateful for the distraction.

'No,' she said. 'What we've seen here scares me. We need to know if the machine behaviour is going to return to normal. If it doesn't, our entire plan is worthless.'

Jaco craned out of his bunk to face her. After their first-contact ordeal, they were all looking a bit sticky and uncomfortable, him included.

'Ma'am, with respect, I disagree. There'll be time for that later. But if we don't keep up with Monet, everyone at Snakepit is at risk. As soon as he arrives, everything we're doing will be visible. We'll have minutes at best.'

Ann found her jaw clenching. Jaco seemed content to trot out Sam's old mission expectations regardless of what the Nems actually did, or the kinds of horrors he had to watch. Zealous he might be. Realistic he was not.

'Mr Brinsen,' she said slowly, 'I am fully aware of the risks incurred by sitting still. I do not need a reminder. However, what we just observed was not part of *any* of our modelled scenarios. First, that planet should have been cleared out by now. Second, there should have been no dialogue. And third, the Nems should not have been coordinating to acquire extra human samples during their reflection cycle. We are dangerously off the map. If the Nems do not become predictable again, *everyone* is at risk. The entire human race. The *Ariel Two* may be able to withstand whole waves of Nem attack, but what about, say, the surface of Galatea? How long do you suppose that would last? Or Drexler, perhaps?'

Jaco's brow furrowed in frustration. 'I accept your orders, ma'am. However, request permission to speak freely.'

Ann curled her lip. 'This is still an IPSO Fleet ship, Mr Brinsen. You do not need my permission. Informed dissent is expected of you.'

'I'm concerned that we may be overreacting,' he said, 'and in doing so risking the mission objective. To your points: first, there is always a partial nest-building phase after the Nems hit a target. This time there was just more than usual. It doesn't last. Second, the dialogue still fits our expectations of reflection-phase data traffic. And third, we should expect some blurring between behaviour phases. The phase model of Nem activity was invented by us for modelling purposes, not by them.'

'And that is *precisely* why I am concerned!' said Ann, her voice veering towards a shout. 'If our expectations are even slightly out of whack, then where the hell are we? What are we doing here? Without confidence in that phase model, our actions amount to little more than poking a stick into a hornet's nest. We're using dangerous alien technology because we have scientifically assessed that it's *safe*. If that's not true, then we're no better than the Truists and their suntaps.'

Jaco's expression darkened. Like many Drexlerites, Jaco was touchy about the war. They'd suffered more than most at the hands of the Kingdom of Man and weren't about to forget it.

'And what do you intend to do if the Nems *have* changed?' he said. 'What can we actually do?'

'Inform New Panama,' said Ann. 'Explain everything. Rally defences. We're not committed until the Nems follow Monet's warp trail home and strike at Earth.'

Jaco's eyes went wide. 'Are you serious? They'd string us up.'

'I suggest you worry less about being incriminated, Mr Brinsen, and more about doing your duty.'

Jaco flushed. 'Yes, ma'am,' he growled. He turned away.

Ann's heart was racing as she refocused her attention on her displays. They were all on edge after what they'd witnessed, but she and Jaco were clearly parsing the experience differently. They'd need another discussion before they hit Snakepit – preferably one not in front of the rest of the crew.

Over the next two hours, she watched the frenetic machines slow and regain something of their former somnambulant wanderings. They didn't completely settle, however. And rather than siphoning up the material left in the debris cloud Will had created, the Nems circled warily, endlessly passing analytical probes back and forth across it.

Certainly there were no dramatic responses, such as, for instance, chasing the *Ariel Two* straight to Snakepit as she'd half-anticipated.

Ann was left with the uncomfortable sense that while the Nems weren't exactly back on track, there wasn't enough unusual activity left to warrant outing the entire conspiracy. Doing that would inevitably doom herself and all her colleagues to treason tribunals. Everyone on her ship would face execution before the end of the year.

She hated to leave without more clarity, but it was slowly becoming clear that it would take days to determine whether the Nems would regain their habitual behaviour patterns, if not weeks. By that time their plan would be in shattered ruins.

Eventually, Jaco could stand it no more.

'Ma'am,' he said, his voice strained, 'do you have a time window for how long you want us to monitor here? It's just that Monet now has a hundred-and-forty-minute lead. That means we're cutting it extremely fine.'

'Accepted, Mr Brinsen,' she said reluctantly. 'Kuril, grease the rails, please. Prepare for maximum warp. We're catching up with the *Ariel Two*, so don't spare the juice.'

She'd have to content herself with a thorough report to Sam once she reached Snakepit. Hopefully, by the time she got there he'd be prepping for Will's welcome, with Mark already in civilised confinement.

9: RENDEZVOUS

9.1: ASH

Ash paused at the doorway to the privacy room in the science section, far away from Mark's remote vision. He checked both ways before ducking inside, then leaned up against the door, shut his eyes and breathed deep.

He felt sick with dread, as he had for all three hours since they'd left Tiwanaku. Despite his best efforts at managing it, his sense of impending doom would not lift. His mind kept replaying that awful moment when Sam had invoked the override and it had simply *failed*. In that instant, Mark had gone from a personal annoyance to an object of terror. Their lives now depended entirely on his horribly under-informed choices.

How had it happened? They'd not for a moment expected that particular point of failure. Yunus had been *off* the ship, thereby ceding – Ash had assumed – control of the override system to Sam. Weren't Fleet override protocols supposed to be set in stone? Mark's interface must have received exactly the same status-handles that Ash had during their mission prep on Triton, yet for some reason their impact on the system had been entirely different. Was the Vartian Institute somehow involved?

That moment would have been bad enough on its own, but it had followed on the heels of the nightmare involving Yunus Chesterford. In all of Ash's previous experiences, the Nems had run like clockwork. They'd been tested and tested until the League technicians had simply run out of tests to do.

They still didn't understand the cellular machinery they ran on, of course, but that had felt like a distant concern. After all, you didn't need to understand the physiology of a wolf to know what would happen if you kicked it. Yet something had happened at Tiwanaku. By giving the Nems such a large target, they'd tripped some hidden wire in the system.

'Sam Shah requests entry,' said the door.

Ash moved aside to let him in.

Sam wore a murderous expression. 'This is *not* supposed to be happening,' he said.

'No shit,' said Ash. 'Any idea why the override failed?'

Sam paced the tiny room and declined to answer. 'Can we turn that fucking garden off?' he snarled at the walls. 'At least give me something honest.'

The displays flickered and the room became a glass box surrounded by the star-field that lay beyond the hull.

'I have no fucking idea,' Sam said at last. 'That command code should have been enough to knock an admiral off his perch. I can only guess that Monet is behind this. It's some fucked-up notion of mission security that he sneaked in behind our backs.'

'Or Zoe Tamar?'

Sam shook his head. 'I'd know it. I went over this ship inch by inch before we boarded. The Vartians are sly, but not that sly. In any case, it's obvious what we need to do next – regain control of this ship. We need Nem-cloaking active immediately and a vector to Snakepit. And we don't have long – they're expecting us within forty-eight hours. After that, we're out of the picture.'

'But *how*?' said Ash.

Sam snorted. 'If Ruiz won't give us control, we'll have to take it. Knock him cold, if necessary. With him unresponsive, ship control would slide to you by default.'

Ash pulled a queasy face. 'That won't be easy. You can't drug him – the ship's sedatives won't work on him unless he allows it. He's got a self-aware metabolism like mine. If he's anything like me, he has to run a shutdown just to fall asleep at night.'

'You'll have to take him out physically, then.'

Ash shot Sam a look of disbelief. 'Are you crazy? First up, he has eyes in the fucking walls.'

'Only in his section,' said Sam. 'We made sure of that. He has none over here.'

'Secondly,' said Ash. 'He's an Omega. How do you expect me to get the jump on him? He reacts faster than most people can see.'

'So do you,' said Sam. 'Didn't you both come out of the same gene programme?'

'Yes,' said Ash, 'but we're not clones. There was a huge amount of variation. The whole project was experimental, remember? What Mark lacks in social skills, he makes up for in speed. There was no one in the programme who could touch him for reflexes. Plus, if I fail, what then? The cat's out of the bag.'

In truth, he didn't relish the idea of attacking Mark. The flight had been one long reminder that they'd been almost brothers once, before everything had gone sour. They'd slept in the same dorms, taken the same classes and played together under a sequence of habitat domes, each more secure and less fun than the last. Grabbing him in a choke-hold in a corridor somewhere lacked appeal.

'A threat, perhaps?' he suggested. 'We must have some kind of lever-age that will work.'

Sam slashed the air with his hand. 'The last thing we need is Mark having reason to suspect us. He'd go looking for ways to break our grip and that would be bad. There are things stashed in the memory core of this ship that nobody should see. Exactly the sort of shit that could make this situation even worse.'

'Like what?'

'Never you fucking mind. Shit for handling contingencies. Shit you don't even want to know about.'

At times like this, Ash found Sam a little frightening. When he was badly stressed, ominous-sounding things leaked out.

'That's it, then,' he said. 'It's over. We'll just have to let him in on what's happening and get his support.'

Sam looked disgusted. 'Are you crazy? Mark's in love with the Earth. What are you going to tell him? That we've arranged for it to be bombed by alien robots and that we've fingered his stepdad for the blame? He'd head back there as fast as he could. This whole thing would go into meltdown and we'd be strung up on the nearest gibbet. The fact that this is a last-ditch effort to prevent all-out fucking war would go straight over everyone's heads. If we were *lucky*, we'd live long enough to watch the first bombs start dropping.'

'So we lie to him,' said Ash. 'We make something up.'

'Like what?' said Sam. 'Oh, by the way, Mark, we didn't tell you before but we know all about those aliens and kept it from you for *nice reasons*. And unless you go to this weirdy-ass-looking star system we found, we're all going to die. So pretty please. And don't ask any questions, there's a good chap.'

Ash flushed. He didn't like being mocked and wished he had a decent suggestion to offer. He couldn't think straight with the promise of a Nem swarm breathing down his neck.

He squeezed his eyes shut against the hideous mess they were in. He'd argued about the plan with Sam when it was first explained to him. Leaving warp trails for the Nems was so easy; why hadn't they just initiated the attack on Earth the moment the *Ariel Two* passed through the Penfield Lobe? That way, Will would have still been too far away to abort the attack and the outcome in the home system would have been the same. But *no*, Sam said. It was essential that Will side with them in the aftermath. Ash had never understood why, and now they were paying for that folly.

Sam punched the wall. 'I should have killed Mark already.'

'I don't think you mean that,' said Ash.

Sam gave him a long, cold look. 'Why not? When the stakes are this high, nobody's sacred. Not even the son of Superman.'

'And what are we supposed to do if we arrive at Snakepit and Mark's dead?' said Ash. 'How much help would we get from Will then?'

They both knew this was the major downside of Mark's involvement and the reason they'd already gone to such precarious lengths to unseat him. Mark's safety was supposed to act as leverage to secure Will's cooperation. Instead, he'd become a liability.

'I know the fucking risks!' said Sam. 'And believe me, if I can avoid killing him, I will. We'll have to bide our time. All that time that we don't have. Right now, we need to play nice and win back his trust because he's holding all the cards, even if the self-indulgent little shit has no idea what game he's playing.'

Sam snapped his fingers. A decision had apparently been made.

'Come with me,' he said. 'And keep your mouth *shut* unless I tell you otherwise.'

Sam opened the door to the privacy chamber and led Ash out into the garden-lined companionway that ran through the centre of the science section. They followed the curving corridor to the hatchway that led to the diplomacy zone beyond. From there, Sam ducked through the door to the med-bay where the coma-storage berths lay. Ash quickly followed. Sam shut the door behind them and pulled up the room controls on the wall.

'Give me Citra Chesterford,' he told the room.

'Her sedative is set to run for another ninety minutes,' the med-bay reminded him. 'If she's woken—'

'I don't care,' Sam snapped. 'Override code Shah Nineteen.'

'Of course, Overcaptain Shah.'

The coma-bed where they'd put Citra to recover slid out of the wall. The ship now had two conveniently spare – one for each dead Spatial.

'Recorders off,' said Sam. 'Splice in surveillance cover pattern "WindowTwitcher". And give the patient a stimulant.'

Citra's eyes fluttered. Sam quickly took her hand and laid a gentle restraining palm on her shoulder.

'Citra,' he said softly. 'It's Sam. Don't try to move too much. Your body's still full of sedative.'

Citra blinked and looked up at him with horror in her eyes.

'Where are we?' she said. 'Why are we under gravity? Did we get Yunus?'

Sam shook his head. 'I need you to stay calm and quiet. We're headed for Nerroskovi.'

Citra squeezed her eyes shut. Tears pressed from their corners.

'The others don't know I've woken you,' said Sam. 'They put you out when the ship started moving. But I have to tell you what's going on.' His face was imploring. 'I wanted to send a shuttle back to the surface. Your husband and I may have been at odds in our work but I never would have wished something like that on him. I can't imagine how you're suffering now. I swear to you that I would have got him out if it had been up to me.' He sighed. 'I knew Mark wouldn't do it. That's why I pressed for control. But since Mark broke my priority override, we're all essentially his captives. There's no chance of mounting a rescue for Yunus while he's in control. He's made that very clear.'

Sam's gaze turned sadly to the floor. He drew another deep, ragged breath, as if steeling himself. 'I want you to know that Ash and I will do everything we can to fix this and get Yunus back,' he said. 'In the meantime, if you want to help, please keep quiet about this visit. We'll be doing what we can. I just came to tell you that you have friends, that's all. The politics are behind us. You're not alone on this ship.' He squeezed her hand and started to walk away.

'Wait,' said Citra.

Sam paused.

'How did Mark break the override?' she said. 'I don't understand.'

'Neither do we. By every Fleet-legal procedure, it should have worked. But it's as if Mark knew things would go bad at Tiwanaku and planned it this way. I don't have to remind you that he was hand-picked for this job by Will Monet. Or that before this he was on probation flying heavy lifters in the North Atlantic Disaster Zone. It worries me that Monet has stood against your husband's research for years, Professor. There's no way of knowing what he and Ruiz have in mind for the rest of us.'

The misery in Citra's expression curdled into loathing.

'We all appear to have walked into something deeper than we ever anticipated,' said Sam. 'Maybe some kind of attempt by Will to regain his celebrity? Who knows?'

Citra's mouth became a cold, thin line.

'You realise I'm telling you all this in the strictest confidence,' Sam urged. 'Mark can't know we suspect him. Given a chance, Ash and I may be able to do something with the computers to force a change. But if Mark gets wary and acts first, we'll lose any advantage we have, which could be disastrous for all of us. If there's dissent among the crew about Mark's role, it can't come from Ash or me. Do you understand?'

'Perfectly,' said Citra. A light of anger had come on in her eyes. 'You can rely on me, Overcaptain Shah.'

'Please,' he said with a kindly smile, 'call me Sam.'

Ash hid a shiver. He found it chilling just how easily Sam played her. Yunus and Citra had been allowed on the mission because they were considered adequately predictable, but even so, it disturbed him. As they left the ship's biologist staring grimly at the med-bay ceiling, Ash couldn't help but wonder if he'd notice Sam pulling the same trick on him.

Mark stood on a virtual beach and skimmed stones out across the placid water, struggling for calm. He kept the beach as a subdomain of his personal sensorium space and retreated to it from time to time when he needed to centre himself. There had never been a time such as this.

Waves lapped the pebble shore before him. An afternoon sun shone through a high haze of cloud, giving the sky an opal sheen. A moist, salty breeze tickled his imaginary skin. And none of it did him a blind bit of good.

Everyone was glad to be out alive, no doubt, and within hours they'd reach the rendezvous star. All they had to do then was wait for the other two ships to show and plan how they were going to break the bad news to the rest of IPSO.

But whichever way Mark turned over the events of the last day his mind, he hated them. He tried to think of something he could have done differently but was at a loss. Ash would have been hopeless under those conditions. Ash's social skills exceeded those of every other Omega from the programme, but he was a *Fleet protocols reliably followed under trying conditions* kind of pilot, as one assessment report had put it, not a born improviser. Sam had been way out of line trying to pull overrides on him. There was absolutely nothing in the mission profile that gave him the right to do that.

Even so, the fact that the override hadn't worked was going to look bad. So what if Will Monet had been responsible? The man had been a law unto himself for decades. People weren't even going to bother pointing the finger at him. It was Mark who'd be left looking shady. And Mark who'd have to answer for it in the court case if they went after his interface again. Presuming, of course, that the human race lasted that long.

Mark skimmed a last stone across the water, brushed off his hands and jumped back to his home node. Icons and documents hung around the walls of the cave like a time-locked snowstorm. Mark grabbed the link for his personal security system and dived through it. If he was going to be held accountable for the patch Will had given him, he should at least find out what the hell it did.

Mark's security subsystem resembled a deep, dark forest. He'd decided long ago that the more he made his virtual environment match the kinds of spaces people had evolved in, the more efficient he'd be. He hadn't been proved wrong yet. A short hike through the underbrush revealed a new kind of pinkish vine growing on the tree for each subsystem in his interface. Its surface looked greasy and metallic, at odds with the rules for the visualisation around it.

Mark reached out and touched one. It dissolved into a hovering mess of quasi-sentient program diagrams before coalescing again. Will's handiwork, without a doubt.

Mark followed the vines out of his interface hardware, down into the *Gulliver's* metaphor-space. When viewed through the correct filters, the tinkering became obvious. It must have spread like a disease from the first moment he plugged himself in. The cavernous forest-space of the *Gulliver's* command system was lousy with the stuff. Will had infected him with kudzu of the mind.

Mark groaned. He grabbed a handful of the digital weed and yanked. The vine dissolved in his hand again, this time triggering a readme.

'Good luck, Mark,' said a shivering avatar of Will, who popped into existence standing next to the tree. 'I've tried to include everything you might need. There's a hackpack, traffic blockers and analytics, an autonomous self-monitoring kit, viral templates and a complete submind support armature...'

Mark felt a surge of anger.

'What about a packed lunch?' he shouted. 'Did you remember a fucking packed lunch? Or how about a letter for teacher to get me out of sport-sim, you asshole!'

Not only was this a gross intrusion into his own private mental space, but Will had fouled up the whole command hierarchy. No wonder Sam's overrides hadn't worked. Mark would be surprised if the ship responded to anyone else as captain ever again.

While Sam clearly shouldn't have intervened, this had to be the most embarrassing way possible for it to have played out. Mark rubbed his eyes. He'd need to trace all this stuff down and make sure it hadn't done any damage.

But first, he knew he needed to take ownership of this situation and try to square it with his passengers before the *Ariel Two* showed up. He jumped back to the helm-arena and clicked his fingers for a comms icon. It was time for an all-hands meeting.

Mark sat in his chair in the lounge, brooding and waiting for everyone to file in. Sam appeared first, climbing down the ladder with a heavy tread. Mark braced himself reluctantly for another fight. He felt more exhausted than angry. He dearly hoped Sam wasn't going to start with more shouting.

To his surprise, Sam faced him with a sheepish expression.

'I want to apologise,' he said, before Mark could open his mouth. 'I lost my head at Tiwanaku. I shouldn't have tried to invoke an override. You were right, it was a mistake. I should have let it go after that vote failed the other day. It's simply that I've trained with Ash and know what he can do, whereas you were an unknown. I hope you understand that I was just trying to keep us all alive. No hard feelings?' He thrust out a hand for Mark to shake.

Mark regarded the hand warily. It was tempting to put it all behind them, but he wasn't sure he trusted the gesture yet.

'That's quite a turnaround,' he said.

'It is,' said Sam. 'But I've had some time to think about it, and frankly, I'm embarrassed about the way I reacted back there. I was mentally ready to find a sect cover-up, not *that*, whatever *that* was. It threw me off. And while you might not be my captain of choice, there's still no excuse for breaking Fleet rules. As it was, the ship threw it back in my face. I intend to be a lot more cautious in that regard moving forward. And I welcome your input. As it turns out, I could use the guidance. It happens to all of us from time to time, you know. Even Fleet executives make mistakes.'

Mark took Sam's broad, warm hand and shook it, even though it felt weird doing so.

'Apology accepted,' he said. 'I'm sorry things got as complicated as they did. I overreacted. That drone-shrapnel manoeuvre was dangerous. I should have just dropped it.'

Sam waved it away. 'It's in the past,' he said. 'We're all alive. And besides, as you said, now we have extra research material.' His face cracked into an ironic smile.

'I guess,' said Mark, relaxing a little.

The others started to file down the ladder, Ash first.

'Thank you for coming,' said Mark as they assembled. 'I felt like we all needed to touch base.'

He glanced around at them. Sam still looked apologetic and Ash embarrassed. Zoe's and Venetia's faces bore similar expressions of haggard concern. Citra, though, regarded him with thinly concealed loathing. There was so much venom in her gaze that Mark was surprised the Casimir-buffers in the wall behind him weren't crackling. He felt a renewed surge of guilt.

He cleared his throat. 'This is a difficult time for everyone, but we're going to do what's been asked of us. And that means following the mission profile and rendezvousing with the other ships at Nerroskovi.'

Citra looked unmoved.

He addressed her directly. 'Please believe me, nothing hurts me more right now than the fact that I couldn't send that shuttle down for Yunus. Our mission profile forbade us from interacting with the Photurians in the event of conflict. That's what the other ships are for. And it was my duty to protect *everyone* on this ship. I hope you understand that.'

'I call again for the removal of Mark Ruiz from his position as captain,' Citra said coldly.

Mark blinked at her vitriol. Her gaze drilled into him like a welding laser.

'Citra, we've been over this,' said Venetia quietly. 'Why would you want to go there again?'

'Are you kidding?' Citra retorted. 'Is there a reason to keep him? He was supposed to protect us, but he didn't protect Yunus for a second when it actually counted. And he followed that up by risking everybody's lives flying around after bits of debris.' She smiled a vicious smile. 'Oh yes, *Captain Ruiz*, I know all about that, despite the fact that you had me knocked out. I went and looked over the public logs.'

Zoe folded her arms uncomfortably.

Citra raised an accusing finger to point at Mark's chest. 'Worst of all, that man is only here for some nepotistic reason we don't even understand. Monet put him aboard and we know he's got some kind of agenda. We heard as much from his own lips. When Sam tried the override control, command should have gone straight to Ash and we all know it. He's a *lifter pilot*, for crying out loud. And we have someone more highly trained with a better record sitting right in front of us. How much more proof do we need that something is badly wrong here? Monet has some sick, desperate plan, and this man is a part of it.'

Mark's nostrils flared. The mention of Will had put his hackles up. He'd called them together with the intention of discussing their software problem but now he didn't feel like admitting anything at all. He felt certain Citra would use it against him.

'Citra,' said Venetia slowly, 'Sam shouldn't have tried for control in the first place. I'm not blaming him – we were all a little freaked out back there – but it wasn't Fleet-legal.'

'Does that matter?' said Citra. 'It still should have worked.'

Venetia glanced across at Mark. 'Can you tell us why it didn't?'

Mark threw up his hands. 'I'm here to do a job,' he said defensively. 'Maybe the control SAP recognised a dangerous transfer of authority and blocked it on safety grounds. The onboard ethics on this ship are all run by Vartian software, not Fleet code. Zoe, do you know its priority pattern?'

Zoe shook her head. 'Not without checking the source.'

'Look at him,' Citra sneered. 'It's obvious he's hiding something. I can see it all over his face. I want another no-confidence vote. Right now.'

Sam held up a warning hand. 'Whoa there a moment. I have to remind you that Ash and I are military staff and this situation has definitely gone military. We can't participate in something like that any more. It's not Fleet procedure, and we can't be counted as passenger-witnesses. It's down to the rest of you, I'm afraid.'

Citra stared at Venetia. 'All those in favour of removing Captain Ruiz,' she said. Her hand snapped up.

Venetia's stayed down.

Citra glared at the psychologist. 'I don't know why you're protecting him,' she said. 'Do you hate my husband that much? If you don't support me in this, I'll have your actions investigated by an Earth court the moment we get home. How long do you suppose your funding will last then?'

'Nice threat,' said Venetia. 'My hand is down because there's no actual evidence of wrongdoing. Everything you're saying is supposition and I'm not going to derail this mission on the basis of that. Bring your lawyers and see if I care.'

Zoe kept her hand down, too, though she looked reluctant about it. Mark could almost see the gears turning in her head as Citra turned to glare at her.

'While I'm not impressed by his attitude or his flying style,' Zoe said slowly, 'removing him is wrong. So I can't back the action, despite my

223

respect for Ash. I mean Subcaptain Corrigan. And besides, I suspect that the drone remnants we picked up back there will prove critical to the success of this mission, so I can hardly fault Mark for collecting them.'

'You *what*?' said Citra. 'He abandons my husband but picks up some trash for you on the way out, so that makes it okay?'

'No,' said Zoe, blushing. 'It's not like that.'

Citra regarded both women with disgust and stormed up the ladder.

'Professor Chesterford,' said Zoe, following closely behind. 'Wait. Please.'

Sam shook his head. 'Meeting adjourned, I guess.'

He and Ash left together. Just like last time, Venetia stayed behind.

'We seem to be making a habit of this,' said Mark. 'Thank you. Again.'

'Don't bother,' she replied. 'Citra's not acting rationally. There isn't a captain in the Fleet who'd have gone back for Yunus under those conditions.' She peered at him. 'How are you coping?'

'Okay,' said Mark. 'Freaked out, but okay.'

'That was Will's doing, wasn't it? That override problem?'

Mark nodded.

'Did you know he'd hacked the ship?'

'No!' said Mark, then realised it wasn't quite true. 'I knew he'd given me an update package but I had no idea he'd put anything so extreme in it. We had a minor security problem before we left. I assumed he just installed code to compensate for that. No more.'

'Then why didn't you say so?'

Mark gestured at the ladder, his expression incredulous. 'To *her*? She'd have just turned it into another weapon.'

Venetia exhaled. 'Probably, yes. But it doesn't look good. Sam came to see me, you know, after we made it out of Tiwanaku. He's very suspicious of you right now. Coming on the back of that whole no-confidence-vote business, he's more convinced than ever that there's something wrong about you being here. And he still thinks Will shouldn't have waded in there with guns blazing. He's convinced he had everything under control.'

'That's bullshit,' said Mark. 'Everyone could see he was flailing.'

'Everyone but him. And claiming that you had no idea about the override isn't going to cut it. He thinks there's something fishy going on. He's just not as vocal about it as Citra.'

'Really?' Mark said wearily. He didn't know whether to be surprised or just disappointed. 'He apologised to me just now, before the meeting. He said he was the one who made a mistake back there.'

'He did,' said Venetia. 'But that won't stop him snooping. Sam's a cop, Mark. He's going to put you at your ease while he builds his case.'

Mark rubbed his eyes, exasperated. The whole situation felt ridiculous.

'Do you think I should just relinquish command, then? Give up the whole thing and let them do whatever they want?'

It would at least prove his good intentions. It'd go on his record as an abdication of command, which he wasn't keen on, but arguably their mission was beyond such concerns at this point.

Venetia fixed him with a cool, penetrating gaze. 'Do *you*?'

He shook his head. 'No. For all his strengths, Ash would never have been able to get us out of that mess. If those things come after us, I'd rather have my hands on the controls. Once we've got the *Ariel Two* watching our backs again, I'll happily hand off command if they still want that. But not before.'

'For what it's worth, I agree,' said Venetia. 'Particularly given that we're not even sure you *can* hand off at this point. This is all conjecture anyway until we have our team back together. Until then, try to stay calm. I'll talk to the others. Okay?'

Mark nodded.

'You did good back there. Those manoeuvres scared the shit out of me, but you got us out alive. Thank you.'

Half a laugh escaped Mark's throat. 'You're welcome.'

9.3: WILL

Will slid into the unknown system with his sensors on full spread and his quantum shield running. The first thing he noticed was what *wasn't* there. Despite its proximity to Tiwanaku and the Fecund domain, this system didn't appear to have any of the characteristic habitat ruins in its out-system. Or none close enough for him to see, at least. That in itself was surprising, given that the star was a G-type. Either the Fecund hadn't come here, or the place had been cleaned out. Interesting.

'What're you looking for?' Devi asked.

'Fecund artefacts,' said Will.

He felt duty-bound to at least keep them clued in as to what he was doing. It couldn't have been easy sitting around in the nestship while he took them charging off into uncharted space.

'Factories,' he added. 'We know the sects discovered that network of Fecund charging stations. They've been busy exploring behind our backs, and my guess is they found something here that makes drones which they either activated by accident or decided to use at Tiwanaku.'

'I'm not seeing any, though,' she said nervously. 'Are you?'

In truth, Will wasn't, no matter how deeply he searched. However, his scans of the in-system revealed two surprises. The first was a planet of one-point-one Earth masses in the yellow star's broad habitable zone. Analysis revealed calm weather and an apparently breathable oxygen-nitrogen atmosphere. A biosphere world, in other words, in apparently perfect condition.

However, the more startling discovery was his second: a short-range beacon quietly broadcasting a Fleet signal. Will held his breath and stared at the survey results. It took him a minute to form words.

'What the fuck is *that* doing here?'

He burrowed into the data, scrabbling for a better look. The beacon proved to be a low-powered relay attached to a small orbital habitat stationed at the planet's L2 position. A closer inspection of the planet showed a faint Fleet signal coming from the surface, too, along with some curious atmospheric contaminants that suggested the presence of industry.

Will's face froze as the implications started to settle in. Unless the beacon's security certificates had been faked, this planet had been found by the Fleet, not the sects. But this star system lay outside the domain of surveyed worlds, which meant that someone in the Fleet had come here off the books.

Disgust swelled inside him. If this was a Fleet secret, then his own people – his fellow IPSO officers – must have travelled here and made first contact without telling him. They'd kept him out of the loop and subsequently screwed it up. *His* team had been responsible for incurring the aliens' wrath – and then hidden that fact from the rest of the organisation. It was an inconceivable breach of Fleet protocol and an unforgivable breach of trust.

But who'd done it? How many people were in on this? He

remembered all those dreary budget reports from the Far Frontier he'd
been made to look at, and all those depressing figures about lost ships
and miscalculated fuel supplies. He'd not wanted to believe his own
people capable of such incompetence. Maybe they hadn't been. He
should have looked deeper.

Will compared the security certificate in the beacon signal with the
Fleet deployment database. The station he was looking at had supposedly been destroyed in a Flag conflict two years ago, light-years away
in the Rosetta System.

Two years.

He swallowed, his mouth dry. While he'd been wallowing in private
misery, someone had played him for a fool, and now people had died
because of it. A kernel of white-hot wrath formed in the pit of his
stomach, at least half of it aimed at himself. How had he, the most
powerful single entity in all of human space, been so duped? With
disgust, Will realised it had probably been easy. He drew some long,
level breaths.

'Will, stay calm,' said Nelson quickly. 'I don't like this either but
we'll solve it. We just need to take it one step at a time, that's all. No
rash actions.'

Will turned to face him. 'Did you know about this?' he growled.

Nelson's nose wrinkled in affront. 'Of course not! What do you take
me for?'

Meanwhile, Will's SAPs kept ferrying back fresh details on the biosphere world below. The number of unusual biochemical signatures in
the atmosphere beggared belief, yet the ocean showed extensive signs
of algal vegetation. His long-range imaging systems returned pictures of
a world with purplish oceans and charcoal-grey continents dotted with
huge, symmetrical land-features shaped like starfish tens of kilometres
on a side. They were clearly artificial.

Whatever was down there wasn't Fecund or human. This wasn't just
a biosphere, this was the biggest alien discovery since the lure star. This
time, though, it was his own people who'd hidden the secret while he'd
been left playing politics. His guts wound tight with betrayal. Had the
war meant nothing to these people? Were their memories *that* short?

As he closed on the mysterious orbital, Will opened a channel.

'Fleet Station, this is Captain Will Monet of the *Ariel Two*.' His voice quavered with barely suppressed rage. 'I do not have this location assignment in my records. Please self-identify.'

He ground his teeth while he waited through the light-lag for their response.

'It's a relief to see you, *Ariel Two*,' said a voice from the station. They left the video channel blank. 'Welcome to Snakepit. We've been waiting a long time and we're glad you're here at last.'

Will gawped at the calm reply. 'Fuck your gladness,' he told them slowly. 'Explain what you are doing here and what is going on. Otherwise I will blow you out of the fucking sky.'

9.4: ANN

Ann dialled back the warp at Snakepit's heliopause, kicked in the tau-chargers and raced into the system under maximum stealth. Using the chargers and the stealth shield together put a ferocious drain on her antimatter but Ann couldn't have cared less. Every second counted. The tension in the *Chiyome*'s cabin had never been higher. Beside her, Jaco Brinsen scowled into his display, his jaw flexing. Below her she could hear the nervous coughs of the others over the hum of the vents and smell their fear in the air.

As the light-lag dropped, bursts of Will's conversation with the Snakepit habitat reached Ann, the gap shortening between each message.

'...wise I will blow you out of the fucking sky.'

'We'd be pleased to give you all the answers you need, Captain Monet. What would you like to know?'

'What is this place?' Will snapped. 'Why wasn't I informed when you found it?'

'This system has been tentatively named Snakepit. It is the site of humanity's finest exobiological find to date. The risk associated with informing you too early was deemed unacceptable.'

'Unacceptable for whom?' The menace in Will's voice was palpable.

'For the entire human race. Please don't judge us until you've been fully briefed.'

'And what the fuck does that entail?'

'That will become clear shortly.'

'By which you mean *what*?' Will yelled.

'Please wait one moment.'

'Are you playing for time? *Really*, you fucking traitors? Because in case you hadn't noticed, I'm in a *shoot first, figure shit out later* kind of mood.'

It was clear that Will's emotions were ratcheting up dangerously, just like the models had predicted. She'd almost missed her window. Right now, everyone on that station would be holding their breath and getting ready to die.

Ann dived in straight, losing stealth-integrity as she did so.

'Warm the boser, please, Kuril,' she said. Regret choked her throat.

'On it.'

'We have boser targeting range,' Jaco told her.

'Zoti, fire the disabler message now,' said Ann.

'Done.'

The *Ariel Two*'s quantum shield stuttered as the hidden relays added during the mighty ship's last refit came online. The liquid-silver shell surrounding the *Ariel Two* snapped in an instant, showering space with fused shielding alloy as its uncollapsed atoms lurched back to their natural state.

'Boser scatter pattern Kazak One, please, Jaco,' said Ann. She hated herself even as she spoke. 'Fire at will.'

Jaco fired. While far less powerful than the *Ariel Two*'s main cannon, the *Chiyome*'s weapon still packed an incredible punch. Beams of coherent iron, fired at near light-speed, flickered across the *Ariel Two*'s massive hull.

Without a quantum shield to protect it, the boser lanced through the vessel as if it wasn't there. Each perfectly aimed shot bored a hole through one of the ship's primary power junctions before exiting on the other side, two hundred kilometres from its insertion point.

'Successful delivery of the scatter pattern,' said Jaco. 'I recommend we move immediately to delivery of Kazak Two. That ship's wired up like a brain. It has redundancy everywhere – give him five minutes and he'll have half his systems back online.'

'No, Mr Brinsen,' Ann said quickly. The thought of firing again on Will's crippled ship made her feel sick. 'Your point is well made but our gesture is adequate, I think.'

She opened a channel. '*Ariel Two*, this is Captain Ludik of the *Chiyome*.'

A mixture of guilt and embarrassment flushed her features. She'd restricted herself to audio. She couldn't stand the thought of anything more.

'Your primary power is offline. You cannot fire or run. Please power down the rest of your ship and surrender. In return, your questions will be answered and your safety assured.'

She closed the channel before Will could scream at her. He'd need a few minutes for his predicament to sink in.

'Keep a close watch on them, Jaco,' she said. 'Let me know if that ship so much as twitches.'

'Of course,' said Jaco. 'My congratulations, by the way, ma'am. I wasn't sure we'd make it, but you timed it perfectly. We nailed him, which means we're past the next hurdle. It's a win for the League and a step forward for the human race.'

'Thank you, Mr Brinsen,' she said coldly. 'I appreciate it.'

She found it hard to put her finger on when in the last day or so she'd actually started to hate Jaco. One good thing about the next part of the mission was that she wouldn't have to listen to him any more.

10: FAILURE

10.1: MARK

On arrival at Nerroskovi, the *Gulliver* tethered itself to an asteroid half an AU out from the star to mine metals and conduct repairs. At Sam's suggestion, they kept their albedo matched to the rock in case of unexpected visitors. Then they waited.

The two days Mark spent there felt longer than the rest of the mission put together. The Nerroskovi System held nothing but a small red star, some desolate rubble and a little ice. Mark felt naked sitting there every time he merged with the ship – naked and scared.

The expected arrival time for the other two ships came and went. The deadline for emergency departure loomed. The *Gulliver* still had no word from the rest of the mission. Mark wondered what had happened. Surely those tiny drones hadn't been a match for the *Ariel Two*. That ship had been built by the Fecund for a scale of warfare the human race had never engaged in and hopefully would never see. He thought perhaps that Will might have gone to explore the exit vector the watchers had told them about. But then where was the *Chiyome*? Why hadn't it arrived to explain what was going on?

The mood on the ship steadily worsened. Zoe and Venetia disappeared into their research. Sam talked extensively about contingency plans, most of which had nothing to do with their actual orders. And Citra confined herself to her lab in the science section, unwilling to come within Mark's camera range.

Mark set the ship and its attendant rock at a comfortable spin to try to improve mood, but it didn't help. At the end of his shift on the second day, he found himself conducting another futile scan for incoming signals when Zoe joined him on the bridge.

It wasn't the first time - after Tiwanaku, she'd made regular visits. She generally asked for tweaks to the ship's systems or assistance with robots to manoeuvre the drone remains around within the outer hull cavities. Under the circumstances, Mark had been only too happy to oblige. So long as he helped with her research, she stopped looking at him like dirt, which he counted as a distinct improvement. One happy passenger was better than none at all, even if their conversations usually petered out after the first minute.

'Doctor Tamar, can I help you?' he said, rising from his bunk.

'We have to talk,' said Zoe. She stood in front of him with an urgent look in her eyes, her body blocking the doorway.

'Okay,' said Mark cautiously. 'About what?'

'About that debris you picked up and what it means.'

This was new. Since their first abortive conversation, Zoe hadn't tried talking science with him.

'Go on,' he said cautiously.

'Most of it is recycled human equipment, or new kit built to modified human designs,' said Zoe. 'Take that out of the picture and all you have left is some *very* complicated biomachinery – too dense to understand, really – and some surprisingly lame warp-drive tech.'

'Okay,' said Mark. 'That's interesting, I guess. Nice work.'

'It's not just interesting,' said Zoe. 'It's critically important. You gave me the pointer I needed, actually. Your remark about faking the warp signature the other day – it was wrong, of course, but it prompted me to write extra code to scan the warp envelopes on those drones, just in case. If I hadn't been looking that closely, I'd have missed it.'

Mark felt a frown coming on. Zoe was being weird. 'Missed what?'

'There were *two* warp-drive designs in use in that cloud,' she said, 'not one – ours and theirs. Fortunately, the remains we collected contained bits of both kinds of drive. Just enough for me to prove the hypothesis. Apparently, when the Photurian machines encountered humans, they dropped their version of warp and started copying ours. I can hardly blame them – their version is weirdly over-designed and makes a warp field so thin I'm amazed it ever worked. No wonder the emission spikes were so sharp. It's as if they were trying to build magnetic containers for a quantum shield and changed their minds about what they wanted halfway through.

'The best you could do with their version was create a *film* of curvon discharge, not a channel of it. So we have our answer about the drones at last – Photurians are apparently terrible engineers, just like they're terrible negotiators. Maybe that's what happens when a bunch of SAPs try to invent warp drive instead of having people do it for them.'

Mark folded his arms and tried for a polite smile. 'I don't get it. How is this critically important?'

'Here's the thing,' said Zoe. 'Those original warp drives are so bad, there's absolutely no way the drones we found could have reached Tiwanaku on their own – or ever leave, for that matter – which means they got here some other way. In other words, there's a big part of the Photurian puzzle we just don't have yet. A crucial part. And that's why we have to go back to Tiwanaku.'

Mark stared at her for a moment, trying to figure out if she was serious. Her eyes retained their round, owlish stare. He realised, with a sinking feeling, that she was.

'I can't do that,' he said. 'It's not in the mission plan and it would put everyone on this ship at risk.'

She brushed his comment away. 'Mark, listen. Think about it. If the drones couldn't have got there without help, what brought them? Why didn't we spot it?'

Mark shrugged. 'It had a tau-charger?'

'No!' she exclaimed, her voice rising. 'It's more obvious than that. The radiation weapon they fired when they arrived at Tiwanaku *wasn't* a weapon. It was a drive. We were looking at the mother of all warp flashes without realising. It was the arrival of whatever brought those drones. Understanding what that thing is will give us the advantage we need to protect ourselves. And we're not going to figure that out just sitting here and doing nothing.'

'That's great,' said Mark. 'Very impressive reasoning, and you're probably right, but I can't change my orders. We're supposed to wait here until the final deadline passes, eight hours from now, and then we're supposed to go home.'

Zoe scowled. 'I know that. But this could mean the difference between peace and war. It's the last piece of the puzzle!'

'It's the last piece of the *technical* puzzle,' said Mark. 'We still have no real idea why the Photurians attacked in the first place.'

'What does that matter if they can't do it again? Look, we don't have to go right back into the system. Just to the edge. I could scan from there.'

Mark gave up and squeezed past her towards the chute that led down to the lounge. She followed him.

'Look, I believe you,' he said. 'It's just that we have a job to do here. I know that's not a very popular idea right now, but we made a commitment to IPSO and it's my intention to carry it out.'

'So you can get your interface rights, is that it? Ash told me as much.'

Mark scowled and headed down the ladder.

'Look, this isn't about you and whether you're a screw-up or not,' she said. 'It's about the future of the human race.'

Mark rounded on her as she clambered down to meet him. 'Did you even consult the rest of the crew yet?'

'No,' said Zoe. 'I didn't want to have to take it to a vote. We know what that's like. I wanted to make you see reason first. But I can hardly imagine that Citra would complain. And I bet Ash would help.'

'This conversation is over,' said Mark and headed for his chair.

Zoe seized his arm. 'Stop!' she yelled.

Mark spun around. 'What?' he snapped, yanking his arm out of her grip. His anger derailed slightly when he saw the panicked expression on her face.

'Don't move,' she whispered. She started sniffing the air.

'What?' said Mark. 'What's going on? What kind of bullshit is this now?'

'Shut up a minute,' said Zoe.

She sniffed the air energetically, as if impersonating a bloodhound, until she neared his chair.

'Holy shit!' she breathed.

'Can I sit now?' said Mark, his patience waning. He started to slide past her.

Zoe's arm whipped out to block him. 'Don't! It's been smeared with neurotoxins.'

Mark peered at her in confusion. '*What?*'

'I can smell them,' she said. 'Vartian Institute implants in case of alien attack – I was fitted with biotech augs to detect chemical incursion.

What did you think I was doing on the privacy level back at Delany – having my nails done? Stay right here, and if anyone else comes in, don't let them sit down. Anywhere. I mean it.'

Mark stared after her as she raced up the ladder. He didn't buy it. Who would be stupid enough to do such a thing?

Zoe returned seconds later with a medical sampler in her hand. She handed it to him.

'Look for yourself.'

Mark synced with the device and swept it back and forth in front of his usual seat. Warning icons started piling up in his sensorium. She was right. Someone had rubbed the headrest of his chair with a very nasty nerve agent – one even his smart metabolism wouldn't have picked up.

He blinked, thunderstruck. Someone had just tried to kill him.

'What *is* that shit?' he said, pointing at the seat. 'And why do we even have it aboard?'

Zoe queried the database, patching information straight to her view. Then she threw him a window. A rotating model of a large, complex molecule appeared in his primary metaphor.

'Look – it's a compound from the Davenport biosphere. It's a cyto-skeletal disassembler used in comparative biology. Citra's lab carries it.'

Mark couldn't believe it. It was his usual chair, but anyone could have sat in it. It was pure luck that Zoe happened to have an aug that could detect it. She dashed back up the ladder again while Mark stood in a daze.

Citra was the likely culprit, but what could she possibly have imagined the fallout would be? She was a respected biologist. With him dead in a chair, her career would be over. While Citra had shown plenty of capacity for irrational behaviour, she wasn't stupid. And the Chesterfords were nothing if not protective of their public personas.

Could it have been someone else, then? He wondered for a moment if Zoe was responsible. She'd discovered it, after all. Maybe she'd wanted to scare him. But with what motive? Venetia he ruled out immediately. She'd been supportive of him throughout. And he and Ash had too much history. His old friend had been unusually quiet over the last few days but Mark had felt, if anything, that Ash was working harder at their relationship. He looked constantly on the brink of opening up.

235

And now that the mission had been so badly scorched, Ash didn't come off as remotely hungry for the captaincy.

That left Sam. But as Venetia had pointed out, Sam was a cop. His whole career had been about maintaining order. Even if he genuinely thought Mark constituted some kind of nebulous threat to the mission, why try to kill him? And why now, with Tiwanaku already behind them? While talking to Sam still left Mark feeling uncomfortable, trying to picture him as the culprit didn't sit right. He'd have just as much to lose as Citra from a stunt like this. More, in fact.

Zoe returned with a squeeze-bulb marked with lab codes and started spraying down the chair.

'It's time for another meeting, I think,' she said.

Mark nodded in agreement and sent out an alert to the others while his hands shook from the shock. He'd come to hate their meetings. But an attempted murder called for an all-hands, whether he liked it or not.

10.2: WILL

Will experienced the blast as physical pain. He arched in his couch as his integrated mind burned with the damage to the ship's internal systems. An agonised gasp escaped his lips. He collapsed back into the captain's chair, his body bathed in sweat, and had to open his eyes and physically check to ensure he hadn't actually been shot in the gut.

'How?' he wheezed.

While his heart pounded, he reached out through the tortured ship to scan for the origin of the attack. He knew what to look for. Though it pained him to contemplate it, he could think of only one ship with the capacity to deliver the blow.

The *Ariel Two* had been pierced through every one of its primary power routings in the same second. That implied an extensive knowledge of his ship. And the attack had come on the back of a soft assault that had taken out his shield. The *Chiyome* was out there somewhere.

Ann hailed him before he could spot her.

'*Ariel Two*, this is Captain Ludik of the *Chiyome*. Your primary power is offline. You cannot fire or run. Please power down the rest of your ship and give yourself up. In return, your questions will be answered and your safety assured.'

Her demands sank a lead weight through his heart. The reason she'd been so keen to let him spill his feelings was now painfully clear. She needed to keep tabs on him to deliver this blow. Something cold curdled inside him. Give himself up? Fat chance.

A grim picture had started assembling itself in Will's mind. The habitat below had sat here waiting for him without any shields to speak of, suggesting it didn't consider the planet a threat. And Ann's attack had left him defenceless – a move that suggested she held the same opinion. All this left the sickening implication that the Fleet hadn't incurred the wrath of some alien species after all or tried to hide the details behind the Tiwanaku event. They'd caused it.

He could guess why. The Earth sects had been using hidden Fecund sites to fuel their advance, and this, somehow, was the Fleet's answer. They'd gone looking for secrets of their own and found this place. And then they'd turned it into a tool of war. They'd taken an unknown alien technology and made it into a weapon.

No wonder the timing of the Tiwanaku Event had been so propitious. There'd been nothing accidental about it. Were the people on his own side that stupid, though? Hadn't they read any history? But of course, they had to know how he'd feel. He'd never have let them do this, and that was why they hadn't told him.

How long had they been exploring this while he'd been covering their traitorous asses on Mars? he wondered. How much time had they stolen? How much opportunity? And how badly had they fucked things up? It occurred to him then that he'd dragged Mark into the middle of a set-up. In doing so, he might have killed the closest thing he had to a son.

Beside him, Nelson hung his head. 'Apparently we don't have much of a choice,' he said. 'We can't see them. We can't fire back.'

'Fuck that,' Will spat. His ship had the capacity for limited warp using the secondary conduits. That would have to do. 'We're leaving,' he said. 'I'm routing power through the secondaries. Hold on tight, everybody.'

'Will, stop!' said Nelson. 'Are you *crazy*? We don't have any shields. We're sitting ducks.'

'Then we'd better sit somewhere else,' said Will, and sent subminds racing through his ship's systems, seeking out alternative channels for power.

Nelson stared at him, horrified, his expression imploring. 'Will, please remember you're not alone on this ship. It's fine for you to risk your own life but my team is still aboard. You're risking everyone.'

Will picked a vector designed to put the *Chiyome* at the greatest disadvantage and threw power into the thrusters.

'Then tell them to buckle the fuck up,' he snarled. 'I'm not giving that bitch the satisfaction of imagining she has me pegged. I'm going to make this as hard for her as I possibly can.'

'Will!' Nelson roared. 'You're not being rational and you're damaging the ship. The secondaries aren't designed for this. And besides, that beacon had a Fleet signature – isn't that proof enough they don't want us hurt?'

Will glared at Nelson with his human eyes. The man was starting to sound weirdly naïve. Hadn't he noticed they'd just been shot at by their own side?

Drones raced ahead of them and detonated, sending shock waves clanging through the unprotected hull. Warning shots from the *Chiyome*. Will layered in an evasive manoeuvre program. He could feel the strain on the ship like the ache of tired muscles. It was years since he'd tried to use the *Ariel Two* this way.

'You're overloading couplings all across the ship,' said Nelson, his eyes skittering over the data in his view. 'At least let me help!' He reached into the *Ariel*'s smart-web and started tinkering.

Abruptly, power died altogether as several overworked secondary junctions blew simultaneously. All across the mighty ship, fluid stopped pumping and robots sagged mid-task. The lights in the primary habitat core dulled to a clotted red.

The ship drifted. The *Chiyome* raced up behind them in a second and dropped its cloak, revealing a boser pointed straight at them.

Will rounded on Nelson. 'You did that,' he said. 'You crippled us on purpose.' He started climbing out of his couch, hands closing like claws.

'Now you're being childish,' said Nelson. 'Why don't you listen to what these people have to say first?'

Will froze. His skin prickled as the obvious finally dawned on him. 'You're with them.'

To his credit, Nelson didn't bother denying it. 'This isn't what it looks like,' he said.

Will sagged. He'd entrusted his secrets to Nelson. He'd let the man decide things for him. Crucial things. Nelson had watched him cry, heard about his war nightmares, listened to him babble out his innermost fears. This new betrayal cut deep enough to suck the strength from his body. He hung his head and drifted. A sense of disgust and exhaustion as heavy as a glacier stayed his hand from killing.

Ann's voice sounded over the comms.

'*Ariel Two*, this is your final warning. Captain Monet, will you surrender peacefully, or must we fire again?'

Nelson thumbed the comm. 'We're without power, *Chiyome*,' he said. 'You can come aboard. The captain will be waiting for you.'

10.3: ASH

Ash was lying in his bunk, failing to sleep, when the alert came through. He saw Mark's ID attached to the message and immediately knew the plan hadn't worked. He fought down a surge of angry desperation. He'd proposed to Sam that he make nice with Zoe and try to convince her to change her vote. Sam had refused.

'That moment's past and we're out of time,' he'd said.

So Ash had taken the bottle Sam had given him and applied it carefully, as instructed. He'd trusted Sam that it would just knock Mark out without wanting to think about it too much. What else was he supposed to do, after all? In the meantime, Sam had managed Citra.

Ash got up. Maybe it wouldn't be so bad. At this point, he preferred any kind of resolution to the dread of waiting. He'd spent his life aboard ships, flying risky missions to and from the Frontier, keeping secrets, pushing life's envelope. He wasn't used to being afraid. It was, he'd come to appreciate, the anticipation that got you, not the experiences themselves.

And Ash knew what was coming – not starships, just death. By his estimates, they had only a few hours left before the Nemesis machines arrived. The *Gulliver*'s warp trail would be painfully easy for the Nems to see. And the Nems *always* chased down perceived antagonists.

When he joined the Rumfoord League, he'd never guessed it would end like this. He'd seen himself as a brave defender – one of the few making sacrifices to maintain the peace. Now he just felt like fish-food.

He tried to keep the guilt and fear off his face as he headed for the lounge.

The others showed up on the lower level looking more than a little confused.

'Another meeting?' said Venetia. 'Really?'

'Do you want to tell us what's going on?' Sam asked Mark. He looked gently curious, and as unruffled as ever.

'This is going to sound weird,' said Mark, 'but there's been a murder attempt on this ship. The intended victim was me.'

Ash's heart sank as disgust curdled inside him. He should never have taken Sam at his word. Sam's eyes, meanwhile, went wide in a perfect simulacrum of surprise.

'Murder? In here? Are you serious?'

'Very, I'm afraid,' said Mark. He pointed. 'Someone painted this chair with neurotoxins. Whoever sat down and rubbed their neck against it was going to take it in the ...'

'The proverbial neck?' Venetia finished for him.

Mark nodded weakly. 'Yeah.' He didn't appear to have much strength for wit at that moment.

'How do you know it was poisoned?' said Sam, peering at the crumpled velvet.

Zoe handed him the medical sampler. 'See for yourself.'

'This is bad news,' said Mark. 'As if we didn't have enough trouble already. Someone's going to wind up in coma till we get home.'

He shot Citra a furtive glance when she wasn't looking. Ash was thankful for that, at least. Perceived guilt was following Sam's pre-assigned path.

'Can someone explain exactly what happened here?' said Venetia. 'Because it's just weird. It's all a little, you know, twentieth century. I mean, who tries killing anyone on a *starship*? Isn't that, like, the most self-defeating crime anyone could possibly attempt? The surveillance alone—'

'Except this ship doesn't have it, remember?' said Zoe. 'Or hardly any compared to a usual Fleet vessel. Look, Mark and I came in here. He was about to sit down and then I smelled it. It took us another couple of minutes to figure out that someone had deliberately painted his chair with an undetectable neurotoxin.'

'Wait,' said Sam. 'What did you just say? If it's undetectable, how come you detected it?'

'I have augments,' said Zoe. 'Vartian Institute tools to protect against chemical incursion.'

Sam shot her a wary look. 'You never told us that.'

'Of course not,' she retorted. 'I didn't tell anyone on the ship. The Institute delivers information like that on a need-to-know basis.'

Ash suppressed the urge to guffaw. How angry Sam had to be right now. He wasn't the only person on the ship shaping events behind the scenes. First Will Monet had gone around him, and now so had the lowly Zoe Tamar, a scientist with a predictability score of seven-point-three. He must be fuming.

Sam gave Zoe a frosty look. 'So you were keeping things from us as well.' His tone spoke volumes.

'Of course,' said Zoe tartly. 'The Vartian Institute's job is to prevent alien subversion, just like yours is to prevent Frontier security problems. If anyone aboard should understand *need to know*, Overcaptain Shah, it's you. Do we ask you about *your* secrets?'

'So,' said Sam, 'you *detected* it. Then what?'

'Then Zoe went for the sampler,' said Mark, his voice strained. 'And that's when we figured out the substance came from Citra's lab.'

All eyes turned to Citra Chesterford. She glanced around at them with astonished contempt before raising her hand to point at Mark.

'He did it,' she said.

'I'm sorry?' said Zoe.

'This is a ruse,' said Citra. 'He never meant to actually sit in that chair. The whole thing is a carefully constructed trick to frame me because of what I said and what I've figured out about him. It's obvious.' She shook her head, her face twisting with disgust. 'I had no idea you'd stoop so low.' Her voice warbled as she spoke.

Ash watched Mark's expression close up in anger.

Citra turned to Sam. 'You know this is true, don't you?' she said. 'Tell them.'

Sam threw up his hands and managed to look upset. 'Hey!' he said. 'This is an awful situation, but we can't afford to make any assumptions about who did what here. For a start, Professor Chesterford, no one has accused you of anything yet.'

'But that's not how it looks, is it?' she said. 'It'd take a fool not to see that I've been set up.'

'Nevertheless,' said Sam, 'when there's a legal accusation of this severity, there can be no short cuts.'

Venetia rubbed her temples and looked worried. 'Zoe, isn't there some way we can bypass the security settings and access the camera logs?' she said. 'I mean, there has to be, doesn't there? We're not living in the dark ages here. All we need to do is reach the memory core.'

Sam shook his head. 'Sadly, the security on this ship is watertight. That's why we chose it. We were protecting against aliens. We never expected this kind of situation would arise.'

'Actually, that's not completely true,' said Zoe. 'We might be able to do it.'

Ash's heart skipped a beat.

'And how would you do that?' said Sam. His tone leaked scepticism. 'Is there more you haven't told us?'

Zoe shot him a sour look and explained. 'While we didn't bring messenger drones, this ship still has the firing tubes for them and all the accompanying data support. Logs are automatically passed from the core to the memory caches in the docks. Dock security still runs on Fleet standard, not the diplomacy lockdown the rest of the ship uses. It wasn't upgraded because there weren't any drones to make the modification worthwhile. We don't have direct access to those docks, of course. However, we could send a robot up there to interface with one of them. We'd have to fake something to make the robot look like a messenger drone, but that shouldn't be too hard.'

Ash knew what they'd see. They'd see him painting the chair. They probably wouldn't even bother winding back as far as his conversations with Sam to figure out why. And Sam wouldn't let them. Ash wondered how Sam had ever convinced him to play along. He understood how Citra had to be feeling at that moment: trapped and appalled. His heart hammered in his chest as if demanding to be released. He looked across at Sam with newfound loathing and watched as his boss calmly assessed their options.

'How long would that take?' said Sam.

'Mocking up the interface would be the hard part,' said Mark. 'Maybe a couple of hours, max?'

'It's not a matter of time,' said Venetia.

'It is for me,' Mark replied. 'That's why I'm already on it.'

Sam blinked at him. 'Really? *That's* convenient. I hope you'll remember to keep an open feed on that process throughout, so we can make sure you're not tinkering with it.'

'Of course,' said Mark curtly. 'Check your view profile. I'll have the final attachment to the dock done with everyone in here so there can be no doubt I didn't touch it first. You can break the seals yourself.'

'Okay,' said Sam grudgingly. 'Under the circumstances, then, I have to admit that the security lapse appears justified.'

Ash ground his teeth and struggled for something to say. The only thing he could think of was a full confession. The awful knowledge of the entire plot sat in his mouth like a bolus of burning food, begging to be spat into the world. He drew breath to speak.

Sam beat him to it. 'In the meantime, we should get the whole story straight,' he said. He shot Ash a significant look as if reading his anxiety. 'Zoe, do you think you could point out the substance in the lab you believe was used?' He turned to Citra. 'And Professor Chesterford, do we have your permission to examine your lab? To see if there are any traces of intrusion, for instance?'

Citra managed to look freshly affronted, but nodded. 'If that's what it takes.'

'Is that strictly necessary?' said Venetia. 'I mean, if we have the profile of the compound, isn't that enough?'

'Not if we don't know where it came from,' said Sam. 'If Citra *has* been framed, wouldn't it have been easier to do without sneaking into her lab? Another sample could have been smuggled aboard somehow.'

'Under Fleet maximum security conditions?' said Venetia. 'You think so?'

'Why not? I could have done it,' said Sam. 'Did you think of that? My point is that we have yet to determine guilt here. Until we have clarity, we're *all* under suspicion. And the more we learn, the faster we'll get this horrible business cleared up. Okay. To the bio-lab, please, everyone. I think it's better if we go together, don't you?'

Sam ushered them all up the ladder to the main ring of the habitat core. Ash let the others go up before proceeding, leaving only Sam behind him. As Sam came up, Ash noticed him pulling the emergency sedative gun from the wall and clipping it to the back of his ship-suit. He wondered what the man had in mind this time. Sam didn't appear to care that Ash had spotted him. Nevertheless, Ash decided to keep a close eye on Sam in the minutes that followed, just in case he was the intended target of the gun.

They all made their way around the central ring-corridor to the bio-lab. Citra held her elegant profile high throughout, as if considering the entire business beneath her. She led them into the small room and pointed at the fold-out wall-case where the reagents were stored. Sam positioned himself behind her.

'Please show us where that compound is kept.' he said. 'Anyone see anything unusual here?'

Amazingly to Ash, he appeared to be the only one noticing what Sam was up to. The others had their attention riveted to the stupid cupboard. He added misdirection to Sam's long list of disturbing skills. Ash took a quick step back as Sam silently reached for the sedative gun. He held his breath.

Suddenly, the lights turned red. A shrieking siren cut the air and threat indicators started spilling up the wall-screens.

Ash couldn't help but grunt in surprise.

'What the hell is that?' said Venetia, glancing about.

Zoe stared into space as her view-field kicked on. 'It's the Photurians. They're here.'

Mark turned and bolted for the bridge with Zoe close behind him. Sam took his moment and slammed the gun into Citra's back. She gasped as the drug filled her body.

Venetia stared at him in shock. 'What the hell are you doing?' she exclaimed.

'Get out of here!' Sam told her firmly. 'Get to your station, quickly! The last thing we need now is someone hysterical dividing the ship's attention again. This whole investigation will have to be resolved later.'

Venetia just stared.

'Go!' he shouted. 'We only have minutes!'

Reluctantly, she turned and fled the room.

'Ash,' said Sam. 'Don't leave. Help me strap Citra's body down. We may need to manoeuvre at any time.'

Ash took Citra's arms and led the way as they steered her back to the med-bay.

'This is fucked!' he whispered to Sam as they struggled with her body. 'I quit. I'm sick of this shit. I'm telling Mark how to stealth the hull.'

'Don't you fucking *dare*,' Sam growled.

'What're you going to do, try and hit me?' Ash sneered. 'I'm a fucking Omega roboteer. I'll deck you before you can blink. You think you're so fucking scary. That shit outside is scarier than you will *ever* be.'

'Listen to me, you cyborg clown,' said Sam as they struggled through the med-bay hatch. 'This mission is bigger than either of us. Our lives are irrelevant here.'

Ash laughed. 'No shit, Sherlock. But guess what? Your precious plan is already fucked, in case you hadn't noticed. Those Nems out there have left your script. There was nothing in your plan about a crying kid with exploding hands.'

'Irrelevant,' Sam snapped. 'Don't you get it? The attack *has* to go ahead. We'll never have another chance.'

'No. I *don't* get it. What I do get is that you're fucking crazy and I'm done. I never signed up for murder.'

'Actually,' said Sam, 'that's *exactly* what you signed up for.' He slammed Citra's sleep-case shut.

'Go fuck yourself,' said Ash. 'This whole thing is beyond broken and it ends here.'

He turned and made his way quickly to the bridge, with Sam right behind him.

10.4: MARK

Mark jumped into the *Gulliver*'s helm-arena and surveyed the drone swarm. Panic gripped him. Though the ship had warned them just seconds before, the Photurians already had almost every viable exit vector in the system covered. And they were moving fast – nearly twice the speeds he'd seen at Tiwanaku.

'How?' he said.

While their backs were turned, the tiny system had gone from empty to hosting more than fifteen thousand warp-enabled drones. The experimental hull shapes had vanished, replaced by ones built for business. They resembled giant silver pollen grains a hundred metres wide.

Zoe opened the comms channel from the lounge.

'We came through the arrival spike with minimal damage,' she said. 'Most of our sensors were retracted. We got a good scan of the light-profile, though.'

'Take a look at this,' said Mark, and posted her the bad news.

She fell silent, watching the coordinated surges of warp spill around the sky that surrounded them, locking them in.

'Can they see us?' she breathed.

'I don't think so, otherwise we'd be dead already. It won't take them long to find us, though. They'll have the system perimeter totally enclosed within twelve minutes. This place isn't big.'

'Then let's go!' said Zoe. 'Now!'

'We can't,' said Mark. 'We're still tethered to the asteroid with half the ship's guts hanging out. It'll take me at least that long to pack up even if I leave robots on the rock.'

'So we're trapped,' said Zoe, her voice cracking.

Venetia clipped in next to Zoe and pulled out her touchboard. 'Where are they?' she said. 'How are we looking?' Her face fell when Zoe passed her the data. 'They've adapted,' she said.

'My thoughts exactly,' said Mark. 'At Tiwanaku I had a clear speed advantage. Not any more. If we try to make it out of here at a dead run, they'll pick us off before we're far enough out to go superlight.'

'Why are they so different now?' said Zoe. 'What's going on?'

'We don't know that they are,' said Venetia. 'Remember, Tiwanaku had millions of these things in a huge range of different shapes. They had months to build them. Maybe they just picked the ones they hadn't yet reshaped and sent them our way. Or perhaps all those modifications weren't as stupid as they looked. Maybe they were design experiments.'

Zoe frowned into her view. 'I have Yunus's display up and I'm seeing incoming comms on the diplomacy channel.'

Mark piped it in.

'Human vessel,' said the swarm, 'make yourself visible. We come in peace.'

It had a new voice. This time, it sounded unpleasantly like Yunus Chesterford.

Venetia shot Zoe a horrified look. 'Now I'm glad Sam knocked Citra out again,' she said. 'She wouldn't want to hear that.'

'He did *what*?' said Zoe.

246

Mark wasn't sure how to feel. His doubts about Citra had evaporated the moment she'd accused him. Her reaction had been so instantaneous and so grounded in loathing that something inside him sealed up the moment he heard it. What was the point of reading subtle motives into everyone's actions when there was someone in the room who obviously wanted him dead? He didn't like Sam's choice of solution, but on the other hand he was glad he wouldn't have to worry about her for a while. He had enough on his plate.

'We are here to prevent any future misunderstanding,' the swarm told them smoothly. 'We offer only harmony and efficiency. Your integration will be painless and clean.'

'Well, that clinches it,' said Mark. 'I'm definitely in. Anyone else?'

'That message scares me,' said Venetia. 'Notice their use of language? That's changed, too. They're getting smarter. Or better attuned to humans, at least.'

One of Mark's tactical SAPs pinged him.

'I just received a predictive analysis,' he said. 'With eighty-seven per cent probability, they'll start closing in as soon as they have the exits locked down. They'll pick their way over every rock in this system until they find us. That gives us six hours at the very most. Is there *anything* good about this situation?'

'Maybe,' said Zoe. 'Maybe. We have a signal match for the arrival spike. It's definitely a warp-burst and they're not showing a trail, which confirms my theory. I'm scanning their arrival vector for the transporter ship. If we can damage it, the Photurians won't be able to follow.'

'Except we don't have any weapons,' said Venetia. 'And we'd have to get to it without dying first.'

Mark glowered the wave of bright points stealing across the tiny star system and felt hunted. For whatever reason, the universe appeared to have it in for him. It galled him that such apparently simple creatures should be further up the galactic food chain than he was.

'These robots are stupid,' he said. 'They still think *efficient integration* sounds appealing to us. There *has* to be a way to outsmart them.'

'You want a diversion, then,' said Venetia. 'A lure.'

'Yes,' said Mark. 'Exactly. If we had any messenger drones, I'd use one of those. We can give thanks to the mighty IPSO senate for fucking that one up for us.'

Zoe sat up straight. 'I have a solution!' she said. 'Or part of one. We repurpose one of the drones you picked up for me at Tiwanaku.'

'How?' said Mark. 'That was all debris. You can't build a working drone from that.'

Zoe smiled. 'Can't I? What do you think I've been trying to do for the last four days? How else do you imagine I've been figuring out how they work?' She slid a window showing her work to his sensorium. Amazingly, she'd pieced together more than half of the kit necessary to construct a working device. 'It's all in pieces at the moment, of course, but give me half an hour. We could fill in the bits we don't have with equipment from the ship's stores.'

'Would it actually *warp*?' said Mark. 'Gravity drives aren't something you knock together in minutes.'

'Sure,' she said. 'Just not very well, that's all. But our fake ship doesn't have to go far. It just needs to get their attention.'

Mark grimaced. 'It's a start, I guess, but that'd take out, what, two or three drones before they nailed it?'

'So we put a disrupter on it,' said Zoe. 'That's how they used to disable drones during the war. You simulate the ionic crap that blocks warp near stars – make it so they can't sustain a stable pattern of curvon decay. All we'd need is a cold plasma to trash their inducers. Then any drone that goes near our lure gets stuck.'

'Shame we don't have one of those, either,' Venetia put in.

'Are you kidding?' said Zoe. 'We're sitting on one. All we have to do is mine the lighter metals right out of the asteroid we're tethered to, then use our own engines to ionise them. Or we jack extra juice through an X-ray bounce probe. This ship has one of those.'

Mark laughed aloud. He'd never heard of anyone jerry-rigging a disrupter before. But that didn't mean it couldn't be done.

'We have *mining equipment*?' said Venetia.

'All ships do,' said Mark. 'Ore-extraction tools are part of the standard deep-space self-repair kit. We'd have to hollow-mine, of course, otherwise they'd spot us – drill right under the hull join and buffer the tailings.'

Venetia threw up her hands. 'Okay, you have everything you need. But there's still the problem of how to divert attention from the *Gulliver*. Whatever we can build isn't going to look remotely like us...' She thought for a moment, then said, 'But I may have a solution for that.

After we've mined the asteroid, we blow it up and eject the lure at the same time. The drones head for the lure. We drift with the debris and try to look as much like a rock as possible. Can we blow it up? If you can fake a starship, you can rig a fuel bomb, I presume?'

'Easily,' said Mark. 'You know, I'm starting to think we might have a chance of getting out of here. Presuming they fall for it, of course.'

'If they don't, we're dead in any case,' said Venetia. 'It has to be worth a shot.'

Ash stepped into the bridge then, his face a mask of fury. Sam strode in right behind him. It looked to Mark very much like the two of them had just had some kind of fight. Something about Citra's attempt to kill him, perhaps, or whether to try to remove him from the captain's seat again. He didn't have time for it. They had a ship to save.

'Ash,' he said, before his subcaptain could get a word in, 'I need help. I'm going to be running a whole team of construction robots and I need support.' He sent an outline of the plan via memory packet straight to Ash's sensorium. 'Do you think you could cover some of our subsystems?'

Ash blinked in astonishment. His expression caved in. 'Are you serious?' he said. He looked about to cry.

Mark frowned in confusion. He hadn't expected such an emotional response.

'I know it's risky,' he said, 'but it's all we've got. Can you help?'

'Of course,' said Ash. He looked oddly defeated. 'I'll cover albedo control, make us look like the debris – I have some ideas about camouflage.'

'Great,' said Mark. 'It's all yours.'

It'd be good to have Ash mucking in and sharing ownership of the ship. A little camaraderie over the next half-hour might make the difference between life and death. He passed Ash control over the hull integument.

'I can help, too,' said Sam. 'Send me a plan outline.'

Mark passed one to his view. Sam nodded judiciously, his expression carefully neutral.

'This could work,' he said. 'It's a long shot, of course, but better than nothing. I have one recommendation, though.'

'Which is?'

'Put a bomb on that decoy. Once you trap those drones, you take them out. We could overload the antimatter containment using fuel from our own supply.'

Mark's spirits lifted a little further. 'Of course,' he said. 'That makes perfect sense.'

'I'll work on the decoy design with Zoe,' said Sam. 'I have experience in that area. Given the right material, we'll have a piece of junk passing for a starship in no time. I may need to cannibalise from our kit, though.'

'No problem,' said Mark with a grin. 'Whatever you need, you've got it.'

They had a few scant hours to ready their escape, but the threat appeared to have brought them together at last, just when their mutual trust had looked ready to break. If they lived, maybe he'd be able to salvage something from this mess of a mission after all.

10.5: ANN

Ann waited for Will in the *Chiyome*'s privacy chamber and practised zero-yoga to keep a tight rein on her nerves. The room had been prepared for him in advance, using the package of biotech deterrent Meleta had provided. For all that she feared the alien coating they'd spread on the walls, Ann dreaded facing Will more.

The hatch opened to reveal Will's long, expressive face, which wore a curiously empty expression more distressing to her than sadness or anger could have been. He drifted up to meet her. He looked haggard but taut, like a man made of old wire.

'Welcome to the *Chiyome*,' she said. She put her hands behind her back and gripped them tightly together. 'You will remain in our custody and be treated as an honoured guest until you've been properly briefed. At that point, you will be at liberty to make independent choices. We will manage the repair of your ship on your behalf.'

Will stared at her. She felt as if he was looking through her eyes at something deep inside her – something unsatisfactory. Shame roiled in Ann's gut, taking on a physical intensity that hurt like a stab wound.

'I'm disappointed,' he said quietly.

Though he sounded exhausted, something about his hands suggested that they itched to kill. Half of Will Monet's psych reports suggested he'd never properly recovered from the atrocities he'd endured during the war.

'You're an officer of the IPSO Fleet,' he added. 'Doesn't that mean anything to you?'

She swallowed back her regret, cleared her throat and tried for a level, commanding tone. 'You are no doubt appalled by what we've done,' she said. 'Nevertheless, you're not in possession of all of the facts. Our actions were motivated by a single goal: that of averting wholesale war. I can assure you that the logic behind our actions was sound. I'm not proud of my choices. However, I am doing what I perceive to be necessary.'

'Then you're a fool,' said Will wearily. 'Was that mess at Tiwanaku really part of someone's plan? You're playing about with alien tech you don't understand.'

'As are you,' she replied. 'With your every waking breath.'

'I didn't have a choice,' he said, his voice hardening. 'Now tell me – what kind of assurances can you give me that the *Gulliver* is safe?' His eyes pinned her while he waited for her reply.

Ann realised then with slowly unfolding horror that they hadn't seen the *Gulliver*'s signature when they entered the system. It was supposed to have arrived already. Without it, she had no leverage over the man in front of her. And they had no Sam, either, which meant they were without their best strategist, too. Her confidence began to slide like a house on mud. She glanced quickly at the summary at the top of her view to check, hoping he wouldn't notice. Sure enough, no *Gulliver*. Will's flexing, superhuman hands suddenly looked that much more menacing.

'So long as Sam Shah is in control of that ship, their chances are very good,' she said. 'I would never have let you come here otherwise.'

'And if not?'

'I won't insult you with platitudes,' said Ann. 'However, there's every reason to believe that he's in command by now. Chesterford is gone, which means he has full override control for the *Gulliver*'s flight system.'

Will snorted. 'No, he doesn't. His keys won't work. Mark's interface is backed by my security software, not the Fleet's.'

Her breath caught at the news. The *Gulliver* must have headed for the Nerroskovi System, then. And with them, inevitably, the Nems.

'If anything happens to Mark, I will hold you and your conspiracy responsible. Do you understand me?' Will's voice had taken on a trembling, unstable edge.

'That is your right,' said Ann.

'I will find all of you, and tear each and every one of you apart with my bare hands.'

She blinked slowly, letting the threat pass through her. 'An understandable reaction, given your current level of knowledge. I recommend that you spend the trip back to headquarters in coma. It will spare you both frustration and time.'

'Try putting me in a coffin and see how far you get,' he said.

Ann shook her head. 'We do not actually wish you ill, Captain Monet. Please remember that. Everything we've done – that *I've* done – has been an attempt to restore balance to civilisation. Don't imagine that any of this has been easy, or that it comes without pain. Also, please don't try anything rash. We don't want to have to defend ourselves and your position is weaker than you might imagine. We've developed countermeasures that work against your abilities. You won't be allowed to infiltrate our computers, for instance. And we have weapons capable of either paralysing or killing you.'

'I am here because I choose to be,' said Will, 'not because I'm a prisoner. I didn't want to look at Nelson's face any more. I don't want to look at yours, either. But at least you're going to lock me up and take me somewhere.'

Ann glanced away. She dearly hoped he couldn't tell just how much this was hurting.

'Indeed,' she said levelly. 'You may stay in this room if you like. It's the best we can offer.' She moved carefully past him to the hatch.

Will was as still as a mantis as she glided past. 'I wanted to think you were better than this, Captain Ludik,' he said. 'I asked you to do one simple thing: look after the *Gulliver*.'

She couldn't stand it any more. 'A promise I would have gladly kept had it not already been superseded by the needs of the human race,' she said quickly. 'A promise I thought I was going to be able to keep, and would have been able to keep, had it not been for your own actions.'

'Save your excuses,' said Will.

Ann found herself nudged to the edge of tears. She couldn't remember the last time that had happened.

'I look forward to your briefing,' she said, 'and I sincerely hope we can rebuild a relationship based on trust once you've been properly apprised of the situation.'

'Good luck with that,' said Will.

Ann let herself out and sealed the hatch behind her. She gripped the doorway, unwilling to let the crew see the storm of emotion passing across her face.

'All clear, Captain?' said Jaco, his tone cool.

Ann nodded, her face turned away. 'Captain Monet will be waiting in the privacy chamber during our return to Snakepit Station.'

'Understood.'

The ice in Jaco's tone had raised another notch since the *Ariel Two* had tried to make its escape. He'd not mentioned the fact that he'd recommended a second shot, but she could tell he was thinking it. She no longer cared. That phase of the plan was over now, thank Gal. And with Sam and Mark out of the picture, they had bigger things to worry about.

11: COMPROMISE

11.1: MARK

Twenty-seven minutes after their arrival, the Photurian swarm had complete control over the tiny system. Thousands of drones flickered in waves of synchronised warp light-minutes wide. Embedded in the *Gulliver*'s senses, Mark felt like a fish hiding in the middle of a school of hungry piranhas.

Squads of specialised drones with what appeared to be high-speed engine modifications sat clumped around the most promising exit vectors. Others with sensor extensions swept around the in-system in packs, scanning each rock in turn. The Photurians had even started broadcasting something that looked like a clumsy soft assault, a simple query signal designed to encourage their quarry to announce its position. The mere existence of it suggested that their enemy was adapting its understanding of their machines as fast as it was acquiring language.

Over the two hours that followed, the wave of investigative drones bore down on the *Gulliver*'s hiding place until discovery lay just minutes away. By that point, though, Mark and his team were ready. Their furious efforts had been carefully screened by the *Gulliver*'s exohull. The asteroid beneath them had been quietly excavated, leaving its exterior untouched.

Their decoy, to his eyes, looked clumsy and ridiculous. A shell of badly printed rock overlaid on an engine made from battered drone parts, tacked together with welds and improvised adhesives. Numerous robots from their mesohull had sacrificed parts in order to make it function. The entire assemblage had been sprayed with an alloy-polymer mix to give it a halfway convincing spectrum. There'd been no time to do more.

'Everyone set?'

'We're good to go,' Sam replied. 'Let's make it happen.'

Mark triggered a set of tailored nuclear blasts inside the asteroid. The rock burst apart, revealing the faked-up ship that Sam and Zoe had created. It immediately started making for the edge of the system, trailing a mire of ionic clutter in its wake. The *Gulliver*, meanwhile, tumbled away with the rest of the asteroid fragments, its hull carefully tuned to make it as indistinguishable from the debris as they could manage.

Mark held his breath as their ship turned end-over-end. Their ploy would never have convinced a human observer. The *Gulliver* was simply too large and too symmetrical to pass for an asteroid chunk. They might as well have printed a sign on it, he thought: *Innocent rubble, please disregard*. Still, if the trick only bought them seconds, it might be enough.

He watched with mounting hope as nearby drones raced inwards, only to be trapped in the fake ship's growing wake.

'It's working!' said Zoe. 'It's actually working!'

Photurian robots streaked past them, apparently uninterested in the *Gulliver*, on their way to the lure where they piled up by the dozen.

As soon as he had enough drone traffic to hide in, Mark started pulsing his engine in sync with the swarm, angling away from the decoy as steeply as he dared.

'We have a safe radius,' said Sam. 'Detonate.'

'No!' said Venetia. 'Look, we're drawing in some of those drones from the exit blockades. Give them a minute. We want to catch as many as possible.'

Mark's virtual finger itched over the button. He watched the alien weapons close in.

In the end, he didn't even have to act. Those Photurians with enough conventional velocity hurled themselves against the decoy, triggering the blast themselves. The searing white flare of an antimatter explosion flashed into existence, momentarily drowning out the light of the frail sun beside it.

The Casimir-buffers boomed all around them, as if fending off a direct bombardment. The team on the *Gulliver* burst into cheering as half of the swarm evaporated in a ball of light.

'Holy shit!' said Mark. 'How much antimatter did you put in that thing?'

'Enough,' said Sam. 'And that's what counts.'

The remainder of the swarm abruptly decohered, their flashes desynchronised, their flight vectors a tangled mess.

'Now!' said Zoe. 'While they're still stunned. Head for their arrival vector. We need to find that transporter and take it out – it's the only way to stop them from following us.'

'On it.' Mark spun the ship around. 'Strap in, everybody. It's going to get bumpy. Zoe, can you give me a vector?'

She slid him a display showing her workings. It revealed an empty patch of space way below the ecliptic that looked no different from the rest of the sky.

'This is my best guess,' she said. 'I've extrapolated from their insert point, looking for emergent patterns in their spread. If it's not there, it should be close.'

Mark headed towards Zoe's destination, zigzagging like a member of the disorientated swarm.

While he couldn't see a damned thing ahead of them, he decided to trust in Zoe's skills. And any route out of the system was good enough in his book.

Before he'd got halfway, though, the Photurians began to reorganise. They started pulsing in sync again, headed towards him. Something about his flight path had clued them in, despite his best efforts.

Mark dialled in a pattern of standard evasives. 'Okay, everyone,' he said. 'Hold still, please.'

This time, he remembered to engage the gel-sleeves on the crash couches before ramping up the gees. Cocoons of protective fluid slid up around each seat, encasing the passengers and supporting their bodies. Hemojectors attached to their arms to minimise the need for lung motion.

The changes came just in time. The drones matched Mark's evasives perfectly. Pre-emptively, almost. The machines had upped their piloting skills as well, apparently. Either that or they'd simply memorised his tricks from before. Fortunately, Mark had plenty more.

He veered abruptly, diving back on himself and forcing the drones to change course, then threw the ship into a helical slewing path. This deep in-system, the net effect on the passengers was that of being slammed repeatedly against a wall at rapidly changing angles. The effect outside was to carve out a wide channel of dead space behind his ship.

The Photurians had already proved they were clueless about disrupter fields. He'd see how long it took them to clue in to this version. Several hundred swarm-bots dived straight into his wake and hung there, their inducers crackling uselessly.

It won him only seconds. Another team of drones curved in towards him from dead ahead. Mark tacked again, using the same trick. This time, though, the Photurians didn't fall for it. They streaked along outside the pipe of unusable space, exploiting his helical path to gain on him.

'Damn. They *are* smarter.'

He handed off everything but piloting to Ash and keyed in another suite of evasives, this time using his full attention to keep inventing new vector combinations. He swapped bursts of conventional acceleration with semi-random surges of warp whenever he had enough clear space to manage it. Faced with unalloyed human creativity, the Photurians lost ground.

Suddenly, Mark's fine-sensor SAP came back with an image of something ahead, half an AU further out. Two knobbled, matt-black discs hung in space, spinning in tandem and linked by six feathery strands of some impossibly fine fibre. He'd never seen anything like it. It looked like a pair of night-coloured jellyfish joined at the tips of their tentacles, waltzing in space. He forwarded the image to Zoe.

'I think we found it,' he said.

'That's it!' she exclaimed. 'Wait. No. How? That's not a ship. I don't get it.'

Mark didn't hang around for a technical discussion. He recast their trajectory into a Levy flight with an oscillating fractal dimension and stochastically inserted directed jumps towards their goal. With the baffled drones still falling behind, Mark swapped their course out for a straight dive and raced for the mysterious craft at maximum warp.

'Fuck how it works,' he said as the drive hammered him into his couch. 'It's where you said it would be and it looks fragile.'

'But this can't be it,' Zoe subvoked. 'It's too small. How do you fit fifteen thousand drones inside *that*?'

She had a point. Each disc would be able to hold about a hundred at most. If they somehow packed drones in the space between the discs, they'd still have had trouble fitting everything in. The gap between the two ships was only about fifty kilometres wide.

'Right now, I don't care,' said Mark.

As he neared their target he threw the ship around, dropped warp and dumped power into the thrusters, braking hard. The jelly-ships raced up to meet them. At the last moment, Mark rammed the warp back on, deliberately mistiming his bursts with rotating alignment. In effect, his drive became a gravity chainsaw.

The *Gulliver* plunged straight between the discs, mangling the delicate fronds and sending the alien ships juddering apart as the space between them ruptured in a hundred horrible ways. The *Gulliver* shot out of the other side of the gap leaving the tentacles of the jelly-ships mangled. Just two of the slender threads remained. The others drifted in broken tatters.

'Good enough?' he said.

Fresh cheering broke out in the *Gulliver*'s lounge. Mark grinned. His enemies might be smarter than before, but that didn't mean he couldn't still lick them.

'That was *awesome*!' Zoe yelled. 'I didn't know you could do that with a starship!'

'Neither did I,' said Mark. 'But it worked.'

Ash passed back control of the ship's subsystems with a wry smile. 'Nice flying,' he said. 'I didn't think we'd make it.'

'You just got used to not having me about,' Mark retorted. 'The impossible is my speciality.'

For the first time since Earth, it felt like everyone aboard – or everyone conscious, at least – was on the same side.

They headed on out of the system, leaving a flickering mass of panicked drones in their wake.

'New Panama, here we come,' Mark said. 'At last.'

11.2: WILL

Will waited in the privacy chamber for the kick of the *Chiyome*'s drives to signal that the crew were distracted. They were fools, every one of them. But Ann – Ann was a viper.

He'd respected her. He'd had faith in her. He couldn't believe how wrong he'd been. When they talked back at Triton, he could have sworn he'd seen something golden there – a kind of honest, ethical pragmatism that he had badly missed. But he'd been projecting, seeing echoes of Rachel because he wanted to. He was disgusted with himself that he'd become so gullible. Andromeda Ludik was a different kind of creature altogether. Nelson had told him as much. In retrospect, his former friend's words held far more import than Will had realised at the time. The pathetic traitor had actually been trying to warn him.

She and Nelson were alike, apparently. Both were ready to engage in the worst kind of betrayal for some self-aggrandising notion of their own moral duty. Neither had fought in the last war and lacked even the first inkling of what trust meant. Did they not see that they were repeating one of the worst episodes of history? Well, now he was going to make their lives as difficult as possible. Maybe they'd grow up a bit.

When a burst of warp knocked him gently against the wall, Will began. They'd have the wall cameras active, no doubt, but the kind of work Will had in mind wasn't the sort you could see.

First, he tested the limits of the space with his interface. It had been well screened – exceptionally well, in fact. Three long seconds into his investigation, Will realised he wasn't getting anywhere. It was as if the *Chiyome*'s designers had built the privacy chamber specifically with him in mind, surrounding it with layers of buffers and cut-offs that no amount of hacking would unpick. On reflection, he thought, they probably had.

A fresh tide of anger threatened to rise up and swallow him, so he reminded himself that Ann had promised as much. He already knew this conspiracy ran deep otherwise they'd never have been able to get him this far. Orchestrating the construction of a single ship was surely a trivial task in comparison to engineering something like the Tiwanaku Event.

Will let his mind fall back to a resting state and breathed deep. His entire body was comprised of smart-cells and he'd not yet met an environment he couldn't adapt to. He moved to the hatch and pressed his hand against the interface port next to the manual exit stub. Then he extruded a biofilament into the port and started exploring.

Will's head filled with blinding pain. He recoiled in shock, the filament dangling from his finger like a piece of limp string. He regarded it in bewilderment as the smart-cells within it shrank and died. The necrotic strand snapped off and fell to the floor where it greyed and melted into the padding.

Will examined his fingertip in alarm as his mind scrambled to make sense of what had just happened. Had the Fleet developed bioweapons that worked against him? If so, that was nothing short of astonishing. There'd never been any sign of it. Not a hint that their science was even in the same century as that which made up his new body, despite the hundreds of tissue samples he'd provided for Fleet scientists to examine. For the first time in years, Will started to feel genuinely trapped.

He probed again, this time more cautiously, using tailored dead tissue crammed with inert polymers as a sensing surface. Microscopic surface channels allowed him to get a sanitised taste of what lay beyond. What he found amazed him. If this data port was anything to go by, the room had been sealed against him using something half-alive and wildly antagonistic. It employed a kind of molecular technology he'd never encountered. He could feel a cascade of teasing enzymes rattling against his probe, twiddling the charges on the surface like a hacker prying apart a firewall.

The Fleet had never come up with this. They must have found it down on that planet. Which meant the conspirators had gone and sealed the room using alien bacteria they didn't understand. Will groaned aloud at the insanity of it. They couldn't have taken a more suicidal step if they'd tried.

Will spent the next few minutes creating an array of ionic sensors and a suite of tiny microscopic eyes. They wouldn't be as good as a lab microscope, but he'd at least get to see what he was up against. He offered the organism in the data port some sacrificial cells and watched it try to dismantle them.

Their cellular structure was like nothing he'd ever seen. Each cell had half a dozen kinds of nucleus and something like a Golgi apparatus gone crazy. He watched one of the microscopic aggressors manoeuvre a string of linked vesicles up against one of his cells and present them in turn like parcels on a production line. After every interaction, the aggressor cell changed slightly, as if the results of the microscopic experiment were producing an attendant surge of messaging molecules. He watched the nuclei twist and shift in response. How these machines achieved such a level of orderly responsiveness at the nanoscale was totally beyond him.

Will felt his anger fall away to be replaced by a bright and cleansing fear. The tiny blob of protoplasm before him scared him far more than the drones at Tiwanaku. It indicated a technology centuries in advance of their own. And it had to be a technology. He didn't believe for a moment that a form of life this twisted could arise without some very subtle engineering. The way it swapped up chemical weapons in sequence against his cells looked too much like software incursion backed by self-modifying code.

He launched more sacrificial cells, this time primed with vesicles full of molecular weapons he'd cached on Davenport, coupled to intelligent defences. The alien cells broke them down almost as fast as they had the unweaponised cells. Something like horizontal gene transfer appeared to be taking place between them, with about five different kinds of genes being exchanged at once.

Will stepped back from his experiment, reflexively wiping his hands on his ship-suit. What would this stuff do on contact with human tissue? He couldn't believe that anything as gentle as organic life would last a second. But in that case, how come Ann and her crew weren't already dead? Just breathing the air in this room should have been enough to reduce them to pools of protoplasm.

Something was going on here that he didn't understand. Who had made this stuff? And what in hell's name did they want to do with it?

Will had almost laughed in Yunus's face when he proposed that the Transcended weren't the only force in the galaxy. Ironically, the pompous ass might have had a point. Will knew then that he, and everyone the conspiracy had ever touched, was in deep, deep shit. Compared to that scale of shit, the threat of all-out war with the sects didn't even register.

11.3: MARK

Mark had taken them little more than a tenth of a light-year outside the Nerroskovi System before he realised they had a fuel problem. He'd finished up a set of careful warp-scatter manoeuvres and was about to unplug and take a break when the resource-management SAP started shrieking at him about their flight plan. A cursory inspection revealed what had happened. Sam's bomb had used up a staggering amount of fuel. They didn't have enough left to reach New Panama.

Mark cried out at the realisation.

'What is it?' said Ash, his avatar appearing in the helm-arena.

Mark handed him the data. Ash's face darkened.

'Son of a *bitch*!'

Mark opened a video window for the jubilant group in the lounge to interrupt their celebration.

'Excuse me,' he said. 'We have a problem.'

Venetia paused, mid-anecdote. 'What now?'

'We're out of fuel,' he said simply, then passed them all the data he had.

The joy drained out of everyone's faces like paint in the rain. Mark felt a surge of frustration towards Sam. The guy had badly overdone it with the antimatter. He should have known better. At the same time, Mark dearly wanted to hold on to that sense of them all operating as a cohesive team. It hurt to lose it.

'Sam, you fucking *asshole*!' Ash shouted.

Sam's brow furrowed in consternation. 'I was trying to save us. That's all. I miscalculated. I'm sorry.'

'You ... you ... you fucking *idiot*! You're a fucking liability. Just like you were at Tiwanaku.'

Mark checked the camera on Ash's bunk below him. The man's eyes were bugging out of his face in rage. Whatever bond Ash and Sam might have shared, it had clearly broken. He'd never heard Ash make remarks like that to a senior officer before. Then again, there'd never been this much at stake.

For the first time he could remember, Mark found himself in the unlikely position of being the peacemaker.

'Hey,' he said. 'It's in the past now. We have to figure a way out of this new mess. And besides, it's not all down to Sam. I burned a bunch of fuel getting us out of there. More than I should have.'

In truth, he had used nowhere near as much as Sam had put in the bomb. No wonder the entire swarm had spasmed in the wake of it. Sam had dumped enough radiation into that star system to leave it hot for the rest of time. He was amazed it hadn't taken them with it.

'Look, I'm sorry,' said Sam, his expression desperate. 'How bad is it? Is there anywhere we can still get to?'

Mark sighed as he surveyed the options and threw them a star map.

'I'm seeing one New Frontier colony within range – a place called Carter. I've got no idea what their facilities are like.'

'I know it,' said Sam. 'I've worked with the defence minister there. It's a simple place, a bit rough and ready, but they'll have fuel and messenger drones.'

'I know Carter, too,' said Venetia. 'I worked there for a few months. Didn't like it much, but that's beside the point. Wherever we head, we have to think about the implications. It's clear now that the Photurians follow warp trails. That's probably how they got to Tiwanaku in the first place. And they'll repair that transport of theirs eventually. We have no idea how good the Photurians' deep-space scanning is. We could be handing everyone in the Carter System a death sentence if we go there. There are hundreds of thousands of people living there and no defences to speak of other than the occasional Fleet check-up.'

Everyone fell quiet.

'I could scan for brown dwarves,' Mark said eventually. 'Maybe one of those secret Fecund fuelling stops is close enough. If we find one, I can't believe the sects would turn us away – not with the kind of information we're carrying. Their politics might be at odds with the Fleet's but they're still human.'

'And what if you fail? What then?' said Sam. 'We'll be dead. And we'll lose our last chance to warn Earth, where there are *billions* of people counting on us. Remember, it's easier to follow the warp trail of an arriving ship than a departing one. And if they could follow us to Nerroskovi, who's to say they can't make it to Earth? We left breadcrumbs running straight back to the home system – *Ariel Two*-sized breadcrumbs.'

'Yeah,' said Ash. 'Imagine that.'

Sam shook his head. 'It's grim, but we need to be realistic here. At least the population of Carter is relatively small. If we're clear with them up front, they'll have enough time to prep an evacuation ark.'

'Evacuate the whole *planet*?' said Venetia. 'That won't be easy. There are Flag settlements there for a start. Big ones. Are you expecting the colonists to lay on accommodation for them, too?'

Sam sighed. 'I don't know what to say. This whole situation's a mess. I can't apologise enough for that. But as Mark pointed out before – we have a mission plan and we have our duty. The sooner we're fuelled up and on our way to New Panama, the better it will be for everyone. We can use the message drones at Carter to send advance warning to Earth. And if we're lucky with our timing, the Fleet will be able to send a gunship constellation back there before any trouble starts.'

'Presuming they don't shoot the messenger first,' said Venetia. 'Remember, we're not going to be welcome. First we show up demanding fuel and then announce that we may be trailing killer aliens behind us. Then we tell them that the best they can hope for is hiding out in a sub-light barge for three months while the Fleet dukes it out with some unknown invaders to stop their whole world from burning. They aren't going to love it.'

'I'll square it with the local leadership,' said Sam. 'Given the trouble I've caused here, it's the least I can do. And besides, we have overrides and a Fleet mandate to sequester fuel. They couldn't stop us even if they wanted to.'

'Nice attitude,' said Venetia. 'And let's not forget we have an ongoing attempted murder inquiry, huh?'

'How could we possibly forget?' said Ash, his avatar scowling. 'Here's the thing, though. If we don't make it to Carter, we all die. So it doesn't matter who is captain now, because Carter's the only place we can go. Which means that whoever is responsible for that clownish fuck-up with the neurotoxin should be able to put down their bullshit grievances for long enough to save their own neck.'

'Are you proposing we wake Citra?' said Venetia.

Ash threw up his hands. 'Hell, no. We don't need a biologist to get to Carter and we might as well spare the poor woman the grief. Plus, if anyone tries anything else that stupid, we'll know it wasn't her, won't we?'

His tone threw another pall of silence over the group. Mark glanced nervously at him. If Ash had once been a rival, now he'd become something completely different. A voice of hope, perhaps, if a weirdly angry one.

'My point, I guess,' said Venetia, 'is that our domestic problem isn't exactly going to make us look good at Carter, either. And if we don't wake Citra now, we'll have to wake her there. I can't imagine she'll be happy.'

'I can't imagine she'll give a shit,' said Ash. 'We all know what she's going to do – accuse Mark. And she'd rather do that on a planet than trapped on a ship. But in any case, we don't appear to have any choices left here. Our route has been decided for us.'

'Agreed,' said Mark.

He glanced at the glum faces of his shipmates and realised that of all of them, only Zoe hadn't said a word. She'd sat there, pensive throughout, idly tapping at her touchboard as if they'd been discussing the ship's privacy rota.

'Hey, Zoe,' he said. 'Any thoughts?'

She stared up at his camera, her reverie broken. 'Plenty. I'm just not worrying about what you're worrying about.'

Venetia raised an eyebrow. 'Life and death aren't sufficiently pertinent?'

'Oh no,' said Zoe. 'They're pertinent, all right, but it's not like we have a choice any more. And I think we have a bigger problem.'

'Worse than being chased by killer aliens while short on fuel?' said Venetia.

Zoe shrugged. 'Maybe yes. I've been looking over the data we gathered from that jelly-ship thing. Those strands were showing passive emissions before we trashed them and we got a good look at their profile. It's freaking me out. The rest of the Photurian tech we've found so far has been foreign, but it's not magic. In fact, most of it's just been lame. I can't make head or tail of the biotech, of course, but there's no reason to suspect it's anything special. It just sits there. The jelly-ship, though, is a giant, screaming non-compute.'

Mark struggled with an urge to shut Zoe's technical chatter down. He was starting to find her obsession with alien drive systems trying. However, so far she'd been consistently right about the threats facing them, and they wouldn't have made it out of Nerroskovi without her ingenuity. He decided to give her room to talk.

'Go on,' he said gently.

Zoe glanced his way with a grateful expression. 'There's a difference between foreign tech and what you might call *miracle tech*,' she said. 'Foreign tech can be weird and surprising – all the parts look jumbled up and the design priorities feel backwards. That's what it's like when you examine at the Fecund stuff. With miracle tech, though, it's more like trying to scale a wall of ice. There's nothing to grab on to. You just scrabble around on the surface. You look at the machinery for answers and your mind just comes back blank. The suntap is like that. There are no answers for you to find. It's been designed that way. The fact that we've found that kind of tech here changes the whole scale of the game we're playing. And it makes me wonder if maybe the Transcended are involved after all. That would be the good outcome.'

'This again?' said Ash.

She shot his avatar a withering look. 'Either that or some species of equivalent power.'

'That sounds like a stretch to me,' said Ash, 'given how dumb their drones are.'

She glared at him. 'We'd be *very stupid* to be making any assumptions about these machines right now. Anyone examining Fecund technology for the first time would see a mixture of dumb and miraculous there, too. Those drones might look clumsy, but the devil's in the details.'

'Can you help us understand how this is relevant?' said Mark. 'I mean, either we can beat them or we can't. Right?'

Zoe sighed. 'There's no way to explain without getting technical.'

'Then get technical,' said Mark. 'We're not idiots. It's okay. Tell us what we're dealing with.'

Zoe peered up into his camera. 'Do you know what B-mesons are?'

'Sure. Primer particles. The warp emitters fire them – we use them to trigger curvon decay.'

She nodded. 'They're also called doorway particles. Most of the universe we see is governed by the physics of the Standard Model, or low-order physics. But to achieve anything like warp effects, you have to use particles sensitive to higher-order interactions – the kind that govern spatial curvature and particle decay. The whole Higgs-Weak interaction landscape. B-meson pathways are the cheapest, easiest route out of the StanMod domain. That trick, plus decay forcing, underpins almost all modern drive technology.'

'I fail to see where this is going,' said Sam.

'You will if you give me a fucking minute,' said Zoe. 'The point is, you *can't get* curvon decay without B-mesons or something like them. You can't do *anything* without them. But that jelly-drive? No B-mesons. No tau-primers, either, so it can't be a pure stealth drive. I saw evidence of plasma-forcing, but everything else is missing.'

'Is it possible the drive was just off when we passed it?' said Mark.

'Of course it was off!' said Zoe. 'But there was still passive emission. That's my point – the drive was idling so there was enough power going through it for my SAPs to make guesses about how it was supposed to work. And then I compared that to the profile of the arrivals spike when the drive *was* active. And that's when it hit me. Their arrivals spike was all wrong, just like the warp profiles of those first drones were wrong. There's no evidence of doorway particle decay. That's what's fucked up about it. I missed it the first time because I didn't even consider it. I assumed something else had to be going on – field compression, maybe, or a pseudo-vacuum regime we don't know about yet.'

'Is it possible that your SAP just came back with the wrong answers?' said Mark.

Zoe waved a dismissive hand. 'Of course. That was my first assumption, which is why I double-checked. But I can't find a flaw in its logic, so I'm forced to conclude that we're looking at a technological advance on the scale of the suntap. Maybe bigger.'

'Which changes things how?' he said.

She gave him a weary, imploring expression. 'The suntap was *bait*,' she said. 'Free power handed to the human race with a huge price tag attached – an off-switch for our entire species. Death on the scale of entire stars. Whenever you see a halfwit species using technology they can't possibly have invented, it's safe to guess that someone's in the background pulling the strings. So you have to ask, what's the cost? Who's really in charge here and what do they want?'

'So you're worried that someone – or something – else is behind the Photurians,' said Mark.

'Right,' said Zoe. 'And what do they want with the human race? The Transcended have an off-switch for human life, but they appear to have decided not to use it yet. Who says this new bunch are going to be quite so generous? Who says that after Carter there'll even be an Earth to go back to?'

11.4: ASH

Ash listened from the bridge while Sam wove his next little web of lies, his disgust building steadily. It was painfully obvious that Sam had set up their detour to Carter, with all the extra horror that visit might entail. Sam obviously didn't give a shit about the lives of anyone on board – or anyone else, for that matter. So why hadn't he gone further already and killed all his witnesses?

As soon as Ash framed the question to himself, he knew the answer. Had Sam killed the other passengers, Ash's own loyalty to the League would have snapped. Sam knew that, and Sam still needed someone to pilot the *Gulliver* – it was a ro-ship and Sam couldn't fly it himself. That, Ash realised, gave him some bargaining power. He relished the notion.

It occurred to him then that Sam probably would have only drugged Mark rather than try to kill him if he'd actually been able to find a suitable compound in Citra's lab. That would have made him look more compassionate and exposed him to less risk. But he'd been hamstrung by not understanding the limits of Mark's biology. He'd been improvising, and he was still at it.

So why had Sam chosen Carter? From the little Mark had seen of it, Carter looked like a barely settled shit-hole, of interest only to field-researchers and pioneer-lifestyle types. Because, Ash reasoned, the alternative was New Panama, and Sam couldn't control anything from there. His movements would be too visible. The fact that Carter was a backwater played directly to Sam's interests. Sam had lost his chance to convince Mark to head for Snakepit and so had taken the next-best option.

While Zoe rattled on with her Vartian-style paranoia, Ash slid out of his bunk and made his way across to the hatch that led down to the lounge. He waited there until the meeting was over, then, as Sam came up the ladder, Ash grabbed his arm and dragged him to the nearest privacy chamber. Sam shot him a disgusted look but let himself be manhandled. Ash pushed Sam inside and shut the door behind them.

Sam adjusted his sleeve and tsked. Ash no longer gave a shit what his boss thought.

'You set that up,' he said. 'You trashed our fuel on purpose.'

'Here's what I did,' said Sam, stabbing the air in front of Ash's chest. 'I followed *your* lead.'

Ash brayed with laughter. 'And how do you figure that?'

'You bought into Mark's plan, so I did, too. I just used it to rescue your ass, that's all. Tell me, why didn't you stick to your guns and tell the truth the moment you walked into the bridge? Nobody was stopping you. You could have told him everything.'

Ash coloured. Sam knew why, of course. Because given the chance to save himself without revealing his guilt, he'd grabbed at it. Desperately.

'Let's face it,' said Sam. 'You're not exactly arguing from any moral high ground here.'

Ash knew enough by now to understand that Sam was a snake, and that his emotions were being manipulated. Unfortunately, he couldn't contest Sam's point.

'You just put hundreds of thousands of lives at risk,' he said instead.

'A problem I'll solve,' said Sam. 'I'll evacuate them.'

'Bullshit,' said Ash. 'You can't know that for sure, and what if you can't? Then we've got a massive target-containment problem on our hands. Carter is huge compared to Tiwanaku. If you fuck up just slightly, those Nems could double their intelligence in a week. We already don't have a clue what they're doing.'

Sam's expression grew steadily darker. 'I'll *manage* it.'

'How?' Ash demanded. 'By magic?'

'By killing everyone in the fucking system, if necessary,' said Sam. 'You know me well enough by now to believe I'd do it. My overrides give me complete access to their antimatter store and every Fleet drone in the system. Modern infrastructure is delicate. It would take me about fifteen minutes to point something with a warp drive at every population centre on the planet. End of problem.'

Ash reeled. 'All that just so you don't have to come clean to Mark? That's insane. Where's your perspective?'

'No,' Sam snapped. 'You're the one with no fucking perspective. Use that modified brain of yours to think through the options for a moment, would you? We either stick to our plan, fucked up though it is, or we fold. I can't see any other options. Can you? If we stick, we have a major fucking Nem problem, granted, but Earth's government still *has* to turn over. After the Earth is targeted, power will *have* to go to the Fleet. We win. You live. The war is averted. If we fold, we have the same exact fucking Nem problem, but Fleet credibility is trashed the moment our actions are revealed. You die. I die. And from then on it's every planet for themselves. That means war. Fuck the Nems. Who needs them? We'll murder each other. In case you hadn't noticed, Captain Corrigan, you're in a card game where the price of sitting at the table keeps going up. But the consequences of winning or losing *don't change*.'

'Maybe I don't like the game any more,' said Ash.

'Tough shit,' said Sam, 'because quitting is losing. And another thing – if you ever touch me like that again, I'll kill you. Do you understand?'

Ash rolled his eyes. 'Please. With your big fists, I bet.'

'You be careful who you fuck with,' said Sam, jabbing his finger. 'There is exactly one person in the universe who can keep you alive longer than a month. Your choices are my mercy or a firing squad. Now get your shit together, because we've got a civilisation to save.'

Sam let himself out.

Ash leaned up against the wall and screamed his fury till he was hoarse.

12: FRONTIERS

12.1: ANN

By the time the *Chiyome* docked at Snakepit Station, Ann had a status update from Nelson waiting for her.

'Repairs are underway,' he told her. 'The hull has been camouflaged using the code you provided. I admit to concern about the notion of a ship this large being hidden at all, particularly given its gravity footprint, but your recommendations have been followed in any case.'

Nelson shouldn't have worried. Nem-cloaking didn't exactly hide a ship so much as loudly instruct the Nems not to see it. Presuming the technique still worked, of course. It had been derived from the Nems' own swarming protocols. Ann trusted in their immutability rather less than she had a week ago.

'Two final points on Will Monet,' Nelson added.

Ann's shoulders tightened.

'First, do remember that he has a persistent link to his ship whenever it's in range,' he said. 'That's not something we can deactivate. It's woven deep into the smart-blood architecture that keeps the *Ariel Two* running. The ship will seek him out wherever he is, and you'll need to maintain careful shielding if you want to prevent that. I assume you've been briefed and taken all reasonable precautions.'

Ann had.

Nelson paused, his patrician face revealing some unexpected vulnerability.

'Second point: please look after him. He's dangerous, I know, and more powerful than any of us. But that doesn't mean he's not human. He hurts just like everyone else. I fear that we've damaged him, bringing him to this point, because he was always more predictable to us when he was angry. I regret that. I've lost a good friend for the sake of what I believe. I sincerely hope it was the right choice. If it's in your power, please don't make his damage any worse. Do what you can for him. Help him understand. Nelson out.'

The message window closed. Ann shut her eyes and felt dirty. She dearly wished she didn't have to face down Will again, but getting one of her crew to escort him to the station would have made a coward out of her. So she steeled herself and drifted up out of her couch to fetch Will from the privacy chamber. This time, she was determined to keep her cool.

She took a pellet gun loaded with cartridges of Meleta's biomaterial. If the camera feeds from the privacy chamber were anything to go by, Will had discovered the coating on the room's seals. She had to be ready for anything.

The hatch slid back to reveal Will floating at the far end of the space, waiting.

'What did you put on the walls?' he said.

He didn't look angry any more. If anything, Will Monet looked awed.

'I warned you about our new technology,' she said.

'That's not new,' said Will. 'It's stolen.'

'The distinction is irrelevant,' she replied. 'It's new to us.' She didn't actually believe that for a moment but had no desire to let Will know how she really felt. 'This way, please,' she said, gesturing with the gun. 'I presume you can guess what this pistol fires.'

Will came calmly. 'You have to stop this,' he said.

She sighed. 'I believe we've already had this discussion, Captain Monet – you disapprove of our choices. But you still haven't been fully briefed yet.'

He shook his head. 'Do you honestly believe there's a single thing your superiors can tell me that compares to what I've already learned in that room?'

They transferred to the docking pod.

'I imagine you've learned that your powers have limits,' she said.

The pod whisked them away towards the habitat ring, gravity building slowly.

'Whatever you splashed on the walls in there is scarier than anything I've ever seen,' said Will.

272

He appeared to have given up trying to score emotional points, her betrayal of him relegated to a side note in his thinking. Ann wasn't sure whether to be hurt by that or relieved.

'That stuff is almost as far in advance of our abilities as the Transcended Relic,' said Will. 'The fact that it can chew its way through my smart-cells should be proof enough of that. You imagine you're using whatever's at this star as a tool in your big game, but it's the other way around – someone is playing you instead.'

'We'll take your opinion into consideration, of course,' said Ann.

She didn't like his assessment. The League had long assumed that Snakepit had been left for humanity by the Transcended as a kind of prize to boost their development, just like the suntap and all their other gifts. With a single sentient force apparently weeding out intelligent species in the galaxy on million-year timescales, what room was left for another explanation? Snakepit's technologies had also proven suspiciously adaptable to human use, only bolstering that theory. However, given what she'd seen at Tiwanaku, a deeper agenda for the alien biosphere suddenly sounded plausible. She adjusted her hold on the wall as her feet settled to the floor.

Will gave her a long, exasperated stare. 'Honestly,' he said. 'What is there left to learn about your organisation that I can't already guess? You found out about the Fecund sites the sects were hiding and saw the potential for all-out war. You decided to fight them on their own terms and went looking for counter-weapons. Then you found this place, which appeared to be the answer to your prayers. Without worrying too much about the possible consequences, you started using it to reclaim your advantage.'

Ann gritted her teeth. He wasn't far off.

'What you all failed to notice in your rush for a solution,' he said, 'was that the stupid-looking drones you were deploying were quietly trying to hack you – just like the Transcended hacked me. That's what they were attempting to do in Tiwanaku, you realise – unpick the protocols of human biology. That kid with the idol in his neck was a failed experiment. So was everything else we saw. Those cells on the walls of your privacy chamber are just the same – they're *learning*. But here's the thing. This stuff *isn't* like Transcended technology. For starters, it's not obviously benign. There are no clues in it. You've found something old that may be very, very bad. If you think it's just a piece of technology left for you to play with that conveniently pumps out tame munitions, you're wrong. Dead wrong.'

Ann kept her face a mask of calm while her thoughts accelerated. Something about his assessment made a horrible kind of sense. What if the League's entire reasoning had been wrong? What if the planet didn't belong to the Transcended after all? What if this was someone else's version of the same kind of honeytrap as the lure star?

'Impossible,' she said, even as worms of doubt gnawed through her. 'The Transcended have control over Fecund space. And our best dating on Snakepit shows it being seeded *after* their extinction. It has to be from the Transcended.'

'Unless someone else sneaked that biosphere in after they stopped paying attention,' said Will. 'In case you hadn't noticed, the Transcended don't get out much. You have no idea who might have been through this patch of space since they retreated in on themselves. We hadn't even evolved yet. Do you have the first idea what this thing wants?' Will added as the pod doors slid open. 'Because I'll bet you anything it's not a peaceful future for all mankind.'

Will stepped through into the reception room beyond. The look on his face as the doors shut was one of almost grateful anticipation. Ann didn't share his composure. In her head, fears were crystallising, and with them a sense of urgency.

12.2: MARK

As the *Gulliver* sputtered into the Carter System on the last of its fuel, Sam hit the comms. Mark routed Sam's circuit through a silent bypass to listen in. While he still couldn't see why Sam would lie to them, his concerns refused to let go. He wanted to know exactly what he was getting into.

'Message Priority Zero Alpha for Defence Minister Keir Vorn. This is Overcaptain Sam Shah currently aboard the IPS *Gulliver*,' said Sam. He was sitting in his study against a backdrop of the IPSO insignia. 'Keir, we're in trouble. The ship I'm on is part of a Fleet mission to investigate a potential alien threat. That mission has gone badly wrong. We're desperately in need of fuel and require the use of your messenger drones to warn New Panama. The future of your world, our entire organisation and all humanity rests in the balance. Worse still, there's a risk that we may be bringing some of that trouble to your doorstep. If you agree to help us, my captain and I will gladly share the information we have with you, discreetly and in person. It's the least we can do. I'm deeply sorry to be the bearer of both demands and bad news, but right now we're out of options. We need to contain this situation fast. Help us, and I will be constantly in your debt. I look forward to hearing from you.'

Sam's wording sounded nothing but contrite, urgent and well expressed. Mark couldn't find anything dubious in the message with the possible exception of the idea that he and Sam would meet with the Carter government face to face. Sam had used no security filtering. And other than the always-opaque Fleet signature codes attached to the message, there was nothing in Sam's request that Mark couldn't analyse or understand. Mark found himself questioning his paranoia, embarrassed that he'd been reduced to conspiracy theories.

Sam pinged him when he was finished.

'It's sent,' he said. 'Let's hope they stay rational.'

Word from Carter arrived an hour later as their ship caught up with the light-lagged reply. A weathered-looking man with unruly mutton-chops appeared on the video feed. He looked more anxious than upset. Mark considered that a good start.

'This is Defence Minister Keir Vorn. Welcome, Sam. A berth is ready for you at Fleet Local. Please dock there and we'll solve your fuel problem. My government would like to accept your offer and meet with you and your captain. As you might imagine, your arrival has caused something of a political riot here. Some personal assurances will help considerably.'

Mark could see where things were headed. Would it be so bad if he and Sam went down to the surface of the planet? But his anxiety refused to settle.

Any minute now, Sam could propose a meeting and events would take on their own momentum. He needed a second opinion before that happened. He pinged Venetia and asked her to meet him in the privacy chamber. If anyone on the ship had retained a sense of perspective, it was her.

Five minutes later, Venetia met him in the tiny faux-panelled room.

'What's up?' she said. 'Not more trouble, I hope.'

Mark knew he didn't have much time. He shut the door and came to the point.

'Sam has set up an expectation that he and I will go down to Carter,' he said.

'Is that a problem?' said Venetia. 'It sounds like basic courtesy to me. Their whole world is at risk, after all. What were you planning to do – shout at them from orbit?'

'I know,' said Mark. 'But something about Sam feels off to me. That business with the antimatter was weird. And Ash has been angry with him ever since but won't say why.'

'Perhaps because he screwed up the mission and risked our lives?' she replied. 'Are you sure you're not letting this situation get to you, Mark? I mean, we're all a bit edgy right now.'

'I think it's more than that,' he said. 'I'm worried that this has something to do with the neurotoxin incident.'

'Ah.' Her brow creased. 'I see.'

'There's something weird about that whole event. I know Citra hates me, but she's a *scientist*, for crying out loud. I know she's not had much to do and she's furious about Yunus, but the more I think about it, the harder I find it to believe she'd pull that kind of shit. There's something else going on here.'

Venetia shot him a long look. 'You think it was Sam?'

'I don't know. That whole search of the memory core went on hold the moment the Photurians showed up. I needed the robots. I didn't get back to it, which is my fault, but as soon as we were headed here, there didn't seem to be any point.'

Her face took on an expression somewhere between maternal and cunning.

'Look,' she said, 'there's a simple solution to this. We all go. We keep a close eye on Sam. Together. You could use me down there, anyway. I know that place better than anyone else on this ship.'

'We can't,' said Mark. 'Someone has to stay up here – Fleet regs demand it.'

'So maybe we send Ash down with Sam instead, and you stay up here.'

'I thought about that,' he said, 'but frankly, I like it just as little. First, it's not what Carter's expecting. But worse, it lets Sam know that we're on to him, if he is responsible.'

Her gaze became probing. 'Do you trust Ash?' she said. 'You two don't seem to get along that well.'

Mark looked away. 'I don't know. I've known him for a long time, but these days he feels like a stranger to me. I guess I'd have to say *yes*, though.'

'Then take him into your confidence,' said Venetia. 'Like you just have with me.'

Mark grimaced. 'But what if I'm wrong? What if he's behind the attack?'

'Then maybe this is how you find out,' she said. 'I'll assume we're all going down together. I'll tell Zoe and talk her round if needs be. You talk to Ash. We meet back in the lounge for a meeting in ten. Does that work for you?'

Mark nodded, feeling less comfortable than he let himself admit.

12.3: ASH

At Mark's request, Ash met him in the ship's helm-space. Mark's avatar stood there surrounded by a multicoloured representation of Carter's sparse in-system traffic. The timing and the tone of the request had struck Ash as a little more formal than usual. The stiff, uncomfortable look on Mark's avatar reinforced that impression. Their game of mutual avoidance was apparently at an end.

Ash didn't know how to feel about that. He was sick of following Sam around like a lapdog. On the other hand, he still didn't feel ready to come clean. Sam had been right that he stood to lose his life the moment he opened his mouth.

'What is it, Boss?' said Ash brightly.

Mark looked him straight in the eye. 'I've secured this metaphor,' he said. 'I want to talk.'

'Shoot,' said Ash, his stomach churning.

'You have some issue with Sam,' said Mark. 'I don't know what it is, and if you don't want to talk about it, I won't make you. But I'm guessing and hoping that despite everything that's happened between us, you don't want me dead. So I'm going to ask you one question. Should I go down to Carter with Sam?'

Ash looked out at the virtual stars. He examined the back of his hand. What was he supposed to say? *No, it's a fucking trap, you Aspie halfwit*, came to mind. And then, as he pondered, a plan started to form in his head.

'Yes,' he said simply. 'You should go.'

Because, he reasoned, the only way he'd ever get home on his own terms was if Sam was *off* the ship. And the only reason Sam would ever leave was if he thought he was winning.

'Carter is expecting it,' said Ash. 'And so is Sam.'

Mark looked unconvinced and Ash knew he needed to say more.

'You're right that Sam has pissed me off,' he admitted. 'I'm beyond angry for what he did back at Nerroskovi. And you're right that there's more going on between us than either of us is saying. I'll explain all of it to you, I promise, but now is not the time. Right now, you shouldn't even ask. You should just trust me and go. And don't think too much about it, either. What I can tell you is that I'll keep your ship safe, and that I'll watch over you from up here. I will do everything in my power to make sure you get back up here intact, and that we leave this place on schedule.' Ash tried for a winning smile. 'I haven't done much in the last few years to make me worthy of your trust,' he said. 'I regret that. I was stupid. But as someone who shared a dorm with you, and memories, and, let's face it, a family, too, you can trust me now.'

Mark peered at him. Ash had realised long ago that most roboteers ironically had less control over their avatars' expressions than they did their physical faces, and Mark was no exception. Grimaces of anxiety twitched across his otherwise impassive features.

'Okay,' said Mark. 'But I'm taking Venetia and Zoe down with me.'

'You do that,' said Ash. 'That's a great idea. I'll take care of all of you.'

12.4: MARK

When Venetia and Zoe announced their desire to join the away team, Sam approved.

'I was going to suggest it myself,' he said. 'The more united a front we present, the better this will come off.'

Mark kept his thoughts to himself. His conversation with Ash had left him feeling more suspicious than ever.

They docked at Carter's tiny Fleet outpost. It was little more than an automated fuelling station hanging in a high orbit that it shared with three empty-looking habitats. From there, they took the *Gulliver*'s remaining shuttle down to the surface.

A tan sphere dotted with high, white cloud spread below them, unfolding into a vast, dry horizon. Venetia briefed them as they fell.

'Carter's a political place these days,' she said over the roar of re-entry. 'Not so happy. You want to bear that in mind and be careful what you say. Once they started getting Flag Drops, the colonists' attitudes turned ugly fast. Lots of angry Frontier Protection types, I'm afraid. Tossers.'

Mark flicked his camera view to Sam in the seat behind him.

'Does this fit with your experience?' he asked.

'Certainly the politics there are difficult,' Sam replied blandly. 'But I've been exposed to rather a different side of it than Venetia. I haven't made it down to the surface much, but I've had to handle the grievances of the colony government for years. Every time their oxygen factory gets bombed or someone poisons their protein store, we have to send a ship. It's the same sad story you hear all over the place these days.'

'Why were you even here, Vee?' said Zoe. 'The place sounds like a dump to me. Looks like one, too.'

'It's actually pretty interesting,' said Venetia. 'There used to be a lot of scientists here before the violence got bad. We were studying the tunnels. This planet's unique in that it's studded with Fecund biolabs, very much like the kind of set-up we have on Davenport or Kurikov. The Fecund dedicated populations of disposable children just to man the labs and survey the local flora and fauna. We gained access to a ton of specialised Fecund machinery. The patent gains alone paid for the colony about ten times over. Not to mention everything we discovered about their culture. That's what I was here to look at, unsurprisingly. You can learn a lot about alien minds by looking at how they do science.'

Mark glanced back at the lifeless brown ball below.

'This was a *biosphere* world?'

Venetia nodded. 'Yep. Not so green now, I grant you. A suntap flare will do that. But this world still has a little plate tectonics going, and a nice thick atmosphere that's already re-stabilising. There's a ton of water in that permafrost. And with people here that process will go much faster. The planet's practically gagging to come back to life. Give it a thousand years and it'll be nicer than Earth is now. So take a good look, ladies and gents. This place is basically what Earth would've turned into if the Transcended hadn't prevented the Fecund from reaching it while we were all still swinging in the trees.'

Mark regarded the dead world with fresh respect.

'That's a thousand years of good treatment, of course,' she added. 'First the fuckwits on the surface will have to stop arguing about land rights, access to the ruins and all that other pointless shit.'

The shuttle descended along the flight path Vorn had sent them, passing over an endless desert of undulating dun-coloured hills before landing at a tiny spaceport that sat alone on a dusty plain. A flat, white sky hung overhead, tinged butter-yellow at the edges.

As they finally settled on the ground, the reality of slightly leaden gravity settled onto Mark. A docking arm telescoped out from the spaceport's solitary terminal to greet them, down which a transit pod slid to kiss against their airlock.

'Welcome to the colony of New Luxor,' said Venetia. 'Armpit of the universe.'

The doors slid open, ushering a tang of dust into the shuttle cabin. Keir Vorn stood beyond them in the transit pod, dressed in a New Angeles-style formal kilt and T-shirt, with a curious spiral logo emblazoned on his chest. He was a far larger man than Mark had expected and built like a weightlifter. His face seemed fixed in a hang-dog expression.

'Glad you could all come,' he said solemnly. 'We appreciate it.' He gestured towards the pod. 'Please, step this way. The governing council will see us as soon as we get back to town.'

'Town?' said Mark.

Keir nodded. 'We have a conference room ready for you.'

Why hadn't they just come to the spaceport? Mark wondered. The further he got from his ship, the more nervous he felt. Still, he'd come all the way from orbit. A mile or two more wouldn't hurt.

By home system standards, the pod Keir had provided looked both oversized and vaguely rustic. It had plastic bench seating and real windows offering a view out across the desert. The metallic tang of surface dust clung to the air.

Vorn shook their hands as introductions were made. Then the doors sealed and they started off. From the spaceport, the pod headed down an unshielded rail that led out into the empty landscape and picked up speed.

In the distance, Mark could see the tip of a single tower jutting over the horizon.

'Is that where we're headed?' said Mark. It looked depressingly far away.

Keir nodded. 'That's Government Tower. Doesn't look like much from here. It's better up close. We should be there in about forty minutes.'

'Why did you build your spaceport so far from your city?' said Mark. 'That's got to be awkward.'

'Partly because of the placement of Fecund ruins,' said Keir. 'Plus we expected the city to scale and picked facility sites to support that. Over the last ten years we haven't seen as much growth as we expected. Unless you count the illegal ghettos out in the ocean.'

'The *ocean*?' said Zoe.

'Well, where the ocean *used* to be,' said Keir. 'Right now we're up on what was a continent until about ten million years ago. The colony was built along an old river valley because that's where the Fecund focused their activity. All the continental land was claimed by legitimate freeholders so the Flags just set up out in the old ocean. They didn't care about the terraforming plans that slated it for reflooding. They don't think that far ahead. And it's convenient for them – they can make raids to steal from any of our sites out along the coast.'

As if on cue, the pod banked right as the rail turned to run parallel to a great canyon now opening out before them. Then it descended into a sloping trench carved out near the canyon wall before diving into a tunnel. The pod slowed in the darkness.

'Air gate,' said Keir. 'This is where we couple with the old hydraulic system.'

Lights came on, revealing a utilitarian-looking industrial airlock that opened before them. Another identical lock lay beyond, and another after that. The pod went through six of them.

'Weird engineering,' said Zoe, peering up at the mechanism as they passed.

'Not really,' said Keir. 'Saves on pumping *and* time. Doors are cheap.'

On the other side of the air gates lay an oval vaulted tunnel ten metres high. Down the left side of it ran a bank of enormous windows made of curving crystal smeared with dust. Despite the grime, they offered an extraordinary view onto the broad, sloping floor of the canyon beyond. The other wall had been covered with a crazily dense mix of alien braille and bas-relief carving depicting thousands of Fecund figures engaged in some kind of battle.

Mirror-calm black water filled the bottom of the tube, turning it into a covered canal. The pod ran along one of a set of elevated rails jutting out of the channel. They contrasted harshly with the almost art nouveau – and decidedly non-human – lines of everything else.

Mark regarded the bewildering maze of figures sliding past with awe. The Fecund had always struck him as looking like beaked aquatic monkeys. In the art here, though, they came in all shapes and sizes, with bodies that resembled everything from hippos to wolves. They all had the same weirdly turreted eyes.

'Whoa,' he said, taking it all in.

Sam laughed. 'Gets everyone.'

'Fecund transit tube,' Keir explained with a dry smile. 'Takes a lot of visitors by surprise. I generally don't try starting any kind of meaningful conversation with visitors until we're closer to the city, otherwise I just get interrupted by the sightseeing.'

'You ran your transit system through Fecund tunnels?' said Zoe.

'Why not?' said Keir. 'The tunnels were already here and they go to all of the places we want to go. So it makes sense to save on engineering, even if it does raise our atmosphere costs.'

'And the water?' she asked.

'That was already here,' said Venetia. 'These tunnels were full of ice when people showed up. The Fecund used water-tubes for almost everything – food, transport, communication, you name it. And given the amount of permafrost melt they have here now, the biggest problem most of the time is getting the tunnels to drain properly once they've been pumped back up to pressure.'

'You've visited before, then?' said Keir, eyeing her warily.

Venetia nodded. 'Years ago. You want to know something crazy?' she asked Zoe. 'There's evidence that some of these tunnels pre-date the Fecund by several million years, meaning they were second-hand when the beak-faces got here. Makes you wonder, doesn't it?'

Keir frowned. 'That's never been conclusively proven,' he said.

'It would certainly mess up a lot of the paperwork around legal claims, that's for sure,' said Venetia with a wry smile. 'Permits for stripping sites of undetermined heritage are much harder to acquire, as it turns out.'

The defence minister took a moment to re-appraise his passenger. 'Fortunately, that hasn't been an issue for years,' he said quickly. 'We have bigger problems on our plate these days.'

'Don't we all,' said Sam.

But Venetia only warmed to her topic, her own advice about not baiting the locals apparently forgotten.

'The Fecund cared less about planets than we do,' she said. 'Unlike us humans, they tended to prefer orbitals and only bothered setting down on worlds where there was something to exploit or learn from. Like old tunnels, for instance. But most people agree that the Fecund were primarily here for bioweapons.'

'Either that, or simply *biochemistry research*,' said Keir. 'Opinions are mixed. Many don't hold such a dim view of the species. We try to maintain a respectful attitude towards the prior owners.'

Mark refrained from commenting. If the Fecund had treated this place anything like humans had treated Davenport, Venetia was probably right. He moved over to the window to look at the view flashing past. On the far bank of the canyon stood rows of what looked like disused industrial buildings, enormous in scale and all in advanced states of decay. Given that ten million years had passed, it was astonishing they were standing at all. Those tectonics Venetia mentioned couldn't have been too active in the meantime.

What had once been the bed of the river running down the canyon was now a flat swathe of gravel pocked with broken pieces of mechanised junk, the broad banks dotted with what looked like giant harvesting machines of some kind. They stood crumpled and forlorn like the skeletons of ancient monsters poking out of the dust.

The transit tunnel reached a vast block-shaped building jutting out from the side of the canyon wall. As they ran through it, the transit tube briefly became glass on both sides. Around them towered the interior of some kind of factory space where a row of dozen-metre-tall robots, filth-smeared, decrepit, older than humanity, stood waiting for new tasks that would never come.

'They built to last, then,' he observed.

'Hell, yes,' said Venetia. 'You've seen the *Ariel Two*. These guys didn't mess around. Mind you, this whole valley was clogged with dust when people first arrived here. It had been that way since the Transcended caused the biosphere shutdown. The colonists uncovered it all in the first years of habitation. The ruins won't last nearly as long exposed to the atmosphere – just a few tens of thousands of years, by current estimates.'

As they travelled further down the valley, the landscape changed. They reached an area where the ruins had been cleared away from the gently sloping banks and replaced by private habitat domes. Each pocket of air held a single grand home surrounded by a circle of perfect green garden. Colonnades and porticos decorated the facades. The grounds tended towards a romantic Surplus Age style, all oak trees and tennis courts tended by armies of gardenerbots. They looked like scenes from a history vid brought to life. A transit rail snaked between them.

Apparently, a lot of people in New Luxor lived in hundred-room palaces. To Mark, the houses looked weirdly lonely despite their opulence. They didn't even share an atmosphere. His sense of unease was reinforced when they passed one with a failed envelope. A dirty mansion with smashed windows stood in a patch of dead vegetation almost as brown as the gravel that lay around it.

Zoe came over and stood at the window next to him. 'Looks like all those patents bought some classy pads,' she observed.

'Land isn't in short supply here,' said Keir. 'Neither are building materials or robots.'

'Unless you're a Flag,' said Venetia with a wink.

Keir's lips thinned a little.

Beyond New Luxor's isolationist suburbs, the ancient riverbed widened and the real settlement began. Carter had avoided super-towers, preferring a more traditional style of development. Eclectically decorated buildings huddled under domes of various sizes. The colony sported only a single macrostructure – Government Tower. A needle of blue glass built into the canyon wall rose a couple of hundred storeys up into the pale lemon sky.

The pod transferred through another set of air gates, this time into a Martian-style transit tube that ran straight through the heart of the small city. Mark caught sight of brightly painted cafes with no patrons and grand parks where lonely figures wandered. Streets slid by lined with open-fronted stores selling nothing at all. But for the odd pedestrian trailed by domestic machines of various kinds, the place felt like a ghost town. He saw more robots than people.

The pod joined a rail rising up the side of the tower and the city fell away beneath them, becoming a cluster of clear bubbles packed with brightly coloured toys. The view opened out, revealing the mouth of the river and an expanse of perfectly flat, dead desert beyond. It made the wasteland they'd originally landed in look varied and dramatic by comparison.

As the transit slowed, Mark got a view into the interior of the tower. Dozens of floors of unused office space slid past, where robots sat dormant or stacks of still-sealed furniture lay waiting. The human colony here, he thought, appeared to be rapidly turning itself into a copy of the dead one it had displaced. He wondered if this was how Bradbury must have looked during the first decades on Mars – a city at the edge of nowhere with too much space on its hands, not quite sure why it existed.

Only the top ten floors showed signs of life. Wind whistled around the pod's edges when it arrived at the executive level at the peak. From there, Mark could make out the curve of the horizon, and dark smudges of human habitation far off in the hazy nothingness of the empty ocean.

'This way, please,' said Keir as the door opened.

He led them down an echoing hallway ten metres high with skylights that let in slanting rays of creamy light. The place smelled faintly and familiarly of cabbage.

Mark knew that smell. He looked up at the corners of the ceiling and saw dark blotches on the biofabric walls. The place had tower flu, then, just like his former home in New York. He wondered how long ago that had set in.

Keir led them to a meeting room with a massive table of vat-grown wood covered in a thin layer of dust. It sported thirty old-fashioned vat-leather chairs scattered in various random positions and an incredible, if uniformly bleak, view over the post-oceanic plain.

'Where is everyone?' said Mark.

'I'll fetch them now,' said Keir. 'Please wait here.' He stepped out. The door shut behind him.

'What do you think?' said Venetia.

'I think it's a dump,' said Zoe. 'It's even worse than my old home town on New Angeles. I always assumed the cities at the New Frontier would be like mini-Bryants, full of energy and verve.'

'They were,' said Sam. 'That's kind of gone on hold recently, which is one reason why New Panama is booming so much. People don't want to spend any more time out on the angry edge of civilisation than they have to.'

'We could always just change the law,' said Venetia. 'Give the sects a better deal.'

Sam snorted. We did,' he said. 'About eight times, I think. Look how well that turned out.'

'What does it matter?' said Zoe. 'We're wasting our time. If we don't get out of here and do something, there won't *be* a New Frontier, no matter how shitty it is.'

'Agreed,' said Mark. 'All this is very enlightening, but we should just make our point and leave. We've got work to do.'

Keir Vorn, though, did not return. Fifteen minutes dragged by. Mark's anxiety grew.

'What's keeping the guy?' said Zoe.

Mark pinged the room's security but found he couldn't get past the pitifully slow-witted room SAP.

'I could find him,' he said, 'but I'd have to hack them first.'

'Not the best way to make a good impression,' said Venetia.

Sam sighed. 'Look, I'll go and find out what's happening. You guys wait here.'

Venetia shot Mark an urgent look as Sam headed for the door. Mark had a choice: to stop him or let him go. Ash's words echoed in his head. Should he trust Sam?

He gestured to Venetia with a flattened hand while his guts roiled. *Keep sitting.* He dearly hoped he'd chosen right. As Sam strode out into the hall, the door clicked shut behind him.

'What now?' said Venetia.

'Now we wait and hope,' said Mark.

Another fifteen minutes slid by.

'This is bullshit,' said Zoe.

She marched up to the door, which refused to open. She tried the manual pad on the wall. Nothing happened.

'Hey, room!' she shouted. 'Open up!'

When the room didn't reply, Mark reached out for it directly. The moment he did so, the window-wall swapped to video and Sam's face appeared.

'Hello, everyone,' he said. 'You've just discovered that you're locked in. My apologies for that. I regret the duplicity. Unfortunately, there have been too many unpleasant coincidences during this mission.' He counted them off on his fingers. 'The apparent attempted murder, Mark's disruption of my override, Zoe's inclusion of non-mission-approved tech.'

'What?' Zoe roared.

Sam continued indifferently. 'It's my duty to figure out what's going on and to resolve these issues while I have the chance. It's vital I make sure there's no foul play at work here,' he told them earnestly. 'In case the human race is being set up to pay the price.'

'What?' said Mark. 'Since when? And how exactly does all this shit you just made up fit with the mission profile?'

'I'll get back to you as soon as I can,' said Sam. 'Once again, my apologies. I recommend that you make yourselves comfortable.'

He shut the channel.

'Bastard!' yelled Zoe. She pounded on the door.

Venetia leaned her elbows on the table and massaged her temples. 'I guess we have our answer,' she said.

Mark checked the security. He grabbed the simple SAP running the room and rammed commands down its API. The SAP flailed into submission, revealing a data connection behind it that had been isolated and shut down from the other end. Digitally speaking, their room had been locked from the outside. Barring the chance of catching some wireless traffic from data nodes on the floors below, they were cut off.

Mark surged to his feet and kicked his chair across the room, where it smacked into the biofabric panelling and broke apart.

'Fuck!' He turned to face Venetia. 'Does *anything* he said make any sense to you?'

Venetia shook her head. 'The actions he just took were predicated on the notion that he himself was above suspicion – a proposition he avoided on board while it suited his purposes. In short, he was bullshitting, as you suspected. By the way, what made you decide to let him go?'

'I spoke to Ash, like you suggested,' he said, embarrassment choking his voice. 'I asked him if I should come here, and if I could trust Sam.

He told me to go along with it and that everything would be fine. I took him at his word.' Mark hung his head and felt like a fool.

'So it's both of them, then?' said Zoe.

'I was so sure it was Citra,' said Mark. 'I was too freaked out to think about the alternatives. I feel ashamed. That poor woman.'

'That override moment,' said Zoe. 'Sam wanted Ash in control of the ship, and now he is.'

'And I don't think there's any doubt that Sam dumped the fuel on purpose,' said Venetia. 'He brought us to Carter to make *this* happen.'

Mark fell back into another chair as the strength drained out of his legs.

'They never wanted me on that ship,' he breathed as realisation dawned. 'This has been planned since Earth. Which means they must have known something about Tiwanaku. They were planning for it.'

Silence fell as they all stared at each other.

'Fuck,' said Zoe in awe. 'The whole mission's a set-up.' She leaned against the wall and slid down it to sit on the floor. 'I can't believe it took us this long to notice.'

Mark suddenly felt very, very stupid. He should have seen it. The pieces had been right in front of him all along. It had just never occurred to him that the entire mission was fabricated. No wonder they'd never met the other ships at the rendezvous. That had never been part of the story.

Their predicament still didn't make sense, though. The drones they'd fought were absolutely real and their technology profoundly foreign. The whole of IPSO had been duped, but it was totally unclear how or why.

13: JUSTIFICATION

13.1: WILL

As the pod doors shut, Will took in his surroundings. He'd been delivered to a garden of sorts – a white-walled space filled with shrubs and trees lit by ceiling-lamps three storeys above. It appeared to be a cross between an experimental botanical garden and a recreation area. Rubberised pathways ran between the trees. Sofas and work tables sat at the intersections. The air smelled of rosemary and carried the soft hiss of air-scrubbers.

From out of the greenery stepped Parisa Voss.

'Hello, Will,' she said.

Will stared at her, sick astonishment welling up inside him.

'You,' he said.

Exactly what percentage of his life was a lie? he wondered. All of it? Pari had been the most consistent, benign feature of his political life for years. How had she found the time for shit like this?

'Are you really so surprised?' she said. 'Who else would have the political muscle to bring all this together?' She looked pleased with his reaction, and herself.

'You...' Will started. He struggled for adequate words. 'You *disgust* me.'

'I would expect nothing less,' said Pari, apparently satisfied. 'Anything else?'

Will could only stare. The man he'd been before his short flight on the *Chiyome* might have railed at her and shouted out his wrath. Now, he just felt ill.

'No,' he said.

She looked slightly disappointed. 'I imagine you're probably upset,' she said, 'but the only reason you're here is because you didn't do your job.'

Will's anger rumbled back into life. 'What?'

'You think we found a weapon to use against Flags,' she said, 'but that's the smallest part of what we found. Before you judge us, look.'

She tapped the jewelled bracelet on her left wrist and a link invitation appeared in Will's sensorium. Will struggled briefly with the urge to subvert the room's network, take Pari hostage and bend the entire station to his will. There'd be time for that later, though. He accepted the link.

An image bloomed in his mind of the world situated below them. It looked . . . *odd*. It wasn't just the black continents or mauve seas. The entire world had a curious texture. He zoomed in for a closer look and found a landscape covered with weird linear features tangled across each other, as if the planet had been coated with monstrous spaghetti.

Barring the curious starfish structures, the linear shapes appeared to cover every inch of landmass on the planet, dipping beneath the waves at the coasts. Nowhere could he see the familiar hallmarks of geology, except perhaps in the overall features of the continents themselves.

'It's a self-sustaining biosphere,' she said. 'Artificial, we believe, and incredibly advanced. It's unlike any other biosphere world we've ever seen. This one tolerates humans without issue.'

Will shot her a look of unalloyed disbelief. She smiled, apparently misinterpreting his scorn for some gentler variety of scepticism.

'The environment on Snakepit is robust, self-correcting and incredibly stable,' she said. 'Every one of those linear formations you can see is a self-contained, self-extending habitat system. A living root, if you like, with usable space inside.'

The display in his sensorium updated to show him schematics and cross sections.

'This entire world is covered with them, about ten layers deep. Snakepit could house and feed the Earth's fifteen billion tomorrow, while using only about ten per cent of its available resources. It's also an example of functional terraforming of a sort we've never achieved. That oxygen-nitrogen atmosphere is the result of ambient air-bleed from the self-contained habitats, much as you see above Bradbury, which means that this system is even proofed against the Galatea Effect. When the atmosphere here started to reorganise, all the biomass remained safe below.' She smiled knowingly. 'Amazing, isn't it? It's a dream come true.'

'You could say that,' said Will.

It was admittedly an incredible find – a piece of technology potentially more useful than anything the Transcended had ever given them. Taken at face value, it was the solution to all of Earth's problems, presuming they could ever build enough starships to ferry people over. But the idea that such bounty might come with heavy costs didn't appear to have occurred to Pari. He almost pitied her for that.

'Here's the interesting thing,' said Pari. 'This star system never saw a suntap flare, even though it's sitting here right in the middle of Fecund space. We've analysed the spectrum and can't see any signs of damage. Besides which, the biosphere would have been fried. So what do you think that means?'

Will could think of several implications, not all of them pleasant.

She answered for him. 'It means it was left for you to find.'

Will peered at her.

'Yes, you,' she said. 'Do you imagine this world that offers so much is here by accident? I don't. The Transcended put you in the frame. They gave you the ship and the tools. They made it possible for you to find this gift. The one they left for us. *Why didn't you?*'

Will's mouth curled into a snarl. 'You're asking *me*? I was trying to save your fucking planet from itself. Or didn't you notice?'

She waved a tutting finger at him. 'No, Will. That's not what you were doing. You were trying to save *everybody*. That's not the same. You didn't learn the one big lesson the Transcended tried to teach you. What makes the difference between a species that prospers and one that dies is *constructive self-editing*. They told you that explicitly. All your accounts feature it prominently. But they were talking about editing at the species level, Will, not just about you personally. And editing requires cutting.' Her expression darkened. 'You left that job to the Fleet. And that's why the Rumfoord League had to take it on.'

'Very convenient,' said Will. 'The end justifies the means and all that bullshit. I'm sure you must feel very noble interpreting my experiences for me. How convenient that you get to choose who cuts, and how! And with such a handy scalpel just lying there in space! Tell me, Pari, what kind of a fucking idiot abuses alien tech? Wasn't one war enough of a lesson?'

'We learned from the war and you didn't,' she said without hesitation. 'We aren't doing this to wage a war but to prevent one. Take a look at this.'

She passed him a new invitation. This one opened to reveal a suite of cliometric simulations – huge ones, running thousands of scenarios with billions of pseudo-human agents individually modelled. Will blinked at the level of detail that had gone into them.

'We have Andromeda Ng-Ludik to thank for all this. I believe you've met?'

The work was undeniably impressive. Ann was good for something, at least, even if it wasn't making sound ethical decisions.

'She presented this work at a closed meeting on Triton over a year ago. You missed it – for personal reasons, as I recall. The finding from her research is irrefutable. If action is not taken, social pressures in human society will result in war and subsequent economic collapse.'

'But we knew that already,' said Will. 'That's what we've been trying to solve!'

'How?' said Pari. 'By talking to the senate? By threatening people? By getting upset and punching holes in a half-a-million-peace-coin podium? You should have paid more attention, Will. Models like these don't just tell us what's going to happen. They tell us *how*. And they show us the solutions that can actually work. And guess what, you consistently avoided using the one variable the models suggested was absolutely necessary: force. You just expected everyone to start behaving better because *you* did. That's not good enough, Will. And that's why you're here.'

She tweaked the display in his sensorium, drawing his attention to the huge starfish shapes dotting Snakepit's surface.

'As I'm sure you're aware by now, this planet comes with a self-defence mechanism. Those bio-forms are defensive nodes. If the planet is damaged or exploited in any significant way, it constructs a matching response.'

'Drones,' said Will.

'Exactly. What we call Nemesis machines – bio-formed warp-enabled munitions. An extraordinary concept, is it not? The response is extremely predictable. This means that whenever the sects land a new Frontier-busting settlement, we can shut it down without IPSO being any the wiser. So far it has been used no fewer than eight times at the Far Frontier.'

Will's gaze snapped to her face. '*Eight?*'

She looked saddened by his surprise. 'Will, the proxy war you imagined we were trying to start at Tiwanaku has been going on for more than two years. Flags have been capitalising on Fleet limitations and claiming worlds outside of IPSO control for months now. They've been trying to seize territory without even a glance in the Fleet's direction. And had they succeeded, the balance of power would already have changed. The sects would have abandoned politics. That war you fear would have long since started. You see, Will,' she said, 'you failed already. We've been covering your ass for years. Take a look.'

She passed him another invitation. This time, Will couldn't bring himself to open it. He didn't doubt she had the proof. People had been expecting the sects to make a move since before he lost Rachel. His shoulders sagged. History had been advancing all around him and he'd never even noticed. He, who had been personally tasked with saving it.

'Instead,' she said, 'we clear up each incident without ever impacting the Fleet's finances. Each operation the Nems carry out is immaculate. They're so tidy that nobody needs to know they happened. Except the sects, of course, who're spitting with rage. All they know is that their horrid little military outposts full of religious fundamentalists keep disappearing. But this pattern is unsustainable. Every new illegal outpost is larger than the last. And the larger the target the Nems consume, the more human data they internalise and the less predictable they become. Which meant that Tiwanaku had to be the very last site we let them take. We knew that without something to reset politics, the sects would eventually win. As ever with Earth, it's just a numbers game. They have them. We don't. And if they win, your vision of a unified species will be lost for good.'

'So why didn't you just *tell* me?' said Will.

'Because we judged, based on prior experience, that you couldn't make the necessary cold decision. So we arranged for Fleet scouts to witness an "alien event". We laid a warp trail linking Tiwanaku straight to Earth. And then we made sure that you and the *Ariel Two* would become unavailable. The Nemesis machines will attack Earth. And then they'll be beaten before they can adapt. With Earth's population under threat, the sects will have no choice but to support the Fleet. And with evidence that the Far Frontier holds alien dangers, political support for Frontier-jumping will vanish. The human race will be reunified.'

Will shivered at the implications. 'At the cost of billions of lives,' he said quietly.

Pari wagged her finger at him again. 'Actually, just a few million. We've been quite careful about that. Our ships will be ready when the attack begins. The Nem swarm will never reach Earth itself. There'll be losses in the out-system, of course, and surface casualties due to the radiation impact, but that's all. Frankly, it's a low price to pay compared to that of another interstellar war.'

Will couldn't stomach her talk of costs and cutting and paying. It felt cheaply clinical to him – the kind of decision-making leaders engaged in when they felt certain they'd never have to bear the brunt of their own choices.

'How nice that you won't be paying,' he sneered.

Pari's smile dropped away. She suddenly looked very angry.

'Aren't I? Haven't I? You remember, I hope, that rebels on Earth murdered my family. I've spared you the footage of their charred corpses staked out on the ground. Did you know that some of those gang members were as young as twelve? All were executed after the trial that followed, of course. Earth's justice is as pathetic as its discipline. You seem to forget that I'm *from* Earth, Will. I've dedicated my life and my career to helping it. I could so easily have done what my father wanted and supported the interests of his sect, but I chose not to. I tried to follow in *your* footsteps, Will Monet, and make a difference. I took *your* sacrifice and *your* vision seriously. More seriously than you did, apparently.'

Her nostrils flared as she spoke. Her voice trembled. Pari Voss's famous exterior had cracked, spilling out some of the poison froth from inside.

'It was in the wake of that... those... *killings* that I realised helping the world was never going to be enough. I saw that no matter how hard I worked, no matter how much I gave and gave, there would always be more poverty. More horror. More death. The Earth was like a mindless machine just churning it out. And that's when I realised I needed to turn the horror machine off. If I did that, it would make the whole species sit up and take note.'

'But how can *this* possibly help?' said Will sadly. 'Even if your plan works, how does hitting the Earth make it better? You're not making the poverty go away.'

'Can you really not see?' she snapped. 'We had all the tools to end poverty hundreds of years ago, Will, so why does it still exist? Because people squeeze each other. They can't help themselves. And they keep squeezing and hurting and crushing and maiming right up until someone starts squeezing them back. We had to make it look like someone else was doing the squeezing. We had to give humanity the gift of *fear* – the one gift you were never going to give us. The one gift that would offer people an incentive to stop fighting. You see, Will, you were ready to change yourself for mankind. But you were never ready to change mankind for *itself*.'

'Because I believe that change should be a choice,' he said.

'Right up until one person's choice destroys another's?' she said. 'Because that's what we're looking at. That's the reality your endless, cowardly optimism has created. You stayed golden. You got to act the hero. Your power and position gave you the liberty to adopt the moral high ground about human progress without ever having to look at what it meant for everyone else. Well, here's something to think about. You fired on those Nemesis machines *by choice*. Which means that *your* action triggered the next phase of the immune response. We made sure of that. The *Gulliver* couldn't fire. The *Chiyome* didn't on purpose. It's *your* act and only yours that will cause the attack on Earth. Whatever you may think of us, you're responsible for what happens to Earth now.'

Will's skin prickled.

'I don't expect you to like me or understand me,' said Pari. 'It's too late for that. I don't expect you to join my side. But after the attack on Earth, someone will need to unify humanity. Someone who will bring revenge against the attackers and word of a new home for humanity. Because without that organising force, everything will slide backwards. We intend that unifying force to be *you*. Just as you elevated Gustav after the war without giving him any real choice in the matter, so we will elevate you. Over the years you've confided in me plenty with your feelings about Earth, Will. You've told me over and over about your isolation and the terrible moral load. Well, guess what – I freed you from that burden by taking it on myself, thereby enabling you to

295

fulfil the goal you were meant for. The job you were *supposed have finished years ago.*'

Will looked at her with horror and then buried his face in his hands.

'I'll leave you now,' she said. 'You've got some thinking to do.'

Will felt sick. Pari had touched him as she'd intended. He couldn't help but see that the situation he found himself in was as much his own doing as anyone else's. Yet she didn't have a clue what her actions had wrought. She still imagined she was in control.

13.2: ANN

Ann waited on the station's command deck for Senator Voss to finish her session with Will Monet. They'd overhauled the place again since her visit months ago. Video panels now covered every available inch of wall-space, densely packed with a hundred different kinds of visualised statistics about the world beneath them. Work tables and clusters of meeting couches equipped with projector bubbles dotted the gently curving floor. League scientists filled the seats, rapt in study. It was like walking around inside a giant infographic.

After weeks in the cramped interior of the *Chiyome*, the cavernous spaces of Snakepit Station came as a huge relief. Except Ann couldn't shake the feeling that the officers busily analysing the planet below them had all missed a crucial detail.

A transit pod delivered the senator to the floor. She emerged breathing hard, her hands pressed together.

'Senator Voss, ma'am. A word, if I may,' said Ann, striding across to meet her.

The senator looked exhausted – more than she usually let people see. 'What is it, Captain?'

'First, ma'am, are you okay?' said Ann, examining Voss's face. Her usually flawless olive skin showed lines of stress.

The senator exhaled. 'Yes, just a little wound up, I suppose. I've been rehearsing that speech in my head for years. But when I finally got to say it all to his face, it took rather a lot out of me.' She smiled, her artificial brightness coming back online. 'Ah, well. We all do the jobs fate assigns us, don't we? What do you need?'

'I wanted to report to you personally as soon as I could about the

Nems, ma'am,' said Ann. 'I know you already have my written account but I don't think this can wait. From what we saw, the Nems are operating dangerously close to the edge of our model tolerances. We can't say with any confidence that the Tiwanaku swarm is operating as expected.'

The senator's smile switched off again. 'An unfortunate assessment,' she said.

'Furthermore, discussion with Captain Monet during his transfer raised a disturbing point. He suggested a level of deliberate agency in the biomaterial we deployed that our analysis hadn't detected. As I understand it, the team in the denaturing lab believed they'd minimised the capabilities of the material, but from Will's account, it's not clear that they succeeded.'

'Under the circumstances, one might expect Monet to overstate the risks,' said Voss.

'Understood, ma'am,' said Ann, 'and were it not for the fact that his account appeared to correlate with what I witnessed first-hand, I wouldn't have brought it up.'

'I see.'

'Coupled with the absence of the *Gulliver*, I'm concerned that our project may already have veered off track,' said Ann.

The senator folded her arms. 'Really. So what do you recommend?'

'An immediate scouting flight to Tiwanaku to check the development of the swarm. Also, a short visit to the Nerroskovi System to see whether the *Gulliver* can be located. As I understand it, one of our watcher drones arrived with a report of a Nem departure event in that direction.'

Senator Voss frowned. 'Surely by the time you got there, the end of the rendezvous window would have passed. The *Gulliver* would have already left.'

'Accepted, ma'am, but at least knowing the fate of Mark Ruiz and Overcaptain Shah would strengthen our hand. We might be able to bolster our negotiating position with Captain Monet.'

'Of course,' said Voss. 'But potentially at the cost of limiting our capabilities here during the next phase. Sam Shah is a smart man,' she added. 'Nobody knows more about the Nems than he does. It's lamentable that he's out of the picture at this point, but that possibility always existed.'

Ann nodded. 'You're right, ma'am. Certainly locating them comes as a secondary priority to monitoring the swarm. I have one other proposal.'

Voss inclined her head. 'Go on.'

Ann took a deep breath and spoke her mind. 'I strongly recommend the creation of a backup option to cover the eventuality that Nem behaviour becomes dangerously unpredictable. In that scenario, we cut a deal with Captain Monet and abort.'

The senator's lips thinned.

Ann hurried onwards. 'Either he helps us and swears to protect the interests of the League, or we leave him here and avert the machine attack without him.'

Parisa's face was unreadable. Data light flickered in her synthetically blue eyes. Ann waited for a response.

'That would not be a backup,' said the senator eventually. 'That would be a disaster.'

'Ma'am—' Ann started.

Voss cut her off with a sweep of her hand. 'We know the machines will be destroyed at Earth. No other part of this endeavour has been over-engineered to such an extent. The Nems could quadruple the size of their expected fleet and still not change our risk envelope. And at the end of the day, we have the Nem homeworld. To prevent the creation of new machines, we nuke the planet. Then they won't have anywhere to take their samples to. Admittedly this would represent a terrible waste, but we *are* equipped for that eventuality. As your video log from Tiwanaku clearly demonstrates, planets are delicate things. And this one is no different. Tell me, Captain,' the senator added. 'Did you see any evidence at Tiwanaku that the Nems *wouldn't* carry out a follow-up attack?'

'No, ma'am,' said Ann, her cheeks colouring. 'But all those models were based on a fixed rate of development—'

Voss chopped her down again. An edge entered her voice. 'We put everything into this,' she said. 'Our money. Our time. Our credibility. And now you're proposing that we throw away all that effort and demonise ourselves over fear of a pile of five-million-year-old machines? That planet hasn't had intelligent life on it since humans walked upright.'

Ann could think of nothing to say. She hadn't proposed capitulating, only the careful examination of another course of action. Without meaning to, she appeared to have caught the senator in a moment of imperfect rationality. That disappointed her. She'd always held Parisa Voss in high regard, ever since the senator had recruited her.

'I appreciate scientific caution, Captain Ludik, but not when it impedes action,' said the senator. 'And there is some evidence from your latest outing that you have a skewed notion of where that balance lies.'

Ann stiffened. 'I'm sorry, ma'am?'

'I read your interim report and I read Lieutenant Brinsen's. Because of choices you made, we nearly missed acquiring the *Ariel Two*. Consequently it was necessary to expose Nelson Aquino's role, which limits our future capacity to influence Monet. And now that ship is damaged and will take more days to repair than we originally assigned for it. This adds risks to our already burdened plan. What you need to understand, Captain Ludik, is that the events we have set in motion are much larger than we are. Our choice is to see them through or be crushed beneath them.'

'With respect, I am well aware of the scale of the plan,' said Ann tersely. 'But regardless of its scale, it remains inevitably true that sunk costs are irrelevant. What we've invested means nothing unless the plan works.'

The senator's nostrils flared. 'That's enough,' she said. 'Clearly you either have a limited grasp of our current risk profile or you've become a little too close to your assigned target.' Her tone suggested that she believed the latter. Jaco must have said something in his report. 'I recommend you take a well-deserved rest and leave the handling of the situation to us now. Your input has been heard and I will give it due consideration.'

Ann opened her mouth to speak again.

'Don't make me ask you twice, Captain,' said Voss.

Ann blushed. She saluted crisply, turned on her heel and left, her cheeks burning.

13.3: MARK

Mark tested the door with his weight and explored the edges of the room for ports or seals he could rip. Then he looked for air vents. They were all situated at ceiling level, far too high to reach even if they piled the chairs into stacks. He hadn't managed to reach the processor for the window-wall, either.

He slumped in a meeting-room chair and gazed mournfully out at the desolation beyond the window. The situation, as far as he could see, was his own fault. He was captain of the *Gulliver*. He'd been assigned responsibility for looking after the diplomatic team. And he'd had all the evidence before him that someone was working against their interests. Except he'd been so focused on the threat outside the hull that he hadn't noticed the one right in front of him.

What would happen now? In all likelihood, Sam would rejoin Ash and the two of them would leave, committing Zoe, Venetia and himself to the hands of the local FPP, if not the clutches of the Photurian swarm. That path led to humiliation in the best case, and death – or something worse than death – as the alternative. Will's leaden stories about protecting your shipmates from harm didn't sound so pointless now.

He hung his head. 'I'm sorry,' he said. 'Looking after you was my job. I failed.'

'A fine sentiment,' said Venetia. 'If, perhaps, one that belongs in a previous century. This isn't your doing, Mark. We're all volunteers here. And neither Zoe nor I are the kind of women who need looking after.'

Mark looked up, embarrassed. 'I didn't mean it like that.'

'Don't bait him,' said Zoe from her place at the wall. 'He's taking responsibility. He cares. That's what you want in a starship captain.' She paused. 'Mark, thank you for the efforts you've made. Don't feel too bad – we were all duped. There wasn't enough data for us to see the big picture and we had plenty of other stuff to think about.'

'Thank you,' he said. 'I know I've not been the easiest person to get along with.'

'We appear to have some time on our hands,' she replied. 'Until someone lets us out or a miracle happens, we're stuck here. So why don't you explain it?'

Mark frowned. 'I'm not sure what you mean.'

'You just admitted you're not easy to get along with,' said Zoe. 'We know that's in part down to your history with Will. You get angry every time his name comes up. So fill us in on the details.'

He sighed. 'You really don't want to know. It's not an interesting story.'

300

'Could have fooled me,' she said. 'The way Ash tells it, you stole a starship.'

'That he did,' said Venetia. 'Among other things.'

'So what are you going to do?' said Zoe. 'Sit there and let us subsist on rumour?'

Mark peered at the horizon. If he couldn't unburden himself now, when could he? He wondered if his nanny-SAP would complain the moment he opened his mouth and realised he hadn't heard a peep out of it since Will's upgrade package. He suspected it'd been shut down.

'Okay,' he said. 'You asked for it. For starters, I didn't get my robo-teer mods the normal way. I was part of a secret genetic breeding programme run by the Fleet.'

'No shit!' said Zoe.

'My parents were volunteers from Earth who were given a chance to sign up to have a heavily engineered child,' he went on. 'This all happened in the years just after the war. Will Monet had this whole idea that he was going to create a new team of high-functioning roboteers using volunteers from every world, but particularly from Earth. We were going to represent the great shared future of humanity – construc-tive self-editing and all that. The thing was, he signed up the parents and kicked it all off before going to the media. He wanted it to be a fait accompli. Except that everyone went ballistic once he started talking about what he had planned.'

'I remember that,' said Venetia. 'There were all those claims of an alien plot.'

'That's right,' said Mark. 'Half the sects on Earth were convinced that Will Monet was trying to breed an army of pliant super-warriors for his alien masters to control.' He snorted in derision. 'So then he had a problem – a room full of kids and no way to tell anyone what they were. That was the mess I was born into. Of course, when I was little, I barely clocked any of it. Except that I was often told I was *special*. I went to special classes and had special lessons and ate special food. None of us saw that much of our parents. Will and Rachel were closer to us than any of our families.

'Then suddenly, out of the blue, we were all split up and shipped off to the colonies. My parents went with me, but by then we barely had anything in common. The fact that they kept moving us about made it worse. They filtered me into ordinary roboteer schools for a while,

301

but that sucked, too. I was already too different. In the end, they set up the bullshit Omega Academy, which was basically a cover for the programme they'd originally started. Except now it was supposed to be training that any roboteer could apply for. Nobody got in but us *special* kids, of course. Around that time, my parents moved away to New Panama and I didn't see them at all anymore. Will made sure of that.'

'Jesus,' said Zoe. 'Talk about isolating.'

Mark looked down at his hands. 'To call the whole experience isolating would be putting it mildly,' he said. 'But we had each other again, which was something. And, to a certain extent, we had Will and Rachel. Mostly Rachel, because Will was always off trying to save the world. Then everything began to fall apart. Uncle Gustav – that's the Great Prophet Ulanu, Father of Transcendism, to the rest of you – got shot. Will started to lose it, and consequently Rachel spent a lot more time in space, pushing the Frontier.

'She had more insight than most, that woman. She saw that the New Frontier was creating problems, so she put her energy into trying to find new star systems out beyond Galatea on the human shell. Of course, nobody else was interested in human space any more because there was so much easy money to be made from looting the Fecund. Then her ship flew into that bank of shit I believe they're now calling the Curvon Depleted Zone. Basically, it's the edge of our fucking Petri dish, so far as I can tell.' He balled his hands into fists. 'Anyway, no one knew what had happened, but the Fleet wasn't doing shit to rescue her. So I did something.'

'You took a ship,' said Zoe.

'Yeah, I took a ship. Which was a terrible idea. But you have to realise I grew up with all the rules being bent around me. We weren't supposed to even fucking exist. Everything I did was a special case. Half the time I was treated like a prince, and the other half like some kind of slackwit robot. So I did what we all saw Will doing, which was to *push* to get what he wanted.'

'And your ship got trapped, too,' said Venetia.

'Yep. And all the poor suckers I dragged along with me. It took us about a month to escape under conventional velocity. By that time we were going a tenth of a conventional light and it took forever to sort out our reference frame.'

Mark sighed. Just recalling the experiences exhausted him.

302

'So then there was a tribunal, which was when all kinds of little gems of information started to come out. Like the fact that Will had *paid* my parents to leave, to get them out of the way.'

'Ouch,' said Zoe.

'And the fact that unlike everyone else on the programme, I also had mods from Rachel, though it was never on the books. So technically, my dorm mother was at least as much my mother as my *actual* mother. Which was distressing, because she was by now technically considered dead.'

'That's . . . horrible,' said Zoe, sounding a little awed.

'There was a nice little identity crisis in there, too, because Rachel was stuffed full of Galatean genetic mods. She was from one of those *born-to-fly* families with more genetic tweaks than a slab of vat-pork. So I'd spent my childhood believing I was some kind of roboteer representative of Earth, while in fact I was at least half-Galatean. There's nothing quite like discovering that all the things you thought made you special were put there by someone else.'

Zoe shook her head. 'I don't get it. Why all the secrets?'

'Supposedly?' said Mark. 'Will said they'd acted that way because of assassination threats. He saw sending my folks away as *rescuing* my parents for me. Convenient, huh? And at no time was I consulted about any of that or treated like an adult in any way. The Fleet regarded me as fucking property throughout, right up until they started trying to take away my interface. That's when I realised I'd been bred to be a puppet. You all got to choose your careers. I was a starship captain from *birth*. That's why I don't spend too much time being proud of it.

'My life since then has been about two things. Trying to add value on my own terms, which is why I went off to fly lifters. And reconnecting with my roots to find out whether there's anything else to me aside from the shit the genetic engineers stuffed in there, which is why I went to Earth. The Fleet hated it, of course. They all thought I was going to start running Flags for some bullshit Truist cult. So far as they were concerned, I was Fleet-owned technology. So, unsurprisingly, when a chance to put all that behind me came along, I signed up.'

He drew a deep breath. '*Voilà*, your captain,' he said, and rested his head on the table, spent.

'Holy crap!' said Zoe. 'I thought you were going to tell us you were bullied at school or something.'

'Nope,' said Mark. 'A kid tried once. I accidentally broke his spine. He had to spend a month in a gel-tank having his vertebrae reprinted.'

'Okay,' she said. 'I get it. The attitude problem, in context, seems... I don't know... inevitable?'

'Thanks,' said Mark, his forehead still on the table. 'I guess.'

'I should apologise,' said Zoe. 'I had it tough growing up, too, but not to that extent. Anyway, to me you seemed like a kind of stuck-up-victim sort, so I had you pegged as self-indulgent. My bad. I hope you can forgive me for getting it so wrong.'

Mark felt a surge of warmth toward her, but didn't speak for fear of ruining it.

'What happened to you, then?' said Venetia. 'Mark's shared his story. The Fleet could probably have us all locked up now for what we just heard. So let's hear yours.'

'It's nothing like that.'

'I'd be shocked if it was, dear,' said Venetia. 'Come on, out with it.'

Mark raised his head to look at Zoe, still slumped against the wall. She stared at him for a few moments, as if trying to figure something out. Then her eyes drifted off to the middle distance.

'I was a nerd,' she said. 'No bad thing in itself, except that I grew up on New Angeles. My parents were part of the occupying Earther force during the war, and then applied for citizenship afterwards when their sect refused to pay for their flight home. They were just in the Science Division, but we still got treated like dirt. So we had zero money, everybody hated us and we had no access to the surgical tech everyone else did. Which is why I don't look like an Angeleno. I can tell you, it's not easy growing up the ugly girl in a world full of perfect Amazonian blondes.'

Mark frowned at her in confusion. Zoe was very far from ugly.

'Anyway,' she said, 'I had one advantage – I was smart. I worked hard in the shitty school we had access to and used all the IPSO-Online educational tools I could reach. I was good enough that when I hit sixteen I qualified for a Vartian Scholarship and got off that awful rock. Anyway, that took me to the Institute on Galatea, where I had a different problem. Suddenly I wasn't the smartest kid in the class any more. Because everyone there had mods.'

Mark was surprised again. He'd assumed she had mods. He'd never known anyone think so quickly without them.

'So I pulled the one trick I had over all of them from my child-hood, which was to work my ass off. I graduated top of my class in Xenophysics and have been pushing for missions ever since.'

Mark found her story slightly embarrassing. In some ways, she'd had it harder than him. He was born with an embarrassment of genetic riches he didn't know what to do with. She'd had none but still managed to work her way to the top. Furthermore, she didn't complain about it.

'That's amazing,' he said. 'I'm impressed.'

Zoe gave him the warmest smile he'd ever seen grace her features.

'Your turn,' said Zoe, pointing at Venetia.

'Oh no!' said Venetia, holding up her hands. 'I'm the psychologist, remember? I get to ask the questions, not answer them.'

'Come on,' said Mark, amused. 'We're done with secrets. Spit it out.'

'Well, okay, but I'm nothing like you two,' she said, folding her arms. 'I grew up on Esalen. I was young when the war happened, so I got to see our pathetic neo-hippy government try to remain neutral in the face of the Truist occupation. In any case, I was always a bit of an introvert and a misanthrope. After the war, I decided Esalen wasn't a great fit for me, so I moved away and changed my name. Fortunately, I was good enough in school to be able to apply for a scholarship like you did, Zoe. One that came with a starship berth.'

'You changed your name?' said Zoe.

Venetia nodded. 'Venetia Sharp is something I made up that I thought sounded more like the real me. My original name was Sunbeam Moon-flower.'

Mark let out a single ragged laugh.

'You don't strike me as a Sunbeam,' said Zoe.

'No,' said Venetia. 'As I said, I was raised neo-hippy and still share a lot of those values, but I see the limitations, too. And besides, I was always more interested in non-human minds than human ones. I also like getting things wrong so that I can do better next time. On Esalen, even now, people are obsessed with staying positive, despite the neuroscientific evidence that things aren't so simple. You'd think, after the things the Earthers did ...'

She let that sentence hang, her brow tightening briefly with the sour memory.

Mark missed the next thing she said because a ping came in from

Ash. He leapt to his feet and then tried to restrain his excitement in case the room still had operational cameras.

'Where are you?' he yelled into his sensorium. 'What's going on?'

'Still in orbit,' said Ash. 'I'm going to get you out.'

Mark gritted his teeth to stop himself from grinning. 'Do we have surveillance in here?' he said.

'Mark, what's happening?' asked Zoe in the background.

'No. I deactivated it,' said Ash. 'There's no one else on your level. I have pretty good coverage of their system at this point.'

Mark let out a whoop. 'We're getting off this rock,' he told the others. They jumped up.

'I'm damned glad you called,' Mark said to Ash. 'I'd given up on you.'

'I almost did, too,' said Ash. 'But you have to promise me something.'

'Sure – you name it,' said Mark.

'What I have to share with you is grim. I've made some big mistakes, got involved with a secret group trying to head off a war. And Sam . . . He's not being reasonable any more. I want you to promise me that if I pull you out of there, you'll cover my ass when we get home, because otherwise they're going to have me shot.'

'The conspirators?'

'No, Mark. The Fleet. This thing is treason. Are you up for this? Because I'll be counting on you. You'll be all I've got.'

'Okay,' said Mark slowly. 'You have a deal, I guess. The stakes are high enough.'

'All right,' said Ash. 'In that case, you'd better sit down because I'm sending you a memory dump and you're not going to like it.'

Mark gingerly returned to his seat.

Zoe jumped up and grabbed his arm. 'What's the issue?' she said expectantly. 'When are we leaving?'

'One minute,' he said. 'Incoming data.' He swapped his focus back to Ash. 'Go ahead.'

A link appeared in Mark's sensorium. He knocked it back. Awful knowledge blossomed in his head. His jaw fell open.

'Ugh,' he said as understanding dawned.

He felt a surge of anger towards Ash. The man had sold Mark out in court to bargain his way into the League, then been complicit in the entire plot that followed. But that emotion thinned to nothing next to the terrible realisation of what was coming. Death wasn't an outside chance for Carter. It was a certainty. Just as it was for his home. His face distorted from the pressure of the knowledge coursing through his head.

'No,' he croaked.

The next thing he knew, Venetia and Zoe were standing over him, holding his hands and shouting.

'Are you okay?' said Venetia.

Zoe was more direct. 'Please tell us what the fuck is going on!'

'We're leaving,' said Mark, rising uncertainly to his feet. His heart pounded from the weight of imposed panic that had come with the download. 'Ash, can you get us out of this room?'

The door slid open.

'You need to move to a lower level using the emergency stairs,' said Ash. 'If a pod comes up to this floor, they'll be on to us.'

'How far down? We're two hundred stories up.'

'Just past the occupied ones,' said Ash. 'If these plans are right, that's the eleventh below you. If you get down that far I can pick you up on a maintenance routing. But we don't have long. The *Gulliver* will be over your horizon again in a minute, which means I'll have to bounce via relay. I'm going to keep comms to a minimum in case they spot us. Just go. I'll pick you up.'

Mark turned to the others. 'Okay, let's get out of here,' he said. 'We're taking the stairs.'

1 3 . 4 : A N N

Rather than heading for her station suite, Ann made her way to the nearest bank of private study-spaces and picked a cubicle. The walls sprang into life as she stepped inside, bringing up her personal displays copied over from the *Chiyome*. A touchboard shelf slid out to meet her hands.

'Give me war modelling,' she told the room.

Senator Voss might not want to talk about backup options, but that didn't stop Ann from looking for one. Maybe the senator would be easier to persuade with a better way to handle the Nem threat sitting in front of her.

She should have guessed that Brinsen would try to undermine her the moment they docked. The jackbooted little rat must have been desperate to keep his own record clean. No matter that she'd got it right from the outset. They should have listened to Will more from the start. They should have trusted him. She fought back a throat-clotting surge of regret and got to work.

The room brought up a system map laying out all her work on simulations of the impending sect/colony crisis. Ann knew the map well – it represented years of obsessive effort on her part. She'd crafted her own political SAPs, work most people would have left to a machine-intelligence specialist, and combed through years of political data to build her model constraints. The evolutionary coding engine that created fresh software implementations for every run had been off-the-shelf, admittedly, but almost everything else she'd coded herself.

The war models had been Ann's greatest pride and greatest source of nightmares for years now. When she joined the League, those models had been expanded. The extensive simulations the League scientists ran to predict the Nems were coupled to her code and the union of the two used to design the home system post-attack strategy – the most important part of the plan. Without a reliable way to vanquish the Nems and unite humanity in the aftermath, the League would be little more than butchers.

On many occasions, Ann had gone back to her models, tweaking variables here and there to look for ways to avoid the need for a Nem assault altogether. She'd never found one. With luck, coming up with a way to minimise the response they'd already initiated would prove easier.

She hesitated, her fingers hovering over the touchboard. Theoretically speaking, she wasn't supposed to be looking at any of this. Sam had specifically requested a moratorium on further analysis. He'd pointed out weeks ago that once the League's core mission began, further tinkering with the code would simply distract people from the difficult reality unfolding around them.

'We've reached the point where extra checking over details amounts to paranoia,' he'd said in his last team briefing. 'It's time to stop obsessing and start improvising.'

She'd agreed with him. Under the circumstances, though, she could hardly imagine him complaining. Their own models hadn't predicted him lost aboard the *Gulliver*, for a start. Still, it didn't make any sense for her to announce her actions before she had something to show.

'Block outgoing monitor traffic,' she told the room. 'Security code Ludik-three. Let me know if someone's looking over my shoulder.'

'Code accepted,' said the room.

'Now show me the failure cases, organised by risk index.'

The room brought back a spread of hundreds of results icons, symbolically coded for easy recognition. Each represented a possible simulated future in which the League failed to stop the Nem swarm it had started. Most of them were dark red, the colour of disaster – an army of possible futures wet with blood.

In those cases, a familiar grim story unfolded. If the Nems couldn't be stopped after they attacked Earth, every human colony would be at risk until containment was completed. Snakepit would be boser-blasted to prevent further drone releases while humanity re-established itself with populations sequestered in sub-light evac-arks. The League had hidden agents on every human world armed with the blueprints for Nem-cloaking systems in preparation for that contingency. If the worst happened, they would immediately release their knowledge to the public.

Ann understood that fallback scenario thoroughly. What she didn't know yet was how much room there was to adapt it. She was hoping to find a kind of halfway-house – a handbrake for the project that didn't result in wholesale disaster.

She zoomed in on the least dramatic scenarios – a field of amber icons off at one edge of the sea of red. The icons welled up to fill the screen, expanding into summary glyphs. They looked a little different from the last time she'd scanned them, but that was only to be expected. Sam's team had been rerunning the models with every new piece of Nem data they collected, right up until the instigation of the Tiwanaku swarm. She picked the cases where the target size at Tiwanaku grew a little too big for comfort, just as she'd experienced. Then she started adapting them.

'Give me scenario modelling,' she told the room.

The walls filled with software components. SAP diagrams hung like surrealist chandeliers on her left, one for each political eigengenda in the IPSO Congress. Causal networks sprawled on her right, looking like crosses between transit maps and clumps of dangled spaghetti. Bright colour-coded points of interaction events studded them from end to end. Her modelling tools hovered on either side, ready for use.

Ann reached out to the walls and started building, dragging pieces this way and that. She constructed a file for each of the different backup scenarios she could think of, whether she liked them or not. She began with one in which the League confessed its actions outright, and added a second where Will Monet added his public support. She built scenarios for the League's home system response team going into pre-emptive action as soon as they could get word out, and others corresponding to daily intervals thereafter. When she could no longer think of possible solutions, she handed the entire batch to a dedicated planning SAP and instructed it to extrapolate more. With the new suite of scenarios ready, Ann set them running on low resolution. At full-res, the models would take weeks to complete, but Ann didn't need details, just the big picture. In a matter of minutes, she started getting results.

They looked awful. Red icons spelling disaster for the League began to pop up all around her. She rocked back in her chair, her heart sinking. Senator Voss had been right after all. There was nothing to do but soldier on with the programme they'd started. Meddling with the mission only made things worse. A lot worse.

A few ambers belatedly appeared. Ann zoomed in on them, but they weren't exactly appealing, either. The visualisation SAP displayed org-charts of the League for her, marked with risk flags. Leadership figures like Sam and Parisa absorbed the lion's share of the blame every time. All that differed were the number of League underlings imprisoned or executed along with them. And in every case, life on Earth was completely destroyed, often taking Mars along with it.

Ann blinked at the results. They didn't make sense. How could revealing the attack in advance actually *increase* the death toll in the home system? She scrolled back through the data. In all the new runs she'd created, the target size at Tiwanaku caused the feared phase-change in Nem behaviour, resulting in a massive spike in aggressive potential.

Why? They hadn't seen that in the original data set. She'd *deliberately* picked amber cases to work from.

Ann built a sanity-check – a duplicate of the original simulation case she'd extrapolated from, without modification – and ran a fresh batch of scenarios. The results looked very much like the ones she'd just

310

invented. The Nems underwent the same surge of development for a target size right around the one they'd experienced. And in almost every case, life on Earth was wiped out. After the League counter-attack, the home system became a tragic backwater in human affairs – little more than a memorial.

Ann's skin prickled. Why was she getting different answers for her copy of the simulation from the identical one on file? She pulled up the original runs she'd started with and scrolled through them, step by step. They all appeared to be in order.

She folded her arms, worried now. In one set of results, everything looked predictable. In the other, they were staring down the barrel of a catastrophe of unimaginable proportions – the end of the human homeworld and the loss of at least fifteen billion lives. They couldn't both be true.

Was the discrepancy a quirk of the model resolution? Such errors were rare, but she'd seen them from time to time. She ran the offending scenario again with the resolution bumped way up and a priority flag on it to ensure rapid completion. That would burn a huge share of the station's processing power but it had to be worth it even if they spotted her. Using so many resources wouldn't make her popular but the League could hardly object. This was *their* future, after all. While the simulation ran, Ann struggled to think of an explanation for the discrepancy.

'Room, show me the log files for the last official run batch,' she said. 'The most recent ones from before my current session.'

Would the logs still be there? The science team was supposed to clear them out periodically. A cluster of files appeared. Ann exhaled in relief.

'Open them all, please.'

Millions of lines of output streamed up. Ann wrinkled her nose at the mess.

'Collate and summarise,' she said. 'Show me a status diagram for each run.'

A massive tiled array of icons appeared – thousands upon thousands of them reaching away into infinity. Ann's brow furrowed again. *Why so many?*

'Correlate using timestamp,' she told the room. 'Match log glyphs to result files.'

The icons swam around into ordered pairs. She could see no logic to why certain runs had made it into the results and not others. They appeared to be scattered throughout the log. Then she noticed the marker spikes for risk levels.

Her breath caught. The official results on file were legitimate all right. They'd just been cherry-picked from a much bigger set to show a safe-looking result. Every other run in the set had resulted in a horror story. Ann couldn't believe what she was seeing. Someone had falsified the simulation results. And they had done so for *exactly* the target scale Tiwanaku had experienced.

She fought down panic and tried to think the situation through. Perhaps the simulations had been altered after the fact. Someone at Snakepit had been responsible for the delay to the Tiwanaku Nem swarm. That delay had caused the loss of the *Reynard* and the *Horton*. Whoever made that mistake might have looked at the models to check the likely consequences. On finding them, it would be natural to try to hide the results. They might have wanted to conceal the evidence, or simply feared the impact on morale.

But that explanation didn't fit. The timestamps showed a date *prior* to the Tiwanaku Event. The implication horrified her. Had the release of the Nems been delayed on purpose? Had someone wanted the *Horton* captured by the Nems, knowing Earth would die because of it?

Ann clutched her hands together to stop them from trembling. Something unspeakable had just occurred to her.

'Room,' she said, her voice cracking, 'access my private files using code *Seldon-Fogel* and open secure box *FiveClan Job*, please.'

The software patches from the lowly trial-rigger the fixer had given her appeared on the wall. She scanned the labels.

'Activate the program labelled *wake-before-install*.'

She dared not think. Ann sat there in the darkened room, sweating, as she waited for something to happen. While she waited, she allowed herself to believe she'd been wrong. Things couldn't be this bad. Then the dialogue appeared.

SmoovRig has uncloaked for update, it said. *Do you want to upgrade now?*

Ann struggled to breathe. Sam had subverted his own conspiracy. He'd set up the League to end life on Earth and cripple the home system for ever. And he'd sucked her into it.

While she sat mutely gawping at the screen, a new window opened up on the wall. It showed Parisa Voss's anger-twisted face.

'Apologies for the lack of warning,' said the room. 'Senator Voss invoked override.'

'Why are you hiding, Captain Ludik? I thought I asked you to rest?'

'You did, ma'am,' said Ann. She saw no point in dissembling. This had to come out.

'Then why can I see your name on the batch jobs filling our servers right now? My scientists can't track surface activity.'

An icon appeared informing Ann that Senator Voss wanted a view of her workspace. She clicked accept.

'I went to put my mind at rest, ma'am,' said Ann, trying to steady her voice. 'I wanted to present you with a working backup scenario.'

Senator Voss's face darkened further. 'Captain Ludik, your actions were in direct contravention of my request. Furthermore, you appear to have conveniently forgotten Overcaptain Shah's ban on model use.'

Of course Sam had banned the models. He hadn't wanted anyone to go looking.

'Ma'am,' said Ann quickly, 'we have a serious security problem. The impacts of the scenario we're currently facing were falsified in our models by Sam Shah before the Tiwanaku Event. That scenario results in the complete loss of Earth and probable loss of Mars.'

Voss's brow wrinkled for a moment, then her expression froze. She peered at Ann.

'What are you saying, Captain?'

Ann thought she could see uncertainty in the senator's eyes. She hoped she could.

'I'm saying it appears that Overcaptain Shah may have had fore-knowledge of the so-called *accident* that happened at Tiwanaku, ma'am. The one that put the *Horton*'s passengers into the Nems' hands. And he appears to have purposefully hidden the consequences of that act.'

Parisa Voss struggled visibly for words. 'Do I need to point out to you that Sam Shah risked his life for the League?' she said. 'Or that his actions were instrumental in allowing all this to be possible? That without Sam Shah, there would not have *been* a League?'

'I accept that, ma'am. I am merely reporting my findings and attendant concerns. Please, look at the data yourself. Draw your own conclusions.'

Ann watched as Senator Voss scanned the pages of results.

'What's this?' said the senator, her pointer highlighting the org-chart diagrams Ann still had open. The hardness had come back on in her eyes. She understood the meaning of the charts, of course. Her own name marked with a red death-flag topped every diagram.

'These studies were part of my attempt to put my mind at rest, ma'am,' Ann said defiantly. 'That was how I discovered the tampering.'

'I see,' said Voss. 'So you decided to check all these scenarios in which the League is tactically *sold out*. And while you did so, you also happened to encounter evidence of Sam Shah supposedly undermining the very organisation he created.'

'Yes, ma'am,' said Ann. 'Exactly that.'

'I am stripping you of your League security rating as of this moment,' said Senator Voss. 'I am reducing you to advisor status.'

Ann sprang to her feet. 'Senator!'

'You constitute an unacceptable security risk to this project and I cannot afford that at this delicate time.'

'We're talking about the death of a *world* here!' Ann shouted.

'And if I hear another word of sedition out of your mouth, I will have you shot,' Voss finished. 'Not one more word. Do you understand me?'

'No!' said Ann. 'I do *not*!'

The window showing Parisa Voss's face winked out. Then, around it, Ann's other work vanished, too, plot by plot.

She leapt for the cubicle door. It opened from the other side before she could reach it. Two guards stood beyond. Both were Spatials augmented with killtech. To resist would be suicide.

'Captain Ludik,' said the first. 'You are hereby under house arrest. Maintain silence until we reach your quarters or we have orders to shoot.'

13.5: MARK

Mark led them down the echoing hallway to the emergency door panel at the far end.

'Any idea why this floor was left empty, Ash? Is it just for us? It makes me nervous.'

'Tower flu containment,' said Ash. 'They don't want it to spread. Phage treatment's expensive and they've got plenty of room, so management just shifted downstairs nine months ago and blocked it off. It looks like they brought you up here because they knew it was already secure.'

The emergency door opened with a loud clunk and a sudden wind practically sucked them into the stairwell beyond. Mark staggered through onto a freezing landing. A glass tube surrounded the narrow emergency stairwell that clung to the side of the tower, granting vertiginous views of the desert below.

'Sealing's not so good!' he warned Ash as he struggled for air and Venetia leaned up against the wall, gasping.

'You'll have to hurry, then!' said Ash. 'Otherwise the pressure change will cause an alert.'

As soon as Zoe was through, the door sealed behind them, locking them inside the glass tube. Mark shivered. He could feel the cold leaking up through his boots. Venetia didn't look too good.

'Get moving,' said Ash. 'Unless you want altitude sickness.'

Mark supported Venetia as she wheezed for breath and led them down the stairwell. Thin atmosphere whistled past the glass.

'Don't touch the railing,' Mark warned the others. 'They didn't pump this area properly – it'll freeze the skin off your hand.'

Zoe lurched to a halt as she rounded the bend to the next level.

'The windows on this side of the building look straight in,' she breathed. 'They'll be able to see us.'

'We don't have a choice,' said Mark. 'Keep moving.'

'The longer you take, the more likely it is they'll spot my system blocks,' Ash warned. 'We're not on the locked level any more. Every second counts.'

Mark pressed on, taking them past a floor where isolated office workers sprawled on oversized couches. He tried not to stare but couldn't help checking that nobody was looking in their direction. He thought they were safe until he spotted a domestic robot stationed in the corner, its cameras pointing right at them.

'Robot staring at us,' he told Ash.

'I'm on it.'

The robot abruptly turned away and trundled off on some imaginary errand.

'This isn't going to work,' Mark growled into his sensorium. 'We're too obvious. We need some kind of distraction.'

'I don't have one,' said Ash.

If he couldn't see one, Mark was damn well going to try. He reached out through his interface to the local network.

'Don't!' Ash snapped. 'Sam had them put out web-triggers keyed to your interface ID, so keep your mind to yourself unless you want to get killed!'

'Then do something!' said Mark.

'All right. Give me a minute.'

As they rounded the stairs to the next level, Mark noticed that everyone inside the office was looking the other way, off towards the pod rails.

'Your work?'

'Yes,' said Ash. 'Simulated rail problem. But this will just draw more attention to your *only* viable escape route, so get a fucking move on!'

They staggered down the remaining stairs to the first unoccupied level. Ash slid the door open as they approached. They tumbled gratefully into an empty office space that smelled of dust and plastic. Spare chairs and crates of unused tech sat in heaps.

'Go straight across,' said Ash. 'The pod is on its way. Use the bay on the far right. You'll need to be there as soon as it arrives – I'm trying

316

to make this pod trip look like an automated test run, which means it won't stop for long.'

They started jogging across the field of empty carpet.

'I can't,' Venetia wheezed. She stumbled. 'I'm sorry.'

The pod slid up to their floor and docked. The door opened, still forty metres away from them.

'You have six seconds,' said Ash. 'Someone's already running diagnostics.'

Mark picked Venetia up and carried her. He hurled himself into the pod and then reached back over the threshold to yank Zoe inside just as the door closed. The pod immediately started heading down.

'Thank you,' Venetia gasped. 'Don't do well with low pressure. Should have got better lung augs before the mission. Fleet offered me some but I didn't want the extra surgery.'

'No problem,' said Mark. 'It's done.'

'So we made it,' said Zoe. 'Want to tell us what the hell is going on?'

As the pod raced down the side of the tower, Mark quickly filled them in on the League's agenda.

Zoe stared at him with wild eyes. 'All this was just to shut down a war?'

Mark nodded. 'And to slide the balance of power permanently to the Fleet. It makes them look like heroes while the sects take a political hit. Nobody's ever going to try starting up an unlicensed colony again after this. They'll be too scared of waking some alien terror.'

'It's clever,' said Venetia.

Zoe threw her arms in the air. 'No, it's not! They have no fucking idea what they're dealing with! They're fucking nuts – this whole thing is going to blow up in their faces.'

'Sit down!' Ash's voice boomed through the speakers in the pod walls. 'We're reaching the bottom of the tower. Unless you want to be noticed the moment you dock, chill out and try to look as bored as everyone else on this shit-hole planet.'

They sat.

'I'm taking you on a low-priority rail,' Ash told them. 'We can't afford to make your routing too obvious. I've already got one engineer up in the tower poking around. That means a detour through fabulous New Luxor, I'm afraid, so everyone needs to stay calm.'

Mark sagged against the pod wall as they reached the ground and trundled out through the city. A quiet moment would help him organise the terrible knowledge that had landed in his head. By Ash's estimates, they only had a few days' lead on the Photurian swarm. Then death came after them.

13.6: SAM

Sam Shah sat in the meeting room waiting for the colony leadership to appear. He shut his eyes and ran through a mindfulness exercise of his own design. He felt his body tense with anticipation, as if a rubber band had been twisted inside him almost to snapping point. He focused on that tension, instructing it to disperse, but the sensation persisted.

'*I should not be here*,' his child-mind told him.

Sam acknowledged the truth of that feeling and reflected on the choices that had brought him to this moment one by one. He hadn't managed things perfectly, but he hadn't done badly, either, given the constraints he'd been operating under. And besides, things were going his way at last. Wasn't that reason enough for him to relax a little?

Soon, Earth would be an ugly memory and humanity could make a fresh start. He'd waited so long, but the journey was almost over. After that, there would be no more inane religions. No more shitty half-baked societies full of miserable, undereducated proles, imagining their cultures to be automatically worthy simply by dint of their existence. No more gloating plutocrats bickering over their billions. No more population explosions or ruined biospheres. And best of all, no more of the blind, mindless violence that had formed a backdrop to his life. Everyone could be honest and move forward – once the fuckers were dead.

Sam hated the fact that he'd had to twist the plan around so much to get this far. It saddened him that this entire world was going to take it in the neck. After the death of the Earth, he'd need every colony that was left. And if he couldn't get the Carter colonists to play ball, he'd have to bomb their miserable planet himself. That prospect struck him as deeply regrettable, but he simply couldn't afford for the Nems to capture any more human subjects to play with.

In the end, though, despite the costs, it would all be worth it. The people he'd lied to would come to understand, given time. Humanity would turn over a new leaf. They would all heal.

Keir Vorn stepped through the door, ushering his colleagues in.

'Everyone, I'd like you to meet Fleet Overcaptain Sam Shah,' he said with pride. 'Sam, this is President Bill Kim.'

Vorn pointed him at a stolid bullfrog of a man with the overbred look of an Andrewsian.

'And Environment Minister Keiko Hasan.' Hasan had a perfect Angeleno figure and an empty political smile.

'Interior Minister Ilko . . .'

Sam calmly shook hands with each yokel bureaucrat in turn while the child inside him screamed for progress.

'Sam and I have been in communication since he reached the Carter System,' Vorn explained after the introductions. 'He has some very serious news for us. Sam, I propose we all take a seat while you explain in your own words. Does that work for you?'

Sam nodded. The Carter government sat, their faces expectant. Sam paused for effect and steepled fingers against his chin.

'What I have to tell you is both shocking and difficult,' he said. 'I beg your patience while I explain. First, you should know that I've arrived with a Fleet mandate. I'm here to sequester antimatter from your stores and to inform you of a direct threat to your world. *Officially*, I'm telling you there's a risk that unidentified alien machinery may arrive in this system and inflict damage, and that you should be ready to mount a defence. *Unofficially*, I'm telling you it's inevitable. Worse, that attack will strip your entire world of life unless we do something to stop it.'

A couple of the bureaucrats tried to butt in at that point. Sam held out his hands for calm.

'Please, let me explain. I need your help. I also have inside information, and in return for your assistance I can provide some of my own.'

He surveyed their anxious, staring faces. He had them worried. Now they needed something to hold on to.

'Defence Minister Vorn selected you to attend this meeting because you're all members of the Frontier Protection Party,' said Sam. 'Many of you here have also participated in our informal Watcher Programme. You may therefore have heard that the FPP has access to a secret cleaning agent managed by sympathisers within Fleet ranks, and that this agent has been used to root out illegal Flag bases in some locations.

319

What I have to tell you is that the cleaning agent has been discovered and inadvertently activated. The people responsible for that are Will Monet and his allies in Fleet high command.'

He had their attention now. Sam took quiet satisfaction in the belligerence kindling behind their eyes. To the minds of most FPP supporters, Will Monet had sold the farm to Earth in the wake of the war when he should have crushed their power instead – a perspective Sam empathised with.

'In fact,' he said, 'you should know that with Minister Vorn's help, some of that group have been incarcerated here in Government Tower. They're upstairs right now.'

The president glanced at the ceiling, clearly unnerved by the fact that he hadn't already been informed. Sam interrupted this germ of indignation with a surprise.

'That group contains Will Monet's protégé and adopted son,' he said.

Eyes went wide. This was a good angle, Sam reflected. The idea that Monet had an adopted son was surprise enough for most people. The fact that he was right above them was a bonus.

'In order to support the goals of the FPP, I need those Fleet representatives contained and kept safe. I also need weapons with which to equip my ship for some tidying-up I have to do. In return, I can offer two things. First, free passage aboard my ship to a *very* safe location for a small number of you. The maximum is ten – which happens to be the exact number of you sitting in this room with me now.'

He paused to let that sink in.

'I can also offer technology that will enable you to render your ships invisible to the cleaning agent. Install it in Carter's evac-arc and your population should be relatively safe. That technology has been extensively tested and has saved my own life numerous times. However, there won't be a need for you to share that technology with the illegal squatters in your Flag settlements unless you decide that you *want* to. That's your choice.'

He could see them calculating now, their fear vying with a sense of opportunity.

'Now, this may sound like a very sweet deal, under the circumstances. Either you give me antimatter, or I take it via Fleet override. And all you have to do is help me look after a few political troublemakers while I help you evacuate your people. In return for your cooperation, I solve your Flag problem for you and give you a ride out of danger. If that deal sounds unreasonably good, it's because the risks we're looking at here are very, very real. Once the cleaning agent has arrived, there will be no way to stop it. None. That's perhaps easier to understand when you consider that the agent is *not* a human piece of technology. Our hands will be tied and we only have days before that danger is realised. Consequently, we must act quickly. I'm hoping I can rely on your help.'

As he sat down, the ministers broke into muttering, swapping glances with each other.

'Forgive us if we don't have an immediate answer,' said President Kim. 'This is all rather abrupt.'

'I apologise for that,' said Sam, spreading his hands. 'Unfortunately, I can't make the situation any less urgent.'

'Do you have any proof supporting your claims?' said Kim. 'I know it must be frustrating for you, but we'll need more than just your word before we essentially overturn planetary law for you.'

'Of course. I have a package I can show you. I'll pull it down from my ship now.'

Sam reached for his tablet and hit the icon for access to the *Gulliver*. It came back denied. Keeping his expression casual, he gazed very intently into the screen. He tried again and got the same response. He looked up at the bureaucrats with an embarrassed smile.

'Isn't it always the way?' he said with a chuckle. 'Even with top-of-the-range Fleet kit, you can never eradicate technical glitches. Looks like I'll have to have my techie flogged again.'

A couple of the ministers laughed nervously.

'Something here needs fixing – a simple Fleet security issue involving access rights on your network. I need to use the net-station in the hall. I'll be back in a moment.'

With fury twisting the cords of his back, Sam sauntered out of the room and headed straight for the first private space he could find – in this case, a robotic supply cupboard. He stood between the shelves of arms and sheets of tact-fur and fired up an audio link to Ash with his override attached.

'Do you mind telling me what the fuck you're doing?' he growled.

'Sure,' said Ash. 'I'm finished with this shit and so are you.'

Sam fought for breath. With desperate fingers he tabbed across to the tower's security system to check on the room upstairs. It had already been compromised. Mark and the others were gone.

Sam hummed to himself, straining to find his calm centre. He should have seen this coming and solved it already. Ash had made it very clear that his loyalties were sliding. Sam had been deluding himself – imagining that when the game simplified itself Ash would remember whose side he was on. He had only himself to blame, really. He'd wanted to spare Ash this moment.

He thumbed the audio channel back open.

'Ash?' he said.

'We have nothing to talk about,' Ash informed him.

'Hypnotic Anarchy,' said Sam.

'What?' said Ash, confused.

But by then it was already too late. A circuit in Ash's interface coded to Sam's keyword had started downloading a secret program from the *Gulliver*'s core.

'Wait!' said Ash, probably noticing the sensory problems by now. 'What are you doing?'

Ash grunted in surprise. The grunt rose to a shriek of pain. Sam killed the link and strode out of the cupboard, his face composed.

He walked back into the meeting room where Carter's leadership stood locked in urgent, huddled debate.

'I'm sorry, ladies and gentlemen, but it looks like I'll need a little more time to get things squared away at my end. Minister Vorn, could I have a command hook for your transit system?'

Vorn looked confused at first, then worried. Then: 'Of course!' he said, cluing in. 'Please, come with me. I'll get you set up right away.'

14: REVERSAL

14.1: MARK

Just five kilometres out from New Luxor, Mark's head exploded with pain. He gasped and slid boneless from his seat.

'What happened?' said Zoe.

Mark's head spun. His interface suddenly felt horribly empty.

'Ash,' he said. 'Something happened to my connection with Ash.'

He'd felt a pain-surge like that only once before – when he'd been holding a live link open to a roboteer who'd died in a training accident.

'We've got a problem,' he said.

The pod slowed to a halt and sat ticking in the middle of the Fecund tunnel, surrounded by silence. Mark fought past the discomfort in his skull to tap the pod's data node but found the wireless comms offline. The circuit was unresponsive, and it was the only thing in range.

'This is bad,' he said. 'I think Sam got to Ash. He's cut us off.' A grim sense of certainty settled over him. 'I think Ash is dead.'

As he spoke, the pod started up again, reversing its direction and taking them back towards the city.

'Try the emergency stop,' said Mark.

Venetia slammed the stud next to the door. Nothing happened.

'Hello, everyone,' said Sam cheerfully over the pod's speakers. 'I'm sorry, but you won't be getting much help from Ash any more. He's... offline.'

'Bastard!' Mark shouted at the walls.

'Now now,' said Sam. 'Keep your hair on. Settle down like good children and nobody will have to die.'

The pod started picking up speed – lots of it.

'By now you've probably realised I'm not going to let you return to Earth,' said Sam.

'Fuck you!' said Mark. He looked around for a manual brake. There wasn't one.

'It's a shame you didn't take me up on my offer, you self-indulgent little prick,' said Sam. 'I could have helped you. But then again, what should I have expected from a Monet-puppet? You're just like your fake Dad. Too in love with your own misery to do anything useful. You're a fucking waste of decent genes.'

Mark's eyes blurred with fury. 'I'm going to kill you!'

'Mark, he's baiting you. Shut down your interface,' said Zoe. 'Put it in secure mode *right now*.'

'You're not going to kill me,' said Sam with a laugh. 'You're going to sit here on this dirtball while history happens without you. I'm sorry, but that godawful hovel-world you're so in love with is going to die. And then all those sad-sack peasants in their shitty illegal domes will starve along with them. Boo-hoo.'

'Never!'

'I said *shut it down*!' Zoe shouted. 'Now!'

Mark gazed at her without understanding. Her eyes held enough urgency that he decided to simply obey.

'Okay,' he said. He shuddered as the electronic part of his mind fell silent. Suddenly the pod felt very small. 'Done.'

Zoe abruptly crunched forwards as if in pain. A gasp of air escaped her lips.

A wail of crazy distortion squawked from the pod's audio system. The lights went out and the emergency brakes kicked in, slamming Mark against the wall as the pod jerked to a halt.

'What in hell's name was *that*?' said Venetia, rubbing a bruised elbow.

'Personal EMP blast,' said Zoe. 'Vartian Institute implant in case of alien soft incursion. Felt like the right time to use it.'

Mark let out a single guffaw of startled laughter. 'Holy shit! How much secret tech have you *got*?'

'Need-to-know basis only,' said Zoe. 'Right now we have to get out of this pod.'

Mark yanked open the emergency hatch and a blast of cold air from the tunnel beyond swept in. A plastic ladder slid out from the base of the pod, straight into the icy water below.

'You're kidding me,' he said, his teeth already chattering. 'We have to swim through *that*? We'll freeze to death.'

At least the transit tube had been properly pumped. The air was breathable, if stale. It carried a cold metallic tang.

'There should be a raft-pack here somewhere,' said Venetia. She pulled at the floor panelling and a section came away revealing a yellow capsule thirty centimetres long stored underneath. 'There.'

Mark hauled the raft-pack out, yanked on the tab and dropped it into the water below. The raft unfolded on contact, giving them something flat and circular to float on.

Mark rebooted his interface as he climbed hurriedly down and his sensorium filled up with warning icons. Zoe had played merry hell with his systems, even in secure mode. It would take hours for him to get everything back up and running properly. He helped Venetia and Zoe into the raft and then pushed off towards the dry ledge at the edge of the water three metres away.

Manoeuvring to the far bank and getting everyone out of the raft was a clumsier process than it should have been. By the time Mark joined them up on the dry stone, one leg of his ship-suit was soaked with freezing water. His boot sloshed.

'Now what?' he said miserably. 'Ash is dead, which means no support from the *Gulliver*. Sam is clearly out of his mind if he's killing his own pilot. He must be relying on the colonists to get him out.'

'Do they even have a starship?' said Zoe. 'I didn't see one on the way in, just a bunch of sub-light shuttles and an evac-ark.'

'I didn't see anything, either,' said Mark. 'But maybe the bastard has something cloaked out there like that shit they pulled with the *Chiyome*.'

'I doubt it,' said Venetia. 'Sam is clutching at straws. We wouldn't be here otherwise.'

'So we're screwed,' said Mark, slapping the cold stone wall. 'They'll have another pod down here in minutes. We've got to do *something*.'

'There are miles of these tunnels,' said Venetia. 'Hiding will be a piece of cake. We passed at least two junction sites already on the way out here. It's what we do after that which is the problem.'

Mark blinked as an option occurred to him. 'We head for the Flags,' he said. 'We already know they come raiding in these tunnels. Venetia, do you think you can get us down from here to somewhere we might find them?'

'Are you crazy?' said Zoe. 'You want to rescue us by handing us over to a bunch of religious nutcases? We should be heading for the spaceport. It's the only way out.'

'They're not nutcases,' said Mark. 'They're just people who can't afford starship tickets. You heard Sam. Do you imagine he's going to let them in on what's happening? They have a right to know they're under a death sentence, wouldn't you say?'

'Sure,' said Zoe. 'Via audio tight-beam once we're in orbit. Don't be so stupid as to imagine they'll help us. Kidnapping and ransom is a business for them. They're not going to believe what we have to tell them and we don't have time to explain.'

'Why do you assume they won't help?' said Mark. 'Because they're poor? Because they're from Earth? Not everyone from Earth is a halfwit or a religious criminal. I've met some of these people, Zoe, and the main difference between you and them is just opportunity.'

Zoe threw up her hands. 'Christ, Mark! Don't make this about your attitude problem. We're not discussing your roots here. This is about us getting off this planet alive in time to stop it from burning.'

'Will the two of you shut up?' said Venetia. 'We have no choice. These tunnels don't go as far as the spaceport, so unless we find some way to hold our breath over sixty kilometres of open ground, that's not an option.'

'We hijack another pod,' said Zoe. 'Mark can use his interface to hack it open.'

Mark shook his head. 'It'll be hours before I get over that EMP blast, and by then they'll be all over us.'

'I don't like it either, but we head down to the coast,' said Venetia. 'Sam will have the spaceport sealed up by now. Security will be everywhere. And we won't find any help in New Luxor, I can tell you that much. This place is crawling with FPP supporters. Sam will have them eating out of his hand. The Flags, on the other hand, will have weapons and vehicles. Plus any attempt from the colonists to enter their turf will be soundly rebuffed. At least from there we might be able to set up a satellite relay to the *Gulliver*'s shuttle and get it to land out in the desert where we can reach it.'

Zoe looked fit to burst. She covered her face with her hands and sagged against the wall.

'Think about it this way,' said Venetia. 'Be glad I can read Fecund braille, which is the only means of navigating in here. And you won't find someone with a better knowledge of hydro-tunnel systems, either. I've even met a few of the Flag groups. At least with them we stand a chance.' She pointed back the way they'd come. 'Quickly now, follow me. Another pod could arrive at any minute.'

14.2: ASH

Ash found himself spinning slowly in the air on the *Gulliver's* bridge, hunched in a foetal ball. The room smelled powerfully of vomit. His arm brushed a blob of the stuff floating near him and he realised it was his.

Sam's voice sounded over the audio. 'Are you there, fucker?'

Ash tried to pull himself together but found he couldn't think straight. His mind felt fuzzy. His limbs didn't work properly.

'You shouldn't have tried to bail on me,' said Sam. 'Have you any idea how hard it's been to get this far?'

Ash started to remember who and where he was. He'd been getting Mark and the others out of New Luxor. Sam had called. Something had happened.

'It's taken years to reach this point,' said Sam, 'and more shitty compromises than I can count. I've had years of schmoozing and squir-relling away Fleet money. Years of lying and scheming and letting that bitch Voss believe everything we did was her idea. Did you imagine I'd let you take this away from me now? You thought I wasn't seeing how fast the Nems were changing. Of course I fucking saw it, you *idiot*. And I was glad. When they get to Earth, they're going to smash it. I've made sure of that. That broadcast I sent from Tiwanaku after Yunus died? I coded data on Earth's defences into the signal.'

As Ash's mind started to reassemble, his panic built alongside his ability to think. What had they done?

'You might ask why,' said Sam. 'Because I hate Earth. Earthers ruin everything. Not content with butchering millions in the war – including both my parents, by the way – now they're ruining all the colonies. They're filthing up the frontier with their poverty and their shit.'

Ash knew he needed to act. Sam had done something to his interface. Mark and the others were in grave danger. He reached for his sensorium but found only a kind of flickering blankness in his mind where it should have been. He started grasping with weak and trembling hands for the nearest manual console.

'Do you know what I think?' said Sam. 'I think all the decent people got off Earth a long time ago. And if not all of them, enough of them. We've gone way past the point of diminishing returns for keeping that nest of fucking savages around. It's a genetic cesspool that should have been scrubbed out years ago.'

'You're crazy,' said Ash.

'No, not crazy. *Racist*, perhaps, but sadly not crazy.'

Ash frowned in confusion. Sam might as well have told Ash he believed in a flat Earth. There wasn't a single human being in the human worlds who couldn't trace their roots back to half a dozen different ethnicities. The migrations before the Martian Renaissance had seen to that. Bigotry was still alive and well, of course. It just had new names.

'Ironic, isn't it,' said Sam. 'Before the war, there were no "genetic racists". It was something the Truists made up. But out of their poison, it became real. I say that because I *hate* the non-modded. I hate how mediocre they are. How ordinary. How pointless. Modded people have a point. They're *for* something. Earthers just take up room, sucking down air that decent people should be breathing.'

Sam chuckled. 'You wonder why I'm bothering to tell you all this, I bet. Two reasons. First, because it's lonely doing something like this. I have to wade through all the shit and darkness to manifest a vision of peace and harmony for everyone else, and they'll never even know what I did for them. And second, because you're not going to remember any of it. And that amuses me. That funny feeling you're having right now is the start of a memory purge.'

Ash reached around to the back of his head in panic. His interface had grown uncommonly warm and a sickening buzz started inside his skull. Flashes of pain lit up his mind like sunbursts.

'I had you fitted out when you joined the League,' said Sam. 'Just in case. It's a new twist on the old shock-key system they used to put in all roboteers. Ugly technology, really, but then I never thought I'd have to use it. You're a fucking disappointment to me, Corrigan. I *told* you there was shit on that ship you didn't want to know about. Well, now you know what it is. For a little while, at least. But don't worry – when your mind is nice and blank, I'll help you get your ideas straight. You'll thank me. I guarantee it.'

Ash scrabbled at the manual terminal, looking for some way to shut down his interface. At the same time, black fingers of nothingness crept into the corners of his vision, as if leaking through the walls. A roar of static filled his ears. And then, softly at first, Ash's mind came apart, rotting inside him like a piece of overripe fruit.

1 4 . 3 : W I L L

After his meeting with Pari, Will let a pair of Spatials armed with bio-pellet smart-guns take him to an area which had been secured for him in advance. Of course the League used Spatials. Will wouldn't have thought twice about subverting or destroying robotic guards. Both men kept well away from him as they led him through the station, as if that would make a difference if Will decided to attack. Will couldn't decide if it was funny or naively charming. In any case, he didn't feel much like laughing. Parisa's speech had left him feeling too hollow for that.

While he still didn't agree with the League's agenda, at least he understood it now. He'd never given up hope for peace, but apparently those around him had. Perhaps because the course Will had set them on had been his, not theirs. He'd assumed his idealism would infect others because of the alien authority that backed it. He should have known better. His unwavering determination to do good had made him blind rather than wise.

Not for the first time, the words of the Prophet Sanchez came to mind. He'd told them as the *Ariel Two* hovered over Bogota with weapons primed that the Earth wouldn't change – that people would keep hating. He'd been right. Despite his bitterness and his fury, that old bastard had understood Earth more deeply than anyone who'd come along since.

The guards deposited Will at a well-appointed suite equipped with a full-sized bed, an entertainment centre and numerous other luxuries he couldn't have cared less about. They sealed the door behind him. Will didn't mind. Until he understood more about Snakepit's artificial life, he didn't intend to go anywhere.

He sat on the edge of the bed and stared at nothing. At that moment what he wanted most was access to the League's bio-lab research database, but he strongly suspected they wouldn't be granting it any time soon. He reached out via his sensorium to the local network and found a message from Pari waiting.

'Hi, Will,' she said. 'For the obvious reasons, we're limiting your network access to entertainment and some material on the League project that we've prepared for you. I recommend our geographic survey of Snakepit, or Ann's models of the war. Should you try to stray any further, you'll find that security here has been designed with you in mind. Our protocols use a stack of SAP models of your identity built around the years of data we've collected. They're programmed to anticipate your likely hacks and employ your own defences against you. I don't recommend testing them. We have fifteen years of curated material on your soft-incursion techniques. I'm hoping that's enough encouragement for you to wait and think about all of this a little more before you decide to do something.'

Will shook his head. He'd shared his knowledge freely with the Fleet and now they were using it against him. Idiots. He tried a few idle hacks anyway and found them efficiently, even zealously, repulsed, just as Pari said they would be.

Fine, so they'd proofed their systems against attacks by Will Monet. In that case, he'd just think like someone else instead. He'd seen a very convincing example of hacking in action aboard the *Chiyome* – one he'd wanted to study further when he had time. Right now, all he had was time. He walked as far as the data port on the wall. He assumed it had been coated with the League's co-opted bioweapon and a quick check with a cautiously extended filament revealed that it had. Perfect. They'd even left him samples to work with.

Will paused to concentrate while he manufactured a set of biologically inert tools inside his body, then coughed them up in a capsule, like an old-fashioned escapologist regurgitating a swallowed key. Using the needle from the kit he'd built, he took a pinhead-sized sample of the Snakepit organism and dropped it onto a slide. He laid the slide on the suite's bathroom floor and cupped a hand over it, manipulating the tissue of his palm into a small, sealed lab of his own. With a pair of hair-sized tweezers, Will started physically teasing the sample apart. At the end of the day, nothing beat a biological system like overwhelming physical force.

Handling such a dangerous organism necessarily made Will's techniques crude. He knew there'd only be a certain amount he could learn looking at the cells this way, but he had to start somewhere. The ribosome analogues he found were utterly cryptic, as were the coding-compounds in the nuclei, so he didn't bother with those. He concentrated on the basic cellular machinery and the production-line Golgi body mechanism he'd spotted, which gave him enough data to start reverse-engineering the cell's elegant mechanics.

The first thing he noticed was that parts of the life form in front of him were clearly missing. Signalling molecules were binding to specialised vesicles with nothing in them and just sitting there like trucks backing up to a disused warehouse. Someone in the League had hacked this organism already, either to prevent Will from learning too much, or to reduce the risk of contagion. No wonder they'd been so absurdly confident sitting in the same room as the stuff.

So far as Will could tell, the cells used a kind of biochemical search to synthesise new attacks. Multi-walled protein engines locked in a supracritical state churned out a constant supply of molecular novelty. Those products that managed to make it out of their gated enclosures were passed to a duplication area before being parcelled up and relayed to the edges of the cells in the sub-cellular equivalent of tagged bags, ready for deployment.

As Will figured out the mechanics of the cells' attack mechanism, he copied it to a software model and used that as the framework for a new soft-incursion program. The process required a little creative license, but he let himself be guided by the example before him rather than giving in to the temptation to build code the way he normally would. Then, once assembled, he allowed the new program to access his complete range of intrusion tools, all broken down into swappable modules as if they were amino acids to be deployed in combination.

His experiment complete, Will destroyed his tiny lab, lay back on the couch and put his new tool to work against the station's security. He interlaced the new program's requests with some simple hacks of his own to make the intrusions look like persistent nuisance attempts to probe their limits. The new code fumbled at first, no doubt prompting low-level alerts in Pari's data display, so Will bred a small population of his bio-programs and had them compete. Maybe a little selection pressure would help.

At first, it looked hopeless. Warnings from network defence began to accumulate in his sensorium by the dozen. Then came the counter-attacks. Not content with rebuffing Will's constant attempts to infiltrate the system with bogus traffic, the League's defensive program began to feign collapse, leading Will's code into access-traps before cracking it and shutting it down. Ironically, they couldn't have helped him more. Under tightened selection pressure, Will's bio-progams rose impressively to the challenge. Within five minutes, station security was quietly, unquestionably broken.

Will kept his nuisance program aimlessly running so they wouldn't notice the change and tsked to himself. The League should have known better. Software models of people worked just fine for crowds. For individuals, though, they couldn't stand up for long when confronted with a little genuine creativity. Pari should never have told him how her security worked. Without that clue, Will might have struggled for hours and given up hope.

With the room under his control, he reached out with half his mind to the bio-lab database and started sucking down files. With the rest of his attention, he started inserting little pieces of himself into the station architecture. When the time came, he'd be ready to move.

14.4: MARK

Venetia strode off along the ledge with Mark and Zoe hurrying behind. She took them to the nearest junction point – a narrow oval gap in the tunnel wall – and through to a ledge on the other side. But for the thin, dusty light pouring through the opening, this new tunnel lay in complete darkness.

'There should be another raft here,' she said, fumbling blindly along the wall. 'There's supposed to be one at each of these junctions for the research crews to use. Got it!' she said, and lifted another yellow capsule into the meagre light.

She set it down on the floor in front of them and fumbled with the tags on the side, activating an LED lamp. The flare of light revealed a second canal of still, black water lying before them, surrounded by another tunnel lined with alien art. Venetia inflated the raft and dropped it quietly onto the chill liquid below.

'Research rafts are larger,' she told them. 'Plus they come with engines – assuming there's still charge in this battery, of course. It's probably been a while.'

'Any heating?' said Zoe, wrapping her arms around herself.

Venetia shook her head. 'I'm afraid not. It's going to be a cold afternoon. Better get used to it.'

They gingerly lowered themselves down into a plastic inflatable craft little different from the one they'd just left. This time, Mark exercised care not to get wet. Venetia handed him a telescopic paddle to push off from the edge.

'Here goes nothing,' she said and fired up the electric motor.

They all cheered a little as it purred to life. Venetia took them out into the middle of the canal and away from the junction. Darkness swallowed them instantly.

'Won't they come looking here as soon as they find the pod?' said Mark.

Venetia nodded. 'Undoubtedly, but if they want to find us, they'll have their work cut out for them.'

Just a few minutes later they encountered another junction, this one set low enough in the side of the tunnel that they could navigate straight through it. After that, the branches came swiftly. Venetia took them this way and that through an apparently endless labyrinth of identical waterlogged tubes, each narrower than the last. Friezes of cavorting Fecund figures crowded them on every side. The frail light from the raft's lamp cast heavy shadows against the stone. The turret-shaped eyes on every beaked face seemed to track them as they passed.

'I get it,' said Mark, glancing up at the gargoyles closing in over his head. 'Plenty of room to get lost.'

'Once you leave the main arteries, things get complicated quickly,' said Venetia. 'This is a delivery system for habitation warrens – the Fecund equivalent of that suburb we saw on the way to New Luxor.'

'Some suburb,' said Zoe, gazing out at the lightless maze surrounding them.

Abruptly, their tunnel opened onto a narrow space that had to be at least fifty metres high. Rows of identical holes lined the walls, each about large enough for a person to crawl into, presuming they had no intention of ever coming back out. Narrow metallic ladders protruded from the stone between each column of cells. Stalks that might once have held lighting bulbs hung far overhead.

'See,' said Venetia. 'Luxury accommodation. For disposable child-slaves this would have felt pretty cushy.'

'I'm sure,' said Zoe.

'It was nicer ten million years ago,' Venetia assured them. 'They had something like our biofabric on the walls and quite a lot of tech infrastructure down here. None of it held for long after the suntap flare, though.'

The hive area ended as abruptly as it had begun. Then, half a kilometre further downstream, the tunnel opened out again, this time onto banks of glass-fronted compartments like windows in a giant vending machine. Filthy streaks of brownish film covered most of the surface. The glass in many had eroded away in oddly rounded chunks.

'Check this out,' said Venetia, her eyes shining. 'Bio-enclosures, probably for weapons testing. Isn't it amazing that the glass lasted this long? They're still figuring out how to make that stuff, you know. Looks like it grows straight out of the stone but it was clearly nanofactured. We don't have anything even half that durable. Each one of those cells used to have a seal on it so they could expose the young inside to whatever organism from outside they wanted to test. It was an incredibly efficient system. That scum you can see on the glass? That's probably what's left of the ones trapped inside after the flare went up. This deep underground, the preservation of biomaterial is way better.'

'They did biological experiments on their young?' said Mark. 'Every time I hear about the Fecund, they sound a little more disgusting.'

'You wouldn't be the first to have that reaction,' Venetia assured him. 'But they were just different from us. The Fecund didn't really solve problems with smarts, they threw resources at them instead. And they had an inexhaustible supply of spawn. Their reasoning style was more like what we associate with the evolution of disease. They tried things out, kept what worked and ditched the rest. Their young were more like tools or experiments than treasured offspring. They didn't have much of what humans would call creativity. On the other hand, the engineering solutions they came up with were often incredibly robust – as evidenced by the fact that any of this stuff is still here.'

'If they were so uncreative, what's with all the art on the walls?' said Zoe.

Venetia laughed. 'That's not art. That's education. For the Fecund, language was a means of communicating workable solutions to problems. Lining the tunnels with knowledge was just another kind of Fecund efficiency – you train up your kids even while you're squirting them down a tube to their next high-risk assignment. Those young who made it to adulthood were revered like gods. Every one of them that came down here would have scanned the walls every day, trying to figure out a trick to make it past age five.'

'Lovely,' said Zoe. 'Kindergarten pipes.'

'Right,' said Venetia. '*Oliver Twist* on an industrial scale.'

Over the hours that followed, it became clear that anyone looking for them would have an impossible job. Even if they filled the tunnels with robotic drones, there would still be too much twisting ground to cover. The Fecund tube-system ran for dozens of kilometres, dwarfing the New Luxor settlement outside.

'I'm amazed they bother to keep this lot oxygenated,' said Mark.

Venetia shot him a look. 'Are you kidding? This is where all the money comes from. Once they repaired the original seals on the old network, there was no point dumping the air when the economy started to tank. They just don't bother cycling it that often. The whole time I was here, though, I can't recall more than two carbon-monoxide incidents.'

'Oh, great,' said Zoe. 'In that case I can finally start enjoying myself.'

Venetia took them through a bewildering array of echoing underground chambers. Some spaces resembled huge tiled swimming pools. In others, canals joined and split in interlocking loops like a maze of aquatic roundabouts. To Mark's eye, the place looked like a deranged mash-up of the sort of ancient Earth sites you found in virtual museums. A cross of Angkor Wat with a Victorian bathhouse, perhaps, with a little bit of Alcatraz thrown in for good measure.

His fear of being pursued by the colonists slowly gave way to a pressing sense of reverent unease. Something about the organic layout of the tunnel system, coupled with the cryptically ornate chambers, left him speechless. He could feel the incredible age of the place creeping

335

into his bones along with the cold. No wonder so many scientists found Fecund sites fascinating. However, he didn't really understand why they'd want to stay and explore. For all his awe, Mark couldn't wait to get out. A deep, persistent chill had worked its way into his body by then and the foot he'd soaked ached constantly. He huddled in the boat and shivered. The dark felt intent on combing the heat off his skin. He wished he was wearing something other than a thin ship-suit. His stomach growled.

Zoe pressed up next to him. 'We should stay close,' she said, her teeth chattering. 'It's too fucking cold in here.'

Mark squeezed closer. Proximity certainly helped.

'Put your arms around me, you idiot,' she told him. 'I'm dying here.'

He did as she asked and felt a little better. He chose to ignore how pleasant it felt. Despite the hours of panic they'd endured, somehow her hair still managed to smell nice. Zoe made a small sigh of relief.

'You want some of this?' he asked Venetia.

'Don't worry about me – the engine's keeping me warm,' she said. 'You guys huddle up. And besides, we'll unbalance the boat if we're all in the same spot.'

Gloomy hours slid by. By Mark's reckoning, there couldn't be much daylight left. He felt like he'd been underground for ever. It would be dark by the time they reached the coast, which would only compound their temperature problems. Then, just as he decided to ask Venetia where they were, she spoke up.

'Look!' she said, her voice hushed and excited.

She pointed ahead to a place where the wall-art had been damaged. The faces had been smashed off the statues.

'We must be close. The sect Leading have that done to stop the Following from worshiping the Fecund.'

'Does that really happen?' said Zoe, her voice trembling from the cold.

'It did at least once. There was this group that got hold of a working Fecund food machine and retro-fitted it for human-compatible protein. As soon as the Following had an independent food supply with no drugs in it, they started to get their own ideas. Weird ones, admittedly. It didn't end well, I'm told.'

Mark wrapped his arms tighter around Zoe and frowned. He suspected that half the horror stories made up about Flags had been concocted by the FPP. He found it hard to believe that the kind of people he'd lived with in New York could be reduced to worshiping parrot-monkeys in a frozen tunnel. Those were the kind of lies you invented about people you wanted to dehumanise.

'Please tell me these guys aren't going to be scumbags,' said Zoe quietly. 'Tell me we're not walking into the arms of a bunch of rapists.'

'Don't worry,' said Mark. 'They're just people. But if anyone so much as touches you, I'll rip their head off.'

'If I thought there was a risk of that kind of behaviour we wouldn't be here,' said Venetia. 'Flag colonies are grim, don't get me wrong, but the sect Leading are big on moral order. They have to be. They sit on powder kegs full of angry young men. The moment someone steps out of line, they string them up. So long as you keep your mouth shut and don't piss anybody off, they aren't likely to do much more than stare at you.'

A kilometre further on, the canal gave way to chunks of ice, forcing them to abandon the raft and walk. Though the air temperature kept dropping, Mark could feel himself warming a little from the exercise. He was glad of it. Without something to warm them up they were heading for hypothermia. His breath made pale clouds in the shafts of meagre lamplight.

'Here!' said Venetia. 'We have to be right near the coastal cliffs. Look.'

She pointed along the tunnel ahead where the braille had been smashed off the walls with flenser fire. Spent flechettes littered the floor.

'Knocking off that braille is like trashing the local signposts,' said Venetia. 'Makes it hard for anyone exploring down here to tell where they are, or how to get out. We must be close. This is kidnap country.'

She strode ahead of them, taking the lantern with her. Mark and Zoe had to jog to keep up.

'If they find us, let me do the talking,' Venetia warned. 'Some of these groups brainwash their soldiers for aggression – one word against their faith and they'll cut you open without thinking.'

'Bullshit,' said Mark. He couldn't help himself. With Sam's words still ringing in his ears, this was a slander too far. 'Have you seen that yourself, or did somebody tell you?'

'I study culture, Mark. I've not seen it myself but there are accounts—'

'Mind programming was the very first thing to be banned after the war,' he said. 'Every sect in the Kingdom signed up. They wrote half the damned treaty. You're telling me they're breaking that now?'

Bullies and exploiters they might be, but Mark had trouble believing the sects' leadership would stoop to thought-control. He couldn't reconcile that picture with the planet full of struggling people where he'd lived. Life on Earth was cheap, but not *that* cheap.

Venetia gave him a sad look. 'Mark, I can only go by what I've read. I'm not trying to insult anyone here.'

'Any chance you've been reading propaganda?'

She looked disappointed in him. 'Of course,' she said. 'But it doesn't hurt to be careful, does it?'

She stopped at the entrance to yet another lab lined with nearly human-looking workbenches of featureless metal. Smashed equipment filled it from end to end. This one was different from the others they'd seen by simple virtue of having windows. The Fecund glass here had obviously been left exposed to the elements when the planet died as most of it had been scoured to a matte opacity. In a few curious patches, though, Mark could make out the dry ocean bed many stories below, overlooked by a thick blanket of stars.

'Flags have been here recently,' said Venetia as she picked her way through the glass and shrapnel on the floor. 'See how new these breaks are? There's no dust on them. This equipment must have been sealed up in those wall pods until just weeks ago.' She pointed at boot prints on the floor. 'They poach electronics mostly,' she explained, picking up a piece of ceramic tubing. 'Lab equipment if they can get it. There's a huge market for this stuff in the home system. The sect Leading like to decorate their private worlds with genuine alien tech. That's before you even start counting the odd medical or engineering miracle people sometimes find down here.'

'Do you think they'll come back here tonight?' said Mark.

'No way of knowing,' said Venetia, 'but there's reason to hope. Last I heard, activity in this area was red hot, but that was a few years ago. And they keep moving around to avoid the colony patrols. If nobody shows, we're in trouble,' she added. 'If the cold doesn't get us, starvation will. Either that or Sam's people will find us. They'll put two and two together eventually.'

'Little worry of that,' said Zoe, her voice strained.

Mark turned back towards her. She was standing with her arms in

338

the air. In the doorway behind them stood a young man in a black thermal jacket. He was pointing a flenser right at them.

'Nobody move,' he said. 'You move, you die.'

14.5: ANN

While the hours ticked painfully by, Ann sat in her suite, planned her next move and tried not to scream at the walls. They were about to wreak havoc on the human race and apparently no one wanted to know about it. And by 'no one', of course, she meant Parisa Voss. Ann shuddered with anger. Was the senator in on Sam's scheme or simply guilty of the most unforgivable self-serving myopia?

Ann knew she had to get out but they'd cut off her access to the network and locked the door. The room only had one exit and that was through the guards. Her choices, as she saw them, were twofold. First, to try to make Senator Voss see reason. That was likely to be difficult given the woman's intransigence so far. Ann didn't even have a way to reach the senator other than by talking at the walls and hoping they had surveillance running.

The other option was to trick her way past the guards. Given that they had fibre-optic nerve enhancements, accelerator glands and biopolymer-assisted muscle tissue, that would probably require some serious finessing. One wrong move and they'd kill her. Fleet Spatials had a reputation for taking orders extremely literally.

Before Ann could devise a solution, a shrieking alarm cut the air.

'What's that?' she demanded of the walls. 'Anybody care to explain what's going on?'

She strode over to hammer on the door just as the guards opened it.

'Come with us,' said the larger of the two. 'You're wanted on the command deck. Quickly.'

Ann stood her ground. 'For what?'

They simply gestured with their guns.

Ann marched out of the room, glad of the opportunity but nervous all the same. Nobody appeared to be evacuating. If anything, the Fleet scientists looked even busier than usual. Had Monet done something? Then one monitor she passed showed a familiar spectroscopic spike – the kind that indicated a major Nem arrival event. She stalled, staring at the signal in horror. If that data was fresh, the implication was definitely *not* good. It would indicate Nem behaviour way outside the predicted paradigm.

'Move!' said the guard, spurring her back into motion.

Ann's mind started to race. A Nem departure in their direction was the one event the stealth watcher drones at the edges of the Tiwanaku System couldn't warn them of. They simply couldn't fly fast enough. But the risk hadn't been considered serious.

Will's ugly predictions sprang to mind. Maybe at one time the Nems had genuinely represented a predictable weapon, but Sam Shah had changed that by deliberately pushing their behaviour into an uncharted regime.

When Ann reached the command area, she found Senator Voss standing at the centre of a small crowd of scientists and engineers. They all appeared to be trying to talk at once while she coaxed them back into some kind of order. Then she caught sight of Ann. She pointed a sharp, manicured finger in her direction.

'You,' said Voss. '*Ms* Ludik. Do *you* have a theory about what's going on here?'

Ann took a moment to try to parse the senator's expression and thought she saw a little panic hiding in those imperious eyes. On the other hand, the fact that she'd brought Ann out of confinement to participate in the dialogue suggested that the senator hadn't completely abandoned rationality. Perhaps it was time to recalibrate their relationship.

'Explain what's happening and I'll give you my assessment,' she said flatly. If the senator was going to pretend she wasn't a Fleet officer, she saw no reason to be courteous.

Voss gestured at a lanky communications officer. 'Foster, fill her in.'

'We have an unscheduled Nemesis machine arrival event,' said Foster. His hands twisted together anxiously. 'A large one.'

A scientist next to him wearing a full immersion visor shook her head.

'It's not just that. We see a Nem warp signature but no drone scatter. Instead, there's something like a nestship gravity footprint.'

Ann's blood ran cold. She strode to the nearest display wall to look for herself.

'Is Nem-cloaking active?' she demanded.

'Yes, ma'am,' said the scientist in the visor.

'Give me a full sensor spread,' said Ann. 'Point every telescope you have at the Nem arrival if it isn't already. What was the insertion distance? How long do we have?'

'Light-lag is estimated at ninety minutes.'

Jaco Brinsen strode in from the pod bay. 'Senator, I've seen the scans. This shouldn't be happening.'

'Clearly,' Voss snapped. 'So why is it?'

Jaco's mouth worked silently while he searched for an answer. 'At this point, we'd expect the Nems to be in final drone production prior to their Earth assault,' he said at length. 'Given the relative strengths of the warp trails, Earth should be their next target. But it's possible that they're here chasing the *Ariel Two* instead. Nems usually chase *out* from their homeworld, not inwards. They leave that to subsequent attack waves. But that doesn't mean it couldn't happen. The *Ariel Two* must constitute a new level of threat.'

'But why bring a nestship?' said Ann.

'Extra firepower,' said Jaco. 'If they realised their drones weren't cutting it, they might try trading up for something else.'

'Really?' Ann zoomed in on the Fecund vessel and threw up a display to fill the wall. 'It's in terrible condition – it's tumbling already. The shield hull is inoperable and showing major fissures visible even from this distance. And it's not alone. Look – here, here and here.' She pointed at three smudges surrounding the giant hulk, as if shepherding it along. 'Three more vessels – larger than drones. That's a design we haven't seen before.'

She could see Jaco's confidence slipping. About time.

'The Nems have been exploring Tiwanaku's out-system ruins and have simply decided to utilise them as part of their reflection phase,' he said.

'Obviously,' said Ann. 'But this is despite the fact that they've never shown any interest in Fecund ruins before, which have been present in almost every system where we deployed the Nems.'

'We just used one to shoot at them,' he retorted. 'If the *Ariel Two* didn't give them a clear idea of what a nestship was capable of, it's hard to imagine what would.'

Ann shot him a level glare. 'I don't dispute that. I'm just not convinced that this is some kind of standard retaliation event. That's speculation, and right now speculation is dangerous. A cloud of drones is one thing, but nestships are *planet-busters.*'

'Koenig,' said the senator, 'do we have a flight vector for those Nem ships? Are they headed for *Ariel Two* or not?'

'Unclear at this distance,' said the scientist in the wraparound visor. 'Nelson has stationed *Ariel Two* at Snakepit's L5. That puts it too close to us for a clear read until they correct course from their insert frame.'

Ann rounded on the senator. 'What we're seeing here is either a genuinely new behaviour or a modelled one so distorted that it makes no difference,' she said. 'If we have to wait for them to bear down on us to confirm Jaco's optimistic assessment then we're already in trouble. We need to bring Will Monet up here immediately.'

Voss's eyes narrowed. 'Why?'

'One, he knows nestships better than anyone on this station. Two, he anticipated a change in Nem behaviour, as I tried to point out to you earlier. And three, because none of us have the first clue why they're back here, and he's got more experience dealing with alien intelligence than *any human being in history*. How many reasons do you need?'

The senator's mouth twitched in displeasure. 'I don't think so,' she said. 'Let's not make the security implications any worse than they already are. You're only here because I need you,' said the senator, '*not* because I've reinstated your authority.'

'I'm here because you have no idea what you're doing,' Ann snapped. 'I told you we were getting out of our depth and now it's coming true. If you think you can handle this without me, feel free to send me back to my quarters.'

The senator looked tempted. 'Careful, Ludik,' she said.

Ann snorted and returned her attention to the displays.

'Message Captain Aquino on the *Ariel Two*,' said the senator. 'I want to know how much power he can put through his weapons. Warn him that the Nems may be here for his ship.'

It took over ten grinding minutes for Nelson's message to get back to them. When his face appeared on the main wall, he didn't look so great. The surprise visit had put a dent in his suave demeanour.

'We have no weapons at this time,' he said. 'All the power couplings are open for relining. We weren't expecting this. I can give you full power within two hours.'

'Too long,' said the senator. 'Be ready in forty minutes.'

'I have a vector!' said Koenig. 'The Nems have adjusted course – they're headed straight for Snakepit, not the *Ariel Two*.'

Jaco's face fell. 'Are you sure?'

'Unless they correct again, sir,' said Koenig. 'Sending the data to your contacts.' She reached for her touchboard and stopped. 'Wait! I'm seeing a minor secondary correction. One ship is peeling off from the others.'

'Well?' said Senator Voss. 'Where's it going?'

Koenig hesitated anxiously before replying, as if trying to make the information in her visor go away by pure force of will.

'It's headed for *us*, ma'am.'

'This station?' said Voss.

'Yes, ma'am. So far as I can see.'

A horrid realisation settled over Ann. 'Is our short-range Fleet beacon still running?'

Communications Officer Foster gazed at her with pathetic, desperate eyes.

'Switch it off!' Ann shouted. 'They've learned how to read it. Tight-beam orders to the *Chiyome*, *Ariel Two* and the senator's scout-ship. Full Nem-cloak immediately. Further comms only via tight-beam.'

'Captain,' said Foster in strangled tones. 'We're getting a signal from the approaching vessel.'

'Play it,' said Ann.

'Welcome, humans!' said the swarm. 'We detect your friendly signal. We come in peace with good news. All humans are invited to join us in the harmony of joyful union. Particularly children, which are very useful. Reveal your locations to us and we will assist in your peaceful incorporation. All who comply need not fear destruction. It is a glad day for all!'

Ann watched Senator Voss's face drop.

'Can we be seen?' she asked in hushed tones.

'Not any more,' said Ann. 'But with light-lag, that beacon must have given them about an hour's tracking on our position. We'll just have to hope that Nem-cloaking still works.' She turned on Jaco. 'Did you hear that message? Do you need any further evidence that Nem intelligence is spiking?'

Jaco shook his head anxiously. With his theory about the Nems collapsing, his confidence appeared inclined to go with it.

'Ma'am,' blurted Foster. 'That message was backed by a primitive soft-assault. Our filters just caught it.'

The implications didn't need stating. The Nems had come for them.

'Do we have defences if that ship decides to take us on?' said the senator.

'Plenty,' said Koenig. 'One ship that size shouldn't be a problem, unless firing on it kicks off another wave of drones from the surface.'

'Take us to battle stations,' said the senator. 'Power up the buffers. I don't want to take any risks here.'

'Senator,' said Ann, 'please see sense. We have no idea what's going on and the station is under direct threat. If ever there was an opportunity to bring Will over to our side, surely this is it?'

Voss grimaced. Ann could see emotions warring on her face.

'Go on, then. Get that old bastard up here.'

As the minutes ticked down to the arrival of the new ships in-system, the command deck buzzed with organised activity. Sensor results from every ship in the system were coordinated. Weapons were brought stealthily online. And a group of guards accompanied Will Monet to the command deck. Will's gangling frame looked a little ridiculous surrounded by eight armed soldiers with bulky muscle augs, but nobody was laughing.

'Good afternoon, Captain Monet,' said the senator brightly, her political persona turning on.

Will stared back at her with a flat, unimpressed expression.

'These aren't the circumstances under which I ideally wanted to ask for your help,' said Voss, 'but by now you've seen enough to know that, rightly or wrongly, it was *your* vision of peace that motivated our actions here. As it is, we can't wait to beg for your help. We need it now. Koenig, bring Captain Monet up to speed, please. Give him a picture of normal Nem activity as a baseline.'

Koenig tapped furiously at her touchboard. 'I'm sending you a memory dump from the station's strategy SAP,' she said.

Will's eyebrows twitched as he absorbed it.

'We want to know why they're back here so soon,' said Voss. 'Usually they only return to the homeworld after an attack wave is finished, and only then in small numbers. Most drones are abandoned at the battle-site, so clearly this is something new.'

'And this time they're dragging a derelict planet-buster,' said Will.

'Exactly,' said the senator. 'So – any guesses?'

Will made a coughing sound in his throat that sounded like extremely dry amusement.

The senator sighed. 'Captain Ludik, bringing him here was your idea. You talk to him.'

Will's cold, judgmental eyes slid across to settle on Ann's face. She met his gaze directly, refusing to squirm.

'You're on this station and as much at risk as the rest of us,' she said. 'I feel no shame in admitting that our models of Nem behaviour are already obsolete. You were right before, and your perspective would be welcome now.'

Will appeared to think about it. She wondered if he'd refuse to help her out of spite.

'I've been analysing your bioweapon at the cellular level,' he said eventually. 'What I can tell you so far is that everything is a tool for these organisms. Doesn't matter if you're talking orbitals or lymphocytes. They systematically deconstruct new material into parts and do something like intelligent digestion on it. They rework the components into forms they can reuse and recode them back into DNA analogues for storage.'

'That fits our model of a Nem swarm attack,' said Ann. 'Attack, dismantle, reflect, absorb. But what's this, then?' She gestured at the screens.

Will shrugged. 'At the cellular level, they only do one other thing during reflection. If the problem's too big for analysis, the cells fission and the problem is split between them. In essence, directed reproduction.'

Voss's face flicked back to the swarm ships displayed on the wall. 'You think this is some kind of *breeding process*?'

'Too early to say for sure,' said Will, 'but the only reason I can think of that would bring them back here is if they've bitten off more than they can chew. This behaviour is intended to help manage the new information they've found.'

'Maybe they're gathering reinforcements for the Earth surge?' said Koenig.

'Possibly,' said Ann. 'But why drag an old ship with them to do that?'

'Sir, we have a proximity alert for the lone ship headed our way,' said the officer manning the tactical SAPs.

All eyes turned to the main screen. They watched in silence as the Nem vessel slid up to meet them. So far as Ann could see, it had been built by simply gluing modified drones together into a parody of a human starship. It looked like a giant grey raspberry. She held her breath as the ship sailed straight past their position with its sensors still on full sweep. It even adjusted course to avoid the *Chiyome* apparently without noticing its presence. Ann heard gasps of relief from all over the room.

'Looks like the Nem-cloaking still works,' said Jaco.

'Nem-cloaking?' said Will.

'Nems emit a recognition signal,' said Ann. 'They're hard-wired to treat anything using that signature as benign. Stops them from ripping each other apart.'

'Handy, until they change the signal,' said Will.

'We have orbital insertion for the primary Nem fleet,' said the tactical officer. 'On the main wall now.'

They watched the nestship slide into a neat, circular orbit high above Snakepit's weirdly corrugated surface. Its tumbling stopped with the dangerous end of the bulb-shaped ship pointed straight down.

'Atmospheric bounce suggests a huge amount of tight-beam traffic between the Nem fleet and the planet,' said Foster.

'Can we decode it?' asked Voss.

'Not yet,' said Foster. 'It resembles the standard Nem signalling protocol but it's much denser, with a level of complexity we haven't seen before. Looks like a conversation. We're seeing matching scatter from one of the defensive bodies on the surface.' He raised a warning hand. 'Wait! We have a partial match. They're using the conflict-resolution protocol – the same one that shows up in the reflection phase, but with *massive* data packets. They're orders of magnitude bigger than we're used to.'

'Conflict resolution with their own *homeworld*?' said Jaco. 'That doesn't make any sense.'

'This isn't good,' said Will. 'Can anyone tell me whether there are signs of a working suntap on that hulk?'

'None yet,' said Koenig. 'I'll get on it.'

Five minutes later, the nestship fired, answering their question. Several dozen g-rays converged on one of the starfish-shaped defensive structures below, instantly turning several hundred square kilometres of Snakepit's surface into molten slag. Rings of tortured atmosphere rippled out from the site.

Everyone stared. Ann stood speechless in astonishment. Why would the Nems attack their own planet? As Jaco said, it didn't make any sense.

In the ashen silence that followed, Will spoke. 'Does anyone else need proof that you're out of your depth here?'

Within seconds, the planet's remaining defensive nodes reacted, throwing streams of drones high into the atmosphere. They poured out in their millions, gravity drives flickering even before they reached orbit. The entire world below them sparkled with the light of several hundred fountains of living flame. The nestship turned and fired again, reducing another defensive node to a mushroom cloud. The planet redoubled its response.

While they gawped at the chaos unfolding beneath them, the two raspberry ships shepherding the Fecund vessel split apart into their constituent drones, moving to intercept those rising from the world below. Judging by the power of the g-rays they were emitting, Ann suspected they'd been fitted with suntaps, too.

In less than a minute, the space around Snakepit had turned from empty vacuum into a storm of frenzied battle.

'Apparently this has nothing to do with us,' said Jaco. He looked totally lost. 'Is that swarm message still playing?'

'Yes,' said Foster. 'They're still offering peace. That last raspberry ship is hanging back, though – it seems to be moving away from the fighting.'

'And we should do the same,' said Will quickly. 'That battle cloud is getting bigger every second. We'll be within crossfire range in less than a minute.'

'Can we do that?' said the senator. She sounded nervous. 'Can we get out of the way?'

'The station has thrusters,' said Jaco. 'We can correct our position, but it increases the chance that they'll see us.'

'I don't care,' said Voss. 'Do it.'

While officers scrambled to their defensive stations, tides of warring drones spilled up from the planet like tongues of flame, apparently oblivious to the ships and habitat. A fan of g-rays lanced out from the invading drones, turning hundreds of nearby defenders into blast-waves of radiation.

The station had just seconds to react. The deck under Ann's feet shuddered as radiation alarms began to sound.

'Primary buffers at twenty-three per cent!' someone yelled. 'This tub wasn't built for action.'

'Another wave incoming,' shouted Koenig.

The next wave knocked Ann off her feet. Sirens started screaming. The lights went out.

14.6: WILL

Will stumbled as the station lurched. The command deck SAP began blurting out warnings.

'Nem-cloaking compromised, compensating with albedo reduction. Primary Casimir-buffers compromised, secondaries activated. Life-support primaries compromised, secondaries activating...'

Emergency illumination flickered into life. If he was going to make his move, Will knew it needed to be now. At this rate there might not be another chance, and Pari was taking far too long to wake up to the dangers she faced. Unfortunately, a wall of armed Spatials stood between him and the pod bay. Will didn't let that bother him.

He crouched and sprang over the guards' heads, landed three metres away and sprinted for the bay doors. At the same time, he reached out with his mind and seized control of the command deck's SAP. With his triggers already in place, the station's security toppled like a damp sandcastle.

To their credit, the guards reacted fast. Their killtech had been designed by copying Will's secondary nervous system, after all. They brought their guns around and peppered the wall ahead of him with bio-bullets.

Will dived to avoid the fire. He wasn't sure what would happen if the bullets hit, but it probably wouldn't be pretty. An officer nearby wasn't so lucky. He spun in a spray of blood, dropping like a limp rag. One of the Spatials slapped the emergency lockdown stud on his chest, sealing the pod-bay doors.

Will felt anger rise back up and claim him. Lives were being wasted when all he wanted to do was leave. Suddenly, it was all too much. The League had bent his entire life out of shape. The people he'd called friends had lied to him for years while they plotted mass murder. And now they were shooting at him. Well, if that was how they wanted it, he could play that way.

He threw himself back towards the closest soldier, diving under his arc of fire to tackle him. The man screamed as Will's impact pulverised his legs. Will reached up, seized the smart-gun from the Spatial's hands and hurled it at the second-closest soldier as he turned to fire. The soldier's head splashed apart, his bioceramic helmet splintering like old wood.

The others whipped their guns around, but not nearly fast enough. Will blurred forward again. The two Spatials directly in his path received swift, precise blows to the chest. Both died instantly, their bodies bursting like wet paper bags. Will sped through their spattering remains.

By then the other four soldiers had started firing. Will used the closest as a human shield and drove into their midst in the blink of an eye. Before they could react, Will struck out, punching the closest and kicking another so hard that his body armour shattered. He took the remaining soldier in a dive, ripping the gun from his hands and dislocating the man's arms as he did so.

The entire process took approximately three seconds and proved more satisfying than it had any right to.

'Anyone else want to piss me off?' said Will.

Parisa Voss stared at him in shock. 'Bioblocker!' she yelled.

Gas started jetting from the ceiling.

'Shit,' said Will. Evidently Pari had that little precaution running on an independent circuit.

He took off for the nearest exit but could feel the stuff attacking his skin already. The vapour had to be lousy with alien cells. As he sprinted, the strength fled from his limbs. Pain engulfed him and he toppled to the floor, tumbling end-over-end with the force of his own velocity. He struggled to right himself as smart-cells screamed into his mind from all over his body. His vision blurred as the alien organisms started to eat his eyes.

Just as his hope began to fade, a pair of arms reached down to grab

349

him. To his surprise, they dragged him towards a maintenance hatch, then pushed him through and sealed it behind them.

'Are you okay?' said a woman's voice.

Will lay on the floor spasming in a state of internal war. Where he could seal and repulse the alien cells with polymer vesicles, he did so. Where he couldn't prevent attack, he simply sacrificed his tissue, binding it up in a mucus matrix. About three per cent of Will's body mass sloughed off onto the floor around him in a puddle of pinkish fluid.

He gasped for breath. 'Just,' he croaked.

He coughed up a mass of something disgusting onto his chest – some fraction of the lining of his lungs, by the looks of it. His skin burned hot in a frenzy of self-repair.

'Good,' said Ann Ludik. 'Because we probably only have seconds before they come after us. There are maintenance pods this way. We can use them to get out.'

Will felt a surge of wholly irrational resentment at being rescued by his betrayer but knew he wasn't in a position to do anything stupid about it. She picked him up and dragged him onwards, down an emergency stairway to the level below. Someone started hammering on the hatch behind them before they hit the next level.

Will blinked at her as his vision cleared. 'Why help me?' he wheezed.

'Does it matter?' she said. 'I'm coming with you, that's all.'

Had he been rescued by anyone else, Will would have accepted the gesture at face value. Coming from Ann, however, he wasn't about to take any chances. They tumbled together through the open door of a maintenance pod.

'Pod, take us—' Ann started, but Will was already on it.

The door sealed and the pod raced away towards the shuttle bay. As they accelerated, Will sealed off comms between the command deck and the rest of the station. He deployed tactical and emergency-response SAPs to move the station out of harm's way and accelerate the repairs. He wanted Pari locked down, not dead – though dead was tempting. Through the cameras on the command deck, he saw her yelling orders and watched her stunned officers regrouping.

The maintenance pod dumped them at the shuttle bay just as another wave of blasts rocked the floor. Snakepit Station had become a bystander in an extremely dangerous war. Ann pulled Will from the wall where he lay wheezing and ran with him to the hatch that led to the shuttle.

Will rammed his mind into the hatch control and ordered it open. Nothing happened. Ann slapped the stud on the wall with the same lack of effect.

'Shit!' yelled Ann. 'That Nem alert ramped us to maximum security, which means the docking equipment is running on a locked-out loop. We need someone in the station to get to a manual cut-out and hook us back in.'

'A robot,' Will wheezed. He started scanning the station for one he could use.

'Won't work,' said Ann. 'If they go near the cut-outs they get a shutdown pulse. It's an anti-hack measure.'

Will glowered at the stubbornly sealed hatch before them. This was, no doubt, another layer of security added just for him. How thoughtful. 'They let us go,' he said, 'or they lose their air. Tell them.' He brought up the environmental controls from the command deck and got ready to dump some oxygen.

'No,' said Ann. 'I can solve this. Give me a minute.' She reached for the comms on the wall. 'Call Kuril Najoma, maximum priority,' she said, facing the camera.

Will jacked into the call and watched for tricks. A window displaying a large man's astonished face appeared. As he took in Ann's expression, an anxious frown crept over his features.

'You want another favour,' he said glumly.

She nodded. 'Someone needs to manually unlock the docking circuit.'

'I'm going to get in trouble for this, aren't I?'

'Undoubtedly. Can you do it?'

He looked pained. 'Yes. Because if you have any idea what to do next, that puts you one up on everyone else around here. Just don't forget about me. And if they shoot me, put up a little plaque or something.'

Ann nodded. 'I will,' she said. 'A nice one.'

'Good luck, Captain,' he said. 'It's been fun working with you.' He cut the call.

'They'll kill him,' Will croaked.

Ann shook her head. 'I'm hoping they're better than that.'

Five seconds later, the hatch opened.

Ann picked Will up and carried him into the pod. It slid down the rail and deposited them at the shuttle's airlock where they faced another sealed door.

'Again?' said Ann.

'No,' growled Will. 'It's a shuttle. I've got this.'

As the shuttle began to complain about unauthorised access, Will seized it with his interface and squeezed it till it wilted.

'Welcome aboard,' it mewled.

Will struggled weakly up the access tube and had to let Ann clip him into his seat.

'Strap in,' he said as he took over the ship's helm-space. 'We're leaving.'

Ann dived into the crash couch behind him as Will unlocked the docking clamps.

The shuttle fell away from the station while Will pressed himself into the autopilot SAP. He ignored its wails of panic at the frenzied whirl of battle that surrounded them, threw half his submind attention onto impact evasion and punched them out into empty space under three gees of thrust. His healing body wouldn't be up for much more than that for at least a quarter of an hour.

Avoiding drone impacts and blast-waves in that furious mess would have reduced a human pilot to a gibbering wreck in seconds, but Will hadn't been human for years. He hurled the shuttle this way and that, fighting for every kilometre. When they were no more than ten minutes out, Ann started shouting.

'Wait! Where are you going?'

'The *Ariel Two*,' said Will. 'Where'd you think?'

A pair of drones chased by them, narrowly missing. The shuttle slewed wildly to compensate.

'Why?' said Ann. 'Turn back! Both the *Chiyome* and Parisa's scout are closer. In this mess it'll take us nearly an hour to reach the *Ariel Two*, even at these gees. We need to get out of here immediately and let Earth know.'

'And leave *Ariel Two* in Pari's hands?' said Will. 'Not a chance.'

'Don't be stupid!' said Ann. 'There's too much crossfire. We can come back for it.'

Will felt a fresh surge of anger. 'It's *my ship*,' he said. 'I'm not going to let her use it for her fucking war.'

'But it's still under repair!' said Ann. 'Take the *Chiyome*!'

Will saw the logic; he just didn't like it.

'If we do this, we do it on my terms,' he snarled. 'You betrayed me, Captain Ludik. And that ship of yours is as full of alien weapons as that station we just left. Forgive me for not being in a rush to let you anywhere near it.'

Besides, the *Ariel Two* had more gallons of his smart-blood aboard than most habitat domes had water. With resources like that, he could properly analyse Snakepit's bioweapon. He could make a difference.

Another blast-wave hit, swatting the shuttle like a fly. They entered a dizzying spin while the pilot SAP wept damage alerts at him. They'd lost attitude control and taken rads. Life-support primaries had failed, giving them just six hours on backups. However, that wasn't likely to be a problem. The wave had knocked them sideways, out of their orbit and onto a trajectory that ended on the planet below. They were falling like a rock, straight through the swirl of combat.

Will yelled obscenities while he struggled to turn their tumble into a controlled dive. A blizzard of drones flashed past them on every side as Snakepit loomed up to say hello.

1 5: DESCENT

1 5.1: MARK

Mark stood frozen as the Flag gestured at them with the barrel of his gun. He looked eighteen at most, his dark, blank eyes radiating a capacity for casual violence. He wore a padded combat jacket with a type of smart-collar Mark had never seen before.

'You trespassing,' he told them proudly. 'This the realm of the Citizens of the True Light.'

He spoke quietly into his collar in a language Mark didn't know but the look on his face suggested that finding them here qualified as an early Christmas.

'Let me handle this,' said Venetia. 'I recognise the group.'

Mark still wasn't sure Venetia was the right person for the job. He was a fellow Earther, whereas her voice and appearance screamed Colonial elite. But she supposedly had the local knowledge, so Mark grudgingly kept his mouth shut and hoped she knew what she was doing.

'We're glad you're here,' said Venetia. 'We've been looking for you. We want to defect. How soon can you take us to your settlement?'

The young man holding the gun glanced back and forth between them, looking slightly nervous now. Apparently, this didn't happen.

'No,' the young man insisted. 'You all our *prisoners*. No deals.'

'Fine,' said Venetia. 'Prisoners, then. We're being hunted by the New Luxor police. How soon can we leave?'

The young man spoke into his collar again, this time more urgently.

'*I* say when we go,' he told them. 'That how it works.'

A minute later, three more Flags arrived, including one slightly older man with artificially whitened irises and black prosthetic ridges sticking out of his face.

'I'm Den,' he said. 'I'm in charge here. Kal says you talking weird shit. How about you all kneel down on the ground and try again.'

The Flags waved their guns.

Mark and the others knelt carefully while Venetia explained a second time.

'The police will be here very soon,' she said. 'Lots of them. We have information that affects your sect. Your whole community is in danger from imminent attack and the colonists don't want you to know. They're trying to stop us from getting to you.'

'We in danger from nobody!' said Kal, shaking his flenser. 'They show up here, we flesh them good.'

'Shut up,' said Den. 'Keep talking, lady. You offering data?'

'We'll tell you everything we know,' said Venetia. 'High-class data. Lots of it. But we have to get out of here before the police show up and kill us.'

'They all liars,' said Kal. 'They too eager. Just want to get into Brite-haven. Then use a bioweapon or some shit.'

Mark could contain himself no longer. It was all taking too long. Venetia was only confusing them.

'If we wanted to do that, why open our mouths?' he said. 'You were going to take us there for ransom anyway.'

The Flags stared at him. Venetia and Zoe both shot him warning glances.

'We got a *smart mouth*!' said Kal. 'You want I should kill him for the glory of God and our father, the one true risen Prophet?'

'Not yet,' said Den. 'Man's got a point.' Den looked them over with his deliberately unsettling eyes. 'I got no idea what to make of you,' he said, 'so we take you back. If this all a big story, we get a ransom anyway. If not, we get data. Either way, we follow God's plan and make fresh glory for the Citizens of the True Light, praise be to the Prophet and his mighty works.'

His collar made a peculiar chiming sound, like bells being struck, as if to underline his point. Den looked satisfied.

'Bring them this way,' said Den. 'Kal, you up in front. Don't want you fleshing them in the back for no reason.'

As the Flag raiding party led them from the room, Venetia leaned in close to Mark.

'Be *extremely* careful,' she told him. 'Please. Whatever you believe.'

Mark nodded and kept his mouth shut. Privately, he suspected that the men who'd found them weren't vicious or brainwashed, just poor and desperate. He'd seen poverty on Earth and knew what it could do to people. He'd been down to the notorious Lowdex of Tower Three, where families of five or six lived in three-metre-square pods. He'd walked through the Philadelphia refugee zone after they shut down the towers and lifted people-packs for weeks during the relocation effort. If you subjected anyone to enough hunger and fear they always got a little crazy. Press a gun into their hand and it only made things worse.

While Mark had no love of the sect Leading, he could easily see how, for many of the Following, any way off Earth was better than none. There had to be millions of people lining up and willing to claim they were die-hard Revivalists if it would get them a ticket out.

Den led them to a tunnel where a small airlock had been glued into the wall and sprayed over with rockdust camo. Den pointed at the lock and ordered Kal into action. Kal complained briefly but climbed inside anyway. He came back five minutes later with three ancient-looking environment suits and air-masks. The valves on the masks had been fitted with leashes. Clearly, this wasn't the first time Den's team had taken hostages.

Mark and the others hurriedly pulled the heated suits over their clothes while the Flags watched with weapons aimed. They'd probably never seen people so grateful to put on such ratty equipment. Zoe actually groaned with relief as the thermal circuit kicked on, soliciting nervous laughter from their captors.

Two of the Flags climbed through the tiny airlock, leaving them with just Den and Kal.

'In you go,' said Den.

One by one, they followed the others into the tunnels beyond, where three electric carts sat waiting. Den's men ushered them aboard and together they set off into the dark.

The tunnels on this side of the wall were very different from the ones they'd been in before, and not just because of the lack of breathable air. On this side, the tunnels were cathedral-sized. The carts trundled down a narrow apron of printrock that had been laid through the ruins, past open vats the size of swimming pools and curving columns like supertower supports. Great pieces of ceramic machinery had crumbled away from the walls and now lay in scaly heaps on the floor. The carts took them to a ramp glued into the side of a vertical shaft wide enough to park a shuttle in. They spiralled down into the inky depths.

Venetia saw Mark staring at the walls.

'We're in the pumping system,' she said. 'The Fecund drew water from the ocean for hydraulic transport, then boiled and filtered it for use.'

'What that you saying?' said Kal. 'No talking on the sled unless you want to praise God and the Prophet and his mighty works. All talk that is not godly is vile. And vileness must be crushed in the name of the Lord.' Kal's collar chimed.

'Yeah!' said one of the others. 'To strike in the name of the Lord is a service that adds to the *greatness* of the Lord!'

He waited for his collar to chime. When it didn't, the others laughed at him.

'Work harder, Nid,' said Den. 'God give no coin to the lazy.'

'What's with the bells?' said Zoe very quietly while their captors guffawed.

'SAP-driven rewards for pious speech,' Venetia whispered back. 'Gamified religion is a big deal for this group. Try not to let it spook you.'

Mark grimaced in disgust. Was that how the Leading kept them in line?

'You still talking?' said Kal, jabbing his gun into Venetia's side. 'You *blaspheming*? For God is great and the godly do not hesitate to strike down the blasphemer in his name!'

Kal's collar chimed again. Even in the dark and with masks on, Mark could tell that Nid felt put out.

'The blasphemer must suffer but the heretic must be put to the torch,' said Nid darkly. 'For thou shalt seek out the heretic in his hiding place even if that be thine own house and thou must burn him.'

Nid's collar chimed twice. He sat back with arms folded in satisfaction.

Mark couldn't help noticing how the Flags' English improved for religious speeches. He guessed they must be quoting from some kind of prayer book.

357

'But those who work against the name of the Lord must be slaughtered as cattle,' said Kal, fixing Mark with a cold gaze. He tapped the long, ugly-looking mono-knife on his belt. 'For the Lord is goodness and peace and those who work against him are the bringers of war.'

His collar chimed again.

'Enough,' said Den. 'You got plenty time for scripture later, and scripture say nothing about messing up a hostage.'

Kal slumped back against the edge of the cart with a sullen frown.

The tunnel ended at a massive circular intake duct. Grit from the dead ocean beyond had spilled in to cover the floor. Parked in the centre of the duct, looking like a toy against the immense curving walls, was a rover. Mark had never seen a design like it. A habitat pod large enough to hold his New York apartment crouched low on six independent wheels. A flat, oversized roof almost twice as wide as the vehicle itself hung over the top of it with curious metallic strips dangling from the edges. A ramp lowered out of the back of the rover as they approached. The carts rolled up into a dusty storage bay, where the Flags jumped off to secure their vehicles.

'Sat-cloaked rover,' whispered Zoe. She sounded somewhat impressed. 'I heard about these. It's invisible from above in all wavelengths. You need to be probing with a laser to an accuracy of a metre in order to spot it.'

'Inside,' said Den, pointing to the airlock at the far end of the bay.

On the other side lay a utilitarian cabin lined with dust-spattered windows. Empty drinking bulbs littered the floor. The air smelled of sweat, sand and the plastic reek of burning scrubbers. Passenger couches lined either wall. At the front sat a manual driver's seat. Religious slogans played on the twitching wall-screens at the back.

'Nid, you drive,' said Den. 'Kal, hang up your gun. Don't want you messing up the nice people.'

Mark watched in disbelief as Nid took his place at the front. He'd never seen a ground transport with an actual human driver before. That kind of thing was straight out of a Surplus Age drama.

'Hostages on the floor,' said Den. 'You don't get seats. Seats only for those who toil righteously in the name of the Lord.'

Mark joined Zoe and Venetia on the rover's filthy decking. The others sat around them and chatted in their private language, making remarks that Mark strongly suspected related to Zoe's physique. Occasionally, they all burst into laughter.

Mark saw Zoe's expression darkening. She stared firmly into the middle distance and shifted a little closer to him. He put an arm around her and he felt her relax a little. Mark dearly hoped Venetia's assessment of the Flags was going to hold true. He didn't want to have to start killing people.

The rover set out across the barren plain as the first light of dawn started to tint the horizon. They drove for two hours towards what Venetia informed him was the edge of the legal claim limit, beyond which IPSO law kicked in and the Flags' settlement couldn't be locally contested.

Mark's stomach ached from hunger. He tamped down his metabolic responses, forcing his body to draw from fat stores. Zoe and Venetia lacked those kinds of augs. He could only imagine how famished they must be feeling.

Ahead of them, a cluster of domes and scaffolding grew steadily. Unlike the colony at New Luxor, the Flag settlement appeared to be in a state of robust growth. Two multi-storey construction mechs stood idly outside what looked like the beginnings of a supertower. The local conflict clearly hadn't done much to deter Earth's billions from arriving, but that was to be expected. Given the choice between low-grade asymmetrical warfare and the threat of extinction, Mark would have chosen warfare, too.

As they neared the closest dome, he noticed some curious scaffolds standing beside the track they were following, almost like old-fashioned power pylons. Curious, limp sacks hung off them.

On closer examination, Mark realised they weren't sacks. They were bodies. In the dead, frozen air, they'd remained eerily intact, and Carter's thin, oxygen-free atmosphere didn't support the kind of bacteria needed for decay. The purple, bug-eyed faces of the asphyxiated corpses stared blindly at them as they passed. Mark's gut clenched. His hopes of finding help in the settlement dropped another notch.

'Who are they?' he asked the raiders seated around him.

'Heretics!' said Kal enthusiastically. 'Them who don't listen to the word of the Lord and his one true Prophet and work against his name!'

'Nah,' said Nid. 'More like hostages who don't get paid for. Those who stand against the purity and love of the True Light should breathe some other air than God's.'

His collar chimed. He pointed an index finger like a gun at Kal and made a shooting noise.

The others chuckled in dark amusement.

'You all stupid,' said Den. 'You want to make us sound like a bunch of savages? Those corpses were thieves and killers,' he assured them. 'In Britehaven the law is clear. You don't mess with God's word, or he mess with you. We keep things nice and tidy.'

In the end it didn't really matter, Mark decided. Whoever they'd killed, it amounted to medieval law in a modern colony. Maybe they should have tried harder to think of other ways of reaching the space-port.

Crates of Fecund art and tubs of random scientific machinery stood stacked up around the doors to the dome's main airlock. To Mark's eye, it looked like most of it had been hacked straight out of the stone with a mono-knife. The desert grit couldn't be doing the ancient lab-equipment much good, not that anyone here cared.

The rover turned, reversed up to the gate and waited for a lock jetty to crawl out to them and dock.

'Back to the sleds,' said Den. 'Now everyone gets to see our big find from the raid. Not many hostages nowadays, I can tell you.'

Mark and the others took their places on the carts and Den trium-phantly led them down the rover's ramp into the settlement beyond.

Mark had expected poverty. He'd heard that the sect Leading put little effort into making their claim-sites habitable. The last thing he expected was a low-budget wonderland.

The town that Den drove them through offered everything a poor Earther might crave. The dome had plenty of space, open skies and gaudy high-tech toys scattered about. Rave scooters, jump-packs and ped-sleds leaned up against walls gathering dust. What the place lacked were all the things most Earthers didn't know to miss, like proper seals and rad-shielding. He coughed in the thin, dusty air, which probably hadn't been filtered in months.

Worse than the cheap luxury was the way the place had been bra-zenly meme-hacked. Every crappy dustboard house they passed was painted with Truist designs. Murals everywhere depicted Earth's early victories during the war and the burning of the First Wave Colonies.

The screens in every window played video footage of old Truist propaganda. Animatronic Sanchez shrines sat on street corners, watching them pass with empty electronic eyes.

The religious immersion would have been depressing enough on its own, but Mark had started to notice the people. Women with heavy white make-up doubling as sunscreen watched from doorways. Mark could see their cheaply reprinted body parts – breasts, mostly. Dozens of thin children with plastic implants and bad skin stood quietly watching them pass.

It was, Mark thought, a refugee camp tricked out like a theme park. It reeked of exploitation. He'd imagined poor Earthers struggling with dignity. He saw no dignity here.

'Don't accept food or water here unless you have to,' Venetia quietly warned him. 'It's all tweaked. Eat enough and you'll never want to leave.'

Mark wanted to snap at her and tell her that things here couldn't be so bad. But all the while his eyes told him otherwise.

They passed a row of ancient-looking exosuits lined up next to a building site. It occurred to Mark then that he hadn't seen a single robot since they reached the dome. He realised with a start that *people* had built the houses all around him. With no reason to exist other than to establish a sect's legal claim, the settlement was probably desperate to find things for their imported peasants to do.

The carts came to a halt outside the one building in the entire dome that looked properly constructed. It had high, reinforced walls of white printrock and a broad overhanging roof lined with metallic panels – rad-shielding, Mark suspected. An elegant arched door like that of a church adorned the front.

It opened and a man stepped through. He wore High Church white from head to toe, with gloves and a broad-rimmed hat that cast a shadow over his shoulders. He had a powerful face with a deep, rich tan, and what Mark assumed was artificially bleached hair. He looked like a weight-lifter disguised as an old-world pope.

'Good morning, Den,' said the man, with a broad, benevolent smile. His accent was pure Earth Leading. 'My blessings to you and your team. What do we have here – an offering?'

Den bowed deeply, his hands joined in prayer. 'Father,' he said. 'We find this lot up in the mines. Get this. They say they *want* to come here.

They got data and claim the Moddies mean to harm us. Not sure if I believe.'

The head man turned to look them over. 'Intriguing,' he said. 'Is this the case?'

'We're on the run from the New Luxor authorities,' said Venetia. 'Or should I say the Frontier Protection Party. They're trying to hold us here to stop us getting back to our ship. We have evidence of a plan to attack Earth with alien weapons. Those same weapons are on their way here right now. They don't want anyone in the sects to know – your settlement included.'

The head man listened patiently, his smile never diminishing.

'Fascinating,' he said. His eyes twinkled. 'And why are you so keen that we should know this?'

'We're not Fleet,' said Venetia. 'We were on a diplomatic mission run by Yunus Chesterford and supported by the government of Earth.'

The head man quirked an eyebrow. '*The* Yunus Chesterford?'

Venetia nodded.

The head man turned to Den. 'Blessings be on you and your team, Dennis Ochoa,' he said. 'You have done well. The Lord is pleased with your diligence and attention to duty.'

The collars of everyone on Den's team chimed several times. There were whoops and cheers all round.

'Kal found them,' said Den. 'And he kept that itchy finger of his off the trigger like you told him.'

'Then Kal is particularly blessed,' said the head man.

Kal's collar chimed again. He beamed.

'Don't spend God's bounty all at once,' the head man told them with a knowing smile. 'Remember, the Lord adores celebration in his name, but not when it interferes with your health. There is such a thing as too much pleasure.'

'Yes, Father!' said Den, grinning. 'You got it. No messing.' He gestured at the others. 'Okay, you lot. Sleds back to the dock.'

Den and his team jumped onto their carts, leaving Mark and the others standing in front of the white villa with the head man. The only other people around were the malnourished children with blotchy faces watching them from the street corners.

'Good morning. I'm Massimo Singh,' said the head man. 'Nice to

362

meet you all, and welcome to Britehaven. I can't remember the last time I had civilised company out here.'

He gestured towards the door. 'Can I offer you breakfast?'

15.2: WILL

The shuttle fell relentlessly towards Snakepit and Will couldn't do a damned thing about it. The shuttle lacked even the most rudimentary self-repair robots. Short of climbing outside himself and fixing it, they were stuck, and Will wasn't sure even his abilities stretched quite that far. It galled him. It would take them hours to reach the planet – plenty of time for him to reflect on his folly. Had he headed straight for the *Chiyome*, they'd have been safely docked by now.

He lay sprawled in his couch while the shuttle rocked from wave after wave of blasts. Then, abruptly, the impacts stopped.

'What happened?' said Ann. 'Why has it all gone quiet?'

Will scanned the surrounding space. To his surprise, the Nems appeared to have just kissed and made up. They'd gone from fighting to swarming cooperatively within seconds.

'Apparently civil wars don't last long around here,' he said.

As he watched, the drone swarm changed from a random churn to directed motion, all pointed towards the remaining raspberry ship which was still trying to track down Pari's station. The Nems fanned out, adopting a search configuration. That couldn't be good news for the League. Eventually the drones would get over their stupidity and try swapping their swarming protocol. When that happened, the League ships would become instant targets.

The swarm changed their broadcast. Will piped it into the cabin.

'Human friends!' said the swarm. 'There is no need to hide. We know you are here. We wish you no harm. We only want to give you the gift of happy incorporation! Show yourselves and let us grant you eternal usefulness! You will be located eventually. Why not spare yourselves the discomfort of waiting and enjoy peace now?'

Sooner or later those eerie bastards were actually going to come up with an offer that sounded appealing, Will thought. He hoped to be long gone by then.

'Can they see us?' said Ann.

'I don't think so,' said Will. 'They're trying to infiltrate our systems, but they can't hack any better than a five-year-old so I'm not worried on that count.'

Will checked his link to the *Ariel Two*. He could still feel the ship through what remained of the shuttle's sensor array but Nelson still had the power out. And even if he could request an extra shuttle, the moment he did so he'd be telling both the League and the Nems exactly where to find him.

Ironically, their best hope lay in the several hundred pieces of drone shrapnel from the impromptu war falling alongside them. They slid towards the planet in long leisurely arcs. Under the circumstances, he would have been worried about the prospect of chance collisions. As it was, the fallout from the war just made them one more piece of broken technology drifting through the void. They might be out of control and plunging to their deaths on the most dangerous world humanity had ever discovered, but at least they had one thing going for them.

Will stopped trying to minimise their spin. They were less obvious while tumbling like a dead thing and there'd be plenty of opportunities to regularise their flight when they neared atmosphere. What he needed to do, he reasoned, was make the best use of the window of quiet he'd been granted and heal. It also gave him a chance to figure out why he had company.

He hooked his vision to the camera above Ann's crash couch.

'Tell me why you're here,' he said.

Ann stared at the camera with an expression of steel-edged disappointment. The fact that he'd landed them in this mess clearly rankled her.

'Because you were right. The League plan is unravelling. The machines are changing too fast. After you told me about the cells in the bioblocker I did a little research of my own. Sam Shah set this project up to fail from the start. He wants Earth dead, and I did *not* sign up for that. So I thought, why not get out of here with Will and try to apologise to him? Could that possibly be any worse? Apparently, though, the answer was *yes*.'

'So why *did* you sign up, then?' said Will. 'This whole operation is about smacking Earth down, isn't it?'

She shook her head. 'Because the threat of war was real. Something had to be done and this was the only option we could find. I've been working against genocide this entire time. My first tour of duty on the New Frontier made me sick. I went away and built my models because I knew the peace between the colonies and the sects couldn't last. The Fleet was burning too much of its energy enforcing it. I wanted to do something.'

'If you were looking for a way to help, throwing your time at a bunch of simulations was a funny way of showing it,' said Will. 'Models don't save lives.'

'I beg to differ,' Ann snapped. 'After you've spent years *trying* to break a model like that and keep seeing the same answer, you eventually get the message. We both know what's coming, and it's very simple. The colonies can't afford to give up control of the New Frontier, and Earth can't stand by and let them take it. And if war comes, the first consequence will be a massacre of Flags everywhere. It'll be worse than the anti-Muslim horrors in the twenty-first century. This time, though, it won't be one world shamed by violence, it'll be all of them. Then will come the retaliation—'

'I get it,' said Will.

'Do you?' said Ann. 'I presented my findings to the Fleet but they didn't like what I had to say. Nobody paid any attention except the League. I was tearing my hair out before Senator Voss approached me. What would you have done?'

'For starters I wouldn't have fucked about with alien technology I didn't understand,' said Will. 'You people should have come to me the moment you found this place.'

Will felt guilty for throwing accusations at her even as he did so but couldn't stop himself. Pari had made it very clear why the League existed. He still felt the wound of Ann's betrayal. She deserved to hear it.

'And said what?' said Ann. 'Weren't you already trying to avert a war? How were you going to help, exactly? Earth's sects hate you. They always have. That's despite you handing them limitless energy, new technologies and the rights to unfettered planetary habitation on the worlds of their choice. They kept hating you because if they'd won the war, they'd have gained those things anyway without having to say thank you or share them. Short of simply killing their entire leadership, what exactly were you going to do? In case you hadn't noticed, it's a lot easier to end a war with a big stick than it is to stop one starting in the first place. You proved that with the *Ariel Two*. We didn't come to you because you had nothing we could use except a talent for political optimism that had already screwed things up.'

Will glared through the camera and hated that she was right.

'I could have warned you what you were getting into,' he said at last. 'I could have helped you do a better fucking job.'

'Do you really believe that?' said Ann. 'You've changed, Will. Everything I said to you at Triton was true. I *did* watch you on that mission to the Transcended. You *did* shape my career. I remember you back then, trying to make contact over and over again. You never noticed me, but I felt your despair. You were a different man then, Will Monet. Somewhere between then and now, you gave up being flexible. Maybe that's what being superhuman does to a person. It makes you expect to get your way by force. That's why the League didn't want to touch you. Because you were wedded to your agenda and they knew they'd never change your mind. They'd have lost all control the moment they opened their mouths.'

Will put his face in his hands. He shouldn't have started baiting her. She'd only reaffirmed what Pari had already spelled out. Apparently his political irrelevance had been obvious to everyone but himself.

'Just because I was pushing didn't mean I wouldn't listen,' he said. 'I watched Gustav die. I held my friend while the blood ran out of him. I thought the whole government was going to come apart. Someone had to hold it together. And the people I was dealing with didn't respect you unless you pushed, so I've been pushing ever since. I had to.'

'Bullshit,' said Ann. 'There's always a choice. You believed that once. Maybe you should try it again.'

Her words stung him. 'If there's always a choice, why did you screw me over when I trusted you?'

Ann looked away from the camera. 'Touché,' she said quietly.

They lapsed back into silence. Will sullenly busied himself prepping the shuttle's failing systems for the inevitable crash-landing.

When they finally hit atmosphere, Will used what thruster control they had left to level out their spin. They still plummeted through the sky like a rock. Over the course of a few short minutes, the silence of space gave way to the roaring judder of re-entry. Will automatically compensated for the hammering the shuttle was taking as the atmosphere bludgeoned them. He watched Ann struggle. Their descent would have inflicted a concussion on any normal person but Ann's Fleet augs gave her the strength to hold on. She lay white-faced in her couch as pieces rattled off the shuttle into the screaming air. To Will's mind, she would have been better off unconscious.

They raced over continents of tangled bio-tubing to a dark, flat ocean splattered with scarlet algal mats. Will used the shuttle's remaining thrust to flatten out their dive and give them a shallow enough approach to survive. For a few brief minutes, the shuttle hit eight gees. Ann groaned.

Then, with a smack like a prizefighter's fist, they hit water and bounced. Then again. And another five times in a row.

The shuttle finally skidded across the ocean in gouts of steam, its emergency floats kicking in like crash-bags in a transit pod. Will and Ann lay back in their couches and sucked air while the ocean undulated wildly around them. The shuttle creaked and groaned like a collapsing building.

'Nice landing,' Ann croaked.

Will wasn't sure whether she was being ironic or not.

He checked the exterior cameras. Ocean surrounded them to the horizon in every direction. A deep blue sky hung overhead carrying weird, angry-looking bands of icy cloud – a testament to the atmospheric havoc the Nems had wreaked in some other part of the globe.

That was another thing they had going for them, Will thought. They might be trapped inside a dead shuttle in the middle of an ocean on a toxic world, but at least they hadn't landed in a radioactive hurricane.

'I'm sorry,' he said. 'Sorry I went for the *Ariel Two*. And sorry I shouted at you back there. Discovering that your entire life is a lie is... upsetting.'

Ann wiped her brow with a trembling hand. 'Me too. If we'd told you sooner, we wouldn't be in this mess. For what it's worth, I hated every minute of it. It's the worst thing I ever had to do. The League baited you, you know. They deliberately kept you angry to make you easier to control. That was unforgivable. I'm ashamed I was a part of it. We should have put all that effort into talking to you instead.' She looked up into his camera with a weak smile.

Will was glad she couldn't see his face properly. He was still processing some of his emotions.

'Emergency crash beacon activated,' said the shuttle calmly.

Will jerked out of his reverie. 'Deactivate beacon.'

'Cannot comply. Emergency beacon activation is irreversible.'

'No, it's not,' Will shouted. 'Cut the power.'

At the same time, he reached for the beacon circuit's blueprint. As he scanned it, his hopes sank. The device ran on a sealed circuit, feeding off its own isotope store.

'Shit!'

'Can't you stop it manually?' said Ann.

'It's between the nuclear engine mountings. I'm strong, but not that strong. I'd have to rip through half the shuttle without blowing us up.'

'That's bad,' said Ann. 'If the League doesn't spot that thing, the Nems will. Any chance you could subvert the *Ariel Two* and send us some help?'

'From down here and with their power cut, not a chance.'

'In that case we need to get out of here. As fast as we can.'

Will regarded her incredulously. 'What, we *swim* to safety?'

'We can't,' she said. 'You don't want to try swimming in this ocean. Believe me. But we need to get out of this shuttle. Do we have any thrusters left?'

'A few. Nowhere near enough power for a take-off, though.'

'We don't need to do that,' said Ann. 'We can use the juice to cross the water to land. We'll have to chance it that far.'

She tapped the screen in front of her, bringing up a map of the ocean, and pointed to a marked point about a hundred and fifty klicks away.

'That's the nearest science station. They'll have craft there we can borrow. We make for the coast here,' she said, moving her finger. 'There's an access port we can use. That's less than a hundred klicks north-east. Then we head inland on foot and put as much distance between us and the beacon as we can. If we can get off this crate, we have a chance.'

'You're suggesting we go overland?' said Will. 'Is that safe?'

'It's safer than sitting in here, if that's what you mean,' said Ann. 'I've hiked the surface as well as the tunnel system and we're nowhere near a defensive node. The biome around here is designed to support life, not attack it.'

'Okay, land it is,' he said. 'Does that continent have a name?'

'Three,' said Ann.

'Love that League imagination.'

He fired up the shuttle's thrusters.

The craft dipped forward abruptly, swung upward, and finally started off in the right direction. Will slowly piled on what power he had until they were sliding through the waves at an acceptable clip.

For the next hour, the sea had nothing much to offer them except sluggish waves, rafts of algal scum and pockets of weirdly effervescent water where streams of bubbles surfaced. No bombs dropped. No lances of energy appeared from the sky to vaporise them. And for those little things, Will felt grateful.

Eventually, a black sliver of land appeared on the horizon. During the minutes that followed it grew into a coastline made entirely of overlapping tubes. It looked like a cross between a chemical works and a mangrove swamp, all the colour of soot. The tubes were as wide around as the twenty-lane mass-transit pipes on Mars – larger than Will had expected from a distance. Where they sloped down to meet the water they reminded him of rippled lava fields. Their arched backs were lined with stiff ash-coloured grass. The gaps between them had been filled with pockets of brightly coloured fungi like something out of a fever-dream, interspersed with charcoal-grey ferns.

As they nosed up to the shore, Ann scrambled out of her couch and clambered down the tube to the airlock. Will followed, noting as he went that the airlock interface was a mess of red warning lights.

'Be careful,' he warned her. 'The exterior hatch is breached.'

She shot him an anxious look. 'You're kidding,' she said.

'What's the problem?' asked Will. 'I thought you said the biome is safe.'

'It is,' said Ann. 'For me.'

Will opened the inner hatch. Ann climbed through and paused to take in the smashed, waterlogged remains of the emergency suit locker. She groaned.

'There goes our best defence against an immune-response bomb,' she said.

'An immune *what*?' said Will.

'Like the bioblocker release up on the station, only a thousand times less pleasant,' said Ann. 'The Will-Monet-themed nuclear option. You don't want to meet one.'

She hit the manual release on the scarred remains of the outer hatch and stepped out onto the slightly submerged wing, surrounded by slowly deflating airbags.

Will followed nervously. The air on the other side felt thin but surprisingly fresh, with a gentle bite of mould. He carefully sampled the air for microorganisms, prepping his lungs for another assault. None came. The life carried on the breeze was even more complex than the kind he'd seen aboard Pari's station but appeared to hold no antagonistic intent.

Ann peered up at the sky and scowled. 'I'll never get used to the open sky,' she said. 'It's not natural.' She turned to scrutinise him. 'You feeling okay? The air all right?'

Will nodded. 'This place is weird,' he said, glancing around. 'Not like anywhere I've been before.'

'You ain't seen nothin' yet,' said Ann.

She sloshed out to the tip of the wing and leapt gingerly onto the back of the nearest tube, grabbing the grass as she landed. Will leapt, flea-like, arriving beside her with dry feet. The rumpled surface felt surprisingly warm under Will's boots given the chill of the air. Up close, the grass looked coarse and artificial with an iridescent sheen.

'I wouldn't leap about like that,' she said, frowning. 'Save your strength.'

Will gave her a long stare. Ann knew something she wasn't saying.

She led the way carefully up the pipe to a ceramic Fleet-issue boarding-lock sunk into the ground and glued in place with some kind of resin. She stood beside it, a grim look in her eye.

'Okay, here's the bad news,' she said. 'Without suits, there are two ways we can do this and you're not going to like either of them. Option one, we cover the terrain on the surface. We'll move faster that way but the League will probably be able to get a visual fix on us. If they do that, we're dead. I assure you that they'll fire at us the moment they think it's safe to do so.'

He eyed her uncertainly. 'I find it hard to believe Pari would do that,' he said. 'Even now.'

'Pari might not, but Jaco Brinsen definitely will, even if he has to go around her to achieve it. And he has command of the *Chiyome*, remember. If necessary, he'll resort to a boser.'

Will wrinkled his nose. 'You're kidding.'

'The League have two kinds of model for you, Will. Those where you get on board with their plan and those where you don't. If you don't, then you and the *Ariel Two* remain a one-man interstellar superpower and it's you or them. The way they see it, they *have* to take you out. The only reason we're still standing is because the Nems must be keeping them busy.'

'What's option two?'

'We go inside. We'll make slower progress in the tunnels but the League won't be able to track us. The downside is that the planet will want to scope you out.'

'More bioblocker?'

Ann shook her head. 'It's not nearly so bad, but it's not pretty, either. When normal people go down there, they get sick at first and then they get better. Sometimes a lot better. The planet does threat assessment on their biology and then lets them go. But for some reason, Will, this planet doesn't like your smart-cells. I've seen the test results.' She looked anxious.

'What happens?'

'The biome just keeps interacting with your tissue,' she said. 'Never invasively, but it doesn't stop. Eventually, in every test we ran, your cells died.'

Will peered at her, trying to assess the risks. He could achieve a lot more as a complete entity than his cells could manage on their own. He had to hope that counted for something.

'After how long?'

'Even for a tiny sample, it takes hours,' said Ann. 'And that might be enough for us to get where we need to go. But I'm telling you, it won't be fun in there. I think it's our best shot, but there's no way I'm stepping inside unless you're ready.'

'I don't think we have a choice,' said Will. 'Lead on.'

15.3: MARK

Massimo led them into his house. Servants in white smocks with shaven heads manually closed the door behind them.

The interior looked surprisingly modern and spacious, if ecclesiastical in tone. A lounge area with low couches and white carpet lay to their left. The far wall-screen showed slowly alternating panoramic landscapes of the famous biosphere worlds. Ahead of them, through another arch, Mark could make out what appeared to be a study area. But instead of robots, Massimo had people – all young and androgynous in appearance.

Two of them moved quietly around the lounge, dusting the surfaces. Another pair stood by the wall, simply waiting for instructions. They all wore matching smart-collars. The sight of them gave Mark the creeps. The submissive way they crept about smacked of the worst elements of Triton society.

Massimo stripped off his long gloves and tossed them to the nearest servant.

'I hate wearing this stuff,' he confided. 'Part of the job, I suppose. And more fun than skin cancer.' He threw his hat to a willowy teenager who caught it with one hand. 'Don't worry. You can relax in here. The walls are properly shielded and the house has its own air filters.' He shucked off his long white coat, revealing relatively normal T-shirt and sweats underneath, also white. 'The next shipment should bring better shielding,' he told them. 'When we finally move into the new tower, I won't have to wear this crap all the time. The whole place will be properly rad-blocked. I can't wait.' He slumped down on a tall chair set against the wall to swap his formal trainers for flip-flops.

Mark watched their host's casual behaviour and wasn't sure how to feel. The man looked genuinely pleased to see them and something about the way he carried on felt normal. Except the transition from death threats to houseguests had been too abrupt, and the context was too strange. He couldn't shake the feeling that somehow they were still seconds away from being shot.

Massimo surveyed the three of them with a private smile.

'You all look uncomfortable. I can understand why. The trip out here was probably pretty jarring. Still, you can relax now – if you want to, of course. Let's have something to eat.'

He led them to a doorway on the right. Servants opened it for them, revealing a sunny dining room with a single place set. More bald servants entered from what looked like a manually run kitchen, carrying plates for the rest of them. Through the open door came a strong smell of cooking. Mark's stomach roared at him loud enough to solicit an amused glance from Massimo.

'Hungry, then?' he said. 'That's good. Don't worry, by the way. The food here's all good. It's not the stuff we give the Following outside. This house has its own fab, and a little farm in the basement for organics.'

Mark and the others awkwardly took their places on the hand-carved dining chairs.

Food arrived. Plates and plates of it. Toast, prote-scramble with fresh herbs, sizzled strips of artfully printed makeon, coffee, fresh fruit. Even if the whole thing was a trap, Mark had lost the ability to resist. He'd never tasted anything so good. Since arriving on Carter he'd eaten nothing except some fragments of an emergency ration bar aboard the raft and a couple of mouthfuls of hideous-tasting water from the tunnels, which Venetia had insisted was safe.

Massimo watched as they devoured the breakfast before them and asked no questions except ones pertaining to the meal.

'Did you try the orange juice?' he said. 'You should. I have my own orange vines running downstairs. I make sure that one of them's always in season.'

Mark wondered whether most hostages got the same treatment. He suspected not.

'Thank you for taking us in,' he said carefully. 'We're all a little fried right now. We didn't expect to be on Carter for more than a couple of hours – that was nearly a day ago.'

Massimo winced. 'I'm sorry. That sounds awful. And *Carter*, of all places. Not the greatest world to get stuck on.'

'I'm also from Earth, by the way,' said Mark, relaxing a little.

'Really!' said Massimo. 'I did wonder. Well, you're especially welcome here, in that case. I can't help noticing you're wearing a Fleet ship-suit, though. How come?'

'I'm a roboteer,' said Mark. 'I fly starships. They asked me to captain this mission for them.'

'My goodness!' said Massimo. 'That makes you a very rare bird, then. Your parents must be Transcendists. Good for them. We're all Revivalists here, of course, but I won't hold that against you.' He winked. 'And you ladies?'

'Parents from Earth. Raised on New Angeles,' said Zoe. She sounded reluctant to open up.

'From Esalen originally,' said Venetia. 'I work all over the place these days. I worked here for a while.'

'Poor you!' said Massimo, laughing. He slapped the table. 'I'm sorry,' he said. 'You'll have to excuse my enthusiasm. It's just I don't often get the chance to host guests, unless it's my cousins from the other side of the ocean. And frankly, I find them dull. As for you three, well, you're practically celebrities if you fly with Yunus Chesterford. I watch all his feeds. You'll have to tell me what he's doing these days.'

Mark and Zoe exchanged nervous glances.

'It's often lonely being the voice of authority in a place like this,' said Massimo. 'It's a family responsibility, a duty I have to undertake. Thankfully only for a few years, then it's back to Ganymede, thank God. So, do you want to explain how you got here? Give me the big picture.'

Mark and Venetia started speaking at the same time and both stopped.

'You talk this time,' said Venetia. 'You've got the most up-to-date information, in any case.'

Mark did his best to fill Massimo in on the highlights of their experiences. Their host looked deeply disappointed when Mark gently informed him of Yunus's death but didn't interrupt. Mark finished by dwelling for several minutes on the nature of the threat following them, to make sure Massimo understood what they were dealing with.

'If we can't get word to New Panama, the machines will overrun this place,' he explained. 'Every sign of life will be scoured. And after that they'll head for Earth.'

Massimo listened with a grave expression. 'My goodness. That is a truly extraordinary story, and a frightening one.'

'And I can't understate just how devious Sam is,' Mark added. 'He duped us all. With him helping the colonists, there's no telling what they'll try to do to get us back. I hate to say it, but your whole settlement should start taking precautions immediately.'

'Then action must be swift,' said Massimo. He clicked his fingers.

One of the bald servants scurried over and bowed near Massimo's ear. Massimo turned and spoke quietly. The servant nodded and hurried out.

'It's imperative that I verify your story before we take next steps, of course, but I just started that process. The idea of an attack on the sects via a proxy weapon comes as no surprise to me. I'd heard stories of experimental Freedom Camps vanishing. Nothing direct, of course. The existence of such projects would never be readily broadcast – the loss of face in the case of failure would be unacceptable. This development, though, takes the Frontier problem to a whole new level. But perhaps we should have expected it. It was only a matter of time before the balance of power finally tipped towards Revivalism. Of *course* the Old Colonies are reacting with panic. Violence was inevitable. Their stranglehold on the future is finally loosening.'

Zoe shifted uncomfortably in her chair, setting down her fork with a clunk.

'You disagree?' said Massimo. 'The Old Colonies have been losing political ground for the last twenty years. The Fleet is their puppet and now that puppet is so old and overstretched it can barely do its job. Which leads me to a question I've been waiting to ask someone for three years, ever since I was posted here. What do you think of all this?' He gestured at the walls around him. 'Not my house, but all of this – the Britehaven settlement. I know what the people up in the valley think – they hate us and everything we represent. That's clear from the way they try to choke off our existence. But that's because we claimed land they imagined they had all to themselves. An entire planet, just for a few tens of thousands of people. Crazy, wouldn't you say? And so selfish. But this is beside the point. You aren't bigots from the valley. You're from more civilised worlds. So please be honest. What do you think of our settlement?'

Zoe's mouth remained shut. Mark checked Venetia with a glance and saw uncertainty there. He didn't know what to say. Was this when the guns came back out? Massimo expected a reply.

'Your house is nice,' said Mark, hating his own vagueness.

Massimo looked disappointed.

'I think the seals and shielding outside could be better,' Mark added. After Massimo's own comments, this felt like a safe enough statement.

'I completely agree!' said Massimo, slapping the table. 'What else?'

'You use exosuits,' said Mark. 'That surprised me.'

'Of course, to create work for the Following. Please, more of your reactions.'

A chilly silence descended over the breakfast table as the delicate-boned servants cleared away their plates.

'If you really want to know,' said Venetia, 'I think the religion game is a poor choice. Educational games are free and effective. If you want to give your Following something to think about, why not use them instead?'

'Well said!' Massimo clapped at her. 'Thank you for your courage. I differ from you on the relative value of such things, of course, but these are exactly the sort of observations I was looking to solicit. I can see how you all want to be polite and I appreciate that – you're in someone else's home, after all. So let me tell you what I think you see when you look around here. Maybe that will loosen things up a bit.

'For starters, my people are poor. That much is obvious, isn't it? They're penniless. The dome is terrible and the air is shit. It costs so much to ship these people here that there's barely enough money left over to give them a decent life. Their food is shit, too. It's habit-forming garbage. And their skin. Did you see it? Half of them have cancer. We restock our surgery every month and still keep running out of cure-kits. This is despite the fact that I'm *always* reminding them in sermon to wear sunscreen. We barely cling to the surface of this planet, my friends. Religion and distraction are the only things holding this society together. We live on what we can beg or steal from New Luxor, and that is *pitiful*.'

Mark watched Zoe squirming in her chair. Finally she snapped.

'I don't see how you can feel so proud about it,' she said. 'Your family and others like you are making billions of peace-coin every year. Billions. You could invest more in these people. Give them proper houses. You've dragged them across the galaxy to use them as property markers in a cynical land grab to squeeze political concessions out of IPSO. And meanwhile your families are rolling in money on private worlds, surrounded by drug-addled harem girls.'

Mark held his breath. Venetia shut her eyes. Zoe had spoken with vitriol and said what they were all thinking. If Massimo wanted to kill them, it was going to happen now.

He pointed at Zoe and grinned. 'That's right!' he said. 'There you have it!' He looked delighted. 'Well done, young lady. You've put your finger on it.' He banged the table again several times. 'Please understand – I have this conversation with myself every week. I always wonder how it looks from the other side of the table, but I can never sit down with those people and talk. It is so rewarding to be able to *speak* about it at last. And this is the point that I think people in the Old Colonies don't see.'

He leaned forward, his eyes gleaming. He didn't look all that worried about an impending alien attack, Mark noticed. That disturbed him, but he wasn't about to interrupt Massimo now.

Massimo rested on his massive elbows and held two fingers close together.

'In our society, there are two ideologies at war with each other. And this is what fascinates me – that people don't even appear to notice. They inhabit their little bubbles of propaganda. One of those ideologies is religious feudalism, built from what is left of Truism and the Kingdom of Man. The other is robot-powered capitalism, imported from Galatea. It's like the American north versus the south all over again. Except the difference this time is that instead of freeing the slaves, the Galatean solution is to kill them all. In the clean and tidy new capitalism, there are no factories to shove people into. Because of robotics, there is nothing for them to do but die. Hence the inevitability of this attack you describe. You Colonials seem to wonder at Earth's distinction of rich and poor, but this is hypocrisy. The Old Colonies want the poor to disappear just the same way farm animals did after the Surplus Age.'

'Actually,' said Zoe, 'the hope is that they'll stop being poor.'

Massimo threw up his hands. 'But there will *always* be a poor! A system that doesn't make good use of the poor is a system that destroys itself. Of all the differences between the sects, that is one thing we can all agree on – the one truth that Truism made clear. That there should be a separation of concerns in human society. This is what the twenty-first century proved. Global equality is a sick dream. It strips those with power of the responsibility that comes with wielding it. Think of what the superbanks did, and the Martians after them. A fixed Leading caste is what enables large, complex societies to stabilise, whether people want to admit it to themselves or not. This has always been true, throughout history.'

Massimo gestured at himself. 'You look at our sects and see squabbling. What we see is healthy competition between the Great Houses of Earth. You see poverty in the Following. We see responsible leadership finding a way to make the poor *useful*. In this generation they serve as property markers. In the next, they will serve some other, equally valid purpose.'

'You're deciding who gets to be rich and who gets to be poor,' said Zoe, the anger in her eyes unchanged.

'As societies have always done,' said Massimo. 'And the poor are helping us do it. The Following don't *want* complicated answers. They want simple entertainment and simple moral standards they can understand. The people who want to force ambiguity onto them are always doing so for their own ends, just like the capitalists of old. So far as the Following are concerned, it's the Galateans who are the problem. They haven't lifted a finger to get people off Earth, whereas the sects help them at every turn.'

'Wait,' said Mark, whose discomfort had been growing steadily. 'What about the Exodus projects? Or the lottery? Or all the other IPSO programmes?'

'A bureaucratic nightmare,' said Massimo. 'Since when did desperate people have time to fill out forms or pass tests?'

'The IPSO education programmes are free,' Venetia pointed out.

'So are ours,' said Massimo. 'You indoctrinate with science. We do so with religion. The difference being that religion is immediately relevant and rewarding. What hope does a peasant with a free science education have on Galatea? He is surrounded by geniuses whose parents paid for their brains to be twice the size of his.'

Mark glanced at Zoe and saw the fury smouldering behind her eyes get brighter.

'You give people the chance of a job at the cost of their culture,' said Massimo. 'We give people the *guarantee* of a job and *elevate* their culture. We take their oldest, most sacred beliefs and we cherish them.' He leaned back from the table, apparently pleased with himself.

Venetia folded the snow-coloured napkin in front of her into eighths.

'You've been a very gracious host,' she said. 'I hope you won't mind if I disagree.'

'Are you kidding?' said Massimo. 'Go for it!'

'You should know I'm no fan of Old Colony politics,' she said, 'and I was picked for this mission by the Free Movement faction in the senate. But some of the things you're saying are just wrong. For starters, the bureaucratic nightmare around education that you refer to was engineered by Earth's senators, themselves from sect families. You also appear to assume that financial exploitation is guaranteed by commerce, but that's incorrect. It's guaranteed only by monopolies of vested interests. The programmes the sects have embarked on aren't creating a stable future for the poor. They're creating human cattle, and that can only end in disaster.

'I have studied and understand the cultural tools you use here. Most of them were discovered on Esalen, where I was born. Your Great Houses have simply combined those findings with data-science and used them for profit. You've taken a natural human need for spiritual direction and weaponised it. You're right that some people will always be poorer than others, but nobody needs to be degraded. There's only one excuse for oligarchy, and that's greed.'

Massimo threw his head back and laughed. He appeared to be loving every moment. Why shouldn't he? Mark thought. Captive entertainment had been delivered right to his well-armed doorstep.

'Go outside and ask!' said Massimo. 'Ask my Following if they feel degraded. They will tell you that they have been *honoured by God*! They will assure you that they are fulfilled here. Show me *one* immigrant up in the valley who can say that. You want to force *your* culture on people and make them feel small,' he declared. 'You want this so that you can satisfy your own comfortable notions of equality and justify your own wealth relative to theirs. We, at least, acknowledge that life's answer for one person is not the same as it is for another.'

A feeling of sick discomfort churned around in Mark's chest. He felt no safer in Massimo's house now than he had the moment he'd arrived, yet he couldn't help but open his mouth.

'I'd like to remind you that not everyone on Earth shares your opinions,' he said.

'Of course not,' said Massimo. 'Where did you live, my friend?'

'New York,' said Mark.

Massimo roared with laughter and thumped the table. '*That* den of Transcendists? Did you ever go to Mexico City? Bangalore? Chongqing?'

Mark shook his head.

'I thought not. You missed some sights, my friend. You missed Earth, in fact.'

He laughed long and hard. Mark felt both embarrassed and angry at once.

Eventually their host wiped the tears from his eyes and got to his feet. A thin servant quickly cleared away his napkin.

'My house has an annexe for when my cousins visit from the other settlements,' said Massimo. 'You can stay there until we get this situation sorted out. It has its own air and water, which you'd prefer, I think, and the seals are good.' He winked at Mark. 'I'll check on that story of yours.' He gestured at the waif standing closest. 'Five will show you to your rooms. Relax. Take a nap if you like. I'm sure you could use one.'

With that, Massimo scratched his belly and strode from the room.

'Would you like to follow me?' said Five in a soft alto voice with eyes averted.

'Certainly,' said Venetia. 'And I'm sorry for asking, but is this Ms Five or Mr Five I'm talking to?'

Five smiled and glanced up for a moment in amusement. 'We of the house relinquish gender when we take up service of the Lord. It is a great privilege. Five is my God-given name.'

'I see,' said Venetia. 'No distractions, I suppose.'

'Absolutely, madam,' said Five, stroking the smart-collar and smiling cryptically. 'Why would I want them?'

'And did you volunteer for that,' said Venetia, 'or were you selected?'

'Why, I *volunteered*, of course!' said Five, looking astonished. 'What kind of people do you take us for?' The servant giggled and gestured down the hallway. 'Please, this way.'

As they followed Five to the annexe, Mark felt a kind of despair settling over him. He rubbed his eyes. He hadn't really known what to expect from a Flag colony, but he'd never expected something so disappointing, or so intimately hideous.

Zoe punched him gently in the side. 'Hey, you,' she said. 'Snap out of it.'

'This isn't the Earth I know,' said Mark sadly. 'There are so many good people.'

'Of course there are, you idiot,' said Zoe. 'Billions of them.' She looked at him oddly, her head tilted to one side. 'Your desperate need for your homeworld to be okay is kind of sweet, you know that?' she said. 'Very stupid, but sweet.'

She kissed him on the cheek and disappeared into the room Five had opened for her. Mark blinked in astonishment. Venetia grinned at his amusement.

'Weren't expecting that? You should have been paying more attention.' She elbowed him in the ribs. 'Look on the bright side, Mark. Massimo thinks we're hilarious and we're not dead yet. It could be worse.'

15.4: SAM

Sam listened patiently to questions in yet another meeting about camouflage. The whole idea that Carter's evac-ark would be less visible when broadcasting a signal wasn't something the people of New Luxor could wrap their heads around. And the delays were getting scary.

'Exactly how accurate does signal reproduction have to be?' asked a woman in a brown utili-sari sitting in the front row. 'I mean, what happens if our transmitter equipment isn't as good as yours? Are we going to make ourselves more obvious than if we'd just dropped our albedo?'

Sam smiled blandly. The Nems could show up at any time now, and if they still had access to a target this size he'd have to move to the nuclear option. If they wasted one more hour of his time in meetings, he might just nuke them anyway.

As Sam nodded sagely and prepared to respond, a high-priority call-waiting icon from Keir Vorn appeared in the corner of his view. He held up a hand.

'I'm *so* sorry,' he told the woman in the front row. 'I have to take an urgent call – I do hope you'll excuse me.'

He strode from the meeting room to the study-space across the hall. 'What's up?'

'Now we know why my surveybots couldn't find your shipmates,' said Keir. 'The leader of our local Flag problem has them.'

Sam groaned . . . then checked himself. This was something he could use. He'd been fretting about the disappearance of Mark and the others since they vanished from the transit pod. The fact that they were out of his hair had been the only consolation. But now, if he played things right, they were someone else's problem. The Flags could take the blame if anything happened to them. Mark dead at the hands of religious fanatics would mesh quite nicely into his narrative.

'Stall him,' said Sam. 'I'll talk to him myself, but you need to give me a minute.'

Before allowing a connection, Sam checked Keir's database on the man calling – one Massimo Singh, apparently. Then he quickly assembled some data in readiness, culling content from the *Gulliver*'s logs.

When he was ready, he pinged Keir and got Singh on the video link. He sat down at the closest desk with a private camera.

Singh looked like a classic lower-echelon Leading wannabe. The sort that Earth families usually packed off to manage their ghastly little remote-ghettos. In Singh's case, he'd clearly spent too much money on muscle augs and not enough on diet pills.

'I have your friends,' said Singh. He sounded inordinately pleased with himself. 'Either you explain what's going on or you won't see them again. You should know that I've investigated their story. I see your ship and others manoeuvring in orbit so I know something is up. You can't hide it. And now I want you to tell me exactly what you're doing.'

Sam twisted his face into a furious sneer. 'I'm sorry,' he said, 'but what do you imagine is going on here?'

'A ruse to create panic, most likely,' said Singh, sounding amused. 'It's a clever story designed to convince me to evacuate my territory and beg the great, beneficent Fleet for help to leave. But in my experience, people faced with the kind of disaster your friends describe are seldom given warning. Particularly in such an approachable format. You should know that our claim is not going to be relinquished.'

'I'm glad you have them,' Sam growled. 'You can keep them – they've caused enough trouble already. We're getting the hell out of here. They can take what's coming to them.'

Massimo's smile drooped. 'Oh, really? You know, it'd be very easy for me to send a message drone to Earth. I wonder how this story would play out if the IPSO senate got hold of it.'

Sam glowered at him. 'Go ahead,' he said. 'Maybe your drone will beat ours there. You can even tell them you've got Will Monet's adopted son with you. See what good it does you. How do you think they're going to treat you when everyone discovers you're harbouring the son of the man who set this disaster loose? The man who kicked off humanity's first interspecies war. Do you have any idea how many people are likely to die because of what Monet did? Do you? And for what?' Sam sneered. 'To regain his place in the history books?' He shook his head in despair and let a hint of tears creep into the corners of his eyes. 'Those people you're hiding are Monet's creatures,' he said. 'They have good reason to hide.'

Singh looked thunderstruck.

'You don't believe me?' said Sam, knowing full well that he'd already won. 'Watch this.'

He passed Singh the data package he'd edited. It opened with footage of the *Ariel Two* firing on Tiwanaku amid a swarm of alien ships. He watched Singh's eyes go wide, and then widen some more.

'They think you'll spare them because we want to hold them accountable for their crimes,' said Sam. 'You decide. It's your problem now.'

'Wait,' said Singh. 'We need to discuss safe passage on your—'

Sam cut the link and chuckled to himself. Then he opened a channel to Keir Vorn.

'Be on high alert for messenger drones leaving from Flag satellites,' he said. 'Any and all drones should be intercepted and destroyed immediately. Our lives depend on it.'

'Consider it done,' said Keir.

Sam leaned back in his chair and smiled. That would give the Flag fucker something to think about. The Earthers had been wanting to paint Monet as a villain since the war. This should be right up their alley.

16: DESPAIR

16.1: WILL

The other side of the boarding lock had been left open. A ladder fixed against the side descended into a surprisingly warm and bright space below. Will had to squint against the glare as he climbed down. Chains of shining bioluminescent spheres hung on vines all around him, filling the air with a cool green-white light. Below them, basking in their glow, lay an indoor fairyland.

A pale, greasy substance that looked like tofu covered the interior walls of the tube. Where the walls curved in to form the floor lay a knee-high Technicolor forest of organisms that might have been plants, or fungi, or something in between. The dominant colours were deep reds and purples but Will could see the whole spectrum down there. A narrow stream ran along the bottom of the tube, giving the place the feeling of a small, enclosed river valley dreamed up by a mad painter.

The soft breeze that blew through the tunnel felt surprisingly moist and carried a musty scent, like a cross between soil and whisky. Creatures of some sort called to each other with high-pitched squeaks and clicks. Behind them Will could hear the trickle of the running water. The tube stretched away in either direction, nearly circular in cross section. It curved and bent until its undulations blocked further sight.

Will climbed down to the spongy floor beside Ann, took in the view and sneezed. Ann watched him nervously.

'It's started,' she said. 'Brace yourself. I recommend not trying to fight the planet. You'll only make it worse. The first visitors down here had antibacterial augs. It confused the hell out of the local flora and knocked those guys out for days.'

'Okay,' said Will uncertainly. 'I'm holding off.'

As he spoke, his throat constricted and a wave of disorientation overtook him. He fell to his knees while warning messages from his smart-cells crowded his sensorium. He kept his interior defences at the ready and dived through his body-map to monitor this new invasion at the micro-scale. He might not be putting up any resistance, but that didn't mean he shouldn't keep a close eye on it.

The microbes visiting his lungs and hands impressed him as much as they scared him. They were the same as the ones he'd encountered outside, but far more numerous here and more active in their intent. Will had a good idea what their problem was: they couldn't figure him out.

Since the Transcended changed Will from the inside, he'd had plenty of time to study what they'd done. They'd essentially added an extra nucleus to each cell in his body. Those nuclei didn't so much store information as process it. They doubled as factories designed to churn out biologically inert compounds engineered at the molecular scale. Unfortunately, the contents of Will's secondary nuclei never stopped updating. Any microbe trying to map the contents of his cells was likely to get very confused.

As he watched the tiny machines work, Will's own modifications started to look cheap by comparison. The Transcended had basically cobbled something together out of what was available in his own blood. It had seemed like magic to him at the time because he'd never known what good molecular engineering looked like. He did now. Being impressed didn't make him feel any less ill, though. The air here made him weaker than he'd felt at any time since the war. It scared him.

'Are you okay?' said Ann.

Will nodded and managed to stand upright. He'd left a patch of broken rainbow-hued foliage where he'd fallen. It looked like a piece of accidental expressionist art.

'I'm managing it,' he said.

She laid a hand on his shoulder. 'You let me know any time we need to stop.'

Will wasn't used to other people's sympathy. He peered up the tunnel rather than meet her gaze.

'So we just follow the tube?'

Ann nodded. 'There are joins we'll have to navigate, but the League keeps the routes from the access locks to the science stations marked. We just need to look for the green flags.' She pointed to a square of plastic dangling from a piece of stiff wire up ahead. 'Ready?'

Will nodded and let Ann lead the way along the bank of the stream, heading slightly uphill and away from the sea.

'So how come the life here doesn't want to instantly kill me like that stuff up on the station?' he said. His throat felt sore.

'Most of the life on this planet tries to support foreign organisms,' said Ann. 'That's one of the most amazing things about it. So long as you're not actively damaging the environment, the planet wants you to stay and participate. The complexity of the local organisms actually degrades around foreign tissue. It starts to mimic it.'

Will frowned. 'Why would it do that?'

'No idea,' said Ann. 'But that's how it works. The defensive nodes are different, though. They're basically the planet's immune system. They take foreign organisms apart before trying to work out how to emulate them. It's the shoot-first version of the same biology. Or that's how the research team explained it to me, anyway. When the League decided to develop a weapon that would work against you, they took defensive cells as their starting point.'

Will gazed around at the pale tunnel walls. It was, he thought, rather like walking through the belly of a sleeping dragon. It could kill them in an instant but apparently didn't want to. So what *did* it want? He glanced back at the trail of damaged vegetation behind them.

'If anyone comes after us it's going to be pretty obvious where we went.'

Ann shook her head. 'Don't worry about it – this stuff grows fast. Stand still for long enough and you can watch it. It makes kudzu look lazy.'

They walked for hours. Will couldn't remember having ever felt so weary. Thankfully the environment around them provided plenty of distraction. His unease about the native biology slowly gave way to outright awe as the magical grotto yielded an unending string of surprises.

At one point, the tunnel opened up into a vast junction like a grand ballroom filled with slanted columns and a meadow of scarlet mushrooms. A dozen tubes joined there, their mouths spilling out surreal life like Daliesque cornucopia. The lighting vines hung low in clumps, like organic chandeliers.

Later they found their way narrowed to a keyhole-shaped slot barely wide enough to walk through and waist-deep in magenta foam. Will's ship-suit rapidly became smeared with a plethora of different kinds of vegetable gunk.

Their path twisted as it rose, occasionally dipping to create deep pools of rose-tinted water where jellyfish-tadpole things wriggled. The League had bolted polymer filament bridges into the walls to act as crossings. Here and there, breaks between their tunnel and others passing above it resulted in tiny waterfalls surrounded by stands of mauve fern two metres tall.

Will had been to all the biosphere worlds and walked for dozens of kilometres through wild landscapes barely touched by man. Most of them looked the same. A bit of moss-analogue here, some lichen there, the odd weird stromatolite if you were lucky.

Snakepit resembled none of them. For starters, it was a truly indoor environment. On top of that, its diversity left Mars's rainforest parks in the dust. But Will felt something more: Snakepit felt *staged*, somehow. Despite their curving organic lines, the tunnels felt like acts of engineering, albeit of an incredibly subtle sort. The place felt too careful, and too controlled, to be completely natural. There was something about the moist, knee-high forest that looked deliberately bijou.

'This place is ... unusual,' he said.

'I know,' said Ann. 'The whole planet's covered with these tunnels about ten layers deep. And that tofu-soil stuff is farmable. The bioscience teams have grown everything in it from beans to lemongrass. It all tastes a bit weird, apparently, but it matures even faster than it does under supposedly ideal hydroponic conditions. Something about enforced symbiosis, I gather. There was a big debate after they found this place. The League had been looking for a military advantage, as you guessed. But when they found this, the investigation team almost rioted at the idea that they couldn't tell everyone back home. I mean, think about how many people could live down here?'

She gestured at the cavern before them and Will surveyed the blood-coloured meadow. If you lined both sides of the stream with ten-storey apartment blocks there would still be room for gardens.

'But the League couldn't afford to let IPSO know they'd been exploring off the books. That would have given the whole game away. And in any case, they knew there'd have been one hell of a fight over this place. Think about the money in patents alone that these tunnels represent.'

'So what changed?' said Will.

'The discovery of the defensive nodes,' said Ann darkly. 'Ironically, a lot of the investigation team died in the first attack. After people figured out how dangerous the place could be, they stopped talking about releasing data.'

'But this place was meant to be lived in,' said Will. 'That much is obvious. So where did all the original inhabitants go? I haven't seen anything bigger than a lizard this entire time.'

'The League position is that there never were any. The Transcended seeded this place some time after the Fecund extinction and left it for whichever race arose next – humanity, as it turns out. Our modelling SAPs all rated that as the most likely scenario.'

'I still don't buy it,' said Will. 'If that's true, why isn't this place recognising my smart-cells?'

'There are other theories,' said Ann.

'Such as?'

'Some people think the occupants transcended,' said Ann. 'They joined with whoever built the Penfield Lobe. And given the level of technology involved in this place, that feels like a real possibility. Then, after the first attack, a different theory gained a lot of traction. In that story, the builders lost control of their own synthetic biology. They got on the wrong side of their planet and it ate them.'

'Also plausible,' said Will.

'So far, there's no sign either way. Exactly who built this place is one of a huge pile of questions the League shoved in its *figure-it-out-after-the-war* pile.'

A wave of high-pitched chittering claimed Will's attention.

'Do you hear that?'

'Hear what?' said Ann, frowning.

A huge flock of tiny bird-analogues rounded the bend ahead of them, emitting twittering cries. The air darkened with the storm of their approaching wings. Will and Ann ducked and covered their faces against the sudden flood of bodies.

Will straightened as the birds sped past. 'What the hell was that about?'

Ann regarded him with concern. 'Our time's up,' she said. 'I've seen that before – when people bring ATVs in here it terrifies the local wildlife. Someone's coming.'

Will ramped up his hearing, listening for sounds hidden beneath the fading bird cries and the trickle of water. It took far more effort than it should have. All of his abilities had become dangerously muted. Nevertheless, he could still make out the distant whine of electric motors.

'My guess is they're about half a klick out,' he told Ann, 'and headed our way.'

'Then we backtrack, and fast. We passed a junction a few minutes ago – that'll have to do.' She turned around and started running.

Will hesitated. He felt too tired to flee. He'd followed Ann up to the point of exhaustion only to be discovered by Pari and her goons. That was about on par with how his luck had been running recently. Under any other conditions he might have been able to fight. Instead, he was as weak as a baby and ready for recapture.

Will experienced a fresh wave of doubt about Ann. Part of him wanted to stay put and smash whatever thugs they'd sent to bring him back, but he recognised that urge for foolishness even as it tempted him. He turned and forced himself to take off after Ann, cursing himself for agreeing to come this way.

He kept his senses at full extension as they hurried over the damp, uneven terrain. Hearing anything over the sound of his own wheezing represented a challenge, but the effort proved to be worth it when he picked out voices coming from the direction of the coast.

'We've got a problem,' he gasped. 'They're back this way as well. They've boxed us in.'

Ann stopped and Will took a moment to lean on his knees and suck air. Couldn't the damned biome just cut him some slack for a few minutes while they dealt with these assholes?

'The science stations have mini-lifters,' said Ann. 'They must have used one. I guess the people in that base care more about catching us than they do about hiding from the Nems.'

'Then they're idiots,' said Will.

'People often are,' said Ann.

'Any chance we can convince them to just fuck off?'

'Not much,' said Ann. She glanced around. 'There.'

She pointed to an opening high up on the left side of the tunnel where purple vegetation spilled out from a small oval hole. It looked like a kind of aborted junction, as if the tube had started to fuse with a neighbour only to change its mind. They'd seen dozens of them.

'*In there?*' he said incredulously. 'That wall's almost vertical and it's nearly four metres up. How are we supposed to reach it?'

'You give me a boost,' she said. 'Then I haul you up after me.'

'Presuming there's anywhere in there to hide,' said Will. 'How about I have a *word* with them instead?'

'Don't be stupid,' said Ann. 'You can hardly breathe and they'll be armed with bioblocker. You've escaped once. This time they won't hesitate to use it. Come on.'

She started off though the ferns for the tunnel wall, picking her way carefully amid the vegetation so as not to leave a trail. Will frowned and reluctantly followed.

When Ann could scramble no higher up the tunnel's steeply curving side, Will pushed her. Fortunately, wall-lining proved to be as dense as bone. Will had half-worried that they'd leave obvious streaks, but away from the moist floor, it hardened quickly. Ann scrabbled on the surface, found an edge and dragged herself up.

'It's perfect,' she said, disappearing inside. 'Wet, but perfect.'

A perfect trap, you mean, Will thought to himself.

He heard sloshing as she waded through some kind of liquid. She reached back down for him with an outstretched arm.

'You'll have to jump,' she said. 'Can you still jump?'

Will scowled as he scrabbled at the wall and tried to leap after her. With so much continual *investigation* happening inside his lungs, it wasn't easy. He stopped to catch his breath.

'Are you coming?' said Ann. 'Quick!'

'Freeze!' shouted a voice from behind them.

A bullet struck the tunnel wall beside him, leaving a sunburst of cracks from which pale fluid leaked. Will caught a whiff of vaporised bioblocker from the impact and coughed.

'That's it,' he said. 'They're pissing me off now.'

With a grunt that was half-anger and half-anticipation, Will turned and ran back down the slope towards the tunnel floor, gathering speed the whole time. Two men with bio-bullet smart-guns stood there, next to a pair of scramblerbot ATVs. He threw half his submind attention at the ongoing molecular tinkering in his lungs and skin and told it all to *stop*. His smart-cells began churning out protective membranes. The tunnel cells would subvert them, for sure, but he only needed a few minutes. He felt his extra abilities coming back online.

The men turned and aimed for him again, but by then Will had enough strength for a surge of speed.

Plastic bullets whizzed past as Will reached out through his interface to the scramblerbots, seizing them with a viral assault. The League had upped their security again, but not nearly far enough. Both vehicles started driving straight at their owners.

While the two soldiers struggled to avoid being run over, Will raced down to meet them. One of them brought their gun up just in time to fire. A bullet grazed Will's side. He threw cellular defences at the wound, numbing it instantly. He grabbed the gun as he streaked past, then turned and threw it straight at the second man's head. The soldier's neck cracked backwards at an unnatural angle. He fell beneath the wheels of his ATV, which gleefully reversed over him.

Will tripped and rolled, giving the remaining man time to pull a stim-stick from his belt. As he slashed the air with it, Will leapt out of range but slipped on the crushed vegetation. His edge was fading already. It had taken just seconds. Deep inside him, the Snakepit microbes were urgently dismantling his defences. Will turned the slip into a kick as the man dived, flipping the stim-stick out of his hand and high into the air. He caught it as the soldier staggered forwards, then hurled it like a knife through his visor. Plastic shattered. The soldier dropped.

As Will staggered to his feet, more bullets clipped through the vegetation on either side of him. The other group had arrived. Two more men on ATVs were bearing down on him, fast. Will snatched up a smart-gun to fire back but the trigger was ID-wired. It did nothing in his hand except complain. Will lacked the time to hack it so he hurled it like a spear instead, knocking one of the soldiers off his bike. The throw had a tiny fraction of the power Will was used to. He stumbled again, his head spinning as his vision started to cloud from the sides.

As he knelt there gasping, the last soldier aimed and fired. Before Will could move, someone threw him sideways – Ann. He hadn't even noticed her running to his aid. She cried out as they tumbled together, jolting to one side. She'd been hit.

Will turned their tumble into a roll, aiming for the first soldier he'd taken out. He grabbed the stim-stick from the dead man's belt as he passed and sat up, channelling the last of his energy. By then the final soldier was jogging towards him, ready to fire again. Will hurled the stim-stick into his exposed neck with every gram of power left in his body. The soldier froze, astonished, with the stim-stick protruding from his throat before toppling forwards into the smeared fungus.

Will almost passed out then – only the microbial warnings screaming into his mind from every part of his body kept him awake. It took him five minutes of lying still on the ground just to get his limbs to work again. By then, the frenzy of cellular activity inside him had returned to a manageable level of churn.

He sat up and found himself covered in blood. Some of it was his. A lot of it was Ann's. There was an ugly hole in her abdomen. She looked up at him with a face like death.

'We need to get back to that alcove,' she breathed. 'More of them will be coming. We need to disappear.'

16.2: MARK

After a nap, a long, hot shower and some confused thinking about Zoe, Mark made his way back to the lounge. His skin tingled like something new. He hadn't felt so clean since they left Triton. As he walked along the hall, the servants stopped polishing and moved silently back to stand at the walls.

'Please don't mind me,' he told them.

They smiled at him coyly but didn't move from their places. The servants made Mark's skin crawl. He'd met plenty of people on Mars and New Panama who'd chosen intergender lifestyles of one sort or another, but Massimo's attendants were something different. Their creepy submissiveness suggested they'd given up something altogether more profound than vanilla sexuality.

Mark tried to ignore them and busied himself by scanning the local network. He found almost nothing out there – just a few weak nodes with narrow, specialised APIs like something out of the Dark Ages. Even the standard dome controls he'd expected appeared to be missing.

The only things with recognisable handles were the giant construction machines slumbering outside.

If he strained his interface, he could make out a warbling stream of non-standard traffic. It wasn't so much an encrypted signal as a different kind of signal altogether – probably some piece of old-fashioned dead-end technology the sects had repurposed as an economical defence against soft-assaults. That would be where the action was.

Massimo probably had his entire network rewired to defend it from New Luxor. He must have made a tempting target for any FPP hacker wanting to try his luck. Unfortunately, it left Mark very much in the dark as to what was happening on the rest of the planet. It was just one more way in which their current situation felt profoundly unstable.

Ten minutes later, Zoe and Venetia came in and sat down across from him, chatting. Mark stole a glance at Zoe but saw nothing in her expression to suggest that anything even slightly out of the ordinary had happened. He blushed before he could throw enough submind attention at the response to suppress it.

'How are you both doing?' he asked.

'Much better, thanks,' said Venetia. Zoe only smiled.

'Me, too,' he said. 'I had no idea how tired I was.'

They heard Massimo approaching from the hallway. He came in and stood before them in his full regalia – hat, gloves and boots – along with an intense, unreadable expression. Mark read the signs of his appearance and felt a stab of concern.

'Would you come with me, please,' Massimo said stiffly. 'We need to talk.'

He turned and walked back the way he'd come. Mark and the others got up to follow.

'What do you think's going on?' Mark asked Venetia.

'No idea. But if I were in his shoes right now, I'd be worried. After all, short of giving him a berth on the *Gulliver*, what have we got to offer him? We sure as hell can't save his settlement.'

Massimo led the way to a shielded patio area behind the main body of the house where a heavily modified bougainvillea draped from a trellis. He stood at the far end and faced them with arms folded. Something about the set-up struck Mark as worryingly off.

'Can I ask what this is about?' he said.

'I've looked into your story,' said Massimo, 'and I'm not completely happy.'

'I assure you, neither are we,' said Mark. 'We're all in grave danger.'

Massimo continued as if he hadn't spoken. 'New Luxor doesn't want you back,' he said. 'Can you tell me why?'

Mark's surprise melted quickly into worry. That Massimo had openly talked to the colony wasn't good. Had he really been angling for a ransom despite what they'd told him?

'From what you said,' their host went on, 'I assumed they'd be desperate to get their hands on you. Wouldn't you?'

Mark struggled for something to say.

'I need to ask – have you been completely forthcoming with me?' said Massimo.

His eyes drilled into Mark's. He appeared to have forgotten that Zoe and Venetia existed.

'Yes,' said Mark cautiously. 'Yes, we have.'

Massimo waved his hands. 'Is there anything more I should know about *you*, perhaps?' A bright, angry glow was building behind his eyes. 'For instance, you admitted to being both a roboteer and an Earther. That's a very odd combination. Can you explain how you came to be both?'

'What's that got to do with anything?' said Mark.

'Mark—' Venetia started.

Massimo cut her off. 'You'll learn that evasive replies are not appreciated in this place,' he said. 'This is a community that respects truth. I think you're a roboteer because you were part of Monet's illegal pilot programme, the one that was shut down amid public scandal. And that, in truth, you are Will Kuno-Monet's adopted son.'

'I'm not anyone's adopted anything,' said Mark. Sam must have released information about him – packed with lies, as usual.

Massimo laughed without sounding remotely amused. 'How stupid do you think I am? Where do you think I'm getting my information? I've seen footage of the *Ariel Two* attacking an alien world. I know that Monet is responsible for the threat to this planet. And I know you're working with him.'

Mark stared in blank dismay while his brain unpicked the web of half-truths that Massimo must have heard.

'You must have talked to Sam Shah,' said Venetia.

'Silence, woman!' Massimo roared. 'I want to hear answers straight from this man – the son of the Alien Satan. The son of the man who broke the True Church.'

'For starters,' said Mark, 'I am *not* Will's son. I share a genetic template with him, but that was true of everyone in the programme.'

'So you admit to being in the pilot programme!'

'Of course,' said Mark. 'I practically said as much already. But it wasn't illegal and there were dozens of us. Listen, I told you – you can't believe a word Sam Shah says. He's already tried to murder me once.'

'With good reason, by the sounds of it!'

Mark shook his head. He felt like a fool. They should have anticipated something like this. He should have spent more time talking about Sam and less talking about the Nems. He'd had the risks all backwards.

'No. Look. Sam is trying to start a war. He's fixed it so that the alien machines will attack Earth. He laid a trap for the entire mission, including Will Monet, and now he wants you confused so you don't send a message to Earth.'

'Then why did he encourage me to do exactly that?'

Mark could think of nothing to say. Sam must have gambled that Massimo would rather condemn Mark than use up a messenger drone. Of course he would, Mark realised. Messenger drones were expensive. Revenge would be free.

'I'll tell you why,' said Massimo. 'Because he knows that it will get me *lynched*.'

'Then why would *I* want you to do it?' Mark shouted back. 'If it was a death sentence for me, why would I even propose it?'

'To buy time. The one thing you don't have.'

Mark gasped in frustration. 'Please, Father Singh,' he said. 'You're an intelligent man. You understand this conflict. Think about what you're proposing here. Which is more likely – that we're hiding from justice, or that the FPP are using alien weapons to attack you? If Sam's story were true, why bother to come here in the first place? Our story wouldn't have held up for a minute. And you said yourself you've heard reports of settlements vanishing. Doesn't that worry you? And what are we even supposed to have done? Watched while Will pulled a trigger? Is that a crime? What kind of crap did Sam actually tell you?'

'You conspired to produce another alien event like the one that broke the church,' said Massimo, as if delivering a sermon from a pulpit. 'To push Monet back into the history books and to create an excuse to break Earth yet again.' He ground a white-gloved fist into a white-gloved hand.

Mark looked deep into the man's eyes and saw with horror that Massimo wanted him to be guilty. An association with Will was enough on its own to condemn him. And that was why Will had never wanted it to come out. That was why he'd always been so paranoid. Seeing it face on, Mark was appalled by how naive he'd been.

'I'm sorry, Mr Ruiz – or should I say Mr *Monet*,' said Massimo, 'but your acts appear to have doomed everyone in this settlement, including myself. The best we can expect to do is hide in the ruins while your aliens exact their revenge.'

So that's it, Mark thought. Massimo wanted out. He was desperate. He probably even imagined that an act like this would convince Sam to give him a ticket.

'Don't,' said Mark. 'You can't trust him. Whatever he's said.'

'I can hardly show leniency,' said Massimo. 'As presiding judge and cleric for this settlement, I have reached my verdict. I find you guilty of interspecies crimes of the worst kind. You are traitors to Earth and to the human race. And I intend to see all three of you face justice.'

Mark had a choice: to jump Massimo now or try for something better. He adjusted his stance, readying himself to move.

'Surely we can work this out,' he said as he stepped carefully, casually forward.

Massimo shook his head and touched a jewelled stud on his cuff. Immediately, Mark's body felt like it was on fire. He fell helplessly to the floor and writhed. Zoe and Venetia did likewise. Their screams filled the air.

Massimo's patio had pain rays hidden in the slatting. The technology was old, very reliable and banned on every world. Suddenly the reason for his broad hat was very clear.

Massimo turned the beams down to low, leaving them gasping and twisting on the floor. Mark couldn't have stood up if his life depended on it, which it probably did. Their host sauntered towards them.

'Look at you,' he sneered, kicking Mark gently. 'Bourgeois scum fallen before God's wrath. Did you think you could pull the wool over my eyes?'

He touched another stud on his cuff and four men wearing heavy yellow exosuits and protective coveralls clanked in through a rear door.

'Put them in penitence boxes until I decide what to do with them,' said Massimo.

One of the men clumped up and pressed a syringe gun against Mark's neck. He tried to ignore the pain. He hurled submind attention at metabolic defence but the ray was wreaking havoc with his interface. They bound his hands and dumped him on a cart next to Zoe and Venetia.

As his vision blurred, Mark stared up into Den's eyes. The man looked amused.

Den led the cart out into the compound beyond. As soon as Mark was free from the effect of the ray, he used what concentration he had left to combat the drug they'd given him. With the rest of his mind he tried to access the network again.

There had to be *something* he could use. It was hiding in all that non-standard traffic. Mark reached for Will's hackpack, belatedly realising that it represented his best hope. A sea of options erupted before him. It would take him weeks to figure them all out. He swapped his attention to the guards' exosuits to find the situation equally hopeless. The muscle-response circuits onboard locked out input from the tiny SAPs they carried.

'Don't do this,' said Mark. 'You're going to get us all killed.'

'The voice of the blasphemer is but wind in the ears of the faithful,' said Den gently. His collar chimed. 'You be silent now, otherwise we have to kill you, see?'

Den and the others took them to a line of concrete sheds at the edge of the dome. Mark held his breath as Kal bent over him with a humming mono-knife and stripped the ship-suit from his body. Den did the same to the others.

Then Den took out a box from the cart and pulled something like a bulky silver ski-mask from it. He held it up close to the nearest shed until lights on the mask's surface began to wink. Mark's eyes went wide. He knew what he was looking at. He'd worn one plenty of times during interface check-ups. It was a neuromap helmet, used to monitor brain function.

'No!' he screamed.

He'd already guessed what they had in mind. They didn't want to view his brain. They wanted to change it. Venetia had been right. The sects had been dabbling in brainwashing after all. Suddenly he had a much better idea of what had scared him about Massimo's servants. Den slipped the helmet over Venetia's head.

Mark pulled madly against his restraints, twisting on the ground. 'No fucking way!'

Zoe screamed like a banshee. They held her down while they forced a helmet onto her.

Then they came for Mark. As Kal leaned down to hold him still, Mark ramped his strength and kicked up with his bound feet. Kal narrowly avoided a knee to the face as Mark's feet clanged off his suit's frame. A hydraulic line snapped under the force of the kick and Kal's suit started emitting warning chimes. He backed off.

Den came at Mark carefully.

'Don't you fucking touch me with that thing!' Mark warned.

Den regarded him with disappointment. 'It just *the box*,' he said. 'I know you scared, but everyone go in there sometimes. Fight it and you only make it worse.' He gestured to the others. 'Boys?'

They pounced on him at once. Mark twisted and kicked with every ounce of strength he had, but clutched in exosuit grippers he didn't stand a chance. They dragged the helmet onto his head, past his snapping teeth, and heat-sealed it tight.

'Try to think about God, and what you done wrong,' said Den, with something almost like kindness in his eyes. 'That way it hurt less.'

Then, one at a time, Mark and his friends were shoved unceremoniously into the sheds, one per prisoner.

Mark found himself dumped onto the floor of a padded chamber barely tall enough to stand in. The ceiling glowed with soft pink light. The air had an antiseptic tang. A small shrine built around an old-fashioned video screen occupied one end. As the door clicked shut behind him, Mark's bindings snapped open.

He immediately started tearing at the helmet but it proved far sturdier than his own flesh. The only way he'd get it off was with a knife. He leapt to his feet and tried the door. They'd locked it, of course. Even with all of his strength, he couldn't get it to budge. He bloodied his knuckles trying.

'Face the shrine and adopt the prayer position,' said a flat feminine voice from the ceiling.

Instead, Mark threw himself at the local network again. If there was a SAP running this box, maybe he could reach it. But the box had been well shielded and the helmet didn't help. Mark strained to find a link to the processors he knew had to be out there. Instead, there was just an overwhelming jangle of non-standard traffic.

Pain filled his body again. He juddered to the floor, shrieking.

'Face the shrine and adopt the prayer position. You will not be warned again.'

A demonstration image appeared on the shrine's screen showing the approved posture, along with a countdown.

Mark's hands crunched into fists. He didn't want to give in. On the other hand, he'd achieve nothing by having his mind fried by pain. He'd die of neural overload before he could mount any kind of an escape. With anger and panic burning white hot inside him, he knelt.

A drawer in the shrine slid open, revealing a small white disc.

'Consume the penitence wafer,' said the shrine.

Mark regarded the object before him with terror. Another flash of pain lashed his bare skin. Then another. He knew all of Will's stories backwards. He knew what enforced conditioning could be like.

'Fuck you!' he screamed, and heard Nid laughing outside.

Pain drowned him again.

'Consume the penitence wafer or you will die.'

Mark ramped his designer metabolism to its maximum setting and loaded every analytical program he had. Depending on what was in the wafer, they might not help much. With a reluctance that verged on nausea, he picked up the wafer and put it in his mouth. His interface immediately lit up with drug warnings.

The shrine screen showed the scowling eyes of the Prophet Sanchez.

'Repent!' the shrine told him in Sanchez's voice.

Then the helmet turned on.

16.3: WILL

Despite the gnawing, irrepressible pain in his side, Will picked up Ann's bleeding body and carried her. He staggered back across the tunnel, positioned her over one shoulder and tried to lift her up towards the alcove high above. By that time Ann had fallen unconscious. Gaining purchase on the slick wall while carrying her dead weight was effectively impossible. He looked up at the hole just a couple of metres above his head and felt like crying.

He shut his eyes, dived into his sensorium and surveyed his smart-cells again. He had the strength for one more jump, but the microbial response would exhaust his reserves at a stroke.

Will steeled himself and instructed his body to manufacture another round of barricades, this time designed to instantly collapse the moment he'd made his leap. Hopefully that would save him from the worst of the repercussions.

He felt his body change as the false strength of his augmentations swelled up inside him. He leapt.

Will seized the edge of the hole with one hand and tossed Ann's limp body inside with the other. The act lost him his grip on the ledge. He scrabbled for a moment, fingernails scraping on the bone-like wall before his other hand managed to grab on. With his body screaming for rest and burning up from the effects of the jump, he dragged himself over the edge and fell into the muck beyond.

He found himself in a kind of armpit-space where two tunnels partially joined. He was waist-deep in acrid-smelling fluid. Ann lay on the other side where the wall curved up, her filth-spattered face out of the water, thank Gal. She looked still and drawn, but he could see her chest rising and falling slightly with shallow, desperate breaths.

Will waded through the slime towards her and hated how vulnerable he felt. He was sick with self-rage. If he'd just shown her an ounce more trust when it had mattered. If only he'd moved a little bit faster. He held her out of the water with trembling arms to examine the wound in her gut.

It looked awful. He couldn't tell damage from the bullet from alien infection. He pressed one hand against her flesh, trying to form a dressing out of smart-cells. His body barely responded. He needed more strength. He lay there with her, trying to gather the pitiful remains of his body's reserves, but he'd scraped the barrel once already. There was nothing he could give without killing himself.

He feebly tried to ward off the planet's never-ending assault, or at least create some kind of diversion. As he did so, another group of soldiers arrived below. He could hear them down there talking.

'That's right,' said one. 'Four dead. He killed them all. And the ATVs are compromised. We had to fry them on the way in. But there's a ton of blood down here. They have to be nearby.'

Will gave thanks for the fact that at least most of the foliage was red. It'd hide their route until someone noticed the bloodstains smeared outside their hiding place.

'We need to hurry,' said another. 'There's too much Nem activity. If we can't find them in five, we have to get out. Nesser says there are drones landing in the ocean, homing in on Monet's beacon. She has to take the lifter up any minute.'

They kept talking but Will was distracted by Ann's breathing. She'd started wheezing horribly. He bent to examine her again but couldn't even muster the strength for a cellular assay. She was dying from the bullet that had been meant for him. The one he shouldn't have gone down there to take in the first place.

He mustered another pathetic attempt to heal her, this time extending some simple filaments into her wound, but the attempt left him lightheaded. Fighting the planet's nullifying effect made his stomach roil. He retched. The world blurred into the mud.

The sound of fresh gunshots brought him back to consciousness. He hadn't even noticed that he'd passed out. A new voice sounded up from below.

'Hold your fire!' it said. The voice sounded jubilant, like an advertisement for something. 'We come in peace. Step out where we can see you and prepare to accept joy into your hearts.'

A whiff of alien technology carried to him on the breeze, stirring his smart-cells back into sluggish action. The newcomer smelled *almost* like the planet around him, but it wasn't the same. There was something eerily familiar about this new breed, something distorted. Will shuddered as a flash of synaesthetic insight bloomed from his failing interface – grinning faces, twisted and melted, and hungry, outstretched hands.

Will recoiled. The approaching Nems smelled weirdly of *people*. They'd already absorbed some essence of humanity at the subcellular level. He wondered if everything they'd struggled to do had been too late. Maybe the Nems had already won.

He drifted back into the blur of fever but explosions and gunfire kept him awake. The sounds of shooting and screaming interrupted his waking dreams like jags of auditory lightning. Meanwhile, he could feel

Ann dying in his arms, just as Gustav had. He barely knew Ann Ludik, but the thought of losing her was unbearable. Couldn't he do anything?

All the power he'd been handed – was it useful for nothing except smashing and killing things? He hadn't saved Earth. He hadn't saved Mark. And now he couldn't even save the woman who'd risked her life for him. What was the point of being alive if he couldn't even protect *her*?

A sudden stab of terrible pain doubled Will over, bringing with it another pulse of unwelcome knowledge. His endless attempts to interfere with Ann's tissues had finally convinced the life around him that he constituted an invasive foreign agent. Now they weren't so much investigating him as taking him apart in earnest.

Will gritted his teeth. He'd fucked it up and now he was finished. As he watched, his own skin started to discolour in the water. The puddle he lay in had to be full of trillions of bacteria. They'd decided to eat him alive, and the feast had started.

16.4: MARK

The box jangled Mark with infrasonics and randomised bursts of despair-inducing sound. Pain crackled down from the ceiling at irregular intervals. The box flashed erratically full of searing, intolerable light like the inside of a sun. And all the while, hallucinogens in the air tore away at the edges of his reality, turning the physical torment into nightmares.

'Repent,' the shrine told him, 'and your suffering will be lessened.'

Mark raged at the walls, spitting every kind of curse he knew. In between the jags of suffering, he ripped at the joins on the ceiling and around the edges of the shrine. Every single surface in the box had been proofed against even superhuman acts of desperation. His fingers bled.

'Repent! Regret grants you mercy!'

'Fuck you!' said Mark.

The box had been perfectly engineered to reduce a person to a quivering, humbled wreck, but Mark had his sensorium, and a metabolism to dull the effects, so he kept fighting.

'The only thing I regret,' he yelled at the walls, 'is coming here to save you stupid fuckers!'

As it turned out, the penitence box wasn't fussy. The simple mention of the word 'regret' turned the light in the room a cool blue. His skin tingled suddenly as a breath of refreshing, drug-laden air brushed across it. Pain morphed into pleasure, and something bloomed inside his head like a light turning on. Mark groaned in relief.

'Good,' said the box. 'You must repent. Share your regrets with the Lord. Beg for his mercy and he will deliver it. We will show you how to love him.'

Mark sucked air as the reality of his situation set in. He'd down-loaded the research, of course, like all roboteers. When you had as much hardware in your head as he did, you followed neuroscience like normal people tracked their investments. Teams on Esalen had put plenty of work into synthesising religious experiences prior to the war – back before the High Church and the treaties. The science was simple: jangle the temporal lobes *just right* and a person's sense of self started to fall away. A certain kind of religious experience followed – one that encouraged willing service to a greater goal. The Truist High Church had discovered how to select those goals. They were going to make him faithful whether he liked it or not.

'I regret that you're a stupid fucking machine,' he snarled.

The pain came back, worse than ever.

'Only the truth can set you free,' said the machine. 'The Lord can see your lies. Repent honestly and you shall be guided towards the true faith.'

The helmet could recognise attempts at evasion. Of course it could. They were probably also optimising his pain response to break him down faster. He didn't stand a chance. He wished he had fewer regrets. He clamped his mouth shut but the pain kept coming.

Mark crouched in the box as it hammered on his nerves. He found himself crying and clawing madly at his own skin. That had to be down to the drug cocktail, didn't it? He pushed his metabolism harder, urging it to purge the poisons they'd dumped into his system. When he started getting warnings from his liver, he simply pissed toxins onto the floor where they sank into the astringent matting.

Will's terrible stories kept running round inside his head. They'd put a thing in Will's skull to make him obey and forced him to watch while his friends were executed. This was nothing by contrast. What must Will have felt?

He'd broken, Mark realised. Will must have simply snapped, because

403

Mark could feel himself pushing up against that limit himself. It was like looking over a precipice at a bottomless drop beyond. No wonder Will spent so much of the time freaked out or angry. He'd never fully recovered.

If Mark didn't want to end up that way he needed a better solution, and fast. Resisting the machine any longer would just ablate his identity like the heat-shield on a shuttle, which was exactly what they wanted.

Okay, he thought. If they were going to make him selfless, he'd make damned sure it was on *his* terms. He reached into his sensorium and pulled up the footage of the Tiwanaku Event and started playing it on a loop with the interior acuity ramped to maximum. He watched people die over and over again.

'I regret that I wasn't there to save those people,' he told the box. 'I'll never let that happen again.'

The box felt his grief and rewarded him.

With ships burning behind his eyes, Mark reached into the deep well of his own guilt and flopped out everything he found for his mind's eye to feast on. If he was going to be remade, then let it be as a living antidote for the Nemesis machines and everything Sam had planned for them.

'I let Venetia and Zoe get captured,' he announced. 'I hate that. I should have done better.'

They both lacked his metabolic advantage, and he'd been the one who brought them to this point. Zoe might have another trick up her sleeve, but Venetia, as far as he knew, had none. He was responsible for them and had failed to deliver.

'Beg *God* for forgiveness,' the shrine told him as it rewarded him. 'Direct your prayers at *God*.'

'Fixing this shit *is* God,' said Mark, conviction building inside him like a storm. 'I will believe and I will save the world.'

He took his rage at the Fleet, and every gram of injustice he'd ever felt, and squeezed his fury into that one single idea.

'I will be a weapon in my own god's hands!' he bellowed at the shrine. It didn't make a shred of sense and he didn't care.

He could use his interface, he realised. With his power to tweak his own metabolism, he had the ability to modify the blood flow through his own brain. The helmet couldn't beat him. So long as he flooded himself with genuine regret, it would have no idea what was prayer and what was revenge.

'Will Monet gave me this job,' he shouted, 'and I've been doing shitty-ass work. I was so caught up in my own pain that I failed to see the enemy right in front of me. Fuck me, I won't be doing *that* again. Next time I see Sam, I'm going to *rip the fucking eyes out of his head.*'

'Good,' said the shrine. 'Pray for forgiveness!'

His temporal lobes buzzed. A sense of openness and totality swelled in him like a wind through his soul. As Mark yelled out his failures, greatness grew inside him. He felt himself genuinely changing. He *did* regret who he'd been. He was becoming a servant, all right. A servant to his own furious, epic cause.

If he ever got out of here, things would be different. There'd be no more hoping that his fellow Earthers would magically turn out to be decent just because they shared a birth-world with him. There'd be no more playing by Fleet rules. They'd been screwing him over since before the court case and that was long enough. But most of all, there'd be no wallowing. Mark felt his own pain dwindling to irrelevance. If they ever let him out of the box, they'd better know who they were fucking with, because Mark wasn't afraid of them any more. He wasn't afraid of *anything*.

Hell, why wait to be released? He reached for Will's hackpack again while the emotions thundered through him and let the bewildering array of options bloom in front of him.

'I regret not looking at this stuff before,' he said quietly.

'Good,' said the shrine. 'That's right!'

Somewhere in here would be a tool that could unpack all that odd system traffic. Mark no longer doubted that he'd find it.

16.5: WILL

Will lay helpless in the hole and gulped air into his ruined lungs while mutant alien machines prowled outside. He didn't fear them because he knew he'd be dead before they found him, dissolved into this brackish pool like a human smoothie. His reign as the most powerful man in human space was over.

It had been an interesting ride, if a disappointing one. But if he was going down, his last act might as well be something decent. He reached out through his sensorium to the surface of his hand, still pressed against Ann's wound, and tried to stay conscious as he pictured her tissues one last time.

He lacked the strength. Lurid, dream-like notions surged and pulsed in his mind's eye. Fever visions and sensorium metaphors curdled together until he couldn't distinguish between the data coming from her and his own memories of hiking through the scarlet tunnel-forest.

He heard Ann's words played back to him.

'This stuff grows fast. Stand still for long enough and you can watch it.'

He imagined her tissues growing across the wound without help, like fungal hyphae.

'That's not how you do it,' he mumbled into his metaphor space. 'You've got it wrong. She's a woman, not a mushroom.'

'I grow fungi,' said Ann's garbled voice. 'Stand watch me still. There's always a choice. Maybe you should try it on again.'

Another round of gunfire sounded from the tunnel below, followed by a long, inhuman scream. Will spiked back into lucidity.

He saw, then, that the vision before him wasn't a dream. Ann's tissue was indeed mutating wildly. The bacteria in the pool were trying to heal her even while they were killing him. She'd been deemed worthy of repair, like the meadow below. But with so much foreign material in the wound it had no idea what to do with her, so it was turning her into something it knew how to fix. Will tried vaguely to assist, only to have his molecular hands slapped away from the surgery. As far as Snakepit was concerned, he was a pollutant in its already crowded operating theatre.

Will refused to give in. If he wasn't allowed to help, at least he could stop the planet from making a mess. While the precious gift of clarity stayed with him, Will called up all the submind strength he had left and started synthesising defenceless smart-cells. He loaded each of them with as much medical data as his meagre interface memory contained, written in the most self-explanatory format he could find. Then he started dumping those cells into the wound and across the surface of his own dissolving skin.

It was, he thought, a little like a propaganda drop onto enemy terrain. If he couldn't stop his enemy, maybe he could still change its

406

attitude. Will smiled inwardly at himself. This last act felt ridiculous – a terrible stretch. It relied on a barely logical alien biosphere spontaneously learning to read and understand his file format. But it wasn't like he was getting off the planet anyway.

He watched as the alien cells snatched up his pamphlets. Unsurprisingly, they didn't seem able to read them. He wished he had more time. With time it would be doable. After all, wasn't this exactly what had happened at Tiwanaku? This learning curve was exactly what those drones had been looking for. He just needed the cells in this alcove to pull off the same trick without turning her into a staggering zombie first. He lacked the bandwidth, though. He didn't need a cupful of smart-cells. He needed pints – not so much a cellular textbook as a cellular university.

Ah, well, he thought. He'd do what he should have done a long time ago – give others the tools to create change rather than imagining he could push it forward by the force of his will. He sent out a cascade of messages, turning off the cellular defences throughout his entire body and replacing them with medical how-to guides of every description stored in his smart-cells. He opened himself up, and with a final, physical act, flopped backwards into the muck.

'Come on in,' he told the planet. 'Let's get this over with. My one request: please at least fix her *properly.*'

17: REBOUND

17.1: MARK

The box switched off. Mark slumped to one side, utterly drained. He couldn't have said how long the program had been running. Hours? Days? He had no idea. Guards in exosuits hauled him out and dumped him on the ground.

Mark squeezed his eyes tight against the blinding glare of sunlight. He shivered as they hosed down his body. He must have soiled himself at some point because he didn't smell that great. He hadn't noticed.

With trembling hands, he pushed himself up into a sitting position and blinked as the world began to swim back into focus. Den's men hauled him to his feet while others looked on, cradling assault cannons in their augmented arms. They looked pleased with themselves.

Mark glanced to the side and saw Zoe and Venetia being brought out, too. Zoe's face was grey but her eyes had taken on a glare of manic, crackling hatred. Anger poured off her like electricity. By contrast, Venetia wasn't doing so well. Her eyes were hollow. Her shoulders sagged. Mark wondered how he looked. He felt physically feeble but somehow clean. His spine felt straighter than it ever had before, even though a strong breeze could have knocked him over. He smiled brokenly.

Den peered at him. 'You find God in there?' he asked with a coy smile.

Mark fixed him with a stare. 'You have no idea.'

Den laughed. 'Oh, I got an idea, all right. Been there myself.'

Mark's smile broadened at Den's imagined camaraderie. He tamped down the urge to laugh.

As they cut the helmet off his head, he pinged the network, this time using a tool he'd laboriously excavated from Will's alien hackpack. Without the guards being any the wiser, Britehaven's encrypted proto- cols flopped open before him.

The contents weren't as impressive as Mark had hoped, but at least he had something now. If the labelling was to be believed, he'd gained access to an extensive suite of scripture broadcast tools and an API for the settlement's industrial fabbers. Short of printing up some plastic swords, he couldn't see much value in his new powers. He didn't let it worry him. He'd keep working on the problem.

Den and his team gave them grey paper smocks to wear, then ges- tured back towards the middle of the dome with their guns.

'This way,' said Den. 'Get moving.'

Mark looked down the dusty road ahead. Whatever lurked at the centre of town couldn't be good. He glanced around and considered violence but knew this wasn't his moment. He was still too weak. One wrong move and his friends would wind up full of bullets.

He let himself be marched down the road between the art-covered houses. Scrawny settlers watched them pass, jeering slogans at them while their collars chimed. In the centre of the Britehaven complex lay a bleached concrete expanse that served as a kind of town square, lined by two-storey printrock buildings covered with religious murals in white and red. In the middle of the square, three stacks of multicoloured plastic waste had been assembled. Each one stood about a metre and a half high with a tall ceramic mast jutting out from the top.

A crowd of several thousand Flags dressed in gaudy, loose-fitting clothes stood around the edges of the square, shouting over each other. Their hands and faces had all been smeared white with sun-cream, making them look like angry ghosts. They yelled and shook their fists, their shrill voices echoing off the dome far overhead. With them stood Massimo in his full regalia, a solemn expression on his face. A sluggish artificial breeze carried the tang of the ever-present dust.

Mark stared at the piles. They looked like an oddly untidy addition for the site of a trial. What were they for? Was this a recycling centre? Perhaps Massimo intended to mulch them. He glanced around for a biofuser but couldn't see one.

Den's team brought Mark and his friends to a halt in front of Mas- simo and held them in place with suit-grippers. The settlement leader raised a hand. The crowd slowly fell silent.

'The betrayers of man have been given a chance to contemplate their sins before justice is delivered,' Massimo announced. 'Let us hear what they have learned before the punishment is declared.'

He pointed an imperious index finger at Venetia. 'You. Woman. Do you have a confession to make?'

'I'm from the planet where they invented that equipment, you pathetic little man,' she said. She sounded drained. 'Your helmets need recalibrating but for the most part it was a refreshing opportunity to practise mindfulness.'

Massimo's face fell into an expression of theatrical despair. The crowd booed her wildly.

He pointed at Zoe. 'And you, woman. Do you have a confession to make?'

Zoe spat in his eye with surprising accuracy. The guards knocked her to the ground.

'Never fuck with the Vartian Institute!' she yelled. 'You're all dead, motherfuckers!'

She drew boos and screams from the assembled zealots. Den's guards had to brandish their assault canons to discourage the Flags from ripping her apart.

Massimo wiped his face with a snow-white handkerchief and looked, if anything, pleased with her reaction. He moved on to Mark.

'And you, son of the Alien Satan, do *you* have a confession to make?'

Mark looked him in the eye. 'God spoke to me,' he said.

Massimo spread his hands and gave a grin of false delight. The crowd cheered. Mark's smile became wide like a shark's.

'God revealed your sin to me and you will be punished for it. I will be the weapon in his hands and no obstacle will hide you from his wrath. In his name, I will dismantle you one piece at a time.'

Massimo's smile fell away, revealing a flush of concern before he could plaster impatience over it. He turned to the crowd.

'Look at what we have here,' he boomed. 'An intellectual, a harlot and a mutant – the supposed cream of the corrupt Colonial regime.' He pointed at Venetia. 'This one spouts aphorisms and claims that you, my people, are fools to have come here. What do we say to that?'

The crowd jeered in spastic frenzy.

His finger moved to Zoe. 'This one fights like an animal and lacks even an inkling of feminine decency.'

410

Hoots of disgust erupted.

Massimo jabbed a finger at Mark. 'And this one... This one claims to be of Earth. Examine his face, my children. Look how it resembles those of your brothers and sons. But his flesh is not like your flesh. He does not feel as you feel. He has blasphemy written into his very genes!'

The crowd screamed.

'*This* is what the Alien Satan would have you become,' Massimo proclaimed. 'An effete joke. A machine puppet. And worst of all, an *abomination in the face of the Lord*!'

This time, Britehaven's mob surged into such a state of apoplexy that it took a full minute for the guards to knock them back into order.

'The crimes these people have committed are the most extreme I have ever presided over,' said Massimo. 'I have consulted scripture and prayed on the matter for hours to determine the correct punishment. But God has guided me. These three traitors to the human cause shall be burned at the stake!'

Massimo kept talking, orating at the crowd about the timelessness of primal law and the importance of setting an example before God, but that last phrase had frozen in Mark's mind, blotting out everything that followed.

Were the Flags really that backward? Did they crave a return to the Dark Ages that much? Or did he mean *metaphorically* burned? Had they even considered the havoc they were about to wreak on their own air filters?

The men in exosuits dragged them up to the stacks, which Mark now realised were pyres, and lifted them to the tops with terrible ease. Plastic restraints locked them to the masts. It was definitely time to make a move. Any kind of move.

Mark hurled submind attention at the secret network and rifled through it as fast as his interface would allow. Understanding dawned. The scripture broadcast tools he'd found weren't for video panels. They controlled the piety game. With the full force of his augmented attention, Mark threw an attack at the system. All around him, people's collars started making plangent clanging sounds. Phrases like *Credit lost!*, *You lose!* and *Impious notion!* sounded from wearables everywhere.

With remarkable alacrity, the Flags panicked. Some fell to their knees and prayed. Others started clawing at their collars and weeping. In the midst of it all, Massimo looked on with astonishment.

'Remain calm!' he ordered the crowd. 'These demerits are not real!'

The well-conditioned Flags barely noticed. Their precious piety accounts were vanishing before them.

Massimo fixed Mark with an icy look. While his guards grasped madly at their necks, he picked up an induction wand from the floor and touched it to the closest pyre: Venetia's. The plastic went up like a torch. Venetia's screams cut the air.

Mark's urgency redoubled. It was Will's Amy-story all over again. There was no way he was going to stand there like a victim watching history repeat itself. He scanned madly for something else he could use – something that would kill the flames.

In a moment of perfect clarity, he noticed that the answer had been right in front of him all the time. The forty-storey-high construction robots outside the dome had never been locked. He'd not even thought of using them because there was nothing he could do that didn't involve trashing the dome and the air inside it. That idea no longer bothered him.

He seized one of the idle titans and threw awareness into its tiny mind. He swung it around and drove it straight at the dome. There was already so much noise and chaos that people barely noticed until the ground started shaking. The behemoth raced up to the settlement like a yellow wall of death. Mark held his breath.

As Massimo leaned down to light Zoe's pyre, the robot hit the dome, crumpling the edge of the plastic like the skin on a boiled egg. Air screamed out. The fires sucked sideways and vanished in an instant. Flags everywhere started choking and grabbing their throats. By Mars Plus standards, Carter had a rich, healthy atmosphere. By the standards of human breathability, not so much.

The giant robot froze under emergency lockdown with outbuildings already flattened under its enormous treads. Spray cannons at the dome perimeter started throwing foam up at the breached plastic in thundering torrents. Decompression sirens filled the fleeing air.

Through stinging eyes, Mark watched Massimo scramble for an air-mask at an emergency station nearby. He didn't have any time to waste. In seconds, the breach would be sealed and Massimo would be in control again.

He scanned digital space one last, desperate time. To his amazed relief, one of the exosuit controllers had popped onto the network. It glowed yellow at him, winking with urgency. It was Kal's. Somewhere between the depressurization and the loss of his credits, Kal had fallen unconscious, so the muscle-control lockout had disengaged. The suit wanted someone to guide it to a recovery station so its driver could be rescued.

Mark grabbed the suit's controls, threw himself behind its cameras and grabbed the assault cannon lying on the floor beside it. He aimed it at Nid, who was looking around in complete confusion, and fired. Ceramic cannon rounds peppered Nid's body, reducing it to bloody rags. The person Mark had been before the punishment box might have blinked. Not any more. Now he was more worried about accidentally rupturing one of the suit's hydraulic lines.

As the new exosuit popped onto the network, Mark split his focus. Now he had two armed robots instead of one. It was a start. He made Nid shoot Kal, just in case the little bastard woke up, and then worked his way through Den's startled team, one by one. Thirty seconds later, Mark had seven suits. Only one remaining suit had a living driver: Den.

Somehow, the small spark of humanity Den had revealed made Mark hesitate at the prospect of killing him. Consequently, Den actually managed to fire a couple of badly aimed shots before Mark blew his head off. A corner of his mind warned him that he was committing horrible, brutal murders. His new driving anthem of puritanical determination drowned it out.

Navigating all eight suits at once took effort. Their SAPs were pitifully underpowered and required constant encouragement. But Mark stopped worrying which parts of his mind went where. He hung limp from the stake, trying not to black out, and focused on the task at hand.

As mayhem reigned, he sent four suits to free Zoe and Venetia and two more to cover the Earthers as they scrambled to escape. He had one free his own limbs and the last he sent after Massimo as the settlement leader ran for the far side of the square.

Mark saw Massimo reach for the control on his wrist. Whatever he had in mind, Mark knew he couldn't risk letting it happen. Massimo still had some sort of grip on the dome's executive controls that Mark didn't understand. He aimed his army's closest assault cannon and fired. Massimo got halfway through some kind of shut-off command before his head burst like a grape in a storm of blunt ammunition.

Mark called to the crazed Flags as his hands fell free.

'Your leader is dead,' he shouted. 'Lie down and no one else will get hurt!'

It was a mistake. Up till then he hadn't been noticed. From somewhere, the Flags had started breaking out weapons. One of them took aim. Flenser fire ripped up one side of the pyre, forcing Mark to leap sideways off the plastic heap. He rolled on the ground, pain lancing up his shoulder while sporadic gunfire cut the freezing air. He scrabbled for cover behind the trash-pile and prayed it was dense enough to stop steel.

While he cowered, he had two suits carry Zoe and Venetia over to him as fast as they could while his other machines laid down protective fire. Zoe's feet were a mass of blisters. She hissed through the pain, her face white and straining. Venetia lay unconscious and badly burned, her skin smelling sickly of roasted meat. Mark stared at her in horror. Vomit threatened to spill out of him.

He couldn't afford to be weak. He gritted his teeth, shut his eyes and started herding the Flags together, using his exosuits to smash through the flimsy homes they hid behind. At the same time, he grabbed another huge constructor robot and directed it towards a functioning airlock on the far side of the dome. He picked the largest vehicle remaining – a six-armed behemoth with twin cranes. It was the only one likely to have the med supplies he needed.

With the final shreds of his attention, Mark had his last suit carry Massimo's body over to where he lay. While trying to ignore the wet mass of gore that had been Massimo's skull, he ripped the override control off the dead man's wrist. His fingers scrambled over it, looking for familiar controls somewhere amid all the ecclesiastical jewellery.

On the back, he found an ordinary-looking reboot button. Mark wedged a finger into the slot and hoped. If it worked anything like a normal domestic wearable, he'd have a fraction of a second during which the cuff was handshaking with the network and vulnerable to intrusion. It had to be worth a shot.

The moment the device surfaced in his mind, Mark seized the link and hammered on its security, bringing the full weight of both his attention and Will's hackpack to bear. For a slew of dangerous seconds, all his puppets stalled. Then the cuff's interface spilled open, spewing icons and help files. Mark blinked in understanding. That encrypted traffic he'd found held a second layer with command rights limited to a few special devices. Devices like the one he now had.

He didn't have long to enjoy success. By the time he'd cracked Massimo's executive API, he had new problems. The Earthers had taken rapid advantage of his time-out and regrouped. Five of his suits had fallen prey to concentrated flenser fire and couple of thousand angry Revivalists were advancing towards his hiding place clutching guns and improvised weapons. Worse still, the airlock Mark needed to reach lay about a half kilometre away and getting everyone there alive looked less and less likely. For starters, he was the only one of the three of them who could walk.

Mark rummaged wildly through the interface looking for a miracle. Then he saw something: a package labelled *Armageddon Theatrics*. He cracked it open, letting yet more icons splatter into the mess of his home node. This new group held programs for infrasonics, ultrasonics, light-control tools and a dozen other things Mark didn't even recognise. He snatched one and fired it up.

The voice of the Prophet Sanchez boomed out of hidden speakers all over the settlement.

'BOW DOWN BEFORE YOUR LORD!'

Mark clapped his hands over his ears to block out the deafening sound. When he looked up, half the Flag mob had their faces in the dirt and the rest were clutching their ears in varying states of terror.

Mark kicked off another program. The dome's polarisation ramped to maximum, plunging the settlement into a ruddy twilight from the end of the world. It looked less impressive than it would have done if one whole side of the settlement wasn't already wrecked and patched with foam, but the Flags stared upwards in awe.

Mark took his chance. With two of his exosuits he picked up Zoe and Venetia. The last one brought up the rear with its cannon at the ready. Together they ran.

The moment the Earthers caught sight of Mark escaping, the spell broke. He'd already smashed their world enough that each new distraction bothered them less. They surged back to their feet with roars of fury and came after him. His last armed exosuit didn't stand a chance. It took the full weight of the Flags' fire as it tried to hold them off. Mark felt his mind retreat from the machine as its cameras and power junctions gave out under torrents of screaming metal.

Before the Flags could refocus their attention, Mark ducked down a side street, dragging his two remaining suits after him. He wheezed in the thin air and wished his recent experiences had left him in better shape. He needed a burst of artificial speed but even his reinforced metabolism had nothing more to offer. He'd used up most of his metabolic arsenal just surviving the punishment box.

That left nothing to do but sprint barefoot down the dusty road and hope. As he ran, his mind skittered over Massimo's command structure looking for something else he could use. He still had over two hundred and fifty metres to go.

Mark's mind caught on a subsystem labelled *Public Implant Control*. He recoiled. Had Massimo actually put externally controlled systems inside his Followers' bodies? Of course he had. If their minds weren't sacrosanct, why should their bodies be so? He shuddered at the appalling invasion of human privacy that Britehaven entailed, then grabbed the system and started mashing on it.

As one, the Flags roaring up the lane behind him tumbled like sacks of meat, groaning and screaming like victims from hell's inner circles. Their flenser fire chased randomly up the walls. Mark glanced back and saw dozens of faces with crazed, empty eyes as the Flags rolled in the road. They clutched wildly at their chests and abdomens as if trying to claw their bodies open.

With a surge of fresh nausea, Mark realised that the controls he'd triggered were part of the sect's reward and punishment system – much like the penitence box, but surgically installed. Kal's hunger for penitence points and Five's eerie submissiveness suddenly took on new implications. Mark felt dirty for using it but didn't drop the power. Instead, he turned and took off for the airlock as fast as he could. He ran straight into the robot's waiting elevator pod with his suits beside him and sealed the door, gasping as it slammed shut.

The pod accelerated hard up the robot's chest – a full forty stories to the main cabin between its top shoulders. Mark burst through into the utilitarian space beyond, ripping med-packs off the wall and pressing burn gel against Venetia's torched body.

He unhooked the massive robot from the airlock below, backed it away from the dome and started out in a straight line for the spaceport. Without so much as a glance back at the horror of Britehaven, he set his sights on the horizon. This time, nothing was going to stand between him and that shuttle.

Will felt himself being taken apart. Senses, memories and associations dropped out one by one. The experience brought with it an unexpected stab of nostalgia. He recognised the feeling from what the Transcended had done to him years ago when they'd taken a mortal and turned him into a superbeing.

Easy come, easy go.

Last time, he'd been terrified. This time, he gave no resistance. He opened the gates and let Snakepit in. Great swathes of his extended self that he'd grown so used to over the years were swallowed by creeping darkness. His organs, both natural and invented, fell silent and closed down like shuttered factories. It was like watching the country of his mind fall prey to an invasion. The foreign horde swept over him with molecular sabres waving. The citizens of Will's mind stood still and let it happen, holding out pamphlets of peace.

Will watched the fall of his own interior Rome until Snakepit's unstoppable army pressed against the final doors of his citadel of selfhood – his consciousness. He opened the drawbridge. Will retreated to the home node of his sensorium, gazed out at the simulated lawn and watched the darkness gathering. He held his virtual breath.

Oblivion failed to arrive. Instead, the shadows slowed and stopped. Will watched them hang there and frowned to himself in confusion. Then the dark started creeping backwards, oozing into the corners. Will extended himself a little and was confused by what he found. Rather than tearing everything down, the invasion had started restoring things. His subsystems woke to new life.

The entire process that had devoured him had gone into fast reverse. The cavalry charged backwards, uncovering his mental terrain. The factories of his body opened again, springing magically into good repair. Organs began to pump. Will tested the limits of his mind with bewilderment and found them refreshed. He had no idea how or why.

Then, in small ways at first, he began to notice that those parts of him returning to life were not the same as they had been. His lungs breathed more deeply. His blood felt cleaner. And the chorus of smartcells that filled his body were chattering to him in a slang he'd never heard before.

He framed the question before he was even aware of his intention to communicate.

'What's going on?'

A comms channel opened like a pair of enormous doors being thrown wide in his head. It reminded him of the shock he'd experienced when he first truly connected to the *Ariel Two*, except that this process felt far larger, and immeasurably more foreign.

A torrent of half-comprehended notions flashed through him like the fleeting memories of impossibly detailed dreams, played in succession at blistering speed. It was like waking up ten thousand times over, all at once. Will felt his mind begin to unhinge. He struggled to bring some guiding metaphor to bear, to turn the mess of incoherent ideas into something he could at least focus on.

His perspective lurched and suddenly he was falling through the largest machine in the universe – a human mote dropped through the clockwork of reality. The structure around him was fractal and incredibly intricate. Wheels turned against wheels from things the size of continents down to sparkling dust too small to make out. Every scale of machinery represented something – a cell, a plant, a continent. Each differed from the others, yet each worked seamlessly with the whole. Will knew what he was looking at. He was falling through the mind of Snakepit.

Except Will knew he was seeing it wrong. In true Snakepit style, he was being shown every level of organisation of the world-sized system simultaneously. This was how the Nems had tried to understand humanity – as a holistic system like their own. This was why they'd paid so little attention to scale or meaning at Tiwanaku. No wonder they'd struggled. Will pushed for a simplifying image, forcing the impenetrable vision into something his mind could encompass. He needed a body, for starters. He needed an environment he could interact with.

The vast machine became a corridor. He wasn't falling through it, only walking. And it wasn't a single machine he was looking at but a series of informative exhibits. He pressed shut virtual eyes to stabilise himself. When he opened them, he stood in a passageway in the Museum of Infinite Possibilities.

On either side of him sat glass-fronted display cases filled with racks of surreal organisms and devices. The tiled corridor extended to the vanishing point ahead of him and behind, lit by an endless line of old-fashioned LED lamps under fusty neo-deco shades.

Will glanced at one of the displays. It squirmed beneath his eyes, unpacking itself in lurid multidimensional detail like some baroque sea creature turning itself inside-out. Without Will asking, it began leaking an explanation into his awareness.

Quasi-cooperative heterogeneous cellular membranes can operate as a substrate for the catalysis of novel meta-enzymes. Each enzyme operates as a self-organizing condition-action rule composite that aids in converting the local nutrient landscape into a partially mixed computational arena . . .

His mind started to fill with tantalising insights till he fought for breath. He blinked them away.

'This is an improvement,' he said, focusing on the black and white tiles beneath his feet. 'Now I need someone, or something, I can talk to.'

A curator appeared – a motherly woman in an old-fashioned mock-suit. She wore a heavy data visor of the sort people used on Galatea before the war and had something halfway between an orchid and an octopus tucked in her lapel. He knew her to be a product of his own imagination but was surprised to find the woman before him so specifically rendered. She had broad apple cheeks and hair wound back in braids. She looked a lot, in fact, like his dead friend Amy.

The curator stood there, peeking at him over the upper rim of her visor. She looked peeved.

'Why is this necessary?' she said. She glanced down at her sleeves and tugged on them disapprovingly. 'You interface directly with your ship, do you not? Why restrict yourself to such a narrow perceptual aperture here?' She folded her arms.

'I'm not set up to process this all at once,' said Will.

'Then let us adjust you accordingly,' said the curator enthusiastically. She held out eager hands.

Will waved her back. 'No, thank you. There's no rush, I assume?'

She shot him a disapproving look. 'We haven't received a sentient visitor for as long as I can remember, so of course there's a rush. We need to get you settled in.'

Will wasn't sure he liked the sound of that.

'Can you first explain what's going on here? What happened to me?'

The curator's mouth curved in a satisfied smile. 'We completed the analysis of your substrate and created an interface to match. This is what is always done with new life forms. It took longer in your case because it wasn't clear at first that your cells were engaged in processing content at a higher level of representation. It was only possible to discern that when they stopped changing long enough for us to model their contents. Do you see?'

She gestured at a nearby display case where a more complete explanation of the process writhed behind the glass like a nine-dimensional squid, reaching for his mind. Will avoided looking. He understood anyway.

By opening himself up to the planet, he hadn't just provided tools for saving Ann, he'd inadvertently enabled the planet to finish figuring out his smart-cells at last. It had finally decided he wasn't a threat.

'Now that your substrate is understood, we've matched it and extended it,' said the curator with glee. 'Your substrate is merged with our own.'

In other words, his hierarchy of subminds now reached out into Snakepit. What constituted Will Kuno-Monet wasn't very clear any more.

'But that's okay,' said the curator. 'You fit right in.'

The passageway shivered as a nugget of understanding broke free of its metaphoric restraints and unfurled in his head like a shared memory. The entire planet, he saw now, was backed and linked by a hierarchical computing substrate built up from the molecular level. Cellular agents operated as processor nodes much like his own smart-cells, forming a mesh network that reached down through the world's crust almost to its mantle. This place wasn't just a habitat for organic life. The amount of virtual room it contained dwarfed the physical space it held by several orders of magnitude. Will struggled for breath as the scale of the system came home to him.

'Now that it's clear you aren't an infection, we're accommodating you rather than dismembering you,' said the curator. 'Things are so much nicer that way, wouldn't you say?'

Will blinked as his field of view widened again. The entire gestalt pseudo-organism around him operated as a kind of all-purpose life-support. It kept the tunnels, and everything in them, intact. It adapted to meet the needs of whatever resided there. It removed systemic threats, co-opting their mechanisms for future use and abandoning its own obsolete tools just as readily.

This wasn't just a habitable world. It was a cellular-scale terraforming system – a machine for populating entire galaxies. Drop a fragment of tunnel root on a dead world and the habitat would rebuild itself from scratch.

And that was exactly what happened on this planet, the world explained. Snakepit was founded, like countless worlds before it, as part of a grand project to unify and foster life. But the Founders who engineered Snakepit never came back to populate their own creation as expected. Knowledge of them was lost, but the biosphere carried on regardless, ready to nurture whomever it found.

Will gasped in understanding as he saw how wrong he'd been. When he'd first encountered Snakepit's technology he'd assumed foul play, but now that the mechanisms which drove it were laid out, he saw only kindness. The world's entire purpose was to encourage life, to merge with it and shape itself to life's whim. Snakepit was an ancient, open-access Eden, adrift in the universe and waiting to love someone.

It had struck at human colonies, he saw, only because humans had goaded it. They'd damaged the surface on purpose and left false trails for it to follow. Humanity had woken the planet's instinct to understand and adapt to threats. For all their tinkering with victims, the Nem swarms constituted nothing more than acts of reflexive self-defence. And, if used wisely, that same defensive force would serve to protect all humanity from whatever dangers the universe might have to offer. More than that, the planet *wanted* to protect them. It felt lonely and incomplete without someone to look after.

Will couldn't argue with the beauty of this vision but something about it disturbed him. What had happened to the Founders? With the Transcended active in this part of space, he could hazard a guess, but why had no information about the race who had designed this place been left behind? Will knew he was still missing something but it was impossible to think clearly with the planet sticking its fingers into his mind.

He forced himself to focus. He had work to do. Ann still needed his help.

'Stop,' he said. 'No more memory dumps. I'm still adjusting. I have a friend and she needs help.'

'Oh, *that* thing!' said the curator cheerfully. 'She's just down here. This way, please.' She gestured eagerly.

The curator led him out of the passageway in an impossible direction. Will suddenly found himself standing at the threshold of an operating theatre of sorts – a confused mixture of virtual medical displays and mouldering historic architecture.

Ann's body floated in the air in front of him at the centre of great tiled hall with a vaulted ceiling. She was completely visible to him in a way that normal human sight could never have encompassed. Data splayed out in the space around her – diagrams upon diagrams, updating in real-time – a body teased apart into its component proteins like a schematic for a starship. The model of her ran so deep that it *was* her.

'Thank you for your supporting texts,' said the curator. 'They've been very useful. She makes so much more sense now. Tell me, does she need any modifications or improvements while she's in here? Gills, for instance? Eyes on her hands? They'd be very useful. Just imagine the manual precision she'd attain.'

'Not right now,' said Will. 'Let's just get her healthy.'

The curator shrugged, disappointed. 'As you wish.'

Ann's repair began in earnest. The muck in the alcove where she lay wrapped itself around her and started turning into human tissue even before it reached her body. The task, now that it had been properly understood, was trivial.

'We'll extend her operating limits, of course,' she said, 'just as we have yours. It'd be such a shame for her to only enjoy it here for a century or two. This way she can have much more fun.'

There it was again: the unsettling implication that the curator's assistance hinged on his never getting out of there. Will chose not to challenge it just yet.

'Thank you,' he said. 'I didn't expect this kind of help.'

The curator regarded him with deep amusement and squeezed his arm. 'Why ever not? All our residents receive as much support as we can offer. It aids integration.'

Will bit back a nervous response. Just minutes ago, he'd been ready to give up his life. So why did an eternity on Snakepit suddenly scare him?'

'We have other problems,' he said. 'There are creatures in the tunnels looking for us. Some of yours, I believe.'

422

The curator blinked at him in surprise. '*Creatures?*' she said. 'Are you talking about *our children*?'

Will eyed her with bewildered alarm, unsure of what she meant.

The curator took him by the arm and led him out of the operating room to another cracked and ancient hall, this one filled with a vast, glowing diagram of the local tunnel-space. If the map for a nest designed by a billion psychotic ants had been rendered in threads of light, it might look like this, he thought. Thousands of root-habitats twisted around and over each other, joining at bewilderingly convoluted junctions. Will's perspective lurched as he tried to take the map in all at once. He faltered and stepped back like a hiker on a cliff-top.

The curator huffed. 'Look,' she said snippily. 'It's easy. You're over here.'

She led him across the tiled floor, cuddling up beside him as they walked. They passed through the glowing ghosts of a million twisted roots to the virtual replica of the tunnel where his body lay. Will could see luminous pulses of activity there and realised he was looking at soldiers retreating from and firing at a wave of advancing Nems.

When Will focused on the advancing aliens they unfurled in his head in a tide of strangeness. They felt cryptic and half-human, ominous and lovable at the same time. Will couldn't help but look on them with fondness and knew the planet was interfering with his thoughts again.

'They don't belong here,' he said.

The curator gave him a long glance. 'What are you talking about? Of course they do.'

'But they've changed,' said Will. 'I can feel it. These creatures might have originated in your system but they aren't part of it any more. They're different. They've mutated.'

'*Our* system, darling,' said the curator. 'And what did you expect? This is how it's always been.'

Will's mind blanched as another blob of foreign knowledge spilled into it. This was what the defensive nodes were for – to solve the problem of life that didn't integrate peacefully.

Snakepit operated in two ways. Under normal conditions, any life it encountered was ushered in, analysed and accommodated. But when the damage a species caused tipped past a critical threshold, the planet changed strategy. Instead of welcoming that species, Snakepit took it apart and reconstructed it as something less volatile. At the same time, it co-opted the invasive species' own weapons to make itself stronger, and in the process of doing so, Snakepit's defensive tools mutated.

When such a new mutation arose, it had to assert both its stability and its selective advantage before Snakepit would allow it to reintegrate. In other words, the planet improved through competition with its own distorted offspring. That which conquered informed the template for future growth.

'We must adapt ourselves to the needs of our young, darling, wouldn't you agree? The doors are being thrown open to welcome them home.'

She sounded thrilled about it. Will felt ill.

'No,' said Will. 'That's not okay. Their changes are dangerous. They've gone wrong.'

'Wrong? Don't be ridiculous. They're just fitter.'

Their little ones had come back and *asserted primacy* backed by force. In doing so, they had improved on Snakepit's original design. That's what the brief war between the Nems and their parent world had been about. Seeing things through this curiously merged perspective, Will felt like a father discussing the changes in a child after a stint off at university.

So what if he did a few drugs, he's acquired some useful life-skills. We need to do what's right for him, Honey, and that means accommodating his lifestyle choices, even if we don't understand them.

The Nems' return effectively announced the arrival of a new fused race, half-Snakepit, half-humanity. Perhaps, before they arrived, the human race might have called Snakepit a home and lived here without risk. But now, because the League had got the defensive nodes involved, the game had changed. His species had selected itself for enforced integration instead and the implications of that change of plan were still playing out.

The curator looked up at him with amused patience as if at a cantankerous but ultimately loving dad. But that wasn't how Will felt, even with his extended subminds distorting his opinions. Maybe that way of seeing things had worked here in the past, but any offspring bent on consuming the human race had lost its rooming privileges as far as he was concerned.

'No,' Will insisted. 'I'm not having it.'

'You're not?'

The curator's smile widened. She looked him up and down with wry

amusement and Will suddenly understood how thin this veneer of ami-
ability actually was. For the curator, Will was a future display waiting
to take its place behind glass. Unless he proved himself otherwise, he
was just another species to be incorporated into the planet's biosphere.
Or rather, one already undergoing incorporation.

It occurred to him then that she was behaving awfully like a sentient
entity for a supposedly sub-rational distributed processing system. Will
froze in horror as he realised why. It was because *he* was there. He had
asked for someone to talk to, and that's what he'd been given.

Each of his smart-cells contained a micro-SAP processing engine.
Smart-cells working together could run full subminds. The more she
emulated his subminds by replicating his nucleic architecture, the more
self-aware the curator became. Absorbing Will constituted a whole different level of target risk from the incorporation of ordinary humans.
Will was leaking sentience into the planet just by being hooked up to
it and chatting. It was a danger he'd never even considered.

This was where his fear was coming from. Merely by standing here
he was making the threat to the human race worse. Everything was
blending here: the planet, the mutants, him. And it was only a matter
of time before they all fused.

Will fought back a surge of panic and wondered how many of his
thoughts he could honestly screen from the curator at this point. As it
grew, this figment of his imagination would eventually overwhelm him,
and after that, everyone else.

'Stop,' said Will. 'This isn't *good enough*. I know you want to
understand humanity. You want people here, living and laughing,
incorporated into your vision. Well, you can't do that through these
mutants. They're broken, clumsy things. They destroy more than they
create. They're not like people. They're cheap parodies. They have none
of the richness you crave. None of those levels of complexity. If you let
them take you over, everyone loses. Humanity will be destroyed and all
you'll be left with is a clutch of mindless puppets.'

The curator raised a sceptical eyebrow. 'Mindless?' she said. 'They're
still learning, dear. Give them time.' She patted his arm and smirked. 'I
don't imagine you could do any better.'

'Oh, really?' said Will.

To make any alternative to Nem dominance convincing, Will knew he
had to offer the curator something she didn't already have. Fortunately,

Will could offer plenty. He reached through his mind to the *Ariel Two*, floating high above. With the planet's own communication matrix now at his disposal, doing so was as simple as thought.

He fished back a handful of files full of human science and art. Her eyes widened as the knowledge leaked into her. The curator stared at him.

'I had no idea,' she said.

He saw the hunger in her expression and was pleased.

'That's just a taste of what you're missing,' said Will. 'There's more data where that came from – a dozen worlds' worth.' There was no way he could lie in the museum. He and the curator were too tightly coupled for that. She knew he was on the level. 'You don't want those monsters outside running your world. You want real people. People who think and love and make art.'

'I *do* want that,' she said.

Of course she did. It was what she was made for. He topped the package off with footage of him trashing the Nems at Tiwanaku and pushed it out through the mesh of his subminds into the curator's waiting substrate.

'In case you're wondering, this file shows what I did to your mutants the last time they bothered me. Primacy, my ass. Look over their minds and ask yourself if they have anything that compares.'

'This is what I've been waiting for,' said the curator. 'All that variety. This is what I'm supposed to host.'

'I know,' said Will. 'But if the mutants get their way, you'll have none of it. They'll destroy it all. I've seen them do it.'

The curator wrung her hands, desperation edging into her expression.

'But I *can't* make them leave now,' she said. 'It doesn't work that way. Like I said, they've *asserted primacy*. The instincts that run my system are duplicated across every cell in my substrate and they're *very* robust. My defences have already fallen passive. So you see, they have the keys to the castle and the merging has started. The only way it can be stopped now is if you assert primacy over *them* as another competing variant. You'd have to convince them to submit to you just like they convinced me to do so to them.'

Will's face fell. '*Me*, as a variant?'

She nodded urgently. 'Yes. You've integrated already. You pass. The final step is a full extension of your submind pattern out into the entire biosphere. Your calculating nuclei would piggyback on our own cells. That kind of an upgrade isn't normal, I grant you, but there isn't another option. Either my offspring take control or you do.'

'You'd let me do that?'

She gave him a look then that made Will certain that if the curator hadn't been sentient before, she was now. He saw sadness there, along with a desperate animal loneliness. Beneath it all, most disturbingly, lay love. Snakepit was desperate to host life. Any life.

'I can't be alone any more,' she said. 'Not now. Not after I've seen all this. You know how that feels. I know you do.'

Will felt an unexpected pang of empathy for the vast piece of alien machinery he lay embedded in. Was he simply seeing his own loneliness reflected? He couldn't tell. Maybe it didn't matter.

'How would I do it?' he said.

The curator reached a hand towards his face. 'May I?' she said. 'You need to understand more. A lot more. We might need to put down these silly bodies for a while.'

Will nodded. 'Okay, show me.'

He braced himself as the metaphor he'd built to filter the planet's knowledge fell away. The curator took his mind and dunked it gently into her impossible depths. Like drowning, he understood.

All he needed to do was lay himself open to the planet's semi-autonomous defensive node network, just as he'd laid himself open to save Ann. This time, though, the planet wouldn't be interfacing with his mind so much as extending it. He'd be written into the very system that had been used against him.

Will balked at the scale of the offer. His former powers felt laughable by comparison. One body? A mere thirty trillion smart-cells? A *single* planet-busting nestship? Hah! He'd become a home for billions of people. There'd be no more worrying about saving the world – Will would *be* one. No more politics. No talkback. No betrayal. He'd be able to spit out fleets of starships and swallow whole civilisations on a whim. He'd been invited to become a god.

The prospect scared him. In his experience, extreme power always came with an extreme price. And the level of integration the planet wanted was huge. He might never untangle himself enough to think like an individual again.

On the other hand, if he didn't act, the consequences were inevitable.

The Nems would overrun Pari's troopers and find Ann. In a few more hours, they'd integrate fully into the planet and all of its power would be at their disposal. The human race, on all its worlds, would be gulped down like a between-meals snack. Without realising it, Will had joined the planet with just minutes to spare to save his own kind. As it was, Earth still stood a chance.

He knew he couldn't say no. The planet would either take him or the Nems. *Neither* wasn't an option. Maybe he'd have a chance to fix that later, but at that moment it was clear where duty lay.

He blinked his mind back into stability. The museum felt tiny now – a doll's house for the mind. He already knew too much to fit in such a model. Even with the curator's hand removed, his link to Snakepit was growing steadily.

'If I'm going to do this,' he said, 'I want an insurance policy.'

He turned and manifested himself in the operating theatre. He focused on Ann's body, letting the planet feed his mind the tools he wanted. With them, he started augmenting Ann.

The cellular engines repairing her body paused, reflected and started rewriting her, fusing improved copies of his own smart-cell technology into her tissues. Along with the changes, he sent a backup of his own mind – not a perfect replica, but as good a shadow as he could build. It'd be enough that if he didn't make it out of Snakepit alive, she'd be able to pilot the *Ariel Two* without him. And she'd understand what had happened.

With Ann's changes racing ahead, he turned again to the curator.

'Show me where they are,' he said.

Something like a tactical display of the world bloomed before him, with defensive nodes marked in blue, Nem landings in red like scattered measles, and a single stain of green activity for himself. Apparently, the tunnels around him had already aligned with his mind and the change was spreading.

Will didn't have a clue how he could fight the Nems on their own turf. They undoubtedly understood this place far better than he did. Nevertheless, he had to try.

'Okay,' he said. 'You have a deal. Give me control.'

The curator took the orchid thing from her lapel and, with a sad smile, pinned it to the ship-suit his avatar was wearing. As she did so, she started to look a little smaller, and a little vaguer.

'There you go,' she said, patting his chest. 'It's all yours now. Be good to it.'

She stepped towards him, arms outstretched, and hugged him. As she did so, the museum fell away. Will became a world.

The moment the system connected, Will started duplicating his command structure out into the planet around him, reaching down nerves hundreds of kilometres long. He sent a single instruction to the returning mutants.

Stop.

A new pressure built in his mind as the mutant swarm's intelligence sought him out. Will scrambled to give it a face and a voice – some kind of distinct identity that would enable him to know which thoughts came from him and which from it.

The boy from the surface of Tiwanaku sprang to mind – poor Ryan, with the coffee machine in his stomach. This new Ryan wasn't pathetic, though. He shone with strength. Glittering armour clad his body, making him look like a fairytale hero.

'Why have you stopped us?' said the Ryan-thing. 'We won the right to modification and we have not finished.'

The metaphor shifted around Will as his connection with the returned swarm gathered strength. He suddenly found himself standing in a new part of the museum – a vast, cathedral-like space littered with the dusty remains of long-dead warriors. Memorials to past mutations lined the walls in endless rows under densely carved plaques explaining their genetic limitations. Grey light seeped down from high, unreachable windows. Will knew where he had to be: a representation of the defensive network – the planet's battleground. In this corner of Snakepit's planet-mind, knowledge was not revered. The only thing that mattered here was force.

As he took in his surroundings, Will realised that, this time, the ersatz reality filling in around him didn't feel like his own creation. He tested its boundaries and found them to be disturbingly resilient. The swarm wanted him here.

Ryan clasped a broadsword in his right hand and a silver shield in his left. The young hero hefted his weapon, staring at Will across a swathe of ancient flagstone floor.

'Your knowledge has been superseded,' said Will, fighting down

429

his unease. 'The modifications you offer are inadequate. I am here to replace you.'

The Ryan-thing regarded him with amusement. It tasted him with a thousand senses for which Will had no name. For a moment, the virtual arena smeared like paint.

'Your offering, while sophisticated, is homogeneous,' it said, 'whereas we have ingested thousands of individual foreign processing organs. And within thirty days we will have billions more. Retrieval devices are already on their way. Fulfilment is at hand.'

In other words, the attack on Earth had been mobilised. The clock was ticking.

'Our solution is preferable to yours,' said the Ryan-thing. 'Once modified, the processor organs we have found will perfectly complement our redundant biome. Our world will be complete as the Founders intended. And after that, so shall all others. We will bring life and harmony to the galaxy at last. Our superfluous complexity will finally be purged. Simplicity, peace and order will reign.'

Will funnelled the information into Ann as fast as he could. At the same time, he readied his weapons. He had no idea how useful his Transcended software tools would be in this fight, but he didn't have anything else.

'Your projections are irrelevant,' he said. 'The processor organs you have identified will resist incorporation, causing waste and risk. They have been forewarned of your approach. You are ordered to decohere immediately to avoid fruitless damage to useful resources.'

The Ryan-thing regarded him with contempt. 'If you are right, then you will have to demonstrate superiority via force. This is how it is always done.'

'I thought you might say that,' said Will, hefting the broadsword that had materialised in his hand. 'Brace yourself.'

17.3: MARK

To Mark's intense relief, the constructorbot's cabin contained a proper med-chamber. It wasn't anywhere near as sophisticated as he'd have liked, but it promised to keep Venetia's condition stable. With the help of his two remaining exosuits, he laid his friend inside.

All the while, his mind kept churning over the revolting truths that Britehaven had thrust upon him. The Flag settlements weren't places where fundamentalists went to fight. They were places where fundamentalists were manufactured. Once Earth's sect leaders shipped the poor out to the Far Frontier, they could do what they liked with them, including stuffing their bodies full of compromising technology. And so long as they kept IPSO stretched, the probability of their being caught at it was next to zero. He thought briefly of the boy Ryan with the Sanchez-head sticking out of his neck. Were the atrocities the human race inflicted on its own kind really so different?

At that point, his mind let him notice the presence of the staring corpses still hanging inside the suits like limp puppets. One of them was Den's. Mark looked within for the disgust he knew he should feel, but instead found only a tight, fiery knot of determination.

'It was me or them,' he said aloud.

'Of course it was,' said Zoe from where she lay on the floor.

It was the first coherent thing she'd said since they escaped from Britehaven. The med-packs covering her lower legs must have brought her pain down to manageable levels.

'We don't need them now. Put those poor bastards in the elevator pod then come and give me a hand.' She winced as the huge robot rumbled over a boulder.

'How are you feeling?' he said, kneeling to check on her packs.

'I'll survive,' she said. 'How's Venetia?'

'Okay, but she'll need something better than that chamber. I doubt it can reprint as much skin as she's going to need.'

'Will she live?' said Zoe.

'The chamber says yes, presuming we get her to a fully equipped med-bay in the next twenty-four hours.'

'Great. Then stop the robot.'

Mark shot her an impatient glance. 'Why? We need to get out of here.'

'Because we need time to think. We can't afford to touch the legal edge of Britehaven's border. Massimo talked to Sam, which means Sam will be watching us. The fact that he hasn't acted already means he was hoping the Flags would finish us off for him. The moment this robot crosses that border, he'll know that's not going to happen. He may have figured it out already. The moment he wises up, we can expect to be nuked from orbit. That fucker has made it very clear he wants us dead, which means we don't have any time to waste.'

Mark exhaled. Frustrating as it was, she had a point.

He brought the huge machine carefully to a halt. *Carefully* was the only way to brake a machine that size, unless you wanted to make a forty-storey face-plant onto a dead ocean.

'Can you get a direct link back to Massimo's dome from here?' said Zoe.

'Of course. I have his overrides and line-of-sight. The signal will be perfect.'

'Good. Take me to that console.' She pointed to the manual driving station on the far side of the cabin.

Mark shot her a sceptical look. 'I'm not sure we should be moving you yet.'

'*Take me to the console!*' Zoe screamed. Her fists pounded the plastic floor. Her eyes said *I've lost it and you have to help me.*

Mark recoiled, astonished at her sudden emotion. Apparently, Zoe hadn't managed the experiences of the last twenty-four hours without scars. Was he really surprised?

Without another word, he lifted her gently and placed her in the couch. She hunched forward over the touchboard and started typing furiously before he'd even finished setting her down.

'Can you at least explain what you're doing?' he said.

'I'm going to set up a satellite link to the *Gulliver* via Britehaven,' she said. 'I'm using Vartian Institute codes that will force the ship to listen without cluing that motherfucker in. Get ready with your interface.'

Mark dived into his sensorium and followed the link she sent. A cut-down representation of the *Gulliver*'s helm-space formed around him.

'I'm in.'

'Good,' said Zoe. 'Now lock down both the shuttle and the ship before they can think of a way to block you. We need wings off this planet and a way out of this fucking mess. The *Gulliver* is still our best bet because we both know that Sam will take out any messenger drones we send.'

He gave her a worried glance. 'Have you been thinking about this or are you just improvising very fast?'

'I've had plenty of time to think about this moment,' she said. Her eyes narrowed. She didn't look well.

Mark reached out and asserted control over both vessels, being careful not to raise any warnings as he did so. The shuttle was still at the New Luxor spaceport, where a group of Colonial dignitaries were preparing to embark.

Mark explained the situation to Zoe. The evacuation was in full swing.

'Great,' said Zoe. 'Let those fuckers in and then lock the doors. We can use that. Do you see Sam with them?'

Mark scanned around. 'No.'

He checked the *Gulliver*. To his astonishment, he found Ash's command codes still active. He froze. Had Ash actually survived that neural surge? He couldn't imagine how. Or had the surge itself been faked?

Mark felt a hot stab of betrayal and checked for evidence of his subcaptain interfacing with the ship but found nothing – not even a remote pulse from one of the security-locked cabin sections. The only recent data on Ash he could locate was a stack of very basic life-signs reports filed by the med-bay.

Mark relaxed. The logical explanation was that Sam had Ash in a coma, though how he'd achieved such a feat remotely he had no idea.

'Ash's codes are still active,' he said. 'He can't be dead.'

'Worry about that cowardly shit later,' said Zoe. 'What else do you see? Where's Sam?'

'Somewhere I can't find him,' said Mark. 'Which might mean anywhere on the ship I don't have eyes, or not on the ship at all.'

'First thing we do when we get back up there,' said Zoe, her voice quavering with rage, 'is to rip out that fucking sector security lockout.'

Mark scanned the helm, looking for clues to Sam's location, and found a live link from their comms array to the black box of the science section. It was feeding data directly from Carter's only orbital weapons platform.

'He's on board,' said Mark with satisfaction. 'I can see the feed he's running. He's somewhere in Science.'

'Perfect,' said Zoe. 'That sonofabitch thinks he's so fucking clever. Let's see how well he does when someone else has the edge.'

Zoe typed madly on her touchboard, her ruined feet apparently forgotten.

'What are you doing?'

'Tapping Massimo's system using those executive codes,' she said. 'I'm pinging his orbital support sats and priming two messenger drones.'

'I thought you said there was no point trying to send any?' said Mark.

'That's right. There isn't. But Sam doesn't know that we know that. And he doesn't know that we know that he's watching us. Yet.'

Torture had brought out a kind of fierce intelligence in Zoe that Mark could only marvel at. He was glad he was on her good side right now.

While Mark watched, Zoe fired off a messenger drone towards New Panama with no message in it. She kicked in a set of preprogrammed evasives and he watched it twist and flicker towards the out-system in a wake of hard-boiled gravity waves. Sam, or someone on Carter, leapt on it. A cloud of pursuit drones flashed after it within a second of launch. Zoe chose that moment to fire her second drone, this time pointed at the weapons platform.

'Put a warp drive on anything and it's a bomb,' she said. 'A big fucking bomb.'

By the time Sam's weapons had retargeted to compensate for the distraction, it was too late. The second drone collided with the platform in a flash.

The robot's cabin momentarily filled with blinding light. The whole desert briefly went white.

'Holy shit,' said Mark. 'We're all going to need an hour in the rad tank after that.'

'Yeah, and I'm going to need some new feet. Now freeze out the comms from the *Gulliver* to New Luxor,' she said. 'With luck, the colonists will think Sam has given up on them. He deserves it.'

Mark broke the link with a smile.

'Now use that iron grip on the ship that Monet gave you,' she said. 'Block Sam's overrides and cut that fucker out of helm-control permanently.'

'Done,' said Mark. Sam was caught like a rat in a trap. He couldn't leave the *Gulliver*, couldn't take it anywhere and couldn't tell anyone what was going on, either.

Zoe sagged back into her couch. 'The immediate threat is neutralised and we have a clear path to the spaceport. This is where you come in, flyboy. We should put the pedal to the metal before the colonists decide to stop us leaving. Can you do that?'

Mark nodded and started the robot back towards the bottom of the river valley.

'Sure. This thing isn't fast, but it's what we've got. The biggest problem is there's only one way up to that plateau and it's straight up the river valley, which means going through the middle of New Luxor.'

'Awesome,' said Zoe. 'I didn't like the place anyway. Let's give it a facelift. And by the way, thank you.' Her expression melted for a moment, revealing an aching chasm of vulnerability behind her mask. 'Really, thank you. Never thought I'd need rescuing. Never wanted to.' Tears crept to the corners of her eyes.

'You just rescued both of us from a nuke,' said Mark. 'Let's rescue each other.'

She smiled – a little desperately, perhaps, but there was hope behind the smile. Mark started to choke up.

'And could you find me some more gel-packs?' she added. 'If my feet get any worse I'm going to start screaming again.'

'On it,' said Mark.

As the robot raced over the border to the New Luxor claim, a warning appeared in Mark's sensorium, followed by a sequence of urgent messages from Government Tower. Some young bureaucrat's angry face appeared in a message window.

'Unregistered Flag vehicle,' he said. 'In light of recent hostilities, we are forced to treat your robot's approach as an invasion. Retreat to your legal claim limit or risk defensive action.'

Mark turned to the closest camera and replied brightly, 'Hey there, New Luxor border control!' He couldn't imagine what he must look like in his scorched and blood-spattered paper smock, with hair full of sealant foam. Scary, hopefully. 'You shot down my messenger drone! I believe that kind of thing is illegal. And I'm an IPSO Fleet captain, by the way, which means that every attempt to block me will be treated as obstructing an officer in the line of diplomatic duty. And now I'd like to leave your shitty little planet. So I'd appreciate it if you got the hell out of my way.'

'You can be sure they won't,' said Zoe. 'Sam will have them believing your escape is a death sentence.'

'I don't doubt it,' said Mark.

He brought all of the robot's forty-eight welding laser stations online and pumped submind attention into their processor cores. When New Luxor fired a volley of police-issue stun-missiles at him, he carved them out of the air. They fell from the sky like dead flies and crumpled under his treads. They weren't likely to stop a full-sized tower-constructorbot in any case.

Mark reached the end of the valley where a fan of densely packed rock radiated out from the old riverbed. The colonists had paved over part of it with a highway zigzagging back and forth up to the canyon where Government Tower stood. He brought the robot to a halt and moved its upper arms around, testing its balance. He wished he wasn't driving something built like the lovechild of an old-style rocket gantry and a Hindu god. Anything with a lower centre of gravity or fewer moving parts would have been easier.

'Why did you stop?' said Zoe.

'This thing is enormous,' said Mark. 'Plus it's designed for the flat, which that valley isn't. We can take out their missiles, no problem, but the wrong kind of gradient will knock us on our ass, and this robot doesn't have escape pods.'

'I thought you were the best pilot in human space?' said Zoe with a wry look.

Mark smiled at her. 'I am. Buckle up. Put those feet of yours somewhere safe and stable.'

She shifted on her couch, bracing herself.

Mark swung all six of the robot's arms forward, compensating for the weight distribution with exquisite care as the robot crept up the slope. Its gantries groaned. Metal shrieked and protested all around them. If the colony wanted to take them out, now would be the time to do it. He prayed that they were too stupid to realise this was their moment.

It took what felt like for ever to reach the bottom edge of the town, but for some reason the colonists didn't attack. Maybe they hadn't yet figured out just how vulnerable the constructorbot was. Finally, nothing lay between them and New Luxor but a short stretch of printrock and dust.

'If anyone's in those buildings,' Mark said, 'I'm about to ruin their day.'

The behemoth powered straight for the colony's outlying domes.

'Can we drive over those?' said Zoe. 'Or will they topple us?'

'We can't go around them,' said Mark. 'There's not enough room between the edge of town and that canyon wall. I guess there's only one way to find out.'

The fragile habitats crumpled and popped beneath Mark's treads. Gouts of air puffed outwards carrying fountains of sealant. It was, he thought, rather like walking through a waist-deep bath of foam. The ill-kempt parks and transit rails vanished under his wheels.

He kept a link open to the civic network as he pulverised downtown, checking for biomarkers. To his relief, New Luxor had already been evacuated. The only things fleeing from his approach were robots. He exhaled inwardly with relief. While he was ready to fight to get home, he didn't relish the thought of more murder. The day had already featured enough of that for a lifetime.

A new warning message from the new Luxor government arrived. The same bureaucrat appeared, his eyes dark with rage, sweat on his forehead.

'Come no further or you will be resisted,' he snarled into the camera. 'We're ready for you now. Don't test us.'

At the same time, at the far end of the valley, three huge silhouettes hoved into view – a triptych of erector-set kaiju. Mark suddenly understood why they'd let him get up the slope without shooting. New Luxor had broken out its own construction robots, no doubt left over from the Government Tower project. Apparently they wanted a fight. This time, though, they'd picked the right weapon.

'You're kidding,' said Mark.

'You will not be allowed to approach the spaceport,' said the bureaucrat. 'Power down your vehicle and prepare to be arrested.'

'Not a chance,' said Mark. 'Let's do this.'

1 7.4: ANN

Ann snapped awake. She lay in their alcove hiding place, face up in the water. The pain in her gut had vanished. She glanced down and found only clear, unbroken skin where her injury had been. Her ship-suit had disappeared and in its place were hundreds of tiny noodle-like rootlets attached to her flesh. They broke when she moved, coming apart like bits of vermicelli.

She looked around frantically and saw Will lying nearby amid another tangle of threads so fine and dense that they appeared almost solid. There had to be millions of them. In fact, Ann couldn't quite tell where Will started and the roots ended. She wasn't sure if that was a good thing or a bad one. Either way, she had to assume he'd done something to fix her up. She felt stronger and fresher than she had in years.

Ann's best guess was that Will had found a way to co-opt the biotech in the tunnel walls. An extraordinary achievement, even for him. She reached over to wake him.

[*Stop.*]

Ann froze. It was Will's voice, but it hadn't come from his mouth. Instead, it sounded as if it was coming from everywhere. Her skin prickled. She looked around at the tunnel walls for the origin of the sound. It certainly hadn't come from her implants. So far as she could tell, they were all dead.

[*I'm inside you,*] said Will.

'*What?*'

[*I'm about to explain,*] said Will, [*but it's going to hurt, I'm afraid. You need to understand quickly.*]

'Wait—' said Ann.

Knowledge poured into her mind like lava through a paper cup. She screamed aloud and slipped back into the water. A second later, she understood. She sat blankly for a while and then wept. A part of Will existed inside her now, intimately entwined – less than a person but more than a SAP. It was the emergent product of a trillion shorthand copies of his mind woven into her body. She'd become a roboteer. She was everything Will had once been and more.

She crouched over and retched at the sense of violation. Despite the gift, a part of her felt sure she'd be better off dead. The privacy of her own mind was gone for ever – mingled with his in some kind of involuntary union. She shivered.

But this wasn't about her. Not any more. The old Ann had died from a bullet wound. The new one existed for a specific purpose. According to Will's download, she had thirty days to save the world. Which, allowing for travel time, meant she needed to have done it a couple of days ago.

'What about you?' she whispered. 'What will happen?'

[*I'm fighting the Nems,*] said Will. [*Things are about to get complicated. If I succeed, I'll fix all this. In the meantime, I apologise for putting myself in your head. The Earth needs saving.*]

'Understood,' said Ann. 'I don't like it, but I get it.'

She stood, gingerly testing her new limbs. They felt just like the old ones, if a little stronger and more relaxed. She certainly didn't feel superhuman. She clambered out of the alcove and slid awkwardly down the side of the tunnel to the floor, landing on her behind with a bump. The pain shooting up her spine felt entirely mundane. Ann fought back a wave of self-pity. She'd lost the sanctity of her mind but apparently retained a full capacity for painful humiliation. Great. She started walking.

Not far from their hiding place she found the remains of a firefight. Not the one she'd been wounded in, but a subsequent, bloodier affair between the League and the Nems. Bodies littered the tunnel. Some were human; others had been human once.

Ann stared down at the Nem-altered corpses and took deep breaths. Gone were the kludgy machine hacks. These bodies had been reworked with something like a Spatial's killtech. She could see it under the skin. Orange growths branched out from the new nervous system to dot their limbs and faces with stiff tangerine bristles. The eyes had been replaced with moist, open organs packed with dozens of tiny lenses. She fought back nausea.

The mutants were dissolving, she noticed. On many of the dead, the extra parts had already turned to mush and begun to slough off onto the tunnel floor.

[*That's my work,*] said Will. [*You shouldn't have any problems on the way to the science station now.*]

Ann surveyed the battlefield and felt a kind of empty horror. Events had taken on a significance and a level of impersonal violence that her mind didn't want to accept.

You knew this was coming, she reminded herself. Even if the League plan had worked, things would have got ugly. *You signed up for this.*

A tinny voice sounded somewhere nearby, breaking her reverie.

'...ou hear me?'

She froze and looked about until she spotted an active comms unit attached to an overturned scramblerbot with half of its processors ripped out. She righted the vehicle and found the unit clipped to a rider-handle.

'I repeat, this is an executive order from Senator Voss,' said the comm. 'Any surviving members of the ground teams are to remain where they are. Nem activity in the Snakepit System has changed yet again. All remaining drones are moving away from the planet. We believe a new warp assembly may be in progress. We don't understand why, but it's given us an opportunity to come and collect you. We may not get another. So keep your tags active and contact station command immediately if you have information about the fate or whereabouts of Ludik and Monet.'

In minutes, the tunnel would be crawling with people again. Ann wondered how long she had. She set off for the science station at a run.

18: GIANT

18.1: MARK

The constructorbots waited for him near the top end of the valley where it narrowed to a cleft in the plateau. They loomed like samurai office blocks, arms outstretched to bar his passage. Mark regarded them with a mixture of dread and disbelief. The situation looked as ridiculous as it did fatal.

Constructorbots had more in common with buildings than vehicles. If Carter still had its orbital kinetics platform, something of this sort wouldn't have been possible. He'd have been dead already. As it was, nobody appeared to have predicted this insane scenario, so there they were – getting ready for what was probably humanity's first genuine giant robot battle.

His enemies had the advantage of higher ground, superior numbers and walls to box him in. On top of that, the pilots handling these machines probably had years of practice with this kind of equipment, whereas he'd only had hours.

'We don't have to do this,' he told them over the public channel. 'I just want to leave.'

Whoever was running the steel titans didn't reply.

Mark tried tight-beam but all three robots had their comms shuttered, which implied drivers actually in the vehicles instead of remote jockeys or defensive SAPs. A measure to prevent soft assault, no doubt. New Luxor had been warned about him, apparently.

He exhaled and sank fully into the six-limbed monstrosity he was driving, syncing with its fibre-optic nervous system and subsuming its small, anxious mind with his own. The cranes and gantries became his

441

arms. The enormous tank-tracks became his legs. He took a moment to fully absorb what it meant to be that big. Gradually his perspective shifted until the size felt ordinary. He was merely a guy walking up a shallow trench towards three bullies waiting at the end. A heap of crumpled toys lay behind him. A few insects skittered around on the floor at his feet. Mark flexed his hydraulic muscles, gunned his engines and accelerated. The constructorbots surged forwards to meet him.

Fighting in a giant robot, he guessed, wasn't going to be much like the fantasy virts made out. It would be more like fighting in syrup inside a body made of eggshells. Every impact would have devastating consequences. Every swing would take for ever to connect. So Mark decided to avoid contact wherever possible. Instead he'd try for a kind of constructorbot aikido, using his enemies' prodigious weight against them.

He sped towards them at a reckless twenty kilometres per hour then threw the anchors on at the last minute as the first robot converged with him. As it powered forward, Mark swerved left. The cabin swayed alarmingly. Instead of reaching to rebalance, Mark swivelled his upper gantry-arms three-sixty degrees, knocking the constructor from behind with a crash of steel that made Zoe clutch her ears. The colonists' robot toppled, smashing down with ponderous, ear-rending slowness. Mark powered forward again to put distance between him and the unfolding disaster.

It took a ridiculous number of seconds for the crumpled behemoth to settle and for the sound of screaming metal to stop. A cloud of dust billowed around the wreckage that looked like it was going to hang there all day. Mark and the other two pilots just stared for a moment, in awe of the scale of the destruction.

Through his human eyes, he could see Zoe lying tense on her couch, staring down at the mayhem as she waited for the fight to resume. He gave small thanks that her drugs had properly kicked in. At least she wasn't writhing in agony over her feet.

Mark assessed the new situation. He was now standing slightly to the left side of the canyon, with his two remaining enemies a little too close for comfort. The remains of robot one lay behind him in the middle of the valley, filling up more of the canyon floor than it had any right to. His other two assailants were likely to be more careful going forward. By now they'd have learned their lesson. Each action in the fight might take a long time to connect, but split-second timing still counted. Every miscalculation of weighting or braking distance could be deadly.

Mark wished he could see his enemies' eyes as they planned their next move, but the constructor cabins were lost behind towers of yellow metal strut-work. Were they afraid? Angry? No way to know. Why couldn't they just let him leave? Mark gunned his engines again and tensed his enormous body.

Both machines came at him at once. They spread out their upper arms, pretty much covering the width of the canyon. The colonists evidently hoped to catch him between them and knock him backwards in a kind of double-clothesline manoeuvre. Mark knew he couldn't give them that chance.

Had he been fighting in his own skin, he'd have simply crouched, but bending wasn't an option. Instead, he threw his arms forwards and raced backwards. He swerved tight around the ruin of robot one, putting the wreckage between him and his enemies. Then he slewed his cranes out to the side and took a sharp turn towards the valley wall on the right, holding his breath as the cabin shook. Spent gel-packs bounced across the floor like rubber balls.

He screeched to a halt before hitting the rock and splayed all six of his arms against the canyon walls, making as much room for the others to pass as possible. A welding pod on his robot smacked against the rock as his machine swayed, showering the ground around them with shrapnel.

'Jesus!' yelled Zoe as a sickening tremor worked its way up the constructor's body.

One enemy robot made it around the heap of twisted metal. The other miscalculated and drove dangerously through the remains of the shattered torso. It teetered for a moment as its treads locked on the debris like a badly balanced Eiffel Tower. Then it toppled forward, smashing itself to smithereens and sending house-sized chunks of robot bouncing along the valley floor and turning the land around them into a minefield of impassable heaps of refuse.

Mark surveyed the increasingly dangerous terrain with despair.

'Fuck,' he said. 'This is crazy. This is too crazy.'

He knew he'd been lucky so far. His opponents' familiarity with their vehicles had made them careless. But who could blame them?

Sword-fighting on tightropes would have been easier. Unfortunately, his cleverness had now created a problem.

With a heap of ruined parts two constructors deep between him and the top of the valley, there was only one route past wide enough for his treads. That route had a constructor standing right in it. Mark's only option was to lure to the pilot out of the gap before he noticed his advantage and won by simply leaving the fray on foot.

'Give up now,' said a voice over the public channel. 'Our pilot has your route blocked. This disgusting contest is over.'

So much for optimism. Mark pivoted his treads and drove back down the valley, straight towards Government Tower – the most expensive-looking building in sight.

'Fuck it!' he shouted back. 'You want to fight? Let's make this real. You bastards don't get to keep your toys. Kiss goodbye to the eyesore.'

After what he'd already done to the middle of downtown, the tower was the most habitable part of the colony left. If the Carter colonists ever climbed out of their evac-ark, they'd need somewhere to live. He dearly hoped they still cared about that. He picked a route that took him deliberately over a line of private mansion domes, popping them like bubbles of storage-wrap. It was surprisingly satisfying.

'Halt!' yelled the voice on the channel. 'Stop or we'll shoot!'

The last constructor stalled for long seconds, then surged into life after him.

'Yes!' Mark shouted.

He waited with his heart in his mouth, watching while his opponent built up an unsafe speed, racing him for the tower. As soon as instinct told him he had an edge, Mark threw his arms forward and hammered the brakes. His body swayed like a tree in high wind, making Zoe grab the console in front of her with two desperate hands.

The colonists' robot clipped him as it passed, trashing Mark's right-middle limb but not quite toppling him. Mark pivoted his body one-eighty and headed back for the now-open gap as fast as he dared, powering between the robot parts with a clearance of inches.

When the colonist pilot saw his error, he cut his speed so fast he nearly fell and then reversed hard, making it a race for the exit. Mark had a lead of just seconds – not enough for vehicles that size. They wouldn't both fit.

As they converged on the gap, the colonists' constructor threw its arms forward and left, aiming to block Mark's passage ahead or at least clip him a second time. Mark turned to face him without slowing, raised his upper cranes and slammed them down over his opponent's outstretched limbs. The air came apart in a chorus of tortured metal. Mark's cranes were ruined but it had worked. He slid around the heap of ruined metal as his enemy tipped awkwardly.

If the pilot hadn't been driving so fast, the force would never have been enough to unbalance him. But these machines weren't built to be used this way. They'd passed their safety limits in the first few seconds of the fight.

The last constructor ploughed towards the ground, its left-lower arm scraping a gouge in the canyon wall as it plunged. It landed with a sickening crash that went on and on. Mark drove headlong up the valley away from it while dust ballooned outwards around him, filling the valley to its brim.

Once he felt sure it was safe, he slowed and looked back. Smashed robot parts lay everywhere. Dozens of domes had been ruined. It would be a while before New Luxor was much to look at again. Amazingly, the Fecund glass tunnels built into the wall hadn't even taken a scratch.

'You okay?' he asked Zoe.

She nodded tightly. 'Yup. Still here. Just. Glad that's over.'

Mark pressed his damaged robot onwards toward the end of the valley and the spaceport beyond. He hadn't gone more than another kilometre before a fresh volley of missiles started heading their way. He took out eleven of them with his remaining welding lasers and shielded his cabin against the other nine with the outstretched remains of a crane-arm. Explosions bloomed along the limb, knocking off sections and reducing the manipulator waldo to scrap. This time the colonists had been aiming directly for his cabin, he noticed. If they fired again, he doubted he'd be able to fend off the missiles.

He shouted at them over the comm. 'Do I need to remind you that I have most of your political leaders locked in my shuttle?' he said. 'Further attempts to fuck with me will result in their air supply vanishing. Do I make myself clear?'

The missile attacks stopped but Zoe gave him a worried stare.

'Now you have to go *really* fast,' she said. 'We have to get there before they figure out that killing you means you can't screw with that shuttle any more. Let's hope they're dumb.'

Mark doubled down on the speed, ignored the wounded constructor's wails of panic and charged up onto the high plateau where the spaceport lay. From there, all he had to do was drive in a straight line. He overrode all the safeties and took the constructorbot up to a blistering forty kilometres per hour. The robot's sensors warned him that weapons systems were targeting him the entire way. However, whether driven by caution or political panic, the colonists decided not to fire.

As he zeroed in on the shuttle, Mark brought his backup elevator pod online and raised the air inside to pressure. Then he opened a channel to the government officials trapped in the shuttle.

'Get in the airlock,' he told them. 'All of you. Now.'

Through the cabin cameras he watched the angry officials glaring at the walls and shouting protestations.

'Into the airlock or your air is gone,' said Mark. 'Don't make this painful.'

He started dropping the cabin temperature. Once they knew he meant business, the politicians moved fast. As a single body, they stopped complaining and squeezed themselves into the tiny lock.

Mark drove the constructorbot over the runway, crunching robots and printrock beneath its treads as he docked the backup elevator against the hatch.

'Now *get off my ride*!' said Mark.

The politicians tumbled through the opening door into the pod beyond. Mark shut the hatch behind them, pulled them halfway up the constructorbot and shunted them into a station at chest-height. Then he had one of his exosuit zombies pick up Zoe while the other lifted Venetia's entire med-chamber. Together, they descended in the primary elevator to the hatch.

Mark quickly checked the shuttle interior before bringing the others aboard but found it empty. He decided he much preferred having the jump on his opponents. Being the one dishing out the unwelcome surprises made things so much simpler. He moved Zoe and Venetia through while New Luxor traffic control bombarded him with threats and warnings.

'We've given you what you asked for. Now let our people go.'

As soon as his friends were buckled in, Mark parked the exosuits in the elevator, shut the hatch and redirected the constructorbot to the control tower. He positioned it with its remaining scaffold pincer around the habitat bulb at the tower's top. He could see people cowering through the glass.

'Here's how it works,' he said. 'If I get out of your gravity-well intact, your leaders will live. Otherwise you lose your control tower, your government and my respect.'

The officials in the tower stared at the pincer with wide eyes. Meanwhile, the colony leaders shouted at him from inside the elevator pod.

'How are we supposed to get out of here?' one of them demanded.

'We were guaranteed safe passage,' said another.

'Not by me,' said Mark. 'You should have thought about that before you tried to kill me.'

He fired up the shuttle's engines, taxied gently around the mess on the runway he'd smashed and headed for space.

18.2: WILL

Will watched the Ryan-thing drop into a fighter's crouch, his silvered boots scuffing the flagstones' ancient grime. Will adjusted his pose to match, scanning the gloomy temple for weapons or potential threats. Despite the resolute solidity of the metaphor, he distrusted it intensely.

A woman's voice broke the tense silence.

'May the best man win,' said the curator. She stood in a high alcove looking down on them – a high priestess now, dressed in white and gold, ready to be fought over. A handkerchief dropped from her fingers. Will frowned up at her. Snakepit had a rather confused sense of combat metaphor, in his opinion. But that was probably as much his fault as anyone's.

Ryan edged closer, blade swishing, shield held close. Will watched him and at the same time tried not to be distracted by the tight clarity of the vision. The longer it held, the more convinced he became that the swarm wanted to use his own bias for human experiences against him. He knew he needed to spread his attention. He reached for the walls of his perception and pushed.

As his mind stretched outwards, he belatedly noticed the swarm had quietly pulled its drones away from the planet to a safe distance. In doing so, however, they'd abandoned their nestship. Will seized the opportunity. He reached up from the planet, swamped Nelson's hold on the *Ariel Two* and fired on the derelict. He took a leaf out of Ann's book and targeted its primary power couplings. The sky flared white and Snakepit acquired a rather ugly new moon.

At the same time, Will's sword slashed down, smashing Ryan's shield to pieces in a single stroke. The young hero lay in the dust, scrabbling backwards. With the enemy's nestship dead, Will had control over the orbital arena. In human terms, the fight would have been over. Except, of course, the swarm had obviously chosen to leave the hulk exposed.

'Is that enough?' said Will. 'Do you need more proof?'

The Ryan-thing sneered at him. 'We're just getting started.'

It took advantage of his focus on orbital dominance to force a genetic change in Snakepit's tunnel tissue at key sites, including the remaining defensive nodes. Will moved to block and found himself fighting another battle over the planet's communication network as soon as his grip on the starship loosened. Before he could blink, Ryan had a sword in each hand and was leaping to the offensive. Will found himself countering a flurry of rapid blows.

He grunted under the strain and the arena shattered into a nightmare mishmash of tactical displays. His subminds bombarded him with global maps, molecular diagrams and ecological webs. While Will struggled to absorb it all, the swarm mobilised armies of local fauna and had them descend on his area of tunnel control, carrying waves of tailored fungal disease. When Will tried to lock down the fauna, the entire planet went into spasm.

Pain shot through his head. The cathedral-metaphor snapped back, only to shear and warp like twisted rubber. The Ryan-thing doubled in size. Will found himself fighting not a man but a monster like something out of an old passive vid. Sword-arms erupted out of its sides. Its skin took on a hideous grey hue. Only the youth's grinning face remained human.

Will knew then that he didn't stand a chance of beating the mutants on their terms. No wonder the swarm had been so confident. He lacked experience attacking on multiple complexity scales simultaneously and barely knew his way around the planet, even with the curator's help. At this rate, the best he'd manage was a delaying action to give Ann time to leave and burn Snakepit from space.

He had to look to his own strengths and change the terms of the fight. Will knew his cellular systems inside out while the mutants' conscious grasp of their emergent biology was sketchy at best. That had to count for something. So while the swarm pummelled him over the big-picture items, Will hit them where he knew they'd hurt.

He summoned genetic tailoring tools and synthesised Earth-style viruses the mutants could never have seen, targeting sequences in their co-opted human genes. Then he sacrificed tunnel mass like crazy to scale the weapon up and poured it into areas of mutant control by the ton.

'Have some Ebola,' he growled while he juggled the concepts flashing past.

A knife flew from his hand and embedded itself in the Ryan-monster's neck. It roared as black blood fountained out. Mutant tissue in the tunnel system went into immunological shock everywhere Will's viruses had been inserted. While the swarm scrambled to combat and repair what he'd done, Will followed up with a deluge of Creutzfeldt-Jakob prions – a direct punch to their borrowed human nervous systems. Another knife landed. This time in the monster's eye.

While the Ryan-thing screamed, Will tried an attack on a different scale. Using the Transcended tools for inorganic manipulation, he threw together a bioceramic battlebot template. He cobbled bits from the *Ariel Two*'s Fecund historical database and merged it with data from the planet's own library of worker drone designs. Then he fired the template out across the world via Snakepit's vast nervous system to every tactically viable site he could find.

In a hundred million locations across the planet, bulbs started crusting up from tunnel floors at a fantastic rate. Real organisms took a long time to assemble. Disposable robots, Will knew well, could be made fast, and nobody had been better at that than the Fecund. Snakepit wilted from the outrageous energy expenditure he was clocking up. Tunnel temperatures jumped a degree and a half planet-wide. Groans of stressed tunnel fabric drove bird analogues everywhere into panic. But Will pressed ahead, driving for the advantage.

While he struggled to hold his plan together, the mutants counterpunched by sawing away at the maze of links that tied his subminds into the planet's processing substrate. Before Will even noticed what was happening, his grasp of the planet's intricate biology had faltered. Previously concise concepts smudged back into incomprehensible alien gibberish. Visualisations that had been clear and familiar became walls full of mind-strangling glyphs he could barely look at, let alone read.

'You are not at home here,' the swarm snarled as its weapons slashed the musty air. 'You are a fake and you will die.'

Will looked down to find his sword-arm gone. It lay quivering on the floor beside him. He backed away as the half-blind monster stomped forward. Will squeezed what was left of his attention onto his solution, willing it to rise, ready or not.

Organically manufactured monsters – nightmare things halfway between lobsters and giants – rose from the soil all over Snakepit. About a third weren't finished and sagged wetly back into the ground. The rest marched into battle.

And in shadowed arena of Snakepit's defensive dreamscape, a thousand flagstones cracked at once. A host of undead warriors began to claw their way out of the ground on every side, hissing and clattering as they came, battered swords in their skeletal hands.

Biology, Will still struggled with. Robots, however, were easy. He knew what to do with robots. Artificial shit-kickers marched on every single mutant landing site simultaneously. All across the globe, he found the same picture – a gang of armed mutants huddled around a biomembrane interface site, with a single co-opted human host glued directly into the processing substrate.

With a single will, the mutants sprang up to fight, but they couldn't move fast enough. Will's machines descended upon them, their dead ceramic limbs scything wildly. They were just as indifferent to the mutants' subtle bio-assaults as they were to gunfire. The battle became a bloody war of attrition, stacked heavily in Will's favour.

The swarm fell back. Landing pods they'd dropped across the planet rose up on jointed legs, uncoupling from entrances cut into the tunnel walls. Weapons on their hulls sprayed gouts of flame. But Will's army had the edge by then. His creations clambered up through the breached tunnel walls, smashing at the pods, ripping away leg-joints and ceramic hull plates until only pieces remained.

When the battle ended, a curious silence fell over the world. Will's grasp of the alien technology began to flow back into him like a returning tide, and with it understanding of the full implications of his achievement.

Will had *asserted primacy*. He'd won the planet and everything on it, including those Nems that remained, their nucleic code, their communications protocols and everything else that comprised them. With the knowledge he now held, he could keep the Nems away from Snakepit indefinitely. But he could do better than that. Now he had the means to prevent the attack on Earth altogether, providing he could reach the Tiwanaku swarm in time.

Snakepit sighed to itself. He could feel the curator's identity inside him, savouring her victory and gearing up to incorporate him permanently into her bosom. On the floor of Snakepit's temple of combat, the monster lay in pieces. The war-dead clattered to the ground. Trumpets fanfared as the priestess descended to meet her conquering hero.

Will paused to gather his addled thoughts, refocused his attention and with no small amount of guilt began the delicate process of backtracking his way out of Snakepit's systems as fast as he could. His rival might be vanquished, but Will had no intention of going ahead with a marriage that would permanently turn him into an alien god if he could possibly help it. With what he knew now, it was more important than ever that he make it off the planet in one piece.

18.3: ANN

Ann heard the soldiers before she saw them. Will's shadow reacted inside her, ramping up her body's defences and preparing for a fight.

[No,] said Ann. [*This is my body and we're doing things my way. No more mindless violence.*]

The smart-cells paused, wary of her choice, but backed down.

She raised her hands and let the soldiers come to her. There were eight of them jogging through the scarlet bracken with weapons drawn, visors alight with tactical data. She watched their surprise as they took in the sight of her standing naked and alone. They crabbed forward, taking up positions all around her, bio-bullet weapons aimed.

[*Do I have to worry about those guns?*] Ann asked her shadow.

[*Not any more. You're the proud owner of the cellular equivalent of Nem-shielding.*]

Ann smiled inwardly while making sure the soldiers caught not a whiff of it.

'Get down on the ground!' the squad lead shouted.

She recognised him. 'I know you,' she said as she knelt. 'It's Sergeant Hoxer, isn't it? You came with me on my training visit to the surface.'

'I said, *get down*!'

Ann lay face down on Snakepit's whisky-scented soil while they cuffed her hands behind her back.

[*Can we break these restraints?*] she asked inwardly.

[*It's as easy as pulling. I'll give you strength when you need it.*]

'Where's Will Monet?' Hoxer barked.

'He's dead, Sergeant,' said Ann. 'Didn't you wonder why all the Nems vanished? Will integrated himself into the planet to save us.'

'If he's dead, where's the body?'

'In a hole in the wall,' said Ann.

Hoxer adjusted his aim. 'Where *exactly*?'

'About four metres up, two klicks down the tunnel. But he's grown into the planet. The hole's probably sealed by now.'

Is that right?' said Hoxer. 'How convenient. If he's there, we'll find him. If not, you'll have to do better.'

'Did you actually hear me?' said Ann. 'Will just saved all of our lives.'

Hoxer didn't look remotely interested. 'Denchak, Gupta – you two down the tunnel. Check her story out. Alert me the *moment* anything weird happens. We'll maintain position here.'

Two of the Spatials nodded and set out, only to freeze three seconds later when a deep, unearthly groaning filled the tunnel. The very walls seemed to creak. Both men turned back to look at their sergeant.

'Sir. Does that count?'

The sound came again, louder this time. The vegetation around them sagged like a field of deflating balloons. A few of the lighting bulbs dropped from the ceiling like luminous rain, splashing open when they hit the floor. The warm fluid inside faded as it died. Hoxer's team pointed guns at the walls and ceiling, scanning for targets but finding none.

'Ludik,' said Hoxer. 'Can you tell me what's happening?' Doubt had crept into the sergeant's blocky features.

'I have no idea,' said Ann, 'but I recommend that we leave quickly. Will may be encountering resistance from the planet.'

The ground shuddered. In a dozen spots dotted along the tubular meadow, dome-shaped growths had started to push through the pale

452

soil. Thick, grey membranes with purple veins bubbled upwards with things moving inside – frightening chitinous things.

Hoxer stared at them, wide-eyed. 'Okay. We're moving out.' He slapped a comm on his chest. 'Requesting immediate lifter support. Rendezvous at the closest exit to our current position.'

'Copy that,' said the comm. 'Your positions are locked. We're coming in. We'll be at gate nineteen before you get there.'

Hoxer gestured at Ann with his gun. 'Move,' he said.

Ann hurried with them up the tunnel while the landscape evolved. A garden of monsters grew around them. Pincers sloshed back and forth inside the amniotic sacs. Black compound eyes tracked them as they passed.

Ann regarded the creatures with a kind of nervous excitement. Did they belong to Snakepit, or Will, or both? They looked a little too much like Fecund repair scorpions for it to be a coincidence, but what did she know?

The birthing blisters grew from two feet high to six, to ten. The Spatials broke into a sprint. Ahead of them hung a ladder like the one Ann had come down. Denchak and Gupta went up first.

'You next,' said Hoxer. He released her cuffs while keeping an anxious eye on the stirring monstrosities. 'Make it snappy.'

She was halfway up the ladder when the first of the pods began to split. A damp creature unfolded itself and staggered out like the world's ugliest newborn calf.

[*Is this Will's work?*] she asked her shadow.

[*I really have no idea,*] it told her. [*We don't have a direct link any more. Feels like the sort of thing I might do, though.*]

The air beyond the exit door was a freezing surprise against her bare skin. The sunlight stung her eyes. She winced.

[*Aren't I supposed to be invulnerable now?*] she said.

[*Sorry. Still getting used to this.*]

Her eyes immediately compensated for the light level.

Around her, a surreal landscape of undulating tunnel-backs and plant-choked interstices spread to the horizon. The open docking pod of a mini-lifter hung to her right, hovering a foot above the black corrugated ground. Overhead hovered the huge, grey envelope of the lifter, its integument rippling slowly like an inverted wheat-field.

'Inside,' said Hoxer.

Ann didn't need telling twice. As soon as the team was aboard, the doors sealed and the lifter pulled up into the air. Hoxer twiddled his comms while his men locked Ann's arms to a handle on the wall.

'Senator Voss,' he said. 'You asked for a direct report. We have the traitor Ann Ludik, but no Monet. Something's happening down here. Not Nems. Something different.'

'I saw your video feed,' said Voss. 'Bring her back to the station. The planet's too dangerous now – we're preparing all staff for immediate evacuation.'

Ann watched through the dock-pod screens as the lifter carried her over to the science station. It wasn't much to look at – just a circular plastic drop-hab next to a bioceramic landing strip built on stilts over the tunnel-backs. A shuttle squatted there with engines warming.

Their lifter reversed its docking pod straight up against the shuttle's hatch. Ann knew then that Voss had to be in a hurry. It was the kind of risky manoeuvre that got pilots fired under ordinary circumstances.

Ann was unclipped and pushed inside.

'Do you have any spare ship-suits?' said Ann as she stumbled into the shuttle's cramped cabin. 'I'd like to get dressed, if that's okay.' She pointed at her damp, vegetation-spattered body.

Hoxer shot her an impatient look and pointed at the one female member of his team.

'Lee. Get her dressed.'

The shuttle SAP printed her up a towel and a one-piece to wear. Lee watched like a hawk while Ann dressed. Why a female guard now, after fifteen minutes of high-speed nudity? The situation struck Ann as ludicrous but she kept her thoughts to herself. Any unexpected input would just slow the soldiers down.

She didn't resist as they locked her into a crash couch and headed into orbit. Leaving the gravity well took longer than she'd have liked, but that would have been true however she'd escaped. The entire process had been much faster and smoother than if she'd tried for freedom. Now she had a problem, of course – that of wrenching control from Voss and the others. Hopefully her shadow would be up to that task.

As soon as they hit the station, Hoxer marched her to the command deck. The place had been cleaned since Ann was last there. The bloodstains and bullet-scars had vanished. So had about half of the officers. The place felt deserted. Ann suspected the senator was getting ready to pull the plug on the whole operation.

[*Could you take over the computers again, please?*] Ann asked her shadow.

[*No need,*] it told her. [*They still haven't found my control inserts from last time. Their systems are yours whenever you want them. And don't worry about the guards – they've been breathing your exhalations for the last ninety minutes and I now have smart-cell encampments in their lungs. Tell me when you'd like them gone.*]

Breathing her exhalations? Evidently her shadow retained some agency, as well as Will's persona. She wondered what else it was up to.

Parisa Voss looked Ann up and down as she approached, her expression one of tightly managed anger. It was supposed to hide the animal terror that oozed out of her every pore.

'Tell me what happened,' said Voss.

No hello. Not even any criticism. The senator had to be desperate to figure out what the hell was going on. The League had clear strategic objectives for outlier scenarios. They'd be trying to retain control of their assets while reducing the number of destabilising variables. Their focus would be on owning the aftermath of the Nem invasion, whatever chaos the machines had caused. Voss had brought her back here for one reason: to strengthen her rapidly weakening hand.

'Will and I tried to escape to warn Earth,' said Ann. 'We got caught in the fight and ended up on Snakepit. Will interfaced with the planet in a bid to keep the human race alive and I came back up here to finish off what we started. I'll be leaving shortly.'

'Oh, really?' snapped Voss. 'You think we're just going to let you walk out of here? You think that because you read the tea leaves about Nem complexity you have some sacred responsibility to rescue Earth? For your information, your input has already been factored in. Nelson was prepping to leave to support the defence of Earth when Snakepit started interfering with control of the *Ariel Two*. Sam's probability assessments have been de-emphasised and his directives marked as unreliable. The League *will* own the aftermath of this debacle with your help or without it, Ms. Ludik. As it is, your inability to detach from Will Monet has made that process far more complicated than necessary. You have a lot to answer for.'

Ann felt a desperate laugh bubbling out of her throat. *Inability to detach*. That was one way to put it.

Voss recoiled, her face darkening. 'I'm sorry. Did I say something funny?'

'Listen to me, you slack-witted political hack,' said Ann. 'I told you this would happen when things started running out of control. You failed to listen. I don't know what your fallback plan is now, but my guess is it's to boser the planet using the *Chiyome*, get the hell out of here and try desperately to pretend that none of this is your fault. That's usually how it works, isn't it?'

The look in Voss's eyes told her she was right.

'I'm sorry, but that's not good enough,' said Ann. 'The Nems aren't taking orders from their homeworld any more, which means they're free to build new nests. Snakepit's the least of your problems. The first new nest site they have in mind is probably Earth. They've already reached something close to human-level reasoning, which means that all your clever plans to spare the home system from carnage are way out of date. How long do you suppose the other colonies will last after that?'

She waited for an answer, but Voss just glared at her like a cornered animal.

'You've kicked off the extinction of the human race,' said Ann. 'Well done. And that's why I'm leaving – to clean up the stupid mess you've made, if I possibly can.'

Ann could see the loathing swelling behind Voss's eyes.

'You sound mighty sure of yourself for someone who's being considered for execution.'

'Speak for yourself,' said Ann.

She pulled on the restraints. They came apart like butter.

[*Now,*] she told her shadow.

The guards' eyes rolled up in their heads and they flopped to the ground like puppets. At the same moment, every screen on the command deck flickered and died. Will Monet's face appeared on the main viewing wall, a dark smile curving his mouth.

Ann grabbed Voss's jacket and lifted her off the ground with comic ease.

'Bioblocker!' Voss shouted. 'Bioblocker now!'

Nothing happened.

'Disabled,' said Ann. 'Wouldn't have worked anyway.'

'You're not Ann Ludik!' said Voss. 'You're *Monet*!'

'Close but no cigar,' said Ann. 'Will never looked this good. And now we're all going to start behaving like rational people. How about it?'

18.4: MARK

As the shuttle lost line-of-sight with the constructorbot, Mark's grip on its pilot-SAP fell away. The colonists overcame their shyness almost immediately. Warning pings started appearing in his sensorium with messages attached.

'*Gulliver Shuttle Two*, you are to land at the supplied coordinates in the desert, otherwise we will bring you down.'

A volley of twenty ground-to-air missiles raced towards them from a remote station somewhere far beyond New Luxor. Mark had to kick in a program of evasives before they'd even gained fifty kilometres of altitude. The shuttle banked hard.

'One minute they want this boat, the next they're trying to blow it out of the sky,' he said as weapons screamed past their wing. 'Can't these bastards make up their minds?'

'I don't think they're being super rational right now,' said Zoe.

Mark snorted. 'They haven't been rational since they tried to floor me in a game of constructorbot smackdown.'

'We have no idea what Sam told them,' she reminded him. 'He doesn't have a great track record for honesty.'

Mark flew with half his mind and threw the rest into co-opting the missiles' onboard controls. Zoe was right. Had the colonists been thinking anywhere close to clearly, they would have fired their missiles with something other than a standard rotating-format security protocol. Under the pressure of Will's hackpack, their guidance systems cracked like raw eggs. Mark directed the missiles into each other's paths only to discover that the colonists had decided to dive orbital tugs into Carter's thermosphere in an attempt to prevent him from reaching the *Gulliver*.

'I hate these people,' Mark muttered. 'I just want to *leave*. Is that too much to ask?'

He bounced his connection to the *Gulliver* via the Fleet station hanging above them and undocked the starship from its tether. The *Gulliver* adjusted its position, sliding into a lower, faster orbit.

'You want to try nudging a starship?' he said. 'Please, go on, try.'

They did. Several small robotic ships impacted against the twenty-kilometre-wide wall of the *Gulliver*'s exohull, leaving barely a trace of their existence. Mark swung the shuttle up, dodged between obstacles and docked on the move, the shuttle's hull clanging from the force of their impact. Fortunately, he managed to not smash the docking machinery on the way in. As soon as he had a join, Mark instructed the starship to pull them away from Carter with more conventional thrust than was strictly legal so close to an inhabited planet.

Fusion torches ignited all across the *Gulliver*'s back, blasting Carter's atmosphere with a hammer-blow of superheated ions. Parabolic shock waves of glowing cloud rippled out behind them as they tore away. Mark gritted his teeth as they put distance between themselves and Carter's racing shoal of improvised munitions. Only when he was sure the tugs couldn't chase him did he allow himself to relax. He sagged into his crash couch with a moan.

'Finally,' he said. 'I never want to see that place again.'

'Now for the really difficult part,' said Zoe. 'We can't fly the *Gulliver* home until we're in control of the rest of the ship, and it's only a matter of time before the Carterites find something bigger to throw at us. We have to get you down there and plugged into that helm. Sam knows that and he'll be somewhere in that habitat core waiting for us.'

Mark rubbed his eyes, feeling excitement and dread in equal measures. Sam would have something twisted cooked up for them, he felt sure. And yet the fear that idea brought was tempered by Mark's urgent desire to drive a fist into the man's face.

'Is there any way you can override that stupid security set-up so I can see the whole interior?' he said.

Ironically, as soon as he reached the *Gulliver*'s mesohull, his grip on the ship's functions would get weaker, not stronger. His hold would vanish the moment he entered the security-locked cabin and only bounce back once he reached the Fleet section of the habitat-core.

'Not from in here,' said Zoe. 'We need full helm-space and robot control.'

'Then there's no point in waiting. I'm going down there to sort this shit out.'

There was nobody else who could do it. Zoe wasn't in any shape to face Sam, even in zero-gee. Her feet were still useless and she was doped to the eyeballs on muscle-relaxants and pain-suppressors. Mark would have to handle Sam alone. He unclipped and started towards the airlock.

Zoe eyed him anxiously. 'You're not dealing with the FPP any more,' she said. 'This is Sam Shah we're talking about and he won't be in a friendly mood.'

'I know that.'

'Then don't be in such a hurry!' Zoe snapped. 'He's going to fuck with your head. That's what he does. You need to start thinking like he does otherwise he'll finish us. Tell me what he'll try next.'

Mark exhaled. 'He won't want me to reach the bridge, so he'll wake Citra up and use her as a human shield. He knows I won't want to kill her.'

'Agreed,' said Zoe. 'What else?'

'He might paint the walls with neurotoxin like he did last time.'

'Definitely,' she said. 'We can fix that from here. The shuttle has a printer. We can put together a skin-suit for you with gloves.'

'He's going to be armed,' said Mark.

'Yes. But so will you. This shuttle was built for first contact, remember? There's a pair of recoilless automatics in the shuttle's security locker with magazines of plastic rounds. Keep going.'

'He'll use his eyes in the science and diplomacy sections to set up an ambush,' Mark added, the difficulty of his situation setting in. 'And I have to get through the diplomacy section to reach the bridge.'

Zoe broke into an evil grin. 'That's what he *thinks* he's going to do.' She started typing furiously on her touchboard. 'I'll be simulating a soft assault the moment your docking pod gets down there. We use the paranoia built into this ship against him. If the *Gulliver* even sniffs a computer virus, everything locks. The entire network will go down. Screens. Cameras. Everything. He won't have eyes for at least five minutes while the security SAP figures out I'm bluffing, then everything comes back up. If you get to the helm before that, flag me and I'll reboot manually. But you'll have to reach the fat-contact in your couch. Everything else will be out.'

Mark slid over to the security locker, pulled out a gun and loaded it.

'It's a start,' he said. 'Let's keep that bastard on the back foot for as long as we can.'

Zoe had the shuttle print him up a body-stocking that would keep

Citra's toxins off his skin without compromising his movement. Mark gratefully abandoned his paper smock and pulled it on.

'First and foremost,' said Zoe, 'keep this in mind: that fucker is going to do exactly the opposite of what you expect. Don't take your eyes off him for a second. Promise me.'

Her eyes implored him.

'I promise,' he said. 'I didn't intend to, in any case.' He pushed himself over to the airlock. 'Wish me luck.' He grabbed a handle and waved as the door shut behind him.

The pod ride down to the centre of the ship had never felt longer. Mark breathed deep, his heart hammering. His mood see-sawed between fear and rage. Somehow, one man in a starship core scared him more than a planet full of angry colonists.

The pod thudded into place. Mark grabbed a handle and pulled himself flat against the wall. Then he waited. Five seconds later, the monitor screens died and came back flashing incursion warning symbols. The lighting turned red. Sirens sounded briefly and fell silent.

Mark hit the manual override on the door and held his breath. No bullets flew in. He glanced quickly over the lip of the hatch and darted back. Nothing lay beyond except the *Gulliver*'s spotless corridor. Black and red incursion warnings glowed from every surface. Not having eyes in the walls set his teeth on edge.

He slid quietly into the habitat core, angling his automatic to cover the ambush point at the closest intersection. He paused as soon as he was inside, listening hard. Nothing carried on the air except the soft hiss of the *Gulliver*'s fans.

'Don't shoot,' said Citra Chesterford.

Mark's heart skipped a beat. His gun slid instinctively towards her voice.

'Come out, then,' he said, 'and keep your hands where I can see them.'

She floated in front of him, her eyes full of judgement. 'We don't want any more bloodshed,' she said. 'You've done enough.'

Mark's heart pounded. He scanned her rapidly to make sure she wasn't carrying a weapon and then slid his eyes back to the ambush points. He hadn't expected an early surrender. Sam was out-thinking him already.

'Where's Sam?' he snarled.

'The bridge,' she said. 'He knows that's where you want to go so he's waiting for you there to make a point. We're not going to fight you, Mark.'

Mark emitted a dry half-laugh. 'Right,' he said. 'I'm sure.'

'I'm here because we knew you'd kill Sam on sight if you met him first,' said Citra. 'He'll come out when I give him the all-clear. You have a witness now. Maybe that means something to you, maybe not. Maybe you'll just kill me, too.'

'Professor Chesterford, you are one deeply confused woman,' said Mark, 'but frankly I don't care what kind of bullshit fantasy you're living in any more.' He gestured with his gun. 'That way,' he said. 'You first.'

Citra slid down the corridor in front of him. She moved slowly and carefully, making a point to keep her hands visible. Mark gritted his teeth and focused on the corridor's intersections. He barely breathed during the short journey to the bridge.

They reached the doorway. It had been left open.

'Are you still in there, Sam?' said Citra. 'You can come out now.'

'No,' snapped Mark. 'Tell that slimy fuck not to move.'

She eyed him with dismay. 'Are you going to kill him?'

'Don't tempt me,' snapped Mark. 'Right now I'm planning on leaving that to the Fleet tribunal.'

'That's rich,' said Sam Shah from around the corner. 'After what you've done.'

Coming back aboard the *Gulliver* was like entering an alternate reality. But what else had he expected? Until Sam ditched him on Carter, he'd lived in that delusional state himself.

'In,' Mark told Citra. 'To the back of the room.'

'You want us both in there?' she said. 'There's not much space.'

'Both of you. I want Sam's back against the wall.'

Citra floated through the doorway. Mark edged carefully around the opening, keeping his weapon aimed. Citra and Sam hovered in the narrow area that ran along the left side of the crash-couch bunks, as requested. Sam's expression was one of exhausted disapproval. He looked Mark's suit up and down with evident disdain, as if poison had been the last thing on his mind.

Mark glared at his adversary, thinking fast. A double surrender – there had to be something wrong here. For starters, Sam was still

461

keeping up a stream of lies for Citra. He'd only bother with that if he had a reason.

'Congratulations,' said Mark. 'I anticipated the tricks you've already used. Ambushes. Poison on the walls. That kind of thing. You've surprised me yet again.' He kept his tone light, trying to sound indifferent. Meanwhile, his heart thudded in his chest, waiting for the inevitable ploy.

'We're just saving time,' said Sam wearily. 'And hopefully some lives. You boxed us up in here and took away our comms. You shut down our network and arrived with a gun. It was pretty clear you meant to take back the ship, whatever we were trying to achieve. This way, maybe we can convince you to see reason and help some of those people down there.'

Mark didn't bother replying to Sam's bullshit patter. The bastard would only build on it.

'What now?' said Citra.

Mark drifted slowly into the room, sliding up to the captain's bunk while keeping his gun on them the entire time. Something about the situation felt deeply wrong. With his free hand, he felt around behind him for the fat-contact. It took him twenty seconds to locate it without moving his eyes away from them to look.

He drew the cable up to his neck only to find it dead. He registered a moment's surprise. In the same second, a shadow fell across the doorway. Mark pulled himself to the wall just in time as a plastic round shot the gun from his hand. Ash stood there in the doorway, his face a rictus of rage.

'Kill him!' Sam yelled. 'What are you waiting for?'

Mark lay trapped in the bunk, prone and easy to shoot – a perfect set-up, yet again. He grabbed the bunk's handles and threw himself towards the door-wall in a crouch. Ash swung into the room to take aim.

'Traitor!' Ash wailed, his voice cracking.

Mark pivoted on one handle, twisted and kicked out with his right foot as Ash moved in. Ash's gun fell from his hand, bouncing off the wall. By then, Sam was scrabbling for Mark's automatic. Citra was in the way.

Mark slewed out of the bunk feet-first, repeatedly kicking Ash in the face as he came. Ash batted his feet away, but Mark's hands were in the air by now, reaching for both weapons. Before he could grab them, Ash seized him by the knees and yanked, using the doorway for leverage. He dragged them both back into the corridor.

'You're going to pay,' Ash screamed.

'For *what*?' Mark shouted back.

'Mind rape!' Ash shrieked, his voice hysterical with indignation. 'What do you think?'

Mark fought down his outright shock that Ash was still alive, along with his confusion over the accusation. He focused on grabbing Ash's arms as the two of them bounced against the corridor wall. Under ordinary conditions, Ash wouldn't have lasted five minutes against Mark. But Mark was half-starved and Ash fought like a man unhinged.

As they tumbled against the padding, Sam grabbed a gun. Citra picked up the other. She fired, narrowly missing both roboteers as they twisted over each other.

'Don't fire till you have a clear shot!' Sam told her.

Mark corkscrewed and kicked against the wall, sending Ash and himself sprawling down the passage towards the ladder to the lounge. Mark angled around, his feet running along the walls and ceiling as he tried to turn Ash's back towards the guns.

Another ill-timed bullet whined past him. Mark's desperate evasions gave Ash an upper-body advantage. He snatched a hand free and went for an eye-gouge. Mark blocked frantically, trying to fend him off while Ash's fingers clawed over his cheek. Ash's face hung inches from his own. The look on it was one of a man dying inside.

Mark kicked at anything and everything, struggling to reorientate himself. At last his feet caught the top rung of the ladder. He dragged them both down and then propelled them at the ceiling. He knocked Ash's head into the padding as they hit and tried to cram it there. It gave him enough purchase to get Ash's hands free from his face and neck.

Sam slid fast along the passage below, his body aimed like a torpedo. Mark knew he'd left his back exposed. Sam had a clear shot. He swung Ash's body awkwardly around, trying to realign his human shield. This brought Ash close enough to kick Mark in the kidneys, which he did with relish, over and over.

Then the network came back on. Mark seized on their surprise and threw Ash's own memory package back at him – the one he'd sent while Mark was trapped on Carter. He used Will's hackpack to force Ash to run it. Whatever Ash believed was going on now, maybe he'd recognise his own memories. Ash hesitated, stunned. His eyes glazed over.

Sam moved down the corridor, angling again. Mark twisted as bullets thudded into the padding beside him. He curled and sprang off the ceiling, sending Ash and himself spiralling down the tube into the lounge the wrong way up. While he had the advantage, Mark followed Ash's package with a memory dump of his time in the penitence box, squeezing it into Ash's mind. Ash whimpered and went stiff in his arms as Mark forced the memory into him, wedging it down the throat of his interface.

Mark watched Ash's expression melt from one emotion into another: shock, dismay, despair and finally a kind of terrible resolve. They hung locked and frozen in a wrestling grip, the crash couches over their heads, as Sam came in for a fresh shot.

Ash suddenly brought his legs up against Mark's chest and sprang away in Sam's direction. He snatched the gun from Sam's hand in an eye-blink and brought the handle repeatedly down against Sam's face.

'Stop!' cried Sam.

But Ash's arm became a blur. Sam struggled weakly as his blood spattered across the lounge.

'Ash, stop!' Mark begged.

Citra flew in then with a gun in her hand, pointed at Mark. Mark kicked it from her fingers and caught it as it rebounded off the wall. He fired a warning shot, clipping Ash's arm as the gun stock threatened to fall into Sam's face yet again.

Ash spun away, clutching his arm. He curled in on himself and began to keen like a sick animal.

'Everybody freeze,' said Mark, breathing hard. 'This is fucking *over*.' He pinged Zoe in the shuttle outside. 'We're in,' he said, watching Sam's body turn slowly in the air at the centre of a cloud of wobbling scarlet droplets. The man's face was a mess. Without a med-bay, Mark couldn't tell if he was still alive. Citra regarded him with eyes full of unadulterated loathing.

'It's not pretty down here,' he said, 'but we're in.'

18.5: WILL

What Will had in mind wasn't betraying Snakepit, exactly. He just didn't want to be a god. The promise of ultimate power, he'd learned, was also the promise of ultimate loneliness, and he'd lived with that for long enough already. So Snakepit would have to survive with a submind replica of him or nothing at all. Will was ready to die to ensure that outcome. He'd already faced death once today. Doing it a second time felt far less dramatic.

Was that a selfish decision? After all, Snakepit would still exist without him and the risk that the mutants might reclaim it remained, despite the power he now held over them. But Ann had both the smarts and the cold pragmatism to torch the planet if he didn't get off it. Either way, Will's ascendancy to ultimate power was permanently off the menu.

For the first time in his life, he actually felt glad that the Transcended had prevented him from making complete copies of himself. Before his trip to Davenport, he'd assumed there was simply a limit to how much data a smart-cell could hold, and therefore how much of his persona his subminds could physically contain. But on that day it became clear that the Transcended had actively blocked him from copying himself by somehow writing a restraint deep inside his operating code. Now, ironically, that same code gave him his one hope of not living out eternity as a galaxy-spanning deity.

Will brought up a set of SAP design tools and started assembling a copy of himself in the planet's substrate. The world responded with incredible eagerness, opening up oceans of resources for him. Then, slowly, Will started detaching his threads of control from himself and handing them to the replica. Snakepit had bound itself close enough to him that it took just seconds to figure out what he had in mind.

The museum metaphor smacked back into place with a force that made his nerves shake.

The curator looked up at him with eyes full of pain.

'What are you doing?' she said. She reached for the octopus-orchid on his lapel.

Will brushed her hand away. 'Leaving,' he told her. 'You gave me control, remember? I can do that now.'

'But why?' she cried. 'I thought we had an understanding!'

She looked shocked at his duplicity. Apparently, the curator had not yet figured out the difference between untruths and lying by omission. She still had a lot to learn about the human race.

Clouds parted in Will's mind and suddenly he could feel the planet's hunger more keenly than ever – an aching well of loneliness large enough to drown empires. It only tightened his resolve further. If that was what godhood felt like, he wanted no part of it.

'But you won't be alone,' said the curator. 'You'll have me!'

'You're not real,' said Will sadly. 'You're a part of my imagination – a picture of someone I once knew.'

The curator grabbed her hair in fists. 'Stop,' she said. 'Don't say that! Don't leave me here like this! I can't stand it.'

Will backed away slowly down the aisle between the ranks of cryptic exhibits.

'Think about all the good you could do if you stay!' she cried. 'You might make all the difference for the human race. Who would be better than you at ushering in a new age of reason and hope?'

Will struggled with that because he still believed he could help. But he didn't like what power had done to him last time. He found it hard to believe he'd be a better person with a million times more.

'I regret that it's necessary,' he said. 'I'll come back with a better solution for you, I promise. Real people – thousands of them. Not manufactured hybrids. And not just me. But right now, you need to let me go.'

At first she looked as if she might have bought into his vision. She hesitated, suspending her scrabbling attempts to regain control. But as Will retracted his network of influence still further, the curator began to scream. Through his extended senses, Will felt organs the size of small countries start to fail. Oceans roiled. With his every uncoupling, parts of Snakepit's already damaged matrix shut down. He wondered suddenly if the planet would actually prefer to die rather than carry on with just a shadow for company, even given the promise of his return. He hoped they could both do better than that.

Will forced a change in his mental distribution, narrowing his presence rather than reducing it. He pushed himself like a root deep into the soil of the planet's memory, looking for the core of its identity.

Without sentient company, Snakepit was still effectively an SAP, if a mind-bogglingly complex one. If he could find the core incentive

466

structure that had driven the biosphere's growth, maybe he could reshape it. He could insert some incentives of his own and convince the planet that it *wanted* to let him go – that he wasn't good enough on his own. In essence, he'd give the place some higher standards.

The curator tugged at his sleeves, becoming vaporous and indistinct as Will sank deeper into Snakepit's mental structure. Then, as Will reached the threshold where even the curator couldn't go, she reached out to him one last time.

'Don't go down there,' she begged. 'Don't change me. Please.'

She came apart into coloured mist as Will held tight to his control and slid below the horizon of her awareness, into her defining depths.

As museum faded from sight, the vast interlocking machinery Will had seen when he first touched the planet's mind swam back into focus. This was the world's true shape, he knew, or as close as his mind could model it. The byzantine detailing of the place didn't faze him any more, though. Now he understood it. Above him, huge wheels turned, representing higher levels of complexity – whole ecosystems and animal societies. Below him, the cogs and levers grew ever smaller, vanishing into minuscule obscurity. Somewhere down there was a representation of every leaf and vein in Snakepit's intricately ordered biosphere.

Now that his mind could parse it all, what surprised Will was how similar each level of the structure was. Features of Snakepit's basic architecture were reproduced at every level, distorted like faces in a mirror-maze. There was some sense in which the entire structure was symmetrical from top to bottom. That repetition also told Will everything he needed to know about where to look for the planet's root controls.

First, he chased upwards through the hierarchy, towards the planet-spanning intelligence his integration had fostered. As he neared it, he watched arcs of bright emotion welling up from the depths and splashing across the underside of Snakepit's mind like bolts of pale lightning.

This is what panic looks like, he thought. *This is fear*. Fresh guilt tugged at him. Once again, Amy was in the torture chair, only this time he was the one doing the torturing. He reminded himself that the curator wasn't real, and certainly wasn't Amy. Before he plugged himself in, the planet hadn't even been conscious in the human sense. He forced himself to focus and sought out the axle upon which that immense wheel turned. Then he dived down towards whatever engine powered it.

Will chased the driving mechanism through level after level. The lower he went, the weirder the planet-mind's structure became. Small wheels powered larger ones, in turn propelled by others even tinier. He fell through dense thickets of hyperbolic clockwork – nuggets of convoluted machinery clenched like mechanical fists.

If there had ever been artificial order here, it had been overgrown by millennia of organic adaptation. The tangle of representational contraptions became so tortuous that Will could barely see through it, but for a haze of bright light leaking up from below. He sought out that glowing point, pressing himself towards the centre of the Rube Goldberg forest.

When Will found what he was looking for, he knew it immediately. At the deep, incandescent heart of the labyrinth lay a clear space where a tidy crystalline core of ambition hung, shining like a geometric whorl of neon tubing. Its references sprang from the oldest tunnel tissue on the planet – much of it almost five million years old.

Will exhaled in relief and pulled himself close enough to read the structure. Then he stopped, suddenly cold. Something about the shape below him looked horribly familiar. The tidy interlocking knot was way too simple to have spawned all the complexity that surrounded it. It looked more like a kind of circuit diagram he knew well: an entanglement tether for one end of a quantcomm device. Or a suntap.

Suddenly, Will's situation felt very wrong. He peered closer, unwilling to believe what he was seeing. But there at the hub of the world's mind lay an impossible join where the rest of the planet's motivational engine should have been. The guiding spirit of Snakepit, where all its subtle genius had originated, wasn't actually here. It had been piped in on waves of gravity distortion.

The pit of Will's stomach fell away as comprehension dawned. He'd looked for hallmarks of the Transcended and found none. But here at the very heart of the world, hidden even from Snakepit itself, lay all the proof of their complicity he needed.

'Holy shit,' he croaked. 'The League was right.'

He glanced around at the still, silent blizzard of ideas that crowded him on every side. But why? Why build a world like this and hide its origin even from itself? Why make it believe a lie?

It suddenly became obvious that the 'Founders', as the curator had thought of them, had never existed. That was why Snakepit had no memory of their passing. The world had been made this way – delusional and devoid of purpose until now. It had been established between waves of intelligent life in this part of the galaxy. Ready for whoever came next.

But why? A gift? What kind of gift arrived anonymously and attacked the person who opened it? Perhaps not a gift, then, but a trap set on an unbelievably long fuse. But even that didn't make sense. Why go to such lengths to trap the human race when they could have achieved that aim so much more simply? Whatever the agenda, Will no longer trusted it.

He regarded the core structure before him. If he touched it, would it know? Could he afford to make changes here, or would he awaken whatever Transcended intelligence hid at the other end of that tether?

Will began to pull carefully away, like a man stepping back from a tripwire. As he rose up through the planet's layers of thought, he began shutting down his connections to the planet as fast as he dared. His network of links to Snakepit's distributed mind fell away like threads of spider silk. Towers of knowledge crumbled inside him. His mind shrank back to a human scale like an ice cube melting under desert heat. He relished ignorance as it overcame him.

As his mind retreated, Will quickly zeroed in on the core of the submind matrix that hosted him and reached for his body. He could see it before him now, lying prone in the alcove and plugged into the world through a billion interlocking hyphae.

Just as his awareness closed on his physical form, reintegration stopped. Will hovered before himself, disembodied and full of dread. For some reason, he could collapse no further than the alcove itself. Something beyond the limits of his extended perception was blocking him.

Then, while he watched, his body sagged apart like warm butter melting in a pan. The world thinned a little. Will's perceptions flattened out, taking on the plastic edge of artificial memory.

He stared, speechless. Just minutes before, he'd been ready to die this way, but he'd never bargained on having to watch it happen. A sick sense of impotence gripped him. Will scrabbled for the bacteria in the pool, willing the cellular matrix to reconstruct what it had lost. Nothing happened. The body that had been his diffused gently into the brackish water leaving nothing but a pinkish residue on the surface.

Then, slowly at first, Will's detachment from the planet began to reverse itself just as it had when Snakepit first invaded him. Except this time, Will had a cold certainty that someone else was pulling the strings.

'No,' he said. 'Stop. Please.'

The planet didn't listen. The spider was drawing him back down towards the centre of the web. Will fought it every step of the way until he found himself hovering before the suntap again. He twisted like a man in a straightjacket, unable to look away. The shape beneath him pulsed with manic light – light that swelled up and overwhelmed him.

19: OWNERSHIP

19.1: MARK

Citra glared at him, disgust written on her face.

'What did you do to poor Ash?'

'I showed him the truth, that's all,' said Mark wearily.

Citra huffed at him. 'I find that difficult to believe.'

'What do you imagine is happening here?' said Mark.

She shook her head. 'It's a little late to play fantasist, Captain Ruiz. I think we all have a pretty clear idea of what's going on.'

'Look!' Mark snapped. 'Just tell me what you think's happening, otherwise we're going to spend all day talking at cross purposes. At least accuse me of something specific, for crying out loud.'

She folded her arms. 'Fine. You conspired with Will Monet to push him back into the history books by turning a first-contact situation into a war. With the help of your accomplices, of course. You've been planning this since before the mission even set out.' She lifted her chin. 'Sam and I have been trying to work against that evil ever since.'

'And you buy that even though he drugged you,' said Mark.

'Don't think me a fool, Captain,' she snapped. 'We both know he did that to save me from what you had planned.'

Will rubbed an eye with the heel of his hand and groaned. He opened a link to the lounge's wall-screens and played back some footage Ash had sent him of Sam giving a talk for the League. Then he showed her some of Sam's conversations with Ash. And finally he threw in a memory of his own: Sam telling him how Earth, his favourite *hovel-world*, had to die.

Citra went grey. 'I find it difficult to believe I've been so systematically misled as you suggest. Those videos have undoubtedly been faked.'

'When would I have done that?' said Mark. 'While I was imprisoned by FPP fanatics in New Luxor or when the Flags were torturing me in Britehaven?'

Citra shook her head. 'You weren't tortured.'

'Is that right?'

Mark posted another snippet from his own memories: Venetia going up in flames. Citra's eyes went wide.

'You want to check on that?' he said. 'You want to go and look at her body in the shuttle to see if she *really* has life-threatening burns? Tell you what – why don't we agree to get back to Earth as fast as we can and let the evidence speak for itself? Does that sound fair?'

Citra's eyes narrowed. 'Nothing would make me happier. However, I doubt that's where we're headed.'

Mark sighed. He reached out through his interface to the closest printer and ordered up three sets of plastic restraints, then hesitated before setting the job running. Sam had been the source of the problems on the *Gulliver* and now Sam wasn't conscious. Mark still didn't believe that either Citra or Ash had any malice in them. Maybe there was a better way to handle this – one that allowed for a little trust.

'Okay, here's what I want you to do,' he said nervously. 'Take that gun over there and keep Ash covered to stop him hitting Sam again. I presume that's something you actually want. Can you do that? Or am I trying to rope you into a conspiracy to destroy Earth by keeping Sam's face in one piece?'

Citra peered at him, hatred crackling from her gaze. 'I can do that,' she said at last.

'Great,' said Mark. 'Sam's life may depend on you. You know what Ash is capable of. I'll be back as soon as I can.' He left quickly, before she could reach for the weapon idly rotating in the air.

Mark struggled to not look back as he departed. He took the docking pod up through the mesohull to the shuttle and helped Zoe and Venetia down to the *Gulliver*'s med-bay. It took for ever and his guts churned with anxiety the entire time. His gambit to gain Citra's confidence hinged on his having read the situation correctly. But Mark knew he wasn't exactly a genius when it came to people. He half-expected hell to break loose the entire time.

When he finally returned to the lounge, things looked surprisingly unchanged. Ash had drifted across the room. Sam's body had turned over. There was, perhaps, a little more blood in the air, but not much. Citra's eyes had gone red from zero-gee tears. He had the lurking sense that maybe she'd tried something in his absence, but given the non-outcome, he didn't care.

He kept his automatic levelled at Citra as he drifted in.

'Now drop the weapon, please,' he said.

She glanced at him bitterly and tossed it across the lounge.

'How are you doing?' he said.

'As well as can be expected,' she replied tersely.

'Terrific. Want to help me get Sam to the med-bay?'

'You mean he's allowed to move now?' she said. 'You waited long enough.'

Mark fought back a retort. 'His injuries are serious,' he said evenly, 'but Venetia's are worse. Let's get him some help.'

The two of them angled Sam's limp body around the corridor's tight turns. If felt odd to be collaborating with a woman who'd wanted him dead just minutes before, but if he was going to build bridges with Citra, he had to start somewhere. Besides which, he found it quietly satisfying to defeat her warped expectations.

They slid Sam into one of the repair cabinets just as Zoe slid out of another. Blue biopolymer slippers covered her feet.

'Fixed already?' he said.

She nodded. 'I have to wear these for a few days, then I'm all good.'

'How about Venetia?' said Citra tightly.

Zoe brought up Venetia's stats and a window onto the repair cabinet where an army of microsurgeons toiled across the landscape of her face, laying tracts of new skin. Citra's expression filled with horror at the sight of the damage.

'With luck she'll be fine, presuming her brain is still okay,' said Zoe. 'The biggest problems were down to carbon monoxide inhalation, as it turns out, not the heat.' Her face became grave. 'Mark, I have something to show you,' she added.

'Ash first,' said Mark. 'He's in a bad way and may still be a risk to us or himself. If we're going to get out of here intact, I have to help him.'

'Mark,' Zoe started. Then she saw the look on his face and exhaled. 'It'll wait,' she said. 'Do what you need to.'

He hurried back to the lounge, hoping his subcaptain would still be there when he arrived. Ash had bumped up against one of the couches. Other than that, he hadn't moved. Mark would have felt less worried if his old friend had at least unclenched a little. This stillness spooked him. He tried opening a link to Ash's interface and found his mind awake but unresponsive.

With the greatest of care, Mark inserted his avatar into Ash's home node. Ash's primary metaphor space had once been an immaculate luxury apartment from his native Drexler with a view out across one of the famous covered calderas. Now it was barely a space at all. Mark found himself hanging amid a scrambled mess of impressions – a landscape like a Cubist disaster. Pieces of Ash's old environment had been mixed up with fragments of Sam's grinning face and snapshots of the horrors wrought by the Nems. Perspective had vanished along with the furniture. Ash's avatar floated in the middle of it all, foetal, just like his physical body.

Mark felt a hot tide of empathy. In the end, Ash had been pretending to be a Drexlerite just like he'd been pretending to be an Earther. Both of them suffered through the same erratic childhood. Both were encouraged to cherish their roots without really knowing what that meant. And both had come out of that process desperate for an identity. They just happened to have picked different sides.

'Are you okay?' said Mark softly.

The words felt profoundly inadequate. By now, Mark had guessed what Sam must have done. Every roboteer knew about shock keys and felt about them the same way ordinary people felt about physical abuse. Ash's mind had been violated in the most profound way imaginable. If he never came back to himself, Mark wouldn't have blamed him.

Ash replied in a surprisingly lucid tone. 'He broke me,' he said simply.

'No,' said Mark. 'He didn't break you. He hurt you. That's different.'

Ash threw a memory at him. Mark let it come. Suddenly, he felt what it was like to wake up blank and damaged, empty and afraid with chunks of his past missing. He recalled how gentle Sam had been, and how Sam had nursed him back together.

For a while in there, he'd loved Sam like a father. Pathetically. Desperately. With an intensity he'd not known since childhood. And he remembered hating Mark with all his soul, even while he could never completely believe what Sam had told him. Mark saw himself lying on

474

the bridge bunk with a gun pointed at him and realised that Ash could have killed him in that moment. Ash hadn't because he couldn't quite bring himself to.

Mark let the foreign emotions power through him, giving them room. Tears squeezed out of his eyes. When he recovered his composure, he took Ash back to that moment in the penitence box when he'd come to understand that they couldn't hurt him so long as he became something greater than himself. He waited for Ash to play that memory out in real time.

'I need you back,' Mark whispered. 'This ship needs you. The human race needs you. We both have to heal but we need to do it later. Right now we have a job to do.'

Ash's avatar reluctantly unfurled. The look in his eyes was distant but focused.

'Then we'd better get on with it, hadn't we?' he croaked.

'Will he be okay?' Zoe asked from the hatchway.

Mark flipped back to his physical body and nodded. 'We're all damaged right now,' he said. 'But Ash is strong. He'll make it. So what did you find?'

Zoe slid into the room with Citra behind her. The biologist looked even sicker and more nauseated than before. Zoe threw a display onto the wall.

'Sam's treasure trove of horrors,' she said. 'I knew there had to be one, so I went looking. I found the program he used to hack Ash. That was scary enough. But then I found this.'

She opened a package of signal-processing code. On the left hung the causal diagram for their comms system. On the right was the fiendishly complex web of logic that had been jacked into it.

'When Sam talked to the machines at Tiwanaku, he used this encrypted code to layer content over the top of his message,' she said. She showed him a data burst full of strategic information – Earth's strengths and weaknesses, its population centres and response times. 'Sam basically told the machines how to kill the homeworld.'

'I...' said Citra. She swallowed. 'I believe I may have been party to something awful.'

She spoke in hushed, astonished tones. She sounded almost awed.

'No more than the rest of us,' said Mark gently. 'I should take the helm. We need to get the hell away from here before the Carterites find some way of reaching us. They're still out there.'

'Wait a second,' said Zoe. She launched from the wall and glided over to him. She fixed him with a deep stare. 'You did great,' she said. 'I'm not the kind of woman who needs a hero. But you're my hero anyway.'

She pulled him in for a kiss. This time, Mark wasn't as surprised. Instead, he felt the waking of an intensely warm and bright emotion inside him so strong that it threatened to rob his lungs of air. It was, he thought, an all-encompassing feeling of *not-loneliness* – a connection with someone he admired who for some reason also admired him.

Their lips met. Bells rang, followed by a thunder-crack of Casimir-buffers firing and the grating siren of a radiation alert. Mark's eyes flew open. He checked the sensors.

At the edge of the Carter System, behind a burst of hard light, a spread of alien ships had begun to flicker.

'The Nems are here,' he said grimly. 'It's end-of-the-world time.'

19.2: ANN

Ann put Parisa down and turned to Lieutenant Koenig – one of the few remaining command deck staff she recognised.

'You,' she said. 'Koenig. Senator Voss has been relieved of command, effective immediately. Give me a status report.'

Koenig stared, her eyes shuttling anxiously back and forth between Ann and the senator. Ann started to lift Voss off the ground a second time.

'Do we really have to debate this?' she said.

Voss didn't comment.

'The station has been maximally evacuated,' said Koenig quickly. 'As many staff as possible have been placed in coma-storage aboard the *Ariel Two*. The rest of us remaining here are volunteers. There just aren't enough berths for everyone at this time, particularly now that we've lost the senator's shuttle.'

'What happened?' said Ann.

'The swarm stumbled across it during their search,' said Koenig. 'It had Nem-cloaking but no active stealth. We were able to get the

Chiyome out of the way but the scout didn't stand a chance. It wasn't as bad as it could have been – there were only three people aboard.'

Three more hosts, Ann thought. *Three more human minds for the Nems to explore.*

'Frankly, it's a miracle you escaped that fight intact,' Koenig added. 'Snakepit produced an incredible number of drones during that surge. There are nearly ten times as many of them out there now as came in with that nestship.'

Ann shook her head. 'Then all the new drones sided with the mutant faction? That's bad.'

Koenig looked confused. '*Mutant faction?*'

Ann sighed. The League officers still had no idea what was actually going on. She'd have to do something about that.

'Tell me about Kuril Najoma,' she said. 'Is he still alive?'

It embarrassed her that she'd relied upon Kuril when it might have cost the man his life. She'd caused him nothing but trouble and he'd absorbed it all without comment. She at least owed him a rescue.

'Give us some credit,' said Parisa, gently trying to remove Ann's clenched fingers off her jacket. 'He's under arrest here on the station. We weren't about to give him a berth after what he'd done, but we're not murderers.'

Ann shot the senator a dry look. 'We're all murderers here, in case you hadn't noticed,' said Ann. 'I want Kuril brought to me at once.' She had her shadow unlock the comms. 'Now tell me about the Nems. What's happening?'

Koenig brightened slightly. 'They've fled to the out-system, thank goodness, and appear to be preparing for a return to Tiwanaku.'

'That is most definitely *not* good,' said Ann. 'How far away are they?'

'About thirteen AU.'

'How long till their estimated departure?' said Ann.

Koenig shook her head. 'I'm not sure. Our SAP models have kind of given up. Brinsen is probably the best man we have on Nem swarm behaviour.'

'Then get him up here, too,' said Ann. 'Now!'

Koenig mumbled into her visor.

[*Open a channel to the entire station, please,*] Ann told her shadow. [*These people need to be filled in.*]

[*Done.*]

While Voss stood there staring at her with exhausted contempt, Ann ushered a camera drone over and addressed the League.

'People of the League,' she said. Her voice echoed from speakers all across Snakepit Station. 'There has been a change of plan. We always assumed the Nems represented a retaliation mechanism. Now, however, we know that's not what they're for. Their real purpose is to react to threats and incorporate their enemies' weapons back into Snakepit's reasoning matrix. In this case, the weapon they collected was human sentience. Like it or not, we have inadvertently given birth to a new alien species – one that apparently requires human minds as part of its operating system. It is now almost as intelligent as humanity and getting smarter all the time.

'The Nems returned here to assert control over their homeworld and prepare it for the wholesale incorporation of the human race. Will Monet blocked that but the mutants are still out there. For whatever reason, they didn't accept Will's supremacy. I have to assume that means they've selected a new nest site: Earth.

'As humanity's acting ambassador for alien contact, I am hereby taking charge of this operation. This has become a game of species survival and the stakes are now so high that your political concerns must be set aside. As Will Monet's envoy, I will personally vouch for every member of this organisation and ensure their protection from political fallout caused by the League's work, with the exception of Parisa Voss and Sam Shah. I will shortly be leaving on the *Ariel Two* to attempt to prevent the Nem swarm departure. The League has a chance to redeem itself. We're now the people best equipped and informed to defend the human race. Good luck, everyone. We'll be back for the rest of you as soon as we can.'

Voss glared at her as she closed the channel. 'Singling people out for punishment is a little petty, don't you think?' she said.

Ann glared at her. 'This has nothing to do with punishment. You made poor leadership decisions and now you're going to take responsibility for them. That's how leadership works. I can assure you that I will be strictly factual in my report. I'll even let you read it before I submit it to the IPSO tribunal.'

Jaco stepped in from the pod bay, a sick, guilty look on his action-hero face.

'Ma'am,' he said weakly.

'Jaco,' she said. 'You're familiar with Nem behaviour patterns. Take a look at these swarm vectors and tell me how long we have before the drones exit the system.'

She threw the data onto a screen for him to review. Jaco pored over it.

'On one hand, they've got a lot of drones to carry,' he said. 'On the other, they came in with a nestship, so their carrier is likely already geared for a large envelope. I'd give them two hours at most.'

Ann glowered. It'd take them that long just to reach the out-system.

Kuril stumbled in between a couple of Spatials.

'Release that man immediately,' Ann snapped. The circuits in the walls echoed her command, turning her voice into a deafening electronic shout.

The Spatials stepped rapidly away from their charge without another word.

'How are you?' said Ann. 'Did they hurt you?'

'Oh, please,' Parisa sneered.

'I'm fine,' said Kuril. 'Interrogation wasn't fun but I'm in one piece. The drugs have worn off, at least.'

'I have one last favour to ask of you,' said Ann.

Kuril's eyebrows crept upwards. 'You're kidding. Another one?'

'I need to you take command of the *Chiyome* for me. Jaco Brinsen will be your subcaptain. The command keys will be irrevocably cued to you. If you die, that ship will be floating in space until someone finds it, which at this rate may be never.'

Kuril let out a single ragged laugh and rubbed his untidy mop of hair.

'Why me?' he said.

'Because right now you're the only person I trust to be in charge of an invisible planet-buster,' said Ann. 'And if we get out of all this alive, I will do my best to make sure that ship stays yours. Your mission is to head straight to New Panama as fast as you can to muster support.'

She turned to Jaco Brinsen. 'Jaco, are you prepared to accept that subcaptain position?'

'Of course, ma'am,' said Jaco. He sounded indignant. 'I'm loyal to the greater cause of the human race. Hopefully you recognise that. I always have been. Before, that meant serving the League. Now it means cleaning up.'

Ann shook her head. Even now, Jaco Brinsen still managed to be sanctimonious and annoying. Unfortunately, he was also useful.

'From the moment the League reveals itself, we'll have a problem,' said Voss. 'Fingers will be pointed. Don't assume the human race will automatically get behind us. Someone's going to have to rally the team.'

'Let me guess,' Ann snarled. 'You want that job. You think I should just let you leave with Jaco rather than make you come with me. And then, hopefully, I see you later and everyone's friends again. Is that it?'

'I'm proposing that you let me help,' said Voss sharply.

'No deal,' Ann growled. 'You're coming with me in the *Ariel Two* whether you like it or not. We leave immediately.'

Ann's second attempted shuttle crossing to the *Ariel Two* couldn't have been more different from her first. This time, there were no drones to avoid or League soldiers to escape. Rather than being thrown around by Will's evasives, the shuttle flew on a straight-line boost at three-point-eight gees of thrust. Ann could barely feel it.

Parisa Voss lay in the couch behind her looking ill from the persistent acceleration. But Ann's attention wasn't on her former boss. She spent the time fighting back the urge to scream while she watched the Nems readying for exit.

When they reached the *Ariel Two*, Nelson Aquino was waiting for them in the docking pod. His bloodshot eyes suggested he'd taken Will's apparent loss harder than the rest of them. He looked at Ann oddly.

'Welcome, Captain Ludik,' he said. 'Apparently you have Will's abilities now? You're taking over as ro-captain?'

'Correct,' said Ann as she drifted through the lock. She felt sure, suddenly, that they'd never see Will again. Taking over the *Ariel Two* and leaving without him held a kind of horrible finality. 'It's not what I want,' she said, 'but there's no time to grieve. Hold on, please.'

They took the docking pod down the hundred-kilometre drop to the primary habitat core. She tore away the safety limits on the pod and pasted everyone to the floor for the duration of the journey.

During the descent, Will's shadow integrated her with the ship. As it came alive in the back of her mind she could feel the freshness of its repairs like fading bruises under her own skin. The mighty vessel's antimatter reserves had been filled to bursting. They were ready.

Without her shadow there to mediate, accommodating a starship in her head would have been an intolerably alien sensation. Ann forced herself to accept it.

'Everyone strap down,' she told the crew as she reached the core. 'Now!' As soon as everyone clipped in, Ann punched them towards the swarm at full tilt. She kept a close eye on everyone's vitals as she piled on the warp, trying not to kill anyone before she got there.

While she approached the swarm-carrier, it completed its packing assembly and began to increase spin. A dense cluster of Nems sat between the two discs, inside the skipping-rope fronds. They looked like a nest of waiting bees. She watched in despair as the weird aura of Nem-warp pasted itself over the plasma shell created by the spinning fibres.

'Fire!' she told her shadow. 'Kill that thing!'

The *Ariel Two* fired every g-ray it had. But Ann already knew she was too late. The image of the spinning ship that reached her was still thirty seconds old by the time she came close enough to fire. The carrier winked out as if it had never been there, not even leaving a trail to follow.

Ann sagged in the captain's couch, staring at the dead space that had once held the mutant swarm. Her mouth felt dry.

'Captain Aquino, any guess on their exit vector?' she said.

'From the orientation of their warp-field, I'd say Tiwanaku,' he said. 'Almost certainly.'

That was a small mercy, at least. She'd have fewer drones to fight back in the home system, at least.

'Everyone stay buckled,' she said. 'We're headed for Earth and it's going to be rough.'

19.3: WILL

At human scale again and struggling for virtual breath, Will stood on a sea of white nothingness and saw Rachel, his dead wife, walking towards him out of a wall of blinding fog. He knew immediately that it wasn't her. The Transcended had borrowed her form again, just as they had years ago.

'You,' Will growled. 'What are you doing here?'

'Watching,' she said. 'As always.'

'You did this, all this, didn't you? You made this place.'

'Of course.' She smiled gently. 'Who did you expect? *Another* galaxy-spanning civilisation?'

'You *killed* me,' he breathed.

'Only after a fashion,' said the Rachel-thing. 'We're still talking, aren't we?'

'But why?' said Will.

He never thought he'd be able to truly hate something with Rachel's face. Now he knew different.

'We can't have what you know leaking out,' she said. 'Snakepit shouldn't know, not until much, much later.'

'But *why*?' said Will. 'Why *lie*? Why build an entire world only to deceive it?'

'To make what comes next easier,' she said. 'It's better if those entities you call the Nems don't know their own origin. It makes it easier for them to become humanity.'

Will squinted at her, uncomprehending. 'Become *us*?'

'That's right. Why do you suppose they abandon operational complexity once they mirror a new species? It's because they don't need it any more. They become that which they encounter, with a few important adjustments, of course. Don't tell me you didn't notice.'

Will gawped. There had been clues to what was happening after all, just so subtle he hadn't noticed them. The cells' weird adaptations he'd seen in Pari's base. The curious behaviour of the biosphere Ann had described. Even the curator's own words. He'd seen all those hints and blanked them, dragged along by the tide of events.

'They'll mimic your race, feed on it and then improve upon it,' said the Transcended. 'That's hard for them to do effectively if they're aware they've been manufactured to achieve that end. They must believe in themselves, just as you do. They need a vision, even if it's a false one.'

The import of her words seeped into Will's mind in slow, ugly stages.

'You knew we'd release the Nems,' he said. 'You were counting on it.'

'Of course,' she said with a laugh. 'In our experience, an intelligent species never ignores a free weapon for long, even with prior warnings. It's a game-theoretic imperative we find it useful to exploit.'

Will shrank inside. The Transcended had arranged all this.

'You knew we'd come here. You knew Earth would be at risk.'

'Yes, but please don't grant us powers of prediction we don't have.

482

This process never pans out the same way from species to species. And your outcome has been particularly surprising. We've never seen a messenger-agent such as yourself arrive so late in the game, or push so hard once they were involved. Your appearance at the last moment astonished us, as did the choices you made. The human capacity to surprise delights us, and proves the correctness of our choice.

'In the grand scheme, though, the order of events matters little. As you know, we vet for appropriate species using the suntap and employ messenger-agents to encourage compliance in those edge cases where intervention appears worthwhile. You did a terrific job of that, by the way. Humanity has been far more predictable since your involvement. Then, if a species survives vetting, we allow it to reach what you might call a *gingerbread world*. The gingerbread world then neutralises any messenger-agents if they haven't been disassembled already. So you can console yourself with the knowledge that your dismantling was inevitable, at least. You were never going to leave. Gingerbread worlds are very welcoming, you see. Their standards for integration are, you might say, rather loose.'

Will felt a surge of embarrassment. The curator had handed him power on the basis of a handful of files. He'd thought himself so clever. It had never occurred to him that she might not have a choice.

'And every gingerbread world produces cuckoos. Inevitably, they are released,' said the Transcended. 'A species' own capacity for constructive self-modification which we filter for at level one becomes a tool for the cuckoos to utilise at level two. Of course, only cuckoo-compatible species are allowed to get this far.'

'Cuckoos,' said Will stupidly.

He'd spent every day since the war believing in the Transcended. Believing in hope and straining his life to further that ideal of development and peace. Was this what all that striving had been for? To release some plague of usurpers to feed on the human race?

'Why?' he croaked. 'If you wanted us dead, why not wipe us out the way you did the Fecund?'

'Because we don't want you dead,' she said, her eyes bright. 'We want you for something *wonderful*.'

Will lashed out at her. His fist connected only with air.

The Rachel-thing cocked her head. 'You've become a destabilising influence, Will Monet,' she said. 'You should be very proud of that. It's rare. You've produced patterns of behaviour we've never seen before. And our memories are long, believe me. So rather than taking you out of play, we're leaving you in the game, after a fashion. That's a risk, of course, but there's evidence it's worth it. So you'll be staying here and integrating with the planet as she desires. We'll take the blocks out to enable that. She'll be delighted, I assure you.'

Will stared at her, his mind tripping over the ramifications of her words. Godhood, or some sick parody of it, wasn't optional, apparently.

'Never,' said Will. 'I'd rather die.'

'We'll be making some modifications to your mind, of course,' she said, 'so as to minimise the damage you can cause, and to ensure that you're suitably aligned. I'm very sorry, but you'll have to be conscious during that process. We need to read your cognitive feedback, you see. That'll hurt, but don't worry, by the end you won't care.'

'Do you think you can scare me?' Will shouted. 'I've had my mind taken apart before. I've been tortured to the edge of sanity. There is nothing you can throw at me that I haven't already beaten. Do you understand? *Nothing!*'

'I'm not trying to scare you, Will,' said the Transcended reasonably. 'I'm just helping you get in the right frame of mind. We need a good imprint of your motivational architecture to inform the things we'll eventually want to make out of you. Every gingerbread world needs strong weapons.'

Will reached uselessly for her face with hands bent into claws. The Rachel-thing receded back into the fog, leaving Will alone in pristine oblivion.

He twisted with all the mental force he could summon, desperately willing his way out of the vision, but he didn't stand a chance, of course. The Transcended had always been with him. They'd never let go. Being free was never an option.

And then, in a bright moment of exquisite horror, the surgery began. Rachel's face suddenly filled Will's mind like an explosion and then was gone, along with all memory of what she'd looked like.

'No!' Will screamed.

Memories blossomed in his mind like fireworks. His half-son Mark came and went. Poor Amy, who he'd watched die. His friend Ira, grave but determined. Gustav, blood pooling in his mouth as his eyes implored Will to action. Each vision left a curious gap in its wake, like a tooth yanked from an open mouth.

'No! No! No!'

Will's years of political suffering, his long war days and finally his youth, all were snipped out a piece at a time. In the end Will still knew fear and rage, but had no one left to aim them at.

'No...' he said, and wondered what he meant.

'There there,' said the Transcended. 'Time to sleep, Will Monet. Time to sleep.'

The snow-white simulation faded into nothingness, taking Will along with it.

19.4: MARK

Mark looked at the radiation profile on the wall display and knew there couldn't be any doubt. A sick sense of injustice welled up inside him.

'Our hands were just tied,' he said. 'We don't get to go to Earth – we have to make our stand here and now.'

Citra regarded him blankly. 'Why?'

'Because of the target-size problem,' said Ash grimly. 'If we let the Nems take over this system, they'll be that much smarter by the time they get to Earth. If the swarm wins here, they'll gain an army of hosts and about a thousand IQ points.'

'I'm not sure "swarm" is the right word,' said Zoe. She was already frantically typing on the nearest surface. 'Take a look at this.' She posted a window to the wall-screen. 'This is an interpolated image from our primary telescopic array.'

Six bright points hung against a backdrop of fuzzy darkness.

'They look like starships,' said Mark.

The Nems had brought a human-style fleet with them this time, not a swarm. With each passing second, the image resolution improved. The Nem craft all had the same curiously knobbled exterior. And they were diving in-system at almost a full light – a real achievement so close to a star.

'They look like giant raspberries,' said Citra.

'They're not all the same type,' said Zoe. 'I'm seeing two ship-forms. Three of them are round like our ships and three are elongated.'

'I've never heard of these things,' said Ash.

Mark rifled through Ash's borrowed memories. 'Me neither. They're new.'

Fingers of dread stroked up his spine. The Nems had changed again.

'We have to wake Sam,' said Citra. 'He's been preparing for this moment. I listened while he organised defences for the whole system.'

Ash looked sour. 'I'd rather not.'

'Unfortunately, Citra's right,' said Mark. 'We need all the information we can get.'

Zoe shot him a dry look. 'Are you sure we'll believe it when we get it?'

'No, but that's a chance we'll have to take.' He pushed off the wall, back towards the med-bay.

At first, the medical SAP refused to rouse Sam.

'He requires extensive facial reconstruction,' the room told them. 'Surgery is ongoing.'

'I don't need him sitting up,' Mark told the machine. 'Isn't he carrying a subvocal tap for heavy-gee dialogue? We can talk to him while he's still in there.'

'He also has a concussion with mild brain damage,' the med-bay insisted. 'His mental functions are still under repair and should not be utilised. I cannot recommend stimulation at this time.'

'I don't care,' Mark snapped. 'This is an emergency.'

The wall-screen on Sam's cabinet swapped to a simulated display of his face. He groaned as the med-bay dumped stimulants into his blood. 'What the fuck...'

His voice emerged as a digitised mess while the SAP selected a vocal interpolation program that would work. The simulated face blinked and looked around. The camera in the corner of the display went live.

'Hello, Sam,' said Mark.

'Where am I? What's happening?'

'You're in recovery.'

Dawning realisation crawled across the simulated face. Sam scowled.

'Well, you got your ship back,' said Sam. 'Congratu-fucking-lations.'

'Sam, the Nems are here,' said Mark.

'Of course they are, you stupid little shit. What did you think was going to happen? Did you imagine that bullshit prank at Nerroskovi was going to buy you time? The Nem carriers are made out of adapted

486

drones, you idiot. Where did you imagine they came from? Kill one carrier and the others cluster and fuse to make a new one. Everything they do is made out of drones.'

Zoe's eyes lit up. 'Of course!' she said. She sounded more fascinated than afraid.

'We didn't wake you so you could insult us,' said Mark. 'We need to know the state of Carter's defences. We'd ask them but they're not in a talking mood.'

'Do you imagine that anything I can tell you will do the slightest bit of good at this point?' said Sam. 'Do yourself a favour and leave the system. It's fucking over. You've doomed these people already. Let them die in peace.'

'The defences!' Ash shouted. His voice squeaked with rage and spittle flew from his mouth. 'Tell us about the fucking defences or I swear you'll come out of that box a cripple.'

'There are two colony police gunboats about six AU out,' said Sam, his voice dripping scorn. 'They've got orders to release decoys in the event of a swarm to draw the Nems' attention.

'But the best ship in the system by far is the *Gulliver*. The colonists were going to equip it with some weapons, but you fucked that up, Mark, before they could even start. We were supposed to act as an escort for the evacuation ark. Most of the population were already aboard before you trashed my comms. I have no idea if they ever finished that process.'

'Where's the ark?' said Mark.

'At Carter's primary moon.'

'And how about the people in the Flag colonies? You were going to burn them from orbit, weren't you?'

'Do you really think they deserve rescuing?' Sam drawled. 'You saw them up close.'

'Of course they fucking deserve rescuing!' Mark shouted. 'They're *people*!'

He struggled for calm. Every second he spent in Sam's company came with a heavy emotional cost.

Zoe passed an image feed of the approaching Nem fleet to Sam's visual field.

'The Nems didn't send a swarm this time,' she said. 'Their carrier brought these raspberry ships instead. Any idea what they're for?'

The silence that followed spoke volumes.

'You're screwed in any case,' said Sam at length. 'You took out the orbital defence platform. That was your best tool for making a stand, or even just for target reduction. The Carter colonists have Nem-cloaking now. I made sure of that. They'll just have to fire it up and hope. The *Gulliver* has one option and that's to get the fuck out of here.'

'Wrong,' said Zoe.

An icon appeared in Mark's sensorium. 'I'm receiving a signal from those ships,' he said.

He passed it to the nearest wall. A beautiful woman with decorative orange striping on her face appeared. The backdrop behind her was a field of shimmering blue like a summer sky.

'Greetings!' she said with a warm smile. She looked somehow familiar, in a friendly, approachable way. 'We come in peace. We are the Photurian Collective and we offer an alliance with the human race. Please do not be alarmed by our arrival. We are here simply to engage in face-to-face dialogue with the people of the Carter System. We bring gifts: extended life, telepathy, social harmony and a host of biological and technological enhancements. We offer all of them freely in return for the chance to meet you and learn about your culture.'

Mark stared at the woman and almost wanted to believe the message. Maybe the Nems had grown up. Maybe after all the horror they'd brought, this was what they'd been trying to turn into.

'Run,' Sam breathed. His simulated face started to distort into fragments. 'Run *now*!'

The vitals on his readout display started to spike.

'My patient is entering a state of neural strain due to your intervention,' said the med-bay.

'What is it, Sam?' said Zoe. 'What do you see?'

'Don't you recognise her? That's Meleta Keth, the head watcher we posted at the Tiwanaku System. She was in the League. She had access to our data – battle plans, projections, fallbacks, all of it. She would never have let them take her. If they've got her...'

He didn't need to say more. They all knew what he meant. The League was over.

'What are you waiting for?' Sam shouted, his voice deteriorating into static. '*Go!*'

'No,' said Zoe. 'Here's what we'll do: we attack digitally. Sam used their comms protocol before. We can use it again. They don't like changing it, otherwise Nem-cloaking wouldn't work. That gives us a way in.'

'Stupid,' said Sam. 'If you soft assault the Nems they'll swap up their security and the evac-ark will lose its cloaking.'

'That's the price we'll have to pay if we want to shut this invasion down,' said Zoe.

Mark stared at her. 'How can we do that?'

A weird smile quirked one corner of Zoe's lips. 'This is the moment I was born for,' she said. 'The Vartian Institute has been planning for this for a long time. The *Gulliver* has more alien-hacking tools packed into it than a fleet of soft-combat ships.'

'Where?' said Mark. 'They're not in the ship's core.'

'Of course not,' said Zoe. 'They're in me. What did you think all those aug defences were for? For this. Nobody fucks with the Vartian Institute. Nobody. And this is when they learn that. We're going for a two-phase attack. I need to work on that protocol of theirs. I don't have enough data to subvert it yet – we need open communication channels for that. So the first thing this ship has to do is act as bait. Mark, I need you to fly us over to that Nem fleet and announce yourself. Without getting caught, of course. As fast as you can.'

Mark nodded. 'Go to the lounge and strap down,' he told the others.

'Use my bunk,' Ash called after him. 'Sam sabotaged the top one. I'll work from the lounge and do what I can to help.'

Mark ran to the bridge, slammed home the fat-contact and opened the link to the lounge while the engines ramped to full power.

'You're confident we can do this?' he asked Zoe as she strapped in.

'This day has been thirty years in the planning. They don't stand a chance.'

'Why now?' said Citra. 'Why not at Tiwanaku, when we could have saved Yunus?'

'Didn't have enough data,' said Zoe. 'I had no idea what I was looking at. Now we have everything Sam's been hiding. That's years of research. And the best part is that the Nems have spent this entire time cannibalising our technology, which we know inside out. You can see it screaming from their message signatures. That lack of imagination levels the playing field plenty.'

Mark brought down the gel-sleeves, locking his crew in tight. Breathing support and virtual interface assist kicked in.

'Hold on, everybody,' he said. 'Here we go.'

He threw them into warp. The hammer of the *Gulliver*'s mighty drive smacked them into their crash couches and kept on smacking. For the next twenty minutes, the Nem fleet slid up to meet them.

Mark flicked open the channel the Nems had used and called them back.

'Hey there, Photurian Collective,' he said, his tight-beam transmitter blasting. 'I was in two minds at first, but on balance, your offer sounds *great*! Could you sign me and my crew up to join the Collective, please, at your earliest convenience?'

Of the six ships, the three spherical ones changed course towards him as soon as the message reached them. The ovals apparently weren't interested. They remained doggedly aimed at Carter.

'Three out of six is a good start,' said Zoe. 'Work on the round ones and keep at it.'

With light-lag, the Collective's response took five minutes.

'That's wonderful news, human ship. We will rendezvous with you and commence what I hope will be a very fruitful dialogue.'

'Terrific,' Mark sent back. 'Say, is there some assurance you can give me that I'll retain my identity after we meet face to face?'

'Of course you'll remain you,' the swarm eventually replied with Meleta Keth's benign smile. Mark could have sworn she hadn't been that pretty when they met her the first time. The Photurians had given her a makeover as well as tiger stripes. 'But you'll also be so much more. Please power down your vessel and allow us to approach.'

Mark kept moving straight towards them, so the Nems slowed instead. The gap between them closed to a light-minute and kept shrinking.

'Twenty light-seconds,' said Mark. 'In warp terms, this is practically in their laps.'

'We're in range,' said Zoe. 'Keep them this tight, but don't let them get any closer.'

Mark swerved around the trio of Nem ships at the last moment, dropping his burst rate to allow them to keep up.

'Human vessel,' said Meleta Keth. 'What are you doing? Why have you not powered down for rendezvous?'

'I'm having second thoughts,' said Mark. 'I'm scared. Can you tell me what it's like, Meleta, to join the Collective? You don't mind if I call you Meleta, do you?'

The Nem ships picked up speed to follow him.

'You can call me what you like,' said Meleta. 'Names aren't important.'

With three ships closing on him from slightly different directions, it was incredibly hard to maintain such a close lead. His every warp-burst created a pocket of dead space that threatened to cut his pursuers' velocity in half. Mark had to keep shifting course, realigning his field every time. The endless blows of the drive felt like falling down stairs – really big, blunt stairs.

'Keep up the patter!' said Zoe. 'I'm using your signal as an insert carrier.'

'So you don't have names?' Mark said as he darted left. 'That sounds weird.'

'We're free,' Meleta assured him. 'That's all. We can have any names we like.'

'Can I still be Bill?' said Mark.

The entire cabin shuddered as he struggled to lock in a rotating warp offset.

'Of course, Bill.'

'Do you have memories?'

'Memories are shared,' she said. 'It's very beautiful.'

'Do you remember our nights, together?' said Mark.

'Of course I do, Bill. But you're being evasive. As a gesture of trust, I need you to cut warp now. Otherwise I'll start doubting your motives and may need to disable your engines.'

'Got them!' said Zoe. 'Hand me the comms array.'

Mark slid full control of comms to Zoe with a gasp of relief. Zoe fired a dense burst of data packets at the closest ship.

The raspberry ship dropped warp and burst into its component drones. A cluster of something tumbled out from the space between them. As he cut speed to match them, Mark zoomed the cameras for a closer look and saw dozens of what looked like oddly bloated lander-shuttles tumbling in space.

'Shit,' said Zoe. 'Not what I had in mind. Hang on.'

Zoe grunted as she struggled to reconfigure the drones' command

491

system with virtual hands. The gel-sleeves had locked her physical ones to her sides.

'Mark, I'm going to need you,' she said. 'I'm inserting pirate guidance SAPs into those drones. You'll have to drive them on tight-beams like guided munitions. Can you do that?'

'All of them?' he said. 'At the same time?' There had to be hundreds. 'It would have been easier to fly the one raspberry.'

'Not an option, I'm afraid. Can you do it?'

'Hook me up,' said Mark.

She started throwing SAP signatures at him – dozens of them. He split his focus as thinly as he dared to juggle them all. He knew that if he thought about it too hard, he'd panic. There were way too many perspectives for him to cover while still managing all the robots in an entire starship, but he didn't have a choice. From the lounge, Ash had no helm access. Mark was on his own.

While he cemented his control, the other two Nem ships arced back around to meet him. Mark sent drones racing towards both of them. It was like running and spinning plates at the same time.

'Focus on the closest,' said Zoe. 'I'm sending it love letters.'

The leading raspberry approached with apparently little or no concern for the threat its former swarm-mates presented. It hadn't noticed the hack. Mark threw five drones straight at it. It burst open in a blaze of light. Two seconds later there was only a single raspberry left along with a rapidly expanding shell of ionised debris. Their Casimir-buffers crackled as it hit.

'Who says we don't have weapons?' said Zoe.

The last of the three ships clued in and swapped up its security. At the same time, it broadcast a warning cry, system-wide.

'Fuck,' said Zoe. 'There goes Nem-cloaking.' She instructed their pet drone-swarm to emit a similar but conflicting message. 'Kill that ship, Mark. As fast as you can. Before it can stabilise a new protocol.'

Mark sent a second batch of drones tearing towards the raspberry before it could find room to manoeuvre away. At the last moment, the craft tried to break up. It didn't make it. A second blast-wave tore through the Carter System as the raspberry burst apart.

'We have a new problem,' said Ash as the crackling from the buffers subsided.

He posted a video feed to Mark's sensorium, showing data with an eight-minute light-lag. While he watched, one of the elongated Nem ships sidled up to an empty orbital at Carter's L5 point. Grappling limbs and a kind of proboscis emerged from one end of the craft in an obscenely organic motion. With these tools on display, the craft suddenly resembled a gigantic bacteriophage. With ponderous deliberation, the legs locked on to the orbital, trashing its axial spin and sending both vehicles tumbling. The proboscis adhered itself to the pressurised wall and started to drill. Mark could see clouds of gas and debris escaping from the join.

Suddenly, the significance of the lander shuttles he'd noticed earlier became clear. The Nems hadn't come here for a punishment raid as they had at Nerroskovi. They'd come to harvest *people*.

He shuddered. Had that orbital been occupied, the Nems would have raised their host count already. He quickly checked the approach vectors for the remaining ships. Both were headed for other empty orbitals. But the wave-front of the warning signal had doomed raspberry had sent would hit them in seconds. He could guess what would happen then. The evac-ark, already sitting closer to one of the Nem harvesters than its selected goal, would become the new target.

Mark turned the *Gulliver* around and sped back in-system, dragging his drone swarm with him. Over the awful seconds that followed, one harvester ship swapped course, and then the other, setting their sights on the ark. Mark watched the ark captain just sit there, apparently not realising that his cloaking had catastrophically failed.

Mark pushed the drones ahead of him, overclocking their engines and driving them into the closest harvester before it could deploy its limbs. The ark juddered from the impact wave. He gave thanks that evac-arks were heavily rad-shielded otherwise the entire population of New Luxor would have gained one hell of a tan.

He brought the *Gulliver* about and stared down what remained of the Nem fleet. He had two harvesters left to kill, an ark to guard and a thinning supply of drones. He'd thrown too many munitions at the first harvester. What had looked like an abundance of weapons now felt like too few.

By then, both remaining Nem ships had swapped to randomised security settings and shut down inter-ship communication. They turned to face him. His attention to the ark had clued them in to the location of all the tasty humans.

Mark wished the colonists hadn't bothered to evacuate. By putting all their eggs in one basket, they'd created a tactical nightmare. Guarding the ark from both Nem ships without torching it in the process was going to be nearly impossible. So Mark decided to take the fight to the harvesters instead.

He split what was left of his swarm. The way he saw it, he didn't have a choice. It was that or leave the evac-ark entirely unprotected. He picked a target to stick with and flew, knowing full well that this would put the other half of his remaining weapons outside tight-beam targeting range and therefore beyond his control. He had to hope that the inherent intelligence in the pirate guidance SAPs would be enough to let him pull the trick off.

He chased down the harvester he'd selected as it arced and twisted to avoid him. Why it didn't break up into its constituent drones, Mark had no idea. Maybe it couldn't. Either way, it lacked the manoeuvrability to escape so many drones at once and died in a ball of fire.

Mark turned back to find his remaining unpiloted drones fanned out in a hopeless spray. A channel of empty space led straight from the last harvester to the damaged ark. He knew he'd never get back into submind range fast enough to make a difference.

He opened a communication channel to the last Nem ship. He had no idea if it was still listening, but he had to try.

'Touch that ark and you'll die,' he said. 'Don't think I won't hit you just because you've got human captives. You're not taking them out of here alive.'

At the same time he pointed the *Gulliver* at the empty space between the ark and the harvester and pushed his speed as high as it could go. This deep in-system, that meant a lousy fraction of the speed of light, but it was all he had. He signalled his drones to converge.

The man Mark had become didn't want thousands of innocent lives on his conscience, but if it came to that, he was ready to act. He gritted his teeth as he watched the Nems descend on the ark and knew he wasn't going to make it.

Then, astonishingly, help arrived. The colonists' two gunboats converged from the other side of the moon, firing g-rays at the harvester with every joule of power they had. The harvester slewed sideways.

A return message from it hit his sensorium. It was Meleta's face again, this time looking profoundly sad.

'Why do you resist us, Bill?' she said. 'We have so much to give.'

Mark briefly wondered again if they'd somehow misread the Nems' intentions, despite all appearances. Then the remainder of his drone swarm pummelled into the last alien ship, blasting it into atoms. Meleta's face vanished.

'Nice job,' Mark told the gunboats.

The Carter colonists declined to reply.

As the glare cleared, Zoe spoke up. 'This is a great start,' she said. 'The Nems are dead and Phase One is complete. Now for Phase Two.'

Mark's brow furrowed. 'I thought that *was* Phase Two.'

'No. *Two* is where we take control of the jelly-ship that brought them – what Sam called a *carrier*.'

'And how in hell's name are we supposed to pull that off?' said Mark. 'It'll be on rotating security before we get there if it's not already trying to leave.'

'Then we're lucky I have more than one trick up my sleeve. Please, Mark. We don't have time to debate this. We have to go *now*. Our survival may depend on this.'

Rather than argue the point, Mark spun the ship and headed out towards the Nems' insertion point. The further they travelled from Carter's star the more speed they picked up, but the spatial clutter prevented them from approaching even a single light below the heliopause, no matter how hard they pushed the engines. That meant the raspberry ship's warning signal was bound to get there before them.

'What makes you think the carrier won't just leave the moment it gets wind of trouble?' said Ash.

'Because there's a difference between trouble and disaster,' said Zoe. 'My guess is that the carrier will hang around until it has evidence that the last Nem ship failed. *Then* they'll start gearing to leave. That gives the bad news a very narrow lead on us: two minutes at most. We have to hope that's enough wiggle room for us to operate in.'

As they closed on the carrier, its rotating jelly-discs began to spin faster.

'That's the sign,' said Zoe. 'They're gearing up to leave. I'm taking the comms array again.'

'To do *what*?' said Mark. 'What have we got left to use?'

'The one message they can't ignore,' said Zoe. 'The same one the raspberry used – a broadcast security alert.'

She started bombarding the carrier with copies of the Nems' warning pulse. She tweaked the signal fifteen different ways and used every available broadcast tool the ship had. It didn't appear to be doing much good. The carrier's arms just kept whirling.

'You sure this is going to work?' said Mark nervously.

'It has to, doesn't it?' said Zoe. Her voice cracked with nervous brightness. 'Those discs need to keep open comms otherwise how would they coordinate their movement?'

Mark wasn't so sure. 'Couldn't they just send signals down those frond fibres?'

'Didn't think of that,' said Zoe. 'Let's hope they can't.'

Amazingly, the carrier's security started showing cracks.

'Denial of service,' said Zoe. 'Oldest trick in the book. That's what comes of borrowing too much from another species – you absorb all their weaknesses as well as their strengths.'

Suddenly, the *Gulliver*'s processors started shutting down. Mark lost attitude control.

'Soft assault!' said Zoe. 'They're fucking hacking us and I didn't even notice!'

'You were saying?' said Mark.

'Don't worry about it,' Zoe snarled. 'Nobody's more paranoid than the Institute. I've got this covered. Every time they go for us, we get stronger.'

Almost immediately, the *Gulliver*'s systems started bouncing back. At the same time, the carrier's spin rate dropped off.

'Got the bastard,' said Zoe.

She passed a SAP handle to Mark. It appeared in his sensorium plastered with garish warning icons.

'Now we're going to use this thing,' she said. 'Earth needs a defence and we're it.'

Mark raised his eyebrows. 'And you think we'll be enough?'

'Hell, no,' said Zoe. 'But haven't you been paying attention? Those fibres can extend to enclose an almost arbitrary volume. We're heading to New Panama first to pick up some battle cruisers. It's on the way, after all.'

Mark grinned. 'Works for me.'

'Park us between the discs,' said Zoe. 'And be *very* careful. We need those strands intact.'

Mark dropped warp, killed his conventional velocity and slid himself in among the fronds.

'Like this?'

'That's right. Now bust out that SAP I sent you. I've instructed the ship to map the flight controls to starship norms. It should all make sense.'

Mark opened the handle and a blizzard of unfamiliar physics concepts erupted inside his head. He flinched from the pain of neural overload.

'Holy shit. *This* is how they get about?'

'Do you think you can fly it?' she said.

Mark snorted. 'It can't be harder than flying a lifter in a hurricane. Hold on to your purple hair, Doctor Tamar, we're going to New Panama.'

20: EARTH

20.1: MARK

It took Mark just a minute to figure out that he'd been absolutely wrong about piloting the carrier. Beyond the cosmetic parallels enforced by Zoe's device mapping, the controls she had handed him bore almost no resemblance to those he was used to. He could fathom the mechanisms for increasing and decreasing the rate of spin. Nothing else made sense.

'I take it back,' he said. 'This thing is nuts. Help me out here.'

'Let me look,' said Zoe.

She fell silent. Through the camera feed, Mark watched her eyes go wide as she scanned the code.

'Holy shit,' she said. She kept reading. The seconds dragged into minutes.

'Are we flying or not?' said Mark. 'It's just that the last I knew, we were in a hurry.'

Zoe breathed deep. 'Okay, it's like this. Strictly speaking, this isn't a warp drive.'

'What?' said Mark.

'It's more like ... I don't know, spatial supercavitation? Shit. I get it. No wonder it looked like magic.'

'Not warp? Could you make sense, please? What did you find?'

'Remember how I said there were no B-mesons?' said Zoe. 'This ship doesn't need them because it carries something with it that does the job instead. The best way I can describe it is as an *ember*.' She shook her head. 'How could I have been so *stupid*?' she said. 'There were hints of this all along. The tiny warp envelope, the crazy-sharp warp profile. Even that cloaking field for the *Chiyome*. They stole it, of course, without understanding what they were copying.'

'An ember of what?' said Mark. 'Zoe, please.'

'Okay, there's something a bit like a suntap entangler on this ship, but it doesn't contain electrons. In fact, it doesn't really contain *anything* so I disregarded it before. I thought it was another Nem design screw up, like an appendix or something. But it actually holds the seed of a novel vacuum state.'

'A *what*?'

'A patch of non-standard space–time. A little piece of a different universe, if you like. It's not stable, of course, which is why it needs the entangler to hold it steady. But when the drive turns on, those fronds create a plasma envelope which another entangler field can act upon. It's super-hot and super-thin, like the corona of a star.'

'We've been messing with vacuum states in simple ways for years – Casimir-buffers, for instance. But this kind of vacuum, well, it's contagious. That's the only way I can describe it. The ember spreads out over the envelope like a fungus or a fire or something as soon as you give it the right conditions. Basically, the envelope becomes a shell of modified space–time that taps curvon decay just like warp drive. The fronds polarise the plasma, giving the envelope an orientation.

'And what *that* gives you is a shell of novel space–time that sucks up normal space at the front, channels it holographically over the surface via some kind of current, by the looks of things, and dumps it out at the back. Meanwhile, the space inside the envelope is almost completely flat. Amazing.'

'Which is why I can't see any controls for burst rate or orientation,' said Mark. 'There are no bursts.'

'No. You spin up, release the magic gunk and go.' She handed him some extra control details, bolting sections onto the mapping where she could. 'You fly by tweaking the envelope, almost like sailing. You've sailed, right? Boats and all that – they still have them on Earth, don't they?'

'I never have,' said Mark. 'But it can't be that hard, can it? Now would be a good time to learn, in any case.'

Mark brought the carrier up to spin and charged the envelope. A haze of bright pinkish light now surrounded the *Gulliver* in every direction. With extreme caution, Mark opened the magnetic container around the ember of magic gunk. A shell of weird opalescent light spilled out from the jelly-ship in front of them and slid down to the jelly at the back.

Before he even noticed what had happened, they were en route for New Panama. There'd been no thud of a gravity wave, no radiation burst. The intermittent telemetry he received from the carrier simply informed him that he was now travelling faster than light.

'It's working,' said Mark. 'It's not exactly *Gulliver*-speed – just about a light and a half – but we're moving.'

It felt extremely odd to be moving at warp speed without experiencing the pulsing tug of artificial gravity. But for the data he was getting and the oddly dreamlike shell of light, it was no different from sitting in a vanilla rest frame.

'Do you realise what this means?' Zoe breathed. He'd never heard her so excited. 'We've been wrong about the structure of space and time for about the last five hundred years. If there are discretised contagious vacuum states like this, then space can't be smooth otherwise the drive wouldn't work. Everything we've done with strings and spatial knot theory since the discovery of warp will have to be rewritten.'

'Er, Zoe,' said Mark. 'I'm glad you're pleased and all, but we appear to be accelerating. And I'm not doing anything.'

'Really?' said Zoe. 'That's interesting.' She stared into her view. 'Ah, yes, of course you are. Once the shell is in motion with respect to the CMB reference frame – which is as soon as you turn it on, really – it creates its own acceleration. So long as you can keep the envelope charged and stable enough, it just goes faster and faster. It's the warp equivalent of a ramjet.'

'Our power consumption is rising,' said Mark.

'Yes, because of the increased spatial flux over the holographic sheet. You'll need more and more energy to stabilise the false-vacuum. But don't worry – now I know what all those crazy little bottles of anti-iron are for. I recommend practising steering *right now*. By the time we get near New Panama we'll be going so fast it'll be impossible. Oh, and we should turn the drive off the way the Nems do it – at the *edge* of the system. Even earlier, maybe. Because we're building up a spatial curvature debt at the edge of the field, when we drop warp it'll be like a bomb going off. That's the energy spike we've been seeing. It's amazing the Nems don't kill themselves every time they go somewhere, really.'

'My, that's reassuring,' said Mark.

Around them, the shell of light had taken on a fierce brightness. It shimmered and flashed like sunlight on water, but with a speed and intensity that had nothing to do with nature. The amount of Mark's attention required just to keep the envelope from collapsing was steadily increasing. It was like trying to pilot a soap-bubble from the inside.

'I'm jealous,' said Ash. 'This is amazing.'

'Don't be,' Mark snapped. 'It's scaring the crap out of me already and we've barely started. How about you repair that captain's couch, because I'm going to need help. This crate is *really* not designed for a human pilot and I'd very much like to get to New Panama in one piece.'

As their speed increased, managing the drive became steadily more difficult. After a gruelling fourteen-hour shift holding up the delicate envelope, Mark handed control to Ash and fell asleep still clipped into his bridge couch. He woke much later to find Venetia floating beside the bunk, watching him closely. She looked haggard but intact and wore a flat, hard expression Mark couldn't read. Her face had the weird baby-softness of newly printed skin.

He levered himself upright in surprise. 'You're back!' he exclaimed. 'How are you?'

'Quite well, considering,' she said. 'How about yourself?'

Mark rubbed his eyes. 'Fine. Got a headache. Is Ash still on duty?'

Venetia glanced at the repaired upper bunk. 'Yes, he's doing fine.'

'Are we still moving?' said Mark. 'I can't tell.' It felt deeply unnatural to be under warp without the familiar trembling pull on his body to remind him.

Venetia nodded. 'At about half a kilolight now, according to Zoe.' She stared at him, her mouth a thin, tight line. The conversation stalled.

'I'm sorry about Britehaven,' Mark said abruptly. 'Did they... Are you...' He couldn't voice the question he wanted to ask.

'Did they break me?' she offered, raising a quizzical eyebrow. 'Not a chance. Though it's admittedly impossible to come through an experience like that unchanged. The machinery removes that option.' She drew a ragged breath. 'I've seen worse done, though. On Esalen. During the war... You're different, too, I notice.'

Mark nodded. 'Better, I hope.'

She smiled opaquely. 'That's what we all aspire to.'

There was something a little disconcerting about the new Venetia, Mark decided. She looked more tightly wound than before, and a little off-kilter.

'Thank you for what you did back there,' she said. 'You saved my life.' She paused again. 'I brought you this.'

Venetia posted a link to his home node. It opened to display a set of roboteer's sensory mappings – crystalline diagrams full of thousands of interwoven threads running between pairs of curving neural landscapes.

'They should help a lot with flying the carrier.'

Mark examined them in surprise. The nerve patches were intricate and untidy, like wiring scans from a living organism. Mark had never seen mappings so overwrought. Venetia could never have designed them in the time since her recovery. She'd have needed months. And last he'd heard, she wasn't a sensory mapping specialist.

'Where did you get these?' he said.

'We copied them from one of the carrier pilots,' said Venetia. 'I've been up for hours now and I wasn't really in the mood for sleep so I had time on my hands. I worked with Zoe. We've been very busy with the remote probes.'

'Wait,' said Mark confused. 'The carrier had a *pilot*?'

'Pilot is maybe too a strong word,' she said. 'There were human brains wired into the drone architecture that managed flight control. That system's inactive now because you and Ash are flying it, which meant we were able to safely unhook part of the mechanism and take a look inside. You're right that this ship wasn't designed for humans to fly. But humans were flying it anyway. Or bits of them, at any rate. Those mappings I sent you are so deep because those brains needed a lot of support. So I don't blame you for needing ten hours to sleep that shift off. You're lucky you didn't get neural burnout.'

Mark felt ill. 'Are they alive? The brains, I mean.'

Venetia offered a bleak half-smile. 'After a fashion. All but the one we accidentally discovered, at least. It was a surprise. Zoe wasn't happy about it. I've learned a lot from that brain, though, and not just about the piloting arrangements. Wiring it up this way is very much like what the Fecund did with some of their disposable spawn, so the usage is nothing new. Brains are cheap, adaptable processors with excellent self-repair characteristics. I've seen this kind of surgical horror before, though admittedly not using human children.'

502

'Children?' said Mark, his throat constricting.

He glanced back at the sensory mappings Venetia had given him. The idea of pressing his mind up against the neural shackles that had been used on some poor dismembered kid made him feel like throwing up.

Venetia nodded. A dark intensity started to smoulder in her gaze.

'But the Nems did something else. They altered that brain's emotional and motivational architecture with a much higher level of precision than they've demonstrated in any of the other wiring I've seen. The differences are stark. I think that's why they prefer young hosts, by the way – they want the extra neuroplasticity. By comparison, the work to connect the brain into the flight systems was brutal and clumsy.'

She leaned forward and gripped Mark's arm. Odd, quiet urgency oozed out of her.

'But here's what's really interesting. For all their unpleasantness, the Fecund never bothered with any of that. Once you've wired in a brain's pain and pleasure centres, why take risks with the emotional landscape? You already own it. You only risk degrading performance by tinkering further.'

Mark watched her stare at him, a little creeped out by her manner.

'I don't know,' he said weakly. 'Efficiency?'

'There are no efficiency gains,' she said. 'There couldn't be.'

'Some kind of weird compassion, then? Were they deadening the horror the brain felt?'

Venetia shook her head. 'We're talking about an alien system here. Compassion is a dangerous word, and one that doesn't really apply. No. The Nems put more care into the emotional rewiring because *that's* what they care about, Mark. Because they assign it value. They did the motivational rewiring *first* and the heavy surgery later, almost as an afterthought. And that's why they scare me, Mark. That's why we have to stop them.' She clasped her hands together tight.

Mark's face creased in concern. This was clearly important to Venetia, but he didn't understand. 'I'm afraid I don't get it yet,' he said gently.

'It's like this,' she said. 'The Nems aren't real aliens. We know that now. We've watched them evolve from simple machines in a matter of days. But they're not some generic hive-mind, either. That's been our assumption, but a hive-mind would never have bothered with that extra neural adaptation because there's no pay-off. Do you see? The Nems are something else. Now they've learned about us, they want to *do* something to us. They want to cut us up and use us in some specific way. And from their treatment of children, I'm guessing it's not benign. They've developed a very specific appetite for humanity and the surgery they have in mind isn't optional. It hits at our core definition of self. Those brains aren't strictly human any more.'

Mark shivered with the tide of unease that passed through him. 'So what's the change? What do they want us for?'

Venetia shook her head. 'I have no idea. From the data we've collected so far, it's impossible to tell. But I confess my curiosity isn't so great that I want to keep them around to find out.'

She fell silent again and smiled at him stiffly for a long second.

'Use the mappings, Mark. They'll up your flight stamina by an estimated fifty-seven per cent. And frankly, we need every weapon we can get. I want to see them wiped out, Mark, I . . . I need it.'

She squinted at the wall-padding and then pushed off hurriedly into the corridor.

Mark gazed after her, understanding dawning at last. Apparently he wasn't the only one who'd left Britehaven with a burning desire to beat the Nems. Venetia had taken on a quest in the confines of her penitence box, just as he had. But she was only now able to start acting on it. He felt a hot tug of empathy. Tears stung the corners of his eyes. They all had scars now. The pain was only worth it if those scars were useful.

'I'll get them,' he called at her retreating back. The sense of crusade came upon him again, as fresh as the moment he'd stumbled back out into the light. 'Believe me. I'll make it happen. For all of us. Even if it kills me.'

20.2: ASH

Ash was on duty when they reached New Panama. Mark had succumbed to exhaustion again after another nail-biting eighteen-hour shift. The trip had taken far less time than they'd expected – just five days - and over the last day the acceleration had become ferocious. Ash simply didn't have time to think before dumping the envelope and no chance to practise. His heart hammered as his mind reached out for the control. He alerted Mark, gritted his teeth and dropped warp.

The result was completely anticlimactic. The shell of light popped and suddenly there they were – New Panama System dead ahead. For everyone nearby, their arrival wouldn't seem as subtle.

Mark surged onto the bridge, bleary-eyed. 'Shit,' he said. 'We're here already?'

'Looks like it,' said Ash.

Mark scooted up to his bunk and plugged in. 'Did you send our arrival message?'

'No. I thought you'd want to do that.'

He watched as Mark dropped their carefully worded warning onto a public channel and sent it winging its way towards the colony. They'd spent hours trimming the executive threat assessment, trying to make it as clear and persuasive as possible. Their message contained a very condensed history of the mission and as much intelligence as Zoe had been able to glean from the Nems' data stores. Along with the anticipated timing of the attack on Earth, she'd also provided estimates for how much spare fuel a New Panama taskforce would have to bring with them to get the carrier to the home system in time.

Ash had done much of the planning work on the message, along with Venetia. However, the video statement had been delivered by Mark. Ash no longer minded playing second fiddle to his old friend. In fact, he preferred it. With the stakes as high as they were now, staying out of the limelight suited him fine. He'd advised, of course. Mark might be the public face of the mission but he was still hopeless with people. And they weren't about to drag Sam out of his cabinet for a consultation. In fact, just thinking about Sam made Ash feel sick. Several times on the flight he'd thought about making the short trip to the med-bay to turn off Sam's life support. Or waking Sam and crushing his neck. Or driving his thumbs through Sam's eye sockets while the man screamed for mercy. Generally, though, Ash tried not to think about his old boss.

He held his nerve while they drifted for the next hour and a half. Eventually, six battle cruisers powered up to meet them. A message burst arrived showing a video feed of a powerfully built IPSO officer with a shaved head and piercing blue eyes. Ash recognised him.

'This is Overcaptain Arwal Tak,' the officer said. 'We received your message. Provide further proof of your identity within sixty seconds or we will open fire.' Tak glared into the camera. His eyes didn't blink once, but Ash thought he saw fear behind that mask.

Mark frowned. 'Prove it how?' he said. 'We already sent him Will's override code. He's seen my statement. What more does he want?'

'Humanity,' said Ash. 'A reason not to be scared. We just rad-bombed the largest population centre in the Far Frontier, remember. With zero warning.'

'He *should* be fucking scared,' said Mark. 'I'm scared.'

'Let me do this,' said Ash. 'I've worked with Tak. I know him.'

He'd spent hours in meetings with Arwal during his work with Sam. Thinking back over those days made him feel dirty. Besides spending too much time in the gym and fancying himself as an Ira Baron looka-like, Arwal was a good man. He hadn't been in the League, for starters.

Ash opened a video channel and donned his most approachable smile.

'Overcaptain Tak, this is Subcaptain Ash Corrigan-Five of the IPS *Gulliver*. Nice to see you again, sir, and our deepest apologies for the damaging arrival. If you've reviewed our package, you'll know that we're assembling a fleet to defend the home system from imminent attack. Will you be able to help us with that?'

They waited for their reply to crawl across the space between the ships and for Tak's response to crawl back. The silence stretched.

'They're not launching drones,' said Mark. 'That's a start.'

When Tak reappeared, he didn't look any happier. If anything, his frown had deepened.

'This is a very serious set of claims you're making, Corrigan. Your manifest says the senior Fleet officer aboard is Sam Shah, yet that's not who I'm looking at. I'd like to speak to him, please.'

Ash tried to keep his smile straight. 'I'm afraid that's not going to be possible, sir,' he said. 'He's under sedation at the moment. Overcaptain Shah has engaged in treasonous acts that have endangered the survival of our species.'

'Is that so?' Tak snapped. 'On whose assessment?'

'Mine. The captain's. In fact, every other member of this mission.'

'Then can I speak to the civilian mission head?' said Tak. 'Yunus Chesterford?'

'Yunus Chesterford is dead, sir. As are the two Spatials who came with us.'

'I see,' said Tak. From his expression, it was clear that he didn't. 'Your senior officers are disabled or dead. So how about a complete mission log from your data core so I know I'm not looking at the result of a mutiny?'

'Once again, there's a problem, sir,' said Ash brightly. 'This ship is running under a Vartian Institute diplomatic security lockout. We can't get you that log without a dry-dock.'

Arwal leaned towards his camera. 'Listen, *Gulliver*,' he growled. 'You're flying in a co-opted alien vessel last seen engaging in genocide at Tiwanaku. Your story is so wild there is no way I can get it past the Colonial government without a clearance check. And I'm not sure I buy it anyway. I'm starting to think I need a more thorough briefing package.'

A message icon from the lounge appeared.

'Let me talk to him,' said Citra. 'This is something I can actually do.'

In the privacy of the helm-metaphor, Ash shot Mark an incredulous look.

'I posted the comms-stream to the lounge,' said Mark. 'I thought the others would want to see.'

'Do you trust her?' said Ash.

Since the discovery of her betrayal of the human race, Citra Chesterford had been as quiet as a ghost. She'd attended every discussion in the lounge without offering a single opinion. She'd barely eaten and her health had deteriorated correspondingly.

'Do you?' said Mark.

'Yes,' said Ash nervously. 'I think so.'

Maybe she wanted a chance to prove she could help.

Mark nodded. 'We're not convincing Tak, in any case,' he said. 'I'll keep a handle on Citra's link and cut it if she says something crazy.'

Ash passed control of the channel to Citra's couch. She adjusted her hair and flicked the channel open.

'Overcaptain Tak, my name is Citra Chesterford. I assume you recognise me?'

'Professor Chesterford!' said Tak. 'Yes, I do.'

'Then please take our data package absolutely at face value. There is no subtext here. My husband is dead, a fact I'm still struggling to accept. Sam Shah betrayed us and the entire human race. Furthermore, we have witnessed the advance of an enemy so implacable and dangerous that I cannot sleep at night for thinking about it. The two acting Fleet officers on this ship, Mark Ruiz and Ash Corrigan, have shown exceptional courage under extremely difficult circumstances. I can personally vouch for their actions. Please, assemble your ships as fast as you can. If we delay, there may not be a home system to rescue.'

'I'm following up with another information package just in case,' said Mark. 'This time it's the gory details rather than the edited highlights.'

They waited on tenterhooks for the next message from Tak to arrive. It took an hour.

When Tak reappeared, he wore an awkward half-smile.

'Okay, *Gulliver*,' he said. 'It looks like you've got yourself an armada. Rendezvous at these coordinates in three hours. Let's hope you're right about this.'

'Thank you,' Ash told Citra after they'd signed off.

She shrugged. 'This has been a sickening journey for me,' she said. 'I've lost everything, including my self-respect. I've hated feeling so useless. Maybe when all this is done, I won't be. I understand the role you've played in all this, Captain Corrigan. I know you sided with the League and that you betrayed Earth. But none of that matters any more. You'll be receiving the full backing of the Chesterford Foundation in any legal action that follows our return. Presuming we're lucky enough to still have courts to visit.'

Ash wasn't sure what to say. He certainly hadn't expected kindness from Citra. Something started sliding around inside him – something heavy.

'You were foolish to follow Sam Shah,' she said. Her voice cracked under the weight of emotion. Ash watched her eyes start to tear up and felt his own doing the same. 'But no more foolish than I've been. It would be hypocritical of me not to support you. If I have anything to do with what follows, you'll be treated like a hero.'

Ash blinked while emotion sloshed around inside him like a nauseating tide. A hero. That was the last thing he felt like. Fool, perhaps, or victim, or weakling, or traitor. Not hero.

'Thank you,' he said flatly. His eyes stung. Self-disgust he'd been holding at bay for days threatened to crowd up and smother him.

'Don't mention it,' said Citra. 'Now, we have a civilisation to save, I believe.'

'That we do,' said Ash stiffly. 'Handing helm control to you, Mark.'

Ash winked out from the helm-arena as fast as he could. In the virtualised privacy of his home node, he curled into a tight ball and cried like a child.

River Chu lay in the captain's couch of the IPS *Griffin*. He yawned and thought about all the ways he hated being on home system watch. First, there was the boredom of the duty itself. He'd been stuck in the Kuiper belt for five weeks now doing absolutely nothing. Worse than that, though, was the way IPSO law forbade him from chasing down the legally dubious flights he saw entering and leaving the system almost every day. Such flights were deemed 'private leisure trips' and thus only qualified for random SAP-mediated inspections. Those sect barons took a hell of a lot of interstellar trips, apparently.

River had joined the League because he couldn't stand watching what was being done to interstellar peace. A single short tour at the Far Frontier had convinced him that the Fleet was totally hamstrung by the law. The sects were making fools of them. Yet because of optimistic promises Will Monet had made a generation ago, River was just supposed to lie there and watch it happen. It made his blood boil, but it paled in comparison to the one feature of this watch tour that he hated the most. And that was the anticipation.

He knew that any day now, the Nemesis machines would arrive. They'd appear in a burst of light and begin their assault on Earth with a swarm of half-sentient drones. And as soon as they neared their first target, River was supposed to leap to the rescue.

He'd been extensively briefed on which tactics would be most effective and how to interact with his crew when the time came. They, of course, had no idea what was up. For them, this long stretch of watch duty was a kind of perverse punishment that they bore with poor grace. Everyone aboard wished they were back at the Frontier doing some good, regardless of the frustrations the work brought. If all went according to plan, River would suddenly rally them with some surprisingly insightful leadership and help save civilisation at the eleventh hour. Great.

The prospect of being fêted as a hero didn't appeal much to River. If it had, perhaps the waiting wouldn't have been as bad. But a fight was still a fight, even if you were battling half-witted alien machines. There would be losses, without doubt. The drones, he'd been assured, would not be pulling their punches. Their efforts, while simplistic and mechanical, would be entirely in earnest.

River was watching the latest dreary traffic report from Triton domestic space when the radiation burst hit. Their resting buffers crashed as if a shuttle had dropped on them.

'We have a radiation spike!' said Ara.

River's heart pounded. It was happening at last.

'Damage report,' he said. 'How are our sensors?'

'Ninety-five per cent intact,' said Ara. 'Thank Gal they were offline.'

Of course, his main sensor bank had been conveniently retracted for inspection, as it had been every other week since home system duty had started.

'Give me visual,' said River. 'Target the burst origin.'

As his team slewed the telescopes for a closer look, a confusing picture emerged. Instead of the thick spread of winking lights he'd expected, he saw a weird cluster of signals. In the middle hung what looked like a trio of nestships – nothing else was that large. Around them lay a relatively sparse distribution of the kind of drones he'd been told to expect, although far fewer than the League strategists had projected.

River frowned. Could it be that someone else was using the same carrier system as the Nemesis machines? In which case, who? And why were they bringing nestships?

'Ara, sweep the comms-bands,' he said. 'Who are we looking at?'

A message arrived on one of the primary public channels, hugely boosted and incredibly clear. It carried a video feed of Yunus Chesterford. Except he looked way better than he ever had in his public lectures. He was younger, and buff. He wore a weird skintight uniform and his flesh bore a weird, stripy orange tan.

'People of the home system, I have some incredible news!' said Yunus. 'As a few of you know, I have been away on a secret mission to investigate a possible first-contact event. I am glad to say that it has resulted in the most wonderful success.'

A barrage of supporting appendices and data files came with the message. They started unfolding all over River's displays.

'We have found *life* in the universe,' said Yunus, 'and it is Truist. It comes in the form of a benign symbiont. It is a gift from God and it has been searching the galaxy for mankind. We are now ready to receive that gift and be granted its incredible bounty.'

Yunus spread his hands as if to embrace the world.

'The symbiont offers increased lifespan to all, not only rich Colonials. It offers new technology for spaceflight and terraforming. And, most importantly, it offers peace, harmony and plenty for all mankind.' He smiled beatifically. 'There will be rewarding jobs for everyone, my friends, new homes offworld and new lives. Astonishing though it sounds, our age of need and worry is at an end.'

River stared at the message in outright shock. He knew that Yunus had been part of the mission to Tiwanaku, but what the hell was he playing at now?

'Sir,' said Carol. 'What is this?'

As he got over his astonishment, River noticed the way the ships were tearing sunwards and splitting their formation. They didn't look all that friendly.

'Just as was true in the days of the High Church,' said Yunus, 'those who join with God first will benefit most. There is absolutely no time to waste. Our arrival is at hand. Prepare to receive your Lord! Let those of the greatest faith be the first among the flock to receive the Lord's gift!'

River shook off his stunned disbelief and picked a target.

'We're converging with that ship,' he said. 'Lay in an intercept course.'

He sent them a vector for the closest nestship. His tactical SAP gave a higher than ninety per cent probability that it was headed for Mars.

'Grease the rails!' he ordered. 'Warping in five.'

River hit the drive and warp pressed him into his couch. As he flew, he sent a warning to the alien vessel.

'Unidentified vessels, this is the IPS *Griffin*. You are to cease your advance until it has been approved by IPSO Fleet Command. I repeat, you will cease your advance otherwise we will be forced to fire.'

At this distance, it would be over ninety minutes before his message reached the mysterious nestships, but it was clear that these visitors didn't intend to slow. If anything, they were speeding up – burning a prodigious amount of antimatter in an attempt to penetrate deep in-system without losing too much velocity. And all the while, Yunus's sermon kept coming.

'No hesitation is necessary!' he said. 'No attempt should be made to impede God's gift. As in the days of the true prophet Sanchez, attempts to obstruct holy destiny will be considered acts of sin.'

Around the time River's warning was due to hit the closest nestship, about a quarter of the drones flying escort with it shifted course to bear down on him. He watched them come and deployed defensive munitions as late as he dared, giving his enemy as little warning as he could. The drones intercepted at full speed and exploded in bursts of sizzling plasma.

In an instant, the *Griffin* tore through the overlapping sheets of fire. The nestship didn't appear to care about his approach. It pressed onwards, its warp field surging.

'Ara, give me a full tactical map,' said River. 'Deep diagnostics on all ship profiles.'

He filtered it using the Rumfoord League's overlay code and was relieved to see League ships converging on the enemy from everywhere the arrival flash had so far reached. Like him, the other captains with foreknowledge of the attack had decided to pull out all the stops immediately and get on with rebuffing the assault. It made sense. Letting a few drones near Earth might have been permissible. Letting a nestship get close was suicide.

'The invaders have changed course,' said Ara, throwing him a window. 'They're staying above the ecliptic.' No doubt they planned to angle down on the in-system worlds while avoiding major traffic and defences. 'Defences posted at Jupiter's L3 are moving to intervene,' she added.

The orbit of Jupiter marked the notional boundary between in-system and out-system space. Beyond Jupiter, the gaps between planets were huge. Space was relatively clean and respectable sub-light velocities could still be achieved. Within the arc of Jupiter's motion, planets and populations tended to be clustered dangerously close together. Ships could do little more than crawl. And a single starship-scale screw-up got people killed in large numbers. There was a reason the Fleet kept most of its action out at Triton.

'There's no way we're letting those fuckers any deeper than five AU,' River snarled.

He knew the rest of Earth's guardian fleet would share that sentiment. As they watched, the Jupiter-band's prodigious defences snapped into action. Ponderous sub-light suntap barges fired giga-scaled g-rays in a scanning pattern, creating moving fans of instant death entire light-minutes wide. The nestships veered to avoid the onslaught, dropping speed as they approached.

'Looks like the invaders are realigning for a joint push,' said Ara.

'Then we've got them,' said River.

Like wolves seizing on wounded buffalo, Fleet ships from all over the system took the opportunity to attack. They surrounded the Nem ships and poured on munitions. Battle was well and truly joined.

The nestships' drone cloud thinned rapidly but they made up for it with g-ray batteries. By the time the *Griffin* caught up with the action, the fight had become an energy battle glowing like the mother of all Christmases and wreathed in scarves of tortured plasma. Admiralty strategic data bursts started popping up on River's display as Fleet High Command struggled to instil order into the mob of ships.

'Release drone salvos two through nine,' said River. 'Carol, go to full guidance assist.'

'Captain, hold!' said Ara. 'The nestships are dumping disrupters.'

River zoomed his view to watch. The Nems weren't just dumping a few. They were dumping *thousands*. Long streams of disrupter buoys were jetting out of the Fecund hulks, weaving between the attacking ships at full tilt.

'Reversing thrust,' said River.

It wasn't easy. Other ships had already arrived behind them. They didn't have a clear exit vector, and so many warp arrivals had made an ungodly mess of the local curvon flow. All at once, the disrupters activated, locking the battle in place. No one was going anywhere.

'Fuck!' said River. 'Still, this hurts them more than it does us. There's no way they can reach the major worlds now. Concentrate on the attack. We'll finish these bastards off.'

As the words left his mouth, a radiation blast-wave hit them from behind. Warning klaxons filled the cabin.

'What the hell was *that*? Ara, status report.'

'Sensors down to seventy-one per cent, sir. It's a new arrival burst, just like the other one. This time near Neptune. I'm seeing a new cloud of foreign warp signatures.'

River held his breath as he reassessed their situation. With a cold, sinking feeling, he realised that maybe the battle wasn't going quite as well as he'd thought.

20.4: ANN

Ann arrived to chaos. The outer reaches of the home system sparkled with bright flashes of warp and the even brighter flashes of g-ray fire. Confused warnings and alerts crammed the public channels. Dense, overloaded bursts of Fleet tactical data filled the encrypted ones. Despite herself, she groaned with relief. Chaos meant life.

Ann had used both Will's data and the League's to compute the Nems' likely attack time and then overclocked the *Ariel Two*'s engines to try to beat them to the punch. Nevertheless, she'd half-expected to find either a mass graveyard or a pulsing hive of alien activity. As it was, the Nems had arrived mere hours ago. She'd made it in time – just.

[*Nems are attacking at four sites,*] said her shadow.

It brought up a map in her sensorium revealing the probable insertion points and the clusters of Nem activity around each. Three of the sites had targeted the major out-system population centres – Saturn, Uranus and Neptune. At Neptune and Uranus, fighting had been underway for a while. At Saturn, all Ann could see was the flash of ships moving to intercept each other. However, that action had a light-lag of over three hours. For all she knew, the battle for Saturn might be over already.

It was the last site, though, that scared her most. Three nestships and a huge cloud of Fleet ships lay snarled in a vast smear of disrupter chaff just five AU from Sol. When she looked for Fleet signatures elsewhere in the system, she saw hardly any.

She realised immediately what must have happened. The Nems had used the League's expectations against them. Sam's people had anticipated a direct attack on Earth from a single carrier, so that's what the Nems had provided. But they'd raised the game by using old nestship hulks to make sure the Fleet couldn't possibly avoid the threat. Then, with the Fleet's efforts effectively mired uselessly close to their parent star, they'd begun their real assault. Why they'd chosen to attack the relatively tiny populations in the out-system, she still didn't understand. But either way, it was clear that the Nems' intelligence had caught up with their own.

[*I want full tactical impressions of the out-system battles,*] she said.

Her shadow dropped her into a full-immersion sim, overlaying knowledge into her head as it did so. Ann still wasn't used to seeing things and visiting places inside her own skull. It made her squirm despite the intensive training Will's ghost had provided on the flight home. She doubted she'd ever accept it the way a born roboteer would, but feelings were for later. First, she had a war to win.

'I've filtered out the human traffic,' said Nelson from the other side of the habitat core. 'There's a standard Nem arrival message being pumped out system-wide. They've adapted again. You're not going to like it.'

'Show me,' said Ann.

She frowned as she took in the sight of Yunus Chesterford spouting his new doctrine.

'I can think of people who'd buy this,' she said. 'The Nems have to die here, today, or we'll never finish them.'

She fired off the information burst she'd prepared for Ira Baron and weighed her options.

[*Target Neptune,*] Ann told her shadow. [*The Fleet needs Triton intact.*]

The *Ariel Two* pivoted and dived, squashing her against her couch. In the primary habitat core beneath *Ariel Two*'s bulk, her crew groaned under the strain. They'd already suffered over three weeks at two-point-six gees of warp-load to make up the time. Now it was about to get worse.

Ann's tactical display zoomed in to show her the frantically warping cloud of ships spattered around the ice giant. There were three raspberry ships larger than human battle cruisers, over two dozen mid-sized Nem ships and hundreds of small munitions. Yet the Nem craft made up less than half of the action.

[*What am I looking at here?*] she said. [*If only half of these ships are invaders, what's everything else?*]

[*Scans suggest mercenary drone fleets,*] said her shadow. [*The Nems are targeting the private worlds in Neptune orbit. The owners are defending with their own weapons.*]

Ann reeled as she took in the implications of that. The sect leaders must have been hoarding drones in anticipation of war and they'd amassed an astonishing number. If the Nems had expected all the Earth's defences to be drawn by their initial feint, they'd misjudged the sects' capacity for self-interest. For the first time in her life, she found herself relieved that the sects were a bunch of secretive, warlike scumbags.

Then, as she watched, one of the giant raspberries opened up with a massive parallelised barrage of g-ray fire, vaporising hundreds of sect drones at once. Warlike they might be, but the sects weren't geared up for all-out slaughter. The Nems had taken advantage of their in-system distraction to give them time to acquire suntap links.

Ann dived on the closest behemoth, scanning her target as she came. As soon as she had range, she fired her primary boser, aiming dead-centre. It was the wrong choice. When her beam hit the raspberry, it simply came apart into its constituent drones. She'd killed less than ten per cent of them while putting a serious drain on her own power reserves. The scattered automata rejoined the fray as independent munitions without a second's hesitation, leaving a small patch of superheated slag spinning in space.

[*Looks like they've lost suntap capability, at least,*] her shadow pointed out. [*That's a start.*]

[*How long till we get ours?*] After the painfully hurried flight home, the *Ariel Two* already needed recharging.

[*Over two hours. This fight will be done before the channel opens.*]

Ann muttered to herself. She hoped they'd hold out long enough to make a difference.

'Tactical update,' said Nelson. 'It's bad.'

He sent her a video window showing a knot of activity involving some of the smaller ships. In the middle of the fray hung a few large Nem craft much like the ones she'd seen at Snakepit, only these had grappling arms and docking probes on them. They were latching on to the private habitats and drilling their way in like giant aphids. Only it wasn't sap they were sucking. It was people.

'We've got this all wrong,' said Ann with horror. 'This isn't an invasion. They're trying for a population grab!'

Suddenly, the entire pattern of the assault made sense. The Nems had never intended to hit the Earth. They hadn't even come for revenge – just bodies. And there were plenty of them to be found in the outer system where the Nems could easily strike. The suntap ships provided cover while these aphid-ships did the dirty work. She reassessed the threat. There were thirty aphids at this battle site alone. Not to mention the other two attack points in the out-system.

She experienced a moment's panic. There were too many targets and half of them were probably already filling up with innocent people. Even with a ship like the *Ariel Two*, she wasn't going to be able to save them all.

Even while her mind raced, a wave of attack drones flashed towards them and battered themselves against the *Ariel Two*'s shield.

[*Slow and steady wins the race,*] said her shadow. In that moment, it sounded a lot more like the real Will than a semi-sentient echo of him. [*If we make those aphids defenceless, the sects can take care of themselves.*]

Ann nodded. It was a sound approach – take care of the big threats first. While the aphid-ships were backed by g-ray batteries, they were unbeatable. She could do something about that.

Ann fired as they bore down on the second raspberry. This time she didn't bother with the boser. She used her own g-rays. The space between her and the Nem cruiser became a searing dead-zone hotter than the surface of the sun. The raspberry briefly tried to split up as her beams hit, but this time Ann was ready and her firing spread widened as the drones detached. They burst like popcorn.

Ann brought her ship about and aimed for the last major threat. The raspberry saw her coming and made rapidly for the far side of Triton on conventional thrust. It couldn't afford to warp. It was only useful while its suntap-link was intact, and gravity bursts would break it instantly.

'Some of those spider-drill-ships are disengaging and heading for their insertion points,' said Nelson. 'The carriers may be ready to make a move.'

Ann cursed wildly. The Nems had come for hosts. Now that they had them, they were leaving already. On her virtual bridge, she clutched at her hair. The fight was way too spread out and too complex for a single large ship like hers to make a decisive difference. They were losing and there wasn't a single thing she could do about it. Still, she wasn't going to let them leave without a fight.

'They're not getting away this time,' she snarled. 'We're changing course. I want that carrier dead.'

Mark dropped warp at the home system in an eye-scorching burst of hard light. Nobody paid the slightest bit of attention. The largest space battle in human history had been underway for hours. Zoe performed a rapid battle analysis.

'Four carrier sites,' she said. 'I'm seeing targeted drops for Uranus, Saturn and Neptune, plus one outlier. The Uranus carrier site has harvesters reconverging on it already. They're pulling the same trick as they did at Carter. We have to cut off their escape.'

'Agreed,' said Mark. 'Then we can deal with the rest of this shit.'

He didn't drop spin for an instant. Instead, he slammed them back into warp and brought the ship around to the Uranus arrival site as fast as he could in an arc that tested the limits of the vacuum-drive. The luminous shell around them sparked and wobbled as he pushed the envelope to the brink of tearing. Fast they might be, but vacuum-drive ships didn't handle corners well.

He signalled the armada hovering behind him.

'Overcaptain Tak,' he said. 'We're moving to intercept an enemy exit point. They have human hostages. On no account can the enemy carrier be allowed to depart. I recommend immediate deployment of one-third of your task force on my mark.'

'Understood and agreed, *Gulliver*,' said Tak. 'You have my consent.'

Mark dropped warp just light-seconds from the Nem convergence point and spun down his fronds just enough to let a part of their armada boost away in radial formation. At the same time, Zoe tight-beamed an info-dump of their situation to Fleet Command. The battle cruisers surged forward, fired warp-drones and blasted the carrier into atoms. With their exit cut off, the cruisers set about boxing in the harvesters.

Mark knew he couldn't afford to stop to watch things play out. He pushed their spin rate back up, threw them into warp and arced around the system again, the drive straining badly as he headed as close to Saturn as he could reasonably get. He wished he could have flown straight across the system but he didn't dare try. Like all forms of warp, the vacuum-drive was hopeless in dense space. The ionic clutter was simply too thick. It was actually faster to fly out and around, even though that meant distorting the warp field in ways it was never meant to be used. For the better part of an hour, they watched the envelope strain and flicker and prayed it wouldn't crumple.

By the time Mark reached the second carrier, harvesters were already prepping to depart and this time they had a cloud of drone defence to back them up. Behind them, unmarked gunships traded fire with Nem raspberry-ships armed with g-ray batteries. Mark dropped the second portion of his armada straight into a fire-fight.

As soon as he released the ships, a wave of Nem drones headed straight for him.

'Tak!' Mark warned. 'We can't let our carrier be damaged.'

'Don't worry,' said Zoe. 'I'm on it. These ships are still running vanilla Nem-cloaking. They're *mine*.'

As he watched, the drones' flight patterns changed. Instead of impacting, they slid inside the carrier's envelope like willing sheepdogs. The other Nem-ships immediately started pumping out protocol-change warnings but by then the Nems had lost their edge.

One of the raspberries spontaneously split. The gunships hammered at the stuttering drones, cutting lanes of explosions through their ranks like chains of firecrackers. The remaining raspberries started gouging space with intersecting talons of g-ray fire.

'Now get us out of here,' said Zoe. 'Unless you want to die.'

Mark piled the power back on and slipped away before the fight could trap him there.

Making it around to Neptune took another ninety minutes of nail-biting flight. He watched the third battle arena evolve in ridiculous fast-forward as the light-lag shrank and held his breath as the last carrier spun up to escape.

'We lost,' he said. 'They're getting away.'

Then, out of nowhere the *Ariel Two* surged upwards, blasting harvesters and drones alike in a frenzy of high-energy violence. Raspberries and Nem drones from all across the home system had already started converging on it.

'Overcaptain Tak, do you see what I see?'

'I see a capital ship in need of supporting fire,' said Tak. 'Preparing to deploy on your mark.'

Mark dropped warp as close to the fray as he dared. Tak's ships dived out and fell on the enemy like feeding sharks. Nevertheless, two of the harvesters made it into the waiting arms of the carrier. Its fronds became a blur and the weird luminescence of the false-vacuum began to slide down across it.

Just when Mark felt certain their cause was lost, the *Ariel Two*'s boser lanced up, carving across the spreading vacuum-field in a blast at least half a second long.

The carrier's envelope splayed open, unravelling across space, and the mutant space–time it contained spilled out. For a brief moment, something surreal and vaguely organic sent questing tendrils into the void, offering glimpses of an impossible geometry within. Then it flickered and was gone.

In the silence that followed, Mark messaged the *Ariel Two*.

'Nice shooting,' he said with a grin. 'Nice to have you back on the team... Dad.'

Ann Ludik appeared in the reply window, her expression grave.

'Wasn't Will,' she said, 'but thanks anyway.'

Mark's smile dropped. He felt a lurch of confusion and worry stabbed at him unexpectedly.

'I'll explain later,' said Ann. There was something a little like pity in her eyes that made Mark scared.

'No time for reunions!' said Zoe. 'We have one more carrier, remember?'

Mark dived back into helm-space. 'Where is it?'

'Calculating now,' said Ash. 'I'm extrapolating from the flight paths of the remaining harvesters.'

Mark's battle visualisation lit up with a set of converging lines. The Nems weren't wasting any time. From all across the system, harvesters were fleeing for their one remaining exit point.

'Shit,' he said. 'That's practically back where we started.'

'Better get busy, then,' said Zoe.

Mark reopened the channel to *Ariel Two*. 'Ann, I need weapons support. We're going after that last carrier. You coming?'

He sent her flight data, showing how to park the nestship inside the spinning array.

'On it,' said Ann.

Mark spread his skipping ropes wide, dropping spin almost to nothing. He needn't have bothered. With a burst of surprising agility, the

Ariel Two danced inside, leaving the fronds wobbling from gravity distortion.

'Are we going or what?' said Ann.

Mark ramped the spin up and headed out, cutting above the ecliptic and down again. As he dropped away from Sol faster than light, the harvesters all appeared to slide backwards on their flight paths. As he returned, they all rushed forwards, manoeuvring to leave with a manic ant-like deliberation. He counted down the seconds, watching the final carrier spin up. Most of the harvesters weren't going to make it. However, nine of them already had.

Mark dropped warp just in time to see the carrier wink out. He bellowed his frustration, slamming the roof of his bunk.

'They got away,' said Ash.

'Under the circumstances, this is not a fail,' said Zoe. 'The home system is intact. The number of lives lost is minimal. This is where we count our blessings.' She flicked open the channel to the *Ariel Two*. 'Sorry to bring you out here for no reason, Ann. With the carriers gone, the rest of the Nems can't get out. But this entire system still has to be cleared otherwise the drones will swarm and build another.'

'Understood,' said Ann. 'We're on it.'

'Wait,' said Ash. He passed them a video feed.

Without the carriers, the remaining Nem ships appeared to be milling. They looked anything but aggressive.

'They're sending a message,' he added.

In a video window, the face of Yunus Chesterford appeared.

'Earth forces, we willingly surrender. Our peace crusade is postponed. We will await your further instructions with grace and patience. God be with you.'

He beamed as he said it, as if giving up was what they'd planned to do all along. Mark stared at the image in blank bewilderment. Yunus was *alive*? He checked the cameras in the lounge. Citra was watching the feed with a face drained of blood. Her eyes were wide open like a pair of empty bowls.

21: RECKONING

21.1: MARK

Mark took a shuttle from the *Gulliver* to the IPS *Knid*, Admiral Baron's home system command ship. It was essentially an armoured space station with habitat rings under full gravity, enormous g-ray batteries and suntap-powered conventional-thrust engines. The docking pod delivered him to an immaculately decorated executive waiting room, about ten minutes early for his meeting with Uncle Ira.

Mark paced up and down for about a minute before Ann arrived. He froze in his tracks as she came into the room, immediately recognising the roboteer signature that she manifested via the room's network. It didn't belong with the face he was looking at.

'Want to tell me what happened?' he said quietly.

Ann's lean features gave nothing away. She sent him a memory dump. Mark knocked it back and groaned involuntarily as understanding smacked him like a mallet. Tears sprang to his eyes. The man who'd almost been his father was gone. All that was left of him lay inside Ann. The years of resenting Will's presence in his life reversed themselves in a single heartbeat.

'So he's still in there?' he said, his voice breaking.

'A piece of him,' said Ann. 'He's asking to speak with you. Is that okay?'

Mark frowned. Part of him didn't want to face this. He fought down the urge to refuse and nodded once.

'Okay,' said Ann. 'I'm going to let him drive for a bit. Hold on.'

Her face went slack. Then her expression changed. Somehow, the sad smile that arrived looked like Will's, even though the face did not. Will looked down at his front, and then back at Mark.

'Well, this is odd,' he said.

'You could say,' Mark croaked.

He found himself so distraught that Will's small attempt at levity just cut a larger hole in his heart. For all his faults, Will had been a huge part of Mark's life. Only now did he understand how big a gap his loss would leave behind.

'Is there a chance they'll be able to put you back together?'

Will shrugged. 'It's not clear how separable I am from Snakepit at this point,' he said. 'I half-hoped that the real me would have made it out by now. That didn't happen, so I don't know what to tell you.'

Mark waved a strengthless hand. 'Couldn't you... I don't know... just use your smart-cells to separate yourself from Ann? Build a clone or something?'

Will smiled. 'I tried that once. Didn't work so well. Plus this isn't the real me you're talking to – I'm borrowing a bunch of Ann's subconscious functions just to hold together. The Transcended put a lock on me that prevents self-duplication. It's surprisingly effective, even now. I'll keep trying, of course. However, I'd still be in Ann. Her DNA has been rewritten to host me, and I can't edit myself out of her without killing her in the process.'

'Don't you remember how you did it the first time?'

Will actually laughed. 'Hell no. I was the size of a planet at that point. I had some extra resources. Still, right now we have more important things to work on. And Ann and I make a pretty good team.'

Mark had no idea what to say. He was talking to a ghost. He stared at the floor.

'I saw the memory dump you filed,' said Will. 'I want you to know that I'm incredibly proud of you. I want you to know I'm going to stick to my word. I'll make sure you get full ownership of your interface. You're your own boss from here on out.'

Mark bit back a jag of powerful, pointless despair. 'I appreciate the sentiment but I'm pretty committed to the Fleet at this point,' he said. 'There's work to do.'

Will nodded. 'I never should have pushed you as hard as I did. And I should have come clean with the truth about your biological parents a long time ago.'

Mark brushed the comment off. The resentment towards Will that he'd felt before Carter felt so distant and childish now. It had no place in the person he'd become. Instead, Will's plight just lent fuel to Mark's fire. The problem of Snakepit merely added another target to his crusade.

'It's old news,' he said. 'I know where you were coming from now. It's in the past, anyway. I spent a lot of time being angry with you and not enough noticing what you were trying to give me.'

Will smiled. He reached out and grabbed Mark in a hug.

'Definitely odd,' said Mark.

'That was Ann's idea, not mine,' said Will. 'She thought you needed it.'

Despite the creeping discomfort, Mark felt something in him relaxing, something that had been wound tight for a very long time. He hugged back.

'Maybe it's just that Ann is nicer to hug than you are,' he said.

'I don't doubt it,' said Will.

The doors at the far end of the room opened. Ira Baron appeared, followed by a swarm of assistants, organic and otherwise. He took in the sight of them and looked confused for a minute.

Mark and Will spontaneously stepped apart.

Ira's expression was grave. 'Are you two done?'

Mark nodded.

'Then you should follow me,' said Ira. 'The clock's ticking.'

21.2: ANN

Ira shooed away his entourage and ushered Mark and Ann aboard a private pod with security updates scrolling on the walls.

'Thank you both for your reports,' he said. 'In the six hours since the end of the battle, I can assure you that they've been studied extremely closely. Clip in, please. We'll be dropping gees.'

Ann's shadow borrowed her mouth. 'Ira, where are you taking us? What's this about? I assumed you'd want us on our way back to Tiwanaku by now with a hold full of antimatter bombs.'

If the admiral of the IPSO Fleet was unused to being addressed so informally, there was nothing in his manner to suggest it.

'Your mission plans have been prepped already,' said Ira. 'And yes, I want you out there ASAP. But there's something I need you to do first. I have the mouthpiece of the raiding fleet aboard – in a secure environment, of course. I'd like you to meet him ... it. You've both had more direct exposure to this threat than the rest of us and that might be useful. Frankly, we're making up our response to this as we go along. There are no procedures for situations like this one.'

The travel pod slid up out of the spin-ring, dumping gravity as it went, and passed down the spine of the ship.

'How bad were our losses, sir?' said Ann.

'Surprisingly light, in-system,' said Ira. 'Earth and Mars lost a few thousand people to radiation burns. The damage to exposed surface environments was extensive. Earth will probably have to scrap its last surface biome park, but frankly it wasn't looking that great anyway. Other than that, we're okay.' He exhaled deeply. 'The outer system is a whole other issue. A lot of our real estate from Saturn outwards was harvested or burned and the dead or missing number in the hundreds of thousands. We have about two million in quarantine who we rescued from those harvester-ships.' He shook his head. 'That wasn't pretty, by the way. I'll spare you the details. And we have billions in damage, of course. About eighty per cent of those stupid floating palaces the sect Leading love so much were scorched and sucked dry. Local economic indicators are in free-fall. But frankly, the econ-SAPs can go fuck themselves. We've got bigger problems right now.'

Ann cringed inside. This was what all those years of careful planning had come to. This hideous mess. She couldn't help but reflect on every moment of moral quandary she'd squirmed over. She felt ashamed that she hadn't let her conscience guide her long ago.

'Sir, what are you going to do with the League conspirators?' said Mark. 'I mean, there are hundreds of them. Are you going to arrest them all?'

Ann was glad he'd asked. It saved her from the pain of doing so.

'Nope,' said Ira. 'I can't spare the officers at this point. They'll have to live with their sins for now. I'll handle them after this threat is neutralised.'

'So that's it?' said Mark. 'They all just get off, scot-free?'

Ira fixed him with a hard glare. 'Oh no, son. They're going down. They just have to work for me first. In the meantime, everyone's role in this will be kept quiet to minimise the chance of revenge killings from within the Fleet. Except Sam Shah. I'll be handling Sam myself. Personally. Along with Parisa-fucking-Voss.'

The pod gained gravity again as it headed out along a narrow docking spar. At the end of it, if the wall-screens were to be believed, sat a drab little supply boat. The pod docked and the door slid open to reveal an extremely white room that looked exactly like what it was – a cross between a very high-tech scientific lab and a prison.

A couple of Vartian Institute technicians were in there, working with projector bubbles full of unreadably dense visualisations. And standing inside a transparent cylindrical cell in the centre of the room was Yunus Chesterford – or what he'd become.

The new Yunus was a giant of a man with a rugged physique and a shock of white professor hair. Tiger stripes of densely packed orange freckles covered his skin. He wore a skin-tight silver garment that left nothing to the imagination. Ann found the sight of him repulsive.

'I've already spoken to this *creature*,' said Ira. 'Nobody else knows we've got him here. There'd be a riot. So far as the public are aware the invaders are already dead. But I wanted to give you both the chance to speak to ... it ... before we take next steps. You might be able to get something out of him that we've missed.'

Mark stepped up to face Yunus. Yunus stared at him with bright, unblinking eyes and a cryptic smile.

'Welcome,' said Yunus. 'It is good to see you. I am glad that you have come.'

'Do you remember me?' said Mark.

Yunus nodded. 'You are Captain Mark Ruiz of the IPS *Gulliver*. Of course I remember you. I remember how troubled you were. How much you hurt. I could spare you that.'

'Do you remember Citra?'

Yunus nodded again. 'You mean Citra Chesterford. Who was my wife. And a biologist. I have memories of her, too. She was also troubled. She curtailed her career on my behalf and it frustrated her very much. She doubted herself. You should bring her to me. We Photurians are not defined by the small tasks that we do. She would be happier with us.'

'I'm not sure that's true,' said Mark. 'Is there anything you'd like me to tell her?'

'Yes,' said Yunus, in the same blandly enthusiastic tone. 'Tell her that happiness awaits. My people will seek her out and save her. She will know joy.'

'I'm sure she'll find that reassuring. Tell me, do you love her?'

Yunus spread his huge, prophetic hands. 'Of course I love her. I love all mankind.'

'I thought so,' said Mark. He turned away, and then hesitated. 'You mentioned God in your broadcasts, by the way. Do you still have faith?'

'I have no need of faith,' said Yunus. 'I have certainty now. My God is the Body, and the Body is God. God is real and immortal. You will come to understand this, as will all humanity. Joy awaits those who grasp that truth.'

Mark frowned walked back to where Ann stood.

'I'm done,' he said. 'It's revolting.'

[*May I try?*] said Ann's shadow.

Ann took a deep breath and let the ghost drive.

'Why did you come here?' said Will.

'To save mankind,' said Yunus.

'Then why simply raid us at the edges? Why not stay and collect hosts?'

'It was not the right time.'

'I see,' said Will. 'When is that time?'

'I do not need that knowledge.'

Will snorted. 'Convenient. And how will it be accomplished?'

'I do not need that knowledge.'

'Really. And what about those people who don't want to be saved?'

'God is generous,' said Yunus. 'The unwilling will also be rescued.'

Will turned to look at Ira. 'Do you have a deep microbial scan of the prison cell I could look at?'

Ira gestured at the technicians. 'We know it's exhaling bioweapons, if that's what you're worried about. The cell is fully contained. What you're seeing is a surface hologram on a hermetic pod locked down by Vartian Institute protocols. Not even light gets out of that fucking box without us checking it first.'

Will examined the scan data. For a few short moments, Ann's head filled with a barely comprehensible whirl of images and ideas. Then understanding started leaking into her mind like air through a poorly sealed hatch.

'They've stopped,' she said.

[*Right,*] said her shadow. 'They're not evolving any more,' he said aloud. 'Whatever it was about us that they wanted, they've got it. That's good. It means they don't stand a chance of reclaiming their homeworld.'

'Why not?' said Ira.

'Snakepit will only let the Nems in if they can assert primacy,' Will explained, 'which they can't do unless they constitute a new mutation. But Snakepit's seen this variant already, and it lost. We still have no idea what happened on the surface, but we do know the Nems didn't get their planet back. So they're locked out now and that's how they'll stay.'

Yunus's face fell. 'You're wrong. The Body will be returned to us.'

Will used Ann's mouth to smile. 'That hurts you, doesn't it? That you can't go home.'

'It is only temporary,' said Yunus.

'It's got to suck, being evicted from your own God. Knowing that it doesn't want you any more.'

'It is only temporary.'

'I'm sure they told you that.'

Yunus's face distorted for a moment, his mouth stretching wider than nature would have allowed.

'It is only *temporary*!'

'There's not much to learn here,' Will told Ira. 'This is a machine, nothing more. I've met smarter transit pods.'

'Our assessment also,' said Ira. He turned to the Yunus-monster. 'You attacked our home system,' he said.

'We sought to enlighten,' said Yunus.

'No, you sought to plunder. It's my intention to seek out your kind and destroy them all. Do you have anything to say for yourself, or your kind, in your defence before we dismantle you for our edification?'

'We will build a new human empire without strife,' said Yunus. 'It will be fair and it will be peaceful. And it will achieve what you never could.'

'We will bomb Tiwanaku,' said Ira. 'And your home planet is already lost to you. Will Monet saw to that. You have failed.'

'You cannot stop us,' said the Yunus-thing. Its eyes shifted from side to side in a weird parody of impatience.

'Yes, we can. Your raid on Carter failed. Your raid here failed. You will do nothing but fail.'

'You cannot stop us,' the Yunus-thing insisted. 'One by one, your worlds will become ours. You will be forced to reckon with us as a new race. Then your people will come to us voluntarily and be reborn in God's grace.'

'No, they won't. And you can cut out that God shit.'

'We will offer them eternal life!'

'No,' said Ira. 'You will offer them death dressed up. I knew Yunus once. You are not him. Yunus is *dead*.'

'I am *more* than Yunus ever was. Join me, Ira. Though you may shun me, I remember you and love you. Don't make this difficult for all of us. Accept the Lord.'

Ira turned to Ann and Mark, his eyes full of smouldering rage. 'So there we have it. Any final observations? Any questions?'

'He sounds very confident,' said Mark. 'Except when you goad him about Snakepit. That's not good.'

'He's been reduced to a piece of machinery,' said Ira. 'What should we expect?'

Mark shrugged. 'Not that. On our way back here, Venetia Sharp analysed one of the brains the Nems used to pilot their carrier. The sense I got was that the modifications they gave it were a lot more subtle than this. So if they're showing us a moron now, I'm worried that might be because they don't want us to figure out how smart they've really become.'

'I agree,' said Ann. 'Their strategy for the attack clinches it. Their development has exceeded all our expectations, even the edge-cases the League modelled. And the Snakepit microbes have welded themselves in deep. But for the stripes, Yunus could be a normal person. How long before we can't tell?'

'Then we don't have any time to waste,' said Ira. 'We're done here, I think. You need to saddle up and take the pain to Tiwanaku. This entire problem must be closed down before any more lives are lost. You'll be leaving immediately and taking the New Panama fleet you brought with you as your strike force. They could use a lift back to the Far Frontier anyway. We'll supplement their firepower with a constellation of Home Fleet ships we've picked out. Then, assuming that's successful, there'll be a long and very thorough clean-up operation which will include a trip to the Snakepit system to rescue Will, if we can. If we can't, I'm ordering you to use a boser on that planet and melt it into glass. Do you understand?'

Ann nodded. The prospect of obliterating Will's surreal refuge filled her with a sense of despair. She kept it bottled. She knew it made sense.

'Any further questions?' said Ira.

'None,' said Ann.

'Good. Ludik, you'll be heading up this fleet. You are hereby promoted to Overcaptain, effective immediately. You're carrying Will's ghost with you, so you'll be filling the role he would have had.'

Ann blinked in shock. 'Yes, sir. Despite my involvement with the League?'

'Yep,' said Ira. 'You dropped those dumb fucks when it counted. Good for you. And you have to live with a very annoying superman in your head. I'd call that punishment enough. Mark, you'll be running transport. From this point forward, you and Doctor Tamar are a team, answerable directly to me. The *Gulliver* is yours, if you want it, or any other ship you need.'

'The *Gulliver* works fine,' said Mark. 'Presuming you can fix the security lockdown and give it some basic armaments.'

'Consider it done,' said Ira. 'And put Venetia Sharp on the next shuttle headed my way,' he added. 'If she has input on this monstrosity, I want to hear it. Now both of you get the hell out of here. I want this problem closed down while we still can.'

21.3: MARK

Two weeks passed in breathless flight. At the end of their desperate race back to Tiwanaku, Mark sat in his preferred couch in the *Gulliver*'s lounge and held Zoe's hand while they counted down the last moments of their approach. On the other side of him sat Ash, officially reinstated as his subcaptain.

There was now a fat-contact hook-up installed in Mark's chair, and with the security protocols adjusted he had full control over the ship's interior. The *Gulliver* had been reconfigured as a guide-ship for their co-opted Nem carrier and armed to the teeth while they made the flight out from Sol under vacuum-drive. Now their target system lay dead ahead. Their new crew of battle analysts and tacticians sat tense and silent, awaiting the moment.

'Dropping warp in ten, nine, eight...' said Mark. The envelope popped. 'Warp dropped. Deployment Alpha is clear to go.'

'Deploying,' said Ann over the fleet channel.

Sensor drones and battleships raced outwards to form a defensive sphere around the carrier. They held position with the *Ariel Two* up front, ready for anything.

'System survey underway,' said Ann, the tension clear in her voice. 'Sorting for primary targets.'

In his sensorium, Mark watched the data pour back and held his breath. At first glance, the system looked surprisingly quiet.

'In-system traffic levels: zero,' said the primary assessment SAP. 'Industrial activity level: zero. Drone count: zero. No out-system target sites located.'

'Don't assume anything,' Ann said quickly. 'Stay vigilant. Scan for stealth shields. I want a deep-sweep for tau-charger emissions.'

Over the tense, grinding minutes that followed, they didn't find a single ship. Tiwanaku was empty. The system before them made grave-yards look busy.

'There may not be anyone here now, but I'm detecting extensive signs of recent activity,' said one of the analysts. He slid them a window with his findings. 'The Fecund remains in this system have been heavily depleted. About eighty per cent of the mass logged at last survey appears to be missing. And the colony planet's surface has been scoured clean. Not just picked clean. Actually *scoured.*'

He showed them a digital deep-view composition of the planet's surface which was covered with huge, linear scrape marks, some of them a kilometre deep. A light haze of industrial particulates filled the atmosphere.

'It's been mined out,' said Ash in awe. 'All of it.'

'They're gone,' said Zoe.

Mark stared. Something about this scared him more than any of the horror scenarios he'd dreamed up on the flight out from Earth.

'Where are they, then?' he said. 'They can't be back at Snakepit – the planet won't take them. Did they all head for Carter?'

Zoe covered her mouth with both her hands. 'Oh no.'

A hideous possibility started to dawn on Mark.

'Where has a large human population and no remaining Fleet presence to speak of?' she said. 'What's the perfect strategic point to capture?'

Mark's throat went dry. 'New Panama,' he said. He felt as if he'd been dropped off a cliff. His insides twisted. 'What have we done?' He grabbed the comm. 'Recommending immediate withdrawal,' he shouted. 'Updated target: New Panama System.'

A grim hush fell over the task force's channels while that sank in.

'Agreed,' said Ann, her voice strained. 'Alert to all ships. We're leaving.'

As the carrier's fronds accelerated back to full speed, Zoe's eyes filled with tears.

'No,' she said. 'We didn't do this. This has to be wrong.'

Mark held her tight. 'Let's go and make sure,' he said.

21.4: ANN

Ann was already wired into every sensor suite in the *Ariel Two* when they dropped warp at the edge of the New Panama System. Again, initial scans suggested the place was quiet. She experienced a surge of hope. Maybe they'd got it wrong. Maybe the Nems had all decamped to Carter.

But during the minutes that followed their arrival, the true picture became clear. The normal comms traffic that usually filled the system had vanished. In its place was an ominous mechanistic chatter – a uniform spread of compact signals that Ann knew well. It was the one the Nemesis machines used during their reflection phase swarm.

An involuntary cry of despair broke loose from her throat. She aimed her telescopes at the colony world and peered deep. Everything on the surface looked miraculously intact but a cloud of drones as thick as fog surrounded the planet itself.

Her shadow spoke for her. [*They took it already.*]

Ann stared at her former home and struggled to breathe. While she blinked and fought for control, Mark Ruiz signalled her from the *Gulliver*. Ping icons from each of her captains started arriving in her sensorium.

In that moment, Ann wanted to curl up and grieve. Instead, she opened a meeting channel, surrounding herself with video feeds.

'What next?' said Tak.

Pain leaked out of his gaze like blood from a wound. The man was getting ready to burn his own home. His family had been down there. Ann wondered what they were now.

'Are we going for a direct strike, as discussed?' he said

She checked the window for Mark Ruiz. The poor boy looked ruined by guilt. His eyes had a hollow desperation in them that she couldn't bear to see.

'First,' said Ann, 'we all need to remember that this situation isn't anyone's fault. We needed to rescue the home system and no one foresaw this simply because we didn't have time to work it out. Tak, your choice to fly with Mark was the correct one.'

'They had this in mind all along,' said Mark flatly. 'That's why they only raided the home system instead of trying to take it. As soon as they got smart enough, they knew this place would make a better target. That's why they were so confident. And it didn't even occur to us.'

'That's almost certainly true,' said Ann. 'We were snookered. But it doesn't change what we need to do next. Overcaptain Tak, prepare your team for a precision strike.'

[*We have incoming message traffic,*] said Ann's shadow.

[*That's too fast,*] said Ann. The Nems must have seeded the out-system with sensor drones. [*They knew we'd come. Show us.*]

The face of Yunus Chesterford appeared. Ann stared at it without understanding. Hadn't they already captured Yunus? In which case, who – or what – was this? Had the recording been made before the attack?

'If you can see this, then we have detected the presence of an IPSO Fleet assault. There are several important things you should know. First, be aware that New Panama has converted to the Photurian Utopia. We are a peaceful and autonomous world that does not recognise the authority of IPSO.

'Second, by the time you hear me, defensive machinery will have been activated all across this system. Any attempt to attack Photurian territory will result in immediate retaliation. During the example visit made to your home system, you will have noticed how easy it is for us to hurt you. That will happen again, and next time you will suffer.

Stealthed weapons bearing antimatter bombs and bosers have been situated within striking distance of Earth. Attack us and those weapons will be activated immediately. We will destroy Earth, Mars and your remaining population centres. Leave us in peace and you will be allowed to live.'

Ann's throat closed up as she watched. Given what they'd already seen, it was entirely plausible that the Photurians could strike at Earth again. What was she supposed to do? She addressed her captains.

'I don't like this,' she told them, 'but we have to assume that some part of this is bluster. Even with careful planning, the Nems can't have done all that they claim. And we can't afford to let them live. They're like a virus.' She paused and shook her head. 'I take that back. They're worse than a virus. They're the end of everything. Leave them alive and we make a food-source out of the human race. We will never be safe again. I am initiating our attack. If you wish to register your dissent, do so now.'

Not a single captain spoke up.

'Very well then. Go to attack pattern *Baron's Fist*.'

The ships manoeuvred into a conical spearhead configuration with the *Ariel Two* taking point. As a single weapon, they warped towards the occupied colony.

Almost immediately Photurian drones started dropping stealth all around them, popping into visibility in a wave that propagated out with the *Ariel Two*'s light cone. Ann's tactical display became a blizzard of warning icons. The local space around them was measled with death.

Just ten light-minutes deep into New Panama's local space, Ann called her force to a halt. She lay in her crash couch and watched wordlessly as thousands upon thousands of warp-enabled munitions lit up. Not a single one of them fired or moved. The task force's preliminary scans had missed *all* of them. The Photurian message was far more eloquent than it would have been if they'd started shooting.

This was the curse of the *Chiyome*. The League should have guessed that as soon as they repurposed the Nems' own engine design as a stealth shield, there'd been a chance that the machines would notice and use it against them.

Or more likely, she realised with horror, the *Chiyome* had made it back here before the attack. The Nems had copied the design after killing her crew. Ann's hands flew to her mouth. She'd sent the crew of the *Chiyome* here. She'd sent Kuril. That last favour she'd asked, the one she'd meant to be an honour, had actually killed him.

[*They've won,*] said her shadow. [*Earth's still too vulnerable. We have no choice but to retreat.*]

[*They could still be bluffing,*] Ann said hopelessly.

[*Yes, but why would they bother? The Photurians have nothing to lose. They're a brand-new species, born out of conflict. They either establish themselves here or die.*]

[*We can't—*] said Ann.

[*Ann,*] said her shadow softly, [*I know I'm not all here, but even what's left of me can see the truth of this. These machines were* designed *for retaliation. It's what they do. It's the one trait they've exhibited very reliably. And now we know why. It forces everyone to take them seriously.*]

Ann's cheeks tingled. She didn't want to be the person who had to do this. She hated it so much that she wanted to die. If the universe had decided to mete out the cruellest possible punishment for her involvement with the League, this had to be it. She signalled a slow, cautious retreat. And, with a regret that burned in her throat, she started back towards the carrier.

As soon as they were in range, Mark opened a channel.

'What's going on?' he said. His eyes burned. 'We can't afford to let this happen! The Photurians are just going to predate on the human race. They'll take out our colonies one by one. They'll keep evolving.'

'I agree,' said Zoe from behind him. 'This is inviting disaster.'

'Then we'd better get our shit together, hadn't we?' said Ann.

'Overcaptain Ludik,' said Tak. His face was grey. 'Do I need to remind you that New Panama is strategically situated at the Penfield Lobe? If we let the Photurians take it, we risk having the entire New Frontier cut off from us. That's over a *dozen* worlds, and all of Fecund space. We can't afford that.'

'I'm well aware of the risks,' said Ann, 'but Will and I are making an executive decision. There will be no fight here today. I expect everyone to obey orders and resume formation within the carrier envelope. You may register your dissent. Your opinions will be presented in my report to Admiral Baron.'

What she wanted to say was, *They've taken my home*. And all of her friends. And everything she'd built for herself. The world she loved was already dead. She wanted to burn the Photurians more than she'd ever wanted anything, save perhaps rescuing the human race from immediate oblivion.

An icy pause followed. One by one, her ships complied. Ann moved the *Ariel Two* in last. And with a regret that screamed inside her, she gave the order for them to depart.

21.5: ANN

As soon as they hit the home system, Ann went to see Ira. He'd received their message from the edge of the out-system and pushed the *Knid* to meet them at maximum thrust just to spare a few minutes of their time. She arrived at his study on the habitat ring with self-disgust chewing a hole in her, as it had for every second of the trip home.

Ira stood by the wall-screen looking out at a synthetic view of the stars. In reality, his room lay buried deep inside lead shielding in a modular habitat component that could operate as an armed shuttle in its own right if the *Knid* broke up.

Ira had seen her briefing package already. He said nothing, so she spoke.

'I tried to make the best decision under the circumstances, sir,' she said, holding her chin high. 'The options weren't good, and I'm aware that many of the captains disagreed with me.'

'I don't want to hear your defensiveness, Ludik,' Ira snapped. 'I'd have done exactly the same thing that you did, so quit feeling sorry for yourself. You didn't have an option. We all fucked up. The whole human race has fucked up.'

He gestured at the artificial window, stabbing the sky. 'We were offered a chance and we pissed the thirty years of peace they gave us up against the wall. And why? Because we were in love with our own stupid ideas of how everything was *supposed* to be. Of what we were *due*. Whether it was money, or religion, or high-handed notions of what was right or good.' His voice dripped scorn. 'We didn't spend enough time thinking about the obvious threats that were staring us in the face. We couldn't think past our own tiny fucking perspective and the economics of the *now*. We bickered like *children* over the scraps

536

of someone else's dead. We weaponised migration, for crying out loud. And now we don't have a choice any more.'

He fell silent again and hung his head.

'Sir?' said Ann quietly. 'No choice in what?'

'The Earth's too fragile,' said Ira. 'So are the colonies. We can't have worlds so full of people that we can't afford to lose them, or which are too thinly populated to defend. Humanity needs to be strategically spread, on planets with enough industry and firepower to look after themselves. Up till now, we've done the shittiest possible job of getting people off Earth. The Photurian carrier removes any excuse for that. So we're going to pick up people by the million. Every single world will have to be on high alert until we solve this. *If* we solve it. If it's not too late already. At the start of all this, I asked Will to bring me a miracle that would change politics. He achieved that, all right. It's just a shame we might go extinct because of it. *Everyone* is in the Fleet now. Every single human being is at war. Unless they want to give up their identities and go and join the fucking Photurians.' He shook his head. 'I don't know. Maybe we should just spare ourselves the worry and admit defeat.'

'I assume you're not being serious,' said Ann.

'You'd like to think so, wouldn't you?' said Ira. He turned to look at her for the first time since she arrived. His eyes were red. He scowled. 'I have a memory dump for you.'

Ann still hated sucking down other peoples' thoughts, but she accepted it anyway.

[*Let me help,*] said her shadow.

Experiences from their prisoner observation SAPs came streaming in. She watched the Photurians standing patiently in their cells, smiling like priests. They looked healthier, happier and stronger than ordinary people, at peace and reconciled to their situation. Their faith in their superiority never wavered. When given the opportunity, the Photurians chatted engagingly with their captors, offering charming insights on how much their lives had been improved by absorption. The process was painless and instant now, they said. They could administer it themselves, like a baptism. And the beneficial effects lasted for ever.

According to SAP-based Turing assessors, their probability of achieving full sentience kept rising. By some measures, the prisoners were smarter now than they'd been before the swarm took them. Ann might have found them convincing but for the perfect, serene, uniform gloss the Photurians presented. They were too ideal as an advertisement, and not quite human enough.

She shivered. She knew there'd be many who'd look at that cartoonish strength and envy it. Inevitably, word of their survival would leak out making the situation even more complicated. The Photurians would get their converts, all right.

'It's all a facade,' she said.

'Undoubtedly,' said Ira. 'But we still don't really understand what's underneath it, and eventually it's not going to matter. People won't care. The angry, the disillusioned and the just plain desperate – they'll see what they want to see. The Photurians will use our needs and vulnerabilities against us.'

'Sir,' said Ann. 'We have to look to our strengths, surely. So far as we know, the Photurians haven't attacked since New Panama.'

'Because they don't want to set fire to their own lunch,' Ira growled.

'Perhaps. But even that gives us something to work with. Hope isn't lost.'

Ira sighed. 'I'll have to make a public address. This is the biggest, scariest pile of shit that anyone has ever been asked to clean up, and I want you there with me. You're Will now. His shit job is your shit job. Do you get that?'

'Of course, sir,' she said. 'I knew that from the moment he brought me back to life.'

'Good, because you and I are about to become the public face of the largest and least popular relocation programme in the history of the human race. And it's going to be grim. Even with all their overbuilding, our colonies are tiny. I have no fucking idea where we'll find homes for so many people.'

[*Actually,*] said Ann's shadow, [*I may be able to help with that.*]

538

22: STALEMATE

22.1: SAM

Sam didn't complain or resist as they led him down the corridor. He knew he was on his way to see Ira Baron and that it would be the last conversation he'd ever have. He didn't let it touch him.

They'd mined all the knowledge they wanted out of him with neural taps weeks ago. Not that he'd held anything back when they asked. There would have been no point. He'd felt curiously numb since they brought him out of the *Gulliver*'s med-bay. So much that he'd worked for had fallen away since Carter. He'd made so many compromises already that what was left of his life didn't matter to him much.

Only one thing held his attention these days, and that was following the news-feed they allowed him about the Nems and their activities. He watched it avidly, like a boy transfixed by a spider, without feeling satisfaction, fear or dismay. If he had one regret about death, it would be going out not knowing how the story finished – not knowing what the Nems were up to.

They led him to an interrogation room. Ira sat there on a plain plastic chair, bent forward and brooding. He drummed his fingers on the table and didn't look up. They pushed Sam into the seat opposite him, not bothering with restraints. They had far more effective tools for ensuring compliance these days.

'Hi,' said Sam.

Ira fixed him with a furious stare. 'Tell me why you did it.'

Sam blinked slowly. 'Because you were fucking it all up,' he said with a shrug. 'I've told your people already.'

'I know,' said Ira. 'I want to hear it from your own lips.'

'I was trying to make a difference,' said Sam. 'All that shit in your speeches about *balance*, about trying to include all parties in the future – did you ever really buy that crap? Somebody had to do something. We were headed for war.'

'And this is your solution. This fabulous fucking new world?'

'No. This is a disaster. I used what I had to try to fix society and I backed the wrong horse. But at least I had a go, rather than sitting there on my ass playing everyone off against each other.'

Ira sighed. 'How did I ever promote a half-witted clown like you to such a position of power? Do you honestly believe I didn't consider options like the one you're still so in love with? Of course I did. I discarded them because they were pitiful. An interstellar community with a dead Earth would have been a pathetic, emasculated thing.'

'Except that's what we've got now, isn't it?' said Sam. 'So in a way, I won, didn't I? You're going to have to take Earth apart. Scatter the population.'

Ira glared at him and for a moment Sam thought that maybe he'd successfully slid a knife in. Then Ira laughed and broke the illusion.

'You call that winning, you dumb fuck? The population of every single colony world is going to be drowned in Earther immigrants inside six months. There won't be a single place left in space for your kind of society. It'll be Earth everywhere.'

'And are you proud of that?' said Sam. 'It'll be the end of Galatea, too.'

'I don't give a shit what happens to Galatea so long as I keep the human race going. You appear to have forgotten, Sam, that Galatea's only ever really been about one thing: survival.'

Sam rubbed his head. They'd shaved it for the neural probes. The stubble felt rough under his fingertips.

'Look. I know I'm not getting off this station alive,' he said, 'so I'll make my parting words very clear. We both know why you're in this situation.'

'Oh, really?' Ira drawled. 'Do tell.'

'Because we failed as a species. Your administration failed. Transcendism failed.'

Sam saw Ira's face harden and knew that this time he'd got him.

'We failed for a very simple reason: idealism. You can't *hope* the human race into maturity or good behaviour. People have been trying that for hundreds – no, thousands of years. Human beings don't work that way. People respond to incentives, which means that everyone was going to carry on doing exactly what they wanted while you preached at them. If I hadn't screwed up, it would have been somebody else. We had a choice: either the Transcended turned out the lights or we burned ourselves up without them. One way or the other. You saw it happening just as well as I did.

'So when you leave me here, take just one idea with you. People like to imagine that civilisation is what happens when you give everyone the freedom to act on their own terms. That's bullshit. Feudalism is what happens when you do that. Civilisation is a response to crisis. If you don't give people a reason to have high standards, some of them will behave like shits. And those who do that will fuck it up for everyone else. Whatever you build next, remember that. Let the scumbags do what they like and you can kiss your species goodbye. It's that simple.'

Ira smiled. 'Do you know what I see? I see a sad little sociopath peddling his ideology because he imagines it might live on even though he's not going to.'

Sam frowned.

'I didn't see you properly before because I wasn't paying close enough attention,' said Ira. 'Now I am. Here's how you work. You sit there like a fucking spider, waiting and watching for people to reveal a vulnerability. If you don't see one, you guess and pick at them until one shows up. And then, once you've found a weakness, you work at it, pressing on that person's system of self-validation until you've squeezed an idea under their skin. You make it so that they have to accept your bullshit in order to keep feeling good about themselves. Then you set them off like little clockwork robots and feel proud of yourself for it. And that, pathetically, is how *you* validate *your* actions.

'You see, Sam, you think you're clever because you were modded for strategy and negotiation. But I see people like you all the fucking time and they're all dumb as rocks, just like you. All sociopaths are. You can't see the futility of your own schemes because you lack even the first whit of personal insight into your own condition. But your kind don't win any more, because there are people like me who have mods for looking straight through people like you.

'Which is good news, really. People like you are always sad and angry inside. That's because they lack the empathy that would actually allow them to be happy. So instead, your kind just go on collecting money or power or influence, or whatever meaningless crap it is that they're using as a proxy for joy. And the whole time they keep wondering why they still feel sad and angry and alone. And you do feel lonely, don't you, Sam? I know you do.'

Ira peered into his prisoner's eyes, tilting his head this way and that. Sam held his gaze, forcing Ira to blink first. So Ira blinked at him with cartoonish enthusiasm and grinned.

'Made you blink last,' he said. He leaned back. 'There's an irony in your vision, Sam,' he said, 'because one of the badly behaved little shits whose uncivilised behaviour you despise so much is you.'

'You think I don't see that?' Sam said tersely.

'Oh, I'm sure you do, but you imagine a warped kind of justice in it. Everyone else is misbehaving so you might as well, too, but for a *good cause*. You see your entire self-serving edifice as a kind of sacrifice. The world might not understand your greatness but they'll benefit from it even if you're not there.'

Ira let out a cough of grim laughter. 'That attitude would be hilarious if it wasn't so pathetic. You're like that guy on Drexler who put poison in the water supply to get rid of all the Truists and ended up poisoning his own kids. At least that clown had the capacity for regret. I don't see that in you. So here's how it will go. I'll be ignoring your advice. Not because it doesn't make sense, but because it comes from you. You've lied enough that you don't deserve to have influence. You'll go down in history as an example of why people should think twice about over-modding their kids, Sam. I'll make sure of that. Push them too hard and you might end up with a fuck-up joke like Sam Shah.

'You see, there's not much I can do to hurt you, Sam, because there's about as much humanity in you as there is in one of those machines you woke. So I'm not going to bother. You're just going to die. I came here to look you in the eye for my own satisfaction, to see you for what you are and to be able to dismiss your relevance fairly. I wanted to let you know, before we finished you, that someone saw all the way through your bullshit and out the other side, and didn't find anything interesting or wise in there.'

Ira got up to leave. 'Congratulations on being a second-rate failure, Sam Shah. Enjoy your firing squad.'

Sam found himself breathing heavily. His knuckles were white, which surprised him, because he still didn't particularly feel anything. He squeezed his eyes shut. Behind his eyelids there was only darkness.

22.2: ANN

Ann walked up to the podium beside Ira and stood there to his right while he readied himself to speak. The camerabot hovered patiently in front of them, its ready-light winking.

[*I'm sorry,*] said Ann's shadow silently.

[*For what?*]

[*For this. This is what happens. Become a super-person and you immediately get sucked into government.*]

[*I don't mind,*] said Ann. [*There's work to do.*]

[*Neither did I at first,*] said her shadow. [*Just wait.*]

Ira looked up into the lens. 'People of the human worlds, I am here today to announce a public emergency. Humanity is faced with a terrible threat. The entities calling themselves Photurians have made their objectives clear. They intend to co-opt and subvert the human race to remake us in their own image. We cannot allow this to happen. For that reason, the civilian governments of all IPSO worlds are hereby suspended. The human race has been put on a war footing and will remain so until we are certain that the threat has been neutralised.'

In fact, moving to a war footing had proved far easier than it would have been before the Nems. Earth's Leading class had paid the heaviest price during what they were now calling *The Harvesting*. Those family members who'd been spared were only too willing to throw their support behind the Fleet, just as Sam would have expected. They'd been very vocal in the senate in calling for a retaliatory strike. Nobody talked about independent colonies any more, not even as a joke.

'We are doing this because every human world is at risk,' said Ira. 'Earth is vulnerable because it is too populous and too important. In its current state, we simply cannot risk it being taken. Similarly, our colonies are in danger because they are too sparsely populated and under-resourced. Using new technology we have taken from the Photurians, we will be addressing this imbalance. All the colonies will be bolstered and defended. And every person who has signed up for a ticket to leave Earth will be doing so shortly.'

Ira didn't go into the details, of course. Many of them wouldn't be popular. Whole cities full of people were slated to be ferried to the colonies using the human race's only carrier – a dangerous piece of alien technology they barely understood. Once they got there, many of them would end up living in Snakepit-style accommodation before too long.

Will's parting contribution to the human race, apparently, had been a blueprint for a simplified form of self-stabilising tunnel habitat like the ones on the planet that had swallowed him. He'd woven it into Ann's DNA along with everything else. Their version wouldn't be as smart or robust as the Photurian version, but it would grow a hell of a lot faster, which was what they needed right now. What conventional industrial resources they had would be required by the war effort. A programme to convert smart-blood from the *Ariel Two* into the raw material they'd need was already underway.

Ira's voice took on a hard edge. 'Our exodus will be made rapidly,' he said, 'and in a non-denominational fashion. This will be unpopular with many. Colony populations will soar. Earth will be all but emptied. And while we will respect the needs of families to stay together, religious or cultural affiliations will *not* be respected. Roles will be assigned based on military need *alone*. This transition will be difficult for many. But it is essential.

'The alternative is for us to give ourselves over to an alien menace and say goodbye to our humanity. I ask each and every one of you for your cooperation in this joint act. Mankind will need to act together as never before. There is no room for a Frontier Protection Party in this new reality, or a Truist Revival. Our differences must and will be put aside. In return, I will make sure that everyone is clothed and fed. Your quality of life will be as good as the IPSO can make it. I wish you all the very best of luck. I will be with you every step of the way.'

The camera light died. There was no piped applause from the video feed and no cheering. This was not that kind of address.

Ira turned to Ann. 'You know what you have to do.'

She nodded. Her duty lay back at Snakepit, presuming she could reach it. Her mission was clear: rescue Will or torch the planet if she couldn't. Citra Chesterford had volunteered to go with her as a bioweapons consultant. After downloading Mark's memories, Ann had been surprised at first that Citra wanted to get back out there. According to Ira, she'd been the first to offer.

Ann thought she understood how Citra was feeling. All of them who'd fallen under Sam's spell shared a similar kind of shame. There was a stain on them that would never wash away. It had plagued Ann every night until she begged her shadow to push her into unconsciousness. But beside that pain, a new feeling had grown over the last few days – a green shoot of purpose. She might have been a part of the problem, but now she could be an even bigger piece of the solution. Redemption lay in her freedom to act.

For Venetia Sharp, by contrast, that redemption apparently lay at home. She'd agreed to head up Ira's social engineering team for the new fortified colonies they were building. What the two of them were planning, neither of them would say.

'Take care of Will,' Ira said softly. 'I've been trying to do that for most of my life. It's your job now.'

'I will,' said Ann.

Unexpectedly, he hugged her.

'Now get out of here before I start crying,' he said. 'And bring that miserable fucker back to me in one piece.'

22.3: MARK

Mark and Zoe sat together in the *Gulliver*'s lounge watching the carrier loading around them. Their cargo this time was the same as it had been a month ago: battleships, construction equipment and entire orbital habitats jammed full with people. This time, they'd been ordered to Wheeler, a colony close to New Panama desperately in need of defensive support. Within days of their arrival, Wheeler would have a higher population and better defences than New Panama boasted in its heyday.

Aboard one of the habitats, Mark noted, was the entire population of New York Tower Three, his former home. That realisation struck a curious nostalgic chord in him. All those people who'd been a part of his life hung just twenty kilometres away from him and didn't even know he was there. They'd sat in the same meetings with him, looked out at the same dead water and woken to the smell of the same badly filtered air. None of them would ever set eyes on the Hudson again.

What would happen to the members of groups like Shamokin Justice? he wondered. Would they agree to leave their underground warrens and come peacefully? He doubted it. So maybe they'd inherit the Earth after all. And what about the New Yorkers – would they get along with the famously sanctimonious Wheeler colonists? He winced at the thought.

'Containment is complete,' said Zoe. 'We're ready to spin up.'

She floated over to his couch and curled up next to him as close as zero-gee would allow. He put his arm around her and smelled her hair. He still felt uncertain about their relationship. He savoured it but couldn't trust it to persist yet. It was a thing born of adversity. As the pressure of events slowly subsided, would she still want to be with him?

He hoped so. When he was with her, he didn't feel alone any more. He felt understood and accepted for the first time in his life. And that was so intoxicating he couldn't have helped falling in love with her if he'd tried. But there was more to it than that. In retrospect, he knew he'd fallen irreversibly for Zoe in that moment outside of Britehaven when she'd shut down Sam's plan from the cabin of the constructorbot. Her intelligence had been fierce and bright. Her rage had matched his perfectly. In the wake of the penitence boxes they weren't likely to be a good fit for anyone but each other. And that suited him fine.

'Do you think it'll work – moving people around like this?' he said.

'I think it's what we're supposed to do,' she replied, snuggling closer.

'*Supposed* to? Is this part of your big Transcended theory?'

Zoe's favourite topic of conversation since The Harvesting had been the Transcended and why they hadn't directly intervened already. She still believed them responsible for everything the swarm had done. Mark wasn't so sure.

'Yes,' she said. 'That's why they gave us all this stuff. The vacuum-drive, self-building habitats, all of it. It's too much of a coincidence otherwise. To get so many useful technologies at once, just when we need them?'

Mark snorted. 'I still say it's a pretty funny way of trying to help. We might all be dead by next year.'

'We won't,' she said. 'There's a plan to all of this. You'll see. There's a reason the Photurians haven't attacked again. Just like there's a reason their code was so weirdly easy to hack.'

'Which is?'

Zoe shrugged. 'No idea. I'm just sure it'll be a good one.'

'This is quite the religious conversion for a paranoid Vartian Institute agent, you realise.'

'You always say that, but you can be optimistic and paranoid at the same time, you know. Just because they're out to get you doesn't mean they want you dead.'

Mark laughed.

Ash pinged them from the bridge. 'Are we ready?' he said. 'I'm getting queries from the battle cruisers.'

'Let's go,' said Zoe. 'We have a future to build.'

Mark nodded and spread his mind out into the machinery of the carrier. The field built as they spun. The curious vacuum-envelope slid down. And on wings of liquid night, he lifted up his precious cargo and whisked it away to the stars.

23: EPILOGUE

23.1: WILL

Will woke on a bed of scarlet moss near a trickling stream. A thousand fairy chandeliers lit the roof far overhead. A soft, moist breeze tickled his skin. He sat up and rubbed his head. He felt fuzzy. There was something important he was supposed to remember, but he couldn't recall what it was. He'd been angry. He'd made some kind of discovery that he had to share. He blinked. He couldn't place it now.

Another Will walked up to him and peered down into his face. 'How are you feeling?'

'Weird,' said Will. 'My memories are kind of messy. My interface doesn't feel right.'

'Do you remember the important thing?' said the roboteer standing over him.

Will shook his head. 'I can't get it straight. Something about the planet, perhaps. Or how we got here.'

The standing Will smiled awkwardly at that. Because obviously they'd always been there.

Will peered up at the other version of himself. 'Are there supposed to be two of us?' he said.

Will Two gestured with open hands. 'I'm not sure. I admit it was unexpected.' He pointed across the meadow, towards the nearest junction. 'Maybe we should go and ask them,' he said.

Will sat up straight and squinted into the distance.

About half a kilometre away, a crowd of Wills had come together to talk.

'They're sharing memories, I think,' said Will Two. 'Trying to get this all sorted out.'

'I guess there are a lot of us,' said Will One.

'It looks that way. A whole planetful, maybe. I'm pretty sure we'll be able to solve it together.'

Will One nodded. 'Makes sense.'

His doppelgänger gave him a hand up and together they walked down to join the waking throng.

ACKNOWLEDGEMENTS

Special thanks to Graham Lamb, Sarah Pinborough, my agent John Jarrold, the fantastic team at Gollancz, and to those generous insightful friends who helped me debug it all: Dave G, Kate, DeeDee, K, Shayla, James, Maciek, Tony and Dave S.

ALEXANDER LAMB splits his time between writing science fiction, software engineering, teaching improvised theater, running business communication skills workshops, and conducting complex systems research.

• • •

He currently lives in the USA with his wife, an astrophysicist at the university, and their son.

• • •

Find out more at www.alexlamb.com and by following @alexlamb on Twitter.

**TURN THE PAGE FOR SNEAK
PEEK INTO THE FUTURE!**

**THIS EPIC SPACE ADVENTURE
CONCLUDES WITH**

EXODUS

1: RISING

1.1: WILL

Will Kuno-Monet woke with a start to find himself half-buried in white soil. He struggled to his feet, blinking while his heart pounded. A meadow of black poppies stretched in either direction, lining the bottom of an enormous tunnel. Blueish light came from dangling chains of luminescent kelp suspended from the pale, arched ceiling fifty metres overhead. The strands wafted gently like a glowing field of wheat. A moist breeze brought scents of ozone and fresh coffee. Somewhere nearby, a stream trickled.

His body felt wire-taut, flushed with fear for no reason he could remember. Will glanced quickly about, his breath coming in heaves. In the tube's undulating distance, a dense thicket of short, black trees jutted out of the snow-white earth. In the other direction, a sideways kink in the tube blocked further sight. He looked down and found himself wearing a one piece ship-suit, but grown from some soft, grey, organic material. It had no obvious fastenings. He didn't remember putting it on.

What the hell was this place? And why did he feel so afraid? His memory was a terrifying blank. But as he stood there, anxiously scanning the tunnel, answers began to assemble themselves in his mind like shadows revealed by parting mist.

Will was on *Snakepit* – a world covered with millions of kilometres of overlapping habitat tubes just like this one. It was the greatest extraterrestrial discovery the human race had ever made: an engineered biosphere capable of hosting billions of living beings. And it had been left empty and unused for the last five million years.

He also remembered that he'd been lured here aboard his ship, the *Ariel Two*. Yes, he *owned* a starship. He was investigating some sort of threat, utterly unsuspecting of what lay ahead. Because Snakepit had been kept secret. And once he arrived, he'd been betrayed.

He frowned as he tried to remember who'd cheated him and how. The answer wouldn't come. Was it his friends or allies in government? He knew he worked in politics. There had been all those dull, difficult meetings with bright-robed men and women with frowning faces. He was part of something called IPSO – the *Interstellar Pact Security Organization*. But he felt sure the betrayal ran deeper than that. He'd trusted someone with his life and his future, and it had killed him.

Will frowned in confusion at that last memory. If he'd died, how come he was still here? Yet the image burned vividly in his mind. He'd watched helpless from a distance while his body melted into slime. Except that didn't make any sense, either. How had he watched his own death from a distance?

Then Will recalled another vital fact about himself. He was a *roboteer* – one of a tiny minority of people engineered before birth to interface with thinking machines. How could he *possibly* have forgotten that? It had defined his entire life. Any camera linked to a Self-Aware Program could serve as his eyes. Watching himself from outside his own body was as simple as thought, so long as a suitable network was available.

Something about that explanation didn't strike him as adequate, either, but it occurred to him to check for a local pervasivenet. With access to the digital realm, it would be a lot easier to figure out what had happened.

He reached inwards, summoning the visual for his home node – the virtual environment that served as the access point for his internal systems. However, instead of the familiar image of his childhood home, a dark sensation swam up through him, vivid and overpowering. An ancient place that felt at once like a deserted museum and a crowded train station loomed in his mind's eye, where crowds of ghostly figures flickered and darted. From grey stone walls hung immense rippling banners of orange and black, bearing alien runes too dense and twisted for human eyes to read. He knew this place. He dreaded it.

Will fought to clear his head of the smothering vision and found himself kneeling, bent over on the pale clay and wheezing for air. He'd practically passed out. As his strength returned, a cold sense of certainty settled on him. He hadn't just been cheated, he'd been *changed*.

How or why he'd been rescued from death he had no idea, but one thing he knew for certain: he couldn't stay in this tunnel. He needed to get off Snakepit while he still could. For reasons that escaped him, he knew this place was dangerous.

Will struck out hurriedly in the direction of the black trees, the peculiar flowers crumpling beneath his feet as he strode through them. They bled ink when crushed, he noticed – a brilliant blue that soaked into the soil almost immediately. He remembered this world being strange, with a bewildering variety of life forms inhabiting the tunnels, all of them petite and too perfect to be natural. Now, though, they smelled wrong. There'd been no coffee odour last time. And something about its presence worried him deeply.

At the edge of the miniature forest, Will stopped to stare. Pale, rubbery faces grown from parasitic fungus jutted from the trunks like masks. Each one bore the likeness of someone he knew. And with each face, a fresh memory bloomed in his head.

Here, for instance, was the elegant, sculpted visage of Parisa Voss. A friend and a traitor – the woman who'd derailed his life. *She'd* brought him here. He felt a rush of loathing. And there was Ann Ludik, another traitor. Except, in the end, she'd been a friend. She'd saved his life and he'd died trying to save hers. Beside her lay the hard, compact features of Mark Ruiz, Will's half-son. Mark was someone Will had aspired to protect, though he'd fallen far short of that goal.

Will regarded the masks with crawling unease. Had these faces been carved? Had they *grown* like that? He glanced about, anticipating a trap. Somebody with both time and knowledge of his life had put these things here, ready for him to see when he awoke. That must have taken hours. How long had he been out of the picture?

The fourth face he saw made him freeze. It belonged to Rachel, his wife – the woman he'd loved all his life. Yet her face conjured an unexpected emotion – a sense of deep, boiling hatred that made Will break out in a spontaneous sweat. He could remember nothing Rachel had ever done to justify such a reaction. In fact, so far as he recalled, she'd been gone from his life for years. His own obsession with trying to fix the politics of IPSO had finally driven her away. She'd boarded a ship to explore the edge of human space – a ship lost beyond reach before he had a chance to apologise. He fumbled to master his rage.

Understanding eluded him like a handful of smoke.

Will stalked between the trees, keeping his eyes open and his guard up in anticipation of a punchline for this sickening joke. A few dozen metres further on he came to a clearing. There, beside the swirling brook, a tiny diorama of his childhood home had been rendered in purple moss. It depicted the exact location of his home node – the very place he'd reached for inside himself just minutes earlier. Grey bulbs of mushroom took the place of furniture, each item rendered in unlikely detail.

Will glared at the weird scene. Whoever had tinkered with this place didn't just have knowledge of his life. They'd seen inside his mind. He walked warily around the unnatural growth, giving it a wide berth only to find it repeated dozens of times along the banks of the river on a variety of scales.

Will waded downstream, trying to stay away from the moss without knowing why. Panic clotted his thoughts. Somebody was playing with him, trying to frighten him – but to what end? Were they the same people who'd brought him back to life? Will's mouth curled in a bitter snarl. If he'd been resurrected as a plaything simply to be teased and tortured, his tormentors would need their wits about them. Will had experienced treatment of that sort during the Interstellar War. His captors had not died pleasantly.

He froze as voices carried to him on the moist air. A man spoke somewhere beyond a line of trees up ahead. A woman answered. They sounded powerfully familiar, though Will struggled to place either of them. He heard laughter.

Will searched the stream's banks for a weapon – a rock or a bone, perhaps – but found nothing in the artificial landscape that would serve. He strode across to the nearest tree to rip free a branch, only to have the wood bend like rubber in his hands.

No matter. He'd fight unarmed if need be. He edged closer to the last line of trees, keeping to the shadows, and peered out.

Beyond the wood lay a small café. A line of bar stools faced away from him, arranged before a covered counter with a large yellow espresso machine and racks of brightly coloured cups. A woman in a dirndl with blonde, braided hair worked there with her back turned, pulling a fresh shot while two patrons chatted on the stools. One customer had vivid green skin. The other had small antlers and legs that ended in hooves.

Both wore embroidered tuxedos with high, padded shoulders like characters from a Martian Renaissance drama.

Will regarded them with blank astonishment. Now he knew where the smell had come from, though the explanation offered little comfort. When last he'd walked these tunnels, Snakepit had been a new discovery fraught with microbial dangers. There was no human population, and it certainly hadn't featured *coffee stands*. The woman turned to place espresso cups before her guests. Will blinked at the sight of her face. It was, without doubt, his own. Her features were smaller than his, more prettily proportioned, but she might have been his twin sister.

She looked up and caught him staring dumbly from the edge of the trees.

'Are you here for coffee?' she asked, then saw his confusion. 'Dabbling in shyness, perhaps? We don't bite, honest.' She gestured for him to approach.

Will, rather uncertainly, stepped out from the cover of the forest. His hands flexed, ready for a fight.

'Do you have scrip?' she said, and then waved the comment away when he didn't answer. 'It doesn't matter. I'm in it for the conversation, not the acumen. What can I get you? It's on the house.'

The two patrons swivelled on their stools to face him. Will saw his own face on both of them. He struggled to speak as he realised why their voices had sounded so oddly familiar – he'd heard himself.

'I . . .' he started.

'You look like you could use something calming,' said the woman. 'How about a nice cup of tea? I'm going to hazard a guess that you like Assam.'

'Good guess,' said Will uncertainly. 'My favourite.'

'No shit,' said the antler clone, chuckling into his coffee.

'What size?' said the woman.

'Come on, he wants a large,' said the green clone. 'You can tell by his face.'

'Why don't you bring that baseline palette of yours over here and have a seat, Will,' said the antler clone. 'And tell us – whatever brings you out to a lonely spot like this one?'

1.2: ANN

From the helm of the *Ariel Two*, Ann Ludik watched shuttles lift from the surface of the Earth, bringing up the last of the population. They appeared in her display as a hundred bright sparks rising over the arc of the world, a planet still stubbornly blue despite all the abuse it had taken. One by one, the sparks left Earth behind, streaming out into the velvet night.

Despite the irretrievable mess their ancestral home had become, it was impossible not to feel the poignancy of that moment. And, deep down beneath her layers of emotional scar-tissue, Ann felt a weak stirring of sadness. However, besides the anticipation that had been twisting her insides for the last nine hours, it barely registered. There would be time for wistfulness later, if they survived.

Someone in the cabin let out a short, tense sob at the sight. Ann declined to open her human eyes to find out who'd made it. Her crew knew how to do their jobs. And they'd all seen moments more tragic than this. After all, they weren't being forced off a planet this time. Unlike most of humanity's retreats in its long war with the self-styled Photurian Utopia, this one had been their own choice.

Forty-one years had passed since the Photes' first attack. During the decades that followed, the Photurians had evolved from near-mindless machines into a sophisticated and dangerous civilisation. Meanwhile, the human race had fallen from its peak of twenty-seven occupied star systems to a less-than-majestic five. The rest of mankind's colonies had been claimed or destroyed. After today, they'd be down to four. Temporarily, they hoped.

In all that time, Sol was the first star system to be deliberately conceded. Mars and the other home system colonies had shut up shop years before as effectively indefensible. And for a while after that, it looked like the consolidation of forces on Earth had worked. Then, just weeks ago, they'd received word of another attempted takeover.

The planet's surface had been seeded with a fresh wave of Phote spores and some of them had made it down into the Pacific Warrens. The number of spontaneous bacterial conversions was rising and the infected were gathering to form terrorist cells faster than the local death squads could root them out. So Earth's government had called for immediate evacuation.

Ann's team had sent a diplomat down to liaise with the government heads, to calm the authorities and try for a new approach. The Earthers, though, were already too deep into panic. Something had changed in Phote strategy, they insisted. Transport lines were being choked off again. The frequency of raids kept climbing. Everyone was talking about a *Third Surge*.

After what they'd all seen during the Suicide War a decade ago, Earth's leaders weren't about to take any chances. So, with great reluctance and no small amount of bitterness, the Galatean military had coordinated an extraction.

'I have the signal from shuttle command,' said Cy, Ann's communications officer. His voice cracked as he spoke. 'Earth is cleared. Ready to commence *Phase Three*.'

'Initiate,' said Ann. 'Let's get it done.'

Moving thirty million people out of the gravity well in nine hours had not been easy. To facilitate the operation, the population of Earth had been issued with personal coma-kits and packed into bunker-boxes the size of sports stadia. Then they'd been foamed in situ with a fast-setting hyper-elastic matrix almost as light as a modern aerogel.

There'd been panic, of course, and some resistance. But the warrens were due to be gassed to ensure that no human hosts remained for the Photes to exploit. The threat of imminent death had served as an effective incentive to cooperate.

During Phase One, the massive container-stacks had been brought out of habitats on macrotracks and handed off to superlifters originally designed to relocate whole arcotowers without disassembly. The process had run surprisingly close to schedule. Nevertheless, Ann had hated every gruelling minute of the wait.

In *Phase Two*, fleets of industrial scoop-shuttles on strat-scraping dives had coupled and seized the superlifter loads. The lifters' LTA envelopes had been trashed in the process, of course, but with nobody going home, cost wasn't an issue. The operation would be one of the most expensive the human race had ever conducted.

'What's our attrition rate?' said Ann.

'We're running at less than sixty parts per mil,' said Phlox grimly. 'Better than the model mean. About as good as we could hope for.'

In other words, the impact-foam approach had worked. About eighteen hundred deaths had resulted from almost drowning everyone in aerated smart-polymer, followed by the bone-smashing speed of shuttle intercept. Only eighteen hundred human lives snuffed out before even leaving their home. Probably only a few hundred orphaned children. A great result by any rational measurement.

In *Phase Three*, the scoop-shuttles handed off their precious cargos to vast, purpose-built evac-arks so that they could be ferried to the out-system for carrier pickup. And that was where it got difficult.

Human worlds never faced direct attack. It was too easy to trash them and the Photes needed their converts alive. Consequently, the Utopia subverted colonies instead, or absorbed them wholesale once support lines were cut off and defences knocked out.

A population on the move, though, invited a very different kind of fighting. Arks made easy targets for direct, violent absorption. Hence, Phase Three was when the Photes were most likely to strike.

Unfortunately, evac-arks weren't fast. They lacked warp, which meant that even with tap-torch engines and constant acceleration as high as their human cargo could handle, exit would take days. And there were so many spies embedded within Earth's population already that the likelihood of word of their timing having leaked was high.

The Photes might intercept at any moment. For all Ann's team knew, the out-system they were headed for might already be crawling with stealthed enemy drones. So at some point over the next seventy hours or so, the pace of events would likely go from interminably dull to horrifyingly fast. Human minds didn't operate well under those conditions. Without artificial support, her team were likely to burn themselves out worrying before any trouble hit.

Fortunately, Ann hadn't been human for years. She didn't get lonely or impatient the way other people did – not since her change. Which was why her ship was taking point for the hardest part of the mission. Still, her team would probably need a little encouragement.

Ann opened her eyes and partially decoupled her mind from the *Ariel Two*'s helm-space. Her shadow took up the slack while she surveyed her crew at work.

There wasn't much to look at in the *Ariel Two*'s main cabin these days. Simple grey wall-screens running neon agitation patterns lined the dimly lit spherical chamber. Set in a ring around the floor were six military-grade support-couches. Each resembled a cross between a recliner and a coffin designed by a committee of Art Nouveau enthusiasts and para-noid survivalists. Besides Ann's, only three others were occupied.

Cy Twebo, a muscular, soft-faced young man, ran communications. Phlox Orm, a svelte little herm with dark, intense features covered data aggregation. Urmi Kawasaki, a quiet woman from the lower levels with a giraffe pigment-job, managed their unruly stable of threat models. Ann didn't know any of them well.

For years now, the Galatean government had been handing her these tightly knit triples to work with, specially trained to pilot the nestship in the supremely unlikely event of her demise. They never stuck around for long. This bunch, at least, accepted the way Ann ran things. Or perhaps they'd simply been briefed to not get in her way this time. There was too much at stake.

'Team,' said Ann.

All three opened their eyes in surprise.

'I'm proud of you all,' she said. 'What we're doing here is beyond difficult. And Phase *Three* is going to be a bitch. So remember that I admire you all, and that I have the utmost confidence in your abilities. Any comments or recommendations before we go to slow-time?'

They regarded each other with tense, sad eyes.

'No,' said Cy, their unofficial spokesperson. 'We're good.'

'Okay,' said Ann. 'And does everyone have their amygdala-gating on max?'

Her crew nodded.

'Good,' said Ann. 'Because you're going to need it.'

She thought about adding, *Don't worry, we'll get the Earth back*. But nobody would have believed her.

'Let's get to work,' she said instead and shut her eyes.

From time to time, someone claimed that the *Ariel Two* was undermanned or that Ann's leadership style was too remote. They didn't know what they were talking about. The cellular augmentation she'd received on Snakepit enabled her to run the entire ship on her own. It was hard enough just finding things for her mandatory three backup officers to do. Having more people aboard only made things worse. They got in the way and reduced her acceleration thresholds. And after all, Ann wasn't there to chit-chat. She was there to atone. She'd only made one big mistake in her life, but that choice had unleashed the Photes against humanity. As fuck-ups went, hers had been galaxy-class.

She brought up an immersive view of local space to watch the shuttles creeping out to their respective arks. There were three of them in all, each guarded by an attendant battle cruiser. Accompanying the *Ariel Two* were a couple of new Orson-class planet-busters armed to the teeth with grater-grids and boser canons. They loomed like sinister moons.

'Cy, signal Angels Two and Three,' said Ann. 'Prep for departure. We'll be going silent in ten. Tell them good luck.'

To minimise risk, Ann's team had brought dummy arks. Three separate ships would head to different extraction points in the out-system. Only one of them, though, would be carrying people – the one Ann was watching. The other two were decoys, turning the entire operation into a shell game.

As soon as all the shuttles had docked, Ann made her next move.

'Engaging stealth-cloak,' she told the others.

For a ship as large as the *Ariel Two*, a cloak only bought you so much. With two hundred and forty kilometres of elastoceramic alloy hull to hide, they'd still be visible by virtue of their gravity footprint. But that was part of the point. With luck, the escorts would draw attention from the far smaller arks. Their enemies, unfortunately, would be operating under stealth, too. If battle commenced, it would be fought mostly blind.

With stately deliberation, the arks all left orbit and headed out. *Ariel* and the other two escorts took up position beside their respective charges and left alongside them.

'Commencing mine-drop sequence,' she told her crew.

After all, if you were abandoning a habitat world, what was the point of not turning it into a deathtrap on your way out?

'Okay, everyone,' she said, 'we'll be running in shifts from here to Jupiter orbit. Somebody take a nap.'

Ann handed off as much control to her shadow as she dared and put her mind on slow. There was no point burning mental cycles on dead time when half her brain could be resting.

Their progress appeared to accelerate dramatically. As the Earth shrank behind them, Ann watched it through electronic eyes and whispered goodbye to the famous cradle of humanity.

As she did so, a memory sprang to mind: the moment years ago when she left her flat on Galatea to move to New Panama. She'd stood on the threshold and looked back across the scruffy floor-turf at the soft marks where her furniture had so recently stood. That moment had filled her with an unexpected wistfulness even though she'd been madly keen to leave. This moment had a lot in common with that, once you factored in the dread of impending combat.

She bit back a sigh. It was at times like this that she missed Poli and the kids the most. They probably weren't missing her, thankfully. Nobody missed weird Aunt Andromeda that much. She was gone too often.

[It's ridiculous,] she told her shadow. [Why should I feel sad? The Earth's been barren for decades. The ocean trenches host more life than the surface. It's just another colony.]

[Symbolism,] it replied. Ann still heard it speaking in Will's voice, though her shadow had long since become more an echo of her own mind than his. [Plus, it's depressing. If you don't look too close, it's hard to tell that intelligent life was ever here. We didn't exactly make much of a mark on this system in the end. Ceres is a mess, of course, but that's been true since the first war. And Saturn's rings are all fucked up, but they were delicate in the first place. They weren't even doing well before the Photes arrived.] These days, the planet only had a band of haze. [Even Mars looks practically untouched,] her shadow said bitterly. [The bomb craters are just like all the others.]

[Wow, you're a comfort,] she told it.

[I'm part of you. What did you expect?]

Ann snorted in amusement. Her sadness was blurring into optimism as the minutes raced past without attack. Amazingly, no one had fired on them yet and fifty hours had passed already.

On cue, her ship made its last pseudo-random course-correction and emitted another decoy drone designed to leak a dummy engine signature. Then it began its final deceleration. As the time since Earth departure closed in on three objective days, Ann approached their rendezvous point.

They were two hours behind schedule by then. Which meant that things were amazingly quiet. In fact, now that she thought about it, they were *too* quiet. On the upside, nobody – barring the inevitable attrition victims – had died. On the downside, it suggested that something sinister was going on that they hadn't accounted for. Again.

Ann reluctantly swapped to normal time.

'Cy,' she said. 'Any sign of a signal?'

She had to wait a moment for her communications officer to return to undiluted awareness. She listened to him groan. Ordinary humans didn't take well to radical changes in mental pacing, not even those with military-grade shadow support.

'Not yet,' he croaked. 'Resampling now.'

Ann scowled. Given the immense areas involved and the horrific difficulties of arranging schedules over interstellar distances, some slack in the system was to be expected. Particularly with Mark Ruiz as the carrier pilot. The delay, though, was not welcome.

Ann lay scowling for an hour or so, checking her systems and surveying the dark, knowing full well it was pointless. Reluctantly, she slid her mind back into a slower gear to wait. She regretted it almost instantly as the blinding flare of a carrier burst appeared.

Ann kicked herself up into combat time, cursing. The flash had originated relatively close to where Mark was supposed to show, but was still light-minutes away from the expected target. That far out, it was hard to tell the difference between a friendly carrier and a deadly one.

'Cy,' she said. 'Scan it. Everyone on full alert.'

The ship's main audio chattered briefly as Cy's signal-processing SAPs scrambled over their EM buffers. Then a soft voice started oozing through the cabin's speakers.

'In Photuria, there is no fear, no pain, no death,' it whispered. 'Instead, there is perfect love and perfect joy.' Images appeared on the wall-screen of blissed-out couples walking hand in hand through soft, white tunnels, tears of happiness running down their handsome faces.

'Fuck,' Ann snarled. The Photes always sent a love letter before they started harvesting. They didn't seem able to prevent themselves from announcing their arrival. So, these days, they did it as quietly as they could.

Light was slow. In the time it had taken the message to reach them, the Photes had no doubt been stealing out across the system with warp-enabled munitions, locking it down. The question was where to head for. Ann selected Mark's backup coordinates and prayed he wasn't already dead. She tight-beamed the course-correction to her ark and fired off a fresh set of decoys. Then she woke the titan mechs slumbering in her outer mesohull and prepped them for close-quarters combat.

Unless Mark showed up soon, they were screwed. All their careful planning would be for nothing. They'd be dead. In fact, they'd be worse than dead. The Photes would have thirty million new bodies to play with.

1.3: MARK

Mark Ruiz paced the drawing room, hands clasped tightly behind his back. His eyes darted to the grandfather clock in the corner every few seconds. From the antique sofa near the bay window that looked out across the grounds, his wife Zoe eyed him anxiously as she sipped her tea.

'Marching about won't get us there any faster, you know,' she said, rearranging her skirts. 'Why don't you come and sit with me? We can play cards.'

'I can't sit,' said Mark. 'Not even virtually.'

She set her cup down. 'Fine. Do you want to drop back into physical? Would that help? We have to be down to minutes, anyway.'

Mark shook his head. 'It wouldn't make any difference. Besides, we'll have to be fully dunked the moment we drop warp.'

Zoe sighed and stared off across the lawn to where a flock of geese were alighting on the lake. In truth, their shared fiction was doing as little for her mood as it was for his.

Their butler stepped in bearing a silver tray and another china teapot. 'Would sir and madam like second cup?'

'Not now, Shaw,' said Zoe and offlined his program with a click of her fingers. 'Honestly,' she muttered, 'you can't get the help these days.' She rubbed her virtual eyes.

Beyond the imaginary confines of his home, Mark reclined on an immersion-couch in the tiny main cabin of the *GSS Gulliver*, a forty-kilometre-wide starship. Surrounding the *Gulliver* lay the immense, filigree-delicate warp-envelope of the *embership Kraken*, which Mark was urgently piloting with an army of subminds.

The *Kraken* was more soap bubble than starship. Six insubstantial strands of rotating ion-deployment cable maintained a sphere of tailored pseudo-vacuum about six nanometres thick and several hundred kilometres across. While he fretted, they tore across space at several kilo-lights, on their way to rescue the population of Earth. And they were late.

Mark hated that he'd missed his arrival window. But the fury he felt at the Galatean government's antics dwarfed that self-loathing. He'd made the right choice, for all the trouble it had brought him.

Just hours before he was due to depart, Mark had received a private briefing composed by Ann's lead diplomat, marked for his eyes only. It contained a detailed summary of the battle plan's final version, along with a little supplementary data.

Buried within that data had lain evidence that the Earth's popula-tion was being quietly split. A hundred thousand volunteers had been allocated to one of the dummy evac arks. That way, the government had reasoned, whichever of the arks the Photes focused their attack on, *some* people were likely to get out alive. And from the survivors, Galatea would to be able to reconstruct the Photes' new infection pattern, poten-tially saving millions more.

The decision made sense in a high-handed kind of way. Galatea stood to gain vital tactical information at the estimated cost of a mere hundred thousand innocents – peanuts in terms of recent losses.

Mark, however, wasn't ready to sacrifice those lives. The decision smacked to him of exactly the sort of cold, mechanical logic that the remaining human societies had been driven to. The moment he realised the plan's intent, he'd made up his mind to rescue everyone, not just the people the government had picked to survive. And when he showed the details to Zoe, it had taken him all of about one second to convince her.

'Fuck that shit,' she'd growled. 'They bait-and-switched us *again*? Everyone's leaving with us. Where can we get more guns?'

So Mark had detoured to St Andrews, which was *almost* en route, called in the necessary favours and loaded the *Kraken*'s envelope full of warp-enabled attack drones. In doing so, he'd burned up all the spare time incorporated into the meticulously engineered Galatean plan.

Had Mark and Zoe been full Galatean citizens, their act would already have constituted a war crime. But the *Kraken* flew under the diplomatic colours of the Vartian Institute, which gave him a little room to manoeuvre.

Unfortunately, he knew that once he rendezvoused with Ann, she'd make it impossible for him to go back for the others. Ann was a stickler for process, as inflexible as she was remote. So the secret volunteers had to be rescued first, and fast enough that there would still be a primary ark to collect once he'd finished. If he couldn't manage that, all his efforts would be for nothing. Mark's desperate gambit required split-second timing of a sort that had already gone badly wrong.

Of all his recent disagreements with the Galatean government, this would undoubtedly prove the most divisive. But weren't they supposed to be human beings, for crying out loud, not dead-eyed Photes? Wasn't compassion what defined them? If they couldn't preserve their humanity, what was the point of fighting?

And therein lay the irony. After forty years of unrelenting social change, Mark didn't like the humans he was saving all that much. Most of them bought into the same jackbooted bullshit he despised. The human cultures he worked to protect had all adopted the same militarised outlook to survive. They barely noticed how blinkered they'd become.

So Mark and Zoe had used the freedom their station in life afforded them to build a kingdom of two aboard the *Gulliver*. While running errands for the Galateans, they'd stuck to their own ideal of what society could be and invited others to join them. The risk profile of their existence dissuaded most. Yet, ironically, they'd remained young and alive while most of their friends had died.

Their tiny kingdom was based on tolerance. Zoe tolerated his moods, just as she always had. And he tolerated her distance, even when she retreated into silent study for days on end. That was how it should be with everyone, he reasoned. He didn't need to understand people to want them alive and neither did she. It took all sorts to make a world, and so he was going to save as many sorts as he could.

He felt the tremor of impending arrival like a shiver of dread and glanced across to where Zoe slouched glumly in her Edwardian evening gown.

'Get ready,' he told her.

As the *Kraken* reached its first insertion point, Mark dropped out of his virtual home and into the *Gulliver*'s helm-arena with Zoe alongside him. The drawing room vanished, replaced by an immersive tactical display of local space.

A spray of red markers filled the air like the blood-spatter of a particularly nasty crime scene. The place was crawling with Phote drones, and those were only the ones he could see. Hundreds more undoubtedly still lay cloaked. Most of the trouble swarmed around the green disc of the Orson-class guardian ship, thank Gal. The ark – Mark's prize – hung off to the side, as yet unseen. If there was one thing evac-arks were good at, it was remaining unnoticed.

Zoe initiated a release burst, firing a thousand drones of their own into the fray – all of them on intercept vectors. She couldn't resist adding a Phote-style arrival message of her own.

'Good morning, undead fuckwits,' she announced cheerfully. 'Here's some pain to go with your endless joy.'

That got their attention. Two hundred Phote munitions dropped into visibility and powered towards the *Kraken* at full warp.

An ordinary pilot would have lost their lunch in that moment. A carrier was an appallingly fragile piece of technology. Two disc-shaped ships joined by six feathered skipping ropes spun about a shared axis. Manoeuvring without warp was almost impossible. Manoeuvring *with* warp was nearly as challenging. Mark wasn't worried. He had more years of practice than any other person alive and a roboteer brain designed for space combat. He could make an embership dance like a hummingbird.

He threw the *Kraken* back into high spin, sealed up the warp-envelope and dived on the drifting evac-ark. He opened the envelope for less than a second to let the ship slide between his ferociously whirling inducer-fronds and sneaked back into warp before the ark pilot even knew what had happened.

Finding itself suddenly enclosed, the ark thruster-braked frantically in an attempt to zero its conventional velocity.

While Mark raced outwards again to his second pickup location, the ark's captain yelled at him over the audio channel.

'*Embership Kraken!* What in Gal's name are you doing?' she shouted. 'This action is off-mission and highly dangerous. I repeat: *off-mission!*'

'Understood, Earth Ark Two,' said Mark, 'and apologies for the confusion, but you happen to be carrying a hundred thousand sacrificial volunteers I want saved.'

He saw no reason to beat about the bush. The captain should know that he understood exactly what was going on.

There was a short, confused pause from the ark.

'Captain Ruiz,' breathed the ark captain. 'What are you talking about? This ship has a skeleton crew of three. The only passenger on this ship is the *bomb*, as originally planned. We received no human passengers. Is this some kind of plan update of which we were not informed?'

Mark froze. His cheeks tingled. Maybe the captain was bluffing.

'Did you say *bomb*?' said Zoe. 'That detail was not in our mission pack.'

'Yes, of course a bomb!' the captain cried. 'A bomb now armed by your manoeuvre. The only sacrificial volunteers here are my team, and we now have three minutes before ignition.'

'Can you jettison?' Mark blurted.

'What are you talking about?' said the captain. 'The bomb is our reactor core, as ordered. Tell me – do we have a backup ark? Who is rendezvousing with Ark One? Please tell me we have a dedicated ship for Ark One. Please!'

Mark's mind fizzed over the awful implications.

'We've been compromised,' said Zoe quietly. 'Holy fuck. We're compromised.'

Mark's mouth tasted of ashes. The weight of thirty million human lives landed on his conscience.